The Song of Everlasting Sorrow

Weatherhead Books on Asia
WEATHERHEAD EAST ASIAN INSTITUTE,
COLUMBIA UNIVERSITY

Weatherhead Books on Asia

WEATHERHEAD EAST ASIAN INSTITUTE,
COLUMBIA UNIVERSITY

Literature
David Der-wei Wang, Editor

Ye Zhaoyan, *Nanjing 1937: A Love Story*, translated by Michael Berry (2003)
Oda Makoto, *The Breaking Jewel*, translated by Donald Keene (2003)
Han Shaogong, *A Dictionary of Maqiao*, translated by Julia Lovell (2003)
Takahashi Takako, *Lonely Woman*, translated by Maryellen Toman Mori (2004)
Chen Ran, *A Private Life*, translated by John Howard-Gibbon (2004)
Eileen Chang, *Written on Water*, translated by Andrew F. Jones (2004)
Writing Women in Modern China: The Revolutionary Years, 1936–1976, edited by Amy D. Dooling (2005)
Han Bangqing, *The Sing-song Girls of Shanghai*, first translated by Eileen Chang, revised and edited by Eva Hung (2005)
Loud Sparrows: Contemporary Chinese Short-Shorts, translated and edited by Aili Mu, Julie Chiu, Howard Goldblatt (2006)
Hiratsuka Raichō, *In the Beginning, Woman Was the Sun*, translated by Teruko Craig (2006)
Zhu Wen, I Love Dollars *and Other Stories of China*, translated by Julia Lovell (2007)
Kim Sowol, *Azaleas: A Book of Poems*, translated by David McCann (2007)

History, Society, and Culture
Carol Gluck, Editor

Takeuchi Yoshimi, *What Is Modernity? Writings of Takeuchi Yoshimi*, translated with an introduction by Richard Calichman (2005)
Richard Calichman, *Contemporary Japanese Thought* (2005)
Yasuda et al., *Overcoming Modernity*, translated by Richard Calichman (2008)

The Song of Everlasting Sorrow

A NOVEL OF SHANGHAI

Wang Anyi

TRANSLATED BY
MICHAEL BERRY AND
SUSAN CHAN EGAN

Columbia University Press ◆ New York

This publication has been supported by the Richard W. Weatherhead Publication Fund of the East Asian Institute, Columbia University.

COLUMBIA UNIVERSITY PRESS
Publishers Since 1893
New York   Chichester, West Sussex

Library of Congress Cataloging-in-Publication Data
Wang, Anyi, 1954–
[Chang heng ge. English]
The song of everlasting sorrow : a novel of Shanghai / Wang Anyi ; translated by
Michael Berry and Susan Chan Egan.
p.   cm. — (Weatherhead books on Asia)
ISBN 978-0-231-14342-4 (alk. paper)
1. Shanghai (China)—Fiction.   I. Berry, Michael.   II. Egan, Susan Chan.
III. Title.   IV. Series.
PL2919.A58C4313   2008
895.1'352—dc22
2007010812

∞

Columbia University Press books are printed on permanent
and durable acid-free paper.
This book was printed on paper with recycled content.

Designed by Lisa Hamm

Printed in the United States of America
c 10 9 8 7 6 5 4

Contents

Translators' Notes and Acknowledgments

This translation is based on the original version of the novel published in 1995 by the Zuojia chubanshe in Beijing. The translation is unabridged; however, there are a series of stylistic variances from the original. Chief among those are the length of paragraphs and sentences, and the presentation of direct dialogue. Long extended paragraphs and run-on sentences, both of which read fine in the Chinese original, have in many sections been broken up into shorter structures in this translation. As a challenge to herself and the reader, Wang Anyi intentionally refrained from using quotation marks and paragraph breaks to signal direct dialogue in the original, instead opting to embed dialogue directly into longer narrative sections. For the purpose of readability in English, the translators have added quotation marks and paragraph breaks in sections where direct dialogue appears (marked by the use of first-person pronouns). Other dialogue sections that use third-person pronouns have been left in their original form, embedded within longer paragraphs. Italics (which are not commonly used in Chinese text) have also been added as a stylistic device to indicate internal thought.

Thanks go first and foremost to Wang Anyi for her patience and support. The power and beauty of her literary world inspired us, and we thank her for entrusting us with this important work. David Der-wei Wang has been a staunch supporter of this translation project from its inception six years ago. We thank him for his kindness and for his willingness as series editor to include this book in the Weatherhead Books on Asia series. Thanks to Jennifer Crewe of Columbia University Press for seeing this project through. We would also like to thank the two anonymous readers, who provided valuable comments on an earlier version of the text. We appreciate the support provided by the University of

California, Santa Barbara as well as the Weatherhead Foundation and the Chiang Ching-kuo Foundation, which helped make the publication of this volume possible. Special thanks go to our copy editor, Alice Cheang. We feel blessed to have had the opportunity to work with a true wordsmith, whose style, sense of literature, and encyclopedic knowledge have sharpened the literary vision of the text. The editorial support of Kerri Sullivan and Leslie Kriesel has also been extremely helpful. Finally, we thank Ron Egan, Suk-Young Kim, and our families for their forbearance and accommodation during the long period we were immersed in this project.

—M. B. and S. C. E.

The Song of Everlasting Sorrow

Part I

Chapter 1

Longtang

LOOKED DOWN UPON from the highest point in the city, Shanghai's *longtang*—her vast neighborhoods inside enclosed alleys—are a magnificent sight. The *longtang* are the backdrop of this city. Streets and buildings emerge around them in a series of dots and lines, like the subtle brushstrokes that bring life to the empty expanses of white paper in a traditional Chinese landscape painting. As day turns into night and the city lights up, these dots and lines begin to glimmer. However, underneath the glitter lies an immense blanket of darkness—these are the *longtang* of Shanghai.

The darkness looks almost to be a series of furious waves that threaten to wash away the glowing dots and lines. It has volume, whereas all those lines and dots float on the surface—they are there only to differentiate the areas of this dark mass, like punctuation marks whose job it is to break up an essay into sentences and paragraphs. The darkness is like an abyss—even a mountain falling in would be swallowed whole and sink silently to the bottom. Countless reefs lurk beneath this swelling ocean of darkness, where one false move could capsize a ship. The darkness buoys up Shanghai's handful of illuminated lines and dots, supporting them decade after decade. Against this decades-old backdrop of darkness, the Paris of the Orient unfolds her splendor.

Today, everything looks worn out, exposing bit by bit what lies underneath. One strand at a time, the first rays of the morning sun shine through just as, one by one, the city lights go out. Everything begins from a cover of light fog, through which a horizontal ray of light crafts an outline as if drawing it out with a fine brush. First to appear are the dormer windows protruding from the rooftop *tingzijian* of those traditional *longtang* buildings, showing themselves off with a certain self-conscious delicacy; the wooden shutters are carefully delineated, the handmade rooftop tiles are arranged with precision, even the potted roses on the windowsills have been cared for painstakingly.

Next to emerge are the balconies; here articles of clothing hung out to dry the night before cling motionless like a scene out of a painting. The cement on the balustrade peels away to reveal the rusty red bricks beneath—this too looks as if painted in a picture, each brushstroke appearing clear and distinct. After that come the cracked gable walls, lined with traces of green moss that look cold and clammy to the touch. The first rays of light shining on the gable walls create a stunning picture, a gorgeous portrait, bearing just a hint of desolation, fresh and new yet not without a past.

At this moment the cement pavement of the *longtang* is still enveloped in fog, which lingers thick in the back alleys. But on the iron-railed balconies of the newer *longtang* apartments the sunlight is already striking the glass panes on the French doors, which refract the light. This stroke is a relatively sharp one, and seems to pull back the curtain that separates day from night. The sunlight finally drives away the fog, washing everything in its path with a palette of strong color. The moss turns out to be not green but a dark raven hue, the wooden window frames start to blacken, and the iron railing on the balcony becomes a rusted yellow. One can see blades of green grass growing from between the cracks in the gables, and the white pigeons turn gray as they soar up into the sky.

Shanghai's *longtang* come in many different forms, each with colors and sounds of its own. Unable to decide on any one appearance, they remain fickle, sometimes looking like this, sometimes looking like that. Actually, despite their constant fluctuations, they always remain the same—the shape may shift but the spirit is unchanged. Back and forth they go, but in the end it's the same old story, like an army of a thousand united by a single goal. Those *longtang* that have entryways with stone gates emanate an aura of power. They have inherited the style of Shanghai's glorious old mansions. Sporting the facade of an official residence, they make it a point to have a grandiose entrance and high surrounding walls. But, upon entering, one discovers that the courtyard is modest and the reception area narrow—two or three steps and you are already at the wooden staircase across the room. The staircase is not curved, but leads straight up into the bedroom, where a window overlooking the street hints at romantic ardor.

The trendy *longtang* neighborhoods in the eastern district of Shanghai have done away with such haughty airs. They greet you with low wrought-iron gates of floral design. For them a small window overlooking a side street is not enough; they all have to have walk-out balconies, the better to enjoy the street scenery. Fragrant oleanders reach out over the courtyard walls, as if no longer able to contain their springtime passion. Deep down, however, those inside still have their guard up: the back doors are bolted shut with spring locks of German manufacture, the windows on the ground floor all have steel bars, the low front gates of wrought iron are crowned with ornamented spikes, and walls protect the courtyard on all sides. One may enter at will, but escape seems virtually impossible.

On the western side of the city, the apartment-style *longtang* take an even stricter approach to security. These structures are built in clusters, with doors that look as if not even an army of ten thousand could force their way inside. The walls are soundproof so that people living even in close quarters cannot hear one another, and the buildings are widely spaced so that neighbors can avoid one another. This is security of a democratic sort—trans-Atlantic style—to ensure and protect individual freedom. Here people can do whatever their hearts desire, and there is no one to stop them.

The *longtang* in the slums are open-air. The makeshift roofs leak in the rain, the thin plywood walls fail to keep out the wind, and the doors and windows never seem to close properly. Apartment structures are built virtually on top of one another, cheek by jowl, breathing down upon each other's necks. Their lights are like tiny glowing peas, not very bright, but dense as a pot of pea porridge. Like a great river, these *longtang* have innumerable tributaries, and their countless branches resemble those of a tall tree. Crisscrossing, they form a giant web. On the surface they appear entirely exposed, but in reality they conceal a complex inner soul that remains mysterious, unfathomable.

As dusk approaches, flocks of pigeons hover about the Shanghai skyline in search of their nests. The rooftop ridges rise and fall, extending into the distance; viewed from the side, they form an endless mountain range, and from the front, a series of vertical summits. Viewed from the highest peak, they merge into one boundless vista that looks the same from all directions. Like water flowing aimlessly, they seem to creep into every crevice and crack, but upon closer inspection they fall into an orderly pattern. At once dense and wide-ranging, they resemble rye fields where the farmers, having scattered their seeds, are now harvesting a rich crop. Then again, they are a little like a pristine forest, living and dying according to its own cycle. Altogether they make for a scene of the utmost beauty and splendor.

The *longtang* of Shanghai exude a sensuality like the intimacy of flesh on flesh—cool and warm, tangible and knowable, a little self-centered. The grease-stained rear kitchen window is where the *amah* gossips. Beside the window is the back door; from this the eldest daughter goes out to school and holds her secret rendezvous with her boyfriend. The front door, reserved for distinguished guests, opens only on important occasions. On each side of the door hang couplets announcing marriages, funerals, and other family events. The door seems always to be in a state of uncontrollable, even garrulous, excitement. Echoes of secret whispers linger around the flat roof, the balcony, and the windows. At night, the sounds of rapping on the doors rise and fall in the darkness.

To return to the highest point in the city and look down on it from another angle: clothes hanging out to dry on the cluttered bamboo poles hint at the private lives and loves that lie hidden beneath. In the garden, potted balsams, ghost flowers, scallions, and garlic also breathe the faint air of a secret affair. The empty pigeon cage up on the roof is an empty heart. Broken roof tiles lying in disarray are symbols of the body and soul. Some of the gullylike alleys are lined with cement, others with cobblestone. The cement alleys make you feel cut off, while the cobblestone alleys give the sensation of a fleshy hand. Footsteps sound different in these two types of *longtang*. In the former the sound is crisp and bright, but in the latter it is something that you absorb and keep inside. The former is a collection of polite pleasantries, the latter of words spoken from the bottom of one's heart. Neither is like an official document; both belong to the necessary language of the everyday.

The back alleys of Shanghai try even harder to work their way into people's hearts. The pavement is covered with a layer of cracks. Gutters overflow; floating in the discolored water are fish scales and rotten vegetable leaves, as well as the greasy lampblack from the stovetop. It is dirty and grimy, impure, here. Here the most private secrets are exposed, and not always in the most conventional fashion. Because of this a pall hangs over these back alleys. The sunlight does not shine through until three o'clock in the afternoon and before long the sun begins to set in the west. But this little bit of sunlight envelops the back alleys in a blanket of warm color. The walls turn a brilliant yellow, highlighting the unevenness of the rough whetstone and giving it the texture of coarse sand. The windows also turn a golden yellow, but they are scratched and stained. By now the sun has been shining down for a long time and is beginning to show signs of fatigue. Summoning up the last vestiges of radiance from the depths, the lingering rays of sunlight flicker with a sticky thickness of built-up residue, rather dirty. As twilight encroaches, flocks of pigeons soar overhead, dust motes drift, and stray cats wander in and out of sight. This is a feeling that, having penetrated the flesh, goes beyond closeness. One begins to weary of it. It breeds a secret fear, but hidden within that fear is an excitement that gnaws down to the bone.

What moves you about the *longtang* of Shanghai stems from the most mundane scenes: not the surging rush of clouds and rain, but something steadily accumulated over time. It is the excitement of cooking smoke and human vitality. Something is flowing through the *longtang* that is unpredictable yet entirely rational, small, not large, and trivial—but then even a castle can be made out of sand. It has nothing to do with things like "history," not even "unofficial history": we can only call it gossip.

Gossip is part of the landscape in the Shanghai *longtang*—you can almost see it as it sneaks out through the rear windows and the back doors. What emerges from the front doors and balconies is a bit more proper—but it is still gossip. These rumors may not necessarily qualify as history, but they carry with them the shadows of time. There is order in their progression, which follows the law of preordained consequences. These rumors cling to the skin and stick to the flesh; they are not cold or stiff, like a pile of musty old books. Though marred by untruths, these are falsehoods that have feeling.

When the city's streetlights are ablaze, its *longtang* remain in darkness, save the lonely street lamps hanging on the alley corners. The lamps, enclosed in crude frames of rusty iron covered with dust, emit a murky yellow glow. On the ground, a shroud of thick mist forms and begins to spread out—this is the time when rumors and gossip start to brew. It is a gloomy hour, when nothing is clear, yet it is enough to break the heart. Pigeons coo in their cages, talking their language of secret whispers. The streetlights shine with a prim and proper light, but as soon as that light streams into the *longtang* alleys, it is overwhelmed by darkness. The kind of gossip exchanged in the front rooms and adjoining wings belongs to the old school and smacks faintly of potpourri. The gossip in the rooftop *tingzijian* and staircases is new school and smells of mothballs. But, old school or new, gossip is always told in earnest—you could even say it is told in the spirit of truth.

This is like scooping water with one's hands: even though you might lose half the water along the way, with enough persistence you can still fill up a pond. Or like the swallow that, though she may drop half the earth and twigs she is carrying in her beak, can still build a nest—there is no need for laziness or trickery. The *longtang* of Shanghai are an unbearable sight. The patches of green moss growing in the shade are, in truth, like scars growing over a wound; it takes time for the wound to heal. It is because the moss lacks a proper place that it grows in the shade and shadows—years go by and it never sees the sun. Now ivy grows out in the open, but it serves as Time's curtain and always has something to hide. The pigeons gaze down at the outstretching billows of roof tiles as they take to the air, and their hearts are stabbed with pain. Coming up over the *longtang* rooftops, the sun shoots out its belabored rays—a majestic sight pieced together from countless minute fragments, an immense power born of immeasurable patience.

Gossip

Gossip always carries with it an exhalation of gloom. This murky air sometimes smells like lavender in a bedroom, sometimes like mothballs, and at other times like a kitchen chopping block. It does not remind you of the smell of tobacco plugs or cigars, nor is it even faintly reminiscent of the smell of insecticides like Lindane or Dichlorvos. It is not a strong masculine scent, but a soft feminine one—the scent of a woman. It combines the smell of the bedroom and the kitchen, the smell of cosmetics and cooking oil, mixed in with a bit of sweat. Gossip is always trailed by clouds and a screen of mist. Shadowy and indistinct, it is a fogged-up window—a windowpane covered with a layer of dust. Shanghai has as many rumors as *longtang*: too many to be counted, too many to be told.

There is something infectious about gossip; it can transform an official biography into a collection of dubious tales, so that truth becomes indistinguishable from gossip. In the world of rumor, fact cannot be separated from fiction; there is truth within lies, and lies within the truth. That gossip should put on an absurd face is unavoidable; this absurdity is the incredulity born of girlish inexperience, and is at least in part an illusion. In places like the *longtang*, it travels from back door to back door, and in the blink of an eye the whole world knows all. Gossip is like the silent electrical waves crisscrossing in the air above the city, like formless clouds that enshroud the whole city, slowly brewing into a shower, intermixing right and wrong. The rain comes down not in a torrent but as a hazy springtime drizzle. Although not violent, it drenches the air with an inescapable humidity. Never underestimate these rumors: soft and fine as these raindrops may be, you will never struggle free of them.

Every *longtang* in Shanghai is steeped in an atmosphere of gossip, where right and wrong get twisted and confused. In the elegant apartment-style *longtang* on the west side of town, this atmosphere is free of clouds, refreshing and transparent as a bright autumn day. Moving down among the modern-style *longtang* neighborhoods, the atmosphere becomes a bit more turgid and turbulent, blowing to and fro like the wind. Lower down still is the fractious atmosphere of the old-style *longtang* neighborhoods with the stone gates. Here the wind has died, replaced by the vapor of a humid day. By the time one gets to where the slum-dwellers live, all is enveloped in mist—not the roseate mists of dawn, but the thick fog that comes before a torrential downpour, when you cannot see your hand in front of your face.

But regardless of the type of *longtang*, this atmosphere penetrates everywhere. You could say that it is the *genius loci* of Shanghai's alleys. If the *longtang* of Shanghai could speak, they would undoubtedly speak in rumors. They are the thoughts of Shanghai's *longtang*, disseminating themselves through day and night. If the *longtang* of Shanghai could dream, that dream would be gossip.

Gossip is base. With this vulgar heart, it cannot help wallowing in self-degradation. It is like sewer water, used, contaminated. There is nothing aboveboard about it, nothing straight and narrow; it can only whisper secrets behind people's backs. It feels no sense of responsibility, never takes the blame for the outcome—whatever that outcome may be. Because of this, gossip has learned to do as it pleases, running wild like a flood out of control. It never bothers to think things over—and no one ever bothers to think *it* over. It is a bit like verbal garbage, but then again one can occasionally find small treasures in the garbage. Gossip is made up of fragments discarded from serious conversations, like the shriveled outer leaves of vegetables, or grains of sand in a bag of rice. These bits and pieces have faces that are not quite decent; always up to something, they are spoiled merchandise. They are actually made from the crudest materials. However, even the girls in Shanghai's west-end apartments feel compelled to stockpile some of this lowly stuff, because buried deep inside this shamefully base material is where one can find a few genuine articles. These articles lie outside the parameters of what is dignified; their nature is such that no one dares speak of them aloud—and so they are taken and molded into gossip.

If gossip has a positive side, it is the part of it that is genuine. The genuine, however, has a false appearance; this is what is known as "making truth out of falsehood, fact from fiction"—it is always dishing itself up in a new form, making a feint to the east while attacking from the west. This truth is what gives you the courage to go out into the world and not fear losing face, or the courage to become a ghost—to go against prevailing opinions. But there is a kind of sorrow that comes with this courage—the sorrow that comes from being thwarted, from being kept from doing what one wishes. However, there is a certain vital energy in this sorrow, because even in the midst of it one's heart surges with high-flying ambition; in fact, it is because of these surging ambitions that one feels such bafflement and loss. This sorrow is not refined like Tang dynasty poetry and Song dynasty lyrics, but belongs to the world of vulgar grievances aired out in the streets. One can feel the weight of this sorrow as it sinks to the bottom. It has nothing of the airy-fairy—the wind, flowers, snow, and the moon dancing on the water—it is the sediment that accumulates at the bottom. Gossip always sinks to the lowest place. There is no need to go looking for it, it is already there—and it will always be there. It cannot be purified by fire or washed clean with water. It has the tenacity for holding onto life that keeps the muscles intact when the bones are shattered, that enables one to swallow the teeth broken in one's mouth—a brazen-faced tenacity.

Gossip cannot help but be swashbuckling and sensational. It travels in the company of monsters and goblins; rising with the wind, its elusive tail can never be caught. Only in gossip can the true heart of this city be found. No matter how gorgeous and splendid the city may look on the outside, its heart is vulgar. That heart is born of gossip, and gossip is born of the Shanghai *longtang*. Magnificent tales of the Far East can be heard all over this Paris of the Orient; but peel away the outer shell and you will discover that gossip lies at its core. Like the center of a pearl—which is actually a rough grain of sand—coarse sand is the material of which gossip is made.

Gossip always muddles the senses. Starting with inconsequential things, it winds up trying to rewrite history. Like woodworms, it slowly chews up the books and records, eating away magnificent buildings like an army of termites. Its methods are chaotic, without rhyme, reason, or logic. It goes wherever it wants, swaggering like a hooligan, and wastes no time on long-winded theories, nor does it go into too much detail. It simply spreads across the city, launching surprise attacks; by the time you turn around to see what sneaked up on you from behind, it has already gone without a trace. It leaves in its wake a chain of injustices with no one to take the blame and a string of scores with no one to settle with. It makes no big, sudden movements but quietly works away without stopping. In the end, "many a little makes a lot," and trickling water flows into a great river. This is what is meant by the saying, "Rumors rise in swarms"; they indeed drone and buzz like a nest of hornets. A bit contemptible, maybe, but they are also conscientious. They pick up discarded matchsticks to make a fire. If they see a lone piece of thread on the floor, they will take it up and begin to sew. Though always making trouble, they are nevertheless earnest and sincere.

Gossip is never cynical; even if the thing in question is nothing but empty rumors, the utmost care is still put into their creation. Baseless and unreliable as these rumors may be, they are not without a certain warmth of feeling. They mind their own business: whatever others may say, they will stick to their version—to them even settled opinions are taken under advisement. It is not that gossip takes a different political view, but that it does not take *any* political view; in fact, it lacks the most basic knowledge about politics. Always going by back roads and entering through side doors, it does not stand in opposition to society—it forms its own society. As far as society is concerned, these are small and inconsequential things, like twigs and knots on a tree. And precisely because society never takes these things seriously, they are able to maneuver unseen through the darkness and have their way. Combined together, they constitute a power that should not be underestimated, in the way that a butterfly beating its wings here can cause a hurricane in a faraway place.

Rumors deviate from traditional moral codes but never claim to be antifeudal. Like a true bum, they chip away at the foundations of public decency. They wouldn't hesitate to pull the emperor down off his horse—not in order to install a new republic, but merely as an act of defiance. Despising revolutionaries and counterrevolutionaries alike, they themselves are consistently slighted and deserted by both sides. Indeed, there is not a presentable one in the whole lot—if there were, they could be promoted to the level of "public opinion," where they could advance into the open. Instead, they have to be content with making secret maneuvers under the cover of darkness. They care not that they are mere whispers in people's ears; they'll make their home wherever their wanderings take them, having no conception of what it means to build an enterprise. These are creatures without ambition, holding out no hopes; in fact, they do not even have the ability to think. All they have is the natural capacity to cause trouble and make mischief; they grow and reproduce in complete ignorance. They reproduce at quite startling rates, hatching all at once like spawn. Their methods of reproduction are also varied; sometimes linear, like a chain of interlocking rings, at other times concentric, like a suite of riddles. They spread through the city air like a pack of down-at-the-heel vagrants. But the truth is, gossip is one of the things that make this city so romantic.

What makes gossip romantic is its unbridled imagination. With the imagination completely free from all fetters, gossip can leap through the dragon's gate and squeeze through the dog's den. No one is better at making up stories, telling lies, and wagging its tongue than gossip. It also has boundless energy—nothing can kill it dead. Wildfires burn but, come spring, the grass will grow again. Like the lowliest of seeds, gossip is carried by the wind to sprout and bloom in between rocks. It works its way into every crack, even getting behind the heavy curtains of ladies' boudoirs, where it floats amid the embroidery needles in the young mistress's pincushions; and lingers among the tear-stained pages of those heart-wrenching novels the schoolgirl reads in her spare time. As the clock on the table ticks, gossip stretches itself out, even filling the basin where milady washes her rouge away. It thrives in the most secret of places: a clandestine atmosphere is particularly beneficial to its development.

The *longtang* of Shanghai are very good at protecting their privacy, allowing gossip to prosper and proliferate. Deep in the night, after everyone has turned out their lights, there is a narrow patch of light peeking out through the crack under someone's door—that is gossip. The pair of embroidered shoes in the moonlight beside the bed—that too is gossip. When the old *amah*, carrying her box of toiletries, says she is going out to comb her hair, she is actually off to spread gossip. The clatter of young wives shuffling mahjong tiles—that is the sound of gossip. Sparrows hopping around deserted courtyards on winter afternoons chirp about gossip. The word "self" is embedded into gossip; and within this word "self" there is an unmentionable pain. This bottled-up pain is different from what the Tang emperor felt at the death of Yang Guifei or the King of Chu for his beloved concubine. It is not the kind of grand and heroic suffering that moves heaven and earth, but base and lowly, like pebbles and dirt, or the tentacles of ivy creeping stealthily out of bounds.

The *longtang* of Shanghai are incapable of harboring the kind of suffering that inspires legends. The pain is broken up and evenly allocated throughout the city, so that each person ends up with a small share. Even when they suffer deep sorrow, its inhabitants keep it down inside their bellies; they do not put it on stage for people to admire, nor do they make it into lyrics to be sung by others. Only they themselves know where it comes from and whither it goes. They alone carry its burden. This is also where the word "self" comes into play, and herein, incidentally, lies the true meaning of sorrow. Therefore we can say that gossip is painful; even if the pain does not arise from proper causes, it is still excruciating. The pain is suffered individually, eliciting no sympathy—a lonely pain. This is also what is moving about gossip. The moment that gossip is born is actually the moment that people are trying their hardest to conduct themselves properly. The people in Shanghai's *longtang* neighborhoods conduct themselves with the utmost attention and care; all their energy is directed to the way they carry themselves. Their eyes are focused exclusively on themselves, and they are never distracted by their surroundings. They don't want to create a place for themselves in history: they want to create themselves. Without being ambitious, they expend every ounce of what strength they have. This strength, too, is evenly allocated. Everyone has his fair share.

The Young Lady's Bedchamber

In the *longtang* apartments of Shanghai, the young lady's bedchamber is usually located in one of the side rooms, or in the *tingzijian*, the tiny room off the landing. But no matter where her bedroom is, its window is never directly exposed to the sun and the flowery curtains are always drawn. When they are pulled open, you can look straight through to the front living room of the apartment in the rear; you may even see the couple who live there, along with the oleander in their courtyard. This vestal bedchamber is far from cloistered. Living in the adjacent *tingzijian* is perhaps an intern working at a foreign firm, an unemployed college graduate, or maybe even the latest dancing girl on the Shanghai nightclub scene.

The back alleys are the setting for all kinds of unsavory goings-on. The salty language of the old *amah* is heard along with the rickshaw coolie's dirty slang. The shady buddies of the college graduate next door and the dancer's girlfriends pass through regularly. In the middle of the night, listening to the creak of back doors opening and closing, you can imagine all kinds of scandals. Take, for instance, the couple in the living room across the way: who can say for sure that they are husband and wife? They may very well be a pair of illicit lovers on the brink of discovery; a few days later, a knock comes at the door, and all the neighbors will hear the sound of shattering glass and furniture being broken. The worst thing that can happen is to have a rich family at the far end of the *longtang* with a daughter attending Zhongxi Middle School or one of the other prestigious girls' schools in the city. Their private luxury car will always be coming or going through the big black gate, and whenever they have a Christmas or birthday party, piano music will ring out. The young lady's bedroom there will be completely different from all the others, inevitably giving rise to feelings of resentment and desire. One could say that resentment and desire are the root of all evil in a young lady's world. What would be the fate of a girl—as pure and delicate as a flower pistil—whose bedchamber is situated in such a place of chaos, noise, and confusion?

However, the shadows cast by the moonlight on the flowery curtains are always soft and beautiful. On cloudless nights, the moon illuminates the entire room, not with daylight's intense glare, but seemingly through a veil, bathing the room with a gentle radiance. The lilies on the wallpaper and the orchids embroidered on the comforter seem to have been drawn with a fine brush, every line and stroke clear and distinct. The faint sounds of a phonograph playing—what is it?—Zhou Xuan's "Song of the Four Seasons" make their way into the room. No matter how noisy and chaotic it may be outside, the young lady's bedchamber is always quiet. The incense, half burned, leaves a pile of ash in the dish. Only six of the twelve chimes of the clock are heard, for the lady has fallen asleep.

Hers is a silent dream. Behind the cavernous windows of the back *longtang* apartments, who else could possibly aspire to these perfectly pure dreams? They are like clouds drifting over the hectic turmoil below, trance-like and short-lived, yet blissfully ignorant that they are destined to be short-lived, occurring night after night. The stitches in the embroidery frame, the scribbles in the margins of a book—line after line, fine and closely spaced—are the language of the heart. The language of the heart is also silent, steeped in moonlight, eye-catching and yet reticent, full of emotions it cannot even begin to articulate.

The moon begins to descend in the western night sky. The darkest moment comes just before the sunlight creeps up onto the horizon. Then, as the first rays of the morning begin to light up the sky, the dream and the language of the heart vanish, like wild geese in flight disappearing over the horizon without a trace. This was but a flash of gentle activity, soft as water in a night where silence reigns supreme, like a single cloud floating above the moiling world. In the morning, the flowery curtains are drawn halfway to reveal an air of anticipation—as if the window had been biding its time the whole night through. The glass of the windowpane is free from even the slightest smudge. And, although there is not a soul in the apartment, the room is filled with anticipation, a nameless, rootless anticipation that expects to be disappointed. Even so, it is free of resentment or regret. During the bustle of the morning, with everyone as impatient as the crowing rooster, this is the only thing that sits helpless, defenseless, passive, and undemanding, yet still fervent with hope. This hope is a flower that bears no fruit, just as everything else is fruit without flowers. This is the only pristine and incorruptible corner in all the *longtang* of Shanghai.

On the rooftops are young pigeons; in the bedchambers are the young girls' hearts. The last rays of the westerly sun that come through the window seem to be singing an elegy, pouring their hearts out in a final display of emotion. On an afternoon bristling with activity, this is the only bit of helplessness. There is something ancient about this helplessness, reminiscent of classical poetry or a plucked zither—but who is there to listen? It cannot even measure up to a floating cloud. Clouds can transform into wind and rain, whereas this can only turn into mist, to be blown away on the wind, leaving no trace behind. Sadly, the vestal bedchamber in the Shanghai *longtang* will sometimes turn into a mirage, a resplendent earthly paradise that vanishes in one fleeting moment.

This vestal bedchamber has actually undergone a mutation. Drawing whatever it can from its environment, it is always eager to learn, but follows no fixed rules. It builds itself up from scratch on the assumption that everything is up for grabs. Here old Chinese parables like *Tales of Virtuous Women* coexist with Hollywood romances; high-heeled shoes are worn under a *cheongsam* of indigo blue. Elegant verses—"Evening falls over the Xunyang River as I see off my guest, Maple leaves and bamboo reeds rustle in the autumn wind" and such like—are intoned alongside popular song lyrics like "Back when we were young." Confucian homilies on the segregation of the sexes are discussed in the same breath as women's liberation. One exalts Ibsen's Nora as a spiritual leader for having the courage to leave home while deep down inside idolizing Oriole in *The Western Wing,* who finds a strong man she can depend on for the rest of her life.

It is not that there are no rules here, just that these rules are simply too complicated to sort out. In the end, everything is blended together in the bedchamber. You cannot lay a charge of deliberate fraudulence, because the heart remains true and is totally in earnest. Like the farmer who rises with the sun and returns from the fields at dusk, each young lady has also worked diligently on the management of her bedchamber. It is not always easy to distinguish the well-bred ones from the uncouth, or those who are decent from their opposite. The rich girl behind the big black gate at the rear of the *longtang* and the dancing girl in the *tingzijian* next door serve equally as models: sedate and dignified, flirtatious and sensual—it's up to them to choose between these. Their mothers hope that they will find a good husband, their male teachers challenge them to declare their independence, and their foreign priests incite them to follow the Lord. The fine clothes in the store window call out to them, the famous stars on the silver screen call out to them, even the heroines of their favorite novels call out to them. Their bodies may be sitting in the bedchamber, but their hearts and minds are somewhere else. Countless roads lie before them, but in the end all rivers flow into the sea. With Western dress sizes on their lips, they are thinking about fabrics for their next *cheongsam*. Their hearts are wild; they desire to travel the world, but they couldn't be more timid and hesitant, always needing the maidservant to see them off and pick them up when they go to the late movie. On their way to and from school, they cross the street only in large groups. They are so bashful they dare not raise their head in the presence of a stranger. The dirty banter of the streetside bum is enough to reduce them to tears. And so you see, it is a bit of a contradiction. In the final analysis, they have only themselves to blame for the trouble they get into.

The vestal bedchamber could not be more irksome than in the afternoon. During the spring and summer the windows are open and, all at once, the cries of cicadas screeching in the parasol trees, the hubbub of the passing trolley cars, the clapping of the sweets peddler, and the songs on the neighbor's phonograph force their way inside, disrupting your peace of mind. Most annoying of all are the faint and trivial sounds that are barely noticeable. You cannot tell what they are or where they come from—incessant, insistent, ambiguous, and shady. You can neither catch hold of them nor chase them away. These curious sounds fill up your heart, making these idle afternoons doubly tedious.

In autumn and winter the haze can linger for days on end. The haze of the Jiangnan region around the lower Yangtze valley has a weight to it; it presses down upon your heart. But how quiet it is—even a sigh is gulped down and comes back out as mist. The fire in the charcoal brazier, originally placed there to drive away the mist, flickers as it is choked by the thickness of the enshrouding haze. The alternations of dark and light, warmth and cold in these afternoons unite to perturb you. When you awaken, they assault your eyes and ears. They plague your dreams as you sleep. When you are at your needlework, they pull at your needles and thread, and as you read, they play with the sentences on the page. If two of you are sitting together chatting, they twist and tug at your words.

Afternoon comes midway through the day, when all the daily anticipations and hopes are approaching an end, and with that come impatience and despondency. Even hope is a struggling kind of hope. This is the *Götterdammerung* of the bedchamber, when the heart has grown old before life has even begun. Just thinking of this, your heart is rent asunder. But you mustn't tell a soul—even if you did, there would be no way to explain.

It would be cruel to look too closely at the young lady's bedchamber in the Shanghai *longtang.* Oleanders grow in other families' courtyards and pink clouds fill their sky; outside her window is a lonely parasol tree. A sea of neon lights dyes the Shanghai skyline a crimson hue, while a single lamp burns in her room. The ticking clock seems to be counting away the years; the years are good, but they won't stand up to being counted. The afternoons are like an autumn filled with impending catastrophes. There is a panicky kind of energy, like that of a man so hungry he no longer cares what he eats. This leads to ill-considered actions, where one fails to mind the consequences, like a moth throwing itself into the flame without the slightest regret. And so the afternoons lay traps—the more enticing, the more dangerous. The brilliance of the afternoon always has something ominous looming over it, as if it is playing some kind of trick. Tantalized by the wind and the shadows, you let your defenses down. On the phonograph, Zhou Xuan sings her "Song of the Four Seasons," counting out all the beauties between spring and winter to poison and bewitch your mind—because only the nice things are mentioned. The pigeons are let loose to soar over the rooftops, but what has actually been released is the heart of the vestal bedchamber. Soaring high and looking down into the window with the flowery curtains, it seems to be reciting the ancient verses: "Easier to part than to reunite" and "It is cold and lonely in high places."

The bedchamber in a Shanghai *longtang* is a place where anything can happen, where even melancholy is noisy and clamorous. When it drizzles, raindrops write the word "melancholy" on the window. The mist in the back *longtang* is melancholic in an ambiguous way—it unaccountably hastens people along. It nibbles away at the patience she needs to be a daughter, eats away at the fortitude she must have to conduct herself as a woman. It tells her that the arrow is on the bowstring, about to fly, that the gold pin is in the box, and all is ready. Every day is more difficult to endure than the last, but, on looking back, one rues the shortness of the time. Consequently, one is at a complete loss. The young lady's bedchamber embodies the naiveté of the Shanghai *longtang,* passing in a single night's time from being young and innocent to being worldly and wise, in a never-ending cycle, one generation after another. The vestal bedchamber is but a mirage thrown up by the Shanghai *longtang*. When the clouds open to reveal the rising sun, it turns to smoke and mist. The curtain rises and falls, one act follows another, into eternity.

Pigeons

Pigeons are the spirit of this city. Every morning see just how many pigeons soar into the sky over the billowing sea of endless rooftops! They are the only living beings that can look down upon this city. Who can observe this city more clearly and distinctly than they? They are witnesses to unsolved mysteries without number. How many secrets they must hold in their eyes! As they soar above the city with its countless buildings, they gather up the scenes in the windows—these, though only scenes from everyday life, by their sheer mass pile up into a soul-stirring vista. Actually the pigeons are the only ones who can appreciate the true essence of this city. By dint of leaving early and returning late every day, they learn much. On top of this, they all have phenomenal memories and never forget what they see—otherwise how can you explain their ability always to find their way? We cannot ever know just what symbols and landmarks they use to navigate their way through the city. They seem to be as familiar with every dark corner of this city as with the patterned feathers on their own wings. The highest point in the city that we spoke of a little while ago actually refers to their vantage point. Even when human beings climb to the highest summit, our point of view is still no match for that of the pigeons. For in two-legged beasts like us, which cannot move about freely, our hearts too are encumbered—making our horizons so narrow that it is almost pathetic. We live among our own kind and always see the same things, incapable of discerning anything new. Our hearts are empty of curiosity, as if everything is already understood. That is because we fail to see anything that is out of the ordinary. Pigeons are different. Every evening they return home loaded with new knowledge. Imagine how many pairs of eyes like this there are soaring in the sky above the city!

Street scenes are a common sight, replaying day in and day out. They are in part performances, and are therefore formulaic. Though iridescent with color and arresting to the eye, they follow conventional patterns. Everyone goes about on the street wearing a mask, as if attending an outdoor party. Their words and laughter are the politenesses exchanged at a dinner party; their behavior cannot even qualify as conventional, it is but the shell that surrounds convention.

The scenes in the *longtang* neighborhoods are the only real scenes. They are the complete opposite of the street scenes. On the outside they all appear to be the same: the rows of apartment buildings look identical—you can barely tell them apart; like street scenes they seem to be following the same conventional pattern. Look inside, however, and you will discover a world of infinite variety. Each and every one is different, leaving you groping about for the door. Neighbors divided by a single wall may as well be mountains apart; what goes on next door may as well be happening a million miles away. Who can ever know? The world of the *longtang* is rife with unsolved mysteries, one coming hard on the heels of another. These rumors are actually nothing but bluff and bluster; yet serious news does not count—in the end you are still left groping around in the dark. In the *longtang* of Shanghai everyone claims that his version is right and there is never room for arbitration. Even the truth is shrouded in darkness, so rumor becomes an even muddier affair. Thus from the outside the *longtang* appear orderly, but on the inside they are in complete chaos. The people on the other side of the windows—the protagonists—are the most confused of all; as time goes on they grow numb and unfeeling—they may as well be blind.

The only clear-seeing eyes belong to the flying creatures that pierce the clouds and penetrate the mist: there is no place they cannot go—they are truly free! Their freedom taunts men's hearts. Passing over the street scenes as familiar sights, their sharp eyes focus on the most unusual occurrences. Their vision has the ability to distinguish truth from falsehood—they are masters at capturing meaning. Their senses are extraordinarily acute. Unconstrained by outmoded customs and habits, they are nature's sole offspring in the city. They circle above the dense rooftops as if circling over the rubble of ancient ruins, the last survivors of a catastrophe. Wheeling back and forth in the sky, their flight is marked with a trace of desperation, and so the sights and colors that enter into their eyes cannot but take on a gloomy tint.

It should be noted that there is another creature in the skies of this city—the sparrow. Sparrows, however, are always fawning obsequiously. They never fly high, but aim only to perch on someone's balcony or land in someone's courtyard, pecking at the crumbs that have fallen into the cracks in the cement—they abase themselves to the lowest level. Although they are frequent visitors to the *longtang* neighborhoods, they are never welcome. They let people chase them hither and yon and have no self-respect. They are without wisdom, the most vulgar of the birds. Their powers of observation are even less than ours, because their innate ability is inferior and they lack the benefits of human civilization. One cannot mention them in the same breath as pigeons: pigeons are animals of the spirit, while sparrows are animals of the flesh. Their breed is especially suited to living in the back alleys of Shanghai—the *longtang* are their natural home. Petty and frivolous, they are always entangled in gossip. A part of the close atmosphere that overhangs the alleys, they foster vulgarity and baseness here.

Pigeons, by contrast, never linger around the alleys; you will never find them perched on the balconies and windowsills or in the courtyards, trying to ingratiate themselves. They always rise high, the city rooftops at their feet. Flapping their wings as they soar through the sky, they carry with them an expression of disdain. Haughty, but they are not unfeeling—otherwise why would they brave the long flight home? They are humanity's true friends, not the kind that stick around just to share the loot; their friendship is based on understanding, sympathy, compassion, and love. If you have seen that small red cloth tied to a bamboo stick fluttering in the wind at dusk—the beacon that brings the pigeons home—you would understand. The agreement implied in it is almost childlike. The pigeons have compassion enough for all the secrets they carry deep in their hearts, and their trustworthiness is equal to their compassion. Flocks of pigeons are the most sublime displays of comradeship in this city, and they also make for one of the most beautiful scenes in the Shanghai *longtang*. The rooftop coops people build to shelter them, just so they can see them off in the morning and welcome them back in the evening, represent the affection of the city's inhabitants—a soft spot in this city's heart.

Nothing in the city—its most obscure crimes and punishments, comedies and tragedies—can escape their eyes. When a flock of startled pigeons suddenly takes to the air and circles above the city, that is the moment crimes are being committed and punishments meted out, and comedies and tragedies are being enacted. At a hurried glance, they look like rain clouds forming abruptly in the sky, or spots in the sun. Ghastly scenes are being played out in the ravines of this concrete city. One sees them or not, as the case may be, but those scenes cannot escape the pigeons. The shock of these sights and sounds fills their eyes, which have a look of sadness too deep for tears. Under the sky, this concrete city, created from the maze of crisscrossing *longtang*, is like an abyss in which people struggle for survival like an army of ants. The dust, dancing through the air, becomes the lord of heaven and earth. Then there are those trivial sounds and noises that fill every corner of the city—they too are the lords of heaven and earth. Suddenly, a flock of pigeons slices through the air with their chill whistles, like the sound of splitting silk, the only wakeful sound in a drowsy universe nodding off to sleep.

Occasionally another group of flying objects will emerge from the city's rooftops to keep the pigeons company—these are kites. They often get caught on the netlike electrical wires, sometimes breaking their wings from the impact, and end up dangling from the edges of the rooftops and electric poles, whence they stare helplessly at the flocks of pigeons. Kites are created in the image of pigeons, but in the end they cannot compare even with sparrows; even so, humanity invests them with all its naïve aspirations. The hands of children set them in flight, as do the hands of vagabonds, who are, after all, children who never grew up. String in hand, the children and vagabonds run with all their might, trying to send their kites up into the heavens. But, predictably, they meet an early demise on their way up. Only a sacred few actually make it up into the sky. What ecstasy when one finally weasels its way into a flock of pigeons and is able to soar with them!

On the day of the Tomb-Sweeping Festival, the tattered remains of kites whipped by wind and rain present the spectacle of a love suicide on the rooftops. Gradually they disintegrate into the dirt, giving sustenance to a few weak strands of green bristle grass. Sometimes, as kites are ascending, they will break free of their strings and slowly become a small black dot in the sky before disappearing. Theirs is a grand escape, backed by the resolution to die in a worthy cause.

Only pigeons are faithful to humans until death; they fly through the skies as if determined to bring comfort and solace to this city—this city like a dried-up ocean, where the buildings are ships stranded on a forest of coral reefs. How many people are suffering here! How could they simply abandon them and leave? In this godless city, pigeons are the closest thing to a god. But they are a god that no one believes in—they alone understand their sacred signs—all we know is that no matter how far away they may fly, they always brave the long flight home. Men seem to have an eternal soft spot for pigeons deep in their hearts, especially those people living in rooftop *tingzijian*, where pigeons bound for their own nests fly past their dormer windows. Although there are all kinds of temples and churches in this city, temples are temples, churches are churches—the people of this city belong to the alleys. Seen from above, people in the alleys look like little dots drifting on the billows; the pigeons' whistles send their gentle warnings, day after day, night after night, eternally sounding out through the sky.

Presently, the sun sprays out over the unbroken expanse of rooftop tiles, bathing everything in golden light. The pigeons leave their nests, their wings showing white against the sky. The tall buildings resemble buoys floating on the ocean's surface. The city becomes animated with movement and activity, building up into the quiet roar of the sea. The dust also begins to stir restlessly in a hazy cloud. Germs of events quickly brew into causes and conclusions; already intense feelings are running rampant. As densely packed windows and doors are opened and last night's stale air rushes out and intermingles, the sunlight becomes turbid, the sky darkens, and the dance of the dust begins to slow. Something too tangled to unravel begins to grow in the air, choking off vitality and passion. The freshness of morning turns into a depressing gloom, inward excitement is quelled, but all those small beginnings keep on breeding all kinds of consequences—what you sow you shall reap. The sun in the sky traverses its usual path; light and shadow move slowly. All signs of stirring have settled, along with the dust, into their normal state, the way they do day after day, year after year. Every trace of romance has been silenced. The heavens hang high aloft and the clouds are pale as the last flock of pigeons disappears into the distance.

Wang Qiyao

Wang Qiyao is the typical daughter of the Shanghai *longtang.* Every morning, when the back door squeaks open, that's Wang Qiyao scurrying out with her book bag embroidered with flowers. In the afternoon, when the phonograph plays next door, that's Wang Qiyao humming along with "Song of the Four Seasons." Those girls rushing off to the theater, that's a whole group of Wang Qiyaos going to see Vivien Leigh in *Gone With the Wind.* Running off to the photo studio is a pair of Wang Qiyaos, best friends on their way to have their portrait taken. Sitting in virtually every side room and *tingzijian* is a Wang Qiyao. In the dimly lit living room of every Wang Qiyao's house there is almost always a set or two of mahogany furniture. The sun draws circles on the windowsill but refuses to come in. There is a three-mirrored vanity in her bedchamber. The powder of her rouge container always looks a bit damp and sticky in its jar, while the container of hair oil has dried up. The copper lock on her camphor chest shines from repeated opening and closing. Whether the radio is tuned to Suzhou *pingtan* storytelling, Shaoxing opera, or stock market updates, the reception is poor and the broadcast is always accompanied by a buzzing hiss. Wang Qiyao's *amah* sometimes sleeps in the small triangular room under the stairs, which is just large enough for a bed. The *amah* has to do everything—her duties extend even to emptying out the dirty water after the mistress has washed her feet. The family orders the *amah* around as if they are trying to get every bit of their money's worth out of her. Yet, busy as she is from morning until night, she still has time to go out and spread gossip about her employer—and carry on a clandestine affair with the neighbor's chauffeur.

Fathers of girls like Wang Qiyao always end up beaten into submission after years of being henpecked by their wives. This sets an example for Wang Qiyao of what it means to respect a woman. On these Shanghai mornings, that's Wang Qiyao's father sitting in the trolley car on his way to work; in the afternoons, that's Wang Qiyao's mother sitting in the rickshaw on her way to buy material for her new *cheongsam*. Every night, beneath the floor of Wang Qiyao's apartment, mice scurry to and fro; in order to eliminate the mice, they bring home a cat, and so the apartment takes on a faint stench of cat piss. Wang Qiyao, usually the oldest child, has become her mother's closest friend while still quite young. Mother and daughter have their clothes made by the same tailor and always go off together to call on friends and relatives. Girls like her always listen to their mothers' complaints about the incorrigible nature of man—using their own fathers as object lessons.

Wang Qiyao is the typical girl in waiting. The girls that the interns working at Western-style shops ogle surreptitiously—they are all Wang Qiyaos. On the hot summer days when clothing is brought out to be aired, Wang Qiyao stares at her mother's trousseau chest and fantasizes about her own dowry. In the display window of the photo studio, the lady in the floor-length wedding gown is Wang Qiyao just before her marriage. Wang Qiyaos are always stunningly beautiful. They wear indigo blue *cheongsams* that set off their figure and a bang of black hair shyly concealing their eyes, which seem nevertheless to speak. Wang Qiyaos always follow the mainstream, neither falling behind nor rushing ahead—they are modernity in numbers. They follow what is trendy the same way they would follow a recipe: with blind faith, never expressing opinions or asking questions. The fashion trends in Shanghai rely completely upon Wang Qiyaos. But they are incapable of setting things into motion—that is not their responsibility. They lack creativity, because they are in want of an independent personality; but they are diligent, honest, loyal, and devoted, always blindly following suit. Uncomplaining, they carry the spirit of the times on their backs—you could even say that they are this city's proclamation. And whenever a star is born in this city, whether on the stage or on the screen, they all become ardent fans and admirers. They are the captive readers of romance novels serialized in the newspaper supplements. The intrepid among them write letters to authors and film stars, but all they are really hoping for is an autograph. In the world of fashion, they are the foundation.

There does not exist a single Wang Qiyao who isn't sentimental, fashionably sentimental—the kind of sentimentalism that is acquired. Dried leaves are kept in the pages of their books, dead butterflies in their rouge boxes. They may cry, but even their tears follow the mainstream. Their sentimentality is acted out before it comes into existence, the display preceding the feelings. You cannot say that it is completely artificial, only that the order is backward—it is something real that has been artificially produced. Everything in this city has a copy, and everything has someone who leads the way. Wang Qiyao's eyes are a bit dull, as if enshrouded in shadow—it is the shadow of sentimentalism. These Wang Qiyaos often appear sad, but this sadness makes them even more enchanting. When they eat, their appetite is no bigger than a cat's, and when they walk they take feline steps. Their skin is so fair that it seems transparent; you can even see their pale blue veins. In summer every one of them gets sick from the heat; in winter they can never stay warm enough under their quilted blankets. They need to take traditional Chinese medicine to strengthen the vital fluids and nourish the blood—the smell of medicinal brew fills the air around them. Between the media and the stage, there are men working behind the scenes to create a fashion perfectly suited to Wang Qiyao, a fashion that moreover seems to anticipate Wang Qiyao's every need and desire.

Between the Wang Qiyaos is a sisterly love, sometimes strong enough to last a lifetime. Whenever they get together, they regress back to the days before they were married. They are symbols to each other of that innocent period in their lives, living monuments or witnesses on whom to rely when recalling lost times. Many things in their lives are replaceable, but this sisterly love remains until death. Sisterly love is a strange thing indeed: it is not the kind of love that endures through thick and thin and inspires one to help a friend when she is down—it recognizes no attachments, no responsibilities. Rootless and unfettered, it offers no security. You cannot really say that these girls keep each other as confidantes—after all, just how many secrets do women store up in their hearts? Most often they are there to keep one another company, but not in any intimate way—they simply keep each other company on the way to and from school, sporting the same hairstyle, wearing identical shoes and socks, and walking hand-in-hand like lovers. If you should ever see a pair of young girls like this on the street, don't ever mistake them for twins. It's simply sisterly love—Wang Qiyao style.

They depend so much on each other, they treat each other with such exaggerated affection, and their expressions are so earnest that you can't help but take their relationship seriously. But when they keep one another company, all they are doing is making loneliness lonelier and helplessness even more helpless, because neither is in a position to do anything for the other. Divested of utilitarian motives, their sisterly love is all the more pure. Every Wang Qiyao is accompanied by another; some are classmates, some neighbors, and others cousins. This relationship is one of the few social activities in their chaste, simple lives. They have too few opportunities for social interaction and so when an opportunity arises they cannot help putting everything they have into it—and the result is sisterly love. The Wang Qiyaos of the world all place great importance on friendship; beneath a facade that chases after the latest fashions there is devotion and sincerity—albeit a somewhat detached sincerity. When one Wang Qiyao walks down the aisle, another Wang Qiyao is her maid of honor; it is a way of paying tribute to her, a way of seeing her off into her new life. The expression on the face of the maid of honor shows that she is yielding the spotlight to the bride. Her dress is a shade less bright, the style is from last year, she intentionally applies less rouge to her face than usual—everything speaks of her willingness to lower her banner. This attitude of heroic self-sacrifice is sisterly love.

Behind every doorway in the Shanghai *longtang* a Wang Qiyao is studying, embroidering, whispering secrets to her sisters, or throwing a teary-eyed tantrum at her parents. The *longtang* neighborhoods of Shanghai are filled with a girlish spirit—the name of this spirit is Wang Qiyao. There is something elegant about this spirit, not haughty, in fact quite approachable, even adorable. It is modest and gentle, and, though a little affected, the affectation arises from an eagerness to please, which makes it welcome to most. Neither large-hearted nor high-minded—but then again it does not aspire to an epic (charm and sweetness are closer to what people want, anyhow)—it is a spirit that belongs to everyday life. It has the frame of mind, "I'll return a favor with a favor, but I won't take disrespect lightly." This may be lacking in its vision, but it is always reasonable; it is a bit petty, perhaps, but pettiness is always more fun than moral rectitude. Such a spirit knows all about manipulation, which can also be fun—human nature needs a little embellishment. It cannot help but be vulgar, but in a way that has been rinsed clean by civilization. Its vanity rests upon a pragmatic foundation.

The moonbeam writes Wang Qiyao's name on the *longtang* walls; the pink leaves of the oleander spell out Wang Qiyao as they fall to the ground; the lamplight behind the screened window also inscribes her name; now and again a soft voice whispers in Shanghai dialect with a Suzhou inflection, and what it utters is the name of Wang Qiyao. When the peddler of osmanthus porridge sounds his clapper to attract customers, he seems to be counting off the hours of the night for Wang Qiyao. The young writer in the third-floor *tingzijian*, having finished his take-out supper, is busy writing a modernist poem dedicated to Wang Qiyao. The dewdrops on the parasol tree are the traces of Wang Qiyao's tears. By the time the maidservant slips out the back door to meet her lover, Wang Qiyao is lost somewhere faraway in her dream.

If there were no Wang Qiyao, the Shanghai *longtang* would lose all their passion. This passion seems to have been squeezed out from the fissures of everyday life, like the golden dandelions growing out of the cracks in the wall, sneaking out where you least expect them. But this passion also seems to dissolve and spread, like lichens creeping across the wall. It can sustain itself on nothing but wind and dew; this is what is meant by "A single spark can start a prairie fire." However, the process involves tenacious struggle and inconsolable pain. It is because there is passion in the Shanghai *longtang* that there is also pain; as for the name of this pain, it too is called Wang Qiyao. Occasionally one finds in the Shanghai alleys a wall completely covered with a thick carpet of Boston ivy; the ivy, with its old, clinging tentacles, is emblematic of passions that have persisted through time. In persistence is inconsolable pain, on which are inscribed the records of time, the accumulated debris of time as it is pressed down and slowly suffocated. This is the everlasting sorrow of Wang Qiyao.

Chapter 2

The Film Studio

FOUR DECADES THE story spans, and it all began the day she went to the film studio. The day before, Wu Peizhen had agreed to take Wang Qiyao to have a look around the studio. Wu Peizhen was a rather careless girl. Under normal circumstances, she would have suffered from low self-esteem because of her homeliness, but because Peizhen came from a well-to-do family and people always doted on her, she had developed unaffected into an outgoing young lady. What would have been poor self-esteem was replaced by a kind of modesty—modesty ruled by a practical spirit. In her modesty, she tended to exaggerate other people's strengths, place them on a pedestal, and offer them her devotion. Wang Qiyao never had to worry about Wu Peizhen being jealous of her—and she certainly had no reason to be jealous of Wu Peizhen. On the contrary, she even felt a bit bad for Wu Peizhen—because she was so ugly. This compassion predisposed Wang Qiyao to be generous, but naturally this generosity did not extend any further than Wu Peizhen.

Wu Peizhen's carelessness was the function of an uncalculating mind. She appreciated Wang Qiyao's magnanimity and tried even harder to please her as though repaying her kindness. Basking in each other's company, they became the best of friends. But Wang Qiyao's decision to befriend Wu Peizhen meant, in some way, that she was pushing a heavy load onto Wu Peizhen's shoulders. Her beauty highlighted Wu Peizhen's unattractive appearance; her meticulousness highlighted Wu Peizhen's lack of care; her magnanimity highlighted Wu Peizhen's indebtedness. It was a good thing that Wu Peizhen could take it; after all, the weight of everyday living did not rest as heavily on her. This was partly because she had plenty of psychic capital to draw on, but also because she simply did not mind. Things came easy to her and she was willing to bear more than her share. Thus an equilibrium of give-and-take was maintained between the two girls and they grew closer by the day.

Wu Peizhen had a cousin who did lighting at the film studio. Occasionally he would come over to see her. In that khaki uniform of his, with its copper buttons, he came across as a bit flashy. Wu Peizhen really could not have cared less about him; the only reason she kept him around was for Wang Qiyao. The film studio was the stuff of girls' dreams—a place where romance is created, the kind that appears on the silver screen in movies that everyone knows as well as the off-screen type that one hears about in the enchanting gossip and rumors surrounding the lives of film stars. The former is fake but appears real; the latter is real but seems fake. To live in the world of the film studio is to lead a dual life. Girls like Wu Peizhen who had all of their needs taken care of seldom wallowed in dreams; moreover, as the only girl in a house full of boys, she grew up playing boys' games and never learned the social skills and canniness most girls picked up. However, after making friends with Wang Qiyao, she became more thoughtful. She came to see the film studio as a gift that she could offer to Wang Qiyao. She arranged everything carefully, only informing Wang Qiyao after she had already set a date, and was surprised when Wang Qiyao greeted the news with apparent indifference, claiming a prior engagement. This compelled Wu Peizhen to try to change Wang Qiyao's mind by exaggerating the glamour of the film studio, combining stories her cousin bragged about with others from her own imagination. Before long, it was more like Wang Qiyao was doing *her* a favor by going with her. By the time Wang Qiyao finally gave in and agreed to go some other time, Wu Peizhen was acting as if yet another gift that she herself had to be thankful for had been bestowed upon her, and she ecstatically scurried off to find her cousin to change the date.

Wang Qiyao did not, in fact, have any prior engagement, nor was she as reluctant as she appeared; this was simply the way she conducted herself—the more interested she was in something, the more she held back. This was her means of protecting herself—or then again, was it part of a strategy of disarming an antagonist by pretending to set her free? Whatever the reason behind her action, it was impenetrable to Wu Peizhen. On her way to her cousin's place, she was consumed with gratitude for Wang Qiyao; all she could think about was how much face Wang Qiyao had given her by agreeing to the invitation.

The cousin was the son of Wu Peizhen's uncle on her mother's side. This uncle was the black sheep of the family. He had driven a silk shop in Hangzhou into the ground and Wu Peizhen's mother had dreaded his visits because all he ever wanted from her was money or grain. After she gave him some heavy doses of harsh words and turned him away empty-handed several times, he gradually stopped coming around and eventually broke off all relations. Then one day his son had showed up at her door wearing that khaki uniform with copper buttons and carrying two boxes of vegetarian dim sum as if they represented some kind of announcement. Ever since then he would come by once every two months or so and tell them stories about the film studio. Nobody in the house was interested in his stories—nobody, that is, except Wu Peizhen.

Wu Peizhen went to the address in Qijiabing in search of her cousin. All around were thatch-covered shacks surrounded by small unmarked trails that extended in different directions, making it virtually impossible to find one's way. People stared at her. One glance told them that she was an outsider, but just as she was getting ready to ask directions they would immediately look away. She finally found her cousin's place, only to discover that he was not home. The young man who shared the shack with her cousin asked her in. He was wearing a pair of glasses and a set of coarse cotton clothes. Wu Peizhen was a bit shy and waited outside. This naturally drew more curious gazes. It was not until dusk that her cousin finally staggered in with a greasy paper bag holding a pig's head or some other cheap meat he had bought over at the butcher's shop.

By the time Wu Peizhen got home, her family was already at the dinner table and she had to fib about where she had been. But she didn't have an ounce of regret; even when later that evening she saw the blisters on the soles of her feet from all that walking, she still felt that it was all worth it. That night she even had a dream about the film studio. She dreamed of an elegantly dressed woman under the mercury-vapor lamps. When the woman turned to her and smiled, Wu Peizhen saw that she was none other than Wang Qiyao; she was so excited that she woke up. Her feelings for Wang Qiyao were a bit like the puppy love that a teenage boy feels for a girl for whom he is willing to go to the edge of the earth. She opened her eyes in the pitch-dark bedroom and wondered: *Just what kind of place is this film studio anyway?*

When the day finally arrived, Wu Peizhen's excitement far surpassed that of Wang Qiyao; she could barely contain herself. A classmate asked them where they were off to. "Nowhere," Wu Peizhen casually responded, as she gave Wang Qiyao a knowing pinch on the arm. Then she pulled Wang Qiyao aside and told her to hurry up, as though afraid that their classmate would catch up and force them to let her in on their pleasure. The whole way there Wu Peizhen couldn't stop jabbering, attracting curious glances from people on the street. Wang Qiyao warned her several times to get hold of herself. Finally she had to stop in her tracks and declare she wasn't going any further—they had not even set foot in the studio and Wu Peizhen had already embarrassed her enough. Only then did Wu Peizhen cool down a bit.

To get to the studio they had to take the trolley and make a transfer. Wu Peizhen's cousin was waiting for them at the entrance; he gave each of them an ID tag to clip on her chest so that they would look like employees: that way they could wander around wherever their hearts desired. Once inside, they walked through an empty lot littered with wooden planks, discarded cloth scraps, and chunks of broken bricks and tiles—it looked like a cross between a dump and a construction site. Everyone approaching went at a hurried pace with their heads down. The cousin also moved briskly, as if he had something urgent to take care of. The two girls were left straggling behind, holding hands, trying their best to keep up.

It was three or four o'clock, the sunlight was waning and the wind picked up, rustling their skirts. Both of them felt a bit gloomy and Wu Peizhen fell silent. After going a few hundred steps, their journey began to feel interminable, and the girls began to lose patience with the cousin, who slowed down to regale them with some of the rumors floating around the studio; his comments, however, seemed to be neither here nor there. Before their visit all of those anecdotes seemed real, but once they had seen the place everything was now entirely unreliable. Numbness had taken hold of them by the time they entered a large room the size of a warehouse, where uniformed workers scurried back and forth, up and down scaffolding, all the while calling out orders and directions. But they did not see a soul who even faintly resembled a movie star. Thoroughly disoriented, they simply trailed after Wu Peizhen's cousin, but had to watch their heads one second and their feet another, for there were ropes and wires overhead and littering the ground. They moved in and out from illuminated areas into patches of darkness and seemed to have completely forgotten their objective and had no idea where they were—all they did was walk. After what seemed an eternity, Wu Peizhen's cousin finally stopped and had them stand off to one side—he had to go to work.

The place where they were left standing was bustling with activity; everyone seemed to be doing something as they moved briskly around the girls. Several times, rushing to get out of one person's way, they bumped into someone else. But they had yet to lay eyes on anyone who looked like a movie star. They were both getting anxious, feeling that the whole trip was a mistake. Wu Peizhen could hardly bring herself to look Wang Qiyao in the eye. All of a sudden, the lights in the room lit up like a dozen rising suns, blinding them. After their eyes adjusted they made out a portion of the warehouse-like room that had been arranged to look like one half of a bedroom. That three-walled bedroom seemed to be the set, but everything inside was peculiarly familiar. The comforter showed signs of wear, old cigarette butts were left in the ashtray, even the handkerchief on the nightstand beside the bed had been used, crumpled up into a ball—as if someone had removed a wall in a home where real people were living to display what went on within. Standing there watching they were quite excited, but at the same time irritated because they were too far away to hear what was being said on set. All they could see was a woman in a sheer nightgown lying on a bed with wrinkled sheets. She tried to lie in several different positions; on her side one moment, on her back the next, and for a while even in a strange position where half her body extended off the bed onto the floor. All this became somewhat boring. The lights turned on and off. In the end, the woman in bed stopped moving and stayed still in the same position for quite some time before the lights once again dimmed.

When the lights came back on, everything seemed different. During the previous few takes the light had been marked by an unbridled brilliance. This time they seemed to be using a specialized lighting, the kind that illuminates a room during a pitch-black night. The bedroom set seemed to be further away, but the scene became even more alive. Wang Qiyao was taking in everything. She noticed the glow emitting from the electric lamp and the rippling shadows of the lotus-shaped lampshade projecting onto the three walls of the set. A powerful sense of déjà vu gripped her, but no matter how hard she tried, she could not remember where she had seen this scene before. Only after shifting her gaze to the woman under the lamplight did she suddenly realize that the actress was pretending to be dead—but she could not tell if the woman was meant to have been murdered or to have committed suicide. The strange thing was that this scene did not appear terrifying or foreboding, only annoyingly familiar. She could not make out the woman's features; all she could see was her head of disheveled hair strewn out along the foot of the bed. The woman's feet faced the headboard and her head lay propped against the foot of the bed, her slippers scattered on opposite sides of the room. The film studio was a hubbub of activity, like a busy dockyard. With all the cries of "Camera" and "OK" rising and falling amid the clamor, the woman was the only thing that did not move, as if she had fallen into an eternal slumber. Wu Peizhen was the first to lose her patience; after all, she was the more brazen one. She pulled Wang Qiyao away so they could go look around other parts of the studio.

Their next stop was a three-walled hotel lobby where a fight scene was being shot. All of the actors, in suits and leather dress shoes, were standing around when suddenly a poor fellow in tattered clothes walked onto the set and slapped the hotel manager across the face. The way the action was carried out looked a bit ridiculous; the actor produced the slapping sound with his left hand as he slapped the restaurant owner with his right, but his timing was impeccable and one could hardly tell it was fake. Wu Peizhen liked this scene much more than the first. She watched them do take after take without getting bored, the whole time exclaiming how much fun it was. Wang Qiyao, however, grew impatient and said that the first one was much more interesting. She said that it was a serious film, unlike this one, which was pure buffoonery, no better than a circus sideshow.

The two returned to the first set only to discover that everyone had gone. Even the bed had been taken away, leaving only a few workers behind to straighten up the remaining items on set. The girls wondered if they had gone to the wrong place and were about to go look elsewhere when Wu Peizhen's cousin suddenly called out to them. As it happened, he was one of the workers breaking down the set. He told them to wait a little while, and then he would take them to watch a special effects shoot that was going on at one of the other sets! They had no choice but to stand off to one side and wait idly. Someone asked the cousin who his guests were and he told him. But when the man asked where they went to school, the cousin was stumped and Wu Peizhen had to answer for herself. The man flashed them a smile, revealing a set of white teeth that shimmered in the darkness of the studio. He was the director, the cousin later told them. He had studied abroad and was also a screenwriter; in fact he had written and directed the scene they had earlier seen being filmed. The cousin told them all this as he led them off to see the special effects shoot, where they saw smoke, fire, even ghosts. Once again the technical people were doing all the work while the actors did virtually nothing.

Asked by Wu Peizhen if they could see some movie stars, the cousin looked embarrassed. He told them that there was not a single big star on any of the sets that day, explaining that it was not every day that big movie stars had scenes. The studio simply could not schedule things the way they would like—they had to work around the stars' schedules.

Wu Peizhen caught her cousin in a lie. "Didn't you tell us that you are always running into all these big name stars at the studio every day?" she protested.

Wang Qiyao took pity on the cousin and tried to smooth things over. "It's getting dark. We had better come back some other time. Our parents will be worried!"

As the cousin led them toward the exit they once again ran into the director. Not only did he remember them, he addressed them jocularly as "the girls from So-and-so middle school"—Wang Qiyao and Wu Peizhen turned a bright red.

On the ride home, neither was in the mood to talk and they sat silently, listening to the ringing bells of the trolley. The trolley was half empty; the after-work rush hour was over and Shanghai's nightlife had yet to begin. The girls' experience at the film studio was not exactly as expected; it was difficult to say whether it was disappointing or whether they had had the time of their lives—the one thing for sure was that they were both exhausted. Wu Peizhen had never had her sights set on the studio. Her reason for going rested entirely in making Wang Qiyao happy, so naturally she had hoped it would be a wonderful trip. Just what was so wonderful about the film studio, however, Wu Peizhen had not the slightest clue—she had to wait for Wang Qiyao's reaction to find out. The impression the film studio left on Wang Qiyao, on the other hand, was much more complicated. It was not nearly as magical a place as she had imagined, yet because it appeared so ordinary it gave her the impression that it was within her grasp—but just what was it that she could grasp? She had yet to figure that out. Her initial hopes may have been dampened, but the anxiety that came with anticipation had been relieved.

In the days following their visit to the film studio, Wang Qiyao did not utter a single word about their trip, and this left Wu Peizhen quite depressed. She was afraid that Wang Qiyao had not liked the studio and the whole trip had been a complete waste. Then one day she told Wang Qiyao in a confessional tone that her cousin had invited them back to the film studio but she had already declined the offer.

Wang Qiyao rounded on her. "How could you do that? He is trying to be nice to us!"

Wu Peizhen's eyes widened in disbelief. Wang Qiyao felt a bit uncomfortable under her stare. Turning her face away, she said, "What I mean is, you should show the guy some respect. After all, he's your cousin!"

This was one occasion when even Wu Peizhen saw through Wang Qiyao. But far from belittling her friend for being phony, Wu Peizhen felt a tenderness well up in her heart. *Although on the outside she looks like a grownup, deep down she is still a child!* Wu Peizhen thought to herself. At that moment, her feeling for Wang Qiyao approached maternal love—a love that encompassed all.

From then on the film studio became a place for frequent visits. They learned quite a few inside secrets about filmmaking. They learned that movies are never shot in sequence, but are made one scene at a time and only edited together in the final stages. The set locations may have been dilapidated and in disrepair, but the images captured by the camera were always perfectly beautiful. On one or two occasions they actually saw some of those famous movie stars, who sat in front of the camera doing nothing, like a collection of idle props. Films scripts were revised at random, and in the blink of an eye even the dead could come back to life. The girls made their way backstage, and as they rubbed their hands against the mysterious machinery that made images come to life, their hearts seemed to undergo a kind of transformation. Time spent in a film studio is never humdrum; the experience always hints at life's greater meaning. This is especially true for the young, who cannot yet completely distinguish truth from fiction and the real from the make-believe, and especially during that era—when movies had already become an important part of our everyday lives.

Camera

Wang Qiyao had learned that the most critical moment in making a film came the second that the director calls, "Camera." Everything up to that point boils down to preparation and foreshadowing, but what happens afterward? It ends forever. She came to understand the significance of the word "Camera": it announced a kind of climax. Sometimes the director let them look through the camera and what they saw through its lens was always gorgeous; the camera had the power to filter out all of the chaos and disarray. It had the power to make what was dark and dismal glimmer with light. Inside the camera was a different world. After editing and postproduction, only the pure essence would remain.

The director became quite close with the girls and they eventually stopped blushing in his presence. A few times, when Wu Peizhen's cousin was not in the studio, they even went straight to look for the director. He had given them the nicknames "Zhen Zhen" and "Yao Yao," as if they were characters in his latest movie. Behind their backs he described

Zhen Zhen to his colleagues as a graceless servant girl right out of *Dream of the Red Chamber*, a little cleaning maid who thinks she is special just because she is employed in a large, wealthy household. Yao Yao he described as a proper miss who acted the part of a rich official's daughter, like the tragic lover Zhu Yingtai. He treated Wu Peizhen as if she were a child; he loved to tease her and play little jokes on her. He promised to put Wang Qiyao in a scene in one of his movies as soon as the opportunity arose. Who knows? Because her coquettish eyes resembled Ruan Lingyu's, they might even be able to capitalize on the audience's nostalgia for the dead movie star and make Wang Qiyao into a new diva of the screen. Although he seemed to be kidding, this was the director's reserved and humorous way of making a promise. Wang Qiyao naturally did not take him too seriously, but she did kind of like being compared to Ruan Lingyu.

Then one day the director telephoned Wang Qiyao at home to have her come down to the studio for a screen test. Wang Qiyao's heart raced and her hands grew clammy. She was unsure if this was the opportunity she had been waiting for. She wondered: *Could my big chance really come this easily?* She could not believe it, neither did she dare *not* to believe it. Deep down her heart was in knots. At first she did not want to tell Wu Peizhen about it. She planned to sneak off alone and return before anyone noticed that she was gone. In case nothing came of the screen test, it would be her own little secret and she could pretend that nothing had ever happened. But then, just before the day of her screen test, she broke down and asked Wu Peizhen to go with her so that she would not be too nervous. Wang Qiyao did not sleep well the night before; her face appeared thinner than usual and she had dark rings around her eyes. Wu Peizhen naturally jumped for joy as all kinds of wild ideas went flying through her head. In no time she was talking about organizing press conferences for Wang Qiyao, who regretted telling her friend about the screen test.

Neither of them paid attention during their classes that afternoon. When school finally let out the two rushed out of the gate and hopped onto the trolley car. Most of the passengers at that time of the day were housewives with cloth bags in hand, wearing wrinkled *cheongsams*, the seams of their stockings running crookedly up the back of their legs. They either had messy, disheveled hair or, if they had just walked out of the beauty salon, hair that look like a helmet. Their faces were rigid, as if nothing in the world concerned them. Even the trolley seemed to be afflicted with an air of apathy as it rattled along the tracks. Amid this sea of indifference, Wang Qiyao and Wu Peizhen were animated and alive. Though neither said a word, centuries of anticipation and excitement were brewing inside them. At three o'clock in the afternoon, the Shanghai boulevards were suffused with weariness, preparing to sign out and change shifts. The sun hung in the western sky above the apartment buildings, glowing ripe and golden. Their hearts were filled with anticipation as if they were about to begin a brand-new day.

The director led them into the dressing room and had a makeup artist work on Wang Qiyao. Seeing herself reflected in the mirror, Wang Qiyao could not help feeling that her face was small and her features plain—she realized that a miracle would not occur—and this depressed her. She became completely resigned as the makeup man worked on her. She even closed her eyes for a while to avoid looking in the mirror, uncomfortable and anxious only to get everything over and done with. She even got neurotic and thought that the makeup man, impatient to get finished with her, was applying the makeup hurriedly and crudely. When she opened her eyes once again and looked, she saw the awkward expression of someone who had no desire to be there. The harsh, unmodulated light of the dressing room made everything appear commonplace. Losing all confidence in herself, Wang Qiyao decided to simply let everything ride; she focused on watching the makeup man gradually transform her into someone else—a stranger she did not recognize. It was then that she began to calm down and her tensions eased. By the time the makeup man finished his job, she had even started to regain her sense of humor and joked around a bit with Wu Peizhen, who remarked that Wang Qiyao looked like the Lady in the Moon descending into the secular world, whereupon Wang Qiyao quipped that if she were a Lady in the Moon, she was the kind whose image was found on boxes of mooncakes. The two of them had a good laugh. Once this happened, Wang Qiyao's expression relaxed, her powdered face lit up, and she came to life. As she returned the gaze of the beauty in the mirror, the image she saw no longer seemed quite as distant and unrecognizable.

Before long the director sent someone over to escort Wang Qiyao to the set, Wu Peizhen naturally following close behind. The lights were already set up and Wu Peizhen's cousin was up on the scaffolding, smiling down at them. The director, on the other hand, became serious and cold, as if he did not even know them. He had Wang Qiyao sit on a bed. It was a Nanjing-style bed with ornate flower patterns carved into the woodwork, a mirror set into the headboard, and high bed curtains all around—all the signs of rustic elegance. Wang Qiyao was to play a bride in a traditional wedding ceremony. She would be wearing a crimson bridal veil over her head when the groom entered and he would pull it away, slowly revealing her face. The director explained that her character had to be bashful and charming, filled with longing and uncertainty; he unloaded these adjectives on her all at once, expecting her to capture them all with a single expression. Wang Qiyao nodded, but deep down she was completely lost and had no idea where to begin. But having decided to let everything ride, she was actually quite calm and composed. She was aware of everything going on around her, down to the shouts of "Camera" coming from the adjacent set.

The next thing she knew, a crimson bridal veil came down over her head. Suddenly everything was swathed in darkness. In that instant her heart began pounding like a drum. She understood that her moment had come and fear welled up inside her as her knees began to tremble faintly. The set lights came on, transforming the darkness into a thick crimson hue. Suddenly she felt feverish, and the tremors worked their way from her knees up through her body. Even her teeth began to chatter. All the mystery and grandeur of the film studio hung suspended in the light shimmering outside her veil. Someone came and straightened out her clothing and then quickly walked off set. The air whisked against her as he passed by. The crimson veil fluttered a bit, for a moment softening the anxieties of that afternoon. She heard a series of "okay"s repeating in rhythmic succession around her, as if converging upon a common target. Finally came the word, "Camera." Wang Qiyao's breathing stopped. She could not catch her breath. She could hear the film running through the camera, a mechanical sound that seemed to override everything. Her mind just went blank. When a hand pulled away her wedding veil, she was so startled that she shrank back with fright. "Cut," the director yelled. The set lights went dim, the crimson veil went back over her head, and they took it once more from the top.*

As they redid the scene, everything grew fuzzy. Things faded off into the distance, never to reappear, as if they had been an illusion. Then Wang Qiyao snapped out of her daze, her shivering ceased, and her heart rate returned to normal. Her eyes adjusted to the darkness once more and through the wedding veil she could make out silhouettes of people moving around. The set lights came up and this time the shouts of "OK" sounded perfunctory. When the word "Camera" was called out, it too seemed little more than a formality—but this formality still carried with it an air of authority, of unwavering power. She began to prepare the emotions the director wanted to see on her face; the only problem was that she had no inkling of how to act bashful or charming, or what it meant to be filled with longing and uncertainty. Human emotions are not simple symbols that can be called up at will. The crimson wedding veil was lifted to reveal a rigid expression; even the bit of natural charm that she normally had about her was frozen.

As soon as he saw her through the eye of the camera, the director sensed that he had made a mistake; Wang Qiyao's was not an artistic beauty, but quite ordinary. It was the kind of beauty to be admired by close friends and relatives in her own living room, like the shifting moods of everyday life; a restrained beauty, it was not the kind that made waves. It was real, not dramatic—the kind of beauty that people noticed on the street and photo studios displayed in their front windows. Through the camera's lens, it was simply too bland. The director was disappointed, but his disappointment was partly for Wang Qiyao's sake. *Her beauty will be buried and lost to the world,* he said to himself. Later, in order to make things up to her, he had a photographer friend of his do a photo shoot for her—but this photo shoot turned into something quite extraordinary. One of the photos even made it into the inside front cover of *Shanghai Life* with the caption, "A Proper Young Lady of Shanghai."

And so that is how the screen test ended, just another trifling incident in the life of the film studio. After that, Wang Qiyao stopped going. She wanted to forget the whole affair—that it had ever happened. But the image of that crimson wedding veil and the dazzling studio lights were already imprinted in her mind and reappeared whenever she closed her eyes. There was a strange frisson attached to that scene; it was the most dramatic moment in Wang Qiyao's quiet life. The moment had come and gone in an instant, but it added a dab of melancholic color to her heart.

Occasionally, on her way home from school, something would unexpectedly stir up her memory of the screen test. Wang Qiyao was sixteen years old at the time, but that one day's experience left her with the feeling that she had already been through a lot—she felt much older than sixteen. She started to avoid Wu Peizhen, as if the latter had stolen some secret from her. Whenever Wu Peizhen invited her out after school, Wang Qiyao would almost always find some excuse not to go. Several times Wu Peizhen even went to Wang Qiyao's home to look for her, but each time Wang Qiyao had the maidservant say that she was not home. Sensing that she was being avoided, Wu Peizhen felt heartbroken, but she held on to the hope that Wang Qiyao would eventually come back to her. Her friendship changed into a kind of pious waiting; she did not even look for any new girlfriends, afraid that they might take Wang

Qiyao's place. Wu Peizhen had a faint notion that the reason Wang Qiyao was avoiding her had something to do with that failed screen test, so she too stopped going to the film studio, even breaking off contact with her cousin. The screen test became a source of sorrow for both of them, leaving them with a deep sense of defeat. Things gradually got to the point where they were no longer on speaking terms: running into one another at school, each would make haste to awkwardly get out of the other's way. They sat on opposite sides of the classroom, but, though their eyes never met, they could always feel one another's' presence. A wall of pity grew between them. The incident at the film studio ended with the word "camera," and the result was what they call in the industry a "freeze frame." Gone, never to return, but the memory hangs on for all eternity.

Their after-school lives gradually returned to normal; but things were not really the same—something had been snatched away. They were hurt, but neither could say where the pain was. At their girls' school, where rumors usually flew rampant, not a soul knew about Wang Qiyao's screen test; they had succeeded in keeping it completely under wraps. It was implicitly understood between them that they should never broach the subject. Actually, just to be chosen by a director for a screen test would already have been a great honor in the eyes of most girls—any hopes of getting a part would be a long shot in a long shot. This was also what Wang Qiyao thought at first, but once she reached that stage everything changed. Suddenly, a price had been exacted and loss was imminent. Only because Wu Peizhen stepped out of her own shoes and empathized completely with her friend was she able to understand the grief Wang Qiyao was going through.

The Photograph

A month had gone by before the director finally called. Wang Qiyao's voice was stiff and a bit sardonic as she asked him just what business he had calling her. The director explained that he had a photographer friend named Mr. Cheng and wanted to arrange a photo shoot for her. Wang Qiyao replied that she was not very photogenic and told him that he had better have Mr. Cheng find somebody else!

The director laughed. "Oh, little Yao Yao's throwing a temper tantrum!"

With that, Wang Qiyao was too embarrassed to refuse and gave in. The next day the Mr. Cheng in question called to arrange the time and place.

When the time came, Wang Qiyao went to the address Mr. Cheng had given her, taking with her several *cheongsams* and dresses. Mr. Cheng lived on the penthouse floor of a multistoried apartment building on the Bund. Part of his apartment had been renovated into a photo studio, complete with cardboard scenic backdrops of European castles as well as Chinese pavilions. Inside were also a dark room and a dressing room. Mr. Cheng was a young man of twenty-six; he had on a pair of gold-trimmed glasses—he was nearsighted—and was wearing a pair of suspenders over a white dress shirt and a pair of Western slacks—very sharp. He had Wang Qiyao fix herself up in the dressing room while he set up the lights.

From the dressing room window, Wang Qiyao could see the Bund, stretched out like a white ribbon. It was a Sunday afternoon and the sunlight was especially refreshing. The clock tower at the Custom House rang the hour, its chiming gradually spreading through the air as if from someplace far, far away. People down beside the river, the size of ants, shimmered as they moved. Pulling her gaze back into the dressing room, Wang Qiyao suddenly felt flustered. Why had she gone there in the first place? Without being conscious of it, she suppressed all hope, refusing to let her expectations grow. She had already suffered a terrible blow and could not help but be discouraged. At the same time, she took a kind of perverse pleasure in watching her dreams melt away, fancying herself the heroine of a sad story. Her only reason for coming, she told herself, was out of respect for the director; for herself, she couldn't have cared less. She looked herself over in the mirror with a feeling of ambivalence, applied some lipstick, and emerged from the dressing room without even bothering to change her outfit.

Mr. Cheng had already set everything up for the photo shoot; a vase of white calla lilies stood on a stand in front of the orange backdrop he had hung. He asked Wang Qiyao to stand beside the stand while he took a few steps back to see how everything appeared. As he looked her over, Wang Qiyao gazed back at him with indifference, not in the least bit embarrassed. Instead she had a jaded expression that seemed to illustrate "all that she had been through"—but the look that spoke these words was naïve and one could tell that it was a bit forced and exaggerated.

Mr. Cheng had an eye different from the director's; the director wanted character, but Mr. Cheng wanted only beauty. Character has to be created; beauty, on the other hand, does not have any such mission. In Mr. Cheng's eyes, Wang Qiyao was practically flawless, a perfect beauty—stunning from every angle. She did not have any of the incorrigible habits of models who were long accustomed to the camera's eye. She was a blank sheet of paper, an empty palette that could be painted to match the heart's desire. At the same time, there was a certain elegant poise about her and she wasn't a bit shy. Her poise came from her experience at the screen test: it was the result of practice. Failure had given it a touch of bashfulness and an endearing modesty—in other words, she was enchanting.

Mr. Cheng was very happy with his director friend's recommendation. He could not remember just how many beauties had been through the door of his photo studio, but every one had come pre-stylized. They were already like finished photographs; all Mr. Cheng had to do was reproduce them. At that moment he felt a sudden surge of excitement, which communicated itself to Wang Qiyao, and, as the lights went on, a spark of indescribable hope lit up inside her. This ranked as a "second choice" kind of hope but she could feel it rising nevertheless. Of course, Mr. Cheng's photo studio could not compare with the film studio for glamour, sophomoric and rather desolate as it was, but it exuded an air of diligence and sincerity, of honest work starting from the bottom, of active pursuit—and this won over one's cooperation. In spite of herself, Wang Qiyao retracted her indifferent attitude and began to show interest and enthusiasm.

No matter how unaffected they may normally be, girls like Wang Qiyao, who know all too well that they are pretty, cannot keep themselves from striking poses in front of a camera. But the poses are usually not very clever—either exaggerated, or coming across a bit forced—and the girls were shown at a disadvantage. Wang Qiyao, however, was an exception: she did not make these kinds of mistakes. She was wiser and had innate self-awareness; she had also learned from her experience at the film studio and remained calm and reserved. That is not to say that her mannerisms were free from a certain affectedness, but it was an unaffected affectedness. She acted like a somebody trying to pretend to be a nobody, and this somehow created an appearance that seemed perfectly suited to the camera. Mr. Cheng could not help himself. He took shot after shot, and Wang Qiyao in turn took to the attention like a fish to water. She began to feel a bit hot, her eyes sparkled, and her face radiated gorgeousness. One after another, she changed into all the different outfits she had brought along as, one after another, Mr. Cheng changed cardboard backdrops. One minute she would be a Chinese girl, the next she would transform into an exotic maiden from abroad. It was already noon by the time they finished the last shot and she went back into the dressing room to change. The Huangpu River glistened; the seagulls soaring above its waters looked like tiny silver spots. A car drove down alongside the riverbank and turned into a dark and quiet street, which ran straight through the tall buildings like a gully at the bottom of a canyon.

Wang Qiyao took her time as she carefully changed back into the outfit she had came in and meticulously folded up the others. Her mind was clear and gave no thought to the pictures that had just been taken—she looked at this simply as something destined to come to naught. As she gathered up her things, she couldn't help but admire the wonderful view from the apartment. The window, at the corner of the building situated right at the intersection of the Bund and that straight narrow road, was so high up you could see six blocks into the distance. She stepped out of the dressing room, said goodbye to Mr. Cheng before going out the door, and walked down the hall to the elevator. At the press of a button, the elevator silently ascended from the ground floor. As she stepped into the elevator, Wang Qiyao noticed Mr. Cheng standing outside his door, watching her.

The photo later selected for the inside front cover of *Shanghai Life* was of Wang Qiyao wearing one of her casual *cheongsams* with a flowered pattern. She was sitting on a stone stool beside a stone table, her face turned slightly to one side, in a "listening pose," as if chatting with someone outside the camera's frame. Behind her was a traditional-style oval window and the shadows of flowers and tendrils—instantly recognizable as a painted cardboard backdrop. Although the photo was supposed to be an outdoor scene, the lighting was all artificial. Her pose was also patently artificial. In most respects it was a rather mediocre photo, the kind that can be seen hanging in the shop window of virtually every photo studio, a bit tacky; and, though the subject was pretty, she was not a stunning beauty. But there was something about that photo that made its way into people's hearts. There is really only one way to describe the Wang Qiyao in that picture: she was a "good girl." Hers was the look of a girl who alters herself to please other people, men as well as women. "Good girl" was written all over her face, in her posture; even the tiny, delicate flowers on her *cheongsam* reached out to you in friendliness. The background scene was fake, as was the lighting, even her pose—everything in the photo was contrived—but precisely because everything around her was fake, the person became real. She was not part of some conspiracy, she was merely playing out her part like a good girl; all of her cards were on the table. What you saw was what you got.

The girl in the picture was not beautiful, but she was pretty. Beauty is something that inspires awe; it implies rejection and has the power to hurt. Prettiness, on the other hand, is a warm, sincere quality, and even hints at a kind of intimate understanding. Looking at her photo brought a feeling of true comfort and closeness, as though one could call her by name. Movie stars and models may indeed be enchantingly beautiful—but, after all, what do any of them have to do with you? They have their lives and you have yours. Wang Qiyao reached down into the bottom of your heart. The lighting in the picture also had a kind of minute intimacy that seemed to bring the image of Wang Qiyao to life. Images of people seemed to be reflected in her eyes and the pleats in her *cheongsam* appeared to move. It was more like the kind of picture one sees pasted in a family album than the kind seen hanging in a glass frame to be admired. It would not have been found in advertisements for Soir de Paris perfume or Longines wristwatches, but would have been perfect to promote MSG or laundry detergent. Down-to-earth, with no trace of extravagance, it had a touch of resplendence of a commonplace variety; and it had a touch of sweetness, as in the faint sweetness of porridge flavored with osmanthus blossoms. It was not particularly eye-catching and it was far from unforgettable. Yet though the image failed to linger in your mind, you were bound to remember liking it the next time you laid eyes on it. It was the kind of photo you could never get sick of, yet by no means something you could not do without. In short, it was proper, comme il faut, and calming; just looking at it made one feel good. The editors over at *Shanghai Life* could not have exercised more wisdom than when they decided to run the photo as their inside cover spread. The photo and the name of the magazine were a match made in heaven, the photo acting like a footnote to the name. After all, what was *Shanghai Life* but fashion, food, and being attentive to all the details of the everyday? The image of Wang Qiyao seemed to capture the essence of all of this; the editors couldn't have chosen a more suitable photograph.

For her part, Wang Qiyao did not understand why they chose *that* photo over all the others, in which she was gazing straight into the camera. She was even a bit confused as to when exactly that photo had been taken. It must have been when she was not paying attention. She did not like the version of herself she saw in the picture, looking provincial and much too prim—completely different from the way she imagined herself to be. It left her disappointed and a little hurt. Seeing her picture in print should have made her happy, but instead she was left feeling depressed. She wondered why she always failed under scrutiny. First her disappointing screen test, and now this: nothing seemed to work out according to plan. She hid her copy of *Shanghai Life* under her pillow—she didn't even want to look at it, and was overcome with dejection for having made an utter fool of herself. She was now confused as to who she really was, and this drove her to desperation. Sitting back down before the mirror, she tried to get a new perspective on herself. She thought of that photo as something that had stripped her of her identity, so that she needed to start all over and remake herself. *Just what was that thing called a "camera" anyway? Was there another life inside its lens?* Thinking about this made Wang Qiyao even more disconsolate. That *Shanghai Life* should have run her picture brought her little happiness—and that little was mixed with an array of complicated emotions, as if she had not been tormented enough already.

This time Wang Qiyao could not hide what happened even if she tried. The entire school now knew who she was—even girls from other high schools came to her campus in hopes of catching a glimpse of this Wang Qiyao. Wherever she went, people stopped to turn and stare. Schoolgirls were like that. It was as if they didn't believe their own eyes and had to have confirmation from others. All the girls who had never given a second thought to Wang Qiyao suddenly became convinced they had been wrong all along. Those who had always admired her, however, grew suddenly ambivalent, hell-bent on taking the opposite side. And so gossip and rumors proliferated, even one suggested that Wang Qiyao had a cousin who worked at *Shanghai Life* and it was he who had got her into the magazine. But whether it was admiring gazes or fabricated rumors, nothing seemed to get to Wang Qiyao, for in both experience and understanding of the world she surpassed them all. All these rumors and idle words were sheer nonsense to her. Although she was the target of their attention, she had very different things on her mind. *Shanghai Life* may have made her a celebrity on campus—suddenly she was known to every student and teacher—but she was left with the feeling that she could no longer find herself. The photo had ripped away her original face and thrust upon her a new identity that she did not want. It was no longer up to her to choose.

A Proper Young Lady of Shanghai

"A Proper Young Lady of Shanghai" was a title tailor-made for Wang Qiyao. She was not a celebrity of the screen or stage, nor a wellborn woman from an influential family, nor a femme fatale capable of bringing down an empire; but if she wanted to take her place on society's stage she would need a designation. Her designation, "a proper young lady," hinted at a harmonious society where everyone was in their proper place. It was not a prejudicial title—any girl had a right to lay claim to it—but Wang Qiyao had won it with overwhelming support. The floral pattern on her *cheongsam* became popular, and her short perm was all the rage. In her person, Wang Qiyao epitomized "a proper young lady of Shanghai." The designation carried with it a commonplace sort of vanity, evoking the image of a fashionable girl savvy enough to know her proper place. Like the bearer of a philanthropic gift, she became the vehicle for everyone's fantasy.

Shanghai in late 1945 was a city of wealth, colors, and stunning women. After the Japanese surrender, the revelry that took place every evening in its nightclubs seemed justified and appropriate. In actuality, of course, merry-making had nothing to do with the affairs of the world; it stemmed from people's natural affinity for pleasure and delight. The fashions displayed in shop windows, the novellas serialized in newspapers, the neon lights, the film posters, the department store banners, and the flower baskets celebrating new company openings all brightly sang out that the city was beside itself with happiness. "A Proper Young Lady of Shanghai" was part of that music, music for ordinary women. It told everyone in the city that they would never be forgotten, that they were all on the road to glory. Shanghai was still a city capable of creating honor and glory; it was not ruled by any doctrine, and one could let the imagination run wild. The only fear was that the splendor and sumptuousness of the city were still not enough. Like a peasant sowing grain, the city planted all that was sumptuous and splendid—it was truly a city of ornate brocade. The title "A Proper Young Lady of Shanghai" made one think of "the moon rising above the city on the sea"—the sea is the sea of people and the moon lighting up the night sky is everybody's moon.

And then an invitation arrived from a photo salon, asking Wang Qiyao to sit for a photo shoot. In the evening, after the salon closed up shop, Wang Qiyao's mother had the maidservant accompany her daughter there in a pedicab. Off they went, a bag of clothing in hand. The photo salon was much fancier than Mr. Cheng's studio; there were more lights, and different people were in charge of the lighting, changing the backdrops, and makeup. Three or four of them encircled Wang Qiyao as if she was the center of their universe. The stores downstairs had closed and all was quiet, as were the desolate streets outside—they were surrounded by silence, and the atmosphere in the photo salon took on an almost sacred quality. The noises of clappers warning people to be careful with their cooking fires, seeping in through the closely drawn curtain of the back window, seemed to be coming from another world. Wang Qiyao felt the intense warmth of the camera lights shining down on her body, almost toasting her skin. She felt like she could almost see the way her eyes must have been sparkling. Surrounding her was darkness, and she was the only soul in that world of darkness.

The picture of her later displayed in the window was even more glamorous because she was elegantly attired in evening dress. But this was a commonplace elegance; like a rented bridal gown, this pseudo-elegance—as long as everyone knew—was not meant to deceive. The splendor displayed in the shop window hinted at a dream ready to be fulfilled, a dream belonging to proper young ladies. It also hinted at a kind of striving, the strivings of proper young ladies. The Wang Qiyao who appeared on the inside front cover of *Shanghai Life* had been an everyday kind of proper young lady, while the Wang Qiyao who appeared in the shop window was a fantasy version of a proper young lady. Both were quite real. The latter captured your eyes, the former your heart; each had its proper place. The Wang Qiyao displayed in the shop window had taken the "good girl" side of her and buried it deep in her heart, replacing it with an expression of restraint on her face—and she seemed to stand taller than common people. Her face bore a detached coldness, but one knew there was an earnest warmth in her that yearned to be liked. This was the image of herself that Wang Qiyao most adored—it suited her taste perfectly and, moreover, provided her with confidence. After seeing it that first time, Wang Qiyao never walked past the shop window again; this is yet another example of her self-restraint. Displayed beneath that were the words, "Wang Qiyao, the Proper Young Lady of Shanghai." From that point her fame spread like the wind.

But Wang Qiyao was still her old self. The night she went to the salon, she couldn't get to sleep until quite late, yet she still arrived at school on time the next morning. During a PTA meeting, the school elected her to present flowers to returning alumni, but she gave up the honor to another classmate. When curious classmates tried to wheedle the details of the photo shoot out of her, she told the complete story, taking care not to exaggerate anything or make it sound at all mysterious or romantic. Her attitude was the same as it had ever been. She never rushed to finish first and never lagged behind—she always tried to steer a middle course. Gradually, her modest attitude helped to quell the jealous feelings brewing among her classmates.

But, though she behaved no differently from before, changes were taking place inside her. In the past Wang Qiyao had always felt a slight irritation about having to abide by the rules and be a good girl, but now she could accept her role without rancor. With success came poise. And because she had already had a taste of success, she was more than willing to step aside so that others could have their chance. That glamorous night at the photo salon, where everything seemed to revolve around her, was enough to illuminate many a dull and tedious day. With her portrait on display in the salon window, even her silence was articulate. Something about Wang Qiyao caused her to rise above the other girls—had made her, indeed, into the exemplar of proper young ladies. Quiet and reserved, she used to behave like this against her will, but now her reticence was held up by hope. But, both before and after, the same patience was always at work.

Patience—indeed, that certain "something" about Wang Qiyao was patience. Patience is a quality that holds fast no matter what setbacks may await; whether you face gains or losses, it always comes in handy. For someone as delicate and soft as Wang Qiyao, what weapon more formidable than patience? Whatever the outcome, be it success or failure, one cannot go wrong with patience; it is the last to go to the wall. Quiet and poise are the attributes of a proper young lady, and Wang Qiyao behaved exactly in the same way as before. One thing from the past was missing though, her friendship with Wu Peizhen. They had become even more distant than strangers. Strangers have no reason to avoid one another, but these two did. Wu Peizhen even went out of her way to avoid walking past the window that displayed Wang Qiyao's photo—she didn't want to lay eyes on a picture of her. Both were riddled by an unspeakable vexation, but thinking about each other only seemed to leave them more depressed.

In no time, however, several classmates lined up to take Wu Peizhen's place; some came knocking on her door to walk her to school, while others asked her out to the movies after class. Wang Qiyao kept them all at arm's length—neither too close nor too far. After several attempts, they lost interest and gave up. Then one day Wang Qiyao discovered a letter hidden in the pages of her textbook. It was an invitation. Besides a card, there was a letter written in the flowery language popular among young schoolgirls. The letter declared the writer's affection for Wang Qiyao, while the card invited her to a birthday party; both were signed by Jiang Lili. Jiang Lili had never had any real contact with Wang Qiyao, nor did she ever seem to have any close friends. Her family owned a factory and she was one of the wealthiest girls in her class. In school she was an average performer; she loved to read novels secretly in class, so much so that she ended up nearsighted. With her Coke-bottle glasses, she appeared even less approachable. Jiang Lili's homework essays were always brimming with luxuriant and gaudy language that seemed to come directly out of one of her favorite tragic romances.

Wang Qiyao accepted the invitation, primarily because she was unwilling to disappoint Jiang Lili but also out of simple curiosity. This curiosity was divided in two halves—she was curious about Jiang Lili and equally curious about the party. All kinds of rumors spread around school about parties at Jiang Lili's house. She never invited people over, and this created an air of mystery. In the past, no matter how curious she might have been, Wang Qiyao's response would have been to refuse the invitation—she would never give herself over to the excitement of others. But now she didn't seem to care—moreover, who knows? Maybe the others would end up giving their excitement over to *her.*

Wang Qiyao decided that she would go, but when she went to tell Jiang Lili, the latter seemed to go out of her way to avoid her. As soon as the bell rang, Lili rushed out of the classroom, leaving her textbook open on her desk, obviously as a receptacle for a reply from Wang Qiyao. Jiang Lili was behaving like a person so overwhelmed with emotions that she could hardly bring herself to speak, but Wang Qiyao was determined not to humor her: she had never liked playing those artful games, and the content of those types of letters always made her skin crawl. When Jiang Lili returned to the classroom to discover that her textbook was empty, a look of disappointment swept over her face. Wang Qiyao was secretly pleased. As soon as the bell rang, Jiang Lili rushed out of the classroom without looking back. Wang Qiyao ran after her, calling out her name, whereupon Jiang Lili's face turned red: she was obviously very embarrassed, yet also very determined, a combination that showed her hurt. She had never expected Wang Qiyao to come right out and thank her for the invitation, let alone say that she would be sure to attend. Jiang Lili blushed even more hotly as teardrops welled up in her eyes, thick misty tears. The following day, Wang Qiyao discovered yet another note in her textbook. It was written on a piece of light blue stationery, the kind with flowery patterns printed in the corners, in language that was like poetry. The letter extolled the beauty of the moon the night before. Wang Qiyao couldn't help but feel a bit sick.

A few days later, the day of the birthday party, Wang Qiyao prepared a pair of hair ornaments to bring as a present. She put on a light wool checkered autumn jacket over a white *cheongsam* and, as a finishing touch, tied a red ribbon in her hair. She didn't leave home until eight o'clock and only planned on staying a few minutes when she got there. A few days earlier, as the party was approaching, Wang Qiyao felt suddenly unsure of herself and her future. She didn't know Jiang Lili very well; everything would have been fine if only she had Wu Peizhen to accompany her there. But Wu Peizhen was like someone from another lifetime. Just thinking of her filled Wang Qiyao with melancholy. She sat in her bedroom waiting for the clock to strike eight, by which time the *longtang* were shrouded in a lonely silence. The few night echoes stole through: the drip-drip sound of well water, the chiming of the clock, and evening songs being transmitted over the radio. The silence of the night accentuated people's loneliness and exhaustion; the day was over but there was still much to do.

At eight o'clock she went out the door; the electric lamp in the alley projected no light, only the colors of night. The other streetlights were also too weak to drive away the darkness surging out of the *longtang*. Neon lights were clouds floating in the night sky and people were but lamplit shadows. Jiang Lili's family lived on a broad *longtang* just off a quiet and secluded main street. The alley was lined on both sides with two-storey apartment buildings with gardens and garages. Here too it was dark and quiet, but darkness and quietude of another breed. The window curtains were all shut at Jiang Lili's house, but the slivers of light that peeped through made it more alive than the neighboring buildings. Wang Qiyao thought that she would be the only one late, but as she approached the building a car drove past her, stopping outside Jiang Lili's front door. The main entrance had been left open, as if to welcome the arriving guests.

Wang Qiyao walked inside and hung her coat up on the coatrack in the foyer, holding on to her gloves and the present she had brought. There were not a lot of people in the living room and they all seemed to be wrapped up in their own conversations. Fresh fruit and appetizers were laid out on an elongated serving table. In the center of the table was an empty spot reserved for the cake, which hadn't yet arrived. Jiang Lili sat alone in the corner playing the piano. She was wearing one of her usual outfits and had a look of indifference on her face—it might as well have been someone else's birthday. But the moment she laid eyes on Wang Qiyao, her face lit up with a brilliant smile. She got up from the piano bench and walked over to Wang Qiyao, taking her by the hand. Wang Qiyao couldn't help heaving a sigh of relief. Jiang Lili was the one person she knew at the party, the one bit of familiarity and closeness, and so she in turn extended her hand. Jiang Lili pulled Wang Qiyao out of the living room, up the stairs, and into her bedroom.

Everything in the room was pink—from the curtains and comforter to the satin drapes adorning the dressing table mirror—but this only succeeded in making Jiang Lili appear even more conservative and old-fashioned. She seemed set on making a mess of her room. The desk and bed were covered with books, their covers torn and spattered with ink; the cups were covered with brown tea stains; her phonograph records were cracked and scratched; and her wardrobe, all in black and gray, was strewn all over the room. Wang Qiyao had originally planned on complimenting Jiang Lili on her room, but seeing this, she couldn't get the words out. The room looked as if it had suffered some terrible injustice and was holding in a bellyful of discontent. Jiang Lili led Wang Qiyao inside and sat down on the corner of her bed, staring into the latter's eyes for the longest time without uttering a word. Wang Qiyao didn't know how to react; the entire situation seemed so very strange and awkward.

Suddenly a hubbub broke out downstairs. They were probably about to bring out the cake. More people seemed to have arrived and waves of celebratory cries and laughter rang out. Wang Qiyao was about to suggest that they go back downstairs when she discovered that Jiang Lili was crying, the tears flowing past her glasses and down her cheeks.

"What's wrong, Jiang Lili?" she asked. "Today's your birthday, your big day! What's there to be so upset about?"

At this Jiang Lili began to cry even more violently and her tears came streaming down. "You don't understand." she muttered as she shook her head. "Wang Qiyao, you just don't understand."

"Then tell me," Wang Qiyao replied. "Just *what* don't I understand?"

But Jiang Lili wouldn't explain—she simply went on weeping and shaking her head. She acted a bit like a little girl trying to win sympathy. Wang Qiyao was beginning to grow tired of this behavior, but she managed to put up with it and suggested that they go back downstairs to rejoin the party. Jiang Lili, however, refused even more stubbornly. Finally, Wang Qiyao got up to go down by herself. Halfway down the stairs, she heard footsteps behind her and turned to see a teary-eyed Jiang Lili following her down. In her heart, Wang Qiyao thought the whole thing ridiculous, even annoying; she was also a bit moved—but this last emotion was a bit forced.

She turned to Jiang Lili. "Maybe you won't change into a new outfit or put on some makeup, but at least go wash your face!"

Her words had something in them of intimacy, but it was an unwilling intimacy. Jiang Lili did as she was told and went to the washroom, emerging with a slightly cleaner face.

She then proceeded to take the box containing the hair ornaments from Wang Qiyao's hand, saying, "This is for me!"

She acted as though she wanted to press the ornaments directly against her heart. Instead of turning back, Wang Qiyao hastened into the parlor. Jiang Lili tried to follow, but was immediately surrounded by a group of relatives.

The rest of the evening, Jiang Lili tightly held Wang Qiyao's hand, leading her around the party. A few people recognized her and went over to chat and say hello. Wang Qiyao gradually relaxed a bit and started to feel much more cheerful. But no matter what, she couldn't pry her hand free—she felt as if she was handcuffed to Jiang Lili. Meanwhile, Jiang Lili would give Wang Qiyao's hand a little squeeze from time to time, as if there were some secret that only the two of them shared. But such forced intimacy only made Wang Qiyao ill at ease. However, no trace of uneasiness showed on her face and she continued to act as if she and Jiang Lili were the best of friends. That this Jiang Lili seemed to be a completely different person from the Jiang Lili she knew from school was a matter of genuine astonishment to Wang Qiyao, but for the time being she couldn't worry about it—she was too busy dealing with the people at the party. Everyone and everything around her seemed to float past her eyes without leaving any clear impression: all was vibrant and beautiful, an enchanting scene indeed. Guests took turns playing the piano in the corner and the intermittent rhythm of the dancing keys was bewitching. The parlor began to grow stuffy, so someone opened the French window leading out onto the tiled terrace; just a few steps down lay the garden. The terrace light was on and one could faintly make out the intertwined branches of the withering lilac out in the garden. Jiang Lili led Wang Qiyao out onto the terrace. She didn't say a word, but simply gazed out in silence over the darkened garden. Annoyed by this odd behavior, Wang Qiyao turned to go back inside, saying she was chilly.

Back inside, the parlor presented a boisterous scene, as a group of kids surrounded a young couple, grabbing for the sweets they were distributing. What remained of the birthday cake lay under the branchlike lamp in scattered pieces like a dismembered carcass, the whipped filling strewn over the platter. Half-empty coffee cups littered the room. The party was coming to a close; as the evening approached its climax, everyone seemed to be forgetting their manners. A young man came up to Wang Qiyao in an aggressive and rather theatrical attempt at making a pass. Wang Qiyao blushed, not knowing how to react. Instantly pulling a long face, Jiang Lili drew Wang Qiyao away, telling the young man not to make a fool of himself. Not long after that, the first of the guests departed; others quickly followed suit and began to say their good-byes. The area around the coatrack became a confusing disarray of people searching for their coats. Jiang Lili paid no heed to any of the other well-wishers and only said a proper farewell to Wang Qiyao.

Before finally releasing Wang Qiyao's hand, Jiang Lili told her that she considered this day their mutual birthday, a day to be shared together. She spoke these words with a heartbreaking expression and, having let go of Wang Qiyao's hand, rushed upstairs to her room. Feeling like a prisoner set free, Wang Qiyao couldn't keep from heaving a sigh of relief. The crowd around the coatrack had mostly dispersed, and only two or three older guests stood in the foyer talking with Jiang Lili's mother. As Wang Qiyao took her coat off the rack, Jiang Lili's mother turned around to say goodbye and thank her for coming. She told Wang Qiyao how happy she had made her daughter and expressed the hope that she would come again. She saw Wang Qiyao all the way out, and even after Wang Qiyao had gone to the end of the street, she could still see the silhouette of Jiang Lili's mother standing in the doorway.

That night marked the beginning of Wang Qiyao's friendship with Jiang Lili. When they saw each other at school, they acted as before, keeping their relationship a secret. Their relationship was nothing like the friendship Wang Qiyao had enjoyed with Wu Peizhen, or the kind most schoolgirls have with their best friends—always inseparable, with endless secrets to share. Each had her own reasons for not wanting to flaunt their friendship. Wang Qiyao didn't want to give people the impression that she was fickle when it came to friendship, taking up one and then another—but deep in her heart, even though she might not admit it, she actually kept her friendship with Jiang Lili a secret out of pity for Wu Peizhen. Jiang Lili, on the other hand, simply wanted to be different, because she always insisted on going against the crowd and doing things her own way. Her first rule in life was quite simple: everything was based on her formula of taking the road less traveled. Each had an idea about friendship different from that of most other schoolgirls—neither thought of herself as part of the mainstream. Wang Qiyao's reason for wanting to be different came from experience, and Jiang Lili's came from the novels she read. The former had a hint of maturity, while the latter was a kind of literary romanticism. Neither one was entirely on track, but, since they were both deceiving themselves, albeit in different ways, they ended up together.

They kept to themselves at school but were inseparable once outside the campus gate. Jiang Lili insisted on bringing Wang Qiyao along wherever she went and, since it was Lili's mother who usually invited her, Wang Qiyao could never bring herself to refuse. Wang Qiyao virtually became a member of the Jiang family. She went everywhere with them. It wasn't long before their friends and relatives all became very close with Wang Qiyao—she was indeed one of them. Owing to her proper manners and her status as something of a celebrity, people began to treat her better than they did Jiang Lili, so that, before long, the tables were turned and she ceased to be invited out as Jiang Lili's friend, while Jiang Lili was invited out as *her* friend. Wang Qiyao had clearly become the one in favor—but she never forgot her place and took special care to treat Jiang Lili even better than before.

Jiang Lili's birthday party was followed by an interminable series of other parties. Nearly all were hosted by friends and relatives of the Jiang family; one led to another and they seemed never to end. Everyone at the parties looked familiar, as if they were all one big family. Although the partygoers came in all shapes and sizes and engaged in different professions, after a first meeting they were just like old friends. The parties followed the same basic pattern, and it did not take long until Wang Qiyao figured out how things worked. She knew that she needed to maintain her composure in order to set herself apart from the noise and excitement at these parties. She knew that she needed to dress plain and neat in order to show herself off against the rainbow of colors and carnival of the night. And she even knew that she had to maintain a genuine persona in order to create a contrast with the overly effusive people who were always eager to shower one another with compliments and favors. She seemed innately to know that "the string is easily broken when strung too tight." Understanding too that she was not one destined to climb to great heights, she kept to her philosophy of "less is more" and remained calm and composed. The result was not immediately apparent, but as time went by it had its effect and gradually Wang Qiyao began to win over their hearts.

She was the single white peony amid a sea of violet and crimson. Hers was the only unaccompanied vocal piece in a long program of orchestrated medleys. She was a haven of silence in the midst of bombastic debates and ramblings. Wang Qiyao brought something new to those parties—a creative something that carried with it the resolution to persevere—while at the same time she maintained enough perspective to see things as they were. At every party she attended she always felt as if she had to depend on herself for everything. Everyone else seemed to stand in the host's position, coming and going as they pleased while, as the only guest, in her comings and goings she was always controlled by others. She also realized that Jiang Lili was her only true friend at these parties; wherever they went, they went hand in hand. Jiang Lili actually despised parties, but was willing to make this sacrifice in order to be with Wang Qiyao. The two became party regulars. The few times they didn't show, everyone asked about them, so that their names wound up circulating all around the parlor. Being occasionally absent from the parties was also a part of Wang Qiyao's philosophy of "less is more"—a rather extreme part at that.

The party—what the Shanghainese call *paitui*—is the very life of the Shanghai night. Neon lights and dance halls form the outer shell of this sleepless city, but its soul is the party. Parties lie at the innermost core of the city, behind quiet shady boulevards in the parlors of Western-style residences; the pleasure they impart is wrapped in people's hearts. The lights at these parties are always dim, casting shadows that whisper the language of the heart. But this language of the heart speaks with a European accent, in classical and romantic styles. And the life of the Shanghai party is always the proper young lady; she is the center. Myriad passions play out in silence; romance lies deep under the skin. Forty years hence, no one will remember these passions and this romance; in fact, no one will be able even to imagine what it had been like. The passion and romance of that era was a dynasty; splendid and glorious, it was a heavenly kingdom. The Shanghai skies mourn; they bemoan the loss of that passion and romance. The Shanghai wind tantalizes, and the waters surrounding her are a washed-out carmine.

Wang Qiyao is one little piece of that passion and romance, not the part that rivets all eyes and becomes the center of attention, but the part that serves as ballast for the heart. She is the heart of hearts, always holding fast and never letting anything out. Supposing there was no Wang Qiyao, the parties would become nothing but hollow, heartless affairs, perfunctory displays of splendor. She was the most meaningful part of this passion and romance. She was that desire that lurks in the soul; if not for this desire, there would be no reason for passion and romance. As a result, passion and romance have found their roots, coloring Shanghai with that thing called mood. The mood casts a magic on every place and every thing, causing them to speak words more gorgeous than song.

Wang Qiyao strolled into the Shanghai night. The night scene was set against the dim lamps of *longtang* alleys as well as the lights shining on the backdrops of photo salons. No longer was this night an out-of-context photograph—it now had a story behind it; no longer still, it moved. Its movement was not the movement of the camera at the film studio, for the camera's movement told someone else's story. The movement of the night belonged to Wang Qiyao herself. Win or lose, she seemed to be in control of her own destiny—but not entirely. That belongs to the great sky beyond the stars, looming over the Shanghai nightline and enveloping the entire city. Turning white by day and black by night, transforming with the passage of the seasons, this corner of the sky is obscured by buildings and city lights, which serve as its camouflage, yet it withstands thunder and lightning and all the chaos of the world, eternally and boundlessly stretched out overhead.

Miss Shanghai

The peaceful atmosphere of 1946 arrived only after what seemed an eternity of chaos. Suddenly all one seemed to hear was good news; anything negative merely set the stage for good news to follow. Shanghai was an optimistic city that always looked on the bright side, in its eyes even bad news had its good side. It was also a city of pleasure that found it difficult to get through the day unless it could find something to make it happy. When torrential floods hit Henan province and people all over China were donating to the disaster relief effort, Shanghai offered its passion and romance—holding a Miss Shanghai beauty pageant to raise money for the flood victims.

The news of the pageant spread quicker than wildfire and, in the flash of an eye, everyone in the city knew about it. "Shanghai" was already a virtual synonym for modernity, but "Miss Shanghai" captured even better the modern cosmopolitanism of the city—after all, what could be more modern than a beauty queen? It stirred up the feelings of the people, for who in this city did not worship modernity? Here even the sound of ticking clocks seemed to echo the footsteps of modernity. People paid more attention to the election of their beauty queen than the election of their new mayor; after all, what did the mayor have to do with them? Miss Shanghai, however, was a feast for the eyes and everyone got a share. The newspaper that printed the first news of the pageant sold out within an hour of hitting the stands, but there was no time to print more copies, as other papers were immediately reprinting the contents of the article in special edition extras. The news spread along the trolley lines all over the city.

How romantic the whole affair was! It was a scene directly out of a dream, but suddenly that dream was coming true. No one could sit still, and hearts pounded like thunderous drums, dancing to the rhythm of the three step. Even the city lights seemed to grow dizzy with excitement, twinkling and flickering. What besides "Miss Shanghai" could possibly be closer to this city's heart? The heart of Shanghai was like a naive child, shamelessly savoring her own pleasure. Each and every citizen wanted to have their vote, selflessly offering their opinions on the new image of beauty.

The first person to suggest that Wang Qiyao enter the pageant was the photographer Mr. Cheng. After their first session, Mr. Cheng had done two outdoor photo shoots with Wang Qiyao, who seemed to get better each time: always calm and collected, she didn't so much as bat an eye. It was as if she could read Mr. Cheng's mind and knew exactly what he wanted. Wang Qiyao's beauty was the kind that grew slowly over time; it never diminished, only increased. In Mr. Cheng's eyes, Wang Qiyao was a goddess, incomparable, unrivaled. Convinced that the "Miss Shanghai" pageant was being held especially for her, he earnestly suggested that Wang Qiyao try out for it—there couldn't have been a more perfect beauty queen. Mr. Cheng was not the only reason Wang Qiyao signed up. She didn't have nearly as much confidence in herself as Mr. Cheng had. Moreover, *he* wasn't the one who would be auditioning for the pageant. There was no way Mr. Cheng could understand the heart-rending vicissitudes she had been through. She wasn't about to do anything without properly thinking it through. But Mr. Cheng's suggestion did set her thinking. Over time, the endless parties she was going to had begun to blur together; she felt she was wandering aimlessly back and forth, not getting anywhere. Thus Mr. Cheng's suggestion ignited a spark in her heart—even if it was only a dull flash of light.

Then one night, at the wedding reception of one of Jiang Lili's distant cousins, Jiang Lili suddenly announced Mr. Cheng's suggestion to all the guests. A wedding is the last place for such an announcement to be made—it was as if Jiang Lili was intentionally trying to steal the spotlight from the bride and groom. Everyone's gaze immediately fell upon Wang Qiyao, who, although angry, couldn't very well show it. But the announcement of Wang Qiyao's beauty queen bid seemed to be a good omen. Even if the big red lanterns decorating the hall had not been intended for her, the jubilant atmosphere no longer belonged solely to the bride and groom. The newlyweds were a propitious sign, as were the lucky day, the wine in their cups, and the carnation on the bride's breast. Even the streetlights outside were radiant and glowing, and so were the gorgeous images of the billboard beauties; everything was lit up in a mood that was ready for pleasure. Wang Qiyao didn't place too much blame on Jiang Lili for what she did, in fact, some part of her was even thankful. *Perhaps it was all fate?* she thought. Who could know? And so she grabbed the opportunity and never looked back.

Jiang Lili acted as though *she* were the one entering the pageant. The whole thing had barely begun and she was already busy running all over town getting things ready. Even Lili's mother was mobilized, and she promised to make a *cheongsam* for Wang Qiyao to wear the day of the pageant. Jiang Lili dragged her off to party after party, as if Wang Qiyao was on an exhibition tour. Jiang Lili had never learned the art of tact, and when she met people at these parties the first words tumbling out of her mouth always had to do with garnering votes for Wang Qiyao. She didn't care whether they even knew Wang Qiyao, let alone how uncomfortable and embarrassed she was making her friend. Jiang Lili had finally found a channel for her willful and domineering nature, and she used it to get what she wanted. In carrying out her campaign to promote her friend, she behaved as if both Wang Qiyao and the very title of "Miss Shanghai" were her exclusive property and she their sole agent. It was a good thing that she had sincerity written all over her face, otherwise things might easily have gone terribly wrong. Wang Qiyao was a rare beauty: this was her firm belief, and she took it upon herself to introduce this beauty to society and advance her cause. By selecting the beautiful Wang Qiyao as her most intimate friend, Jiang Lili could beautify a part of herself.

The title of "Miss Shanghai" actually meant nothing to her—all that was important to Jiang Lili was Wang Qiyao. She wanted to win over Wang Qiyao's favor; it was, in fact, a little sad to see. Her parents and siblings she treated like enemies, reserving all her affection for Wang Qiyao, who seemed to be the longed-for target of her love. But this love issued not only from Jiang Lili. Much of it came from the novels she had read. Wang Qiyao could hardly bear it. Wang Qiyao pitied her for being caught up in a vicious circle—wanting what she couldn't have, never appreciating what she did have, and becoming a terror to everyone, herself included. It was only out of sympathy that Wang Qiyao let her carry on as she did, but even she sometimes had to step in and say a few words when Lili went too far. At these reprimands, Jiang Lili immediately turned into a naive child uncertain of what she had done wrong, fear and confusion written all over her face. But deep down she never admitted she was wrong.

On one such occasion when Wang Qiyao had lost her temper, Jiang Lili folded her arms and declared, "Wang Qiyao, I just don't know what I can do to make you happy!"

These words made Wang Qiyao think back to Wu Peizhen, and she was overcome with dismay. She couldn't recall Wu Peizhen ever uttering such irritating things—but those words described perfectly what Peizhen had constantly tried to do. Wang Qiyao was standing just inches away from Jiang Lili, but she felt they were so distant that they might as well have been on opposite sides of the world.

Although it was only recently that Wang Qiyao had sent in her headshot, rumors were already starting to spread. Wang Qiyao's original idea was simply to send in her photo and then forget about the whole thing. She had no intention of making a big deal out of the pageant, but how could she remain indifferent in the light of the uproar Jiang Lili was creating? And then there was Mr. Cheng, who seemed intent on bringing the pageant up at least two or three times every day. Mr. Cheng knew a few people in the newspaper business—this was important not only because the Miss Shanghai beauty pageant was a hot topic in all the papers, but also because it was to be judged by representatives from the newspaper industry. Mr. Cheng's newspaper buddies, however, were not terribly close with him, so that one could never count on the accuracy of his information. Wang Qiyao refused to let herself be swayed by rumors; Jiang Lili, on the other hand, found herself on a never-ending emotional roller coaster. On one occasion Mr. Cheng came to them with the news that the head of a certain major industry, who went by the name of the "king" of something-or-other, was entering his daughter in the pageant and had simultaneously decided to make a large donation to the Disaster Relief Committee. Hearing this, Jiang Lili wanted immediately to run off and start raising money in Wang Qiyao's name to match his donation. On another occasion Mr. Cheng told them that a politician was going to sponsor a certain socialite for whom he was about to hold a huge reception at the Park Hotel, to which every celebrity in the city was invited. This set Jiang Lili off on a scheme to host her own reception. Wang Qiyao could not be unaffected by all of this. Even though she didn't want to make a big deal about the whole thing, it was already much too late for that. She had trouble suppressing her excitement as, day in and day out, she waited for the results.

Waiting for the results was like waiting for the dice to turn up in your favor—throwing them down harder doesn't do any good. Fate decides everything. And so Jiang Lili decided to go to church to pray. The words she uttered to God were like a melodramatic essay worthy of publication. At first Wang Qiyao kept her impatience well hidden, but after Jiang Lili started bragging about her to the whole world, what patience she had left began to wear thin. Gradually, impatience became annoyance and Wang Qiyao took to ignoring Jiang Lili. Lili, however, interpreted this coldness as a sign that she hadn't done enough and began to work even harder. This left Wang Qiyao at a complete loss. She knew that Jiang Lili was good to her, but she felt constrained, as if her personal freedom was being violated. The natural reaction was to stand up and resist. Being extra nice to someone can be a form of manipulation—kindness is an exercise of power in its own right. Meanwhile, though nothing had been formally declared, the entire city was already filling up with gossip; virtually everyone in Shanghai knew. Wang Qiyao only wished that there was a place where she could hide, where she didn't have to see another soul. She wished she could be deaf so she wouldn't have to be bothered by all those annoying questions. It was a good thing that by the time of the pageant they had both already graduated and didn't have to worry about school anymore. Wang Qiyao couldn't even imagine how she would have dealt with the stares if she had still been in school. Her relatives were already a handful. And so she had no choice but to spend most of her time at Jiang Lili's house; no matter how much of an uproar Lili made, there was only one of her—outside there were hundreds. Later, Wang Qiyao decided to move in with the Jiang family.

Actually, Lili had been wanting Wang Qiyao to move in with her for some time, but till now Wang Qiyao had always declined. When she finally agreed, Jiang Lili was so ecstatic that she made sure the room was all fixed up a full three days before Wang Qiyao was even scheduled to move in. Seeing how happy her daughter was, Lili's mother was also full of energy, ordering the maid to do this and that to get the house ready for their honored guest. The only people living with Lili were her mother and a brother. Her father had moved his factory to the interior during the war and afterward never relocated back to Shanghai. He had, in fact, taken a second wife out there and rarely came home, not even for Chinese New Year. He only returned to Shanghai twice a year for his children's birthdays—that was his way of showing fatherly love.

Jiang Lili's little brother was attending middle school, but he often played truant and did nothing but sit home and listen to the radio from morning till night, coming out of his room only for meals. Everyone in the family was a bit odd; even the maid had strange habits. Things were backwards in this family; the children did not have an ounce of respect for their mother, while she constantly fawned upon them. They counted every penny when it came to daily necessities, yet could throw away a hundred *yuan* at the drop of a hat. The mistress of the house seemed to have tired of being in charge and let the maid boss them around. After moving in, Wang Qiyao felt almost duty-bound to share the responsibilities of running the household—even though her status was half that of a retainer. She became the one to decide what they should have for dinner the following day; the one to ask when anyone in the house was looking for anything; and when the maid went through the daily accounts, it was always her job to make sure there were no mistakes. After Wang Qiyao moved in, the maid suddenly had someone keeping her in check. Her late night mahjong games in the servants' quarters were at an end, she was no longer allowed to keep guests for dinner, and she had to ask for permission before going out and return in a timely fashion. She was also required to comb her hair and dress more neatly—no longer would she be allowed to go clanking and clacking around all day in those annoying wooden sandals. And so, as she overhauled the household, Wang Qiyao slowly took away the maid's power, bit by bit, until she was the sole mistress of the house. By moving into Jiang Lili's house, she had evened things up with Lili. She had improved the household, thus repaying Jiang Lili for being so good to her, but she had also wrested back some control over her own life. That way, the slate was wiped clean and they could be on an equal footing. It was during this time that Wang Qiyao received the news that she had qualified for the preliminary pageant.

The pageant was swamped. It was as if all the gorgeous women in Shanghai had assembled in the room. Reporters from virtually every newspaper in the city scurried around, fighting to get their stories out first, while they feasted their eyes on the beauties that surrounded them. Their gazes were laced with desire, as were their articles. The entrance to the hotel where the pageant was being held was crowded with pedicabs and automobiles, along with a continuous flow of people coming and going. The girls came accompanied by their maidservants, sisters, or other family members, tailors, and hairdressers in tow. Shanghai girls were different from other girls. Like the men in their families, they too wanted to turn heads and make something of themselves. Moreover, they didn't just talk about it, they took action. In some ways, they were even more aggressive and tenacious than their fathers and brothers, unafraid of losing or getting hurt. At least half of the splendor of Shanghai was built on their desire for fame and wealth; if not for this desire, more than half the stores in the city would have long gone under.

Shanghai's splendor is actually a kind of feminine grace; the scent carried by the wind is a woman's perfume, and there are always more women's clothes displayed in the store windows than men's. The shadows of the French parasol trees seem to carry a womanly aura, as do the oleanders and lilacs in the courtyards—the most feminine of flowers. The humid breeze during the rainy season is a woman's little temper tantrum, the murmuring sound of Shanghainese is custom-made for women's most intimate gossip. The city is like one big goddess, wearing clothes plumed with rainbows, scattering silver and gold across the sky. The colored clouds are the sleeves of her gown.

On that day, more important than the rest, on that special festival celebrating pretty girls, the sun rose especially for them, shining down on them as they left their homes across the city. Every last rose or carnation in the shops was bought up by well-wishers to congratulate the girls. Their bodies were wrapped in the most fashionable clothes, their faces displayed the highest artistry of makeup, and the most stylish hairdos adorned their heads. It was a massive fashion show and they were all models, each and every one a rare beauty—the cream of the crop. Looked at separately, each seemed destined to take the crown; put side by side, each appeared prettier than the last; once the competition began, their collective beauty marshaled up a force capable of toppling mountains and overturning the sea. They were the pith and marrow of this city—its spirit. Normally their beauty was spread evenly throughout the city, diffused in the air; but on the day of the pageant their essence was concentrated into what was the most gorgeous portrait Shanghai had ever painted of itself.

A feeling of relief came over Wang Qiyao when she was selected for the preliminary pageant; she could finally face all those people who had been supporting her, and, most of all, she could face herself. But she was a little surprised when she made it into the second round of competition. Only then did she begin to take the pageant seriously; up until that point she had simply been trying to make Jiang Lili and Mr. Cheng happy. Taking the pageant lightly was her way of building a protective shell around herself—behind that shell reposed her dignity. Wang Qiyao's self-esteem had been injured by Jiang Lili and Mr. Cheng's diligence; the sole course of action she took to protect herself was to assume a thoroughly ambivalent attitude about the whole affair. Thinking back, Wang Qiyao realized that those had indeed been difficult days to get through. When all was said and done, the hope and hard work of Jiang Lili and Mr. Cheng rested entirely on Wang Qiyao's shoulders. Success or failure depended not on them but on her. In a way, they were making Wang Qiyao's decision for her; forcing their own dreams and desires onto her. Had Wang Qiyao taken things seriously, she surely would have ended up angry and perhaps even terminated her friendship with them. It was her ambivalence that saved their relationship. But everything turned out all right once Wang Qiyao made it into the second round. Everyone was happy—including Jiang Lili and Mr. Cheng.

Wang Qiyao and Jiang Lili began to reappear at a new series of parties, each of which one seemed to resemble a press conference where the questions never ceased. Wang Qiyao never failed to answer the questions put to her. Jiang Lili, on the other hand, was extremely reserved and refused to answer certain questions. About this time Mr. Cheng did another photo shoot for Wang Qiyao. He borrowed a friend's photo studio and shot a series of close-ups and headshots. He wanted people to remember her face. Afterward he got a buddy of his who was with the press to pull some strings and the photo was printed in a corner of the page of one of the Shanghai newspapers. It wasn't a big newspaper, but the photo ran alongside an article about the Miss Shanghai pageant—so it was basically free publicity for Wang Qiyao.

Events were now unfolding so quickly that Wang Qiyao began to get scared. Her progress was *too* smooth—there must be some booby traps lying ahead. She had always believed that fortune comes and goes in cycles—nothing good lasts forever. But about this time Wang Qiyao first started entertaining some rather extravagant hopes. She had naturally high aspirations, but having come to terms with the limitations imposed by her environment, she developed a habit of splashing cold water on her hopes. The world is full of opportunities, she knew, but often the harder you try the less you end up with. So she decided instead simply to hold on tight to the little bit she already had. At least it was something and, who knew, perhaps if she didn't think about it things would start going her way. Sometimes the less you try the more you end up with. As it was, things really were going her way, and even if she didn't want to think about it, she really had no other choice. The days became even more difficult to get through. Her earlier difficulties sprang from trying to protect herself and keep people at bay, but now she wanted in. As the semifinals approached, Wang Qiyao started to look thin and fatigued.

Her bedroom, adjacent to the downstairs parlor, had been converted from a study expressly for her. It had a window overlooking the garden, where the moonlight flickered under the night sky. Sometimes she thought to herself, *even the moon here is different.* The moon back home was a small courtyard moon, stained by the smell of kitchen smoke and lampblack; the moon here might as well have come from a scene in a novel, its light shining on flowers and rambling plants. When she couldn't sleep at night Wang Qiyao would get up and gaze through the sheer drapes out her window. She listened to the nameless sounds of the still night, so unlike the night sounds back home, which all had a name. Back home she could always tell whose baby was crying or which mother was berating her child; she could identify the sounds of rats racing beneath the floor, or the sound of a toilet flushing. Here only one sound had an identity. The lord of all sounds—and that was the sound of the bell tower ringing. It overrides all other sounds and voices, which form a bed of echoes reverberating through the night. The echoes are the finest strokes of a huge painting that constitutes the deep thought of the night. This sound has a buoyancy that lifts you up and knocks you around as if you were riding on a bed of waves. When people have floated on the waves long enough, they feel hollow inside and out, thoroughly saturated by the night.

The nights here have a corrosive power; they eat away at people's true feelings, replacing them with illusions. The nights here are clear and limpid. And unlike the nights outside her window back home, filled with muck and impurities, the nights here shine on people, making each and every strand of their hair distinct. If you reach out your hand, the color of the night slips between your fingers, and not even a sieve can sift out a single particle. The night fills the sky, pressing down on the rooftops, but the buildings never feel its weight, because actually it is as light as the wings of a cicada. There is only one thing in the night that has form, and that is shadows cast by moonlight. They stand out in delicate strokes against the invisible color of the night; they are the flesh and skin of the night. The night penetrates through ten thousand things; there is no crevice it does not creep into, and in the end the ten thousand things turn shapeless and colorless. The night is a solvent; it breaks down the structure of objects and replaces them with empty form. The nights here are magical; they confuse the senses, turning everything upside down.

The list of contenders who made it into the semifinals was printed in all the newspapers. Although the final victor had yet to be chosen, Wang

Qiyao was already basking in the attention. Everyone knew that she was staying with Jiang Lili, and their house was a revolving door for visitors. Even their most distant acquaintances suddenly felt compelled to stop by and ask endless questions. Wang Qiyao became a source of glory for the Jiang family. Jiang Lili and her mother spent all their time greeting the never-ending stream of visitors and serving them tea and snacks. Busy as they were, they couldn't have been happier—except for Jiang Lili's little brother, who locked himself in his room, listening to whatever ramblings or songs came in over the radio. Every day the three women would get up, first thing in the morning, dress, make themselves up, and sit in the parlor, waiting for the doorbell to ring. Sitting there, waiting to welcome their guests, they were like soldiers ready for battle. Things were coming to a head, they realized, and there was no room to overlook even the minutest detail. On one occasion Wang Qiyao was interviewed by a reporter for the evening edition of a local newspaper. His article described Wang Qiyao and Jiang Lili as being as close as sisters, and thanks to the Jiang family's notoriety in the business world this helped to inflate Wang Qiyao's reputation.

Jiang Lili's mother had long since come to think of Wang Qiyao as dearer than her own daughter. Her daughter was always rebelling against her, whereas Wang Qiyao was the complete opposite and heeded her every whim. She even went so far as to write to her husband in Chongqing to pressure him to donate money to the Disaster Relief Committee so as to throw some additional support in Wang Qiyao's corner. Normally, Jiang Lili and her mother had nothing to occupy them; now they were not only busy but had a common objective. United by this common goal, they suddenly found themselves getting along quite well.

Although there were still a few days until the pageant, they all had their own secret hunches about the outcome. Some of the candidates were clearly going to end up at the bottom, while for others making it into the final round was a mere formality. Then there was the group of girls who fell somewhere in the middle—they weren't at the bottom, but neither were they assured of making it into the final round. These girls still had a fighting chance—Wang Qiyao was one of them. Actually, they were the ones who carried the burden of the competition, and throughout the pageant were the ones to stand fast amid the rushing currents—it was they who were the true Miss Shanghais. Throughout the drama of the pageant, these were the divas who met all the challenges. It was a question of survival of the fittest. In the end, whoever was able to break out in front deserved to be the true Miss Shanghai.

Among the visitors who came to the Jiang house at this time was one person Wang Qiyao had not expected to see—Wu Peizhen. Wang Qiyao opened the door and, seeing who it was, instantly lost her composure. Wu Peizhen was also flustered; she looked away and didn't know what to do with her hands. At a loss what to say, the two stood awkwardly facing each other, until Wu Peizhen removed an envelope from her pocket and handed it to Wang Qiyao. Wang Qiyao looked over it but didn't seem to take it in, except that it was some kind of invitation from the director over at the film studio. Wu Peizhen said that she needed to know whether Wang Qiyao would be able to make it. Wang Qiyao didn't have a chance to think it over properly but agreed nonetheless. Without so much as a goodbye, Wu Peizhen turned and took her leave. Wang Qiyao followed her outside. Wu Peizhen gradually slowed down so that Wang Qiyao could catch up with her, and they walked side by side down the *longtang*.

After walking for a few minutes, Wu Peizhen paused in front of a mailbox and said, "Go on back. You don't need to see me off."

Wang Qiyao insisted on walking her a bit further, saying that she didn't have any other errands to do anyway. The two of them stood there, neither one daring to face the other.

"I was originally going to drop the invitation right here in this mailbox," Wu Peizhen finally said after a long pause. "In the end, however, I decided to deliver it myself."

Wang Qiyao stared at the mailbox without uttering a word. After a long silence, they both began to cry. They didn't know what they were crying for, or what there was that was even worth crying about, but deep down both were overcome by a sadness for what they had once had and what was now irretrievably lost.

It was ten o'clock and the early morning sun beamed down on them through the leaves of the parasol tree, like shards of crystal or slivers of quicksilver, as dry leaves brushed against their legs while those on the ground crinkled beneath their feet. With their handkerchiefs soaked in tears, they still couldn't say what was wrong, all they knew was that they were profoundly sad. It was as if their girlhood, so carefree and pure, was gone forever, and from that point on their lives would become much more complicated. A sedan drove silently past. The sunlight reflected in the side of the shiny car was also like a ray of quicksilver. They went on crying a while longer before Wu Peizhen slowly turned and, with lowered head, wiped her tears and walked away. Wang Qiyao gazed at her retreating silhouette. Her tears gradually dried, but the blinding sun shone in her eyes, so that she could hardly keep them open. She knew her eyes were swollen and her face felt numb. Eventually, she turned around and began making her way back to the house.

The director had invited Wang Qiyao for dinner at the New Asia Restaurant. Figuring that Wu Peizhen would be there, Wang Qiyao intentionally did not tell Jiang Lili about the dinner, saying instead that she was going home to visit and pick up some odds and ends. But Wu Peizhen wasn't there—only the director. When she arrived, the director greeted her as Yao Yao, which immediately made her think back to what had happened at the film studio—it all seemed like another world.

"Yao Yao is a big girl now! All grown up!"

His tone seemed to hint at the affection a big brother feels for a little sister, almost enough to bring tears to one's eye. Wang Qiyao, however, fought them back and responded with a smile.

"Well, I may be all grown up, but you just keep getting younger."

The director had never expected Wang Qiyao to respond in such a manner and was visibly taken aback.

After a long silence, Wang Qiyao continued, "And so, to what may I owe the pleasure of this meeting?"

The director denied having any special motive for arranging the dinner, but his lips betrayed his heart, and deep down he was uncertain how to proceed. He began to regret not thinking things through beforehand; Wang Qiyao was no longer the girl he used to know. At that moment, the waiter came with the menu. The director asked Wang Qiyao to order, she tried politely to refuse before finally ordering two dishes. Duck feet marinated in wine and Yangzhou shredded tofu were both mid-priced dishes that would neither break the host's bank or make him lose face. Their table faced the window and the glass pane looked as if it was dyed by the color of the neon lights outside—it was like their own private fireworks display. Only a handful of the lights along the wall were lit, while the tables themselves were illuminated by candlelight. The shadows on their faces danced with the flickering of the candle as the two of them wondered just who it was sitting across the table—and what they were doing together. Since the director had already denied having any special reason for wanting to see her, he couldn't very well change his story now. He had to settle for some small talk instead. Wang Qiyao didn't believe that he had invited her for no reason. There must have been something—she just didn't know what. Both were growing impatient as they chatted about all kinds of things. They talked about the past and the present, but when they finally got to "Miss Shanghai," the conversation suddenly stopped.

The food arrived and the director mumbled a few polite words before digging in. Once he started eating, he seemed to forget the business at hand and paid attention only to what was on the table. At that moment, noticing a hole worn through the cuff of his suit and his overgrown fingernails, Wang Qiyao suddenly began to feel nauseous and put down her chopsticks. It was only after a goodly portion of the dishes had been eaten that the director started to loosen up and put on a casual demeanor. As a luster slowly lit up his face, he put down his chopsticks then, as if trying to start over from the beginning, he offered Wang Qiyao a cigarette. She declined but helped to light his. The gesture moved the director and a closer feeling of trust seemed to grow up between them.

"Yao Yao," he said at last. "At your age you should still be in school. Why bother competing in that 'Miss Shanghai' pageant anyway?"

Wang Qiyao explained that it wasn't her idea, that the waters were flowing in the right direction and she was merely riding along with the current, and in any case fate would determine the outcome.

The director continued. "You're an educated girl, so you'll have heard about women's liberation. You should hang onto your ideals. After all, those other girls competing in the 'Miss Shanghai' pageant are nothing more than the playthings of rich officials and celebrities. Is that what you call 'going with the flow?' "

"Well, I have a different opinion about that," Wang Qiyao rejoined. "As far as I'm concerned, competing in the pageant is the very symbol of a woman's liberation. The Miss Shanghai pageant confers social status on a woman. And your theory about all the girls being playthings for the rich doesn't hold water either. After all, several daughters of rich officials are competing. You're not telling me they would take advantage of their own daughters, are you?"

"You're absolutely right," the director went on. "The whole thing is precisely for those big shots' daughters. The entire pageant is one big birthday present from those big shots directly to their daughters and mistresses, everyone else is there to make them look better—it's a game within a game."

Hearing these words, Wang Qiyao's expression changed. She countered with a cold smile.

"Well, that's not how I see things. At home, every girl is somebody's daughter, but when she goes out into society she is a woman; what makes you think that they're good enough to compete, but I'm not? And even if what you said is true, I couldn't drop out of the race even if I wanted to. I'm going to see this out to the end. We'll just have to wait and see who comes out on top."

Seeing how his remarks had offended her and realizing that she had a point, the director didn't know what else to say. He managed to hem and haw his way through a clichéd speech about equality of the sexes and female emancipation, his words sounding like lines straight out of a movie. He even spoke of how it was the responsibility of the young to keep their country's fate within the horizon of their hopes and dreams.

"China today is facing an uncertain future, bullied by America and on the verge of a civil war." His words had the high-minded, arty ring of leftist cinema.

Wang Qiyao decided to stop trying to refute him and simply let him say whatever he pleased. He went on and on and, when he finally paused, she stood up to leave. The director was caught completely off guard. He was about to say something, but Wang Qiyao beat him to the punch.

"Actually, director, you also played a role in my decision to compete in the 'Miss Shanghai' pageant. If you hadn't introduced me to your friend Mr. Cheng, who took those photos for *Shanghai Life,* none of this would have happened. To tell you the truth, Mr. Cheng was the one who suggested I try out for the pageant in the first place."

With that, Wang Qiyao unleashed a mocking smile. This smile provoked the director and he was suddenly struck by an inspiring thought. "Yao Yao—excuse me—Miss Wang, the 'Miss Shanghai' crown is but a floating cloud. It may look enticing, but it will be gone before you know it. It is like mist passing before your eyes, it won't last. You'd be better off trying to fetch water with a bamboo basket. It dazzles your eyes, but in a split second it will all disappear. In my years at the film studio, I've seen my share of glamour, but at the end of the day all that is left of the cloudburst and lightning is a strip of transparent, black-and-white celluloid with a backward image. Talk about emptiness; well, there is nothing emptier than that—*that* is what you'd call vanity . . ."

Wang Qiyao didn't wait for him to finish. She turned away and walked out, leaving him talking to her retreating backside. There was a wedding banquet being held downstairs and the celebratory firecrackers drowned out his voice.

The director felt he had a historic mission to persuade Wang Qiyao to drop out of the pageant and criticize the "Miss Shanghai" beauty contest. In 1946 the film industry was among the more progressive groups in Shanghai. The revolution had already taken firm root in that circle. The director had read about theories of women's liberation, progressive youth, and the elimination of decadence in books, but the latter part of his talk was based on personal experience. He had paid a price in suffering and love for these experiences, so his advice came straight from the heart. He watched Wang Qiyao walk off—not once did she turn to look back. The more truculent she grew, the more uncertain he realized her future was. But if he had wanted to help her, there was nothing he could have done.

Strings of celebratory firecrackers continued to sound as the neon light reflected in the window turned from red to orange and from green to blue. How raucous and colorful were those Shanghai nights.

Miss Third Place

The director's words went right past Wang Qiyao's ears. Since her meeting with Wu Peizhen she had had the feeling that she could never go back to the way things were. This realization only led her to pursue her ideal even more strenuously—there was no turning back now. She wanted to turn herself around overnight, and for this there was a price to be paid. It was unclear, however, what this would entail. Her future was uncertain, but Wang Qiyao's heart was at ease. She was by nature the kind of person who puts action before words. But, owing to setbacks, she had become prone to melancholy when thinking of the past. This sadness was an encumbrance, needlessly adding to her burden; in the end, her instinct to move forward forced her to let that sadness go. Wang Qiyao seemed to fully expect to make it into the semifinals and then into the final round. Neither brought her much pleasure, as if she had bestowed these honors on herself. Because she no longer believed in miracles, the only faith she had left was in herself. Every girl who made it into the final round took it completely for granted. After round after round of competition, they had long erased any notion that it was "just luck that had gotten them this far." Once they got past that, everything was on their own shoulders.

This is what sets Shanghai girls apart from other girls—they believe in the power of the individual and take the initiative into their own hands. Frankly speaking, once you have made it into the final round, you are already halfway there and already qualify as a semicelebrity. Several of Shanghai's well-established clothing stores came knocking on Wang Qiyao's door offering to sponsor her with complimentary tailor-made outfits. When the list of finalists was released, it was simultaneously announced that the final competition would take place in three parts: the first in traditional Chinese *cheongsam*, the second in Western dress, and the third in a bridal gown. In their bridal gowns all the contestants looked as if they were about to go down the aisle. Suddenly rumors started flying around that the girls were all kept women, and people even gossiped about the famous men each was involved with. In the days leading up to the final pageant, the Jiang family refused all visitors, with the exception of Mr. Cheng. He was their sole link with the outside world. With his help, they could sit in their living room and still know everything that was going on.

Wang Qiyao, Jiang Lili and her mother, and Mr. Cheng strategized about Wang Qiyao's wardrobe in the final round. Mr. Cheng felt that whoever had decided to save the bridal dress competition for last was truly inspired.

"Most wedding gowns are relatively similar in design—the bridal photos displayed in salon windows all seem to be of the same person—bridal gowns are the ultimate emblems of purity and elegance. Let's see who can capture the essence of a bride-to-be—real gold can stand the test of blazing fire."

The three women listened spellbound to Mr. Cheng's words. Women wear their clothes on the outside, but Mr. Cheng seemed to know what was going on inside their hearts—he understood them completely.

Mr. Cheng went on, "As for the wedding gown, although it's hard to know where to begin, there are several crucial points. First, we have to take advantage of the power of contrast. The first two outfits should roll out the red carpet for the third. They should make the wedding dress stand out. Aren't wedding gowns white? Well, we'll start out by giving them brilliant colors. Aren't wedding gowns simple and pure? Well, we'll dazzle them with elaborate designs. Aren't wedding gowns right out of fairy tales? Well, we'll show them the way of the world. With the first two outfits we'll put on quite a show—give them quite an eyeful—but then we will end with a quiet echo. This is where our second tactic comes into play. Wang Qiyao will wear the simplest and most completely unadorned wedding gown, of the commonest kind you always see in display windows. By going as simple as we can, we will heighten the contrast. This should produce the strongest effect. The only difficult part lies in deciding just how to make those first two outfits stand out—for that, I'm going to have to rely on you three ladies."

But after all that, how could any of them dare say anything? As women, they all felt ashamed that they had to listen to a man's advice on fashion—it was an utter dereliction of duty. Only Wang Qiyao had a few ideas she was willing to share. After hearing Mr. Cheng's wonderful idea, she said, she had decided to wear crimson red and jade green to set off the white dress. Mr. Cheng knew right away that Wang Qiyao understood where he was going with his plan; they had some minor differences of opinion when it came to the specific colors, but that was all. He felt that, although crimson and jade were two of the most eye-catching colors, it all depended on how one wore them.

"Wang Qiyao's beauty is not the kind that can be flaunted; it's an understated beauty—the kind you come to admire only after taking it in slowly. Crimson and jade, however, are strong, decisive colors; they leave no room for gradual appreciation. The eye of man works hastily, and such strong colors could ruin Wang Qiyao chances—they will not only cover up her subtleties, but completely smother them. We want strong colors, but not *that* strong. What if we tone things down a bit and find colors that compliment Wang Qiyao's strengths? Working with her natural endowments, we could use softer colors to attain an equally powerful effect. I suggest we go with pink: with Wang Qiyao's charm this should create a delicate elegance. As for green, let's go with a warm apple green. It may be a bit rustic, but it will blend well with Wang Qiyao's purity to create a vivacious effect."

By the time Mr. Cheng had finished, there was nothing more the three ladies could say; they didn't dare add anything. And so, the color scheme for Wang Qiyao's outfits was decided in this way.

Meanwhile, rumors were spreading all over the city that the judges had been bought off and the three finalists had already been decided. The winner was to be the daughter of some rich entrepreneur, second place was to be taken by the mistress of some government VIP, and the third runner-up was supposedly a social butterfly, famous throughout Shanghai. Although this was mere gossip, the rumored winners were so much older than the other contestants that a tabloid printed a satirical essay to accuse the judges of selecting a "Madame Shanghai" instead of a "Miss Shanghai." Following this essay came another that ridiculed the pageant, insinuating that the satiric term "Madame Shanghai" meant that anyone with the right connections could become a beauty queen. A third essay appeared to dispel the rumors: the future Miss Shanghai was to be decided by a fair vote, and no bribing or purchasing of votes was allowed. This was in turn refuted by a fourth article, asserting that nothing can be done in this society without money—including garnering votes. If nationalist officials and even anti-Japanese heroes could be bribed, what was going to stop someone from buying off the "Miss Shanghai" judges? This criticism was actually a potshot at the successful bribery by a high-ranking official from Chongqing. Back and forth went the papers and tabloids with their accusations and insinuations. The smell of gunpowder rose, creating quite a show on the eve of the final round; it also brought a new tension to the atmosphere surrounding the pageant.

Mr. Cheng's visits to the Jiang home became even more frequent. He would arrive first thing in the morning and stay until late at night. They were on the eve of a major battle. Once they invited the seamstress in, she never left; she had all three meals with them and even stayed over at night. She was like an esteemed guest, but at the same time she also worked for them, supervising the tailors they had hired. Mr. Cheng was naturally the one in charge; Jiang Lili was another supervisor, as was her mother. Then there was Wang Qiyao, picking away at every little detail—every stitch had to be perfect for her. Deep down she felt rather bad about making a fuss over such minor details—*Is this what life has come down to*? The most infinitesimal matters, and yet she was expending every ounce of her heart and soul on them. She knew only too well that the seamstress's handiwork was beyond criticism, yet she was set on finding fault with her. Seeing the seamstress caught in an awkward situation, Wang Qiyao not only felt worse about herself, but even started to feel bad for the seamstress. The embroidered flowers on the pink satin *cheongsam*, however, still managed to warm her heart. Those minute, closely spaced stitches were woven into her dreams, and the meticulously worked piping was sewn into them; just looking at them brought tears to her eyes. If things didn't work out in the end, one couldn't blame them. The apple green Western outfit had a much more natural feel than the *cheongsam*: its cashmere fabric seemed to absorb the light and let it sink in, where it stabilized her mind. The pure white wedding gown inspired a myriad emotions; there were a thousand words that it was yearning to say even as it remained tragically mute—although, as every one knows, ultimate understanding requires no words at all.

These articles of clothing would venture out into the world with her, companions to her loneliness. Her intimacy with them is that of skin pressed against skin, heart against heart, but in the final analysis nothing and no one would be able to help her. She had only herself. This sadness too she could keep only to herself. During the last days leading up to the pageant finals, having to stay in the Jiang house felt like an insult, and the rumors printed in the papers felt even more of an insult. The kindness with which Mr. Cheng and the Jiangs treated her was insult heaped upon insult. All of this hurt she kept inside; outside she looked the same as ever and no one could tell that anything was wrong. Everyone was filled with anxiety as they busied themselves with their various tasks. The house could not but take on a somewhat chaotic aura, but Wang Qiyao somehow maintained her composure amid this chaos. And in spite of it all, with each hour, with each passing minute, amid the tabloid polemics, her pink and green outfits, and the hurt she carried around inside her, the pageant finals came closer.

The voting method was quite romantic. In front of the stage was a row of flower baskets, each labeled with one of the contestant's names. The judges cast their votes by placing a carnation in the basket of the woman of their choice. White and red carnations filled the lobby of the theater, selling at a hundred dollars a stem, the proceeds to be donated to flood refugees in Henan. Every carnation in Shanghai seemed to have been gathered up into the lobby of the New Heavenly Garden Theater to make a carnation gala. White and red were the colors of romance, and their fragrance was even more intoxicating. That night even the stars in the sky seemed to transform into carnations, spreading romance all around. And oh, how the lights shone! They were incredible, the way they spoke with their brilliance. People became delirious. The parasol trees beneath the lights also had a great deal to say, but they kept quiet. The traffic surged in a continuous flow with the excitement of a cheerleading squad that didn't let up.

This city has more energy than it knows what to do with. It understands neither sorrow nor the affairs of man—all it desires is to taste the full palate of worldly pleasures. Outside New Heavenly Garden, mist rose under the entrance lights. Mist had also risen amid the carnations in the antechamber, merging into a layer of clouds. The flashes of the cameras were lightning amid these clouds, unleashing an instant romantic downpour. One after another, the contestants' cars arrived. Emerging from their automobiles was their first opportunity to strike a pose and show themselves off. There was too much splendor for the eye to behold, and the evening had its first high point amid a fanfare of wild cries and cheers. The contestants were showered with strings of sparkling confetti, surrounding them in a flurry of chaos and colors—a fleeting glimpse of beauty, then the girls all disappeared inside. The people at the entrance to the New Heavenly Garden were volunteer walk-ins, their only purpose to make the atmosphere more exhilarating. A long line of people waiting to buy carnations formed in the lobby. Although each flower had been cut at the stem, they seemed to continue growing. No matter how many were sold, there were still countless baskets of them. In the blink of an eye, everyone had a stem in hand—the foyer had transformed into a soirée for carnations, where they gathered joyfully in all their delicate finery. How truly marvelous! The scent of the carnations would linger as they lay in slumber for the next forty years.

Music and dance accompanied the final round. The contestants' three-part appearances came interwoven with song, dance, and arias from Peking opera; each time they approached the stage the girls were preceded by stirring music, but once they had appeared everything seemed to stop and the audience held their breath. All eyes were on the girls. There was no room for mistakes. After each song, dance, and opera performance, a new queen was born and everyone felt that she was leading the way for the queen of queens. As for her whose fate was to be decided momentarily, what glory lay in store! The flower baskets in front of the stage gradually filled up with carnations. One after another, the flowers were placed inside, carefully and sincerely.

The carnations in the baskets could not know that they were serving to highlight the beauty of Wang Qiyao. The red and white carnations were there to anchor her pink and apple green outfits, otherwise those colors, too light, might flutter away. Amid the sea of red and white carnations, Wang Qiyao stood out, a pistil emerging from the flowers, lovely beyond words. She did not steal the attention from other girls on stage: it wasn't her style to be hostile. Instead, she slowly won the audience over. Bit by bit, as if gathering her crop at harvest time, she drew you in with her sweetness—it was as if she wanted to have a heart-to-heart with you but needed to ask your approval first. The flowers in her basket did not arrive in cascades, but they kept coming. As if by a spring trickling on without end, her basket was filled up. Wang Qiyao may not have been the most gorgeous or the most bewitching woman on stage, but she was the most popular. The three-part fashion show seemed to have been designed expressly for her. They allowed people time to get to know her and let her leave her imprint in their hearts. Each appearance on stage was more magnificent than the last; by the final round Wang Qiyao had won back the hope that she might take home the crown.

When she came out on stage for the last time in her white wedding gown, the white carnations seemed to fade into the background while the red jumped out, leaping directly on to the white gauze of her gown. Before Wang Qiyao had had a chance to become the beauty queen, she was already the queen of carnations. Hers was the most simple and common wedding dress, a step back from the razzle-dazzle of the elaborate and intricate gowns worn by the other contestants. The others were modeling wedding dresses—only she was a bride. The stage was piled up with satin, brocade, crepe, chiffon, and organza. One person only was made of flesh and blood—and that was Wang Qiyao. Charming, but with a hint of bashfulness, she even had a touch of that mild resentment that often afflicts young brides. This was the final round. Everything was coming to a head—all of her effort, all of her hopes—the result of all her ambition and hard work was to be decided. With the splendor of the moment came the pain of loss—tomorrow she would see the withered flowers carried away down the flowing rapids. Wearing that wedding dress, Wang Qiyao felt truly herself; both she and the dress embodied the sentiment that this was going to be the last time. Along with this feeling came joy, sorrow, and a slight hint of being wronged. The dress had been specially designed for Wang Qiyao and it seemed to understand just what she was going through. A tragic feeling built up inside her as she wore that wedding gown.

Reluctant to leave the stage, she slowly turned to bid farewell and in that moment she was not simply beautiful—she was real. The flowers were now falling like raindrops into her basket, but Wang Qiyao didn't have time to look; before her eyes all was a confusing blur. She felt alone and helpless, like a prisoner awaiting execution. She wanted so badly to give her all, but she didn't know where to direct her effort—it was just her and her dress, together until the end. She wanted to cry for her uncertain future. She thought back to the film studio, to the moment when the director yelled "Camera." It was all the same, down to her outfit. Back then she had been wearing a red wedding dress; this time it was a white one. Was this some kind of omen? Perhaps one always came out empty-handed after putting on a wedding dress—perhaps a wedding dress is actually a gown of mourning!

Wang Qiyao had already lost half her hope. Tears clouded her eyes. At this final moment, there seemed to be a downpour of carnations in the theater, and it was difficult to make out who was voting for whom. Some of the judges even seemed to be throwing their flowers in the wrong baskets. The climax was at hand. What followed would be either victory or defeat: a few would be exultant, all others would face disappointment. The girls stood stock still as a sinking feeling descended upon them. The rain of carnations ceased, the music stopped, as did their hearts. Now was the moment when they would be awakened from their dreams.

How quiet indeed that moment was. One could even hear the clapper of a street peddler selling porridge flavored with osmanthus blossoms—a shadow of the everyday world creeping into this peculiar place. The collective spirit began to hang low. A handful of silk-like petals danced in the stage lights, and their lack of direction left everyone with a feeling of sorrow. The faint chime of the clock was the work of the hand of fate reaching out to remind them all—no party lasts forever. There was utmost quiet. One could hear the rustling of the contestants' gowns—it was the muffled cries of their hearts. In this city that never sleeps, this was the calmest moment and the most serene place—all the quiet in Shanghai seemed to gather here. Forced to cease their activities and forbidden to make a sound, in this one moment the whole world dwelt in silence. The carnations in the antechamber and the flower baskets—all were in full bloom, yet they too were silent. From high above, the entire stage could be seen bathed in light, while the audience remained shrouded in darkness like a bottomless abyss. Never had the city been so agitated, nor had it ever witnessed such quiet. But suddenly this quiet was coming to an end and it seemed a new disturbance was brewing. The hearts leapt into the throat; the string was about to snap.

Thunderous applause broke out. The house lights came on, illuminating even the audience. The queen had been announced, with a radiant crown of gold placed on her head. Her beauty was overpowering; in a hairnet woven with shimmering beads, she looked truly regal, unquestionably one of a kind. The gold crown could only be worn by her, for it belonged to no other. Even her flower basket seemed to be larger than the rest, as if it had anticipated extra votes—indeed, in the end it was so crammed with carnations that they hung over the sides. The first runner-up had an irrepressibly coquettish air; the silver crown suited her perfectly. There were more white carnations than red in her basket, as if she had been destined to win the silver crown. She bred desire as she shot forth flirtatious glances, this sensual woman who concentrated in her person the passion of the ages—a rare beauty indeed.

The applause thundered on as the lights turned even brighter, illuminating even the furthest corners of the theater. The show was at an end, and people were about to leave. Wang Qiyao sensed that tonight belonged to other people and that tomorrow morning also belonged to them. It was at that moment that she felt a hand leading her to the center of the stage, and a flower crown was placed upon her head. Her ears buzzed with the sound of applause, and she couldn't even hear the announcement. The gold crown and the silver crown dazzled her eyes and she couldn't see a thing. Stupefied, she was led over to the side of the queen. She composed herself enough to look at her basket and saw it almost overflowing with an equal number of red and white carnations. There, before her eyes, lay the fruit of her efforts.

Wang Qiyao was second runner-up in the beauty pageant; "Miss Third Place," they called her. The title seemed to be custom-made for her. Her beauty and seductiveness, too understated, were not enough to make her the queen, but perfect for Miss Third Place. It was necessary to have a Miss Third Place. She was especially cut out to meet this intrinsic need, to play the supporting role: she symbolized the solid core underneath the resplendent surface, in no way inferior to the others and in fact truly representative of the quiet majority. In this city of romance, girls like her are the most elementary ingredient. The streets of Shanghai are crawling with girls who could have been Miss Third Place. Girls who come in first and second are always busy going to fancy parties and taking care of their various "foreign affairs." We never see them—except when they are trotted out on important occasions. They are a regular part of every grand affair. Girls like Miss Third Place, however, are a part of everyday scenes. They are familiar to our eyes, and their *cheongsams* never fail to warm our hearts. Miss Third Place therefore best expresses the will of the people. The beauty queen and the first runner-up are both idols, representing our ideals and beliefs. But Miss Third Place is connected to our everyday lives: she is a figure that reminds us of concepts like marriage, life, and family.

Mr. Cheng

MR. CHENG HAD STUDIED railway engineering, but his true love was photography. During the day he was on the staff of a Western firm, while at night he took photos and developed them at his home studio. His favorite subject was women—in his eyes the female form was the most elegant composition in the world. He had studied women and believed that a woman's best years were between the ages of sixteen and twenty-three, when delicacy and maturity were equally alluring. He spent his entire salary on his hobby; it was a good thing that he did not have any other hobbies, or a girlfriend. He had never been in love. His love lay under the lens beneath the mercury-vapor lights, always upside down. His love was in the darkroom being developed, bathed in crimson light, floating to the top of the water like a lotus made of paper. Perhaps after gazing at so many women through the lens of his beloved camera, he could not help but assign them a secondary status. Mr. Cheng gave little thought to things like marriage. His parents in Hangzhou would sometimes bring the issue up in their letters, but he paid them no heed. All his energy and emotions were devoted to photography. Merely to touch the equipment brought him happiness. He felt as if each item in his studio could speak to him and understand his joy and pain.

In the 1940s photography was still a modern hobby, which naturally made Mr. Cheng a modern youth. At twenty-six, however, he was already an old youth. When he was a bit younger he had indeed been fascinated by all the modern playthings. Whatever was fashionable in Shanghai, he was sure to give it a whirl. He had been enraptured in turn by the gramophone, tennis, and Hollywood movies, and just like all modern youths, he was fickle in his interests, always tiring of the old and moving on to the new. But once he fell in love with photography, he pledged his steadfast devotion, to the abandonment of everything else. He had first been attracted to photography because of its modern appeal, but once he was hooked, he no longer pursued what was in fashion. Photography enraptured him the same way some people fall head-over-heels in love. Suddenly he realized that his entire past had been squandered in aimless desires and pointless distractions. Yet, though much precious time and money had been wasted, Mr. Cheng congratulated himself for having discovered all this in good time.

Since his discovery of photography, he no longer qualified as a young man in pursuit of the modern; gradually he had gotten too old for that. Surface novelties could not move him any more. What he needed now was true love. No longer did his heart wander as it had in his youth. He felt a hollowness that needed to be filled with something, and that something was true love. From the outside, Mr. Cheng still looked very modern, with his slick hair parted down the middle, gold-rimmed glasses, three-piece suit, shining leather shoes, fluent English, and knowledge of all the Hollywood stars, but his heart was no longer modern. This was something that those modern girls who pursued him did not know—and this was also the reason they always went away empty-handed.

Mr. Cheng certainly had his share of admirers. He was at the suitable age for marriage and the object of attention for numerous romantic young ladies and their parents. He had a proper job and earned a respectable salary, not to mention a very interesting hobby. Poor girls! Little did they know, as they sat before the camera casting suggestive glances, that they were directing these at a cold, unfeeling machine. It was not that Mr. Cheng didn't pick up on all this; he was simply not interested. In his eyes, the girls who visited his photo studio were not real. Their every pout and smile was for the camera; none of it had anything to do with him. It was not that he did not admire their beauty; it simply did not affect him.

At twenty-six there were already some things to which he was impervious; he was quite different from the reckless seventeen- or eighteen-year-old boys who chase after their desires without the slightest regret or worry about what might happen tomorrow. A twenty-six-year-old heart has already begun to grow a shell; the shell may have some cracks and fissures, but by the age of thirty-six any remaining fissures would have been sealed. Who could still squeeze her way into a crack in Mr. Cheng's heart? Finally, a candidate appeared, and her name was Wang Qiyao. On that Sunday morning when Wang Qiyao first walked into his studio, she didn't immediately grab his attention—the lighting had filled the room with a soft darkness. Perhaps it was just this lack of any immediately striking quality that led Mr. Cheng to let his guard down. It was as if she had quietly stolen in on him.

Mr. Cheng was not terribly excited at first. He thought that Wang Qiyao was just like all the other girls you see on the street and it was hard for him to get inspired. But after each photo he seemed to discover something new about her. With each shot there was something more to explore, and so he took shot after shot, completely enchanted by what he saw. Even when he was finally finished, he still felt as if there was so much more to capture on film. Actually, that something was the lingering impression she left. Mr. Cheng suddenly began to feel disappointed by his camera. All it could capture was the "here and now"; it was helpless when it came to capturing that "lingering impression." He began to realize his inadequacy in the face of beauty. *So there is a kind of beauty that can travel through the air*, he thought. *How limited the art of photography is!* After Wang Qiyao left, he couldn't help but open the door to take a last glance at her as she stepped into the elevator. Seeing her figure behind the elevator's closed steel gate was like beholding the luminous moon obscured by a layer of cloud.

That afternoon Mr. Cheng completely lost track of time while developing the photos in his darkroom—not even the sound of the Customs House's bell could break his trance. He anxiously awaited the appearance of Wang Qiyao's face in the water as if he had just learned to develop photos; but this time he wasn't anxious about getting the technique right—he was anxious to see her. An image gradually began to form on the photographic paper and slowly grow darker; it was as if Wang Qiyao was walking toward him. He could feel his heart twitching.

Wang Qiyao had come to divide Mr. Cheng's heart against itself. She was not merely another woman captured by his lens, for she had an added significance that eluded the grasp of his camera. Actually, Mr. Cheng didn't want to grasp anything. He felt he had lost something—something deep inside—and he needed to get it back. And so he tried different tactics, but the whole process took place in the dark because he didn't know what the cause was—just as he could never know the outcome. He submitted Wang Qiyao's photo to *Shanghai Life* magazine, never imagining that they would actually publish it. Knowing that people were handling her picture, however, didn't make him feel good. Not only had he failed to find that missing something on the inside but he seemed to lose something else as well.

The picture had been Mr. Cheng's favorite, but now that it was published, he came to disdain it. Only once did he visit the photo shop that had Wang Qiyao's picture on display in the window, and this was late at night. There were barely any people or cars still out on the streets, the city lights were all dark, and the late-show crowds that had been lingering around outside the movie theater were already gone. As Mr. Cheng stood outside the shop window, an awkward feeling welled up inside him; the image in the window was so close and yet so far. In the window he could see his own reflection, the face under his fedora hat revealing traces of sorrow. Standing there under the streetlights of the deserted road, he felt lonely. Beyond those pockets of excitement animating this city that never sleeps lurks the loneliest breed of loneliness.

After this he did two more photo shoots with Wang Qiyao, but not only did he fail to find what he was looking for, but each time he seemed to come away with an indescribable feeling of loss. At the same time, Wang Qiyao did not even seem to be looking into Mr. Cheng's camera; she was looking into the eyes of the people. Each pout, every smile was arranged for the front or back cover of another magazine; her image seemed to be waving to her readers. Mr. Cheng felt as if his eyes were not his own; they represented the people. That was the last time that he suggested Wang Qiyao sit for his camera.

He thought of asking her out, but couldn't bring himself to. On one occasion he called her up, having already bought two movie tickets, but as soon as Wang Qiyao picked up the phone, he lost his nerve and said he was calling about something else. Although at twenty-six Mr. Cheng had seen his share of beautiful women, he had always viewed them with detachment. In many respects he couldn't even measure up to a sixteen-year-old boy. At the very least, sixteen-year-olds have courage, but Mr. Cheng had neither courage nor experience—he had nothing. Mr. Cheng's dream of having a date with Wang Qiyao was only realized after she became friends with Jiang Lili. He ended up inviting both of them out. That was the only way he could get up the nerve to ask. And although Wang Qiyao didn't say so, she was secretly quite pleased. Not that she was interested in Mr. Cheng, but she was eager to be on a more equal footing with Jiang Lili. Since she had become close with Jiang Lili, the two had spent all their time around the Jiang social circle, and now Wang Qiyao finally had a chance to take her out with one of *her* friends. That night Mr. Cheng invited them to an American film at the Cathay Theater. He arrived first and waited for them at the entrance; the two schoolgirls were in high spirits as they came down the street, chatted animatedly in the sunlight under the parasol trees. The clear sky was festooned with a few silk-like clouds, their shadows dancing on the side of the buildings.

A man taking two girls out is a wondrous sight. It is an event of bashful solemnity, a grand affair that leaves one full of thoughts and questions. Some afternoons are designed especially for these types of dates, afternoons redolent with languor, ambiguity, feigned naiveté, and genuine feeling.

Jiang Lili had heard about Mr. Cheng, but this was the first time they met. Wang Qiyao introduced them before they entered the theater. Jiang Lili sat between Wang Qiyao and Mr. Cheng. Of course there is always something going on between the two who sit on the outside and although the one in the middle acts as a partition, she is also a bridge. When Wang Qiyao offered Mr. Cheng some olives, Jiang Lili had to hand them over. When the film's dialogue got complicated, Mr. Cheng would translate for Jiang Lili, who would in turn pass on the translation to Wang Qiyao. Throughout the movie Wang Qiyao was holding Jiang Lili's hand as if they were trying to isolate Mr. Cheng. And though Mr. Cheng was equally attentive to both girls, Jiang Lili was actually getting in the way. The theater was pitch black, save for the column of rotating light emanating from the hole in the projection room to create an illusionary world. The cinema was far from full at this afternoon show; people sat scattered in twos and threes throughout the theater, and everyone seemed occupied with their own thoughts. The dialogue on the screen reverberated above their heads and buzzed in their ears. Feeling somewhat intimidated, the three of them pressed close against one another. Jiang Lili could hear the sound of breathing and hearts beating only inches away; she didn't catch much of the film, but instead served as a mouthpiece for the two sitting on either side of her. Although Mr. Cheng leaned close, whispering to her, every word was meant for Wang Qiyao, even if his utterings did happen to reach Jiang Lili's ears first.

As they emerged from the theater onto the sunny street, Mr. Cheng appeared a different person. Afterward they went for coffee, the two girls sitting together on one bench with Mr. Cheng on the opposite side. Although Mr. Cheng's words were directed at Wang Qiyao, he kept looking at Jiang Lili. Wang Qiyao didn't answer his questions; Jiang Lili spoke for her. Their conversation was not about anything in particular, just small talk, and either of them could have answered. But gradually Jiang Lili began to say more and hog the conversation. Mr. Cheng would ask a question clearly directed at both of them, but she would answer only for herself, while Wang Qiyao remained silent. Mr. Cheng had no choice but to follow Jiang Lili's lead. In the end the two of them were having a heart-to-heart talk. They acted as if they were close friends who had known one another for years, as Wang Qiyao watched from the sidelines. What a shame that, although Mr. Cheng was completely consumed by Wang Qiyao, he couldn't share a word with her, nor did he dare look directly at her. Jiang Lili's words were like a river overflowing with literary phrases, but it was awkward for Mr. Cheng to let his eyes linger on her, so he stared into his cup of coffee. Reflected there in the cup was Wang Qiyao's image, but still she did not speak. Only when he looked down did Jiang Lili stop talking. She too lowered her head to gaze into her coffee cup—and there was reflected Mr. Cheng's image, looking down in silence.

From then on Mr. Cheng became their regular evening date. He was like their guardian angel, always following close behind them and seeing them both home. Mr. Cheng began to neglect his old hobby of photography. His camera became covered with dust and his darkroom began to grow mildew; whenever he stepped inside he would be struck by a strange, unnamable sensation. The true love that lurked deep in his heart had transformed from something cold into something hot, from something hollow to something tangible.

Mr. Cheng was an ardent enthusiast for their evening dates at first; they filled up many lonely nights for him. Parties had not lost their novelty, but attending them with Wang Qiyao quickly cast a pall over them. The main reason he went to the parties was to get closer to Wang Qiyao, but Wang Qiyao grew even more distant from him. Eventually Wang Qiyao did begin to talk more and acted more cordial—in order to fend him off—but oddly enough Mr. Cheng then found himself at a loss for words. Whatever he said failed to capture his true feelings and ended up being the kind of empty talk he could have said to anyone else. Everything that took place on their dates was shared; when they laughed or got silly they did it together and when they met up and departed it was always as a group. Parties were settings uniquely devoid of personal freedom, and someone like Mr. Cheng, who thought up designs of his own, was doomed to be disappointed. Still he couldn't stop himself from going. Even though Wang Qiyao had become a phantom, he couldn't stop chasing after her. Even when the phantom had disappeared in the wind, he continued to search for her. At parties he would stand in the corner, holding his drink, barely moving the entire evening. Wang Qiyao seemed to fill the air, waiting for him to gaze upon her, but he couldn't see her. The nights were full of dejection. The surrounding excitement mocked him, but still he did not retreat.

In Jiang Lili's eyes, Mr. Cheng also turned into a phantom at those parties, a phantom who had lost his way. She said whatever she could to bring him back into the world, but her loquaciousness irritated him. However, being a soft-natured man who did not like to hurt anyone's pride, he would always force himself to make a few perfunctory remarks in reply, but this left him feeling even more dejected. The gloomier Mr. Cheng appeared, the more Jiang Lili became set on cheering him up. Even if he was as cold as ice, she believed that she could melt him with her warmth. This was where all the novels she had read came in handy. They taught her how to be soft and passionate, how to use elegant words, and how to analyze situations—a pity, then, that she was playing the wrong part. Having started off with an awkward sentence, the rest of the essay had run askew. She was operating under misguided hopes and misplaced confidence. Mr. Cheng was completely at her mercy at these parties. Although he was almost catatonic, even a shell of a man would have satisfied Jiang Lili—and if the shell were smashed, she would have assiduously picked up the broken pieces. Jiang Lili always said she went to these parties for Wang Qiyao's sake, but actually it was for Mr. Cheng. She was like an outsider, always standing in the corner. That wasn't what she wanted, but because Mr. Cheng was an outsider, she had no choice but to go over to the corner to join him. When Mr. Cheng was depressed, she couldn't help being depressed too; her whole heart was with him. A shame, then, that Mr. Cheng couldn't see any of that. The only thing on his mind was Wang Qiyao—only Wang Qiyao and he were real, for everyone else was wearing a mask; only their two hearts were genuine, while the others could not even recognize what was authentic. A pity that those two hearts were not on the same path; the more genuine they were, the more difficult it was for them ever to meet.

Suggesting that she compete for "Miss Shanghai" was Mr. Cheng's way of trying to please Wang Qiyao. When Jiang Lili enthusiastically seconded the nomination, it was only partially in support of Wang Qiyao; the main reason was actually Mr. Cheng. Those days may have been difficult for Wang Qiyao to get through, but they represented the best of times for Mr. Cheng and Jiang Lili. The three of them saw each other almost every other day, but whenever they met they always had an endless array of things to talk about. Once Wang Qiyao moved into the Jiang house and Mr. Cheng started to come around, even Jiang Lili's mother got fired up. Visitors to the Jiang house came in spurts, waves of excitement followed by dry spells of cheerless desolation. But whenever Mr. Cheng dropped by, the desolation would lift and the house took on a warm glow. Though a visitor, he brought a sense of family to this house where there was no man aside from a boorish young son. Furthermore,

Mr. Cheng was the kind of man who could help them make decisions. Even when he was not making decisions, his presence in the living room was a welcome sight.

In the days leading up to the pageant Mr. Cheng and Jiang Lili both found a channel for their energies and a temporary object upon which they could sublimate their respective infatuations. They both couldn't have been happier. Now that they had a common objective, they suddenly found a common language—but Wang Qiyao found herself in the awkward position of being forced to sing a different tune if only to assert some control over her own life. So the more united the other two grew in trying to please her, the more discordant her song became. The three of them ended up on two teams, and for Wang Qiyao it was two against one. In her heart she knew that they were trying to help her, but she couldn't help displaying a bit of guile and stubbornness to boost her own confidence. Thus, though divided into opposite camps, they were united in a common cause; cocooned in their separate passions, they were nonetheless willing to sink their differences and try to make the best of things.

One man and two women was the most common grouping of lovers to be found in 1946. Herein lies the starting point of the comedies and the tragedies, the truths and the absurdities. In the dappled shade under the trees, a pedicab carries two ladies, followed by a second pedicab carrying a man—so begin countless stories like this one. Who can guess how this one will end?

As the pageant drew closer, Wang Qiyao became genuinely excited whenever Mr. Cheng showed up. At this time, when nothing else was certain, he was a known factor. And although he wasn't enough, at least he was something—someone she could rely on. To what extent Wang Qiyao was willing to put her fate in his hands was something to which she gave little thought; she couldn't. Perhaps she was thinking: *Even if I take ten thousand steps back, in the end I'll still have Mr. Cheng; even if everything comes to naught, when all is said and done he will still be there.* Mr. Cheng was her cushion. Staying with the Jiang family had hundreds of benefits, but not a single one rightfully belonged to her. Although she was living the good life, that life lay at the margins of someone else's life. It was as if she were living her own life as a remnant. Returning home meant that she could be a whole piece of fabric again, but her whole piece was smaller than other people's remnants, not even good enough to serve as the lining of a presentable suit. Even though Mr. Cheng was also a remnant, at least he was presentable.

During those times when her spirit was at its lowest, Wang Qiyao went out with Mr. Cheng alone a couple of times. Once he accompanied her home to pick up some things. He did not enter the *longtang* with her but instead waited in a coffee shop down the street. Staring out the window at the passersby, Mr. Cheng would say to himself: *Wang Qiyao should be coming up behind this girl.* Or *Once that guy walks past, I bet she'll appear.* He didn't even realize that his coffee had grown cold. The chimes of the trolley clanking by were pacifying music to his ears, and the sunlight shining through the parasol trees seemed as if it too was playing a silvery tune. Finally Wang Qiyao emerged in the sunlight, which seemed to shine right through her. She was so stunning, as if she had walked straight out of a painting, that he feared she was about to melt into thin air. Mr. Cheng had the sudden urge to run over and save her, no matter what it might cost him. He was so agitated that his eyes grew teary. At the same time, however, he felt somewhat aggrieved. The dust had continued to collect in his photo studio. The container of fixing solution left in his darkroom had become discolored. Countless days had passed since he had even stepped inside! He was aware that he had put himself in an awkward situation, without a backup plan, virtually cutting off any way out. He could only move forward. By the time he realized his coffee had grown cold, Wang Qiyao was already standing before him. But once she was there his rancor was replaced by a wholehearted devotion. Wang Qiyao didn't even sit down; she wanted to leave straightaway, as if sitting down would signal that she had made some kind of commitment. Although she valued him as a fallback in the event of complete debacle, her present circumstances were nowhere near so desperate. Nonetheless, she wanted him around for a sense of security, as well as for Jiang Lili's sake.

Naturally she understood Jiang Lili's heart. As long as she wasn't blinded by passion, there wasn't anything a sensitive girl like Wang Qiyao couldn't see. She even understood the heart of Jiang Lili's mother, an incompetent woman who needed to consult Wang Qiyao on everything, no matter how trivial—at least before Mr. Cheng came along. When Mrs. Jiang had to attend a relative's wedding, she used the pretext that Wang Qiyao wasn't feeling good to get Mr. Cheng to accompany them to the banquet. Her transparent actions left Wang Qiyao feeling at once angry, bemused, and sorry for her. Whenever things like this occurred, Wang Qiyao knew she had to step aside and let the Jiangs have their way. This time the problem was that if she didn't go, neither would Mr. Cheng. In the end, all four of them attended together so that Mrs. Jiang would not lose face. Throughout the evening, Wang Qiyao never left Mrs. Jiang's side, while keeping open the seat next to Mr. Cheng, which Jiang Lili dutifully filled. By bringing together Jiang Lili and Mr. Cheng, Wang Qiyao was partially setting things up for her own retreat. It was also her way of looking out for Jiang Lili and her mother, as well as an opportunity to sit back and laugh at them. She knew better than anyone that Mr. Cheng had already invested his heart in her, which gave her self-esteem a padding she could always fall back on. Although it was painful to see Jiang Lili throwing herself against a brick wall, it was also a means for Wang Qiyao to vent some of her own pent-up resentment.

Mr. Cheng never knew what she was thinking. She had a complicated mind, one made more complex by her situation. Mr. Cheng had unwittingly fallen into a labyrinth, wherein he was constantly chasing after Wang Qiyao, but somehow always ending up in Jiang Lili's company. Mr. Cheng was a straightforward man who never overanalyzed his surroundings. He thought of Jiang Lili and her mother only as warmhearted people and, although they sometimes seemed to go a bit overboard, he never suspected that anything else was afoot. So he repaid their warmheartedness in kind, never imagining his innocent actions would take him down a path he did not wish to follow.

Who knows how many times Jiang Lili shed tears over Mr. Cheng? Mr. Cheng either paying a little extra attention to her or neglecting her was reason enough for her to run back to her room to cry. Her room had been fixed up by then. The books were all neatly shelved and in proper order. The teacups were washed every day. She was constantly replacing her old phonograph records with the latest ones, mostly romantic serenades; Hanging at the head of her bed were a few hand-embroidered fragrant pouches, the handiwork of Wang Qiyao; inside her wardrobe were bright, colorful new clothes, all conforming to Mr. Cheng's tastes. The room had a lively atmosphere, a mild, docile, and amiable temperament, a mood of expectation. She had written many words never to be seen by another, all hidden away in her diary, which she kept bundled in a crimson silk cloth. She could never see things clearly, sometimes because she had been blinded by love, and other times because she was too wrapped up in her own feeling of entitlement. She had power over Wang Qiyao and it seemed only natural that this power should carry over to Wang Qiyao's friends. But even *she* was a bit hazy when it came to this entitlement and couldn't figure out just how much was real and how much existed in name only. Which part was rightfully hers? And which part was owing to a fair trade they had made? Ever since her childhood

Jiang Lili had been accustomed to getting her way, which in the end set her up for a fall.

When it got to the point that Jiang Lili couldn't stand the torment anymore, she would pour her heart out to Wang Qiyao. It was the kind of melodramatic venting one reads of in novels. As she spoke, she often skipped over entire sentences and her words failed to convey what she wanted to say, but those were precisely the moments when she revealed her true feelings. This distressed Wang Qiyao and left her at an utter loss for words. It would have been wrong to rain on her parade at that moment, but even more irresponsible to encourage her. The situation was extremely difficult to negotiate diplomatically, and it was hard too to speak the truth. Wang Qiyao had no choice but to let Lili carry on as she pleased and refrain from taking any position at all herself. However, after Jiang Lili began to incessantly solicit her advice about Mr. Cheng, Wang Qiyao was forced to agree that he wasn't half bad. But when pushed further, she added, "But he is a bit bookish . . ."

"He's not bookish," Jiang Lili retorted. "It's called being *refined* . . ."

Seeing how infatuated she was, Wang Qiyao would sometimes drop Jiang Lili a little hint, telling her things like, "Everything comes down to fate. If you don't have that on your side, all efforts will be in vain."

Hearing those words, Jiang Lili could no longer contain her joy. "That's right," she replied. "I often think about how big a role coincidence actually plays. It was just chance that you and I met, and then you brought Mr. Cheng into my life—this kind of coincidence is fate!"

Sighing in private, Wang Qiyao told herself that she had fulfilled her obligation and that from here on out none of their affairs would have anything to do with her.

Everything boiled down to the final round of the pageant. They felt that as soon as the day came, everything would be clarified. And so their entire focus was on getting to that day. Once it arrived, however, they discovered that nothing was as it had seemed. Looking up, they realized that even though several years, several decades could all be revealed in an instant, they would remain in the dark for awhile yet. That night the three of them—one from the stage and two from the audience—would find that the focus of all their dedication and hard work was now out of their hands and up to the whims of fate; there was something sad and moving about this. The stage was filled with girls, but those two sitting out in the audience only had eyes for one. They had invested so much in this pageant that it was impossible for them to make any objective judgment. They felt like prisoners about to be executed, with no other choice but to wait there helplessly for the end to come, for the hand of fate to descend.

During round 3, Mr. Cheng was nearly brought to tears when he saw Wang Qiyao in her wedding gown. Here was the apparition he had been yearning for day and night, the dream he had hoped would never end. Jiang Lili also became teary-eyed, but in that wedding dress she saw not Wang Qiyao but herself. To Lili this was no dream, but a vision of her own future. At that second, as the three of them, on stage and off, faced one another, their eyes glistening with tears, their hearts were miles apart. At that last climactic moment Jiang Lili impulsively grabbed hold of Mr. Cheng's hand. Mr. Cheng didn't resist, but neither did he reciprocate, as his attention remained fully focused on the stage. His entire body was numb, not to mention his hands. When it was announced that Wang Qiyao had won the honor of third place, Mr. Cheng instinctively stood up. He momentarily squeezed Jiang Lili's hand before withdrawing his own so that he could applaud with all his might. Jiang Lili also applauded. She felt as if she had been struck by lightning, and she blushed.

In that moment the evening seemed to have come to a perfect finish. Although Wang Qiyao had not been awarded the top honor, coming in third place somehow felt more solid. The passionate couple in the audience each seemed to have caught a glimmer of hope. That night Mr. Cheng and Jiang Lili waited in the lobby as Wang Qiyao was being photographed and interviewed. The scent of the carnations in the lobby had begun to wane; the crimson and white colors were no longer quite as bright; the blossoms were beginning to wither, strewing their petals all over the floor. The show was winding down. The lobby lights were the last lingering vestiges of brilliance, and the atmosphere of expectation had dissipated. The traffic on the street had died down, but dumpling vendors had quietly appeared on the sidewalks: a late-night scene.

The next morning a clean-shaven Mr. Cheng, wearing a sharp outfit, arrived at the Jiang house. The girls had already made themselves up and were sitting in the living room. You could tell from their eyes—a bit puffy and bloodshot—that the three of them had been up all night. The sun was slightly wet and sticky, shining down on the waxed wooden floor—the wax itself appeared to be on the brink of melting. Jiang Lili's mother personally prepared tea and snacks; even she was wearing a new outfit. The feeling was that of the morning after a rip-roaring New Year's Eve. The shreds of firecracker paper had all been swept away, and although the New Year had only just begun, a sense of weariness had already set in.

It would be unreasonable to expect the celebratory mood to last for an entire year. They revisited the night before, each adding their own take on what had transpired, constantly expanding on and correcting what the others were saying—as if they wanted to relive that moment. The bright lights and dazzling carnations from the night before were unreal under the muggy sun, everything that had happened seemed faint and distant. And so they tried even harder to recall every little detail.

The morning passed but they carried their conversation over to lunch. The table also made it seem like it was New Year's Day. There was a new tablecloth and the chinaware was the special set reserved for the New Year. However, the excitement at the table barely concealed a feeling of let down; more than half the day had passed and nothing new had yet occurred. Afternoons are always lethargic: it is difficult to get one's energy up and everything feels a bit off. The dust was sticky in the gray light. Having sat in silence for a while, Jiang Lili got up and walked over to the piano in the corner of the room. She toyed with different melodies, off and on, as a kind of encouragement to push them forward. With nothing else to do, Mr. Cheng walked over to the piano and, leaning against it, asked Jiang Lili if she knew how to play this or that song. Jiang Lili used the piano to answer him. She couldn't play all of them, but she knew passages from almost every one. It was as if she was acceding to his every wish, and the two started genuinely to enjoy themselves. A young lady at the piano and a gentleman standing right beside her made the very picture of affluent domestic bliss.

Sitting on the sofa on the other side of the room and looking at them, Wang Qiyao suddenly realized that her days in the spotlight were over. *Oh, the glory of yesterday!* The sound of the piano grated on her ears—it seemed to mock her and pierced her to the heart. Jiang Lili at the piano looked elegant and aloof despite being so plain; even Mr. Cheng seemed to have grown distant at that moment. Wang Qiyao grew depressed—not an unusual feeling in the wake of a grand event with its frenzy of emotions and excessive hopes. She stared out at the garden on that winter day; the branches of the lilac trees were all intertwined, impossible to disentangle; the sun shone brighter and the air grew brisk. No one was thinking about the night before, everything appeared relaxed and free of purpose. That was simply how things went in Shanghai: even the greatest excitement lasted only an instant. Wang Qiyao told herself that it was time for her to go back home. Mr. Cheng turned around at this moment. "Wang Qiyao, come over and sing us a song!" he said.

Wang Qiyao could no longer contain her resentment. She turned red and laughed sardonically, "I'm no artist like Jiang Lili. What am I supposed to sing?"

Jiang Lili continued to concentrate on playing, but Mr. Cheng felt uneasy after hearing Wang Qiyao's response. He came over to her and suggested, "What do you say to catching a movie together?"

"I'm not going!" Wang Qiyao declared in a fit of pique.

Mr. Cheng decided to try something else. "I'd like to invite you two young ladies to dinner at a Western restaurant."

But Wang Qiyao begged off; she turned her head away, tears in her eyes. Mr. Cheng was truly considerate, but it was precisely his consideration that rubbed her the wrong way. The two of them sat in silence. The sound of Jiang Lili's piano playing no longer grated on Wang Qiyao's ears. It had become a soft, heart-rending melody.

From that day Wang Qiyao started to date Mr. Cheng. She would tell Jiang Lili that she was going back home to visit, but she would turn back around as soon as she got to the end of the *longtang*. On two occasions when she came back from the movies late at night she could hear the sound of Jiang Lili's piano ringing out through the expansive night even before she reached the door; it was Lili's way of talking to herself. She had resumed her piano lessons, having finally found something that pleased Mr. Cheng, and something through which she could express her feelings. Wang Qiyao would tiptoe into the house, but Jiang Lili always heard her and stopped her in order that she might share in the latter's feelings. Even the moon outside the window was affected by Lili's outpourings. Jiang Lili had settled on Wang Qiyao as her confidante, and Wang Qiyao could not escape. When she mentioned the possibility of moving back home, Jiang Lili would not hear of it. If Wang Qiyao went back home, she said, then she was going too. There was no way she could stand being separated from Wang Qiyao. Jiang Lili had always been somewhat melodramatic, but her feelings were nevertheless real and Wang Qiyao had to take her seriously. She was also aware that although she had made no promises to Mr. Cheng, she was depriving Jiang Lili of her chances. It wouldn't have been so bad if she didn't know how much Jiang Lili was in love, but Jiang Lili made sure that she knew all about it. Wang Qiyao's ideas about ethical behavior didn't come from romance novels, nor did they involve complicated principles; simply speaking, they were reciprocity, respect, and trust—if you do me a good turn, I owe you one. Wang Qiyao felt guilty around Jiang Lili and behaved even more solicitously to her than before. She began treating her like a real sister.

"How come Mr. Cheng never stops by anymore?" Jiang Lili once asked.

The look on Jiang Lili's face left Wang Qiyao no choice but to stop accepting Mr. Cheng's invitations to go out alone with him. Consequently, he was again forced to visit the Jiang house frequently. Jiang Lili couldn't have been happier; Wang Qiyao felt she was compounding a blunder, but was helpless to do anything else. The only salve to her conscience was that she never made Mr. Cheng any promises. She relied on this to maintain a balance. But a non-promise is a very thin line. She was walking a tightrope. Skill was everything, as was maintaining her composure.

Then one day a shy and anxious Mr. Cheng suggested that she pay another visit to his photo studio. The invitation had an implied meaning—if she pretended not to understand it, they could still keep up a semblance of normality; but should she refuse, then all the cards would be laid out on the table. Wang Qiyao wanted to keep things hazy; it was too early for conclusions. Her ambition had lately been rekindled, thanks perhaps to Mr. Cheng's adulation.

This visit to Mr. Cheng's photo studio also took place on a Sunday. The day before Mr. Cheng tidied the place up, wiping away all the dust. He placed fresh flowers—two roses amid a bunch of baby's breath—on the dressing table, on which a small framed photo of Wang Qiyao was also displayed. In the photo, taken during her first visit, Wang Qiyao appeared several years younger, but it had actually been less than two years. The scene outside the window remained the same. It was as if those two years had left their mark only on Wang Qiyao; everything else was untouched. The flowers and the photo were both there to greet her—especially the latter, which needed no explanation. They were the sincere offerings of an honest man. Wang Qiyao pretended not to notice anything. Emerging from the powder room with light makeup, she sat down before the camera and the lights went up. Their minds flew back to that Sunday afternoon two years earlier. The lighting was the same, but they had been strangers then, two faceless souls like the countless others seen from the window wandering the streets below. Now, though the future was still unknown, at least they had some sort of understanding between them, which was very rare in their world. And even though it had been quite some time since Mr. Cheng had shot Wang Qiyao, they weren't at all uncomfortable; in fact, they behaved as if they were old partners.

Mornings always go by quickly. Time moved briskly beyond the thick curtains, while inside the lights shone bright. Neither of them felt hungry. It was as if they never wanted that session to end. They chatted incessantly; there were so many things that, looking back, seemed terribly entertaining. They started out with shared experiences before moving on to take turns telling stories about themselves. One would talk and the other would listen; gradually they both became spellbound and forgot about taking photos. They sat on the small steps in front of the backdrop, one slightly higher than the other. The lamps were out now, but some natural light crept in from beyond the curtains. Mr. Cheng told her how, when he was in Changsha studying railway engineering, he heard about the Japanese bombing of Jiabei and rushed back to Shanghai to join his family. The journey was long and arduous, and he had never imagined that by the time he finally arrived his entire family would already have moved on to Hangzhou. He thought about following them to Hangzhou, but the situation in Shanghai had stabilized, and so he decided to stay. Thus began what would eventually turn into eight years in Shanghai, eight lonely years—that is, until he met Wang Qiyao.

Wang Qiyao told him about her grandmother in Suzhou, the gardenia in front of her house, and her consummate skills in making sticky long-legged rice dumplings. Her grandmother often went to pray and burn incense at the temple on East Hill, where one could find miniature wooden tea sets carved by hand at the fair; the teacups were no bigger than a finger nail and only held a drop of water. The last time Wang Qiyao had gone to visit her in Suzhou was the year before she met Mr. Cheng.

The novelty of the situation carried them along and their conversation went all over the place—no topic was off-limits. Time stood still and they stopped worrying about consequences; all they cared about was this moment of happiness. Mr. Cheng eventually went on to describe to Wang Qiyao his very first impression of her. Although these words had a confessional side, neither looked at it that way; he simply spoke from his heart and she listened with hers, with a hint of playfulness between them.

"If I had a sister . . . and were able to choose what she was like," said Mr. Cheng. "I would pick someone just like you."

Wang Qiyao replied by saying that if she had an uncle, she wished he could be just like Mr. Cheng. This exchange was nothing more than a playful means of connecting and neither of them took it much to heart. It was just that they felt free to say whatever was on their minds. And then the two of them stood up . . . they were so close. Their eyes sparkled; their glances met for a split second before breaking apart.

Mr. Cheng pulled the curtain open and the sun came streaming in, bringing with it floating stars of dust dancing in light so bright they could barely keep their eyes open. Gazing out the window at the river, they saw foreign ships at anchor, their colorful flags blowing in the wind. The people below were like ants, moving around in groups, breaking up and regrouping, but everything seemed orchestrated and their movements had a definite beginning and end. The Huangpu River rolled briskly on down toward the sea, disappearing at each end on the horizon so that all they witnessed was one moment of the river passing by. As the two leaned against the window, the bell at the Customs House rang out twice—it was already afternoon! They had spent an entire morning baring their souls to one another with little thought for what might be gained or lost. These unhurried interludes that usually lead nowhere—rather extravagant in this fast-paced world—often turn out to be the most precious and unforgettable moments in our toilsome lives.

By the next day Mr. Cheng had already got all of the photos developed. Although not every shot came out well, they were unlike any photos he had ever produced. Taken as they talked and joked together, the photos captured something very rare. In some of the photos Wang Qiyao seemed to be caught in mid-sentence, in others she appeared to be listening; but the exchanges were heartfelt and personal—not intended for other ears. These were photos meant for private enjoyment, never to be displayed to the public. Together they looked over them in a coffee house, chuckling over each image. The scene from the day before was fresh in their minds.

"Look at you here!" Mr. Cheng exclaimed.

Wang Qiyao laughed, "Oh my, how could I possibly look like that?"

Thinking back, they pieced together what had been going on when a particular shot was taken. "Oh, so that's what happened!"

Each photo had a set of circumstances surrounding it, broken, illogical, little events that didn't seem to add up to a story—but then again, who knows for sure? Once Wang Qiyao had gotten through the whole stack, Mr. Cheng had her turn them over to see what was written on the other side. He had inscribed the back of each photo with a poem. Some were classical poems, others were in the modern vernacular, but the majority were original pieces written by Mr. Cheng. They described Wang Qiyao's spirit and appearance and expressed the feelings of Mr. Cheng for her. Wang Qiyao was touched, but she masked her emotion with a joke. "This is more Jiang Lili's style," she quipped.

At the mention of Jiang Lili's name, they both grew uncomfortable and fell silent.

After a pause, Mr. Cheng asked, "You don't plan on staying on at the Jiang house, do you?"

Mr. Cheng was probing her intentions for his own purpose, but the question hit a sore spot. Wang Qiyao's expression changed and she responded with a sardonic smile, "My family calls every day begging me to come home, but Jiang Lili simply won't let me go. She keeps saying that her home is my home. She might not see it, but I realize what's going on. Just what am I staying in their house like that for? Their maidservant? A little country girl hired to keep the mistress company for life? I'm just waiting for the right opportunity to move out without making Jiang Lili feel bad."

Seeing how upset she was, Mr. Cheng blamed himself for not being considerate enough of Wang Qiyao's feelings, but he had no way to take back what he had just said. Wang Qiyao, for her part, seeing Mr. Cheng's uneasiness, realized that she had overreacted and softened up a bit. The two chatted on about some innocuous topics before saying goodbye.

As things turned out, the opportunity for Wang Qiyao to move out of the Jiang household presented itself just a few days later. Unfortunately, the way things came about left everyone upset. One night Jiang Lili went into Wang Qiyao's room looking for a book she had lent her. Jiang Lili didn't find the book, but beside Wang Qiyao's pillow she saw the photos—and the poems Mr. Cheng had inscribed on them. Jiang Lili had been blind to Mr. Cheng's intentions vis-à-vis Wang Qiyao even though they had been right there before her eyes all this time, but the photos forced her to come face-to-face with reality. A suspicion she had long suppressed and buried deep in her heart was suddenly yanked out into the open—all at once the water subsided and the rocks were exposed. This revelation utterly destroyed Jiang Lili's love, as it destroyed her friendship. Jiang Lili had worn her heart on her sleeve in both of these relationships. She had willingly devoted so much of herself to both of them. Never had she imagined that this would be how things would come to an end.

Director Li

A request for Wang Qiyao's presence at a grand opening arrived the day Wang Qiyao moved out of the Jiang house. Wang Qiyao had already stepped into the pedicab when the Jiang's *amah* rushed over with the envelope. Wang Qiyao noticed the unmistakable look of joy on the old

Cantonese woman's face and knew that she was only too happy to see her go. She wondered how she could have earned the enmity of someone she barely even knew. Why would the *amah* hate her for no apparent reason?

Neither Jiang Lili or her mother came out to see Wang Qiyao off; Lili's excuse was that she had to make a trip to the university to register for classes, and her mother had a headache. This left Wang Qiyao with the feeling that she was taking flight amid defeat. Dressed in a beige short-sleeved silk *cheongsam*, Wang Qiyao was carrying a folded fan to block the early autumn sun, in whose rays lingered the last remnants of summer. The sound of cicadas rang out one after another, but the trees stretching their canopies over the street were already showing fall colors. Her spirit was so low that she didn't have the energy to open the envelope in her hand. She had not told Mr. Cheng about what happened: some things are tricky to explain. She was also in something of a pique and rather enjoyed making her situation appear worse than it really was—as if that was the only way to vent her resentment. As the pedicab emerged from the broad *longtang*, a scented mist rose up from the lilacs along the courtyard walls. The street just outside the *longtang* was empty of people and traffic, and the quietude also seemed to send up a mist. When Wang Qiyao finally opened the envelope in her hand, she discovered it was an invitation to cut the red ribbon at the grand opening of a department store. The invitation didn't make her terribly excited. If anything, it led her to ponder sarcastically just what a "Miss Third Place" like herself could possibly bring to such a grand opening. It was probably a second-rate department store and they couldn't get Miss Shanghai or the girl who came in second—so they had to settle for her. It was turning out to be a dreary day. Another chapter of her life was over. Although things had come to a close, the aftermath held plenty of clean-up work for her.

She arrived back at home just in time for lunch, but told her family she had already eaten and went into the small *tingzijian* with a few books. The floor and walls in the *tingzijian* were all a dirty gray, having just been scrubbed with soapy water. Wang Qiyao's mind was unusually serene as she spent the entire afternoon reading. Around dusk she received two phone calls. The first was from Mr. Cheng, who asked her why she had gone home. He only learned of her departure after a trip to Jiang Lili's house, where he was told that she had some matters to take care of at home. When Mr. Cheng asked Wang Qiyao what exactly had happened and offered to help out, she laughed. "Nothing of consequence; actually it was an excuse to get out of there."

Mr. Cheng heaved a sigh of relief and, after some hesitation, asked whether her sudden departure had something to do with what he had said the other day.

Wang Qiyao replied with a question. "Just what did you say the other day? How come *I* don't remember anything about it?"

Too embarrassed to press the issue, Mr. Cheng paused for a moment and then asked if he could come and see her. She said that since she had only just returned home, she needed to take care of some errands, but they could talk about getting together in a few days.

The second telephone call came from the department store, reiterating the invitation. She was informed that a car would be sent to pick her up. The ribbon-cutting ceremony would be followed by a banquet where her presence was also requested, after which the car would see her back to her residence. The tone of the man on the phone was extremely eager and courteous, as though afraid she wouldn't come. That pair of telephone calls brought a great deal of comfort to Wang Qiyao. She felt as if she had sunk to the bottom but was now coming back up to the surface. She had not planned to have dinner, but after those two phone calls, she not only ate but even sat down to help her mother with extracting the plumules from lotus seeds before going upstairs to bed. She slept soundly that night.

The day of the ribbon-cutting ceremony Wang Qiyao wore the same outfit she had worn during round 1 of the beauty pageant—the pink satin *cheongsam*. Her hair had grown out a bit, but she did not get it cut and permed, instead deciding at the last minute to have it combed into an old-fashioned chignon at a nearby hair salon. She took a perfunctory view of the whole thing, as her way of protesting against being ignored for so long. She wondered how they could possibly still remember "Miss Third Place" when she herself had almost forgotten. Her appearance, however, turned out to be a success. Pink was the perfect color for her, delicate and fresh. Her hairdo was also the most fitting style for her mood, with its tantalizing hint of a woman with a past; but hardly anything could hide the blooming youth of an eighteen-year-old. Her shoes were new, a pair of white stilettos that made her appear taller, giving her the stateliness of a proud locust tree in the wind.

As Wang Qiyao got into the car at the front of the *longtang*, she could feel countless eyes on her, peering out from all the windows. Nothing escaped her neighbors' notice. Wang Qiyao felt a bit sad. Riding in the car, she gazed at the street scenes passing by outside her window, as the trolley bells kept clanging, an eternal sound. Her eyes had a blank expression, as if she were indifferent to everything; but in that coldness was a determination to meet all challenges, a resolve to follow her fate through to the bitter end.

Upon arrival her eyes betrayed a gleam of surprise. The department store was the very one advertised in all the newspapers and on the radio in recent days. The grand opening ceremony was also quite imposing, and several dozen flower baskets lined the entrance to the store. Although Wang Qiyao began to regret the casualness with which she had viewed the event, she quickly composed herself, even laughing at herself for getting too excited. After all, however glorious the affair might be, her part was no more than to make the rounds and go home. At that moment Wang Qiyao seemed to see through everything; but that didn't mean that she was going to give up trying. On the contrary, sizing up the situation coolly was just the preparation she needed for the hard work ahead. She reached for her compact to make a last-minute inspection before getting out of the car.

Numerous dignitaries were in attendance at the opening. Many of them looked familiar from their pictures in the newspapers, but because current events and politics were remote from Wang Qiyao's world, she was clueless as to who all these people were. Ribbon-cutting ceremonies always began with a long string of speeches. All Wang Qiyao could do was stand quietly, waiting for her moment to snip the ribbon. Although it was her first time, she had seen such ceremonies in movies and magazines, but now that it was happening for real it somehow didn't seem as exciting; rather, it was as if she was taking part in something routine. Deep down she regretted the outfit she had chosen and could not wait for the whole thing to wrap up so she could go home. It was only during that split-second when she was snipping the bow that her heart fluttered for a moment. After all, she was the center of attention; it was her turn in the spotlight, but it only lasted a fleeting moment.

Before the banquet that followed, most of the dignitaries left to attend to other business, leaving only a small group behind, among whom was a man called Director Li. As everyone went to take their seats for the banquet, Wang Qiyao found him sitting beside her. He had the air of a military man, with excellent posture and a reserved demeanor. The people around him all acted obsequious, some as if they had to be extra careful, and the whole atmosphere was somewhat tense. Wang Qiyao alone was not constrained by his presence, speaking with a childlike naiveté and breathing a bit of life back into the air. She thought Director Li must have been a manager or something there at the department store and asked him a question about the various cosmetic lines they carried. Only when she saw the way he smiled did she realize that she must have made a mistake. It was too late to take her question back, so all she could do was bury her head and pay attention to what was on her plate. Her blush made Director Li smile again. Wang Qiyao later learned that Director Li was a towering figure in military and political circles, and a major stockholder in the department store. The decision to invite Wang Qiyao to the grand opening that day had in fact been made at his bequest.

Director Li had first seen Wang Qiyao during the Miss Shanghai pageant. He had originally gone to support the girl who eventually came in second, but when it came time to vote he threw his flowers into Wang Qiyao's basket. What Wang Qiyao stirred up in him was not passion but a feeling of sympathy. Men of forty carry pity in their hearts; the pity they feel is for themselves but they project it out onto others. Men of forty: is there a single one who does not have a scar in his heart? Time alone leaves its scars, right and left, to say nothing of those chaotic days. Director Li had been through much in his life. On the outside people only saw his power and importance, but few realized how lonely it can be at the top. There were all kinds of conflicts playing out within him, layer upon layer of them. On the outermost layers were conflicts between nations; underneath came conflicts between political parties; beneath these conflicts between different cliques; and, at the core of it all, the conflicts between individuals. He was the kind of man whose slightest gesture held untold implications. All that outsiders knew was that Director Li was important, but no one realized how his stature made him a living target. Everyone had their sights set on him. Director Li lived his life on stage—the political stage—where nothing was what it seemed and he had to be constantly wary of what could happen both on stage and off. He was a political machine, his springs always tightly wound; not even for a moment could they be loosened. Only in the company of women did he remember that he was indeed made of flesh and blood.

Women are not in the least bit political. Even when they plot one against another, it is more like child's play, a form of entertainment. When women scheme, it is always for love; the deeper they are in love, the craftier they become. Their love is eternal and never dies. Women are not that important. They have no power over matters of life and death, glory and decline: they are there to put you in a relaxed mood, to serve as scenery. Women were Director Li's true love, but love was not relevant to the grand scheme of Director Li's life work. For him love was a bit like a luxury item, never something he couldn't do without. But for a powerful man like Director Li, luxuries always lay within grasp.

Director Li's first wife stayed at the old family residence. It was a marriage arranged by his parents through proper matchmakers. Besides her Director Li had two other wives, one in Peking and one in Shanghai. But all told there were countless other women he had played around with. Director Li was a man who appreciated feminine beauty, even to the point of being a judge at the "Miss Shanghai" beauty pageant. At his age, however, he no longer appraised women with his eyes; instead, he used his heart. In his younger days, he too had been enamored of the bright eyes and flashing smiles of conventional beauties—the "good enough to eat" variety that satisfied the senses. But as he got older, and as his senses came to be glutted, his tastes began to change. He began to crave intimacy. He had been to many places and had seen a great many women. Peking women had an endearingly down-to-earth beauty, but this was too fulsome and left no lingering taste to savor; Shanghai women, on the other hand, stayed intriguingly on the palate, but in the end this quality was as nebulous as clouds and mist. You couldn't become intimate with either type. Owing to the social climate in which they lived, women from both places were apt to chase after fashion, as a result of which they looked boringly alike, variations on the same themes. None of them captured his eyes, much less his heart. In the past few years, it appeared as if he had begun to lose his appetite for women, but in actuality his standards had grown stricter and it was harder to find anyone to his liking.

There was something about Wang Qiyao that struck Director Li's fancy. He had never been fond of the color pink, because it was too feminine. A woman in pink was wearing her coquettishness all over her face, parading her sensual allure. But when Wang Qiyao wore pink she managed to make it tasteful. The pink still spoke of coquettishness, but it was honest and straightforward. One could see every stitch and thread that went into the embroidered flowers on her *cheongsam*—all expressions of care and diligence. Director Li realized that he had misjudged pink and decided it was just as natural on a woman as were the wind blowing or water flowing. If anyone was at fault, it was those women who ruined it by wearing it the wrong way; their accomplices, the tailors who ruined it by making awful outfits, were also to blame. But, after all, how pleasing to the eye and comforting to the soul this color really is!

Director Li had dealt with so many women that he was a little dazed, and so he had grown circumspect. He may have thrown his flower into Wang Qiyao's basket, but she was still by no means unforgettable in his eyes. Preoccupied with business matters and entangled by other women, he didn't have much time to think about her. Upon being invited to attend the grand opening ceremony for the department store, he happened to inquire who would be cutting the ribbon. He was told that it was yet to be decided, but that a certain movie star whom he liked—with whom he had once had an affair—had been suggested. Director Li responded by saying, "Why not invite Miss Third Place!" And so Wang Qiyao was invited and ended up sitting beside him. From close up, her satin *cheongsam* appeared as soft as water, as if understanding human desires, and her new hairstyle was youth pretending to be old, sensible, and shrewd. When she asked him her question about cosmetic lines, he broke out in a smile. Not only did he not mind her faux pas, but he liked it very much indeed. *A girl utterly innocent of the world!* And then, when he noticed that having realized her mistake, she kept quiet, a deep pity welled up within him—it was at that moment that he secretly made his decision.

As far as women went, Director Li was always decisive. There was never any dragging out of things or beating about the bush: he always dove right into the heart of the matter. This was partly the result of what power does to a person, but it was also simply because he felt that life was too short to do otherwise. After the banquet Director Li offered to see her home in his car, catching Wang Qiyao by surprise. Watching how the crowd cleared a path for them as they made their way out, she followed him meekly to his car. She noticed the fawning gazes as they approached the car; although she could sense that their reaction came partially out of fear, she kind of liked it. She began to understand just what kind of person this Director Li was. She was a bit taken aback but also pleased when Director Li personally opened the car door for her. He sat beside her, and though not a large man, he radiated an aura of authority with his dignified manners. He was the symbol of power: all one could do around him was to submit and obey. Director Li kept quiet the whole way. The curtains were drawn; off and on, street lights shown through the car windows. Wang Qiyao found herself speculating, *What is he thinking?* It was not until then that a curiosity bordering on hope dawned on her. *How will this day end?* she wondered. The car continued to glide over the road and the lights showing through the white curtains now ran in series. This city that never sleeps is like a riddle, and the answer to the riddle will not be revealed until its time comes. When will the time come? One never knows. Wang Qiyao was a little scared, but she was also calm in the face of fate. She seemed to feel that whatever was to happen had already been decided. What good would it do to worry about it?

Director Li it is, then, not Mr. Cheng. Director Li is the type of man who makes decisions. Mr. Cheng needs other people to make decisions for him. The car had already reached Wang Qiyao's home when Director Li turned his head toward her, "I'd like to invite Miss Wang for a casual dinner tomorrow night. I wonder if she will do me the honor."

The invitation was couched in humble words, but, issuing from Director Li's mouth, the words carried a subtle power. It's your decision, and yet not your decision. Wang Qiyao nodded in some confusion. Director Li proceeded to clarify that she would be picked up at seven in the evening, at the same time reaching over to open the door for her.

Standing in front of her own home, as she watched the car disappear in a flash from the *longtang*, Wang Qiyao felt she was dreaming. It was her first meeting with Director Li, yet he had seemed to know all along what to do with her. *Who was this man anyway?* Wang Qiyao's world was very small, a woman's world, comprised of clothing fabrics, rouge, and powder. Its glory was the glory of makeup and finery—matters that were but floating clouds in the big world. Mr. Cheng was a man, but because of his gentle nature and his eagerness to please Wang Qiyao he had turned into a woman, a slave to Wang Qiyao in her little world. Director Li, on the other hand, belonged to the wide world outside, a world incomprehensible to her. However, she did understand that her little world was controlled by the big world; the big world served as a foundation, with a solidity on which one could rely.

Slowly she pushed open the door. The parlor downstairs was dark. An odor of greasy food wafted out of the lit kitchen, where several maidservants huddled together to gossip about their employers. She climbed upstairs to her bedroom and stayed up for a while, sitting at the window and looking out. The neighbor's window was only an arm's length away. Although the curtains were drawn, one could see clearly into the other room, but everything there was normal.

Wang Qiyao pondered her coming dinner date with vague anticipation. What had happened the day before seemed so distant she could hardly recall it. She put her mind to work planning the clothes and shoes she should wear the following day, and deciding how she was to do her hair. She sensed that Director Li liked her, but in what way she did not know—and that uncertainty left her at a loss as to how she should present herself. However, she had a basic faith in the natural course of events. Come what may, she must be steadfast. Even though she must apply herself with due diligence, she should never try to force the issue, because things had a way of unfolding according to hidden principles. She must put her whole heart and mind—there was no room for error—into doing her share, but always leave herself plenty of space to maneuver for just in case things should fall short of her hopes.

The next day Wang Qiyao kept the same hairdo but put on a white *cheongsam* with white piping, something studiedly casual that she might have even worn around the house. Her makeup was heavier, though, and the bright red lipstick and rouge accented her plain dress. On her arm was a beige cashmere sweater, whose sole purpose was to round out the color palette. The car stopped once again at the entrance to the *longtang*, and the chauffeur came to knock at the door, once, twice, neither too soft or too loud; he was obviously well trained. Wang Qiyao felt a little frazzled when she walked across the courtyard. She had met this Director Li only the night before; before she even knew who he was or why they had met, things had suddenly come a long way. Director Li greeted her with a smile as she got in, as if they had been old friends. Even though they exchanged few words, this was after all their second meeting, so the atmosphere was somewhat more relaxed.

On the way, Director Li looked down at the purse sitting on her knees and pointed to the beads. "What are those?"

"Beads . . ." Wang Qiyao earnestly responded.

"Oh! . . ." Director Li exclaimed in mocking surprise.

It was only then that she realized he was teasing her. Responding in kind, she pointed to the ring on Director Li's finger.

"What's this?"

Without a word Director Li took her hand and put the ring on her finger. Her joke had backfired, but she was helpless to retract her words, nor could she withdraw her hand. Fortunately, the ring was much too large to stay on and Director Li had to take it back.

"Well now, we'll just have to go shopping tomorrow for a more suitable one!" They reached the Park Hotel as he said this. The men at the door all knew Director Li and greeted him as they ushered them inside. They rode the elevator to the eleventh floor, where the staff had been expecting them. They were led to a private dining room with a window overlooking the city lights.

Without consulting Wang Qiyao on the menu, Director Li nevertheless managed to order all her favorite dishes. Apparently he knew what a woman liked. While waiting for the food, he casually inquired about Wang Qiyao's age and education and where her father worked. Wang Qiyao was annoyed at this questionnaire-like barrage, but responded matter-of-factly to all of his questions. Impishly, she asked him the same questions, never expecting him to reply. When he took her seriously she was pleasantly surprised. Next he asked Wang Qiyao what she was thinking. Thoroughly flustered, all she could do was sip tea to hide her face.

Director watched her for a while before asking, "Would you like to continue your education?"

"I don't care . . ." Wang Qiyao answered as her eyes met his. "I have no ambition to have a Ph.D. like Jiang Lili."

"Who is Jiang Lili?"

"She's my classmate," replied Wang Qiyao. "You wouldn't know her."

"That's why I asked."

This forced Wang Qiyao to say a few things about her friend, stopping and starting, in bits and pieces, until, exasperated, she said, "I don't think you would understand."

Director Li held her hand in his. "If you talk to me every day, I will . . ."

Wang Qiyao's heart leaped to her throat. She blushed deeply, so embarrassed that her eyes brimmed with tears. Director Wang released her hand and said softly, "What a child you are!"

She couldn't help but raise her head. Director Li was glancing out the window. It was a foggy night outside, and this was the highest point in the whole city. Once the food was served, Wang Qiyao gradually managed to compose herself. It occurred to her that she had overreacted. She had prided herself on being sophisticated, especially since gaining some experience in dealing with Mr. Cheng, and she thought she should not have been so bashful. Recollecting herself, she cast about for topics of conversation. Her childlike attempts to act grown-up were not lost on Director Li, but he was all too willing to humor her. She asked him how many documents and memos he had to read and write each day, then realized, as soon as she had posed the question, that he might not actually write *any*—it was probably the duty of his secretary to write documents and he only needed to sign them. She hastened to ask how many documents he signed each day. Director Li reached into her purse and took out her lipstick. Drawing a thick red line on the back of her hand, he remarked, "I'm signing one right now."

On the third day Director Li again invited Wang Qiyao to dinner, after which he took her to Lucky Phoenix Jewelers to buy a ring, fulfilling his promise in the car the day before. Then he saw her home. Watching the car as it drove away, Wang Qiyao was dismayed. The Director came when he wanted to come and left when he wanted to leave—she had no say whatsoever. She had known this would happen, but somehow she wished for more. It was a wish ungrounded by any confidence; she was put in the unaccustomed position of having to be totally passive.

For days afterward Director Li did not contact her. It was as if he had never existed, but there was no denying the reality of the jeweled ring. With the ring on her finger, Wang Qiyao could not help thinking about him. She was captivated. Whatever he said came to pass and whatever he forbade became an impossibility. During those days Wang Qiyao did not go out and she declined to see Mr. Cheng. She was not deliberately avoiding him; she just wanted to be alone. In her solitude Director Li's face floated in her mind, hazy, a face that she saw from the corners of her eyes with her head down. Wang Qiyao did not really love him. He was not in the habit of accepting other people's love: what he consented to accept was the responsibility for other people's fate. He took other people's fate and assumed responsibility for them in varying degrees. What Wang Qiyao wanted was for him to become responsible for her.

Wang Qiyao's family tiptoed around her during those days. They were dying to ask what was going on, but they all held their tongues. Their neighbors had recognized Director Li's license plate, which was widely known in Shanghai. The fact that the car had already made several trips to their *longtang* sent rumors flying. That was another reason Wang Qiyao stayed holed up at home. Parents in the Shanghai *longtang* were generally open-minded, especially when it came to daughters the likes of Wang Qiyao. They had no choice but let them do what they pleased. They treated their daughters almost like guests—even before marriage—serving them the best food and indulging their occasional tantrums. Every morning her mother would stand at the window looking out for the car with a mixture of hope and dread. Whenever the phone rang, spasms of alternating apprehension and relief shuddered through the household. And although no one said a word about it, everyone in the family was counting the days.

Several times Wang Qiyao wanted to vent her frustration by calling Mr. Cheng. She impulsively raised the receiver but put it down every time. How could she be so foolish as to toy with her own life? She could lose it all as a result of such childish antics. How could she possibly compare Mr. Cheng to Director Li? She came to terms with the fact that there was nothing she could do except to accept whatever fate had in store for her. She calmed down, albeit with a feeling of helplessness, but also with a resolve to remain steadfast in the face of new challenges. She would simply have to let things take their course, keeping faith meanwhile that when the boat reached the bridge, it would straighten out by itself. She needed patience. She had to wait in ignorance as to whether there was something worth waiting for. What else could she do but wait?

It was another month before Director Li reappeared. By that time Wang Qiyao was thoroughly discouraged and had given up hope. Director Li sent his chauffer to fetch her. As the chauffeur waited in the parlor, she hurriedly got dressed, having time only to change into a *cheongsam*. The *cheongsam* was brand new and a bit too large, but she had had no time to get it altered. A few days earlier, she had had her hair trimmed but not permed, so she quickly curled it with hot rollers. She had lost some weight and her eyes looked larger, a little sunken, betraying a touch of resentment. She was taken to a restaurant on Sichuan Road, to another private room, where she found Director Li sitting at the table waiting for her. As soon as he touched her hand, bitter tears rolled down her cheeks. He sat her down right next to him and held her in his arms. Neither of them said anything, but they understood each other. Director Li too seemed to have been through a lot. The hair around his temples had grown grayer. However, the ordeals they had undergone were different—hers had ground away at her heart, but he had undergone ordeals that crushed him like an unbearable weight and left him ready to give way at any moment. They had both come for solace. What Wang Qiyao wanted was comfort that could last her a lifetime, while Director Li just wanted a smidgen. The things they asked for were different, in quality as well as in quantity, but a smidgen to Director Li was the entire piece for Wang Qiyao—it made a perfect match.

As Wang Qiyao cuddled against Director Li, her heart settled down and she finally felt grounded. By this point Director Li's iron-like will had also turned into mush. He thought to himself, *Women are really the only clear notes amid the cacophony of strident noises in this tumultuous world.* Wang Qiyao had ceased to think. Now that she had Director Li she did not need anything else. After they held each other for a while, Director Li lifted her chin and looked into her eyes. Her face seemed more childlike than ever, with the total trust and obstinacy of a child. Director Li had seen a lot of women, from all walks of life and in all kinds of circumstances. At this stage in his frenzied life a woman looking up at him with unquestioning trust evoked a poignant mixture of sweetness and bitterness. He was enthralled. He clasped her to him again and asked what she had been doing at home.

"Counting my fingers."

When he asked why on earth she would do something like that, she answered, "I was counting the days until you came back."

Director Li held her tighter, and thought, *She may look like a child but she's got all the guile of a woman.* After a pause, Wang Qiyao asked what he had been up to since last they met.

"Signing documents, of course."

At that they both laughed. Wang Qiyao thought, *He even remembers that joke. He must have been thinking about me all this time.*

The nights on Sichuan Road were reassuring in their ordinariness. The lights illuminated clearly all things in their respective orbits. The restaurants served food that one might have found at home, delicious even though a bit greasy. The window, fogged up by human breath, had a warm feeling, seeming to exude sympathy. Director Li released Wang Qiyao and let her return to her own seat. He said he had sent someone to rent an apartment for her. He would visit her regularly. If she felt lonely she could invite her mother to stay with her sometimes. Of course he would also hire a maid for her. If she wanted she could attend college, but only if she wanted—since, after all, she did not want to be a Ph.D.! They both smiled at this allusion to their first dinner alone together.

As Wang Qiyao listened to him, she thought it was a well thought out, almost flawless proposal, yet she did not want to accept immediately.

"I'll go home and ask my parents . . ."

This schoolgirl-like response made Director Li smile at her indulgently. He reached out to caress her head. "From now on you only have to ask me."

Tears streamed out of Wang Qiyao's eyes, and a profound sense of grievance welled up in her. Director Li was silent. He understood even better than Wang Qiyao the source of her grievance. He had seen tears of this kind many times. Even though they always proved to be fleeting, they left a residue, which tended to resurface during times of crisis. When he was young, he thought he could crush anything in his hands into dust. But he no longer had that boundless confidence. Experience had taught him that every person in the world—no matter how great—is always a puppet in the hands of another. Those are the hands of fate. He therefore felt that Wang Qiyao was shedding tears also for him, and he was moved. After Wang Qiyao stopped weeping, she patted her eyes; they were still red, but clear enough that one could see all the way down to their bottom. Director Li saw himself reflected in those eyes. After that she seemed much more relaxed, but at the same time resolute, as if she had finished performing a farewell ceremony. She had now entered a new stage in her life and was ready to go to battle.

"When can I move in?" she asked.

Director Li was taken aback. He had thought it might take some time to get her used to the idea and had not expected her to be so cut-and-dry about it.

"When . . . ever . . ." he uttered hesitatingly.

"How about tomorrow then?"

This put Director Li in a tight spot, because although he had toyed with the idea of getting her an apartment, he had not taken any steps actually to rent one.

"Let's wait a few days . . ." he was forced to temporize.

In the ensuing days Director Li was constantly in Wang Qiyao's company, eating with her and taking her to see Peking opera. Director Li was a southerner, but he had spent a large part of his life in Peking and so had become a Peking opera aficionado. He now found the local operas of his hometown of Shaoxing extremely boring. Movies also bored him. The Peking operas he liked were those featuring female lead roles—and among these he delighted most in the ones where the lead was played by a man. He thought that men in female roles were more feminine than women, because only a man could understand what was so entrancing about women—women themselves would never understand. The female leads played by women articulate the female form, but men could articulate the female spirit. This is a simple case of an onlooker being able to form a clearer picture of what goes on than the parties involved. He especially despised Hollywood movies and the women in them, who displayed nothing but feminine shallowness. Those Hollywood actresses were not fit to hold a candle to men playing female roles in Peking operas. He thought if he were to play a female lead, he would bring to life the most beautiful woman in the world. A woman's beauty is definitely not self-conscious. Women are most beautiful when they are not aware of their beauty—often precisely when they think they are ugly. The feminine beauty articulated by men in female roles is an idealized beauty. Whether moving about or staying still, frowning or smiling, they are interpreting women, as if women are books they have studied. Director Li's love of Peking opera stemmed from his love of women; furthermore, the two were similar in that he looked at both from the perspective of an aesthete. Wang Qiyao came from a generation in Shanghai that grew up watching Hollywood movies; the drum rolls and clanging gongs of Peking opera always gave her a headache, yet she learned to control her personal dislikes when she accompanied Director Li to the opera. After a while she actually began to find it interesting, and was able to make a few intelligent remarks about the performance, allowing her to converse with Director Li on the subject.

Director Li took her to see the apartment a week later.

The apartment was located in an alley off one of those quiet streets that ended at the intersection in front of the Paramount Nightclub in Jing'an Temple district. There were several apartment buildings standing side by side, collectively named Alice Apartments. The one that Director Li rented was on the ground floor, with a large living room and two smaller south-facing rooms that could be used as either bedroom or study. A room designed for the maid faced north. The floor, of narrow teak planks, gleamed with burnished brown wax. The European-style furniture was made of rosewood. Curtains had been hung and the tables were covered with tablecloths. Antimacassars, vases, and other such items had been deliberately laid aside for Wang Qiyao to do with as she liked, to give her the satisfaction of decorating her own home. The closets were also empty, so that by filling them she could fill out her days. The jewelry box was also empty, to be filled with Director Li's riches.

The overall feeling that Wang Qiyao experienced upon entering the apartment was that it was large and empty. Walking around, she felt tiny. She had the distinct sensation of floating on air. She doubted its reality. Was it genuine or fake? The apartment was dark because it was on the ground floor, the curtains were drawn, and also the day happened to be overcast. When the lights were turned on, it felt like nighttime.

Entering the bedroom, Wang Qiyao saw a bed for two, over which hung a ceiling lamp. The scene looked eerily familiar, as if she had been there before, and her heart sank. She was about to turn around to take a look at the other room, but her path was blocked because Director Li stood right behind her. He held her and maneuvered her toward the bed. After a slight struggle, she found herself lying on the bed. It was dark in the apartment, and only the birds chirping outside the window indicated to her it was still daytime. Director Li mussed up her hair and the makeup on her face, then started to unbutton her. She stayed still and even cooperated by getting out of her sleeves.

This moment was bound to come sooner or later, she thought to herself. She was nineteen and this was the right time. No one deserved this moment more than Director Li. Giving this to him felt more right to her than if she had given it to anyone else. She would be able to settle down with no second thoughts and no lingering doubts. She caught a whiff of the lime that had recently been used to whitewash the ceiling—it struck her nose with a certain cold acridity. On the brink of that very last moment, she did feel some regrets. She realized that she had twice worn a wedding gown—once at the film studio and once on stage during the final round of the pageant—but when it came time for a wedding gown in real life, she was not wearing one.

Alice Apartments

ALICE APARTMENTS IS a place unknown to most, a quiet island in the midst of a noisy city. Situated near the end of a dead-end street, it is a self-contained world. The window curtains are drawn, and even the cries of the crows and sparrows seem to be shut out. The residents seldom step outside and even the maids do not stop to gossip. As soon as the sun goes down, the iron gate is clanged shut, leaving a small side door illuminated by an electric lamp as the only point of entry. Who lives here and what do they do? Why is the place called "Alice"? Does the name have any special significance? "Alice" evokes the image of a beautiful young girl in love. The place is a wonderland compared to our philistine world. And although it is right next door it could just as well be at the edge of heaven, each world invisible to the other. Why has it been plunked down into this ordinary neighborhood? What kinds of things take place behind those curtains? The city air is full of beguiling rumors, scandalous rumors, rumors of adventurous women who sail away on their love to faraway places—places as distant as Alice Apartments.

Alice Apartments is the quietest spot in the entire city. This quiet does not resemble the unruffled calm of a maiden. It is the quiet of a woman on shore straining to catch sight of her husband at sea, a forced quiet. Here is a fantasy land purchased at the price of loneliness and relinquished youth. In this fantasy land, one day is a hundred years. The streets of Shanghai are filled with would-be Alices, women who are discontent with being ordinary, women full of dreams. Opportunities are severely limited in this city of freedom. Women who make it into these apartments are the elite corps among Alices.

If you were to take the roof off Alice Apartments, you would see a charming world of satin, gauze, velvet, and tassels. Even the wood furniture glows with a silken light. There is a profusion of soft, bright fabrics.

The footstool standing next to the bathtub, the cushion on the sofa, the bed curtains, the table covers, all are richly embroidered with resplendent threads. The colors are magnificent; of red alone there are a hundred shades. Flowers run riot everywhere: embossed on lampshades, carved on dressers, worked into the glass of the picture windows, and sprinkled all over the wallpaper, not to mention those that stand in vases, hide inside handkerchiefs, and sit submerged in jasmine tea. Violet-scented cologne, rose-colored lipstick, nail polish the shades of impatiens, dresses smelling faintly of chrysanthemum . . . these and more proliferated with all their coquetry at Alice Apartments. Flirtatious in the extreme, and feminine to the uttermost. This is a woman's world. No other place in this city of concrete and steel is so soft, so warm. The light fixtures are shaded to bathe everything in a gentle, dreamy glow. Everything is so supple that you feel that if you were to try to grasp it, it would flow out from between your fingers.

Something else is special about Alice Apartments: a surfeit of mirrors. Mirrors on both sides of the doors, by the bed, next to the dresser, over the sink, on the vanity table; tiny mirrors in powder compacts; and, finally, mirrors next to pillows, to throw light onto the walls for amusement. Everybody therefore appears in doubles at the Alice Apartments, in loneliness or in joy: one is real and the other a reflection; one is authentic and the other an illusion. Songs from the gramophone are also echoed in the apartment in pairs. The needle of the gramophone grows dull from wear—it plays on two grooves at once. Dreams are the shadows of wakefulness, darkness the shadow of light: each is one half of a pair.

Like a woman's heart, Alice Apartments is made up of countless silken filaments: on the walls, the windows, the beds, the floors, the tables and chairs; in sewing boxes, in makeup cases, in the clothes hanging up in the closet, threading in and out of golden and silvery beads. It is rather a nest for a woman's heart. For the heart is like a bird that wants to fly as high as it can, tirelessly, heedless of danger. Alice Apartments is a nest resting on the uppermost branch. Alighting, the bird feels it has found a home.

The women in Alice Apartments are not born, nor have they been brought up by their parents: free spirits, their bodies are the essence of heaven and earth. They are wind-borne seeds, disseminated from the sky, that grow into wild, rambling plants. They spread in all directions, putting down roots wherever there is soil; they do not adhere to principles, nor do they fit any mold; they have an irrepressible urge to live, and dying they have no regrets. However, being untethered and carefree, they often become disoriented; they waver. Birds plunge down from the sky at such moments, as hesitation saps their energy, confidence, and hope. The greater the heights to which they ascend, the greater are the dangers they must face.

Alice Apartments may look quiet on the surface, but underneath it is restive, because the hearts of those who live there are oppressed. You can hear this in the ringing of the telephones behind those heavy window curtains. It reverberates in the large living room, even though, having passed through satin and brocade, the eager sound is muted. The telephone is a crucial item in the Alice Apartments, serving as the artery through which life-force flows. The telephone's ringing runs through the apartments like the undercurrents of a river. No need to find out who the callers are—it does not matter—we need only know that the calls come in the form of summons, or of consent; they have a revitalizing effect on Alice Apartments. The telephone rings out even in the middle of the night, when it is most unsettling. The sound shoots through the heart's loneliness, and the heart remains agitated long afterward. Doorbells ringing are of equal significance. Unlike the lingering notes of telephones, however, doorbells tend to be snappy, assertive, overbearing. They are undercurrents powerful enough to affect the direction of the river. No need to find out who presses the buttons; enough to know that they are people capable of carrying out commitments. These two kinds of sound roam Alice Apartments at will with a proprietary air. Alice Apartments—sumptuous, dreamlike, fabulous—float atop these two kinds of ringing. They are the beads that, strung together, make the necklace.

Alice Apartments have their lively moments, always heralded by a doorbell. When the doorbell rings, the heavy curtains can barely contain their giddy merriment. These festivals occur regularly at Alice Apartments, but not according to the calendar. The merriment may last several months, or only one unforgettable night. Laughter and joviality are suspended during these precious hours, as are tears. Normally the maids have hardly anything to do, but at these festivals they are so busy that they have to have the event catered or bring in outside chefs from the Yanyun Restaurant. For these festive occasions, red lanterns are hung, red candles lit, new clothes put on, and comforters embroidered with mandarin ducks taken out from the chests. Festivals come at different times for the residents of Alice Apartments, but one or another seems to be taking place the whole year round. They take turns being merry. At the Paramount Nightclub, not too far away, merriment is also being had by all, an overpowering merriment, but one does not know what kind of squalor lies behind the merriment there. In contrast, the gaiety at Alice Apartments is genuine through and through. What you see is what you get. The Paramount is like a rushing river, but Alice Apartments is like a harbor, waiting for people to come home. They party all night long at the Paramount, but all that changes the next morning. At Alice Apartments, things are kept on an even keel, day after day, night after night.

Charming and mysterious places such as the Alice Apartments are not unique. Blissful little enclaves like it are scattered throughout Shanghai. To outsiders they look like anthills with thick, shell-like walls; who can guess that behind that gray cement lie beautiful and exotic worlds? Their beauty is the beauty of fireflies, shining brightly during their brief lives, all their energy expended on one flare. Afterward, their decaying bodies nourish the ivy, which mourns their beauty. The residents of these places strive to fulfill their ideal of femininity and keep up their hope for happiness. But the strivings into which they pour their souls do not count for much—they are mere remnants in the hands of fate. Places such as the Alice Apartments are therefore like graveyards. The place locks its residents away so that it alone can enjoy them. The inmates come of their own free will, but their arrival marks the end of freedom. Here is a prison of the heart, a prison of volition, a prison of hope. They become the prisoners of place, putting their vestigial hope into the ivy, for ivy is capable of climbing walls and crawling out through cracks. Thus, the Alice Apartments are also about sacrifices, ritualistic sacrifices offered to the goddess of liberty, and to their own selves. That is what "Alice" means.

There is another name for such places: "society girl apartments." Being a "society girl" is a profession unique to Shanghai, halfway between wife and prostitute. This profession, which dispenses with titles, does not operate according to rules; only what actually takes place matters. It is a livelihood that bears some resemblance to being a free-roaming nomad, who goes from pasture to pasture, seeking shelter in tents. The apartments are the girls' tents, which they make as beautiful as they can. The girls themselves are beautiful, even elegant; their elegance is in a class of its own, judged by its own standards. Having relinquished the roles of wife and mother, they metamorphose into femininity itself. It would not be excessive to declare that their beauty is an asset to the city, the pride of Shanghai. We must express our gratitude to the people who nurture them, for they have performed an aesthetic service for mankind.

These women spend their entire lives trying to display their beauty for a brief season, like flowers that blossom only once every hundred years.

What a splendid sight when these flowers bloom! They have made themselves beauty's emissaries—beauty is glorious, even if the glory is as fleeting as passing clouds, gorgeous dusk clouds that enfold the entire earth. Nothing belongs to them, but they do not mind being clouds. Brief as their time is, they enjoy it up there, looking down on earth. So what if time is transitory, so what if it is illusory, so what if the clouds should transform into ivy, to crawl through the cracks and walls to wait for the next century?

Farewell to Alice

Wang Qiyao moved into the Alice Apartments in the spring of 1948. This was a year of great turmoil and unrest, with China embroiled in a civil war the outcome of which was still poised in the balance. The world within Alice Apartments, however, remained as sumptuous and cozy as ever. Nineteen-year-old Wang Qiyao had settled down and found a home of her own, but when she moved in, she did not let anyone know except her family.

When Mr. Cheng called, he was told that she had left for Suzhou to stay with her maternal grandmother, and they were not certain when she might be back. Mr. Cheng then took a trip to Suzhou, at a time when the gardenias were in full bloom. He thought he caught a glimpse of Wang Qiyao in every doorway by a gardenia tree. He even found teacups no bigger than a fingernail for sale, and all the little girls who played with those miniature tea sets looked just like Wang Qiyao as a child. Wang Qiyao had left her imprint on all the cobblestones, but there was no sight of her. He arrived in Suzhou with a sinking feeling, and with that same sinking feeling he left. On the night train back to Shanghai, his heart was as dark as the scenery outside, and tears rolled down his face. He could not understand why he should be so dejected, yet sadness took firm hold of him.

After his return, he abandoned his search for Wang Qiyao; he also abandoned photography. Every morning and night he walked blindly past his photo studio, and went straight out the door or into his bedroom. There were too many things he would rather ignore. At twenty-nine, he was single and had no thought of marriage. He did not care about his career, and having given up his hobby as well, he seemed to have stopped caring altogether. He roamed the streets of Shanghai with a fedora on his head and a walking stick in his hand, looking like a character in a classical European painting. His despair was part genuine, part performance—for the benefit of himself as well as for others. There was a measure of satisfaction and hope in his acting.

In the days that Mr. Cheng was looking for Wang Qiyao, someone else was looking for Mr. Cheng. This was Jiang Lili. She too ran into one setback after another, but she never gave up. She first went to the Western firm where Mr. Cheng had been employed. They told her he had quit but suggested she try another firm where he might have gone. To the second firm she went, and was told there was no such person. When she returned to the first place to try to learn Mr. Cheng's home address, the secretary decided it was better not to give it out, especially seeing how anxious Jiang Lili was. Stumped, Jiang Lili's only remaining option seemed to be to go to Wang Qiyao for help, even though she knew this was not a smart move. To her dismay, Wang Qiyao had also disappeared. This set her wondering if the two had gone off together. But it seemed unlikely, there being no wedding news from either. It was from Wu Peizhen that she eventually got hold of Mr. Cheng's address. During their meeting, Wang Qiyao's name never crossed the lips of either, but she was on both their minds. Even though Jiang Lili and Wu Peizhen had been classmates for years, they had rarely spoken. Wang Qiyao, a scar on the heart of each, was the only connection between them. Jiang Lili hurried to the address once she had it in hand.

Taking the elevator to the top floor, she found his apartment door shut. No one answered the doorbell. She decided to wait for him, leaning against the banister of the staircase, where she could look out the hall window. The water of the Huangpu River at dusk ran dark crimson. A steamboat blew its whistle. She felt adrift. *When will he be back? How long has it been since she saw him? How did he behave the last time? What was he like the first time they were together?* She was caught in a myriad emotions. Red clouds formed on the horizon and slowly turned black. Pigeons went flying separately, each to its own destination. The light in the building had turned on automatically, but still there was no sign of Mr. Cheng. Jiang Lili's legs had become sore and she felt chilled, though not hungry. The elevator made quiet but distinct sounds as it went up and down, but never rose to the top floor. There was a great deal of activity for a while, as people came home from work, but the elevator never came up. Jiang Lili spread her handkerchief at the top of the stairs and sat down. She firmly believed that, sooner or later, Mr. Cheng would come home—she *would* see him. Outside the misty night shone with lights; inside the building was enshrouded by a tomblike solemnity. One realized that people lived here only when, occasionally, a door flew open, voices were heard, and the smells of dinner came floating up. Jiang Lili hunched over on the cold marble step and wrapped her arms around herself, determined to ignore the passage of time. It was then that she heard the elevator rising to the top floor and saw Mr. Cheng step out. For a few seconds she could not believe her own eyes and failed to recognize him. He had always been slim, but now he was a bag of bones, a hanger for clothes and hat, supported by a walking stick. She felt sorry for him without venturing to guess why he was so gaunt.

Tears streaming down her cheeks, she called out to him. "Mr. Cheng!"

Mr. Cheng was confused and took a moment to recognize her. When he did, past events rushed back in torrents.

Mr. Cheng and Jiang Lili had not seen each other for some time. Each was nursing a wounded heart and felt an instant empathy with the other. After all, in the vast sea of people drifting through this crowded city, the two of them shared something. The reunion was bittersweet. Now they were ready to write a sequel to an interrupted story, even though each had a different version in mind. Mr. Cheng opened the door, turned on the light, and led Jiang Lili inside. It was her first time in the studio, and she was amazed, even though the place had fallen into neglect. She walked around, touching this and that, until her hands were covered with dust. Watching her, Mr. Cheng pulled himself together. He went to lift up the cloth covering the lighting equipment. This sent dust flying all around.

"Have a seat," said Mr. Cheng. "I'll take your picture!"

Jiang Lili sat down, ignoring the dust clinging to her *cheongsam*. During that instant when the lights came on, there was a split second when Mr. Cheng thought it might be Wang Qiyao sitting there before him. Jiang Lili had her hands on her lap; the expression on her face was strained but happy. She dared neither move nor smile, aware that her body and soul were completely enveloped by Mr. Cheng's gaze. How she wished this moment could last forever. But as soon as Mr. Cheng had pressed the shutter, the light went dark. She was still in a daze when she heard the sound of his voice speaking to her. He asked if she had seen Wang Qiyao. Jiang Lili's burning heart cooled instantly.

"I haven't had dinner yet!" she replied, rather stiffly.

Mr. Cheng was confused. He had no idea what her hunger had to do with him.

She continued, "I got here in the afternoon and have been waiting for you all this time!"

At this Mr. Cheng hung his head like a shamefaced schoolboy. Jiang Lili softened.

"Would you accompany me to dinner, Mr. Cheng?"

Mr. Cheng agreed and they filed out of the door.

Outside the building, night lights and starlight sparkled on the river, and the street was alive with people and cars. The excitement infected them.

"Jiang Lili," Mr. Cheng turned to her enthusiastically. "I'm going to take you to someplace special for dinner."

"I'll go wherever you take me," she responded.

He walked briskly ahead, and she had almost to jog to keep up with him until, as if something had come into his mind, he abruptly slowed down. He did not seem to pay too much attention to Jiang Lili's questions. They arrived at a tiny little restaurant nestled at the top of a narrow wooden staircase. It was not originally designed to be a restaurant, just the upper storey of someone's house. Seated at a table by the window, they looked down onto the noisy street below, with its sidewalk lined with fruit stands, where the light was dimmed by the steam curling up from wonton stalls. Mr. Cheng did not ask Jiang Lili what she wanted; he went ahead and ordered several local specialties, including duck feet in wine sauce and shredded pressed bean curd, and then stared blankly out the window.

After a while he began to reminisce. "Wang Qiyao and I were having dinner here one time when she suddenly developed a craving for mandarin oranges. So we dangled a rope down with a handkerchief and money. The vendor took the money and sent up the oranges."

Mr. Cheng had avoided thinking about Wang Qiyao for a very long time—this was his way of punishing himself—but seeing Jiang Lili, he could not help it. He took no thought for Jiang Lili's feelings; in fact he half-consciously exploited the situation, knowing full well that Jiang Lili would listen to whatever he said.

Though Jiang Lili, for her part, was aware that Mr. Cheng and Wang Qiyao had gone on dates, this was the first time she heard him describe their time together. Overwhelmed by a mixture of anger, impatience, and bitterness, she put her head down on the table to cry. Mr. Cheng stopped talking and looked at her helplessly, but offered no comforting words. After weeping a while, Jiang Lili took off her glasses to wipe away the tears and forced a smile.

"I waited half the day for you, Mr. Cheng. Do you think I am here to hear you talk about Wang Qiyao?"

Mr. Cheng lowered his head and stared at a gap in the table.

"Don't you have anything to say that's *not* about Wang Qiyao?" she asked.

Mr. Cheng smiled in abashment. Jiang Lili turned her head to look out of the window. The fruit stands were not selling mandarin oranges, but golden melons. She thought perversely of having a melon pulled up on a rope but decided against the idea. What is the point of imitating Wang Qiyao? All the dishes on the table are apparently her favorites: she had already captured the fellow's heart. But Wang Qiyao was nowhere to be found. Why should Jiang Lili be threatened by a phantom?

She recomposed herself and smiled sardonically. "You, Mr. Cheng, keep thinking of Wang Qiyao, but Wang Qiyao doesn't even remember you. Isn't that a pity!"

That hit a sore spot. However, he was a man after all and did not cry, only letting his head drop lower, and this again aroused Jiang Lili's pity.

Changing her tone, she said, "Actually, I have also been looking for Wang Qiyao, but I have nothing to report. Her family's lips are sealed and I can't pry a word out of them."

Raising his head, Mr. Cheng said pathetically, "If you ask again, you can probably wheedle something out of them. After all, you are her best friend."

Jiang Lili became furious. She raised her voice. "How much is friendship worth? I have stopped listening to friends—they are all cheats. The more I trust them, the more they hurt me."

There was truth in what she said, and Mr. Cheng fell silent. Having vented her anger, Jiang Lili calmed down considerably. She continued after a pause, "Actually, I don't mind asking again. I am curious why they should behave so mysteriously. Perhaps it is something scandalous."

At this Mr. Cheng lost the urge to press the matter.

In reality, Wang Qiyao moving into a unit in Alice Apartments that Director Li had rented for her was a fairly big event in Shanghai society, one of the few notable peaceful events during an extraordinarily turbulent time. However, Mr. Cheng belonged to another world, and because of recent setbacks he had been keeping a low profile. In her search for Mr. Cheng Jiang Lili had been oblivious to everything else, but once she settled down the news filtered through to her. Her source was none other than her own mother.

"That classmate of yours . . . the one who stayed with us," Mrs. Jiang mentioned one day. "She has become an 'apartment lady'! I hear she now belongs to Director Li."

Jiang Lili quickly asked who Director Li was, but her mother had only the vaguest idea, as she was merely repeating what she had heard. She had the impression that he was famous, someone everyone knew. Jiang Lili was stunned. How could Wang Qiyao go down that path? Then she thought back to the awkward expressions Wang Qiyao's parents had greeted her with and suddenly everything made sense.

"You know," Mrs. Jiang added, "it would be better for girls of her class to stick to their own kind. Once they get a taste of the outside world, they all end up going down that path."

Clearly she was prejudiced, not to mention vindictive, but one could not deny that there was truth in what she said. However, Jiang Lili would hear none of it. Waving her hand in dismissal, she fled.

It was true that Wang Qiyao had hurt her, but Jiang Lili still hoped that Wang Qiyao would happily settle down with someone—that would leave Mr. Cheng for herself. Still, she found the news distressing and even secretly hoped that the whole thing was just a rumor. *Wang Qiyao is an educated girl,* she thought to herself. *From her manners and speech one can tell that she usually has a good head on her shoulders. How could she be so foolish as to destroy herself!* Jiang Lili was determined to investigate the matter and refute this story. But everything she learned only confirmed the news—she even found out the address of the apartment. Jiang Lili wanted to see for herself. *I should go see Wang Qiyao. If it is as bad as they say, then perhaps Mr. Cheng will give up on her.* But at that moment she realized that it was only because of Mr. Cheng that she had put herself on the case. *Mr. Cheng will be crushed!* The very idea depressed her, and she spent the rest of the day feeling sorry for herself. Since she was a child, everyone had tried to please her; the only people she had ever tried to please were Wang Qiyao and Mr. Cheng. And in the eyes of these two people, she might as well have never existed.

Jiang Lili had never been to Alice Apartments, though she knew of it by reputation. She felt a certain apprehension, but also a bit of a thrill in anticipation of her adventure. The afternoon was overcast, with dark clouds hanging low. The pedicab driver gave her a strangely appraising look. Once past the Paramount, the streets took on a different air. As Jiang Lili paid the driver and walked toward the iron gate of the *longtang,* she could feel eyes watching her from behind. Inside the complex silence reigned. All the windows were shut and shaded. Jiang Lili thought she could tell which window belonged to Wang Qiyao: it must be the one with the rustic floral pattern. *Could Wang Qiyao really be living here?* It was with some trepidation that she rang the doorbell, not certain whether seeing Wang Qiyao appear was something she hoped for or dreaded. Meanwhile, the sky had darkened further as it prepared to unleash its rain. The door opened a crack, revealing a sliver of an indistinct face. With a provincial Zhejiang accent, the person behind the door asked who she was looking for.

"I'm looking for my classmate, Wang Qiyao," Lili replied. "My name is Jiang."

The door was shut again, but reopened soon after to let her in. The floor gleamed with wax. There, at the other end of the dark living room, in the doorway of a brightly lit bedroom, stood Wang Qiyao. She was in a floor-length dressing gown; her long hair had been permed into large wavy rolls, and she seemed taller. As each stood, backlit, able to see the other's silhouette but not her face, a feeling came over both of them that was at once familiar and strange.

"How do you do, Jiang Lili?" Wang Qiyao asked.

"And how do you do, Wang Qiyao?" Jiang Lili returned.

When they moved over to the sofa in the middle of the living room, the maid had already brought tea, and they both sat down.

"How are your mother and your brother?" Wang Qiyao asked.

Jiang Lili responded politely to her queries and glanced around. A little light had stolen in around the edge of the window curtains, and she could see that Wang Qiyao had gained a little weight and that her complexion was lustrous. Along the bottom of her pink dressing gown was a border embroidered with large flowers. The sofa and the lampshade were also covered with large flowers. She remembered how Wang Qiyao used to favor tiny little flowers in her *cheongsams*, and thought to herself that those flowers had turned grandiose along with their mistress.

Pretty soon they ran out of things to talk about, and simply sat facing each other in awkward silence. They couldn't talk about the past; things had changed so drastically that it was hard even to remember what had happened.

"I have come," Jiang Lili began after a long silence, "because Mr. Cheng asked me to see you."

Wang Qiyao smiled faintly. "What does Mr. Cheng do to keep himself busy these days? Is he still doing photography? Has he bought new equipment? Several lamps burned out in his studio, and he was talking of replacing them."

"He has not touched those things in a long time." Jiang Lili replied. "These days he can hardly work up enough energy to turn on an electric light, much less the lamps in his studio."

Wang Qiyao laughed. "That old Mr. Cheng! Sometimes he really acts like a naughty child." Then she asked, "How about you, my dear? When are you going to get your Ph.D.?"

Having made this first jab at Jiang Lili, Wang Qiyao grew livelier and took aim with another. "And have you written any new poems lately?"

Jiang Lili was livid. *How dare she speak to me as if I were a child?* Rounding on Wang Qiyao, she asked, "What about you, Wang Qiyao? You must be doing *very* well?"

Wang Qiyao raised her chin a little bit.

"Not bad."

It was an expression she had never shown before: the heroic pose of a martyr.

Then she went on, "I know what is going through your mind. I even know what your mother thinks. Your mother is certain to compare me to your father's kept woman in Chongqing. Please excuse my bluntness, Jiang Lili, but if I don't say these things aloud, we shall have nothing else to say to each other. I understand you are avoiding the subject so as not to embarrass me. Therefore let *me* talk about it."

Jiang Lili felt her face turning red and white by turns. She wished a hole would open up in the ground into which she could burrow; at the same time, she had to acknowledge Wang Qiyao's superiority in handling the situation—she had certainly hit the nail on the head.

"I hope you do not mind my making this comparison," Wang Qiyao continued. "How should I put it? . . . Your mother is like the fabric sewn on the outside, to be shown to the world, because she is presentable. The woman in Chongqing is the fabric used for the lining. It mayn't be presentable, but it's inexpensive and serves a necessary function. Your mother and the woman in Chongqing are each mistress of her respective domain, neither taking away from the other. Whether we end up as one or the other is not within our personal control. It is all fate."

Jiang Lili had ceased to be agitated. Even though her parents were being used as examples, she felt she was being given a lecture on life. The matter under discussion bore no resemblance to the relationships in her romantic novels, but it was straightforward and had a ring of truth. Wang Qiyao spoke unexcitedly, as if she were analyzing someone else's affairs with cold detachment.

"Of course, it would be ideal if one could both be presented to the world and serve a real function," she went on to say, "but we all come with our distinct properties. Rather than making do, it's better to put each fabric to its most fitting use. This is to pursue the ideal in a far-from-ideal world. Furthermore, there's an old saying that even the moon goes through cycles of perfection and incompleteness, and when the vessel is full, the water spills over. Who's to say that, lacking the other half, one might not be more secure as a result?"

Jiang Lili listened intently. Perhaps Wang Qiyao was justified in belittling her after all. Putting things this way, her explanation could even make her mother feel better about the woman in Chongqing.

Wang Qiyao was right. With the taboo subject now out in the open—exposed in all its starkness and simplicity—they both felt much more at ease. To Jiang Lili's queries about Director Li, Wang Qiyao answered truthfully, recounting for her an outline of the events that had led her there. She even took Jiang Lili to see their bedroom, but before they entered, she rushed forward, blushing, to stuff something from the bed into the dresser. Jiang Lili realized that Wang Qiyao was no longer the pure young girl she once had been and that henceforth there would always be a line dividing them. After they returned to the living room, Wang Qiyao ordered the maid to go out and buy some crabmeat buns for snacks. As they ate, they gossiped about Wang Qiyao's neighbors, thereby confirming many rumors and correcting others floating about in Shanghai. The sky outside brightened. They seemed to have gone back to old times, putting their differences aside. They acted as if Mr. Cheng did not exist and talked more about Director Li. Wang Qiyao showed Jiang Lili his pipes, large and small, in a metal box. She took one out and clowned around, puffing away at it. When Jiang Lili stood up to say goodbye, Wang Qiyao insisted that she stay for dinner. She even made a show of asking the maid to prepare special dishes. The maid was as enthusiastic as the mistress at the prospect of entertaining their first dinner guest.

Over dinner, Wang Qiyao said poignantly, "I have had countless dinners at your house. Now I can finally have you over to my home."

Jiang Lili was touched and for the first time appreciated how confined Wang Qiyao must have felt living at her house. Darkness had fallen outside, and the lights in the living room were turned way up. A record of the opera king Mei Lanfang singing in his usual falsetto played on the gramophone; the lyrics were difficult to understand but the emotion in his voice was palpable. The chinaware under the lamp had a serene look, the food was delicious, and the warm Shaoxing wine gave off a comforting vapor.

Jiang Lili was uncertain to as how she was going to break the news to Mr. Cheng. She was afraid he would take the blow very hard. She also worried for her own sake—if Mr. Cheng were to become totally despondent, her own dream would have no chance of being realized. She pitied both Mr. Cheng and herself for their lack of control over their own destinies.

She made a date to meet him in the park. From afar, she saw him standing alone and felt sorry to have to bring him such unwelcome news. Mr. Cheng spotted her and came up to greet her as she was getting ready to step off the pedicab. Walking on the paved road that ran along the edge of the park, neither wanted to bring up the subject, so both remained silent. They made a full round before deciding to rent a rowboat. Out in the middle of the lake, facing each other in the boat, they felt the invisible presence of Wang Qiyao between them.

After they had been rowing a while, Jiang Lili finally said, "Does Mr. Cheng still remember? The last time we were in a rowboat here, there were three of us."

She meant to prepare him for what was coming with this. Mr. Cheng sensed that she was about to report something devastating. He turned red and tried to push the topic away by calling attention to a willow tree, so pretty it should be in a painting. Ordinarily, this remark would have been pleasing to Jiang Lili, but she was not about to be diverted from her mission today. She tried another opening.

"My mother says, 'Ever since Wang Qiyao stopped coming around, Mr. Cheng has disappeared as well.'"

Mr. Cheng forced a smile but could find nothing to say by way of a response, so he hung his head. Sorry as she felt for him, Jiang Lili was determined to get it over with. She mustered up her courage and blurted it out.

"My mother also told me some rumors about Wang Qiyao."

Mr. Cheng almost dropped the oar in his hand. His face seemed suddenly drained of blood. "Rumors are unreliable," he retorted. "All kinds of rumors go the rounds in Shanghai."

Stung by this absurd remark, Jiang Lili pressed on with some asperity, "I haven't even told you the nature of the rumor, yet you are already refuting it."

Mr. Cheng's eyes blinked behind his glasses. He had long since forgotten to row and the boat was going around in circles. Jiang Lili was almost ready to let the matter drop, but on second thought reflected that there might not be another chance like this. Lowering her voice, she told Mr. Cheng everything that she had heard and seen. Mr. Cheng proceeded to row steadily. He did not shed any tears, but his actions became stiff and wooden, as if he had been transformed into a marionette. On reaching shore, he laid the oar against a large stone, tied the boat, and walked off, oblivious that there was a Jiang Lili still sitting there. Jiang Lili scrambled ashore and ran after him with his walking stick. She found him standing in the woods facing a tree. She walked closer, meaning to complain, but saw that he was weeping.

"Mr. Cheng!" Jiang Lili called him softly. It became apparent that he simply did not hear her. Jiang Lili tugged lightly at his sleeve, but he gave no response.

Sighing, Jiang Lili said, "You're so upset. What should I do?"

It was only then that Mr. Cheng turned around to look at her.

"I may as well die . . ." he mumbled dejectedly.

Jiang Lili found herself crying. So she was not even a worthy rival to death! To her surprise, Mr. Cheng took her in his arms, and put his head against hers. She instinctively returned his embrace. Hope arose in her breast as she sniffed the scent of his hair tonic on his collar. Even though this hope was squeezed forcibly out of Mr. Cheng's hopelessness, it was still hope.

In the days afterward Mr. Cheng no longer spoke of Wang Qiyao, nor did Jiang Lili. They went out every week. Whether they went to dinner or a movie, they always avoided places the three of them had gone to together, or those that Mr. Cheng had gone to alone with Wang Qiyao. They tried to steer clear of Wang Qiyao, but it was not easy. Every time they got together they felt they were doing something behind her back. Wang Qiyao had occupied a large space in each of their hearts, leaving only the edges for their relationship. Nonetheless, the feelings they had for each other were genuine: no deception or pretension there. Needless to say, Jiang Lili truly loved Mr. Cheng while he, at the minimum, did not find her objectionable. On top of that, he felt a certain gratitude, on behalf of himself and of Wang Qiyao. It was the tenderness of a brother toward a sister, a real tenderness.

For a time they saw each other almost every day, even showing up together at parties and gatherings among their relatives and friends, appearing as a couple for whom marriage was but a matter of time. This was a time of healing and calm. There were no extravagant hopes, just quiet planning along sensible lines. Mr. Cheng often dined at the Jiang house, and even the automaton-like young master of the house managed to say a few polite words to him. On Jiang Lili's twentieth birthday her father came out to Shanghai from the interior. Solemn introductions took place, and the two men were left with good impressions of one another. Even though Mr. Cheng had not proposed formally, they spoke with each other as if they were one family. Jiang Lili's mother began to mull over the upcoming wedding, wondering what kind of *cheongsam* to wear at the banquet. As she recalled her own wedding, her joy was mixed with sorrow.

In the midst of these heartwarming activities, Jiang Lili was fretful. Even when Mr. Cheng was with her, he still remained somewhat aloof. The more she got from him, the more dissatisfied she grew. By nature domineering, she had furthermore been brought up with a strong sense of entitlement. Circumstances had forced her to be tolerant for a time, but it was not a situation she could live with in the long run. Her natural tendency was to either advance or retreat; moderation was just not her style. She became extremely demanding of Mr. Cheng, especially in matters concerning Wang Qiyao, whose importance she tended to blow out of all proportion. At first she allowed a fuzzy area to exist around that forbidden territory, only fretting in private. Soon, however, she brought the fight out into the open.

One day, as they headed toward a department store on foot to buy gift certificates for a friend, Jiang Lili, annoyed at Mr. Cheng's inattentiveness, followed his eyes to a pedicab, wherein sat a young woman in a cape enthroned among her purchases. It took her a few minutes to digest what had occurred, but when she did, Jiang Lili suddenly stopped talking. Roused from his reverie, Mr. Cheng asked why she had stopped.

"Oh," Jiang Lili responded coldly, "I mistook that lady for Wang Qiyao and completely forgot what I was saying."

Peeved at having his daydream exposed, Mr. Cheng merely kept quiet. This was the first time Wang Qiyao's name had come up in their conversation since the day on the lake, and over them hung a sense of an invisible line being crossed, of skeletons being brought out of the closet. Taking Mr. Cheng's silence to be an admission of guilt, Jiang Lili became incensed. She lost all interest in gift certificates and immediately hailed a pedicab to go home, leaving Mr. Cheng on the street. Contrite, Mr. Cheng blamed himself for not being more careful. He continued on alone to buy the certificates at the Xianshi Department Store, and, to placate Jiang Lili, also bought some pine nut candies at Caizhi Zhai. He took the trolley to her house. Jiang Lili was sitting in the living room, but upon his arrival ran upstairs to her bedroom and locked the door. Mr. Cheng did not want to raise his voice and spoke softly to her through the door, to no avail. Just as he finally gave up and was about to leave, the key turned and the door opened. There she was, her eyes swollen as large as peaches from crying. Mr. Cheng had to console her a thousand times, and it was dusk before she was mollified.

Once something happens, it tends to happen again. Gradually, Wang Qiyao became a mantra that Jiang Lili invoked all the time. Sometimes she was right—he *was* thinking of Wang Qiyao—but other times she was dead wrong. Mr. Cheng was unfailingly apologetic. After a while, Mr. Cheng himself became confused. Perhaps there was really no room for anyone else in his heart aside from Wang Qiyao. What might have faded away naturally over time became etched in stone. Mr. Cheng had indeed suffered grievously from his love for Wang Qiyao, but he had resigned himself to losing her. Now Jiang Lili practically taught him that he could still think freely of Wang Qiyao and let her presence remain with him day and night. Reclusive by nature, he would let his thoughts wander back to Wang Qiyao whenever he was alone. He resumed his interest in photography, taking pictures of scenery, objects, and architectural structures, but no human figures. That space he reserved for Wang Qiyao alone. He saw less and less of Jiang Lili.

Initially, Jiang Lili would not call him. When he finally came around to phone or visit, she would pretend to ignore him, even declining to see him, partly because she was still sore and partly because she was deploying the old stratagem of disarming the opponent while pretending to let him go. But when Mr. Cheng stopped calling altogether, Jiang Lili panicked. She started to call him. She felt better when she heard his voice, but that did not prevent her from remaining angry. Even when they did manage to get together, they seemed always to part unhappily. After a few instances of this, Mr. Cheng even started to decline some of her invitations to go out. They were thus back to square one—both were discouraged that their sincerity and efforts had come to naught. Jiang Lili, however, could not come to terms with this; she refused to believe that this was happening to her. Rebuffs from Mr. Cheng only provoked her to take further action, propelling her to call him again and again, until she was forced to acknowledge defeat.

In the end, she resumed her humble attitude: she simply had to see him, with no strings attached. This frightened Mr. Cheng, who went into hiding. His "fright" had little to do with Jiang Lili specifically, but with relationships between men and women in general. He had offered up his heart twice—albeit, it is true, each time in a slightly different fashion—the first time he invested his love and the second time his loyalty. Each time he gave himself wholeheartedly to the effort, but what did he receive in return? Nothing but suffering—suffering when he didn't get the girl, and even more suffering when he did. He began to doubt if there could ever be happiness between man and woman, and gradually grew convinced that all attempts were futile.

Jiang Lili's phone calls were going unanswered. Going to inquire after him at Mr. Cheng's new workplace, she was told that he was on an extended leave for a trip to his hometown. They were not sure when he would be coming back. She went to his apartment on the Bund to see if she could track him down. She had a key—which she had hardly used, because Mr. Cheng usually came to her house. There was a desolate look to the place, with its noiseless elevator, few signs of human activity, and domed ceiling. The air was swirling with dust as she inserted the key into the keyhole. Inside, dust danced in the light shining through the cracks between the curtains. After her eyes adjusted to the darkness, she saw that a heavy layer of dust had settled on the floor, the camera, the tables, and the chairs, as well as on the cloth covering the light fixtures. Standing in the middle of the room, she grieved as she recalled how, not too long ago, it had been flooded with radiant light. The chairs and the steps in front of the backdrops were still there, looking cold and indifferent. Jiang Lili went into the dressing room and turned on the lamp on the vanity table, empty now except for dust. Staring at herself in the mirror, the only living being in the apartment, she saw a heartless, hollow shell. She wandered into the dark room, which had a light of unknown source. A string of negatives were dangling from a metal wire. Upon inspection, all were scenery shots, devoid of people. She went into his bedroom, where there were a bed, a dresser, and a rack for clothes and hats. One lone dusty shirt hung on the rack. Other than that, the room was in perfect order, like a man lacking expression or words. Jiang Lili thought she could hear dust descending from the ceiling. She realized that this time Mr. Cheng would not come back to her no matter how persistent she was. She had lost him for good.

As the relationship between Jiang Lili and Mr. Cheng went through its sea changes, virtually all that Wang Qiyao did was wait—wait for Director Li. Right after he put her up in the Alice Apartments, they had spent two weeks together. To Director Li, who usually crowded two days into one, this counted as a honeymoon. After this he showed up only sporadically, sometimes for a night, sometimes for a few hours during the day. Wang Qiyao never questioned him as to where he was or where he was going. She had no interest in, nor any understanding of, politics or business matters. Her apathy pleased Director Li, who saw it as an ignorance that came out of a woman's self-awareness and pathos. He loved her even more and regretted that he could not spend more time with her.

During this period Director Li was like an arrow on a tightly drawn bow, ready to take off at any minute. Even in sleep he would abruptly sit up, ready to give or carry out an order. He was bedeviled by nightmares that made him struggle and cry out. Wang Qiyao could only hold him tight, whispering consoling words all the while, until he woke up in a sweat. He would then turn around and embrace her. Only then would his tense body ease up a bit. Some nights he could not sleep at all. He would sneak out into the living room to listen to a Mei Lanfang record. Even with Wang Qiyao he felt he had to put up a front; only Mei Lanfang could totally disarm him and let him relax. Only Mei Lanfang on the gramophone knew what he was thinking—and Mei Lanfang would never tell. Sometimes Wang Qiyao woke up in the morning to find him gone from her bed. She would find him asleep on the sofa, the tobacco in his pipe turned to ashes; only the record on the gramophone would still be moving, going round and round.

Director Li never told her when he might be back. Wang Qiyao stopped counting the days on the calendar. Time became a straight line, registering neither day nor night. Eating and sleeping, she had only one purpose, which was to wait for Director Li to show up. It was only after she met him that she began to realize just how immense the world really was. A person could disappear without a trace for weeks on end. She also realized how isolated one's world could become. The chime of the trolley cars sounded so far away, as if it had nothing to do with her. She understood what separation meant, and what impermanence meant. Sometimes she said to herself, *Director Li is sure to return the next time it rains.* Then, when it rained, she would say, *He'll be sure to come when the sun comes out.* She would flip coins trying to predict whether or not he would appear. She would look at the flower buds in the vase, saying to herself, *Surely he will appear by the time the flowers have bloomed.* Instead of counting the days, she counted how many times the outside light reached a certain point on the wall, playing on the idea that the Chinese word for "time" is made up of the characters for "light" and "shadow."

Feeling lonely as she waited, she tried to fill her loneliness, but the more she tried, the lonelier she felt. She could have gone to stay with her parents, but she did not want to be interrogated. For the same reason she did not want them to visit her. She had stopped phoning them, effectively cutting herself off. After the first time, Jiang Lili visited twice more, and they went to the movies together. But then she stopped coming. Nobody else called, and Wang Qiyao did not go out. She forbade the maid to go out except to buy food, and even then she severely limited the time the maid was allowed to spend on errands. She wanted the maid, too, to feel what it meant to be lonely. Loneliness added to loneliness. She ate very little, once a day at the most, and was usually oblivious to what she was eating. She sometimes put on the Mei Lanfang record and tried to figure out just what it was that Director Li got out of the songs. She also wanted to be better prepared in case he took her to another Peking opera, but the significance of the lyrics still eluded her. She felt resigned to having always to wait for Director Li. It had been a game of waiting from the outset—the days she waited far outnumbered their days together. She did not realize that waiting was the main activity at all the units in Alice Apartments.

Every time Director Li came back, Wang Qiyao could not help crying. She never complained, but Director Li knew why she was unhappy—although this did not prevent him from leaving again. Director Li too felt helpless. Even he couldn't figure out at what point all those accumulated setbacks began to weigh him down and make him feel helpless—he whose pet phrase used to be "Go for it!" had became "Unfeasible." Because of his willingness to take risks, he had penetrated to the very core of power, but now that he was there, he had run out of room for maneuvering and almost everything became unfeasible. People thought he was powerful, but he knew he was helpless, even when it came to his own fate. He pitied Wang Qiyao as well as himself. His loss of faith in himself only strengthened his pity for her, and he tried to be good to her. Wang Qiyao, for her part, came to yearn for him, and there existed between them the true affection of man and wife. This was a love engendered by waiting, a tenderness that contained more sorrow than joy, an affection that tried to make the most of what they had.

Wang Qiyao was not aware of how desperate the situation had become. She only knew that Director Li was growing more and more erratic, and this left her feeling ill at ease. She also began to notice that at each visit he looked more haggard and aged than the last time. She felt she was living in a cave while a storm raged outside. But what could she do except worry? His was a world in which the clouds and rain contended furiously; in her world, clouds were clouds and rain was rain. What could she do besides wait? All she could offer to Director Li was her waiting. She couldn't even discern his world from afar, much less enter it. She listened intently for the sound of his car starting at the entrance to the *longtang*. It was gone in an instant.

On one of his visits Director Li turned to her after they had made love and said gravely, "You must never acknowledge your relationship with me. This apartment is rented under your name, and no one knows when I come to see you. There may be rumors about us, but they are only rumors."

Lying in bed next to him, she took his words to mean that he wanted to deny any involvement with her. "Of course!" she rejoined sarcastically. "I know very well I am not worthy of being associated with the Lis. I have never fancied myself a member of your family. I have never acknowledged anything."

She spoke as if the precaution was totally unnecessary. Director Li knew she had misunderstood him, but didn't quite know how to explain himself, so he simply smiled a bitter smile. He did not think Wang Qiyao could be petty, but there it was. Realizing her mistake, she was deeply contrite. She managed to force a smile as she looked at his drawn face and white hair, saying, "I was just teasing."

Director Li was moved. He took her in his arms. "My whole life I feel like I have been walking on thin ice and now I'm at the edge of an abyss. This time I'm afraid I may not be able to save myself. I just don't want you to get entangled in my problems. You who are so innocent."

He was almost in tears as he spoke. These words came straight from his heart, and they were words he rarely allowed to escape from his lips. He spoke these words for her, but also for himself. Astonished at what she heard, Wang Qiyao wanted to interrupt him as he made these ghastly pronouncements, but the words stuck in her throat. She started to sob.

In retrospect this was an unusual night. Outside, it was abnormally dark and quiet. Not even the vendors' clappers could be heard, and no music issued from the Paramount. It was so quiet they could clearly hear the maid in her bedroom crying in her dream. Neither of them could sleep a wink. They talked a while before becoming absorbed in their respective anxieties. Wang Qiyao wept quietly, but Director Li pretended not to notice. It was not that he did not want to comfort her, only that he did not know how. Any promise he might make would not be easily kept, so he was better off not making any. Wang Qiyao heard Director Li get up from bed and walk around the living room. She too pretended not to notice. If Director Li, with all his connections, was helpless, who could help him? It was a profoundly lonely night. They were together, yet neither could comfort the other; each was powerless to alleviate the other's anxiety, both tormented by premonitions. Director Li's premonitions were based on what he knew. Wang Qiyao was simply scared, sensing the coming catastrophe. She dared not think further, telling herself, *Everything will be better tomorrow when the sun comes up.*

As she lay waiting for the dawn, she fell asleep and dreamed that she was on her way to Suzhou to visit her maternal grandmother, but was awakened before she could reach her destination. The room was dark, but she could see Director Li's face clearly, hovering over her. He placed a Spanish box of carved mahogany next to her pillow, reached for her hand, and put a key in her palm. He said the car was outside and he had to leave. Wang Qiyao put her arms around his neck and sobbed. She lost all her good manners and reserve, hanging on to him childishly, refusing to let him go. She did not know when he would be back again. Facing her were endless days and nights of awkward waiting, of staring at the light on the wall, which moved fast when she wanted it to slow down and quickly when she wished it would stand still. Outside the window, the parasol trees too had frustrated her wish by shedding their leaves prematurely. Wang Qiyao cried for a long time in a confused welter of misery. She was still crying when Director Li pushed her away and left. That night she soaked herself with tears, until morning came and she was too exhausted to go on crying.

This time Wang Qiyao could not sit still to wait for Director Li's return. She had to get out. She dressed herself properly and hailed a pedicab. She stared absentmindedly ahead at the street scenes, passing from one place to another. The display windows in the shops told her that styles of shoes and hats had changed, but this did not concern her. The new romantic movies advertised outside the cinemas also had nothing to do with her. Nor did the young couples sitting in the coffee shops. She felt she already belonged to an older generation. The silvery sunlight sprinkling down between the leaves dazzled her. Watching the crowd on the street, she thought it unfair that among all of those people there was no Director Li! Stepping down from the pedicab, she realized that she had come out to shop without knowing what she was looking for.

Sometimes Wang Qiyao would go home empty-handed; other times she bought lots of items that she did not want, but piling them into the pedicab made her feel better. She did not know where she wanted to go, but the motion of going forward gave her the sensation that she was getting closer. As the street scenes on either side of her flew past, time was also flying past—that at least was progress.

While Wang Qiyao was going out for her rides, several of her neighbors vacated their apartments. She did not see them go, but only sensed that her surroundings had grown even quieter. To fill the vacuum, she put on Mei Lanfang's records and turned the gramophone up high. The singing echoed and reverberated through the rooms, making the apartment feel emptier. One day she opened the windows to look at the sky, and was startled to see sparrows flocking all over the balcony across from her. The woman who lived there must have moved out. She looked around and realized that many of the apartment windows were tightly shut and leaves had collected around the windowsills, showing that those units too were empty. Alice Apartments was apparently in a slump. Her heart sank but she comforted herself, saying, *As soon as Director Li returns, everything will be fine. But when will he be back?*

She went out more frequently, sometimes three times a day: morning, afternoon, and evening. She would complain that the pedicab was too slow, ordering the driver to go faster, as if she were racing with the cars. She hurried out and hurried back, seemingly on an urgent mission. She scanned the road eagerly, as if her eyes could carve out a Director Li from the crowd. She burned with so much anxiety her lips became parched.

She realized that more than two weeks had gone by since Director Li's last visit; it felt like an eternity. Her patience had run out—she could not stand it another minute. She went out again but, shortly after she stepped out, Director Li arrived. His face was drawn with apprehension. He asked the maid where Wang Qiyao had gone, and was told she went shopping.

"When will she be back?"

"One can never tell," the maid replied. "Sometimes she comes right back, sometimes she's gone all day."

She asked how he would like his lunch, but he explained that he had to leave before noon. The curtains were drawn in the bedroom, but Director Li could feel Wang Qiyao's breath. Going into the bathroom to shave, he felt her breath there too. There were water spots in the basin left by Wang Qiyao, and strands of her hair in the hairbrush. After shaving, he sat in the living room to wait for her, but she did not show up. Restlessly, he paced the living room, looking at the clock. He had come on a whim, but now that he was here he felt as if he really needed to see her. He had never yearned to see her as much as at that moment: it was like an intolerable thirst. Until the very last minute, as he put on his jacket, he was still hoping that Wang Qiyao would miraculously appear. He left Alice Apartments in dejection. When would he get to see her again?

Ten minutes later he spotted Wang Qiyao from his car. From behind the lace curtain in the rear window, he caught sight of a pedicab approaching until it was almost parallel with his car. There was Wang Qiyao in her autumn coat, her hair blown about by the wind as she tightly clutched her lambskin purse. Her eyes were fixed ahead, as if she was searching for something. The pedicab moved forward alongside the car for a while but then got left behind, and Wang Qiyao disappeared from view. Instead of comforting Director Li, this chance encounter filled him with despair. It was a scene emblematic of a chaotic world, one snapshot in a life that was flying past. The thought struck him that they were actually two people sharing the same fate, one with clear understanding, the other without a clue, but neither had any control over their destinies. Two lonely souls, they had no one to rely on other than themselves, like two autumn leaves blowing in the wind, briefly making contact with each other before being blown apart. The car moved slowly through traffic, the driver beeping the horn. Because he had waited for Wang Qiyao, Director Li was now pressed for time. This was the late fall of 1948. Shanghai was about to undergo massive changes, but the city failed to comprehend this. Neon lights continued to light up each night; wine continued to flow; new Hollywood pictures continued to premiere at the local cinemas; and the latest melodies kept on playing at the dance halls. A fresh group of taxi-dancers paraded themselves.

Wang Qiyao also had no idea what had happened. She had been waiting for Director Li, hoping with all her heart that he would appear; but in the end they were like two shadows passing in the night.

That evening someone else came to Alice Apartments. It was Wu Peizhen. Wearing a black coat, with her hair permed and her lips painted red, she looked very much the picture of a well-to-do married lady, more sophisticated and attractive than she had ever been in her school days. Wang Qiyao hardly recognized her as she entered. Even after ascertaining that it was indeed her friend, she was still quite astonished, saying to herself that Wu Peizhen's good looks must have been hidden all along by her excessive modesty. Wu Peizhen, on the other hand, felt self-conscious about her new image.

"I'm married," she said with a blush.

Wang Qiyao felt as if she had been struck a sharp blow. "Congratulations," she murmured as her eyes went blank.

She sat down without offering a seat to Wu Peizhen. At this point the maid came out with tea. "Please have some tea, Miss."

Wang Qiyao scolded the maid harshly. "Can't you see she is a Missus? How can you call her Miss? You must be deaf and blind!"

Stung and bewildered, the maid did not try to defend herself and simply left the room. She knew Wang Qiyao was in a bad mood. Wu Peizhen became even more uncomfortable. She was a sensible person, and being newly married made her particularly sensitive to social nuances. She heard the bitterness in Wang Qiyao's voice and blamed herself for bringing up the subject as soon as she entered the door, as if she had come to flaunt her marital status. In reality, it had not occurred to her that this was anything to gloat about. She recomposed herself and sat up to face Wang Qiyao, to tell her that she was sorry for the sudden visit but that she could not possibly leave without saying goodbye. Once she left, she said, she did not know when she would see her best friend, and her only friend, again. This might not be how Wang Qiyao viewed their friendship, she realized, but she herself had always done so. Apart from her own parents, Wang Qiyao would be the only person in Shanghai she was going to miss; their carefree time together had been the happiest in her life. Wu Peizhen was overstating the case, but it was true for her then and there. There, amid all the turmoil and chaos, as people became sickened with uncertainty, the past presented itself as the best of times.

Wang Qiyao could not focus as she listened to Wu Peizhen. So many things had happened that day. Her mind was reeling. She had been waiting weeks for Director Li, who would not come; then when he finally came, she was out, and when she got home, he was gone. Now Wu Peizhen showed up, saying she was married, and then told her she was leaving.

When Wang Qiyao had finally calmed down enough to disentangle the events, she interrupted Wu Peizhen: "Where are you going?"

Wu Peizhen had to think for a moment before saying she was leaving for Hong Kong with her husband's family. The family owned a mid-scale industrial firm that was relocating to Hong Kong. They had tickets on a steamer due to leave the next day.

Wang Qiyao laughed. "Wu Peizhen, little did we know that you would turn out to be the luckiest among the three of us!"

"The three of us?" Wu Peizhen asked in confusion. "Which three of us?"

"You, me, and Jiang Lili," Wang Qiyao replied.

Hearing Jiang Lili's name, Wu Peizhen was a little upset. She turned her head away. In her heart she had always felt that Jiang Lili had snatched

Wang Qiyao from her. Although she was now married and more mature, she still kept unsettled scores from her schoolgirl days—we tend to keep these kinds of scores well into old age.

Without noticing that Wu Peizhen was piqued, Wang Qiyao continued, "We are no match for you. Jiang Lili will probably end up as an old maid, whereas I am neither a wife nor a concubine. You are the only one who married well, with endless years of pomp and prosperity ahead of you!"

Wang Qiyao became increasingly excited as she talked. Her eyes sparkled as she scratched her nails back and forth against the sofa, so hard that they were on the verge of breaking. Not knowing what to say, Wu Peizhen lowered her head. Then, impulsively, she grabbed hold of Wang Qiyao's hands and said, "Come with me to Hong Kong!"

Wang Qiyao was caught off guard and totally lost her train of thought. When she realized what Wu Peizhen had said, she snickered. "How would I go with you? As a servant? A concubine? If a concubine, I may as well stay in Shanghai. No purpose served by simply moving around."

"Don't you 'concubine' me," Wu Peizhen replied. "You understand perfectly what I meant. I have always regarded you as my better."

A quiver ran through Wang Qiyao and she felt limp. She twisted her head toward the wall, and stared at it for a moment. When she turned her face back toward Wu Peizhen, it was full of tears.

"Thank you, Wu Peizhen," Wang Qiyao murmured through her tears. "But I cannot leave. I have to stay here and wait for him. If I leave and he comes back, what would happen then? He will be back. If he does not find me here, he is going to blame me."

The next day, at the time of Wu Peizhen's scheduled departure, Wang Qiyao thought she could hear the whistle of the boat leaving the shore. The times they spent together scrolled by in her mind, one scene after another. During that period of their lives, they were like white silk, on which words were later to be written; then the words became sentences, and the sentences strung together to become history. Those wordless days had been carefree days. They could do what they wished: they had no responsibilities; even their sorrows were irresponsible sorrows. The relationship she had with Wu Peizhen did not involve responsibility—it was pure friendship. That was not the case with Jiang Lili, where personal interests always had to be considered—this did not mean, of course, that considering such things was anything to be ashamed of. Her friendship with Wu Peizhen was like a plant floating in clear water, whereas her friendship with Jiang Lili resembled a lotus growing in a mud pond. With Wu Peizhen's departure, a large section of Wang Qiyao's life history was snipped off and taken away—the section on which there were no words. The rest of the scroll was full of words, some smudged because they were written when the brush was weighed down with too much ink. The free flow of calligraphy suffers when it is executed with too much earnestness.

Wang Qiyao went on waiting for Director Li. She dared not go out again after having missed him that day. Ever since she started noticing her neighbors' empty windows, she also could not bring herself to open her own windows. The curtains were tightly drawn so that she could avoid noticing the moving lights on the wall. In her apartment the lamps burned brightly both day and night. The clocks were not wound, so there was no sense of time. The only sounds emitted from the gramophone—the voice of Mei Lanfang going, *Yi yi eh eh*, round and round, over and over.

Wang Qiyao wore a floor-length dressing gown all day long, with a belt loosely tied around her waist, looking somewhat like Mei Lanfang on stage playing the female role in *Farewell, My Concubine*. *This thing called time—if you ignore it, it will go away,* she thought to herself. She grew calmer, and found that she had begun to understand Mei Lanfang. She grasped just what it was that Director Li heard in his voice. It was the gentle but tenacious striving of women. The striving was like a needle hidden in cotton. It was directed toward men, and toward the world. While men understood this, women themselves were not conscious of it. This was what constituted that little bit of true understanding between men and women.

Mei Lanfang's singing voice served as a foil to the silence of Alice Apartments. This silence was a feature of Shanghai in 1948. Silence filled many anthill-like concrete buildings, and may even be said to have held some of them up. It was the other, complementary, side of the city's energy, like shadows cast by light. Wang Qiyao had shut off the world outside. She had stopped reading the newspapers or listening to the radio. The news was confusing and unremitting: a crucial battle between the Nationalists and the Communists was being fought in Huaihai; the price of gold was soaring; the stock market collapsed; Wang Xiaohe was shot by the government; the Jiangya steamship running between Shanghai and Ningbo exploded and 1,685 people sank to the bottom of the sea; a plane flying from Shanghai to Peking crashed, and among the dead was an adult male under the pseudonym of Zhang Bingliang, known to us as Director Li.

Part II

Chapter 1

Wu Bridge

WU BRIDGE IS the kind of place that exists specifically to be a haven for those trying to escape from the chaos of the world. In June when the jasmine blooms, its fragrance permeates the whole town. The canals divide themselves into endless configurations as they flow beneath the eaves of the houses on the water. The black-tiled eaves are neatly aligned, as if delicately drawn with a fine paintbrush. Stretching over the canal, one after another, are arched bridges, also delicately drawn. There are many such towns in the Jiangnan region, and they always evoke feelings of nostalgia. But once the turmoil of the day is over, people are always eager to return to the cities and start the race all over again. The scenery in small towns like this comes straight out of an old-style landscape painting; the austere concept of emptiness is incorporated therein. White is the shade of colorlessness, black is the mother of all hues—together, they conceal all things, embrace all things, and bring all things to an end. But the painstakingly applied brushstrokes also suggest a Western-style picture, because in it are people buying and selling, cooking and dressing, going about their daily lives, and enjoying moments of leisure in the middle of their labor. So, beneath the void is solidity, and a multiplicity of actions lie behind the ascetic exterior. These qualities combined are what makes these towns especially suitable for wounded refugees from the cities.

An uncanny wisdom seems to pervade these places—a chaotic kind of understanding, intelligence born of ignorance. The people are all monkish, neither joyful nor sad, not passive, not aggressive; devoid of rancor, their behavior changes with the seasons. Their wordless philosophy is open to interpretation. In the morning, sunlight comes in like a rainstorm, striking Wu Bridge from all directions; smoke rises from kitchens, mist from the trees. The light, smoke, and mist of Wu Bridge blend into a soundless melody.

Bridges are the principal feature of this place, its very soul. To outsiders, they suggest the Buddhist idea of being ferried to the other shore. Wu Bridge is a place of compassion. Beneath its bridges the water swiftly flows, carrying all refuse away. Overhead the clouds glide by, preparing rain for the earth. The bridges let boats pass underneath, and people walk over them to the other side of the canal, where the long eaves stretch out from the houses to shield them from the sun and the rain.

Every grain of rice eaten at Wu Bridge has been winnowed, hulled, polished, washed, and strained in baskets. Every piece of firewood used in cooking the rice has been split into small pieces and placed under the sun to dry. If the firewood, used one piece at a time, is not completely burned, it is set aside as charcoal for the brazier to give warmth in the winter. The stone slab roads of Wu Bridge are covered with the imprints of naked soles; the sides of the canals are crowded with women beating laundry. People live their lives in measured drops at Wu Bridge, neither frittering away their time nor wasting anything. Nor are they greedy. They spend what they earn carefully and make sure there is something left for their heirs. Everything at Wu Bridge—the roads, the bridges, the houses, the pickled vegetables in the pantries, the jars of wine buried in the ground—has been accumulated day by day, generation by generation. You can see this in any early morning scene. Along with the cooking smoke are the enticing smells of sun-dried vegetables and boiling rice, as well as the aroma of rice wine. In this place one reaps what one sows—what can be more satisfying than a beautiful place where the virtuous get their just deserts?

As dawn breaks over Wu Bridge, a rooster opens the chorus of morning cries. Another day has begun, a day of spring flowers or autumn harvests, all clear signs that nothing here ever changes. Never mind the unruly changes going on in the world outside, Wu Bridge remains true to itself. It understands that the multipatterned kaleidoscope of the outside world is only an extension of good, simple living. When the great and the overweening plummet from their heights, Wu Bridge is there to accommodate them. When everything else turns dismal, it remains unchanged. It is the base and the core. It is time itself. Like an hourglass, it renders the flow of time visible. The other shore and the passage there are all contained within.

Water is the reason places like Wu Bridge can exist. The waterways of Jiangnan are like branches on a tree, extending out one from the other, multiplying a hundred times over. Wu Bridge is surrounded by waterways, but it is not isolated, like an island in the sea; it is rather a quiet enclave in a noisy world. The sea is cold, vast, and boundless, whereas these canals and waterways wind through people's lives. The sea is a place without hope: what happens there is dictated by fate. But canals open up a way out of those places that are without hope; setting up a visible truth to stand against fate, they are easygoing and come-at-able. Compared to islands, places like Wu Bridge are more knowing, more prosaic, more willing to compromise. We can believe in them without sacrificing our earthly happiness, a crude happiness far removed from any splendor. This is a happiness that does not require the accompaniment of elegant music, but grows out of the pleasures of everyday living. Wu Bridge hovers, marvelously poised, between the philistine world and the realm of enlightenment. It is hard to tell to which side the balance is tilted. Places like these are here to put a crimp in society's vanity, but also to alleviate its sense of hopelessness, maintaining a delicate equilibrium. Once or twice in our lives, we arrive by some miracle at a place like Wu Bridge, where we can recompose ourselves.

Underneath its serene exterior, Wu Bridge has a strong urge to make its presence felt, just as, under its blanket of smoke and mist, the chickens crow and the dogs bark—what you sow there surely shall you reap. How close to the heart Wu Bridge lies! It caresses all the scars we carry around inside, giving reason to our actions, explanations for our fortunes. It understands that everything boils down to two words that drive us all: *to live.*

All the outsiders who come to Wu Bridge seem to arrive in a miserable condition. Dejected and dismayed, most of them come not of their own volition, but because they have no other choice. Even before learning its name, they start complaining—what a backwater the place is. They either stay indoors, sulking petulantly, or swagger about town, looking down on everything. But whether arrogant or crestfallen, they show themselves to be shallow and boorish. It takes them some time to discover that there is more to Wu Bridge than meets the eye, and when they do, they are only too grateful. The folks at Wu Bridge take their haughty attitude with a stoic resignation. This is a form of compassion, like an adult forgiving the unruly behavior of a child. They view outsiders as part of the scenery: year after year, month after month, there are always one or two meandering down the streets. These are the victims of the incessant combat playing out there. The locals are never shocked or surprised when they encounter these strangers from the cities; their presence in Wu Bridge couldn't be more natural. The locals seem not to understand them, but actually they understand better than anyone.

Folks here know that the bright, colorful clothes the outsiders come wearing are but clouds at sunset, and the hearts inside those fancy clothes are flickering lights ready to fade out at any moment. When outsiders arrive in boats, after a long journey through mazy waterways, they feel they have landed on the outer edge of the known world, a world that they hate and love and that they refuse to let go. Blinded by bitterness, they know not what lies in wait.

Wu Bridge is our mother's mother. But, being once removed, we see her as a stranger. Also, a generation of mixed blood flows between us, so, in the absence of resemblance, she is more distant to us than a stranger. Be that as it may, this is where we all come from. The bridges of Wu Bridge all lead us back to our maternal grandmother—our source—which is why we keep coming back here from the twists and turns of life's journey. Every one of those strangers from the city has his or her own Wu Bridge. Wu Bridge is the closest of our ancestors; ordinary people like us can simply reach out and touch her. She is not the kind of ancestor we think of when we see the ceremonial banners flying on Grave-sweeping Day in the spring; rather, what brings her to mind are the sweet cakes served that day, made of glutinous rice flour dyed with green herbs and shaped by hand. We associate her with steady, quiet effort, with the comforts of food and clothing. She calls out to us from the aroma of dried meat on New Year's Day, and from the warmth of charcoal hand-braziers; she summons us to shoulder the hoe to work in the fields, to cast our nets into the sea. It is her voice we hear calling as we stroll over a bridge, ride in a boat, hurry along on a road, or leap over a ditch. Her calls reverberate through body and soul—you can't hide from them and you can't escape them. Her calls echo in heated wine jugs, in roasting chestnuts, in jasmine blossoms in June, and in the October osmanthus. Her calls enshroud, building inexorably layer upon layer, besieging those outsiders until they are forced to acknowledge her.

Throughout the Jiangnan region, where waterways spread out like nets, places such as Wu Bridge are scattered about, like nests in trees to shelter lost souls. The outsiders come and go like the tide. Their cycle of departure and return mirrors the ebb and flow of affairs in the world outside. Wu Bridge is where they come to recuperate, but as soon as they are rested they leave again. For this we may blame the gentle and accommodating ways of Wu Bridge, which never cures them of their sickness, only the symptoms. Nevertheless, to all the broken-hearted and teary-eyed arriving on its shores in boats with thatched canopies, Wu Bridge offers solace.

As you approach Wu Bridge by boat below a drizzling sky, going under the arch of one bridge after another, you feel as if you have passed through many imposing gates. You will see hundreds of willow trees, their thin, long leaves swaying like bead curtains in the wind. Through the bead curtains, you see houses built right to the water's edge, their half-immersed stone steps covered with velvety green lichen. Bamboo poles, draped with baskets and colorful laundry, stick out from the windows. Galleries lined with stores hang above the water, the columns supporting them overgrown with lichens, and the menu tablets outside the wine-shops look as ancient as the columns. It is not at all unusual, along the way, to come across a wedding boat or two, distinguished by a large red paper cutout of the character "happiness" pinned on its thatched canopy. The boat, festooned with red and green satin ribbons, is loaded with the bridal trousseau. The bride weeps, but those are tears of happiness that she is shedding. On either side of the water are yellow cabbages and green rice seedlings: white butterflies flit among them, a brilliant display of color.

At last you have arrived in Wu Bridge.

Grandma

Wu Bridge was the ancestral home of Wang Qiyao's maternal grandmother. Grandma hired a boat and they left Suzhou in the morning, arriving at Wu Bridge by the afternoon. Wang Qiyao sat under the canopy, wearing a blue twill jacket trimmed with camel hair, a cashmere scarf wrapped around her head; her arms were crisscrossed in front of her, as she kept her hands tucked inside her sleeves. Sitting across from her outside the canopy, Grandma was hugging a brazier for warmth and smoking a cigarette. She too had been a beauty in her time. On her wedding day she had traveled this very same canal on her way to Suzhou, and a light spring drizzle had been falling as she arrived in Suzhou, which was abuzz with rumors of her beauty. It was Grave-sweeping Day and the haze that shimmered through the surrounding scenery had mirrored the haze in her heart. Now, after all these decades, everything was crystal clear.

Looking at Wang Qiyao, Grandma felt as if she could see her granddaughter forty years hence. The poor child had set off on a crooked beginning that would not be easy to straighten out. It was all because she was too pretty. In truth, beauty is deceptive, not because it deceives others, but because it deceives oneself. It would be much better for a woman not to be conscious of her beauty. If only she could be kept in the dark for a few years, by then the danger would have passed. Unfortunately, people in a place like Shanghai are always vying to lavish compliments on pretty girls and tell them how beautiful they are. They seduce you into believing that everything is wonderful, that the good times will never end. They take you with them into this dreamland; but people do not easily give up their dreams, even after circumstances have changed. Grandma pities Wang Qiyao for having been so early, so rudely awakened. It would have been nice to have been allowed to dream on for a few more years. Well, she will just have to take things one step at a time. The advantage of an early awakening is that she still has youth on her side. However, starting out now is not the same as starting out then. One has scars, like a cracked egg. It will be a continuation rather than a fresh start.

The old boatman comes from Kunshan, and he is singing a melancholic song from his hometown. Listening to that Kunshan melody at this moment only makes one feel more desolate than ever. The sun gives off a pallid glow. Only the brazier emits some heat to dispel the cold, but its fumes induce a slight headache. Grandma realizes that it will take some time for Wang Qiyao to come around; like someone who has fallen from a great height, she'll be dazed for a while. Grandma had never herself been to Shanghai but what she had heard was already quite enough. It was a world that cried out with its siren's wail to all who entered. Once stirred, the heart can never regain its calm. The child may look deadened now, but once the pain and hurt abate she will raise her head again. This is what is so dangerous about Shanghai, a place riddled with sin. Yet in good times, Shanghai can be a heaven on earth where twenty years of gaiety are crammed into a single day. Grandma cannot possibly imagine what that means; the most gaiety she's ever known was seeing gardenias and jasmines blooming together, their fragrance a sea of pure white dotted here and there by red balsam flowers. She understood the old adage, "A drop of water will not stir someone who has survived the bitter sea." She knew that this child was in for a difficult journey, and this wasn't even the worst of it. That was still to come.

The fumes from the brazier, the smoke from the cigarette, the tune of the singing boatman merge into a lullaby. Grandma broods over the paths open to Wang Qiyao. The thing to do is send her to a nunnery, where her heart would be forcibly held down and she will at least be able to live out her days in peace. Yet this option was as unsatisfactory to

Grandma as it would have been to Wang Qiyao. Grandma actually appreciated worldly happiness even more than Wang Qiyao. The only kind of happiness Wang Qiyao has known is in large part hollow, made up of finery and fancy food; Grandma has known happiness to its fullest. Grandma loves feminine beauty, which no flower can rival. Often, looking at herself in the mirror, she cannot not help but be thankful that she was born a woman. She prefers the quiet world of women to that of the man, where one has to remain on battle alert at all times, struggling to the death. A man's shoulders are weighed down by the burdens of family as well as business, and he walks a tight wire where the slightest misstep can plunge him into ruin; whereas a woman simply shares the fruits of his labor and if necessary suffers along with him. The agony of childbirth is fleeting. The flesh and blood breaking off from a woman's body remain linked to her forever. This is something that men will never understand. Looking again at Wang Qiyao, Grandma pities her for not having yet enjoyed the benefits of womanhood. These benefits are ordinary yet genuine—solid through and through, from the beginning to the end, in name and in fact. They are the happiness that is enjoyed with an ordinary heart. Unfortunately, the poor child's heart has lost its ordinariness. It has been twisted, and henceforth she will only appreciate warped happiness.

Waterfowl swim in the wake of the boat. *Gu gu*, they cry, before taking flight.

"Are you cold?" Grandma asked.

Wang Qiyao shook her head.

"Hungry?"

Seeing Wang Qiyao shake her head again, Grandma realized that she was scarcely more alive than a marionette. Her spirit had wandered off and Grandma feared that when it finally returned, the child would be a changed person. *How will she be able to settle down again after everything that has happened?* At this point, the boat came to a small town and Grandma asked the boatman to fetch some rice wine. She heated the wine over the brazier and offered some to Wang Qiyao, to warm her hands even if she didn't care for any. From vendors hawking their wares on the dock, Grandma bought some tea-flavored hard-boiled eggs and pickled bean curd to go with the wine.

She gestured toward the people and houses onshore. "Wu Bridge is just like this town, only bigger," she told her granddaughter.

Wang Qiyao's eyes were fixed on the lichen-dappled stone wall where the boat was tied, against which the water was lapping.

Raising her eyes to look at Grandma, she felt no connection to the shriveled and odd-looking woman before her. *How horrible it is to get old!* Yet she knew this was a fate from which no one can escape. All along the winding waterways, she could think about nothing but getting old—the idea tore at her. This whole place with its endless waterways is ancient, including the sky, the water, the lichen on the stone. The Kunshan boatman couldn't be that old, yet he looked like a fossil. She felt as if she had fallen into the bottomless abyss of time: there was nothing to hold on to. Grandma's brazier was antique, the embroidered pattern on her shoes timeless, the wine she drank of indeterminate vintage, even the bean curd she was eating had been pickled in age-old broth. The boats and carts along the interminable waterways crawl on for all eternity. Time is a wall forged of metal that no one will ever break through. No one can withstand time. The earth endures season after season of planting and harvesting. Waterfowl sing the same tune for hundreds of years. And in a scale of time where the units are counted in centuries, people are as ephemeral as fireflies. Succeeding generations appear and disappear like the teeming eggs that fish spawn. *One is no more than a passing traveler, among innumerable others. How old is this boat that ferries people from one shore to another? How old is Wu Bridge, a place that existed even before Grandma was born?*

One by one, the bridges overhead receded into the background; Wang Qiyao felt they must have passed through countless gates to arrive in an ancient world that had been closed to her. She could have cried, had she not been so numb. Her sadness was mixed with a strange sensation that touched her deeply. That day, the scenery was colored in all different shades of grey. The leaves had fallen from the trees, exposing the delicate branches; the surface of the water was wrinkled by tiny waves; the lichen was made up of an infinite number of dainty dots; scratches on the sides of houses, built up line by line, accumulated into a tangled mass. Chimney smoke and the sound of laundry being beaten on fulling blocks are so primordial that one hardly notices them. The only bright spots in the landscape are the fish and the lotus blossoms printed on the aprons and headscarves of the women doing their wash on shore. Although these hand-printed patterns are also archaic, they always appear new. It is as if every era needs them and they become true living fossils. They never age, and even through the passage of time they always appear eternally contemporary. Floating down the river of time, they bob unsteadily on the surface, like water sprites, while all else sinks down to the bottom. They are like a Daoist elixir of immortality: their presence allows the world to endure even longer.

There seemed to be no end to the bridge arches they passed through in order to get into the heart of this ancient world. The chimney smoke grew denser, and the chorus of laundry blocks came at them at shorter and shorter intervals. A new spark lit up Grandma's eyes. She snuffed out her cigarette and began to point things out to Wang Qiyao, who remained absorbed in her own thoughts. The insides of her heart were scattered, its remnants strewn everywhere. Even if she were one day to try to mend it, the scattered pieces could never be completely recovered. The boatman suddenly stopped singing and asked Grandma for directions. He swung the boat around as if heading for home. Not long after that, Grandma announced that they had arrived. The anchor was dropped and the boat drifted toward the shore. Led by Grandma, Wang Qiyao emerged from the canopy to discover that the sun had come out. Its glare made her squint. Disembarking on the arm of the boatman, Grandma paused, brazier in hand, to describe the exciting scene on her wedding day to Wang Qiyao. All the homes alongside the canal had their windows open and people were craning their necks to watch her dowry chests and decorated sedan chair being lifted onto the boat. The blossoming white gardenias set off her red wedding gown. Among the green buds on the trees, the blue water, the black roof tiles and bridge piers, she alone was a splash of red. This red, ephemeral but recurring, is part of a cycle that has been renewing itself since time immemorial.

Deuce

At Wu Bridge, Wang Qiyao stayed at the house of her Grandma's brother, who ran a pickled foods shop famous for its pickled bean curd. Every day a fresh delivery of firm bean curd arrived from the supplier. The supplier had two sons. The elder was married with children; the younger, known to every one as "Deuce," attended school in Kunshan and had been planning to enroll at a normal college in Shanghai or Nanjing that fall, only the unsettled political situation had prevented him from taking the entrance examinations. Deuce sported a look that is best described as "old-fashioned modern": he had glasses, wore a camel-colored scarf around the collar of his school uniform, and parted his hair down the middle. He viewed the women of Wu Bridge with disdain, wouldn't dream of mixing with the men, and spent most of his time reading in his bedroom instead. On moonlit nights, his silhouette made one of the local scenes—the Wu Bridge recluse. Without exaggeration, every part of Wu Bridge had its own recluse, and it was Deuce's turn to take the stage. Recluses were bubbles on the river of Wu Bridge—the river kept on flowing, but each day its bubbles were different.

Deuce was favored with a flawlessly light complexion and delicate facial features. He spoke as softly as he walked. If he were not such a fine boy, his family would have disapproved of him and the town folks would have made him the butt of their jokes, which was what they customarily did with recluses. But Deuce aroused the parental instinct in people, and they happily indulged him. Several families had thought about making him their son-in-law. This may have had to do with the tenor of the time, in which a solitary figure held a certain appeal. People were genuinely fond of him. Deuce held himself aloof from Wu Bridge, sometimes even letting his contempt show on his face, but this only enhanced his progressive aura. He saw himself as a man of the world, and regarded Wu Bridge as a discarded remnant. He would have left if he had had his choice, but his health was not strong enough to confront the turmoil of the outside world, and he was forced to fall back on Wu Bridge. He had now become one of the discarded remnants, but his heart belonged out there.

Accordingly, Deuce was a tormented soul. There is an old saying that a man's shadow was his spirit, but Deuce claimed he was a man without a shadow. On moonlit nights he would glare at his own shadow on the stone slab bridge and reject it. *Is that really me? Clearly, it must be someone else.* One day, walking past the pickled food shop, Deuce saw Wang Qiyao sitting inside. He was electrified. *Now there is my true shadow!* he exclaimed inwardly. From that day on he volunteered to make deliveries for the shop. He had to walk over three bridges, and his heart leaped with joy, higher as he passed over each bridge, although he did not allow it to show. With a tightly drawn face, he would drop off the bean curd, turn around, and leave. On his return trip, his heart sank at every bridge, but there was exhilaration mixed in with that sadness, and he walked with a spring in his step. He was convinced that Wang Qiyao had been mistakenly snipped off from the proper world and that she still carried with her the splendor of that other realm. *Why did she end up here?* Deuce was so grateful that his eyes grew moist. Her presence brought sunlight to Wu Bridge, ensuring that this place would never be lost. Her presence brought a glimmer of hope to Wu Bridge, providing a link between this place and the outside world. Oh, what changes she brought to

Wu Bridge! Deuce had heard rumors about Wang Qiyao, but no matter how outrageous the rumors were, he was not put off. On the contrary, they fed his fantasy. To him, Wang Qiyao epitomized the opulence of Shanghai—even though this was a bygone opulence, a bygone dream. The reflected glory of Shanghai was strong enough to last through another half-century. Deuce's heart came alive again.

Wang Qiyao soon began to take notice of this young delivery man. With his fair skin and effetely persnickety schoolboy style, he seemed to her a character out of an old photograph. When he spoke with her great uncle, she listened closely through the partition, and found that he was so soft-spoken he sounded like a bird. Once she ran into him on her way to buy needles and thread. He fled, blushing, to another bridge. Wang Qiyao was amused and began to take an interest in him. She discovered that he had a habit of walking by himself at all hours, and his silhouette in the moonlight was as charming as that of a virgin. He sometimes leaped with a girlish joy. One day, after he had dropped off the basket of bean curd at the front of the store and was on his way to the back room, Wang Qiyao called to him from behind, "Deuce!"

As he turned his head, she hid herself to watch the agitated and confused look on his face. This was the first time Wang Qiyao had engaged in a mischievous act of any kind since arriving in Wu Bridge, and it was Deuce who brought out this side of her. After looking around, Deuce thought he must have been hearing things, but instead of ignoring it, he shouted back, "Who's calling me?"

Wang Qiyao put her hand over her mouth to conceal her laughter—the first time she had laughed since arriving. This too was because of Deuce.

The following day, running into him on the street, she stood in his path and said, "How come you didn't see me yesterday with those big eyes of yours?"

Deuce was so embarrassed that he turned bright red all the way down to his neck, where a blue artery pulsated wildly. He fixed his eyes on her but did not know what to do with his hands. "Where are you heading?" she asked more gently.

Deuce mumbled that he was on his way to collect bills and showed her the account book. Wang Qiyao glanced at the handwriting on the slips and asked if it was his. Getting a grip on himself, he answered that some of it was. She asked which parts were his, and he showed her several lines of elegant tiny characters. Wang Qiyao, who knew nothing about calligraphy, praised his writing, "Not bad at all!"

The rosiness gradually faded from Deuce's cheeks. "You're mocking me."

"Even the Chinese teachers at my school couldn't have written characters the size of a fly's head with such a fine hand," Wang Qiyao rejoined with a straight face.

"In Shanghai, the entire educational system is focused on the sciences and other practical subjects," said Deuce. "Calligraphy is a pastime that one indulges in during leisure hours."

His range of reference took Wang Qiyao by surprise, and she realized she had underrated him. She tested him with a few other questions, to which he responded intelligently in the tone of a good pupil. Before they parted, she invited him to visit her more often.

Someone else delivered the bean curd the following morning. Deuce himself came in the evening wearing a pair of canvas athletic shoes newly whitened with shoe powder. He still had on his scarf and in his hand was a bundle of books. He came as a visitor, bringing candies for children in the household. The books were for Wang Qiyao, he said; with no movie theater in Wu Bridge, these might serve to entertain her in the evening. It was a random collection of books that included timeworn detective stories such as *Astounding Tales* and *The Cases of Judge Shi*, contemporary romances such as Zhang Henshui's *The Heavy Darkness of the Night*, and magazines such as *Fiction Monthly* and *Panorama*. *He's emptied his bookcase for me,* Wang Qiyao told herself. *Wu Bridge is a simple and conservative town, after all. In Shanghai a boy like Deuce would have learned how to be more cunning and slick long ago, yet how much more dashing and urbane the boys are in Shanghai!* Wang Qiyao looked again at Deuce and felt sorry for him for being buried in the backwoods. Under the lamp his face looked even paler, and a thatch of his very black hair had fallen over his forehead.

She teased him. "So, when are you going to fetch your bride?"

He blushed and said he was only eighteen.

"Your eldest brother is only twenty and he already has several children," replied Wang Qiyao, nothing daunted.

Deuce snorted, "That's Wu Bridge for you."

That he set himself apart from Wu Bridge showed how highly he thought of himself. Wang Qiyao told herself to mind his sensitivity, but she could not help amusing herself at his expense. "Would you like me to introduce you to a Shanghai girl?"

"You are making fun of me." This, with lowered head, sounding aggrieved.

Seeing that she had hurt his feelings, Wang Qiyao went on hastily, "You are at an age when you should be thinking about your career. What are your plans?"

Deuce explained how he had been going to attend a teachers college in Nanjing when his plans were thwarted by the political situation. Mention of the political situation sent a chill down Wang Qiyao's spine and she fell silent. Deuce sensed that he had inadvertently touched a sore spot. Rather than questioning her, however, he tactfully offered comfort by saying that things would have to settle down eventually, life has its ups and downs, and—quoting the *Book of Changes*—when misfortune has reached its limit, good fortune is sure to follow. It was at just such a juncture, when everything seemed uncertain, that Wang Qiyao found herself in the backwater town of Wu Bridge. She had supposed that her life no longer mattered, much less her heart. But suddenly she was struck by a subtle feeling that her heart was coming back to her.

Deuce had the same feeling. Wang Qiyao was like a mirror to him. Only when he sat in front of her did he understand himself. He started to come by every other day and stayed chatting until the moon rose in the sky. Sometimes, when the weather was warm, they walked the streets together. Lights shone out from under the canopies of boats in the canals and from houses along the canals, and the water sparkled with moving threads of light. Their hearts were both clear and serene.

"Hey, Sis, is the moon in Shanghai the same as this?" asked Deuce.

"It looks different," replied Wang Qiyao, "but it's actually the same."

"Actually, there are two moons," retorted Deuce. "One is the moon, and the other is its shadow."

"I didn't know you were a poet!" Wang Qiyao laughed.

She thought of Jiang Lili, who seemed now to be a person from a previous life. She thought that poetry, an affectation for Jiang Lili, came naturally to Deuce. Deuce demurred, "You are the poet, not me."

Wang Qiyao refrained from laughing aloud and said, "How could I be a poet? I can't recite a single line of classical poetry, or even modern poetry, for that matter."

"Poetry is not about any which lines," Deuce replied in earnest. "Some people think that if you cut sentences to roughly the same lengths and arrange them in lines, that's poetry. Others think that poetry is written by linking sentimental words. To them poetry is about striking a pose."

Wang Qiyao felt the latter was a perfect description of Jiang Lili's poetic style.

"Actually, poems are pictures drawn with words," said Deuce. "Take these examples: '*The moon over the land of Qin and the House of Han shines its beams upon the Radiant Palace Lady.*' That's like a painting! '*We called her a thousand times before she came out, still holding the pipa half concealing her face.*' That's another one! Or how about, '*Her jade face is streaked with lonely tears, raindrops glistening on pear blossoms in the spring.*' Isn't that a painting? '*Behold the slender peach tree, its flowers shimmering!*' They are all word pictures, aren't they?"

Wang Qiyao's listened intently. She had not cared much for poetry, but this pricked her interest. Deuce, however, stopped talking.

"Tell me more!" She urged him.

"I have already proved my point."

"What point is that?"

"I've proved that you are indeed a poet."

At first Wang Qiyao didn't understand what he meant, then blushed as she figured it out.

Deuce's Heart

Deuce could not understand it. Why, after being jubilant for a few days, had he become even more morose? Something was gnawing at him. Before, his depression had been diffused; now, it had a focus. Before, he didn't know what he wanted; now he knew, but what he wanted was impossible. Why would he want the impossible? Isn't that the same as lifting a rock to smash your own foot? This Shanghai woman that he called "Sis" was like the multicolored clouds at sunset—she could disappear at any moment without a trace. She was, in truth, a legend. He wanted to add a few lines to the legend, but even before he'd got his writing brush ready, she was liable to be off creating another legend. How distinct she was from the rest of Wu Bridge!—as enigmatic as Wu Bridge was transparent. At his age, however, men prefer enigmas over the truth. After all, once you have arrived at the truth, what's left to wish for? This explains Deuce's despair and Wang Qiyao's allure.

Deuce developed a daily routine of going in to chat with Wang Qiyao while she did her needlework in the back room of the pickle shop; but the closer he got, the more distant she seemed to be. And the more distant she seemed, the harder he strove after her. It was as if she was moving farther and farther away, until all that was left was an indistinct silhouette.

Deuce would occasionally think back to that evening they discussed poetry under the moonlight. The verses he'd recited still rang in his ears and at that moment Wang Qiyao seemed to grow closer. The old familiar verses had come tumbling out of his mouth, but he had since been bothered by their contexts. They felt more like Deuce's own spontaneous creations, inspired by the moment, rather than what they really were—the words of the ancients. Gradually he began to remember the source of each verse, and this made him uncomfortable. "*The moon over the land of Qin and the House of Han shines its beams upon the Radiant Palace Lady*" comes from a poem by Li Bo about the beauty Wang Zhaojun, who was sent off by a Han dynasty emperor to marry a barbarian chieftain. This line seemed to suit Wang Qiyao's present situation as her native moon shone down on her in a distant land. The line preceding this one reads, "*Once on the road to Jade Pass, never from the end of the earth shall she return.*" Was that a sign that Wang Qiyao would stay, never to return to Shanghai? Deuce became excited at this, but then thought perhaps the poem did not quite fit the situation, because Wang Qiyao had not left the country. On the other hand, maybe it did fit after all, because in the poem the Qin dynasty was supplanted by the Han, and China had also just undergone a major change of regime. Then and now, the moon of yesteryear shines on today's people. It follows—in poetic logic—that, as time passes and does not return, neither would she. That the moon of a bygone Shanghai shone on Wang Qiyao—the idea pierced Deuce's heart. "*We called her a thousand times before she came out, still holding the pipa half concealing her face.*" This comes from Bo Juyi's "The Pipa Player," a poignant poem about a woman, once beautiful and much sought after, now reduced to singing for a living aboard a boat. "*Her jade face is streaked with lonely tears, raindrops glistening on pear blossoms in the spring.*" That is from an even sadder poem, also by Bo Juyi, called "The Song of Everlasting Sorrow." The woman is the favorite concubine of a Tang emperor, who is forced to kill her to appease his mutinous army. Deuce couldn't help but grow heavyhearted. He wondered why all the famous beauties named in classical poetry came to a tragic end. It is said that beautiful women lead tragic lives. Is that their inescapable fate? It seems that only in the *Book of Songs* do we have a depiction of feminine beauty ending in happiness and celebration: "*Behold the slender peach tree, its flowers shimmering!*" But even these lines take on a portentous note, as they follow a series of tragic images. With his heart weighed down, Deuce wondered, *Could this really be a sign?* He could see the air of misfortune surrounding Wang Qiyao. *Ah, but how exquisite she is!* Deuce found himself irresistibly drawn to her.

Deuce's feelings for Wang Qiyao were not only love, but a worshipful adoration. To him, Wang Qiyao was not a person, but a spirit that infused the surrounding air with mystery. Her presence overcame him with visions of loveliness—however transitory—and he felt himself vaporized into something akin to smoke or rain. Wu Bridge, with its extreme quiet, its long nights, dense and serpentine waterways, crowded house eaves . . . was hospitable to illusions. Wang Qiyao was illusion incarnate when she, shimmering with the splendor of the big city, walked on the stone slab streets. One could almost hear dance music echoing in her footsteps. Deuce was suddenly convinced: this woman from Shanghai had been sent to seduce him. The riskier the situation was, the stronger the seduction became. Deuce saw himself the martyr to a hopeless religion. He sought not the eternal, but the ephemeral; the pleasure of the moment, that was all he cared for. He was bewitched.

Wang Qiyao took Deuce's affection as mere puppy love. She had grossly simplified the situation, but this was what saved the young man. Their relationship could only go on if seen in such unsophisticated terms. As a matter of fact, his love was pure; he wanted nothing in return—it was enough that he be allowed to love her. When Wang Qiyao went shopping for food, Deuce carried her basket. When the sun came out and she decided to wash her hair outside, Deuce poured water on her head to rinse off the soap. When she shucked peas, he held a bowl to catch them. When she did needlework, he grabbed the needle to thread it for her.

Wang Qiyao watched with pleasure as he crossed his eyes trying to thread the needle. It was a simple, spontaneous pleasure, completely uncalculated. She could not help reaching out to touch him on the head. His hair was soft, cool, and smooth. She ran her finger along the ridge of his nose below his glasses and it too felt cool to the touch, like that of a little dog. Deuce's eyes moistened with agitation.

"Would you come with me to Shanghai?" she asked.

"I'd love to!" he replied.

"And how do you propose to support your 'Sis'?" she pushed him.

"I'll work."

She laughed, a little startled. Then: "The money you earn will scarcely be enough to buy me hair lotion."

Deuce was taken aback. "You underestimate me," he protested.

Wang Qiyao tugged at his dainty earlobe. "I'm teasing you. I don't even know whether *I* can return to Shanghai."

"I'll take you back on my boat!" Deuce proposed with a look of utter seriousness on his face.

Wang Qiyao laughed. "Can you really?"

"All rivers lead to the sea," Deuce responded smartly. "What would stop me from taking you back?"

Wang Qiyao fell silent.

A faint light lit up Deuce's cloudy heart. Confident that he had a rough sense of the terrain, he asked himself what he should do, and decided that it was time to take action. The forsythia had proclaimed the arrival of spring with tiny yellowish flowers on its sparse branches. Deuce thought that he, too, had waited out the winter, and, as he walked along the river watching the boats set out, a plan formed in his mind. Thanks to Wu Bridge's water, he knew what to do. Inspired by a muddled courage, he resolved to move toward the hazy light shining in his future—there is, in truth, no courage except muddled courage. He stopped his daily visits to Wang Qiyao, but, curiously enough, this made her more real to him. She had been absorbed into his plan, and this, to him, was a momentous parting. He was filled with sorrow at the impending separation, but into the sorrow joy came as well, because he knew that somehow this would lead to an eventual reunion. In his heart he sang a song of intermingled joy and sorrow, the song of a child. If people could have seen him wandering around Wu Bridge by moonlight, they would have been deeply moved by his eyes, in which faith and resolve were transmuted to a limpid tenderness.

Wang Qiyao was wondering what had become of Deuce when she heard him knocking at the door. There he was, with his canvas athletic shoes newly brushed with shoe powder, his scarf freshly washed and ironed. Behind his glasses his eyes were glistening.

"Sis, I've come to see you . . ." said Deuce.

"You haven't been coming around. . . . Did you forget about me?" asked Wang Qiyao.

"I'd forget everyone in the world before forgetting you," replied Deuce.

"When men get married, they forget even their own mothers; and I am neither kith nor kin to you," said Wang Qiyao.

"A promise is a promise," Deuce assured her, ". . . the only thing I fear is that one day we'll meet face to face on the streets of Shanghai and you won't even recognize me."

"And what difference does it make whether I recognize you or not?" Wang Qiyao retorted with a laugh.

Clearly hurt, Deuce lowered his gaze and said softly, "You're right . . . I don't know why I ever expected you to remember me."

Wang Qiyao was about to say something to mollify him when he stepped back outside and said, "Goodbye, Sis!"

With that, he turned around and left, his shoes silently carried him away on the stone slabs. His retreating silhouette immediately blended into the Wu Bridge night and he disappeared. Wang Qiyao had more to say and thought about catching up with him, but, deciding it could wait till the morrow, she shut the door.

The nights of Wu Bridge were quiet, so quiet. One could hear the dew fall. Wang Qiyao waited for Deuce the following day, but he never showed. She waited again the next day, but still no sign of him. Then, four days after his last visit, she heard from the bean curd delivery man that Deuce had left town. He had gone to Nanjing to get into a teachers college. Wang Qiyao thought back to the night of his last visit, mulling over everything he had said, and every sentence seemed to take on a new meaning. She was certain that Deuce had gone not to Nanjing, but to Shanghai. She also sensed that he had gone there for her; he was there in Shanghai waiting for her! However, Shanghai was an ocean of people, even if she were to go back there, would Deuce be able to find her?

Shanghai

Wang Qiyao had not thought of Shanghai until Deuce brought it up. All the nights she had spent there, in that city that never sleeps, suddenly flooded back into her mind, but how distant it all felt! In the morning, as she combed her hair, she saw Shanghai in the mirror, but Shanghai had aged, with tiny wrinkles around its eyes. When she walked by the river, she saw a reflection of Shanghai, but it was a faded Shanghai. Every time she tore a page from the calendar, she felt how Shanghai had grown older, and the thought pained her. The days and nights of Shanghai were filled with feelings as magnificent and volatile as the clouds in the sky above Wu Bridge. Amazing and unforgettable Shanghai! Its splendor blazed out radiantly even after all had turned to dust and ashes and creepers. It was just as well if one had never gone to Shanghai; all who had been there were caught forever under its spell.

The image of Deuce under sail, bound for Shanghai, fixed itself in her mind. Wang Qiyao shook her head at Deuce's absurdity in thus acting on a jest. But was it a jest—or a prognostication? It could very well have been a pronouncement. Even a young man such as Deuce in Wu Bridge gets to go to Shanghai—why should she, Wang Qiyao, born and raised in Shanghai, stay away? There was no reason she should settle here, with her heart torn in two, always yearning for Shanghai—a city like a tormenting lover who refused to go away. There was no news from Deuce, no letters for her, nor—according to the bean curd delivery man—any for his family. Wang Qiyao was now certain that he had gone to Shanghai. She sighed as she wondered how he could possibly find his footing in that teeming city. What a rash move that was! But he had gone to create his own legend. She missed him immensely. When she opened the window and saw the moonlight on the ground by the water, she saw the shadow of a faded Shanghai, under the same moon, far away.

Wu Bridge was not totally cut off from Shanghai. The colorful label on Dragon Cure-all Medicinal Ointment came from Shanghai, calendars featuring pretty girls had been produced in Shanghai, the dry goods stores sold Little Sisters cologne and Old Knife cigarettes from Shanghai. Some people in Wu Bridge hummed arias from Shanghai opera. All these little things provoked Wang Qiyao, calling out to her everywhere she went. They scraped at her painful scar, but this was a wound to which she had willingly submitted. Now that the impact of the shock had worn off, she began to view the events leading up to it as inevitable, a kind of baptismal fire. She felt Shanghai pulling at her, but in a way different from what Deuce had felt. He had experienced the pull in an abstract way; to Wang Qiyao, the pull took on concrete forms. She detected hints of Shanghai oleander in the fragrance of jasmine blossom. The sparkling water of Wu Bridge made her recall the night lights of Shanghai. Zhou Xuan cooing "Song of the Four Seasons" on the radio was her homeward summons. When people addressed her as Shanghai Lady, as they often did, she felt they were implying that she did not belong there. Her *cheongsams* were getting old, and new ones had to be made in Shanghai. Her shoes were out of shape from over-wearing, her sweaters had holes, the skin on her hands and feet was cracking. Her entire being felt ravaged and torn; even if she didn't want to, she knew it was time to go home.

There was still no news from Deuce, but then legends tend to have quiet beginnings. Wang Qiyao had no doubt that he was in Shanghai. With him there, the city felt warmer. She could no longer stifle her discontent, and even before she decided to leave, Wu Bridge was already waving goodbye. Every tree, every blade of grass, every brick and stone turned themselves into mist-shrouded memories in her mind. The weeping willows, dancing under sun, under moon, were transformed into dream scenes. She began to notice boats passing swiftly under the bridge arches, and boatmen singing Kunshan melodies. After winter and spring had sped past, by the time the lotus started to seed, Wang Qiyao was on her way to Suzhou in a boat. On both sides the walls of houses changed to stone cliffs, dappled with age-old water marks and lichens. The town stretched away from her like a scroll unfolding. The realities and illusions of Wu Bridge, its reasons and sentiments, its creatures of flesh and of the spirit—all were blended into the boatmen's Kunshan songs and the rumbling sounds of ancient rice mills.

As the boat emerged from Wu Bridge and swung out into the open water, Wang Qiyao found herself in a broad landscape. Waterfowl made black dots in the air. From the fields onshore came the sound of drum rolls and gongs clanging to scare the sparrows away. On the river, the water was as bright as a mirror, reflecting a cloudless blue sky. Countless boats were under sail, as if racing against each other. Wang Qiyao felt a thrill of excitement. Even before arriving at Suzhou, she could already smell the gardenias. Suzhou: a city always associated with Shanghai. Suzhou: Shanghai's memory and dream. The sweet, sticky Suzhou dialect, which can make hate sound like love, is made expressly for romantic conversations in Shanghai. Suzhou gardens, transported to Shanghai, contrive to preserve a measure of leisurely ease in the large city. Having arrived at Suzhou, one is halfway to Shanghai.

Wang Qiyao took the train from Suzhou to Shanghai. The boat had seemed slow to her, but even the train was not fast enough. Outside, the night was completely dark except for an occasional light, gleaming firefly-like. Her heart settled down. Shanghai lies just behind the heavy stage curtain that is the dark night. As soon as the train passes through the tunnel, the curtain will rise and Shanghai will be revealed. The first sign of Shanghai—the illuminated water treatment plant in Zhabei—brought tears to her eyes. Soon the lights came crowding in on the train window like moths against a lamp, but the train heedlessly hurled itself forward, rattling along loudly. Past events overflowed the banks of her memory like a melting river in spring, but she realized the past was gone. As the shadows of people she had known floated across the window, her face was streaked with tears. Suddenly, the train whistle blew, its blast splitting the night like a piece of silk. Brilliant lights flooded in, and the phantoms disappeared. The train entered the station.

Peace Lane

SHANGHAI MUST HAVE at least a hundred Peace Lanes, some occupying a large area connecting two major streets, others connected to other *longtang*, forming a vast network of twisted, dirty lanes where one can easily get lost. As confusing as they may be to outsiders, each has developed a distinct identity simply through having survived for so many years. Under moonlight, these blocks of crumbling wood and brick look positively serene, like something out of a painting executed with minute brushstrokes; they too hold memories and aspirations. The ringing bells make their evening rounds, reminding residents to watch their cooking fires, evincing a trace of warmth and goodwill from those who live there. Mornings, however, begin with night-soil carts, clattering in to collect waste for fertilizer, and the raspy noises of brushes scrubbing out commodes. Amid the smoke of coal burners, laundry soaked overnight is taken out to be hung, banner-like, on bamboo poles. Every action, every gesture comes across to the onlooker as a boastful swagger or perhaps an exaggerated fit of pique; why, the collective provocation would be enough to darken the rising sun.

Each Peace Lane has a few residents who are as old as the neighborhood. Being history's witnesses, they observe newcomers with knowing eyes. Some are not averse to mingling with newcomers, and this creates an impression of continuity. But on the whole they like to keep to themselves, adding an air of mystery to the neighborhood.

Wang Qiyao moved into the third floor of 39 Peace Lane. Different batches of tenants had left their plants on the balcony. Most had withered, but a few nameless ones had sprouted new leaves. Insects swam in the stagnant liquid of moldy jars in the kitchen, yet among them was a bottle of perfectly good peanut oil. On the wall behind the door somebody had written, "Buy birthday present on January 10," and a child had scrawled "Wang Gensheng eats shit." One could only speculate about the birthday celebrant and the object of the child's resentment. Rubbish lay, piled up haphazardly—one could make nothing coherent out of all this. Having put her things down among other people's debris, Wang Qiyao decided to make the place her own by hanging up her curtains. The room did seem different with the curtains. However, with no shade over the light bulb, the objects in the room simply looked naked rather than illuminated.

Outside it was a typical evening in May. The warm breeze carried with it whiffs of grease and swill, which was the basic odor of Shanghai, although the typical Shanghainese was so steeped in it he scarcely noticed. Later in the night would come the scent of rice gruel flavored with osmanthus blossoms. The smells were familiar, the curtains were familiar, and the evening outside was familiar, but Wang Qiyao felt strange. She needed to reattach herself to life here; fortunately for her, the lines where attachments could be made were clearly marked on the fabric. Wang Qiyao was grateful to the large flowers on the curtains, which, no matter where they were placed, remained in full bloom, faithfully retaining the glory of bygone days. The floor and the window frames emitted the odiferous warmth of decaying wood. Scurrying mice conveyed their greetings. Soon, bells reminding people to watch their cooking fires began ringing.

Wang Qiyao underwent three months of training as a nurse in order to be certified to give injections. She hung out a sign advertising injections outside the entrance to her apartment on Peace Lane. Similar signs could be seen along the entrances of other *longtang*—following those signs inside, one could find Wang Qiyaos of all different shapes and sizes eking out a living. They all woke up early, put on clean clothes, and straightened up their rooms. Then they ignited the alcohol burner to disinfect a box of needles. The sun, reflected from the rooftops across the alley, left rectangles of light on the wooden floor. After switching off the burner, they reached for a book to read while they waited for patients. The patients tended to come in batches, morning and afternoon, but there might be one or two in the evening. Once in a while, when someone requested a house call, they hurried off in white cap and surgical mask. Lugging a straw bag containing the needles and medicinal cotton, they looked very much like professional nurses as they scurried down the street.

Wang Qiyao always wore a simple *cheongsam*. In the 1950s these were becoming rare on the streets of Shanghai, a symbol of nostalgia as well as style, at once old-fashioned and modern. When she crossed the streets on house calls, she was often struck by a sense of déjà vu—the places were familiar, only the roles were changed. One day she called on a patient in a dark apartment where the waxed floor reflected her shoes and stockings, and was led into the bedroom. There, under a green silk blanket, a young woman lay. Wang Qiyao had the curious sensation that the woman was herself. Having administered the shot, she put her things away and left, but her heart seemed to tarry in that apartment. She could almost hear the woman complaining to the maid that the shrimps from the market were too small and not fresh enough—didn't she know the master would be home for dinner that night? At times she stared into the blue flames of the alcohol burner and saw a resplendent world in which people sang and danced for all eternity. Once in a while she caught a late movie, one of the ones that started at eight, when street lamps were reflected on the face of the silent streets. Only the theater lobby would be bustling, as though time had stood still. She only went to old movies: Zhou Xuan in *Street Angel*, Bai Yang in *Crossroads*, and others. Although they had no connection to her present situation, they were familiar and they spoke to her. She subscribed to an evening newspaper to fill the hours of dusk. She read every word in the newspaper, making sense perhaps of half the reports. By the time she finished it, the water would be boiling and it would be dinner time.

There was an exciting element of unpredictability to her work. Hearing footsteps on the staircase at night, she would speculate, *Who could it be?* She was unusually vivacious on these occasions and often talked a bit too much, asking this or that as she reignited the alcohol burner to sterilize the needle. If the patient was a child, she would put out all her charm. She would feel sad after the patient left. Pondering over the recent commotion, she would forget to put things away, and then discover that the pot had boiled dry. Such interruptions in her tranquil routine gave rise to a vague feeling of anticipation. Something was fomenting, she felt, from which something might just develop. Once, awakened in the middle of the night by urgent and frightened calls for help at the door, she threw a jacket over her nightgown and rushed downstairs, her heart pounding, to find two men from the provinces carrying someone on a stretcher. The person was critically ill. They had mistaken her for a doctor. After giving them directions to the nearest hospital, she went back upstairs but could not sleep a wink. All kinds of odd things happened in the night in this city. Under the lamp at the entrance to the *longtang*, the shingle advertising "Injection Nurse Wang Qiyao" looked as if it was waiting patiently to be noticed. The passing cars and the windswept fallen leaves hinted at concealed activities in the dark night.

People came to Wang Qiyao in an unending parade. Those who stopped coming were quickly replaced by others. She would speculate about her patients' professions and backgrounds and was pleased to find most of her guesses correct as, with a few casual remarks, she pried the facts out of them. Her best sources were nannies accompanying little charges—these eagerly volunteered all kinds of unflattering information about their employers. A number of patients had nothing wrong with them, but came for routine health-enhancing shots, such as placenta fluid. They became so comfortable with her that they would drop by to gossip. Thus, without going out of her house, Wang Qiyao learned a great deal about the neighborhood. This hodgepodge of activity was enough to fill up half her day. Sometimes she was so busy she could hardly keep up with all the goings-on.

The hustle-bustle on Peace Lane was both invasive and highly contagious. Wang Qiyao's tranquility gradually gave way to frequent footfalls on the stairs, doors opening and shutting; her name was regularly hollered by people on the ground with upturned heads, their fervent voices carrying far and wide on quiet afternoons. Before long, the oleanders, planted haphazardly in makeshift planters formed from broken bricks on balconies, put forth their dazzling flowers. Nothing marvelous had happened to Wang Qiyao, but through careful cultivation her life had also sprouted countless little sprigs that held the promise of developing into something.

People at Peace Lane knew Wang Qiyao as a young widow. Several attempts were made to match her up with men, including a teacher who, though only thirty, was already bald. Arrangements were made for them to meet at a theater to watch a movie about victorious peasants—the kind of thing she detested—but she forced herself to sit through it. Whenever there was a lull in the show, she heard a faint whistling sound coming from the man as he breathed. Seeing this was the best she could do, she declined all further matchmaking efforts on her behalf. As she watched the smoky sky above Peace Lane, she often wondered if anything exciting would ever happen to her again. To charges of arrogance as well as to praise for being loyal to her late husband, she turned a deaf ear. She ignored all gossip and advice, remaining at once genial and distant. This was normal on Peace Lane, where friendships were circumscribed, there being untold numbers of large fish swimming around in the murky waters. Underneath all that conviviality, people were lonely, though often they did not know it themselves, merely muddling through from one day to the next. Wang Qiyao was rather muddleheaded about some things, while she couldn't have been more clear-sighted about others; the former concerned issues of daily living, while the latter were reserved for her private thoughts. She was occupied with people and things during the day. At night, after she turned off the lights and the moonlight lit up the big flowers on the curtains, she could not help but slip into deep thought. There was a great deal of thinking going on around Peace Lane, but much of it, like sediment, had sunk to the bottom of people's hearts, all the juice squeezed out of them, so that they had solidified and could no longer be stirred up. Wang Qiyao had not reached this stage. Her thoughts still had stems, leaves, and flowers, which glimmered in the dark night of Peace Lane.

A Frequent Guest

Among Wang Qiyao's frequent visitors was one Madame Yan, who came quite regularly. She lived in a townhouse with a private entrance at the end of Peace Lane. She must have been thirty-six or thirty-seven years old, as her eldest son, an architecture student at Tongji University, was already nineteen. Her husband had owned a light bulb factory that, since 1949, was jointly operated with the state. He was now the deputy manager—a mere figurehead, according to Madame Yan. Madame Yan painted her eyebrows and wore lipstick even on days when she didn't leave the house. She favored a short green Chinese jacket over a pair of Western-style pants made of cheviot wool. When they saw her coming, people stopped talking and turned to stare, but she acted as if they did not exist. Her children did not play with the other kids, and, since her husband was driven everywhere by a chauffeur, few people really knew what he looked like. There was a high turnover among their servants; in any case, they were not permitted to loiter when they went out for errands, so they, too, appeared aloof.

Every Monday and Thursday Madame Yan would come for a shot of imported vitamins to help her ward off colds. The first time she saw Wang Qiyao, she was taken aback. Her clothes, the way she ate, her every move and gesture, hinted of a splendid past. Madame Yan decided they could be friends. She had always felt Peace Lane was beneath her. Her husband, a frugal person, had bought the property at a good price. In response to her complaints, he had, in bed, promised many times to move them to a house with a garden. Now that their assets were controlled by the government, they felt lucky simply to be allowed to keep their house. Still, as long as she lived in Peace Lane, Madame Yan felt like a crane among chickens. No one there was her equal and, in her eyes, even the neighbors were no better than her servants. She was therefore delighted to see another woman similarly out of place moving into no. 39. Without seeking Wang Qiyao's permission, she made herself a regular visitor.

Madame Yan usually showed up in the afternoon sometime after two o'clock, heralded by the fragrance of scented powder and her sandalwood fan. Most of Wang Qiyao's patients came between three and four o'clock, so they had an hour to kill. Sitting across from each other in the lazy summer afternoon, they would stifle their yawns and chatter on without fully realizing what they were talking about, as cicadas droned in the parasol tree at the entrance to the *longtang*. Wang Qiyao would ladle out some of her chilled plum soup, which they sipped absentmindedly while exchanging gossip. Then, having thrown off their afternoon sluggishness and cooled off, they would perk up. Madame Yan did most of the talking while Wang Qiyao listened, but both were equally absorbed in the conversation. Madame Yan would go on and on, passing from stories about her parents to gossip about her in-laws; actually, all she wanted was to hear herself talk. As for Wang Qiyao, she listened with her heart and eventually made all business concerning the Yan family her own. When, once in a while, Madame Yan inquired about Wang Qiyao's family, she always answered in the vaguest terms. She suspected Madame Yan didn't believe most of what she said, but that was fine—she was free to speculate. Wang Qiyao would much rather that Madame Yan guessed the truth but left things discreetly unsaid; but Madame Yan, who had to some extent figured out the situation, insisted on asking questions point-blank. It was her way of testing Wang Qiyao's sincerity. Wang Qiyao, for her part, wanted to be sincere, but there were some things that simply could not be spoken aloud. So they went around in circles, one chasing and the other evading, and before they knew it, a grudge had grown up between them. Fortunately, grudges are no impediment to friendships between women. The friendships of women are made of grudges: the deeper the grudge, the deeper the friendship. Sometimes they parted acrimoniously, but would resume their friendship the very next day with a deeper understanding of each other.

One day Madame Yan announced that she wanted to set Wang Qiyao up with someone, but Wang Qiyao declined with a good-humored laugh. When Madame Yan inquired into the reason, Wang Qiyao simply recounted the scene at the movie theater with the schoolteacher. Madame Yan laughed out loud but then continued with a straight face, "I'll promise you three things about the guy I want to introduce you to. One, I'll make sure he's not a teacher; two, that he's still got a head of hair; and three, that he doesn't have asthma."

They both collapsed in laughter, but that was the last time Madame Yan brought up the topic of matchmaking. They came to a tacit understanding that the subject would not be broached and they would simply let nature take its course. Both being still young and bright, their sensitivity had not yet been ground down by time, and they quickly understood how each other felt. Although there was a ten-year difference between them, Madame Yan acted a bit young for her age and Wang Qiyao was more mature, so they were well-suited. People like them, who become friends at mid-life, tend to keep part of themselves hidden away. Even Madame Yan, who usually wore her heart on her sleeve, retained certain secrets that she herself might not have understood. It was not necessary for them to know everything there was to know about each other—a little sympathy went a long way. And even though Madame Yan was not satisfied, she could bear it and still treat Wang Qiyao as a true friend.

What Madame Yan had was time on her hands. Her husband left early every morning and did not get home until late at night. Two of her children were grown, while the third was cared for by a nanny. She socialized with the wives of other industrialists and businessmen, but this hardly took up all her time. Dropping by to see Wang Qiyao became part of her daily routine; she sometimes even stayed for dinner, insisting that they simply eat what was already on hand rather than doing anything fancy. Consequently, they often had leftover rice, heated up again with just a dish of mud snails to go with it. Wang Qiyao's near-ascetic lifestyle reminded Madame Yan of her own simple, quiet life before marriage, which seemed so long ago. If a patient came while they were talking, Madame Yan would help by bringing over a chair, getting the medicine out, and collecting the money. More than once the patient thought the well-dressed woman was Wang Qiyao's younger sister, which caused her to blush with pleasure, as if she were a child being patted on the head by an adult. Afterward she would in a self-deprecating tone urge Wang Qiyao to get some new clothes and have her hair permed. She spoke eloquently about how a woman must treasure her youth and beauty, which would disappear before she knew it. This never failed to touch Wang Qiyao, who, at twenty-five, was indeed watching her youth slip by. Madame Yan's outfits were always new and fashionable, but that was all she could do to hold on to the tail end of her youth. At times her appearance startled and touched Wang Qiyao. There was an innocence about her heavy makeup and also a certain world-weariness, blended together to create a desolate kind of beauty. Eventually, unable to withstand Madame Yan's blandishments, Wang Qiyao went out and got herself a perm.

The smell of shampoo, lotion, and burning hair was intimately familiar to Wang Qiyao, as was the image of a woman sitting under the hair dryer, one hand holding a magazine, the other extended to be pampered by a manicurist. The routines of washing, cutting, rolling, perming, drying, and setting had long been imprinted on her mind. She felt like she had been there just the day before, surrounded by faces she knew. When the process was completed, the old Wang Qiyao emerged in the mirror—the intervening three years seemed to have been snipped off along with her split ends. Looking into the mirror, she noted Madame Yan's face, on which was a mixture of astonishment and envy. As the stylist gave her hair a last-minute adjustment with a hand blower, the expression on Wang Qiyao's face, turning slightly to avoid the hot air with just a soupçon of the spoiled child, belonged to yesteryear.

"I had no idea you were so pretty," Madame Yan said candidly.

"I'm sure I won't look as good as you when I get to be your age," responded Wang Qiyao, also candidly.

Her comment was meant to be flattering, but as soon as the words left her mouth, she realized their inappropriateness. Yes, time is unforgiving and she had hit a sore spot. They both fell silent. In a gesture of contrition, Wang Qiyao took Madame Yan by the arm and they walked down Maoming Road together.

After a few steps, Madame Yan suddenly laughed. "Do you know what I like most about the Communist Party?" Caught by surprise, Wang Qiyao did not know quite what to say. "It's the law against concubinage."

Even though Wang Qiyao knew very well that Madame Yan was not referring to her, her heart skipped a beat and she loosened her grip. Madame Yan continued, "If it were not for the Party's prohibition, our Mr. Yan would have taken on a concubine."

"You're being oversensitive," said Wang Qiyao. "If Mr. Yan had been so inclined, he would already have done so. Why would he have waited so long?"

Madame Yan shook her head. "You do not know, Wang Qiyao. It almost happened. He had his eyes set on a taxi dancer over at the Paradise

Club. But then came Liberation and he could not decide whether to go to Hong Kong or stay in Shanghai, and the matter was delayed."

Wang Qiyao tried to recall how they had got onto this topic: was it because she had referred to their age difference? After walking silently for a while, she said comfortingly, "After all is said and done, a man's relationship with his proper wife is the most steadfast."

Madame Yan smiled and nodded. "It's true that it is the most steadfast. But do you know what steadfastness means? Steadfastness means suffering. Only love means happiness. Steadfastness implies suffering together, love implies enjoying one another's company together. Which would you choose?"

Wang Qiyao had to admit that there was a grain of truth in what she said, and was surprised that Madame Yan, pampered as she was, had not been spared from suffering. Madame Yan turned her face toward Wang Qiyao. "Don't you think love is better? No one who has tasted it can ever let it go. What do we women live for anyway? Only for men!"

This time, Wang Qiyao had to disagree. She spoke with some asperity. "Me? I live for myself."

Madame Yan patted the back of Wang Qiyao's hand, which lay in the crook of her arm. "That's even more tiring. A woman who lives for a man saves herself a great deal of trouble."

Wang Qiyao fell silent. Walking in the speckled autumn sunlight, the two ladies became almost transparent to each other at that instant.

After getting her hair permed, Wang Qiyao seemed to have a renewed interest in life. Her good clothes came out of the bottom of the chest and were updated with minor alterations. One by one, she took out her tweezers, eyebrow pencil, and powder compact and laid them in front of her mirror, where she tarried longer and longer. The person in the mirror, an old friend as well as a new acquaintance, communicated with her. Madame Yan took Wang Qiyao's changes as a challenge to herself. Of the two, Wang Qiyao knew more about makeup and was more self-assured. Her appearance was always understated. Madame Yan, on the other hand, tried rather too hard and tended to go overboard. Consciousness of Madame Yan's efforts spurred Wang Qiyao on. With her brilliant sense of style, she achieved far superior effects, and Madame Yan, driven to tears, often went home to throw tantrums at her servants, deliberately mussing up her newly set hair in disgust. But as soon as she had quieted down, she would regroup to do battle anew. For many days running, Madame Yan would arrive at Wang Qiyao's with the sole intention of showing off. Wang Qiyao conceded nothing and quietly trumped her with even more stunning touches. Madame Yan's envy began to show. She remarked wryly what a shame it was that Wang Qiyao was all dressed up with nowhere to go. Wang Qiyao, knowing what lay behind the remark, pretended not to hear, and then upped the ante. Thus the two friends came to view each other as deadly rivals. They could very well have parted ways, but the contest persisted and they felt compelled to check each other out daily.

One day Madame Yan came dressed in a short satin jacket with piping to see Wang Qiyao, who, in a white jacket similar to that worn by physicians, was giving an injection to a patient. She had a large mask on, and only her eyes, firmly fixed on the patient, were exposed. Madame Yan sensed defeat even before she knew what was underneath the white jacket and slumped into a chair. When the patient left, Wang Qiyao was startled to find Madame Yan sobbing in a corner of the room. She went over and supported her by the shoulder. Before she had a chance to ask, Madame Yan said Mr. Yan had been in a peeve that morning, but refused to tell her what was wrong. She carried on about how life was no longer worth living and began to cry. Wang Qiyao said she should stop being so paranoid. There are always ups and downs in a marriage, and she of all people should know better. Madame Yan wiped her tears and continued on to say that she did not know what had happened, but lately she couldn't even coax a smile out of Mr. Yan, no matter how hard she tried.

"Why don't you try ignoring him, then? Let him figure out how to make *you* smile," Wang Qiyao suggested.

This finally produced a grin on Madame Yan's face. Wang Qiyao dragged her to the vanity table to recomb her hair, and showed her some of her makeup tricks. The unspoken words behind their words were how they really communicated, and from that day on they were able to resume their intimacy.

By now Madame Yan had veritably worn down the threshold on Wang Qiyao's front stoop, but Wang Qiyao had yet to step inside Madame Yan's home. It was not for want of trying on the part of Madame Yan. Every time she extended an invitation, Wang Qiyao would always say that she was expecting patients.

One day, Madame Yan asked half-jokingly, "You're not afraid Mr. Yan might eat you up, are you?"

Blushing deeply, Wang Qiyao persisted in declining. But the remark was enough to make her feel that she was not reciprocating Madame Yan's goodwill properly. She insisted that Madame Yan stay for lunch and consulted her on what to do with several dresses at the bottom of her chest. After lunch, sensing she had got the upper hand, Madame Yan again pressed the invitation, which Wang Qiyao finally accepted after some hesitation.

It was around two o'clock when they locked the door and windows and made their way downstairs. Few people were up and about in the *longtang.* As the sunlight streamed onto the pavement, the silence was interrupted only by the music of children's voices from the elementary school next door. Feeling a bit solemn, they did not speak as they made their way toward the back door of the townhouse. Madame Yan called out, "Mama Zhang!" whereupon the door opened and they entered.

As her eyes adjusted to the darkness indoors, Wang Qiyao saw they were in a hallway, on one side of which a window with sheer curtains faced out onto the *longtang.* The formal dining room at the end of the hallway was dominated by an oblong oak table, surrounded by leather upholstered chairs; over it hung an old-fashioned chandelier with light bulbs in the shape of candles. This room was also shaded by sheer curtains, the heavy fringed drapery layered over them now parted and pinned up to the window frame. Across the waxed floor, at the other end of the dining room, a narrow flight of stairs gleaming with brown paint led them upstairs. From the landing, also shaded by sheer curtains, Madame Yan pushed in a door and they entered a room divided down the middle by a portiere. On the far side of the drapes stood an oversized bed with a shirred green satin bedspread reaching to the floor; a light with a green lampshade hung over the bed. On this side of the drapes, a host of floral patterns played over the decor. The armchair cushions were embroidered with flowers, as was the tablecloth covering the round table, which was littered with nail clippers and cotton balls stained with nail polish. A pink glass lampshade hung over the round table. Under the window, shaded with sheer curtains and heavy drapery, was a long European-style sofa upholstered in red and green, with cloud-like patterns engraved in its legs and back. Had she not seen it herself, Wang Qiyao would never have guessed such a luxurious place lay hidden in Peace Lane.

As soon as Madame Yan had sat Wang Qiyao down on the sofa, Mama Zhang brought in tea. Tiny chrysanthemums floated on the green tea, served in fine china cups with gold trim. The light filtering through the curtains was bright enough to see by, but the curtains subdued the hubbub rising up from outside. Wang Qiyao felt as if she had fallen into a fog, uncertain of where she was. Her host pulled out a piece of dark red fabric from the armoire and held it against Wang Qiyao's body, saying she wanted to have a fall coat made for her. She dragged Wang Qiyao in front of the mirror to see how it would look. Looking into the mirror, Wang Qiyao saw reflected a tobacco pipe lying on the chest next to the bed and with a flash thought she was back in Alice Apartments. Everything here was reminiscent of Alice Apartments. She had known all along what she would see here—what memories it would stir up—that was the reason she had resisted coming.

Mahjong Partners

From that day on, in addition to Madame Yan's regular visits to Wang Qiyao, Wang Qiyao would also occasionally call on Madame Yan. If patients showed up while she was out, Wang Qiyao would have her downstairs neighbors tell them to find her at the house at the end of the *longtang.* Not long after this, Madame Yan's second-oldest child came down with the measles. He ran a high fever for days and broke out in a rash that covered his whole body. As Madame Yan had never had the measles and was in danger of being infected, she could not take care of the child and asked Wang Qiyao for help. People coming for shots were told to go directly to the Yan house. Mr. Yan was never home in the daytime and in any case was not the type that minded, so the two ladies made his bedroom into a clinic, setting up the alcohol burner on the round table for sterilizing needles. One of the children's rooms on the third floor became the infirmary. Every hour or so, Wang Qiyao went up to check on the patient; the rest of the time they whiled away by chatting. Mama Zhang served them lunch and afternoon snacks. The Yan boy's bout of measles had turned into a long holiday for the ladies.

During this period, friends and relatives of the Yan family came by with fruits and delicacies, but they did not go up to see the boy, staying just a few minutes in the parlor downstairs. One of the visitors, a cousin of Madame Yan's several times removed, was known to the children and the rest of the household as Uncle Maomao. After graduating from college in Peking, Uncle Maomao had been assigned a job in the remote province of Gansu, where he naturally had no desire of going, so he came back to Shanghai and lived off his father's savings. His father used to own a factory many times larger than that of Mr. Yan. He had received a lump sum in compensation after the government took it over, whereupon he retired with his two wives and three children to live in a house with a garden on the west side of Shanghai. Uncle Maomao was his father's only son, but the child of the concubine. Although pampered as a boy, he had sensed the peculiarity of his situation very early on and this taught him always to calibrate his behavior so as to keep on everyone's good side. Now, as a grown man freeloading at home, he made himself useful. Should any of the women need anything—his sisters or either one of his mothers—he made it his business to get it for them. If they wanted someone to accompany them to the hospital or the beauty salon, or to buy fabric for clothes, all they had to do was say the word. He freely offered advice on a variety of topics. He also cheerfully volunteered to discharge bothersome social duties, of which paying occasional visits to the Yan family was one.

The day that Uncle Maomao dropped by, the boy was feverish and a doctor had to be called in to give him medicine and shots. The two ladies were so busy that they did not have time to take their lunch until well past one o'clock in the afternoon. When Mama Zhang announced Uncle Maomao's arrival, they asked him to join them upstairs. After all, he was family, and Madame Yan had known him since childhood. He sat on one side while they ate. It was a gloomy day, but the alcohol burner was still on and there was a warm feeling in the room. As soon as Mama Zhang put the dishes away, Uncle Maomao joined them at the table, and the three chatted without ceremony.

With Madame Yan guiding the conversation, both he and Wang Qiyao felt quite relaxed even though they were meeting for the first time. The bedroom setting created an atmosphere of easy familiarity, and they talked and laughed with little inhibition. When Uncle Maomao asked if they had a set of playing cards on hand and Madame Yan responded, "You have no adversary worthy of you here today," he whispered to Wang Qiyao in an aside that he was an expert at bridge, playing every Sunday at the International Club. Wang Qiyao hastened to wave her hand, indicating that she was no bridge player.

Uncle Maomao laughed. "Who said anything about bridge? After all, who ever heard of three people playing bridge?"

"Then what did you want a deck of cards for?" asked Madame Yan as she got up to look in the drawer.

"One can do lots of things with a deck of cards besides play bridge," he explained as he began to shuffle the deck she handed him. "Actually, bridge isn't at all difficult. It's fun to learn."

He cut the cards into stacks of four each and explained how bids are made and when one should put a card into play. Madame Yan accused him of seducing them into the game by degrees, but she soon got into the spirit. Wang Qiyao, on the other hand, tried to dismiss his efforts, laughing, "We'll be exhausted before we even get the hang of it, leaving him to play all by himself."

"Is bridge that scary?" asked Uncle Maomao. "It's not a trap, you know."

He gathered up the cards and dazzled Wang Qiyao by shuffling them into a fan, then into a standing bridge. "Perhaps you'll make more money doing card tricks at Great World Amusement Center," Madame Yan teased him.

"I don't know how to do tricks," he rejoined. "But I can read fortunes. Let me read yours . . ."

"You don't get any credit for telling my fortune. You already know everything about me," said Madame Yan tartly. "Perhaps you can prove your ability by telling us a thing or two about Wang Qiyao."

Uncle Maomao demurred at this. "This being my first meeting with Wang Qiyao, I will not be so impertinent as to make guesses about her past or future."

"There, you have already exposed yourself—the rest is all excuses!" Madame Yan snorted. "Real gold is not afraid of being melted in the fire. I don't believe for a second that you can actually read fortunes."

With his cousin egging him on, Uncle Maomao felt he really had to show his stuff. Wang Qiyao begged to be excused from the exercise, but Madame Yan goaded her. "Don't you worry! Let him do it. I guarantee he won't be able to figure out a single thing about you."

Uncle Maomao shuffled the cards again and cut the deck several times, leaving only a few cards fanned out in a row. He asked Wang Qiyao to pick one out and turn it over. But as soon as she did, the patient upstairs rang the bell, and she hurried off. While she was gone, Uncle Maomao furtively asked, "Tell me, has she been married?"

"Ha! What did I say? You're a fraud. You just won't admit it!" Madame Yan chortled. "But to tell you the truth," she continued in a whispered undertone, "Even *I* don't know."

Time flew by that afternoon, and before they knew it, it was dinnertime. They were having so much fun that, when the horn of Mr. Yan's car sounded at the back door, they asked Uncle Maomao to come back the next day. Madame Yan promised she would send Mama Zhang to fetch some crab dumplings from Wang's Family Dumpling House. The next day Uncle Maomao showed up as promised at about the same time, but this time the two women had finished lunch and were busying themselves picking the plumules from lotus seeds with large blanket needles. The alcohol burner was not on, and the air had a crisp feel. Try as they might, they just couldn't recapture the conviviality of the previous afternoon. After the lotus seeds were done, there was nothing else to do and they all felt somewhat let down. Uncle Maomao's suggestion that they play cards with the deck that had been left lying on the sofa went unopposed. He said he would teach them *durak*, a Russian card game, the simplest form of poker, and explained the rules as he shuffled the deck. When he discovered that the ladies did not even know how to arrange their cards, he helped them do that. Then he realized he had seen their hands and had to reshuffle the cards. Their spirits revived as they played.

Playing *durak* with the two ladies demanded only ten percent of Uncle Maomao's attention. Madame Yan kept comparing cards to mahjong as she played, devoting only thirty percent of her mind to the game. Wang Qiyao alone was focused. She fixed her eyes on the cards, considering every card carefully before she set it down. Unfortunately, she kept winding up with the weakest hand and the other two kept winning.

Wang Qiyao finally let out a sigh. "It looks like winning and losing are predestined. One cannot force the hand of fate."

"So, Miss Wang is a fatalist," commented Uncle Maomao.

Wang Qiyao was about to respond when Madame Yan said, "I don't know about being fatalistic, but I do believe things are predestined. Otherwise, so many events can't be explained. There was a ferryman in my husband's hometown. One night, after everyone had gone to bed, someone hollered to be taken across the river. He got out of bed and ferried the passenger across. When they reached the other shore, the passenger placed something hard into his hand and left in a hurry. The ferryman discovered it was a gold bar. He used it to purchase grain and made a fortune when famine struck the following year. He then took his money to Shanghai and bought stock in a rubber company that was just going public. Little did he know that the rubber company would declare bankruptcy within three months, leaving his shares totally worthless. Later, he found out that the man he ferried across the river was a robber with a price on his head."

Enraptured by her story, they forgot about their card game and had to start all over again.

Uncle Maomao said it was mere coincidence. Wang Qiyao disagreed: "I think things had to work out that way."

"I don't know about coincidence" Madame Yan interjected. "All I know is that everything happens for a reason, and those reasons are set and nonnegotiable."

"If you are predestined to have only seventy-percent happiness, and you insist on a hundred percent, you will be in trouble," said Wang Qiyao. "My grandma told me about a courtesan in Suzhou, only moderately pretty, who captivated the heart of a Yangzhou salt merchant as wealthy as a king. He paid a sum of money to redeem her from the brothel. Soon afterward his wife died of illness and he made the courtesan his proper wife, and they had a son the following year. This should all have ended happily, but unfortunately the child began to look strange by the third month, and turned out to be deaf and dumb. Three months later, the woman fell ill with a strange disease that prevented her from eating or drinking, and she eventually died. Everyone said that her life had been shortened by her good fortune. It was not her fate to enjoy so much happiness."

Madame Yan, touched by the story, nodded with a sigh.

"I suppose you believe the old saying, 'When the moon is full, it begins to wane, when water reaches the brim, it begins to spill'?" remarked Uncle Maomao.

At this Wang Qiyao rejoined, "All the saying means is that each individual has a certain amount of happiness he is entitled to, and that amount is predestined and different for each individual."

Uncle Maomao did not contradict her, and they continued to play. He had a story of his own to share with them. An old friend of his father's had died more than a decade earlier. The moment he died, the clock on the wall stopped ticking. It was an old clock hanging high up on the wall and the family did not get around to fixing it for almost ten years. Then about six months ago, his wife passed on from some illness, and at her death the clock started to work again. It had not stopped since. They were quiet after this story. The sun had shifted to the west and the house darkened, but through the sheer curtains they could see the window across the street still bathed in brilliant sunlight. A shadow of foreboding crept into their midst. At this moment Mama Zhang came upstairs to announce that the lotus plumule soup was ready. When she asked if she should go out to pick up the crab dumplings, Madame Yan, suddenly realizing the time, hurried her off. She was instructed to take a pedicab home, not the crowded bus, where she might spill some of the juice. Wang Qiyao lit up the alcohol burner in preparation for the child's next injection. The flickering blue flame instantly filled the room with the color of dusk.

The afternoon had not been as merry as the previous one, but it had nevertheless touched them individually. The hot juicy dumplings Mama Zhang brought back were consumed with relish, along with a fresh pot of tea. They played another round of *durak* until Madame Yan said regretfully, "The days are getting shorter, forcing us to quit just as the fun is starting. What if Uncle Maomao comes again tomorrow before lunch? I shall ask Mama Zhang to roast an eight-treasure duck, which she usually cooks only on New Year's Day. It's her specialty."

"My mother sampled the eight-treasure duck here a few years ago," said Uncle Maomao. "She liked it so much that she sent our family chef over to learn the dish from Mama Zhang. Aren't we lucky to have the real thing!"

"That's right, it has been four or five years," said Madame Yan. "We used to visit each other much more often. Nowadays we hardly see you. When you showed up the other day, I was shocked—you've grown up so fast!" Turning to Wang Qiyao, she went on, "You can't imagine what he was like as a little boy. Even in his short pants, he always wore a Western suit jacket and long white socks, and had his hair parted in the middle. He always looked like a ring bearer at a wedding."

"You mean to say that you now find me disagreeable?" Uncle Maomao asked.

"You are not at all disagreeable . . ." answered Madame Yan, a little despondently. "But your outfit certainly is!"

Uncle Maomao was wearing a well-pressed blue khaki "liberation suit." His shoes were shiny, with slightly pointed tips. His longish hair was combed to one side, in the style of college students, exposing his clear forehead. He presented himself with style and with a studious air calculated not to call too much attention to himself. But Wang Qiyao felt herself growing excited as she imagined what he might look like in a Western suit. Madame Yan made a few more emotional remarks, sighing heavily, before the three parted.

The next day was cold with a slight drizzle. They all put on heavier clothes, and a hotpot was brought in at lunchtime. The coal fire burned bright and over it they boiled a broth with green spinach and thin snow-white noodles. Crackling sparks occasionally shot out from the fire. With the window shades pulled halfway down and the lamp turned on, the room was filled with warmth and cheerful intimacy. It was the kind of moment one wanted to hold onto before it slipped away forever, the kind of setting in which one was apt to offer and accept comfort. The sound of raindrops pattering on the window was the weather speaking its heart, the broth in the pot was boiling with the fire's innermost thoughts, the heavy drapery in the window and the pink lamp were silently speaking their hearts. Wang Qiyao bit into a bone as she was eating a piece of fish; she removed it with her chopsticks and the bone landed on the table upright. Madame Yan insisted that she make a wish on it. Wang Qiyao said she didn't have anything to wish for, but neither Madame Yan nor Uncle Maomao would believe her.

"Well, suit yourself if you don't want to believe me. But I'm telling you there is nothing to wish for," insisted Wang Qiyao.

"You might be able to keep it from me, but it won't be so easy with Uncle Maomao—after all, he knows how to read fortunes," said Madame Yan.

"Not only can I read fortunes," Uncle Maomao jumped in, "I also know how to predict the future based on analyzing Chinese characters! If you don't believe me, write down a character and I'll show you."

When Wang Qiyao refused to write one down, Madame Yan spoke up, "Okay, then, I'll give you one for her."

Madame Yan looked around and, noticing that the sky outside was overcast and rainy, blurted out, "How about *tian,* or sky."

Uncle Maomao dipped one of his chopsticks in the soup and drew the character in question on the table, 天. He then extended the vertical line upward, producing the character for "husband," 夫.

"I've got it," Uncle Maomao declared. "There is a wealthy husband in Miss Wang's life."

Madame Yan clapped her hands in approval, but Wang Qiyao interrupted, "Hold on a minute. It was Madame Yan who chose that character, so if anyone has a wealthy husband, it's Madame Yan. If I have to give my own character, it would be *di,* or 'earth.'"

"Okay, then 'earth' it is!" announced Uncle Maomao as he wrote 地 on the table with his chopstick.

Then he broke the character down into its components, inscribing its right side 也 on the table, before adding the radical for "man" beside it, thereby producing the character for "he," 他.

"It's a 'he'!" he exclaimed, "which also means that you will have a wealthy husband."

Wang Qiyao pointed to the other component of the character for *earth,* 土, "Look, doesn't this show that 'he' is already in the ground?"

She had spoken carelessly and as soon as her words slipped out her heart skipped a beat. She forced a smile to cover up her embarrassment.

Both Madame Yan and Uncle Maomao felt her comment was inauspicious, but seeing how uneasy Wang Qiyao looked, neither dared say anything more. Madame Yan got up to summon Mama Zhang to add more water to the hotpot and make the fire hotter. Uncle Maomao took the opportunity to change the topic by complimenting Mama Zhang's eight-treasure duck. It was only after the hotpot started to boil again and sparks shot out from the fire that Wang Qiyao finally pulled herself together.

As they enjoyed the broth and the eight-treasure duck, Wang Qiyao said casually, "Speaking of wishes, who can say how many wishes there are in this world! In Suzhou there is a temple with a wishing pond where people toss in copper coins. My Grandma told me the monks live on those copper coins, but one wonders just how many of those people's wishes are fulfilled."

Madame Yan and Uncle Maomao thought that Wang Qiyao was through with this topic; when she brought it up again they were uncertain how to react. The broth in the pot was drying up and seemed to have difficulty coming to a boil. Wang Qiyao laughed derisively at herself for being foolish as she sipped more soup. The sky darkened a bit more as if it too had lowered its voice to listen to people speaking their hearts. Uncle Maomao told the ladies about a card game called "bluff." Each player takes a turn setting a card face down on the table, naming the card as he does so. He may be bluffing or telling the truth. Anyone who thinks he is bluffing is free to turn the card over to verify his claim. If the card is what it is claimed to be, the person calling the bluff has to take the card in; if not, the player discarding the card has to take it back, while the person who has successfully called the bluff gets to discard one of his own cards. Uncle Maomao said that even though the game is called "bluff," the winner is not always the person who bluffs. As Wang Qiyao and Madame Yan looked uncomprehendingly at him, he explained, "A player who does not bluff may take a little longer to discard all his cards, but he eventually does, as long as he keeps playing. One other thing: he shouldn't call someone else's bluff either, because that would expose him to the risk of having to take their cards in. He should simply let other people do all the bluffing and the calling while he discards his own cards one by one."

The ladies still looked at him in perplexity, but Wang Qiyao suddenly got it. "You were talking about the game, but what you really meant is much bigger than that, isn't it?"

Uncle Maomao smiled at her.

"If you are talking about life, then the strategy you advocate is much too passive," argued Madame Yan. "None of your card games is as good as mahjong. In mahjong you need luck as well as strategy to deal with the thirteen concealed tiles in your hand. In mahjong, luck always gives you the opportunity to win but also limits your chances of winning. What you have to do is have your tiles all lined up, waiting for that missing piece, like an admiral with his ships lined up ready for the wind to turn. This is how life should be conducted."

As soon as Madame Yan started to talk about mahjong, the glory of her past victories flooded her mind and her spirit rose. There were the times when she had won by a hair's breadth, and others when her luck turned just as she had given up all hope. She reiterated that no Western card games could possibly be more exciting than mahjong. Compared to mahjong, *durak* and "bluff" were all mere child's play—they all boiled down to simple competitions to see who holds the higher card; it was all simple arithmetic, really. "In mahjong, the value of any given tile depends completely on the situation, just like in real life. How do people compete in real life? By comparing their ages? By comparing who has more physical strength? No! You're both smart, so do I need to go on?"

At this point Madame Yan was bristling with resentment, intent on venting her own unhappiness. The broth in the hotpot had evaporated, but she insisted on having some more. Uncle Maomao refuted her, saying there was more to card games than she thought. For instance, in "bluff"—which he had oversimplified in his explanation—a player may believe that the other person is bluffing but still pretend to go along, because he himself wants to let go of a lower card. Thus one person may conspire with another in a bluff.

Madame Yan curled her lip in contempt. "That doesn't make sense. In mahjong there is nothing that doesn't make sense."

Uncle Maomao was piqued. "If mahjong is so interesting, why isn't there an international competition for mahjong?"

Seeing that the cousins were truly angry with each other, Wang Qiyao was both bemused and annoyed. She jumped in to try to smooth things over. "May I invite the two of you over to my home the day after tomorrow? Though I can't offer you eight-treasure duck, I can make a good home-cooked meal. What do you say?"

On the day of the dinner, Wang Qiyao went home and started to cook. By then Madame Yan's son had recovered from the measles: his fever was gone, the rash had disappeared, and he was already back to his old mischievous ways. Wang Qiyao bought a chicken, saving the breast meat to be sliced and stir-fried. She used half of the rest to make soup, and chopped the other half into bite-sized pieces to be parboiled and served cold with sauce as an appetizer. Completing the four cold dishes were sautéed shrimp, pickled egg, and marinated wheat-bran dough; the four hot dishes consisted of stir-fried chicken, carp with scallion, shredded celery with dried tofu, and scrambled egg with shellfish. This was simple fare, making with no pretence of competing with the delicacies served at the Yan household; yet, presented together, the dishes were elaborate enough to show her respect for her guests.

The two guests arrived at dusk. This being his first visit, Uncle Maomao had taken care to bring along some fruit. Wang Qiyao thrilled to the sound of their footsteps on the stairs. It was, after all, her first occasion as hostess in this place—not counting, of course, the many times that Madame Yan had invited herself to dinner. On the freshly laid tablecloth was placed a plate of watermelon seeds that Wang Qiyao had roasted. She herself was in a festive mood, her flushed face beaded with a thick layer of sweat. When she drew the curtains and turned on the light, they noticed the large flower patterns. Wang Qiyao sat them down; as she served them tea, there was a faint trace of tears in the corners of her eyes. She returned to the kitchen—to the pots and pans that, after languishing so long in a state of quiet neglect, were finally bubbling to life—and tears rolled down her cheeks. With chicken broth humming on one burner, she ignited the other to heat up the frying pan, where the oil sizzled raucously. The chattering voices of her guests were immensely satisfying to her, even though it was not a big party.

Dinner was served with half a bottle of rice wine, lending additional warmth to the room. The guests gave high marks to the food, which, though not sumptuous, was just right for intimate friends. Each dish seemed to seek out and gratify their gastronomical desires in unexpected ways, conveying the cook's thoughtfulness and eagerness to please.

"Ah, all we're missing now is a fourth person!" Madame Yan couldn't help sighing, which caused the other two to chuckle. She ran her eyes over the room and, at the risk of being mocked further, pressed on, "Actually, how would anybody find out if we were to play mahjong? With the curtains drawn and a blanket on the table to muffle the noise of the tiles, who could possibly find out?"

Her excitement mounted as she told them about a set of mahjong as lovely as jade that she had hidden away—she couldn't wait to put it to work. But both Wang Qiyao and Uncle Maomao said that they didn't know how to play.

"Mahjong is the easiest game in the world to learn, simpler than bridge or even *durak*, for that matter!"

"And how is that possible?" Uncle Maomao asked mockingly. "After all, you said that card games are all nothing but child's play."

Madame Yan laughed, but ignored his remark and simply started explaining the rules governing mahjong. She explained how the four players sit facing east, west, north, and south. Frustrated again by the fact that they were missing their fourth, she became despondent. The others tried teasing her but were unable to snap her out of her foul mood.

At long last she said, "I feel awfully sorry for you. You've never had a chance to play mahjong."

"Well, if you feel that strongly about it," replied Uncle Maomao, "perhaps I could produce a friend to fulfill the dearest wish of my fair cousin."

"And if you don't mind this place being small, we could have the game right here," Wang Qiyao added.

"It's not like we are having a dance party, so who cares if the room is a bit small?" Madame Yan chimed in, though she expressed worry over whether Uncle Maomao's friend was trustworthy.

Uncle Maomao reassured her. "If he comes, he'll be trustworthy enough." It took a few minutes for the ladies to understand what he meant, and then the matter was settled. Madame Yan worried further that Mr. Yan might find out. Her husband, a cautious person, was not one who relished being involved in anything forbidden by the People's Government, and she had kept her mahjong set without his knowledge. The other two assured her that as long as she didn't tell, there wouldn't be any problems.

Soup was served before the dishes were finally put away, the table wiped, the plate of melon seeds returned to the table, their teacups replenished, and Uncle Maomao's fruit sliced up and served on a plate. As they had all eaten a little too much, the conversation lagged. They could hear the neighbor's radio broadcasting Shanghai opera. The singing resembled everyday conversation, and the subject was the bitterness of not having the necessities of life, such as rice and salt—a far cry from Shaoxing opera, which always revolved around ill-starred lovers, or Peking opera, consumed by lofty ideas such as loyalty and patriotism.

"Your apartment is noisier than my house, but somehow one feels calm here. One feels restless at my house, even though it is quiet there," Madame Yan observed.

Wang Qiyao responded that there was calmness and restlessness everywhere. Uncle Maomao glanced at her and then let his eyes wander round the room. It was quite elegant, but somehow hinted at a hidden sorrow. The old embroidered bedspread with its lotus-leaf border suggested broken dreams, as did the large blossoms on the curtains. The heavy walnut chest of drawers must have been kept in memory of one thing or another. There was an unbearable sadness to those faded cushions on the sofa; they signified time slipping by like water through one's fingers. He was aroused from this reverie by Wang Qiyao, who was handing him a bowl of sweet dumplings. The dumplings, homemade from fermented rice, were as dainty as pearls and free from even a single speck of impurity.

At seven o'clock on the day agreed upon for their mahjong party, Madame Yan arrived first, the mahjong set swathed in a blanket and cradled like a baby in her arms. Having been caressed by countless fingers, the tiles were truly as smooth and cool as white jade and made a delicious clicking sound when they struck against each other. When Uncle Maomao arrived with his friend, however, Wang Qiyao and Madame Yan became subdued; this was not only because he was a stranger, but also because of the reason for his coming. As Uncle Maomao bantered with him, he surprised the ladies with his fluent Mandarin. He was introduced as Sasha, which they thought sounded like a girl's name. He looked somewhat like a girl too, with his fair skin, shapely chin, slender build, and light-colored student-style spectacles. Sasha was his twenties, his hair had a blond tint, and his eyes were bluish. They wondered where he had come from, almost forgetting why they had invited him over. The two men talked about everything except mahjong, and the ladies went along with the conversation.

Suddenly, Sasha stopped in the middle of what he was saying and, flashing a seductive smile, asked, "Shall we start?"

His abruptness stunned them, especially Madame Yan, who blushed, speechless, as though the police were already knocking at the door to arrest them for gambling. Sasha spread the blanket out over the table and, in one swift motion, dumped the tiles noiselessly down on the soft surface. They quickly took their seats and were soon playing as if they had known the game all their lives. As she listened to the mahjong tiles clicking, Madame Yan was near tears. Time seemed to have reversed itself. The only jarring note in the familiar situation was the stranger.

Maybe it was Sasha, or maybe it was because they were too tense: the game did not bring them the anticipated happiness. They spoke in lowered voices and played with solemn faces, as if performing obligatory duties of some sort, and failed to arrive even at the joviality they had enjoyed at cards. Before long, Uncle Maomao, who constantly needed to mediate between Madame Yan and Sasha, began to feel bored. Sasha alone was having a good time, making little jokes that ran counter to the prevailing dreary mood. His overly correct Mandarin was a little alienating, and his jokes struck them as overbearing, although this was offset somewhat by his good manners. At the same time, his fine manners, combined with his youthful gentleness, made them feel deferential, as if he were the real host at the table.

Wang Qiyao was annoyed when she noticed Uncle Maomao fawning over Sasha. She became indignant on his behalf and wished the game was over so that the guests would all go home. She had planned on making a fruit soup for a midnight snack but now had second thoughts. As for Madame Yan, fear gripped her almost as soon as she sat down to play, and her heart was in her mouth the entire time lest a patient show up for an injection, or Mr. Yan come looking for her. With her attention wandering, she didn't win even a single round. Uncle Maomao had come with the intention of pleasing his cousin, but once it became clear that this was not about to happen, he lost interest. Sasha was way ahead in the game and the chips piled high in front of him. He acted as if they were all there to play with *him*, not the other way around. Eventually they completed the minimum sixteen rounds, whereupon Madame Yan claimed she had to go home, otherwise her husband might lose his temper at her staying away so long. Uncle Maomao was only too happy to leave. Relieved, Wang Qiyao only perfunctorily pressed them to stay longer. Sasha was incredulous that the game ended so quickly. Fortunately, the radio next door announced eleven o'clock and everyone commented on how late it was.

"It's so easy to forget the time when you're playing mahjong," sighed Madame Yan, who did feel a tinge of regret when the game was finally over. Soon after she left, Uncle Maomao and Sasha also said goodnight. Wang Qiyao listened to the rattling sounds of their bicycle chains as they receded into the night, until silence once again reigned over the *longtang.*

The next time they saw Uncle Maomao, the ladies scolded him for bringing such a strange fellow into their midst. He appeared so different from them and there was virtually no common language between them; could he possibly be trusted? Uncle Maomao explained that Sasha was his bridge partner, and a very close friend. He was the son of a high official, who had been sent from Yan'an to Russia, and the Russian woman he married there. Didn't they know that Sasha was a Russian name? His father died during the War and his mother returned to Russia, so Sasha had been raised by his grandmother in Shanghai. Due to ill health, he had never taken the college entrance examinations and never left home. Not only did this account of Sasha's background fail to reassure the ladies, it actually made them even more apprehensive about him. This was a source of amusement to Uncle Maomao, who assured them they had nothing to worry about, even though he didn't bother explaining why. In spite of their wariness, Uncle Maomao brought Sasha back to visit. Gradually, the ladies grew intrigued by him and began to let their guard down. They felt that knowing him somehow expanded their horizons, and Sasha's Mandarin became yet another interesting thing about him. Once they had got over their initial prejudice, he really began to grow on them. He was a lively, easygoing fellow, eager to make friends despite his air of superiority. In short, with his knowledge of the game and his impeccable manners, he was the perfect mahjong partner.

Afternoon Tea

Eventually Sasha wound up not only coming to play mahjong at night, but he even joined them in the afternoons when they weren't playing. Their gathering place shifted from the Yan townhouse to Wang Qiyao's place, partly for the convenience of her patients and partly because everyone felt more comfortable there. The sumptuousness of the Yan household made them self-conscious; even Madame Yan preferred Wang Qiyao's place to her own. They came to expect Sasha and would ask after him if he failed to appear.

The four had plenty to do to amuse themselves even when they weren't playing mahjong. The blue flame burning all day on the alcohol burner seemed like a dancing spirit. Wang Qiyao always had some simple but scrumptious refreshments for them—whether Western cakes or Chinese dumplings—unless Madame Yan had left instructions ahead of time for Mama Zhang to buy something from Qiaojiazha or Wangjiasha. Uncle Maomao was put in charge of tea and coffee. This became a way of life. Initially, refreshments were prepared for the gatherings, but now they gathered for the refreshments. Sasha always came empty-handed and left with his belly full, but the others didn't seem to mind. However, one day when he did not show up, the others, assuming that he had been detained at the last minute, started in on the tea and conversation without him. At dusk, just as they were getting ready to wrap it up for the night, they heard footsteps coming from the stairway. Sasha appeared, panting and covered with sweat. He had a bundle wrapped in newspaper, which he opened up to reveal a large loaf of round bread with a crispy crust, still hot and aromatic, obviously fresh out of the oven. Still out of breath, Sasha explained that he had had a Russian friend bake this loaf of Russian bread for them, hoping it would be ready for their afternoon tea, but the process had turned out to be more complicated than they thought. He was like a little boy in his naïve enthusiasm and they were deeply moved. From that day on they looked on him as one of their own, and afternoon tea became a routine that took place at least once or twice a week.

Wang Qiyao straightened up her apartment on these occasions. She would put away the feminine articles that she had always had on the table and set out some snacks, such as hawthorn slices or dried mangoes. Before the guests arrived, she laid the table with the gold- trimmed cups and saucers that she had bought especially for these gatherings. The refreshments for the next gathering were a matter of collective discussion, but since it was always held at her place, more often than not she ended up being the provider. She didn't mind the extra expense, but she did appreciate the dried longans, red dates, and lotus plumules that Uncle Maomao frequently brought along in addition to the tea and coffee for which he was responsible. Wang Qiyao was pleasantly surprised that he had noticed how much energy she put into their gatherings, and was moved by his thoughtfulness. Sasha, on the other hand, did not seem to feel the need to contribute anything more than that one loaf of bread.

After a while, Madame Yan got tired of sending Mama Zhang out to buy refreshments and suggested that they share the food bill equally. Wang Qiyao, however, would not hear of it, saying that this would turn their casual get-togethers into something much too formal. Uncle Maomao came up with a better idea: that they keep track of their mahjong winnings and put them in a common pool for refreshments. This had the added benefit of making the games more exciting. Madame Yan and Sasha were in favor, and Wang Qiyao did not resist, lest Uncle Maomao's good intentions go to waste. So it was settled. From then on a few dollars were handed over to Wang Qiyao after every mahjong game. Wang Qiyao took her responsibility seriously, carefully marking down in a notebook the dates of proceeds and expenses and where the money went—not that she thought anybody would check the accounts, but more for her own peace of mind. Now officially in charge, she tried hard to think of new delights to serve her friends. When she ran out of ideas, she would consult Uncle Maomao, who not only happily offered opinions, but volunteered to make the purchases. Madame Yan and Sasha had only to bring their mouths to eat, drink, and talk.

Some time after Sasha had presented the loaf of bread, he brought the Russian woman who had baked it to meet them. She came in a checked woolen coat and short boots trimmed with fur. Her hair was combed back into a bun at the nape of her neck. Tall and stately, with blue eyes and fair skin, she looked like a movie star stepping out from the screen. In the presence of this dazzling prodigy, Wang Qiyao's apartment appeared small and dark, and Sasha, around whose shoulders she had draped her arm, looked like he could be her son. As Sasha looked at her, his eyes took on a salacious gleam that resembled a cat's. She gazed back at him in fascination. Sasha helped her off with her coat, revealing, under a tight sweater, breasts that stood out like two small mountains. It was only after she and Sasha sat down close together, side by side, that they noticed the pores on her face and the wrinkles and blemishes on her neck. She spoke Mandarin with a heavy accent, using expressions that they found hilarious. Every time they laughed at something she said, Sasha's eyes would scan their faces with a complacent expression. She addressed Wang Qiyao and Madame Yan alike as "young lady," which made the two women blush and giggle. Her appetite was huge: she drank cup after cup of tea with sugar, ate bowl after bowl of osmanthus-flavored red bean porridge, and helped herself to large quantities of sesame candies and mandarin orange cookies from the table.

The pores on her face reddened, her eyes began to shine, and she became loquacious, putting on droll expressions that made them laugh even more. The more they laughed, the more she exerted herself, till everyone was almost on the point of hysteria. When, finally, she decided to entertain them with a dance, they were in positive transports of glee. Crashing into the table and chairs, she shimmied toward Sasha, who had been clapping to keep time, and embraced him passionately as if they were alone. It was all the others could do to avert their eyes as they tittered. Come nightfall, she was still glued to her chair, picking at the crumbs of sesame candies from the plate and licking her fingertips with a famished glint in her eyes, and seemed to have no intention of leaving. Sasha had the good sense to take her home. As they tottered down stairs, hugging each other, her raucous laughter could be heard reverberating throughout the *longtang*. Behind her she left an apartment in disarray, spilled tea and food stains on the tablecloth, and three people sitting in a stupor on the sofa, too exhausted even to turn on the light.

This, however, was not their typical tea party. Mostly they talked quietly as the afternoon sun shifted and the light grew softer. When they were not talking, they would look at each other meaningfully, as if they had a great deal more to say. Wang Qiyao did not bother to make dinner after the guests departed, instead just heating up whatever leftovers were on the table. Her apartment appeared especially quiet and empty after these gatherings, and she felt more restless than usual. At such times everything seemed pointless and she could not summon enough energy to do anything. Sleepless, her mind would be filled with countless things, and even the moonlight was irritating. She wished that someone would show up for an injection. Sometimes she would rise from bed and light the alcohol burner, just for the sake of having something to do; at other times she would try some needlework but then quickly lose interest, oblivious even when the ball of yarn rolled beneath the sofa. She might pick up the evening newspapers and blankly read through them without really taking anything in; or perhaps she would sit before the mirror brushing her hair, not knowing who the person staring back at her was. Her thoughts, incoherent, seemed to come from nowhere. She flipped a coin on the table, forgetting what she wanted to predict and which side she favored; playing solitaire, she forgot which cards should be moved onto which.

In the *longtang* they had done away with the routine of sounding a clapper to remind people to put out their kitchen fires and substituted a bell, which rang much colder in the peaceful night. Hearing that bell, Wang Qiyao realized she would have to live with loneliness until the next afternoon tea. The gaiety of their afternoon tea parties did not seem to make up for the loneliness she suffered afterward. She started to go to the late show at the theater. Late-night movies were the only semblance of a night life that remained in the city, flickering embers of the city that used to never sleep. However, half of the seats in the theater would be empty, and the silent streets she passed on her way home were always deserted. The shadows of parasol trees, the tired faces of people waiting for the trolley, the sound of the bell as the trolley rolled to a stop, the streetlamps and neon lights, all spoke of the lateness of the hour. But even in the dead of night, a feeble light was struggling through, like a hidden current that can be felt only by those intent on sensing it.

Now it behooved Uncle Maomao to consult with Wang Qiyao on refreshments the day before the afternoon tea parties, so that he could make the necessary purchases. Sometimes their discussion lasted late into the afternoon, and Wang Qiyao would ask him to stay for dinner, inviting Madame Yan to join them. After a while, Madame Yan would come on her own accord and Sasha, too, would arrive for the occasion. Thus, dinners succeeding afternoon teas became routine, and they had to raise the ante at the mahjong games to cover the extra expense. In fact, the mahjong games became indispensable. That was fine for every one except Sasha, who frequently made excuses for not showing up. They understood his problem but no one wanted to speak of it. Wang Qiyao began to notice that sometimes, during a game, Uncle Maomao would refrain from declaring victory even when he drew the tile he had clearly been waiting for, instead throwing the game so that Sasha could take the winnings. She developed a new contempt for Sasha and a new admiration for Uncle Maomao for the discreet attempts to help him.

One day, when Wang Qiyao happened to draw a tile that she knew Uncle Maomao had been waiting for, she put it up for grabs at the center of the table, glancing briefly at Uncle Maomao. After a momentary hesitation, Uncle Maomao took it and announced that he had won big. Wang Qiyao was inordinately pleased that she had guessed right and, moreover, that he had let her do him a favor. To her dismay, Sasha pushed over her entire hand for all to see, exclaiming, "How could you give up a tile that you could have used yourself, just so that he could win?"

Hurriedly shuffling the tiles, Wang Qiyao said that she had sacrificed the match in hopes of drawing a new tile that would give her a perfect hand. Inwardly, she was fuming, *Sasha, you have no idea how many times you won at the expense of others!*

Madame Yan, however, was offended. "Everyone here should follow the rules of the game! No playing favorites!"

This embarrassed Wang Qiyao even more, and she reiterated her regret at having relinquished a match in vain. This failed to placate Sasha and Madame Yan, and they stopped the game as soon as the round was over. The next time Uncle Maomao came over to discuss refreshments, Wang Qiyao complained, "Sasha may be a man, but he's pettier than most women."

"I feel sorry for him," replied Uncle Maomao. "The guy's unemployed but bent on having a good time. The government allowance he gets for being the son of a martyr is barely enough for him to play billiards."

"I am not upset about the money," said Wang Qiyao. "It's about playing fair. I didn't want anyone to chip in for the refreshments; they don't amount to much anyway."

Uncle Maomao laughed. "Why should you make such a big deal about it then? Let me apologize to you on behalf of Sasha."

"Sasha's not the only one who should apologize," said Wang Qiyao.

"I apologize for my cousin's behavior as well," Uncle Maomao declared soothingly.

Wang Qiyao's eyes moistened at this. *This Uncle Maomao is quite perceptive. He understands everything.* She wanted to say something else, but stopped herself when she heard Madame Yan coming up the stairs. Once inside the door, Madame Yan plunked herself down in a chair and declared, "What is wrong with Sasha?"

Seeing that they were finally all on the same page, the other two glanced at each other and smiled.

Instead of refreshments, Uncle Maomao proposed that for their next gathering they should all have coffee at the International Club as his guests. Wang Qiyao realized that this was an attempt at smoothing over ruffled feathers and thought to herself, *He means well, but all good things must come to an end.* Nevertheless, she went to have her hair set at the beauty parlor the next morning, and, after an early lunch, she put on some powder and lipstick and lightly touched up her eyebrows. She had planned on wearing a light coat over a *cheongsam*, but then thought this might be too formal and make it look as if she was trying to compete with Madame Yan. Instead, she put on a gray jacket with a poplin facing over a pair of matching wool pants; a subdued floral silk scarf completed the outfit. She was barely ready when Mama Zhang called up from downstairs that the pedicab was waiting in front of the Yan's townhouse. Clasping her handbag, she arrived at the pedicab just as Madame Yan came out in a black wool coat appropriate to her status and makeup that was quite becoming to her. They climbed into the pedicab, which slowly took them out of Peace Lane. The sun was bright red, the leaves on the parasol trees had thinned out, and the sky appeared unusually high. For a moment Wang Qiyao thought that the person sitting next to her was not Madame Yan but Jiang Lili, but this was just a brief lapse. Her face and lips felt dry to the point of flaking, and her eyelids drooped heavily in the sunlight, as though swollen from too much sleep. Display windows scrolled swiftly past; a trolley swung slowly around the corner before hurtling forward as its bell chimed.

Uncle Maomao and Sasha were waiting for them at the gate of the International Club. Standing there at the entrance, ready to greet them, Sasha looked as if *he* was hosting the event, and when they alighted, he told them that he and Uncle Maomao were in fact co-hosting the event.

The two men led them into the lobby, where the floor shone like a mirror. Outside the French window, the lawn had already wilted; only the chrysanthemums were still blooming in defiance of the cold air. Sofas were arranged around low tables covered with white tablecloths. A waiter in a white suit and red tie came to take their order after they had sat down. Sasha picked out several items as Uncle Maomao looked on smilingly; they appeared to be in complete rapport. In the end, Uncle Maomao picked up the tab. Wang Qiyao thought that Sasha's deviousness must have come from being thoroughly spoiled. She averted her eyes and looked at the lotus-shaped lamp on the wall; she felt hot and wished that she had worn the other coat, which she could now have taken off. Not having been to this kind of place in such a long time, she had forgotten how to dress. The coffee and cakes were served in fine porcelain, and the tableware and coffeepots were all made of silver. A man spotted Uncle Maomao and Sasha and came over to greet them. Turning to Madame Yan, he asked, "And how is Mr. Yan doing these days?"

As they chatted, Wang Qiyao felt keenly that she was the outsider, and turned her head away to look at a pot of evergreen with red berries. By this time the lobby was filling up with people, the waiters shuttled back and forth, and the aroma of hot coffee filled the air. Sitting there in her inappropriate clothes in the midst of all the merriment, Wang Qiyao found she had nothing to say to the others and deeply regretted being there.

The newcomer grabbed a chair to sit down with them, ordering coffee and a piece of cake for himself. There seemed to be endless things to discuss. Uncle Maomao turned to Wang Qiyao, explaining discreetly that they knew him from their bridge games. The man was a poor but enthusiastic player. He didn't have any regular partners and had to resort to bribing people with dinner invitations to get them to play with him. Wang Qiyao understood that Uncle Maomao was making an effort to include her in the conversation, but it only made her feel even more out of place. Presently, the man turned around to invite them to dinner at Maison Rouge. Madame Yan and Sasha accepted. Uncle Maomao looked inquiringly at Wang Qiyao, who made a slight bow and said that she had to go home before dinnertime for an appointment with a patient.

"What appointment?" demanded Madame Yan. "How come you didn't mention that earlier? You can't leave just yet!"

Sasha also insisted that she stay; he said that if she wasn't going, then no one was going. Uncle Maomao asked if the patient had a telephone, and suggested that perhaps she could call to tell him she would be late.

Wang Qiyao knew that he was trying to give her a way out of her predicament, hoping that she would be able to come along.

"Let me think about it for a moment," she replied.

Everyone thought that this meant she was staying, but after a short while she stood up and firmly took her leave. Furious, Madame Yan accused her of being inconsiderate of her friends. Wang Qiyao apologized profusely, but deep down she was thinking, *She's only angry at me because I had the gall to rebuff her patronage.*

Uncle Maomao walked out with her. It was already dusk and the wind had picked up. Fortunately, she was able to withstand the chill on account of having been too warm inside. Uncle Maomao was quiet, his head hanging low, so she tried to keep the conversation going by asking about the kinds of services offered at the Club and whether they were expensive. When they reached the gate, she said, "Do go back in, it is cold out here."

As if he had not heard her, Uncle Maomao blurted out, "I was just trying to make sure that everybody had a good time tonight."

He spoke no further, but Wang Qiyao instantly understood what he meant. Her heart fluttered. Is there anything that escapes this man? At this point she saw a pedicab and, quickly hailing it, she climbed in without looking back.

Evening Chats Around the Stove

Winter had arrived. Wang Qiyao discussed with Uncle Maomao installing a stove with a chimney in the apartment so that they could enjoy their tea and play mahjong in comfort. Uncle Maomao agreed to get the stove and aluminum pipes but refused to accept any money from her. He arrived the next day with a worker who had brought the materials along in a cart attached to his bicycle. Under Uncle Maomao's supervision he completed the job in a few hours. The stove worked perfectly and the pipes fit so snugly that not a wisp of smoke escaped into the room. As they warmed themselves at the stove and ate lunch cooked right there on it, Wang Qiyao buried a sweet potato in the embers, and it was roasted in no time. That afternoon they abandoned the other refreshments in favor of the sweet potato and vied like children to pile so much coal into the stove that they nearly smothered the fire. When the room grew dark, their faces, reflecting the fire in the stove, became transformed, like something in a dream or an illusion. The following day it snowed, not the clammy sleet normal for south of the Yangtze River, but real dry snow that accumulated on the windowsill. Even Peace Lane looked immaculate.

This was the winter of 1957. The large world outside was undergoing shattering upheavals, but the small world around the stove existed in a remote corner, or perhaps a crack, of the large world, forgotten and, for this reason, safe. What a lovely scene it was—the snow drifting outside, the stove burning inside. They thought up all kinds of delightful things they could do with the stove, roasting Korean dried fish, baking pastries, scalding thinly sliced mutton in a pot of water, boiling noodles, and so forth. Gathered around the stove, they chatted, ate, and drank. Lunch, afternoon snacks, and dinner rolled into one long meal. The sun on those snowy days was of little consequence, the hours no longer mattered, time became infinite. They dispersed reluctantly only after it was pitch black outside. Barely awake and half-dreaming, they quivered in the sub-zero temperature as they slipped and slid their way home.

Sitting around the stove had the effect of making them feel like part of a family. When Wang Qiyao and Madame Yan knitted, Uncle Maomao and Sasha would hold their yarn; when the ladies made dumplings, the men arranged them carefully in circles, flower-shapes, or pyramids. They bantered a great deal, often ganging up on Sasha. They asked him if he had made a habit of eating Russian bread, meaning, of course, that Russian woman.

"Russian bread's not bad," Sasha replied, "but I can't handle Russia's 'foreign' onions and 'earthly' potatoes."

Everyone laughed at the pun he was trying to make, and he declared brashly that, if they were interested, he could bring them more bread, but only on the condition that they ate it with onions and potatoes.

At the hail of taunts that came in response to this, Sasha lamented, "The proletariat is being assaulted by the capitalists!"

"Who are capitalists?" Wang Qiyao cried in mock indignation. "I am the Number One Proletarian here. I rely on my hands for my living."

"Then why are you on their side instead of helping me?" demanded Sasha.

"I've been forced to give everything my family had to the proletariat," Madame Yan scoffed. "So I am now the real proletarian and you are the rentier."

"Proletarian or not," Wang Qiyao went on, "I'm not going to help you, Sasha! We're rice-eating Chinese, and you're a bread-eating Russian. We belong to two different camps."

The other two applauded her stance. Acting as if deeply hurt, Sasha accused them of bullying a poor orphan boy. At this they felt a surge of real sympathy and tried to mollify him. He grabbed Wang Qiyao's hand and begged pathetically, "Let me call you Mama!"

Aghast, Wang Qiyao flung his hand away, crying, "Stop it, Sasha! Have some respect for your own mother!"

When they saw that he really did not care, they began to rib him about his mother. He said, "What of it? It's only natural that my mother should have looked for another man."

They were quite shocked at this attitude, and, though they laughed, they thought the less of him as a result.

Sasha was pleased that he had got them to laugh, but he was also thinking, *You capitalists, stinking of rot, you dregs of society! You have no idea what awaits you.* Nevertheless, he genuinely liked them, not the least because they fed him an unending variety of delectable foods. Perhaps his fondness for food was an aftereffect of his tuberculosis, from which he needed plenty of nourishment to recover. Over the years, he had developed a discerning taste, and so he readily appreciated the delicacies Wang Qiyao provided. He also enjoyed their company. In contrast to his lack of money, he had endless time on his hands. Every morning, on waking up, he had to figure out how he was to spend the day; in this regard they were all in the same boat. The fact that they viewed life differently was an added attraction, since this could enhance his social experience. Experience was what Sasha valued. He needed experience to understand the world, which he intended to ride as an expert swimmer rides the waves. He was willing to make certain sacrifices in exchange for the benefit of their company. In reality, he did not take them seriously, just saying whatever came into his mind. This, however, did not mean there was no substance to his jabbering. Truth was mixed in with fiction, the genuine jumbled up with the bogus. How they took it was entirely up to his audience. This is what is known as "muddling through." Thus, those in the know pretended that they weren't, and those who weren't pretended that they were. The sun went from east to west, and from west to east, as did the moon. And so the days and nights in this city passed.

One day they fell to teasing Sasha again by telling him they had a girl they wanted to introduce him to. Sasha said he would have nobody—except Madame Yan's daughter.

Madame Yan said she was too young, but he insisted that he would be willing to wait, even if it meant waiting until he was old and gray.

"You'll have to address me as your mother-in-law then," Madame Yan joked.

"It would be an honor to have you as my mother-in-law," he retorted.

The others found this uproariously funny. The broth had spilled out of the clay pot, making a sizzling sound; the dumplings and meatballs were swirling in the broth as if they too were having the time of their lives. Then, suddenly turning serious, Sasha announced, "Now it's my turn to fix someone up."

When everyone asked who, he responded by pointing at Uncle Maomao. Laughing, the ladies asked Sasha who the intended partner was, but in their hearts they were a little uneasy, because they never knew what would come out of his mouth. When Sasha demurred, they mocked him.

"You're going to be mad at me . . ." he warned.

The others became agitated, even as the smiles remained on their faces and they continued to press him.

"You promise not to wring me out for what I say?" Sasha asked.

The smiles instantly froze on the faces of the three. They knew exactly what he was going to say.

"Of course we will," said Wang Qiyao. "We don't expect ivory to come out of a dog's maw."

"Miss Wang must already know who I have in mind," observed Sasha, "otherwise she would not be so upset."

Wang Qiyao was not prepared to be caught like this. Her face turned a bright red, and she could no longer take it lightly. She said, with some asperity, "Every time you open your mouth the most deplorable things come out. You must be looking for a tongue-lashing."

"And what if what I say isn't so bad?" Sasha challenged.

Feeling trapped, Wang Qiyao put down the porcelain ladle she was holding a bit too hard, and its handle broke in two on the edge of the clay pot. Now, no matter how much Sasha abased himself and how hard Uncle Maomao tried to control the damage, the amiable mood was shattered. They sat around uncomfortably and everyone went home before dark. The snow was melting on the ground, and muddy water ran between untidy mounds. Wang Qiyao accompanied her guests downstairs, but there was a forced joviality in their good-byes.

The day after next, Madame Yan had a private conversation with Uncle Maomao.

"It was silly of Wang Qiyao to make such a big deal out of Sasha's jokes, making everyone uncomfortable," she said.

Uncle Maomao, in an attempt to play the matter down, said, "She wasn't really that upset; the ladle broke accidentally."

"I am not referring to the ladle," said Madame Yan. "Sasha was simply making a joke, I thought, but she took it too seriously."

Having said this, she glared at her cousin. Clearly discomfited, Uncle Maomao feigned a smile. "You're making too much of this. There's really nothing to it."

But Madame Yan retorted, "You're a smart person and you know very well what I meant. This is the last time I'm going to say anything on the subject. With time heavy on our hands, it is fine to amuse ourselves with each other's company—but don't you get any ideas."

Uncle Maomao gave a little laugh. "What kind of ideas could I possibly have in my situation?"

"Humph!" sniffed Madame Yan. "Well, perhaps you don't, but there's no telling just what's going through *her* mind . . ."

Uncle Maomao felt Madame Yan was not being fair to Wang Qiyao, but he was in no position to defend her, so he simply kept quiet. Seeing him fall silent, Madame Yan took it as a sign that he had accepted her advice.

She relaxed somewhat and said, "I'm responsible for you when you're over here with me. How could I face your parents if something should happen?"

"I'm a grown man," insisted Uncle Maomao. "What could possibly happen?"

Madame Yan jabbed his forehead with her fingertip. "If anything does, it will be too late!"

With that, they headed over to Wang Qiyao's apartment. Sasha was already there, warming his white, slender hands over the stove as Wang Qiyao filled the Thermos with hot water. The four chatted casually as if nothing had happened. Particles of dust swirled in the air, illuminated by the column of light coming in from the window. Madame Yan and Uncle Maomao sat themselves down by the stove and the unpleasantness of the previous day was forgotten.

As the Lunar New Year approached, Wang Qiyao set a pair of millstones next to the stove for grinding glutinous rice. Sasha carefully ladled out the rice, swollen with an overnight soaking, into the mill along with an equal amount of water; Uncle Maomao turned the mill to grind the mixture. Meanwhile, Wang Qiyao pounded sesame seeds in the adjacent mortar. Madame Yan, in her capacity as supervisor of the entire operation, didn't lift a finger. The aroma of sesame seeds was so tempting that they wished they could just munch on them. Sasha felt a keen sense of the happiness that comes from devoting meticulous care to the details of living. Granted that this happiness, the product of restricting one's vision to one's immediate surroundings, is akin to that of the proverbial frog at the bottom of a well, it is nevertheless a way of stretching one's life out. Moved by this, Sasha, growing solemn, sought enlightenment from the ladies on various fine points of culinary art. They explained things to him patiently, as if he were a naughty child who has decided to reform himself, promising to make New Year's cakes, deep-fried spring rolls, walnut cookies, and pine nut candies for him. Sasha wondered to himself whether there were enough days before the New Year to prepare all that food, and said aloud, sighing, "How true it is that 'Each grain of rice comes with hard work'!"

"That's only half the work," Madame Yan chortled. "The other half goes into making clothing! But I don't believe you would know anything about that."

Once the subject of clothing was broached, Madame Yan and Wang Qiyao immediately launched into an excited discussion about fabrics and tailoring, conjuring up dancing images of gorgeous finery. Sasha was so taken with their exchange that he forgot what he was supposed to be doing, and Uncle Maomao was so dazzled that he didn't even notice that he was grinding an empty millstone. What the ladies discussed was an entire world meticulously woven of needles and thread; how much care must go into creating a single magnificent outfit to adorn one's body.

Madame Yan exclaimed, with infinite emotion in her voice, "Nothing is more important for a person than the clothes they wear; these demonstrate better than anything else a person's spirit and taste."

"What about food, then?" Sasha asked.

Madame Yan shook her head. "Food ends up on the inside, so it's not as important as face, which is what announces you to the world. You rely on it for respect and credibility. One must, of course, live for oneself, but think about how dull life would be if there weren't others to show off to every once in a while!"

At this, she grew sad and her voice dropped. Infected by her sadness, they labored on, but their buoyant enthusiasm had died. The noises they made now sounded hollow, the sesame seeds smelled pungent and greasy, and the paste from the stone mill started to look unappetizing; coal stains showed on the walls, and the air felt dry and dusty. Suddenly everything was musty, tainted, squalid; even the fire in the stove seemed drab.

Soon, however, the squalor was shrouded in darkness, which slipped through the window into the room like a thin but tepid liquid flowing over everything, enveloping space and objects, voices and breath, in a hazy membrane. Only the fire in the stove flared up to warm them with a sudden intensity. At this moment, all desires converged into a longing to nuzzle up to each other; nothing else seemed to matter. The firmament itself might collapse, the earth swallow them up, but what of that? Tomorrow ceased to matter and so did yesterday. As they stir-fried chestnuts in sugar, breathing in the delicious aroma, they exchanged heart-felt words, words carrying the warmth of what was deep inside, albeit only about the most superficial matters. Then, putting an iron pan on the stove, they roasted watermelon seeds, mixing in a few gingko nuts; the nuts gave off a bittersweet scent, a sharp scent compounded of many nameless odors, suggestive of some kind of rebuke, which they conveniently ignored. Putting aside all differences, they luxuriated in their tenderness and affection for each other; what else could they do besides be affectionate? Outside, it was cold and dark, and this only heightened the warmth within. They wished the snow would stay forever, because its melting would be a signal to extinguish the fire burning within their hearts.

They talked, softly and gently, and forgot instantly what they had just said. Words that vanish without a trace and yet are charged with feeling that lingers on—these alone voice what is in the heart. In truth, all they talked about was the sweetness of the chestnuts, the aroma of the melon seeds, the richness of the dumplings, the smoothness of the fermented rice, and the tenderness of the eggs; then conveniently neglected to mention the bitterness of the gingko nuts. The night was pitch dark, but the sky would soon turn bright again. At last their conversation had reached the point of deepest intimacy, where to speak further would only make them grow apart again. They talked about leaving, but their feet lingered. "See you tomorrow," they all said, but none of them wanted that night to end. Tomorrow might be better, but that was unknowable, whereas they could still hold on to today. But even the present slips through one's fingers like the sand in an hourglass.

Somehow they found a way to make it through the days while living for the nights. They gathered around the stove, exchanging riddles and telling stories. Many of their riddles went unsolved, just as their stories often seemed to have neither beginning nor end. Wang Qiyao said they lived as if every night was New Year's Eve. Uncle Maomao said even though they were reversing their days and nights, no matter how hard they tried to go against the grain, some things cannot be changed. Madame Yan said they acted as if they were at a wake, but since the deceased were remote ancestors, they did not feel compelled to grieve. Sasha said it was like they were part of a Siberian hunting party, destined to return empty-handed.

They stuffed the crevices between the stones and the bricks of the world with crumbs from their food and their conversations. They played cat's cradles with a shoestring, passing the string from hand to hand until it unraveled or got all tangled up; they took strands of hair, knotting them and then untying the knots, until the hair snapped or the knots became too tight to undo; they toyed with interlocking links, which ended up either in a jumbled heap or else scattered on the floor; they worked on an old "seven-piece" wooden puzzle and, much as they tried, failed to devise new combinations. They went to their wits' end trying to come up with all kinds of little tricks and clever ideas, all of which came to nothing. However, the small always ends up nourishing the great; big things survive by consuming the carcasses of the little. But do not look down on even the most minute of things; for with the coming of daybreak, even the tiniest particles of dust in this world sing and dance in the sunlight.

Kang Mingxun

DURING THOSE MUDDLED nights when anything seemed possible, people's hearts appeared bright on the surface, but there was also a dark side lurking. Uncle Maomao, whose real name was Kang Mingxun, had a place in the dark side as well as the bright side of Wang Qiyao's heart. She did not dare to think about him, yet could not get him out of her mind.

Once, when they were alone together, Wang Qiyao asked, "So . . . when are you planning to get married?"

"What kind of girl would marry an unemployed bum like me?" Kang Mingxun replied with a wry smile.

It was Wang Qiyao's turn to smile in disbelief. "Who are you kidding? A man of your impeccable character from such a well-heeled family . . . you could have the hand of any girl."

"Then would Miss Wang do me the honor of introducing one?"

"But I don't know anyone in my circle worthy of you."

Kang Mingxun took up her tone. "Now who's kidding? It is plain to see that a woman of your elegance could only belong to the highest stratum of society. . . . How could someone of my lowly status impose such a request upon you?"

"You shouldn't make fun of a girl from a modest background," said Wang Qiyao.

"Just who is making fun of whom?" Kang Mingxun rejoined.

Thus they parried. However, even though Kang Mingxun was responsive to every one of her queries, the two of them were interrupted before Wang Qiyao had ample opportunity to squeeze all the information she was looking for out of him. The next time they were alone, it was Kang Mingxun who reopened the subject.

"When can we expect to hear of *your* wedding?"

Wang Qiyao took up the same jocular tone. "Who would be willing to marry someone like me . . ." but her voice trailed off before she could finish.

Kang Mingxun was poised to pick up the banter when he was startled to discover tears in her eyes. He said hastily, "Forgive me if I said something I shouldn't. He who knows not what he does is innocent."

Unable to speak, Wang Qiyao shook her head. It was a while before she repeated, "Who would marry someone like me?"

"Well, whatever could be wrong with someone like you?" he ventured.

"What do you think?" She threw the question back at him.

"You are so perfect a lady that anything I say would be like adding flowers to a piece of brocade."

"You're teasing me again."

"Clearly, my dear, you are the one doing the teasing this time."

This time Kang Mingxun had been the one to raise the issue, but because he stopped short of asking any pressing questions, Wang Qiyao never got the opportunity that she had been hoping for to give him a direct response.

The repartee between Wang Qiyao and Kang Mingxun was a game of hide-and-seek. The seeker is intent solely on catching his prey. The hider, in contrast, is of two minds, fearful of getting caught but also worried that the seeker might give up the game in exasperation. In concealing himself, he must at the same time keep the other party interested. When other people were present, the two often spoke a language that functioned on two levels. Theirs was a hide-and-seek game played out in the open, with a tacit understanding that left them both plenty of room for maneuvering. They developed a secret code whereby ordinary words took on meanings comprehensible only to the two of them while leaving the others in the dark. Yet, because neither sent any messages openly, these could, if necessary, be repudiated. Hence the alarm when Sasha jokingly announced that he had found a girlfriend for Kang Mingxun—Wang Qiyao was so upset she broke the porcelain ladle she was holding—or what Madame Yan later told her cousin—Kang Mingxun was so flustered he made many a slip in his reply. In both cases, however, they had overreacted; the issues were subsequently dropped. Later, it was Wang Qiyao who brought the subject up again, asking Kang Mingxun who the girl was that Sasha had wanted to introduce to him.

"How should I know?" was the retort. "Why don't you ask him?"

"Sasha surely had someone in mind," she insisted.

It was clear that Kang Mingxun knew who it was, but he only said, "If you really wanted to know, why did you shut him up the other day just when he was about to tell us?"

Mortified, Wang Qiyao argued that she had done nothing of the sort. Why would whatever Sasha said have had anything to do with her?

"If it has nothing to do with you, then why do you want to know so badly?" Kang Mingxun pressed on mercilessly.

His words reopened old wounds: Wang Qiyao felt deeply hurt. Her face turned red. It was only after several minutes that she managed to retort, "You are all in the same league, all black as crows."

"Remember that Sasha is in the other camp," Kang Mingxun joked. "He grew up eating Russian bread."

Wang Qiyao smiled at this peace offering. In reality, they had gone in a circle and ended up where they had started; the feeling that they had actually gotten somewhere after all this running around was but an illusion.

There is, however, something to be said for illusions. Though lacking substance, illusions can serve as the basis on which more substantive structures can be built. Should those structures subsequently collapse, something of substance may nevertheless remain. This situation can be compared to the Viennese Waltz in ballroom dancing: stepping forward and back, back and forward, a couple glides from one end of the floor to the other; when the music stops, they may quite likely wind up in the same place where they began, but they will still have a sense of fulfillment and elation. Playing hide-and-seek with Kang Mingxun created, in part, the same kind of illusion for Wang Qiyao; but she also began deliberately to take the false for the real, twisting meanings to suit her own purposes. Her games drove Kang Mingxun to his wits' end. She would occasionally refer to the two of them as "us" and Madame Yan and Sasha as "them." Although this in itself didn't seem to signify anything terribly scandalous, it still put Kang Mingxun in a bit of a flutter, uncertain whether this was a good thing or a bad thing.

On one occasion, he asked Wang Qiyao, "Why do you put my cousin in the same camp as Sasha? Don't tell me that she grew up on Russian bread too?"

"Isn't he her son in-law?" Wang Qiyao giggled. "Of course they're in the same camp!"

They all laughed, but Kang Mingxun wasn't sure if he liked her explanation. They were lost at a crossroads groping about in the dark, each boldly trying to capture the other without himself getting caught. Whole narratives, protracted and intricate, were embroidered out of these illusions. When they found themselves alone again, Wang Qiyao made the next move.

"What do you mean by accusing me of pushing your cousin over to Sasha's side?" she asked.

"Need you ask?" Kang Mingxun retorted. "It is complicated enough without you sticking your nose in. . . ."

Each question was framed inside another, which in turn led to another. They were like shadow-boxers; it might look as if the two of them were advancing and retreating in an endless cycle, but by the time they were finished, they would know which of them was the stronger, and who was to be the victor.

They both eagerly volunteered to take care of everything for the group's afternoon tea parties, but this was a mere pretext to enable them to carry on with their games of ambiguous repartee; these occasions were the murky waters in which they could go fishing unnoticed. During an afternoon or evening of idle chat, there would always be opportunity for them to sneak in one or two coded messages, veiled words that were indeed as slippery as live fish and just as hard to catch hold of. Back and forth they parried, neither acknowledging the real matter at hand; each feigned ignorance of all innuendo while refusing to allow the other to get away with doing the same. As baffling and complicated as this mode of communication might sound, the parties concerned were not in the least bit confused; to them, everything was crystal clear. In their hearts everything was as clear as a well-balanced account. Well-matched opponents, they moved with economy and precision, bending their wits to the challenge of the game. Every so often they would become momentarily dazzled and diverted by their own virtuosity, but they quickly reminded themselves of their true purpose. For pointless and childish as the game might seem, at its core lay a profound anguish. This anguish was for one's own self as well as for the other; there was empathy and consideration in it, and yet also a relentlessness, because, after all, everyone always puts themselves first.

In truth, Kang Mingxun had discovered everything he needed to know about Wang Qiyao quite early; he was just good at keeping it to himself. The very first time they met, he thought she looked vaguely familiar. His suspicions were aroused when he found that she lived so reclusively and in such straitened circumstances, and the furniture in her apartment certainly spoke of an intriguing past. Living in this time of epochal change, Kang Mingxun was perceptive beyond his years and, wise in the ways of the city, was all too aware that people's lives could be transformed in an instant. Peace Lane was a crevice in the city into which many fragmented lives had drifted. He saw shimmering behind Wang Qiyao an aura of splendor that belied her present ascetic life. One night, as they were playing mahjong, the lamp cast a shadow over her face; her bright eyes sparkling mysteriously in the darkness, she threw down her tiles with a lift of the eyebrows and a coy laugh. Somehow her expression reminded him of a screen diva from the thirties, Ruan Lingyu. Of course, Wang Qiyao was not Ruan Lingyu . . . but who was she then? He didn't know it, but he was teetering on the brink of discovering her secret.

Then, one day, passing a photographer's shop with a picture in its window of a woman in bridal veil, he was immediately struck by a feeling of déjà vu. His mind raced back to another photograph that had hung in the same window long ago. If he had made the connection with Wang Qiyao at that moment, the riddle would have been solved; instead it slipped past. His interest in her seemed to intensify with every moment they spent together. He saw wrapped in her unadorned simplicity a rare beauty that infused everything around her with glamour; but in that austerity he also caught a glimpse of passion, and this too infused itself into her surroundings. *Who was this woman*? Kang Mingxun pined for the city's vanished glory, of which only the trolley bell remained, and it saddened him every time he heard it ring. Wang Qiyao was like a mysterious shadow of that feeling; like a phantom that came and went unsummoned, she haunted him. He swore to himself that he would get to the bottom of this. *I must uncover her past. . . . But where to look?*

In the end the answer simply fell into his lap. One day, while chatting with "Mother," the mistress of the house, and "Second Mother," his father's concubine and his own birth mother, that famous event of a decade earlier came up—the Miss Shanghai Beauty Pageant. His birth mother even remembered the name of the girl who came in third place—Wang Qiyao. To Kang Mingxun it was like suddenly awakening from a dream. Yes, those eyes that recalled Ruan Lingyu, the familiar image he had once seen hanging in the photo shop window, the "Proper Young Lady of Shanghai" featured in *Shanghai Life*, the rumors that she had later become the kept woman of some powerful man . . . it all added up. There it was, the entire story of Wang Qiyao's life, fantastic and poignant.

Out of this puzzle a new Wang Qiyao emerged; her romantic past, alive with enticing details, presented itself before him. The real Wang Qiyao finally rose up from behind all of those secrets; her face, her smile, all came to life for him. This may have been a brand-new Wang Qiyao, but it was also a reincarnation of the old Wang Qiyao. He could barely recognize her, yet somehow seemed to know her only too well. He felt the joy and excitement of having something restored to him. *This is now an entirely different city,* he thought to himself, *the street names have changed, the buildings and streetlights are but the shell of their former selves, their core melted away and replaced.* In the past even the breeze whispered of romantic longings, and the parasol trees told stories as they waved in the wind; now the breeze is nothing but dead air and the trees mere bark and leaves, all their magical charm overthrown. He had tried to keep up with the times, but his heart was still trapped in the past, leaving him hollowed out and empty. But Wang Qiyao was a true relic of the past: she would be able to help him steal his heart back from yesterday.

He didn't go back to visit Wang Qiyao for several days after this. When Madame Yan telephoned, he claimed he was tied up with business at home and couldn't make it. He agonized over what he should say to Wang Qiyao but eventually decided to say nothing and behave as if nothing had happened. When Wang Qiyao asked why he had not joined them, he said he had been busy. When she wondered aloud whether he had found some more interesting places to go, he simply smiled and placed the package he had brought—a box of fancy cakes from Big Chang's Bakery—on the table. Wang Qiyao hurried out to get plates for the cake. She had just given an injection to a patient and still had the scent of alcohol on her hands. Wearing a cardigan over a cotton *cheongsam*, with a pair of old-fashioned cotton shoes with straps, she busied herself getting the tea ready.

Suddenly Kang Mingxun recalled a hotpot dinner at his cousin's townhouse, back around the time they first met, when he had tried telling everyone's fortune based on random words that came to their minds. Wang Qiyao had picked the character for "earth," whereupon he pointed to the right half and said it could be construed as "he."

Impulsively, she pointed to the left half, made up of the "dirt" radical, exclaiming, "This shows that 'he' is buried, doesn't it?" and her face was immediately stricken with grief.

Now he understood the cause of her sorrow.

Pity welled up in him, also a sense of loss, for Wang Qiyao as well as for himself. Feeling depressed, he spoke very little and remained aloof and listless the remainder of the afternoon. His gaze, turned outside the window, happened on the cracks and water stains on the neighbor's balcony. The whole world looked damaged—nothing was perfect any longer. In contrast to the waxing and waning of the moon, this disintegration was unrelenting; the chipped only gets more chipped, the broken more broken, until one day nothing would be left but squalid ruins. Perhaps one day, when everything has completely disintegrated, the cycle will start over again. But life is short, and if it is someone's misfortune to be born in a period of disintegration, he may have no hope of ever seeing perfection.

Kang Mingxun was the son of a concubine but the only male progeny in his family. As a child, he learned that he had to please his father's proper wife, whom he was taught to address as "Mother," as well as his birth mother. His father might take his second wife, "Second Mother," to intimate social gatherings, but on formal occasions the family was represented by Father, Mother, and Kang Mingxun. Mother was by nature a manipulative person. Tradition and common practice already made her position one hundred percent unassailable, but she also had grievance on her side. She therefore claimed one hundred and thirty percent of privilege. The thirty percent extra that was her due naturally got deducted from Second Mother.

Father was conservative, so, as much as he adored Second Mother, hierarchy always came first. Everyone in the household had their proper place according to rank and age. As the male progeny, Kang Mingxun spent more time with Mother than with his own birth mother and thus became much closer to his half-sisters than he ever was to his own sisters. He felt the need to ingratiate himself, as if he would be rejected otherwise. He was vaguely aware that Mother's love had to be won, whereas Second Mother would always be there for him whether he desired her love or not. Consequently, he was much more solicitous of Mother and inclined to neglect Second Mother, to the extent that he would deliberately distance himself from her so as to please Mother. Even as a young boy he had always shown this unseemly tendency to align himself with the strong to exploit the weak—thanks to a healthy instinct for survival.

Once, while playing hide and seek with two of his sisters, he climbed the stairs to the third floor and pushed open the door of Second Mother's bedroom; the bed skirt was moving, so he knew that someone must be hiding under the bed. But, on sneaking in, he saw Second Mother, sitting at the edge of the bed with her back toward him, head slumped over and shoulders shuddering. He stood stock still as his younger sister rushed out from underneath the bed and, jubilant and shrieking, ran past him. But instead of chasing her, he just stood there, transfixed.

It was a cloudy day. The teak furniture was gleaming, as was the waxed floor. Second Mother sat facing the window, her figure delineated against the dim light, her hair messy like a bird's nest, her narrow shoulders pathetically small. Sensing someone behind her, she looked around through her tears, but before she had seen him, he had already run out of the room. His heart was beating wildly, and he was overcome by a mixture of pity, revulsion, and deep sadness. To camouflage his emotion, he emitted a gleeful shriek so loud that Mother came out to scold him. At this moment, Second Mother's tousled head appeared at the top of the stairs, and his heart filled with hatred for her. This hatred grew in direct proportion to his pain. As he slowly matured and became adept at navigating this complicated environment, the pain and the hatred diminished until they were no more than hazy impressions, lighter than dust motes. Yet it was precisely these hazy impressions from his past that would sway the decisions he made during the crucial moments of his life.

Kang Mingxun understood that no matter how lovely Wang Qiyao was, or how much she appealed to him, or how marvelous she had been in bringing back his heart, she would remain a shadowy illusion. However much her beauty might intoxicate him, on this one point he always remained clear. Some things simply could not be done: no two ways about it. Yet he was unwilling to give up. He wanted to proceed, to take matters as far as they would go, and only afterward worry about picking up the pieces. The difficulty was *how* to proceed. How to stake out new territories? How to make his next move? What could he do? Wang Qiyao was infinitely cleverer than Second Mother, and a hundred times more tenacious. He was confronted with nothing but obstacles. However, his feelings for her only intensified when he realized that all her cleverness and tenacity stemmed from being isolated and vulnerable. These were survival mechanisms, but as such only showed up the hopelessness of her situation all the more. Kang Mingxun would never admit it, but he had a special empathy for the weak, otherwise he would not have been so quick to recognize their pathetic readiness to compromise and their convoluted tactics. Like Wang Qiyao, he lived on the margin, on other people's sufferance, with precious little room for maneuver. They should have joined forces, but, sadly, their interests were in conflict, so neither was in a position to help the other. In the innermost recesses of Kang Mingxun's heart there lived a compassion whose seed had been planted that cloudy afternoon in his childhood, and this compassion exerted a strong pull. He saw the specter of pain hovering ahead, but for the moment a happiness, still unexpired, beckoned. As discerning as he was, Kang Mingxun lived in the present—a present in which hope and happiness were scarce commodities. His eyes were forced by despair to turn away from the future and the shadow of pain, allowing him only to focus on the happiness that lay just within his reach.

Kang Mingxun began to call on Wang Qiyao more frequently, at times unannounced. He claimed to be passing by, thereby catching her unaware; her hair was often tied up casually with a handkerchief, and the place somewhat untidy. She would get embarrassed and, all in a dither, pick up various odds and ends, a detail that he always found touching. And so he kept making these surprise visits in the hope that they would lead to something unanticipated . . . something miraculous. Once he came right at lunchtime, when she was eating leftover rice with a plate of tiny little clams the size and shape of watermelon seeds. The shells were piled high next to the plate. Seeing the frugal way she was able to make use of leftovers moved him deeply. On another occasion he arrived just as she was washing her hair, her collar turned down, head upside down in the wash basin, her hair full of bubbles. Under his gaze, her ears and the nape of her neck turned scarlet, like those of a naïve little girl. From the depths of the wash basin emanated what sounded suspiciously like sobs. When she was finished, she dried her hair hastily, with the water dripping down her back, wetting her clothes—this made her look even more pathetic.

Gradually Wang Qiyao came to expect these surprise visits and would get ready for them. She made sure that the preparation was not obvious lest he think the less of her. She still wore casual clothes, but they were neat; the apartment was still somewhat messy, but not too much so. She still had to eat lunch, and the food was always simple, but not coarse. She stripped her life of nonessentials. As to the washing of hair and other such intimate chores, these were performed either very early or very late, at times when Kang Mingxun could not possibly turn up. As a result, his surprise calls ceased to wreak their accustomed havoc—much to his regret. But the energy she had spent in protecting herself did not go unnoticed, and he felt terribly sorry for putting her through that.

Wang Qiyao's pretend act was intended as a screen to prevent him from barging straight in. It was, however, a screen that she was prepared one day to forgo, its function analogous to the red veil worn by the bride at a traditional wedding, which the groom lifts up at the end of the ceremony. During this period, Wang Qiyao became more reticent than she ever had been. The two of them would sit together, speaking little. By sunset they had gone over only the same familiar ground, each anxious not to commit any error. In the past they had had little to say but found plenty to talk about; now they had plenty to say but were unwilling to speak—it was as if both were lying in wait, each one waiting to ambush the other. Day after day, they watched the sun move from one wall to the other, their hearts half-concealed in the dark, with no clue to the present or the future. As for hope, though Wang Qiyao did harbor some, she could not act on it. Any action on her part would be tantamount to senseless sacrifice, a selfless offering of herself. Kang Mingxun, who had no hope, could have launched an attack at any moment, but he was far too afraid that it might end in disaster. They sat in silence, each smiling wryly inside, wordlessly imploring the other to give way. Yet who could afford to give way? With only one life to live, neither was willing to roll over for the other.

The stove had been dismantled, leaving a large mark on the floor. The hole in the window where the flue used to be had been pasted over with paper, a relic of the winter now past. The spring sun was lovely as usual and, as usual, inefficacious. The smiles on their faces barely masked their bitterness. These desperate smiles hinted at a sort of assurance—but not the kind each was looking for from the other. With all paths of escape cut off, they stuck to their guns. Both positions were entirely defensible, but this in no way improved the situation. Each was acting out of self-interest—but a heart driven by self-interest is still a heart and, having a heart, one must feel the joys and sorrows of life.

One night, two patients came for shots, one after another. As soon as Wang Qiyao had seen them off, she heard footsteps again on the stairs. She wondered if this could be yet another patient, all crowded into one evening. It turned out to be Kang Mingxun—the very first time he arrived alone at night, unannounced too. They both felt somewhat awkward. Her heart was throbbing. She offered him a seat, made tea, plied him with candies and watermelon seeds. Hurrying back and forth, she scarcely stood still for a minute.

Kang Mingxun said that he had gone to call on a friend but found the gate at his friend's house padlocked. Then, turning around to go home, he discovered he had forgotten his own house key. His family and all the servants were off at a Shaoxing opera and, although his father was home, he did not want to get the old man out of bed, so he thought he would come by to wait until the show was over. Kang Mingxun rambled on and on; busy getting the snacks ready, Wang Qiyao took in only half of what he was saying.

"What opera did you say you were going to see? Which theater is it at?" she asked.

Kang Mingxun repeated his story, this time even more haphazardly than before. Wang Qiyao got even more confused, but pretended to understand. After a few minutes, she inquired anxiously when the show was to start, afraid that he might be late. Realizing how hopelessly entangled the situation had become, Kang Mingxun gave up trying to explain. Wang Qiyao was simply rummaging around for something to say; seeing no response from him, she too gave up pursuing the matter. They sat in silence and the room grew quiet. They could hear the neighbors moving about. The flame had gone out, and the acrid smell of unburnt alcohol filled the air. Footsteps came up the stairs. Wang Qiyao wondered with a start who else could be coming on this peculiar evening that seemed so full of foreboding. The caller was a party official from the neighborhood coming by to collect the communal fee. He did not even step inside. The two of them listened intently as the man made his way back down the stairs, step by step. He caused them some alarm when he stumbled over a step, and then, after all was well again, they exchanged a smile that seemed to bring them together momentarily. Between them there was a tension, as of an arrow cocked on a tightly stretched bowstring.

Wang Qiyao took Kang Mingxun's empty teacup out to the kitchen. From the rear window she saw in the distance the red star atop the Sino-Russian Friendship Building, and asked herself in a prayerful mood, *What is going to happen this evening?* When she brought the refilled cup back into the room, Kang Mingxun was still sitting woodenly facing the window, rapt in thought. Wang Qiyao placed the teacup in front of him and took a few backward steps to her own seat. She realized they would never get through this night, and even if they did, a day would come that it would be impossible for them to get through. All this time Kang Mingxun sat facing the window, which, with its curtains drawn, made it seem as if he were looking into a wall. His pose suggested that he had something to say . . . if he only knew how to begin. Their silence told of words unspoken; they simply didn't know where to start.

At last Kang Mingxun opened his mouth. "There's nothing I can do," he said.

Wang Qiyao laughed. "Do about what?"

"Everything," he replied.

Wang Qiyao laughed again. "Just what is it that has you at such a loss?"

Her laughter was in lieu of tears. So, these were the words she had been waiting for so patiently! Nevertheless, not only did she find herself perfectly calm; she was even tempted to put him through the wringer a little. She resolved to make him lay everything out in unequivocal terms, even though any explanation he had to make was no longer relevant to her. She wanted the satisfaction of embarrassing him. Having waited this long, she was entitled at least to this much recompense.

Laughing again, she said, "So there's nothing you can do about it . . . does that mean there's nothing you can say either?"

Kang Mingxun did not have the nerve to face her. He turned away—now it was Wang Qiyao's turn to watch *his* neck turn scarlet.

She stepped up the assault. "Really, there is no harm in telling me. I'm not going to use it against you."

But at this point her voice quavered and her eyes filled with tears, even as she persisted in smiling.

"Say something!" She taunted him. "Why don't you say something?"

Kang Mingxun turned to face her and said imploringly, "What do you want me to say?"

Wang Qiyao was stunned. She could not recall, for the life of her, what it was that she had wanted to get out of him. She could no longer keep up her indignation and, in panic, tears came streaming out. Kang Mingxun's heart melted. That cloudy afternoon so many years ago came back to him, and it was as if Second Mother had turned around to face him and he was looking into her tear-streaked face.

"Wang Qiyao," he said. "I shall be good to you."

His words were hardly reassuring, but they did come straight from his heart. Even so, Kang Mingxun realized he had offered her no future to speak of, and he started to weep. Still crying herself, Wang Qiyao saw that he was truly pained, and this made her feel much better. Gradually, her tears stopped. Looking around her, she saw how the single lamp in the room threw off more shadows than light. She had not realized this when she was by herself, but it certainly looked sad and lonesome with the two of them there.

She smiled through her tears and said, "Really, there is no need to hold back. A woman like me is content to be able to simply live in peace. How dare I wish for more? Even if heaven helps me through today, I must still face tomorrow. The monks may have run off, but the temple isn't going anywhere."

"By the same token," said Kang Mingxun, "what kind of man can I call myself? I'm forced to address my own mother as Second Mother as if she's not even my real flesh and blood. I eke out a living anyhow, and have only myself to rely on. How dare I entertain any high hopes?"

Wang Qiyao sighed deeply. "I daresay you men want too much out of life. It is all very well to give up sesame seeds for watermelons, but I'm afraid you might end up giving up watermelons for sesame seeds."

Kang Mingxun also heaved a long sigh. "If men demand a lot from life, then it's because women demand so much of them. Women make demands on us, but where can we men go to make our demands? In reality, men have the least control over their own lives."

She scoffed at this. "Who is making demands on you?"

"Not you, certainly," he said. Then he fell silent.

"I do have one demand . . ." Wang Qiyao spoke after a long pause. "I want your heart."

Kang Mingxun lowered his head. "I would like to give it to you . . . but I'm afraid I may not be able to."

With those words, Kang Mingxun placed all his cards on the table. He had given fair warning and drawn a line between the two of them. Without intending it, Wang Qiyao flashed a frosty smile. "Relax, you needn't worry."

This was the night that the curtain would rise and all would be revealed. Unsatisfactory as it was, it was nevertheless a new beginning. It was a step forward, but also a step backward, as they made concessions to the reality of their circumstances. They had each laid out their conditions before jumping in, but they were also going ahead without considering all the consequences. Their objectives were clear; at the same time they were making things up as they went along. There was a certain amount of self-deception, of taking the easy way out, and compromises were arrived at solely because of a lack of willpower. Alone and at loose ends, with equally bleak prospects, this man and this woman, mutually attracted and sharing genuine sympathy, had chosen to grasp the happiness at hand. They sacrificed their future prospects, knowing full well that their happiness would be empty and transitory. After all, life flows like water through one's fingers, and eternity is but an illusion. Once we have come to terms with that, nothing else really matters.

Having realized that all her hopes were in vain, Wang Qiyao oddly felt a kind of relief. Kang Mingxun's love for her, slight as it was, was like a consolation prize in the midst of complete debacle. By contrast, having won Wang Qiyao's love at little cost to himself, Kang Mingxun felt indebted. His heart was heavy as he emerged from her apartment and rode home on his bicycle through the dark quiet streets. Though he had been planning this night for a long time, its arrival still caught him unprepared. There were many things he had not thought through ahead of time, but it was now too late to make amends. Whatever happened was now water under the bridge.

As they lay intertwined in bed, Wang Qiyao asked Kang Mingxun how he had found out about her background. Rather than give a straight answer, he asked her how she discovered that he knew. Knowing that he would not rest until she confessed, she reminded him of the afternoon tea when he had suddenly brought up, in loving detail, the Miss Shanghai beauty contest of 1946. She knew then that he must know her identity, and that their love affair was doomed.

Clasping her close, Kang Mingxun asked, "But aren't we a couple now?"

Wang Qiyao responded with a chilly smile. "Yeah, a couple of wild ducks . . ."

Realizing his faux pas, he released her and turned away.

Wang Qiyao snuggled against him from behind and asked softly, "Upset, are you?"

Kang Mingxun stayed still for awhile. At length, he told her how, having been brought up by Mother, he was always shy with his own birth mother. He especially dreaded being alone in a room with her, and was always looking for an excuse to get away. He felt terrible whenever he reflected on this. Second Mother had taught him all about suffering. Finally he said that in all the twenty years he spent with Second Mother, he had never talked to her the way he had talked with Wang Qiyao tonight. Wang Qiyao drew his head toward her bosom and stroked his hair tenderly. She not only loved him, she cared enough to put herself in his place.

"I know no one could possibly compare with you," Kang Mingxun said. "But there is nothing I can do."

These words "nothing I can do" took on a new desolation this time. Everyone has an abyss that he cannot get across: he had never dreamt his was going to be like this. He truly had no idea what to do. Wang Qiyao told him soothingly that she would love him until the day he married; on his wedding day she would be a bridesmaid and then never see him again.

"Are you trying to kill me?" Kang Mingxun said. "How could I bear being with someone else the day I part with you?"

Even in jest, they could not avoid hurting each other, and the teasing would always end in tears.

They were extremely discreet, getting together only at hours that did not raise suspicion, but there was no way they could have escaped Madame Yan's detection. She had been keeping an eye on them from the start and had a pretty good handle on the nature of their relationship as it started to develop. She blamed herself for having unwittingly brought them together. She blamed Kang Mingxun for not listening to her. Most of all, she blamed Wang Qiyao for throwing caution to the winds and landing all three of them in hot water. She wanted to scream at her: "Even if Kang Mingxun didn't know what you are, there's no way *you* could pretend not to know!"

Her guess was that Wang Qiyao was a former taxi dancer or a nightclub girl who had to go into hiding now that the world had changed. Madame Yan felt ill-used—she had considered Wang Qiyao a friend with whom she could share her nostalgia for a bygone world, but who now revealed herself as selfish and greedy. At the cost of giving up her beloved mahjong games, she stopped visiting Wang Qiyao, citing different excuses. Needless to say, Wang Qiyao and Kang Mingxun knew why she had stopped coming. Sasha, on the other hand, kept up his visits, whether oblivious of the situation or pretending not to have noticed, and thus became both a nuisance and a convenient smokescreen for the lovers. Once Wang Qiyao asked Kang Mingxun whether Madame Yan might tell his family about their relationship, to which he replied not to worry, that he would simply deny everything and then they would have no recourse. Wang Qiyao greeted this with silence.

After a long pause, she said, "If you deny everything with me too, what recourse will *I* have?"

"Whether I deny it or not, there is still nothing we can do about our situation." Wang Qiyao was disarmed by his candor. Kang Mingxun assured her, "Whatever happens, you will always be in my heart."

Wang Qiyao was scornful. "I am not a phantom that lives only in your heart."

Although she said this with asperity, it was not out of anger but deep sorrow. This is something they had not counted on. They had not known that their happiness would be adulterated with sorrow, nor had they bargained on having to mortgage their future for the present. Life is a series of interlocking links; it is never easy to separate one out from the rest.

In the depths of their despair, hope grew where there was no hope and concessions were made on top of concessions. All this flowed from the initial compromise. In private, they were both secretly waiting for a miracle to deliver them from their predicament. One day Kang Mingxun arrived home to find the whole family giving him the cold shoulder. Second Mother's face was streaked with tears, her nose red and her lips purple—he hated seeing her like that. His father had shut himself up in his room and refused to emerge for dinner. On the living room table was a boxed cake, the telltale sign of a visitor. He found out from the servant, Mama Chen, that the visitor was Madame Yan. The cake, left untouched, looked very much the part of a rejected scapegoat. He dared not leave the house the following day, which he spent going from bedroom to bedroom, paying his respects to all the elders of the house, who snubbed him at every turn. Father kept shutting himself up. Instead of crying, Second Mother took to sighing.

It wasn't until the third day that Kang Mingxun managed to sneak out of the house to tell Wang Qiyao what had occurred. Mingled in her consternation was a new element of elation: now that things were out in the open, and light was shining in through the broken window, one could never tell what might happen next. Old-fashioned families like his cared enormously about appearances, and now that the rice was already cooked, they might just decide to let things pass and swallow their pride. Kang Mingxun also felt more at ease. He had a different secret wish. He told himself that if his father should explode and disown him as a son, he would simply leave home and that was that. On this day, they shared a stirring of hope and were more affectionate than usual. By chance, Sasha had not come by to make a nuisance of himself, which allowed them to snuggle up on the sofa under a blanket, watching silently, hand-in-hand, as the light on the closed curtains turned from bright to dark. The noise in the *longtang* under the window spoke for them, as did the chatter of the sparrows. These fragmentary sounds, scattering like fallen leaves and broken branches over their heads, were minute keepsakes of their love and sorrow. After night had fallen, they did not turn the light on, but let time and space evaporate around them among the dark shades, exulting solely in the solid reality of their warm bodies.

However, Kang Mingxun was to be frustrated in his secret wish. As soon as he reached home that evening, he knew that the ice had melted. Even though it was past eleven, no one demanded to know where he had been and why he was back so late. The door to his father's bedroom was ajar, and he could be seen sitting under a down comforter reading his newspapers, his face serene. From his sisters' rooms came music over the radio—robust modern sounds, indicating that everything had returned to normal. Mother asked him whether he wanted some dim sum. He was not hungry but nodded in acceptance of her gracious offer. As he ate the lotus plumule and jujube stew, Mother and Second Mother sat by him to knit and chat about the latest Shaoxing opera coming to town. They asked if he wanted to see it. He replied that, if Mother and Second Mother wished, he would get tickets for them.

"If you have time, that would be delightful, but don't press yourself if you are busy," they chirped merrily.

Three more days passed without incident. At first he thought they might ask about the affair, but it gradually dawned on him that the subject would never come up. His entire family had agreed to let the matter pass, pretending to know nothing about what had happened. The cake too had disappeared. He did not know how to react to this change in the course of events and avoided Wang Qiyao for an entire week. Instead he spent the time accompanying his two mothers to Shaoxing opera performances, escorting his sisters to Hong Kong movies, and going with his father to the Yude Bathhouse. After their baths, they lay, wrapped in towels, on the bench, drinking tea and chatting like two old friends. He recalled how things used to be when his father was still young and he himself a little boy. But now he had to turn his eyes away, heartsick at the layers of excess flesh on his father's neck.

Day after day, Wang Qiyao waited for him, anxious at first but growing calmer as she consoled herself with the thought that, the more violent the storm in his household, the greater the possibility that a change would come. During this time, Madame Yan came by once to spy on her, but Wang Qiyao was careful not to reveal anything, only showing her the usual hospitality. Madame Yan, however, could not resist asking why Kang Mingxun was not there.

Wang Qiyao laughed. "Since you started keeping your distance, we no longer have a foursome for mahjong. Kang Mingxun also stopped showing up, and now only Sasha remembers me and comes regularly."

Even as she said this, they heard footsteps on the stairs and, as if to confirm the statement, Sasha entered. To vent her anger and bitterness, Wang Qiyao made a show of abandoning Madame Yan, and talked gaily with Sasha instead. But deep down, she was being torn apart. Tears welled up in her eyes as she wondered: *Will he ever come back?*

It was eight days before Kang Mingxun finally came to see Wang Qiyao again. They both looked somewhat haggard. Her heart, which had been floating in uncertainty, sank, but it seemed to have landed on solid ground. This time, they each sat quietly in opposite corners, eyes averted, their faces turned away, as though each was afraid of being ridiculed by the other. The afternoon faded into night.

Wang Qiyao rose suddenly to turn on the light, asking, "How about dinner?"

In the light, they felt as if they no longer recognized each other and behaved rather stiffly.

"I have to go home for dinner," explained Kang Mingxun, although he seemed to have no intention of leaving.

Rather than ask him again, Wang Qiyao went to the kitchen to cook, leaving him to pace by himself in the room. The people across the lane had turned on their lights and he could see them bustling about. He heard the sound of the neighbor's door continually swinging open and slamming shut. Soon came the mildly explosive sounds of food being fried in the kitchen, followed by its aroma. He settled down, and even felt a little happy. Wang Qiyao came out with dinner—soup, a vegetable dish, and a plate of periwinkles to go with the rice. They sat down to dinner, making no mention of the past eight days. It was as if that week had never been. As they ate, they started to chat about the weather, new fashion trends, and what was happening around town. After dinner, they scanned the *New People's Evening News* for a movie. Wang Qiyao suggested a new Hong Kong movie. Kang Mingxun looked at the title—he had just seen that very one with his sister—but he agreed anyway. They tidied up a bit before leaving and then, just as they were about to step out the door—Wang Qiyao already had her hand on the handle—she suddenly stopped, turned, and buried her head in Kang Mingxun's arms. They embraced quietly for a long time. The apartment lights were already out, but the neighbor's light, shining in through the window curtains, cast a filmy sheen on the floor.

From that day on neither of them gave any thought to the future, which was in any case remote. How could they bear to let it corrode the present? They needed to make their lives more substantial, to make all the emptiness around them disappear. With the future no longer a factor, they held the present ever more dearly, dividing each minute into eight parts, treating short afternoons like long nights, the span of a season as if it contained a whole cycle of incarnation. Evidently there are advantages to brevity as well as to a long duration. One tends to waste time when there is a lot of it; when time is short, one makes the most of it. They ceased to grieve over the fact that they could not be united as husband and wife. After all, matrimony is a social convention, whereas they lived only for themselves. It was themselves that they loved, themselves that they reproached; no one else had any say in the matter. This was their own private little universe. Although it was small and lonely, they were free—free to love and to reprove, beyond the control of others. Thus the large and the small too have their respective advantages. There may be more breathing room in the large, but there is also room for inconsequential and impure elements, and for illusions to grow; whereas the small is, by comparison, pure and true.

They would sit by the table, silently watching the blue flame of the alcohol burner with a mix of joy and sadness. From time to time, people with infants needing shots would come knocking. Wang Qiyao would hold the child sprawled on her lap, with the parent standing by to keep it still, while Kang Mingxun, with a foolish smile on his face, dangled a toy to distract it from crying. Each time they conjured a touching scene that was both comical and tender, in this way retrieving what other people carelessly tossed away. They spent countless hours picking edible *malantou* by the stream, gently placing the large leaves in one pile and the young ones in another pile—the care they took was emblematic of the warmth they invested in these fragments of love. Though their efforts did not add up to much, still they were honest efforts. For two people who habitually weighed every move from the standpoint of self-interest, an affair that ran contrary to their interests offered a momentary respite and a lesson in true love.

The days passed, with no hint of when the "future" might arrive. It only seemed more distant with every step they took, so that it felt as if they would never get there. This interlude lasted a long time and, if it weren't for what then happened, they would have thought they could go on like that forever, always pushing the future far, far away, into a dark corner where it would never be seen and not bother them. What happened, however, was a signpost of the future—Wang Qiyao became pregnant.

At first they refused to believe it was true. After it was confirmed, they felt utterly helpless. Afraid to discuss the matter at home lest the neighbors overhear them, they put on gauze masks and went for a walk in the park, where they kept looking over their shoulders apprehensively. The winter trees were bare, a thin layer of ice had formed on the lake, the grass had withered, and the sun shone weakly from behind the clouds. Walking in circles on the grass, they saw no escape from their predicament. The skin lay taut on their faces and their hair was parched from the dry air; they felt they had come to the end of their road. As soon as they left the park behind, they went their separate ways, keeping their eyes straight ahead. The raucous noises of the city hung over them like rain clouds, and they soon lost sight of each other.

The next day they resumed their conversation at a park further away, where the scenery was equally bleak and there were few visitors, and the sparrows hopping on the yellow grass seemed to be the only signs of life. The light of the sun as it shifted gradually through the bare trees reminded them that they could not afford to procrastinate. Their hearts were crushed with anxiety. Still, no solution presented itself, and they fell to bickering. Wang Qiyao, suffering from morning sickness, was cantankerous from the start. Kang Mingxun, who had to stifle his own agitation to soothe her with words he did not mean, felt his situation becoming insupportably awkward. He soon reached his breaking point and exploded in anger. They feuded as they walked down a cement-paved lane, at first in smothered whispers, but soon forgot themselves and raised their voices. Under the empty winter sky, however, their shouts were as feeble as whispers, blown away in the wind. Flocks of birds rose like grains of sand wafted aloft. The two were desperate but not nearly desperate enough—they still clung to the hope that some miracle would befall them. They shared a powerful urge to survive, like weeds sprouting between cracks in the pavement—abusing each other was proof that they had not completely given in and were struggling still. Both had lost weight; they looked pale, and Wang Qiyao's face was all broken out.

After this initial period of agony, they fell into a stupor during which they stopped going to the park and ceased all discussion. Wang Qiyao would sit under her comforter with a hot water bottle to keep her warm, while Kang Mingxun sat on the sofa wrapped in a woolen blanket. They resembled brooding hens, yearning wistfully for the danger to hatch into something else. When the sunlight reached the wall opposite the sofa, Kang Mingxun would use his hands to make shadows of animal figures—a goose, a dog, a rabbit, a mouse—as Wang Qiyao watched from her bed. By the time the light moved away, the show was over and it would be dusk.

Kang Mingxun now did the cooking. He had never touched a frying pan before, but he turned out to be a superb chef. He found he could push his anxieties aside by focusing on culinary techniques. With Wang Qiyao's flowery apron around his waist and a pair of protective sleeves over his shirt, he brought the meal to Wang Qiyao's bedside, his hair mussed up, his forehead oily and perspiring, his eyes aglow with excitement. Tears rolled down her cheeks and into her bowl as she ate. Kang Mingxun watched helplessly on one side, looking very much like a waiter on duty. Soon he too became teary. They could no longer put it off: a decision had to be made. Wang Qiyao said she was going to get herself examined at a hospital the following day. Kang Mingxun offered to go with her, but she declined. She had no way out, she said, but there was no reason why he should be dragged down along with her; this was the direction her life had been taking, whereas Kang Mingxun had other duties to fulfill.

She caressed his hair and, smiling through her tears, said, "While the mountain remains, we shan't lack firewood."

She realized at this moment that she truly loved this man and was willing to do anything for him.

"Who will you say is the father?" Kang Mingxun asked.

Wang Qiyao conceded that this was a sticky point. Even if she did not say, others would guess. As discreet as they had been, they were together a great deal, and Kang Mingxun would be the prime suspect. Even if it escaped other people's notice, Madame Yan would certainly know. But then an idea suddenly came to her. She thought of someone else . . . Sasha.

Sasha

Sasha was a half-breed child of the revolution—a product of the Comintern. He was by right one of the city's new masters, but his heart had no home here. Everywhere he went, he was treated like a foreigner, which always left him confused about who he really was. This city had many people of mixed blood, born largely of fortuitous circumstances—they were the accidents of history. Their half-breed faces betrayed their uncertain fate, a fate that capriciously brings people together and tears them apart. These people spoke in hybrid languages and all looked a bit eccentric, the result perhaps of warring bloodlines, or perhaps of conflicting lifestyles. Their unconventional and rambunctious behavior, charming while they were children, became disagreeable in adulthood. Their unusual appearance made them stand out in the crowd, marking them as loners. One turned upon them the eyes of impudent curiosity. They, for their own part, saw themselves as temporary residents of the city, and that feeling of transience often hung on for a lifetime. They seldom made long-term plans, living one day at a time and never saving for the future. What was there for them to save anyway? Their possessions were not theirs to keep. Some half-breeds disappeared inexplicably without a trace; others put down roots and learned the local dialect; a few joined the underworld and led a life in the streets, in this way helping to lend an air of dark mystery to the city.

Sasha's cockiness in proclaiming himself an heir of the revolution was merely a pose—he needed to compensate for his vulnerability and his inner sense of vacuity—it was a laughable attempt to embolden himself. With neither mother nor father, nor any livelihood, he buzzed around all day long like a headless fly, an ingratiating smile on his face, constantly seeking acceptance. Yet he resented the role that fate had assigned him, and was ever on the lookout for opportunities to get even. He was at bottom amoral and unprincipled, always taking the easy way out for himself, which sometimes worked out to the convenience of others.

Wang Qiyao thought he was the perfect candidate. She would have been racked with guilt doing this to anyone else, but had no such qualms when it came to Sasha. This was a role he had been born to play.

"I've got an idea," she said to Kang Mingxun.

But when he inquired about this, she refused to say more. He was not to worry about it—she would handle everything. Kang Mingxun was disquieted. He had some inkling of what she was up to; he was hesitant to ask but also felt he ought to press her for an explanation. Fortunately, Wang Qiyao was adamant about not revealing her plan, instead simply instructing him not to come around anymore. They embraced as usual when he said good-bye, but on this occasion he felt his heart being torn to shreds and could not let her go. Her body was connected to his very heart and soul, and so could never be separated from him. He wept till he ran out of tears, his throat went hoarse, and he lost his voice. Emerging at last into the street, he was annoyed that his bicycle refused to budge, until he realized he had forgotten to undo the lock. He got on his bike and rode down the street, swerving left and right; it took some time before it dawned on him that the blurry haze of lights shining into his eyes as he moved was headlights, and that he was going the wrong way against the traffic. He experienced what the dying felt in their last moments on earth—while his body still clung to life, his soul had already departed.

Over the ensuing days he wandered repeatedly back to Peace Lane, without knowing what he was searching for—the place was noisy, as usual, with people and cars coming and going. He asked himself if it was possible that Wang Qiyao really lived there and saw at the entrance to the lane, as if for the first time, her sign advertising injections and inoculations—somehow he couldn't quite figure out how the name on the sign related to himself. Spring Festival was approaching and the streets were crowded with people busy purchasing things for the New Year, but he was no more concerned with these things than with a fire blazing on the other side of the river. For several days on end he visited

Peace Lane twice a day—morning and night—but he never ran into Wang Qiyao, nor anyone from Madame Yan's household. Not once did he see a single familiar face: it was as if Wang Qiyao was a drop of water that had disappeared into the ocean. Wandering back and forth, he was consumed by a feeling of emptiness. He promised himself that he would not come back, but sure enough, the next day, back he came. This went on until one afternoon, around three o'clock, he saw Sasha. Bag in hand, Sasha walked at a hurried pace into the lane. Trying to look casual, Kang Mingxun strolled in and out of several stores across the street, all the while peering at the entrance to the lane. It was only after the streetlights came on and there was still no sign of Sasha that he wearily climbed onto his bike and slowly rode away, to return no more.

Sasha had always regarded Wang Qiyao as one of the many women who were fond of him. He knew he had a pretty face that women liked. Their affection for him was always mixed with the tenderness and solicitude shown by a mother toward her child. Over time Sasha grew even more gentle and sensitive, as if he had been born to fulfill their fantasy. He loved women the way children love the parents who nurture them. He loved their generosity and honesty, their simplicity and credulity. They never failed to repay a kindness. Women, how insubstantial they are! Incredibly, they value, above all else, tender feelings. Sasha did not own a thing—in this sense he was a true member of the dispossessed proletariat—yet he had an endless abundance of tender feelings, as much as anybody might care to have. His memories of his Russian mother were hazy, and he had no sisters. His sole experience with the opposite sex was with these older women, who loved him more than they loved themselves. What they asked of him was tenderness, in return for which they showered him with their beneficence. In their arms, Sasha was an adorable little kitten, gentle beyond imagination. He could also be peevish at times—provoked by their suffocating adoration—on occasion he might even scratch them with his claws, but even then he did it gently.

Sasha took to women as a fish takes to water. However, he was, after all, a man with an encompassing worldview, harboring many aspirations, some of which lay beyond his reach, although this did not prevent him from setting his sights on them. Sasha was always awkward and ineffectual around other men. With them, neither his pretty face nor his status as heir of the Comintern counted for much. His attitude toward men was one of diffidence and fear. He was always too tense in their company, and they came to look down on his hypersensitivity. Sasha was a threat to none, but jealous and resentful of all. On this point women's adoration was no help at all. In fact, they only exacerbated his self-loathing. He came to believe that the only reason he hung around with them was that he was good for nothing else. Consequently, Sasha was at heart a misogynist—to him women were mirrors reflecting his own ineptitude. Sometimes he would look for an opportunity to retaliate, but his little acts of revenge were gentle, nothing to raise the alarm. His feelings for Wang Qiyao were, however, somewhat different and had as much to do with Kang Mingxun as with her. Sasha had no doubt that if it had not been for Kang Mingxun, Wang Qiyao would have fallen in love with him. Now that the two had fallen out, as he sensed, he grew excited rather than upset, because it meant that he was now on equal footing with Kang Mingxun.

One might suppose that Sasha was deserving of pity, but Sasha himself had no idea of what he was getting into. Taking Wang Qiyao's sudden affection and Kang Mingxun's retreat as a mark of his victory, his vanity was greatly flattered. As a trophy won, Wang Qiyao took on additional importance to him. When he noticed that she was lethargic and listless in her appetite, he had his Russian friends make bread for her. He willingly played the part of her assistant, making cotton balls and sterilizing needles. This aroused some guilty feelings on Wang Qiyao's part, but remorse immediately gave way to the image of Kang Mingxun, her apron around his waist, protective sleeves on his arms, his forehead oily and perspiring, trying so hard to please her. Her resolve stiffened—she could not afford to turn back, she could only move forward.

The first time she went to bed in Sasha's arms, she noticed, as she caressed his body, how fair his skin was—almost transparent—and that his muscles were slight and soft. *He was only a boy.* Running her fingers gently through his hair as he lay lost in deep sleep, his hand resting on her breast, she was astonished to discover that his feather-light hair was not evenly colored. This amused her, and teardrops fell from her eyes. She saw too—what his eyeglasses normally kept hidden—the long, fan-like lashes over his eyes and the delicate flanks of his nose, which twitched faintly. She felt remorse at taking advantage of him, but, lacking an alternative, she could only apologize to him silently. She comforted herself with the thoughts that he did not have parents to answer to, and that, sheltered by his position as the heir to veteran revolutionaries, he could afford to take this rap. At the same time, though, Wang Qiyao found Sasha intimidating. She had not expected the child-like Sasha to be so experienced with a woman's body; he was obviously well practiced, and she nearly lost control of herself. She was not a novice herself when it came to men, but Director Li was in the distant past, and intimacies with him, always rushed, had left little impression on her. Moreover, she was young then and was much too preoccupied to pay attention to her own sensations. With Kang Mingxun she had had to play teacher. Sasha was the first man who made her feel the thrill of being a woman, yet that thrill was somehow repulsive to her. During those moments a thirst for revenge overrode her guilt and she could only think, *Sasha, you deserve every bit of this.*

When she told Sasha about her pregnancy, suspicion flickered in his eyes. He started to ask incisive questions that showed he knew nearly as much as any gynecologist. Traps were laid for Wang Qiyao, but she was careful to sidestep them, and there was nothing he could do. She marveled inwardly at his calmness. This was certainly no Kang Mingxun. It was fitting that he, of all men, should own up to the responsibility. After all the questioning was over, Sasha still did not believe her, but he kept quiet. They continued their dinner and went on to bed.

Later Sasha, sprawled on the bed, placed his ear to Wang Qiyao's belly. When she demanded to know what he was up to, he giggled. "I'm asking the baby its name."

"Well, you won't get an answer out of her!" Wang Qiyao retorted.

They spoke in double entendres because what they really wanted to say was out of bounds. All Wang Qiyao knew was that this time Sasha came into her with unusual force and her own climax was correspondingly intense—all of which made her feel that he truly deserved what was coming to him, and her conscience was eased.

For the next two days Sasha made no allusion to their discussion, behaving as if nothing had happened. Wang Qiyao could not restrain herself from asking, "What are we going to do?"

"What's the hurry?" Sasha casually replied.

Wang Qiyao was compelled to suppress her impatience and play along with him, but she was determined not to let him get away. Anger allowed her to see matters in simplistic terms, and she was able to joke: "Let's have this child and take it with us to Russia to live on bread."

"And what if the child prefers Chinese pancakes and fried dough to Russian bread?" Sasha rejoined.

Half suspecting that her secret had been discovered, Wang Qiyao did not dare carry the joke any further. However, her resentment gave her strength. Meanwhile, two more days went by. Sasha came as usual and, after lunch, sat picking his teeth. As the sun shone on his face, one could see the tiny blood vessels beneath his skin. After a while he nonchalantly announced that he would take her to the hospital the following day.

"Which hospital?" Wang Qiyao asked.

"The one in Xujiahui." He said he had made a special effort to find a doctor who had studied in Russia. Feeling that an enormous load had suddenly been lifted off her shoulders, Wang Qiyao heaved a sigh of relief, and was then struck with a spell of dizziness.

They took a public bus to the hospital. Sasha—deliberately it seemed—let two buses pass by before taking the most crowded one. Wang Qiyao rarely went out, much less took the bus. Not being used to pushing and shoving, she let other people go ahead of her. The door closed behind her as she got on board, pinching her heels. By that time Sasha had made his way deep into the crowded aisle, out of Wang Qiyao's sight. There she stood at the door, unable to move forward or backward, pushed and grumbled at by all the passengers getting on and off. By the time she got off at Xujiahui, her hair was disheveled, a button had fallen off her dress, and her shoes were dirty from being stepped on; she was beating back the tears and her lips were quivering. Sasha, the last to emerge from the bus, asked her how she was feeling. She gritted her teeth, swallowed her tears, and said she was all right.

Quickening her steps to keep up with him, she made a point of always getting ahead of him, as if to say, "Don't you even think about getting away." Sasha, who had a few more tricks left up his sleeve, was compelled to get down to business. They found themselves at the imposing gate of the hospital, which was marked with a red cross. Sasha led her twisting and turning down many a corridor before they found his friend, the resident doctor, who was resting in his office, having just finished his rounds. He stepped in first to talk to the doctor before motioning for Wang Qiyao to come in. Wang Qiyao, seeing that the doctor was a man, blushed with embarrassment. He asked her several questions and told her he needed a urine sample before the examination. Wang Qiyao wandered furtively around the building like a thief, too intimidated to ask where the restroom was. When she finally found it, a janitor was cleaning it and she was forced to wait outside. As soon as she entered, she was overcome by the harsh smell of Lysol and began to vomit, though nothing but acrid liquid came out. Soiling the freshly scrubbed bathroom filled her with shame and dread. She started to cry, so hard that she was afraid all the pent-up grievances inside her might explode in a scream of anguish. Stuffing her handkerchief in her mouth, she doubled up, racked with spasms of sobs. The back window, on which she leaned to steady herself, offered a vista of undulating rooftops. On some of them, rice was spread out on mats to dry. The sun shone on the rooftops, even on the grains of bug-infested rice. A flock of pigeons rose and glided in circles, their wings flickering in the light. Wang Qiyao stopped sobbing, even though her tears continued to flow. The pigeons wheeled round and round, up and down, growing more distant and then closer, like seagulls soaring over the ocean of rooftops. Wang Qiyao straightened up, wiped away her tears, walked out of the bathroom, and went downstairs.

Sasha did not return to Wang Qiyao's apartment until two o'clock in the afternoon. She was giving an injection to a patient, and had another one waiting. On the table, the blue flame of the alcohol burner was licking the box of needles. Her sheets and bedding had been taken off the bed and were being sunned on the balcony, the floor had just been mopped, and the furniture was freshly wiped. Wang Qiyao herself had changed into a blue smock with white polka dots, her hair was neatly combed and tied back in a pony tail—she looked like an entirely different person. When Sasha entered, she asked if he had had lunch and offered him some water. In the presence of strangers, Sasha had to stifle his anger. He had no idea what Wang Qiyao wanted out of him. As soon as the patients left, he sprang from his chair. He was still smiling as he asked her what she had against that doctor that made her run off as soon as she laid eyes on him, not even bothering to tell him she was going. Wang Qiyao tried to explain by saying that after she had gone to the bathroom, she couldn't find her way back to the doctor's office. Sasha said it was his fault, he should have gone with her to help her find her way. Wang Qiyao insisted that she should take the blame; she always had a terrible sense of direction.

"Getting mixed up about where you are going isn't so bad . . ." replied Sasha, "but you should be careful about getting mixed up about the person you should be with."

At that, Wang Qiyao stopped talking and flashed an awkward smile. She paused for a moment before asking Sasha if he wanted anything to eat. Sasha twisted his head away sulkily and said no. The blue tendons on his neck were bulging. His behavior reminded Wang Qiyao once again that he was still a child, four or five years younger than she and Kang Mingxun, who had conspired to take advantage of him. She went over to fondle his silky, feather-soft hair, which brushed gently against her palm. They were both silent.

There was a long pause. Then, avoiding her gaze, he asked, "Just what do you really want from me?"

These heart-wrenchingly bitter words carried a plea. Wang Qiyao realized that, as much as she had been wronged, she had not been dealt as bad a hand as Sasha. But she was helpless, whereas Sasha had options. Her hand lingered in his hair and she marveled at its colors.

"Sasha, do you know the old saying, 'Husband and wife for a night, husband and wife for life?'" she asked.

Sasha kept quiet.

"Sasha, don't you want to help me?" she prodded gently.

Sasha rose to his feet in silence and left the room, softly closing the door behind him before descending the stairs.

Sasha was truly in a wretched state. He could not understand how everything had happened, but somehow his world had suddenly been turned upside down. One might be tempted to think that Sasha, being a half-breed, was heartless. But deep down, half-breeds also have feelings and know right from wrong. He realized that Wang Qiyao had entrapped him and this enraged him, but he also pitied her. He walked briskly along the street, aimlessly, utterly frustrated. Everyone else looked happier than he was. He could not obliterate from his mind the image of Wang Qiyao's face, bloated, tear-stained, and marred by freckles from her pregnancy. And though he knew that her tears were aimed at trapping him, he still felt sorry for her. Tears welled up in his eyes and he felt haunted by an oppressive feeling.

He eventually grew tired from walking, his stomach started growling from hunger, and his throat was parched. He bought himself a piece of cake and a bottle of soda; he had to return the bottle to the vendor, so he ate standing next to the counter. He heard someone referring to him as "foreigner," which gave him a certain satisfaction. His spirits lifting a little, he returned the bottle and decided to visit a woman from Russia he was friends with. Her place was several trolley stops away. The trolley bell cheered him up. It had turned out to be a beautiful day, the sun still bright at four in the afternoon.

When he got to her door, he was greeted by the odor of floor polish. Inside, all the furniture was pushed against the walls, chairs were placed upside down on the table, and the floor was as shiny as a mirror. The Russian woman was so happy to see him that she lifted him up in her arms and set him down in the middle of the room. She took a few steps back, declaring that she wanted to take a good look at him. Standing in the middle of the shiny floor, Sasha looked small, like a puppet. She commanded him to stand still and, humming a Russian song, danced around him. The whirling and twirling left Sasha a little dizzy and impatient. Laughingly, he ordered her to stop. Then he moved to the sofa and lay down. He was so tired he could scarcely open his eyes. With his eyes closed, he felt the warmth of the sun on his face and the sweetness that comes with fatigue; he also felt the woman's exploratory fingers on his body, but he was too exhausted to respond and fell fast asleep. When he woke, the room was dark; only the hall was lit. Smells of onions in borscht wafted from the kitchen, a greasy, pungent odor. His friend was talking in whispers with her husband to avoid waking him up. The furniture had been put back in place and the floor gave off a dark luster. His nose twitched and large teardrops fell from the corners of his eyes.

The following day, Sasha returned to see Wang Qiyao, They were both calmer. Sasha volunteered to find her a woman doctor if she wanted.

"Let's just stick with that male doctor," Wang Qiyao conceded. "At this point, what difference does it make if it's a man or a woman?"

They exchanged smiles in which there was more than a hint of bitterness. After making an appointment, they returned to the same hospital, but this time they went in two pedicabs, Sasha in one and Wang Qiyao in the other. It was the same doctor, but this time he saw her at the outpatient clinic. He appeared to have forgotten all about the prior visit, asking Wang Qiyao the same set of questions, then telling her to leave a urine sample. As Wang Qiyao stepped out of the clinic, she noticed Sasha behind her.

"You are afraid I'll get lost again, aren't you?" she asked.

Sasha smiled, but did not turn back into the clinic, choosing instead to wait for her outside the door. A parade of women passed before him, some of them pregnant. Perhaps owing to his experience with Wang Qiyao, his mind began to wander and he imagined that every one of those women was dealing with the same unspeakable problems, in the face of which they all stood helpless. The thought oppressed him. Wang Qiyao returned only to say she had to go to the lab, and asked him to wait. She disappeared at the end of the hallway with the air of someone who had already accepted her fate. The arrangements went smoothly and a date for the operation was set. As it was noon by the time they left the hospital, she suggested lunch, and Sasha agreed. Being unfamiliar with the area, they walked around aimlessly for a while. The steeple rising from the Xujiahui Catholic church stood proudly against the blue sky, its sight filling them with solemnity. After walking on for some time, they finally found a restaurant and went in.

Once seated, Sasha said lunch was on him. Wang Qiyao said she clearly should be paying today, why should he pay? Sasha threw her a glance and asked why she should pay—*he* clearly should be paying. She was a little shaken by her own carelessness—she had nearly given herself away. She pretended to yield to him but figured he probably did not have the money anyway. They ordered a few dishes and chatted about nothing in particular.

"Will the operation hurt?" Sasha asked abruptly.

Wang Qiyao was taken aback. She said that she did not know either, but it couldn't possibly be as painful as giving birth.

"How does it compare with having a tooth pulled?" Sasha asked.

Wang Qiyao laughed. "How could you make such a comparison?" She appreciated Sasha's concern, but couldn't pass up an opportunity to mock him. "It's not a tooth, you know?"

At this point, the dishes arrived and they started to eat.

"Of all the food I have ever had, those meals you made for me were the best," remarked Sasha.

Wang Qiyao accused him of only saying such things to flatter her, but he insisted that he meant every word of it—her cooking stood out, not because she used expensive ingredients or made unusual dishes, but because it was home cooking, the kind that one could eat day in and day out and never tire of.

"Of course those dishes were home-cooked, what else could they be? Food made by vagabonds?" joked Wang Qiyao.

"You put it perfectly," Sasha replied. "Perhaps you don't believe it, but people like me lead lives that can only be described as vagabond."

"Of course, I don't believe you," Wang Qiyao said.

Ignoring her, Sasha continued, "I am busy from morning till night, acting like I have a hundred places to go, but that's only because I really don't have anywhere to go. . . . My heart is unsettled; I can't sit still anywhere for long. I feel like there is this fire burning under my seat, and so I have to get up and go. . . ."

"What about your grandmother's place?" Wang Qiyao asked.

Sasha shook his head with a dejected air, but didn't say a word. Wang Qiyao felt sorry for him but could not think of what to say to comfort him. They ate the rest of the meal in silence. When it came time to pay, Wang Qiyao matter-of-factly took out her pocketbook.

To her surprise, Sasha was furious. "Wang Qiyao, do you really think so poorly of me? I may not be rich, but I can still afford to take a woman out to lunch."

Wang Qiyao's cheeks burned and she managed only to stammer, "This is really for me to take care of."

She was taking an enormous risk with those words, and her eyes betrayed a glimmer of guilt. Sasha held her hand with the money in it, his face suddenly suffused with gentleness.

"This is a man's business," he said softly.

Wang Qiyao did not argue with him. After he paid the waiter, they left the restaurant in silence, each barely able to fight back the tears.

As the day of the operation was approaching, Sasha received a call from an aunt in Russia asking him to meet her in Peking. He suggested that Wang Qiyao postpone the operation for a few days until his return, but Wang Qiyao insisted on going ahead with it without him. She told him not to worry, explaining that it wasn't really a big deal.

"Just like pulling a tooth," she added teasingly.

But Sasha would not hear of it. Wang Qiyao lied to him, saying that her mother would go with her. Although he doubted that she would actually ask her mother, he turned a blind eye and pretended to believe her. Before he left, he forced her to accept ten *yuan* to buy something nutritious after the operation. Wang Qiyao took the money but later sneaked twenty back into his pocket. She heard the sound of his footsteps going down the stairs and out the back door, gradually growing ever more distant. She sat transfixed, her mind emptied of all thoughts, as the colors of dusk slowly slipped in through the window, engulfing her like a cloud of dark mist.

That was a night of utter stillness. Everything seemed to be the way it was before—no Sasha, no Kang Mingxun, not even Madame Yan. Wang Qiyao took in even the minutest sounds of Peace Lane: footsteps on loose floorboards, doors being shut, parents hollering at their children, even the whoosh of running faucets. Her gaze settled on the potted oleander plant on the balcony opposite, bathed in cold moonlight. She could almost see the gentle hand that tended the plant. In contrast, the sound of water rushing down the pipes had a preemptory air, as though lodging a protest on behalf of Peace Lane. Even though the patch of sky above Peace Lane was narrow and crooked, it remained, far, far away. On clear nights the silhouettes of the buildings stood against the sky like a paper cutout. The buildings might conceal the moon and stars, but they could not prevent their light from shining through, nor could they block out the warmth and cold. Good: it meant that the seasons were still on schedule and people's lives went on as usual.

Wang Qiyao opened a packet of longan fruit and started shelling them. No patients came on that tranquil night; only the old man from around the corner came around, warning people to mind their kitchen fires, a well-intentioned message coming from an experienced voice. Wang Qiyao had filled a bowl with succulent longan meat, leaving the shells in a heap on the table. The large flowers on the window curtains, somewhat faded, were still distinct. The mice soon kicked off their nocturnal activities, squeaking merrily along. Cockroaches, masters of the night, began scurrying about out of human sight, coming on shift even as people went off to bed. A myriad of insects were astir, drawing the sparrows' attention.

The following day was humid and warm, with a drizzling rain. Wang Qiyao took an umbrella with her. On her way out she looked back at her apartment, wondering if she would be back in time for lunch. When she got downstairs, the unrelenting rain was creating eddies alongside the curb. The seat in the pedicab that she hailed at the entrance to the lane was damp, even though it was shielded by oilcloth curtains hanging down from the canopy. She felt chilly as little raindrops came through and splashed on her face. Through the slits in the curtains she could see the stark branches of parasol trees brushing against the gray sky. She thought of Kang Mingxun—the father of the child she was carrying. It was at this moment that she realized that the "problem" growing in her belly was a child—but that child would soon be gone. Her back broke out in a cold sweat and her heart was racing. In her confusion, she suddenly began to wonder what it was that dictated that this child be removed from the world. Her face was now drenched; the raindrops were deafening as they titter-tattered down on the canopy. *I will be left with nothing—not even my baby.*

Without her realizing, tears ran down her cheeks. Her knees were knocking together. Never in her life had she felt so anxious. One of the most important decisions in her life would be settled in an instant. Her eyes became fixed on a minuscule hole in the oilcloth: the material was about to tear, but for now it was still held together by a thin web of filaments, through which light leaked in. *What could this hole mean*? she wondered. Looking through where the oilcloth curtains met the canopy, she saw another slash of the vast gray sky. She was thirty years old, with nothing to show for all that time; she wondered what there would be to look forward to in the next thirty years. This was real despair, but lurking in the depths of this despair was a glimmer of hope.

The pedicab had stopped outside the main hospital entrance. Shivering behind its curtains, the palms of her hands covered in sweat, she gazed blankly at the throng of people coming and going; she seemed to be standing at the edge of a cliff. The rain came down harder; everyone put up an umbrella. Lifting the curtains, the pedicab driver peered at her with curious eyes. This mute gesture of impatience goaded her to decisive action. Her mind was still muddled, and the driver, his face awash with rainwater and sweat, seemed to be looking at her from far away. She heard herself saying, "I forgot something. Take me home."

Down came the curtain. The pedicab turned around and moved forward with the wind behind it. The rain no longer blew in her face and her mind cleared up. *Sasha, you were right,* she said to herself. *Going it alone is never a good thing.*

On reaching her apartment, she pushed open the door and found everything exactly the way she had left it. It was only nine o'clock in the morning. She sat by the table, struck a match, ignited the alcohol burner, and placed the box of needles on it. Soon she heard the sound of water boiling. She glanced again at the clock. It was only ten past nine—time enough to return to the hospital. Wasn't this what she had been working toward for the past few weeks? Were it not for her sudden caprice, her objective would have been achieved and she would have been on her way back in a pedicab. She listened to the ticktock of the clock, and realized that it would be too late if she didn't leave immediately. As she blew out the burner, the alcohol fumes assaulted her face. Just at this moment someone knocked on the door, asking for an intravenous injection. She opened up the box of needles, but was so preoccupied with the thought of getting back to the hospital that she couldn't locate a vein; each time she poked in the wrong spot, the patient cried out in pain. Forcing herself to calm down, she finally found a vein. As soon as the needle met blood, she was able to pull herself together; as the medicine slowly dripped into the vein, she began to relax.

The patient finally left, holding a wad of cotton to his arm. As Wang Qiyao picked up the used cotton balls and needles, however, her agitation gave way to unspeakable weariness and lassitude. She gave herself up to fate, assuming an attitude of complete resignation. Since there was nothing she could do, she might as well do nothing. Before she knew it, it was already lunchtime. She went into the kitchen and saw the pot of chicken soup she had made the previous night, cold now, a film of fat on the surface. She put the pot on the burner and made rice while she watched the raindrops pelting against the window panes. She told herself she would simply lay it all on poor Sasha: whether she decided to keep the baby or not, it would go down as having been his child. If Sasha was willing to help her, then let him help her all the way! As the aroma of the chicken soup reached her nose, a hope rose up in her—things would eventually work themselves out. It was a hope that spoke all at once of complete surrender and a willingness to put everything on the line.

At that very moment Sasha was sitting on a northbound train, smoking one cigarette after another. He had never met this aunt; in fact, he had only heard of her for the first time a few days ago. His own mother was a stranger to him, how much the more this aunt! Sasha was going to see her because he wanted to explore the possibility of moving to Russia. He was tired of his current lifestyle and wanted a new beginning. He figured that being a half-breed had at least this one advantage—one had a place to escape to. You could call it escape or, if you prefer, exile, but the point is that, whichever way you looked at it, he had the option of disappearing . . . of leaving everything behind.

Mr. Cheng . . . Again

Wang Qiyao ran into her old friend Mr. Cheng at a consignment store on Huaihai Road. Supplies of nonstaple foods were becoming increasingly tight that year; although quotas had not been reduced for staple products, it was evident that they were running low. To limit consumption, the government started issuing vouchers for an ever-expanding range of items. A black market quietly emerged, and food was sold at many times the official price to meet demands. Panic was in the air. People were worried about where their next meal was coming from. Being pregnant, Wang Qiyao had to eat enough for both herself and the baby, and was forced to resort to the black market. But the income from her practice, normally just enough to cover her monthly expenses, couldn't buy two chickens on the black market.

Before their last parting, Director Li had left her several gold bars. She had kept them under lock and key all these years, saving them for an emergency. That time was now at hand. Late one evening Wang Qiyao took the mahogany box from the drawer and placed it on the table. As the light shone down on the wooden lid, the Spanish-style carvings evoked a splendor buried deep in the recesses of her memory. The box remained indifferent to her touch, as if separated from her by thousands and thousands of years. She sat looking at it for a long time, and then returned it to the drawer unopened. To touch the money now, even after all these years, was still premature. Who could tell what future hardships might be lying in wait? Better to take a few of the old outfits she no longer wore to the consignment shop before the roaches got to them. She hauled the chest out of the closet and, lifting its cover, was quite dazzled by its contents. The first item to meet her eyes was the pink *cheongsam*; the silk slipped from her hands like water and lay in a heap on the floor. She could hardly bear the sight of these garments; to her they were not mere clothes, but skin she had sloughed off over time, one layer after another, like the shells of a cicada. She grabbed a few fur pieces at random and closed the lid. Later, rummaging through the chest became a routine. The chest was opened and shut many times as she frequented the consignment shops and learned how they operated. One day, having received notice that some of her things had been sold, she went to the store to pick up the money. She was on her way out when someone called her name. Turning round, she saw Mr. Cheng.

For a moment, Wang Qiyao was so disoriented that she thought time was flowing backward. Mr. Cheng's gray sideburns roused her from her reverie. "Mr. Cheng, is it really you?"

"Wang Qiyao? I . . . I must be dreaming."

Tears welled up in their eyes as all kinds of memories flooded into their minds; it was all too much to make sense of, and they both felt overwhelmed. Wang Qiyao smiled when she realized they were standing next to the counter for photography supplies.

"Are you still taking pictures?"

Mr. Cheng smiled in his turn. At the mention of photography, they had found an entry point into the chaotic past that had come rushing back to them.

"Is your photo studio still there?" Wang Qiyao asked.

"So you remember . . ." At this moment, Mr. Cheng noticed that Wang Qiyao was pregnant, her face a little swollen—and a veil descended between her and the woman he had once known. When he had first seen her on the street, she appeared just as she had ever been; it was as if the past had reappeared. Now that they were standing face to face, he realized that everything had changed. When it came down to it, even time cannot stand up to scrutiny.

"How many years has it been?" he couldn't help asking.

They counted on their fingers—twelve years. Thinking back to the last time they had seen each other—their good-bye—they fell silent. It was almost noon, and they were getting jostled by the crowd in the busy store. Wang Qiyao suggested they go outside, but it was worse in the street, and they kept being pushed to one side, until at last they found themselves beside an electric pole, where they finally began to get their bearings. But once again they were at a loss for words; they stared blankly at the array of notices posted on the pole. The sun was already emitting a spring warmth, and they felt hot in their winter padded jackets, as if their backs were pressed against a stove. After standing there awhile, Mr. Cheng offered to walk Wang Qiyao home, saying her husband must be waiting for her. Wang Qiyao said there was no such person.

"But we should be going anyway. . . . I'm sure that Mrs. Cheng must be worried sick about you," she said.

Mr. Cheng blushed. "There is no 'Mrs. Cheng' and I suspect there never will be . . . at least not in this lifetime."

"That's too bad," Wang Qiyao rejoined mildly. "What have women done to be deprived of this privilege?"

They began to liven up and their conversation grew more animated. Looking up, they saw that the sun was at its zenith, and they realized that both their stomachs were growling. Mr. Cheng suggested lunch. Unfortunately, all the restaurants were full, with lines of customers waiting for seats. The sight of those crowded restaurants only fueled their hunger, and they could hardly tolerate the wait. In the end Wang Qiyao proposed that they go to her place for noodles. Mr. Cheng said that in that case they might as well go to his apartment, because a friend had brought some eggs and salted meat back for him from Hangzhou just the day before. They boarded the trolley, which was always empty at noon, and sat side by side, as the street scenes flashed before their eyes like images from a movie, each image bathed in a flash of sunlight. They had not a care in the world, content simply to let the trolley take them where it might.

Mr. Cheng's apartment was still there, just as she remembered it, only older. The water stains on the outside walls were a bit more pronounced. The interior was darker, due in part to the layer of dust on the window panes, which looked as if they had not been wiped in the last twelve years. The elevator was in bad shape: its iron grating had rusted, and the clanking sound it made echoed up and down the shaft. Wang Qiyao followed Mr. Cheng out of the elevator and stood waiting as he rummaged for his key. A huge piece of a spider web hung from the domed ceiling; she wondered if it had taken twelve years to weave this. Mr. Cheng opened the door and she entered. After her eyes had adjusted to the darkness, she saw that the little world inside had barely changed; it was as if the entire room had been encased in a time capsule. The wax finish on the brown hardwood floor had a lustrous sheen, the lighting frame and the camera stood in their assigned places, the carpeted wooden platform was still there, and behind them the doors and windows of the cardboard backdrop looked at once ancient and naively fresh.

Mr. Cheng went straight to the kitchen and got busy. She could hear the sounds of chopping, followed shortly thereafter by the aroma of rice and salted pork. Rather than offering to help, Wang Qiyao wandered about the studio. She moved along to the back, where she found the dressing room unaltered and saw a pleasing reflection of herself in the mirror, which was too blurred to expose the traces of age on her face. From the dressing room she passed on into the dark room. After groping for the switch, she turned on a red bulb whose rays focused on a single spot, leaving all else in a darkness that hung pensive and yet seemed symbolic of permanence in the face of change. Wang Qiyao failed to understand that it is precisely this myriad of unchanging little worlds that serves as a counterfoil to the tumultuous changes taking place in the outside world. After standing there for a moment, she switched off the light, softly closed the door, and went into the kitchen. Chopsticks and two bowls had been laid out on the round table by the gas range. A pot of rice simmered on one burner while on the other a terrine of egg custard was simmering.

Mr. Cheng served the egg custard along with the salted pork he had cooked in the rice. Sitting across from each other, they picked up their bowls, but were so much past the point of hunger that they almost didn't feel like eating. It was not until each had finished their first helping that they realized how famished they really were. They ate bowl after bowl, as though filling a bottomless pit. After they had consumed all the rice in the medium-sized pot and polished off the entire terrine of egg, they burst out laughing in the realization that, not having seen each for twelve years, they were so focused on eating that they had barely exchanged a single word—they had probably eaten more that afternoon than the sum of all the meals they had shared in the past.

Feeling somewhat embarrassed and sensing Mr. Cheng's eyes on her, Wang Qiyao said, "Don't look at me like that. You only have to eat for one person, but I have to feed two. Besides, I didn't eat any more than you!"

They were both taken aback by the way she had so frankly broached the subject; they immediately lapsed back into silence.

After a long pause, Wang Qiyao said, with a forced smile, "I know you've been wanting to ask . . . but even if you did, I really wouldn't know what to say. At any rate, what you see before you is every bit of me . . . there really isn't anything else to ask about."

Her words were at once defiant and worldly, but they hinted at feelings of resignation and bitterness. Mr. Cheng could sense that she had lived through an epoch of sorrow. Having got that out of the way, they relaxed and were able to talk about the present without any more references to the past. Mr. Cheng said he was now working in the accounting department of a government firm. His salary was more than enough for a single man, at least up until recently, when things had got a bit tight, but he was much better off than his colleagues who had families to support. Wang Qiyao explained that her income was tight to begin with, and that of late she had to rely increasingly on the consignment store to make ends meet.

Mr. Cheng was concerned. "Selling old clothes isn't a long-term solution. What are you going to do once you've sold everything in your closet?"

"What is long term?" Wang Qiyao retorted with a laugh. "How long is long, anyway?"

Seeing that he had no response for this, she said more gently, "I just hope to get through my present situation. . . . That is my sole long-term goal."

Mr. Cheng asked her how she managed. Wang Qiyao gave him a detailed description of how she counted every grain of rice. Mr. Cheng in turn regaled her with tales of his Dao of austerity, learning to get three lights out of a single match. Once they returned to the subject of food, they could talk of little else. Their excitement mounted until each insisted on inviting the other to dinner; it was as if they were engaged in a spirited competition to outdo one another. Wang Qiyao had to excuse herself: she had a patient coming for an injection and then a house call to make in the afternoon. Mr. Cheng saw her to the door, and watched the elevator door close before returning to his apartment.

The spring of 1960 was one in which people could talk of little else besides food. Even the scent of the oleanders aroused hunger. Mice scurried around all night beneath the floor in their hunt for stray morsels; flocks of sparrows took to the skies like migratory birds, searching for food. Saying that the city was in a state of famine would have been a bit extreme, but people were indeed doing whatever they could to satisfy their palates. Prominent figures lined up outside Western-style restaurants, waiting for a seat. Who knows what quantities of filet mignon, pork chops with onions, and fish disappeared into the bottomless pits of their stomachs. The aroma of butter cakes was almost enough to drive someone to murder or, at the very least, to send morality out the window. Street robberies occurred one after another, nothing major, just snacks snatched from children's hands. At bakeries, drooling onlookers vastly outnumbered paying customers. There was a sharp rise in thefts as well.

In the still of the night the city's inhabitants were kept awake not by anxious thoughts but by the rumblings of their stomachs. In the presence of hunger, even the profoundest sadness had to take second place; everything else simply disappeared. The mind, stripped of hypocrisy and pretensions, concentrated on substance. All the rouge and powder had been washed away, exposing the plain features underneath. Under the city's bright lights, people's faces were thinner and sallower, but infinitely more honest. Manners went out the window. Compared to the stark candor of true "famine," a residual layer of extravagance remained; but the water had clearly receded and the rocks were now showing through. And even though the grave solemnity of "famine" was missing—hints of comedy lingered—there were ample occasions for irony. Hasn't it been said that comedy is created by tearing down trivialities? Trivialities were certainly being ripped up in this city, although if truth be told, a good deal of flesh and bone were also involved. Still, the damage was not major, just a little wound.

Mr. Cheng and Wang Qiyao were reunited over food. Their aim, however, was not pleasure in eating, but eating to fill one's belly, unlike afternoon tea and midnight snacks with Madame Yan, whose purpose had been chiefly to pass the time. It did not take the two of them long to figure out that there was economy in joining forces, as well as moral support. Consequently, they had at least one meal together every day. Mr. Cheng handed the bulk of his salary over to Wang Qiyao for board, leaving himself just enough for a regular haircut and lunch at the office. He would come to Wang Qiyao's place right after work, and they would cook together, chopping vegetables and washing rice. On Sundays Mr. Cheng would come before lunch for Wang Qiyao's food vouchers, and then get in line at the stores and purchase what he could—sometimes it was several dozen kilos of sweet potatoes, at other times, several kilos of rice noodles. He carefully hauled the items home, and the whole way back he would ponder all the different recipes they might use them in.

His suits were getting old, the lining torn, and the cuffs frayed. He was also balding around the temples. The rims of his gold-rimmed glasses had lost their luster. But even though his attire was old and somewhat faded, Mr. Cheng was always very neat. His face too was bright and animated, not at all jaded and worn like most men his age. This caused him to stand out in a crowd; he looked like an actor right out of an old 1940s movie. By 1960 there were still a handful of men like him floating around the streets of Shanghai. Their exceptional looks were a living memorial of the past, and they always drew curious looks from the children. He was not like Kang Mingxun, who, though old-fashioned at heart, put on a Mao jacket in an effort to keep up with the times. Mr. Cheng was stubborn, and remained obstinately loyal to the old pre-Liberation fashions. A man like him never did learn how to carry a load of sweet potatoes with grace—the tin bucket kept bumping against his kneecaps, forcing him to switch it from one hand to the other. When he switched hands, he would take the opportunity to catch his breath and enjoy the scenery along the street. The parasol trees were starting to bud, casting shadows underneath. His heart very calm, he would ask himself: *Can this be real?*

Mr. Cheng's regular visits to Wang Qiyao's apartment never became much of a subject of gossip around Peace Lane. The neighbors had long taken note of the way Kang Mingxun and Sasha came and went, as well as the fact that Wang Qiyao's protruding belly was growing more noticeable by the day. Peace Lane was, in reality, quite open-minded and sophisticated. Wang Qiyao had long been relegated to the category of "one of *those* women," and that was enough to satisfy the curiosity of the people who lived there. Every street in Shanghai like Peace Lane had at least one of *those* women. They used to all be concentrated in the Alice Apartments, but had had to disperse due to changing circumstances.

When couples who lived on Peace Lane got into squabbles over everyday things, one could often hear the wife protest, "I might just as well go off and live like that woman Wang Qiyao over in no. 39!"

Whereupon the husband would sneer: "Really? Have you got what it takes?"

That would always shut the wife up.

But sometimes it would be the husband who would instigate things. "Take a look at yourself in the mirror! And then go look at Wang Qiyao in no. 39!"

"Can you afford someone like her?" the wife would retort. "If you can, I'll gladly step into the role!"

That would be enough to silence the husband. It was thus evident that in their hearts Wang Qiyao was viewed by her neighbors not with contempt, but with a smidgen of envy. Once Mr. Cheng began coming around, the aroma of food wafting out of Wang Qiyao's kitchen had become most enticing. People would exclaim as they inhaled, "They are having meat again over at Wang Qiyao's."

Wang Qiyao went to bed early each night, but Mr. Cheng would still be at the table going over their food expenses and planning their meals for the following day. Even though they had just eaten dinner, they would already be going over all the mouth-watering details of what they would have the next morning for breakfast. They talked into the night, as cats in heat began to yowl and Wang Qiyao to nod off. Mr. Cheng would get up from his chair to make sure that all the windows were locked before closing the curtains, tidying up, and turning off the lights. . . . Then he would exit quietly, setting the spring lock and carefully closing the door behind him.

Mr. Cheng never spent the night at Wang Qiyao's. The idea had crossed Wang Qiyao's mind, but she never discussed it with him, afraid Mr. Cheng might be put off by the fact that she was pregnant with another man's baby. But deep down she had already decided that if ever Mr. Cheng broached the question, she certainly would not rebuff him—not because she loved or desired him, but out of gratitude. Twelve years ago she had designated him as her last resort, someone she could always count on. She did not know then how rare and valuable this "last resort" would turn out to be. Her sights had been set on the future, and she never thought she would need to step back. Though not exactly in full retreat at present, she could no longer talk of advancing and was in fact close to having to make use of this "last resort." These days, spending mornings and evenings together with him, she discovered that Mr. Cheng had barely changed—but she was now a different person. It would have been easier on her if he had changed a bit. It was precisely because he had not changed that she felt guilty—as if she had somehow betrayed him by returning to him a fallen woman, while his integrity had remained intact. With this sense of guilt came a new reticence. She believed she had forfeited all her rights, leaving only gratitude in their place. But Mr. Cheng never broached the question, and no matter how late it was, he always went home. There were several occasions when, half-asleep, she sensed him hovering by her bedside. Her heart palpitated, and she thought that he might stay. But after a few minutes, he would always leave. Each time she heard the door closing softly, she would be struck with a combination of disappointment and relief.

Now and then their conversations turned to old friends such as Jiang Lili. Mr. Cheng still had some news about Jiang Lili these days from that film director friend of his. At the mention of the director, Wang Qiyao was transported to another world, and scenes from her confused past emerged out of the recesses of her memory.

"How does the director know Jiang Lili?" she asked.

Mr. Cheng explained that in an effort to locate him, Jiang Lili had contacted Wu Peizhen, who had put her in touch with the director. Wu Peizhen, of course, was another name that brought back a torrent of memories. Mr. Cheng said the director now held a deputy position at the Department of Film—none of them had known it at the time, but he had been a long-standing Communist Party member. It was under his influence that Jiang Lili had joined the revolution. When Shanghai was being liberated, Mr. Cheng had personally witnessed Jiang Lili waving her baton at the head of a parade of girls beating on drums as they marched past. He could scarcely recognize her in that military uniform. She still had glasses, her sleeves were rolled up to the elbow, and she was wearing a leather belt. She could have stayed in college and received her diploma in another two years, but she had decided instead to work in a yarn factory as a common laborer. Being educated and exuding revolutionary zeal, she was singled out to serve as a union officer and before long was married to the factory's military representative. Her husband was a native of Shandong province and had originally come south to Shanghai with the troops. They now lived in a new commune in Dayangpu with their three children.

On hearing the story, Wang Qiyao exclaimed, "Even in my wildest dreams I would have never imagined that Jiang Lili would one day become a cadre! Isn't that wonderful!"

Mr. Cheng agreed that it was wonderful, even though neither really believed their own words; the story simply sounded too much like a legend—something just didn't ring true.

After a pause, Wang Qiyao went back to the previous topic. "So, the director was a Communist all along! Back when I ran for Miss Shanghai, he took me out to dinner and tried to persuade me to withdraw. I wonder if he was following orders from above? Who knows, maybe if I had listened to him, it would have been me joining the revolution instead of Jiang Lili!"

They both laughed.

Wang Qiyao and Mr. Cheng considered paying a visit to Jiang Lili, but they wavered, uncertain whether—under the circumstances—they were still fit to be her friends. Like most Shanghai residents who had lived through such sweeping historical changes, they regarded the Communist Party as unapproachable, and saw themselves as people left over from a previous era. Moreover, living in the heart of society, caught up in the swirl of everyday life, they barely had a chance to develop a coherent opinion of themselves, let alone grand concepts like "the nation" or "political power." They are not to be faulted for their narrow frame of reference, because a large city is like a huge machine that turns according to the principles dictated by its own structure; only its tiniest components have a human texture, and it is these tiny components that people hold onto, otherwise they would fall into the vacuum of abstraction. The residents of Shanghai hewed to the little things of life, which left them stranded on the margins when it came to politics. If you told them that the Communist government belongs to the people, they would still keep their distance, due to modesty as well an overweening pride—deep down they still believed that they were the true masters of the city. Wang Qiyao and Mr. Cheng were all too conscious of the fact that they did not belong to the same class of people as Jiang Lili. The only reason they came up with the crazy idea of paying her a visit was because of their former entanglement. If not for that, they would have never even dreamed of calling on someone like her.

Wang Qiyao's reunion with Mr. Cheng was also a reunion with her past. When she reflected back on her youth, revisiting past experiences, she wondered whether it had all been a dream. *Who can really tell the past from the present*? As she grew heavier and her feet swelled up, she gave in to laziness and ended up sitting around most of the day. Her mind would wander as she sat knitting a wool outfit for the baby with material taken from an old sweater. The yarn came in different lengths, and she had to connect them as she knitted. Progress was painfully slow. Every day, Mr. Cheng would be overwhelmed with work at the office and chores around the house, and it was only after dinner, around eight o'clock, that he would finally get a chance to sit down. By then Wang Qiyao would be so exhausted that she could barely keep her eyes open or get a complete sentence out of her mouth without slurring the words. Mr. Cheng, watching from the other end of the sofa, was infected by her lethargy and they would nod off together until the evening chill snapped them out of their slumber. Mr. Cheng might awaken with a shiver but Wang Qiyao would remain still. She would wait for him to make her bed and help her get in, whereupon she would get half undressed and burrow under the covers. As always, Mr. Cheng would go on to make sure all the doors and windows were locked before he turned off the lights and quietly closed the door behind him.

They had been wondering whether to call on Jiang Lili and had still not made up their minds, when she took them by surprise by unexpectedly turning up on Mr. Cheng's doorstep. Since his reunion with Wang Qiyao, Mr. Cheng was hardly ever at his apartment, except when he went back late at night to go to sleep. There is no telling how many times she must have gone there looking for him before she finally caught him at the elevator. Failing to find him upstairs this time, she was waiting for the elevator to take her back down, when it arrived and out stepped Mr. Cheng. Standing there, face to face, they recognized one another, but there was something about each of them that the other did not recognize. It seemed only natural that they should feel as if their world had completely changed, even though at one level everything seemed just as it was before. Jiang Lili was in a Lenin suit; her khaki pants were a bit baggy around the knees and too short around the ankles. Her leather shoes were covered with dust. Her glasses, also dusty, seemed thicker than before, so that one had to peer through several concentric circles to find her small eyes, and look even deeper into her eyes to find a glimmer of recognition.

"What a coincidence!" Mr. Cheng exclaimed.

"What do you mean? You might think it's a coincidence, but not me!"

Thus brusquely checked, Mr. Cheng did not know how to go on.

"You're not home in the morning, not in the evening . . . you don't even come home in the afternoon for lunch!"

Mr. Cheng apologized as he opened the door for her, even though deep down he wanted to tell her, "Well, I'm here now, aren't I?" It was a Sunday afternoon and, having helped Wang Qiyao settle down for her nap, he had decided to go home to take a shower and pick up some fresh clothes—he had never dreamed that he would run into Jiang Lili. Jiang Lili stepped inside; as she stood in the dust-laden sunlight, her face showed not even the hint of a smile. Her eyes were full of reproach. Mr. Cheng felt uncomfortable and his heart pounded. He was looking for something to say that might break up the tension, but what came out instead was, "Is there anything I can do for you?"

This infuriated Jiang Lili. "You think the only reason I came by is because I have some official business with you?"

Mr. Cheng turned red. He contrived a smile and excused himself to make tea. But the hot water thermos was empty, the glasses were dirty, and the lid of the tea can had rusted shut. Following him into the kitchen, where she watched as he boiled water and washed the glasses, she observed, "This place looks like a chicken coop!"

With that, she turned and went back into the living room. When Mr. Cheng emerged from the kitchen, she was standing there lost in thought. The heavy drapes in the photo studio had been pulled back and the room looked empty and abandoned, with the lamps, platform, and cardboard backdrops all pushed into the corner. Watching her from behind, he did not have the nerve to disturb her, so he withdrew to the kitchen and hovered around the stove, as the kettle whistled louder and louder until the hot steam popped open the lid.

When Mr. Cheng returned with the tea, Jiang Lili was pacing back and forth, with hands clasped behind her back like a man. He placed the tea on the shaky round table that normally served as a prop.

Sitting across from her, Mr. Cheng asked, "How's your husband?"

Jiang Lili frowned. "Who do you mean? Old Zhang?"

This was how Mr. Cheng found out her husband's surname. He deemed it unwise to pursue this line of inquiry and instead asked about her children.

She frowned again. "Always causing a ruckus, that's all they know how to do! What else is there to ask about?"

He considered asking about her work but thought it was not his place to pry into official affairs, so he stifled his words. He truly had nothing else to say, but Jiang Lili would not permit him to remain silent for long. "After all these years, isn't there anything else you want to know?"

At that point Mr. Cheng finally realized that she was simply intent on being unreasonable; he decided to be a bit more brazen and put everything on the line.

"Well, since I keep asking the wrong questions, why don't you go ahead and ask me something?"

"Who said you're always asking the wrong questions?" Jiang Lili warmed up a bit; the cold look on her face had obviously been just a show.

This strengthened Mr. Cheng's resolve to remain taciturn. They had come to an impasse. All Jiang Lili could do now was lower her head and sip her tea. The melodious sounds of a steamship whistling from afar contrasted with the stillness in the room, where a genial warmth was gradually emerging. They were both thinking of the past, which was still heartwarming, despite its unpleasant aspects. It may be true that life goes forward, but it can also be said that life is a series of retreats. As one gets older, one is more willing to make accommodations and less likely to mind things.

"I see not much has changed for you—still here in the same old apartment," Jiang Lili observed.

Mr. Cheng lowered his head and responded sheepishly, "I am a man of few desires."

Jiang Lili laughed disdainfully. "How could you make such a claim? You have very definite desires."

Mr. Cheng didn't have the courage to answer.

It was only after a long silence that Jiang Lili asked, "Where does Wang Qiyao live?"

Mr. Cheng was startled. "You're looking for her?"

"If you don't know, just say so," she said impatiently.

"I know where you can find her," Mr. Cheng hastened to reply.

"Where?" Jiang Lili sprang to her feet, as if about to rush out immediately to find Wang Qiyao.

Mr. Cheng also stood up. "I was just getting ready to go over there myself. I'll take you to see her.... We were actually just talking about you the other day."

Invigorated by this turn of events, he forgot the clothes he had come home to pick up and made straight for the door. In the doorway he turned around to discover she had not budged. She was standing there staring at him. Even at a distance he could see the sadness in her eyes. He had the sensation of having stepped back in time to when they were all young. The two stared at each other, each coming to terms with the other's feelings, before walking out the door.

It turned out that Jiang Lili was completing the paperwork for admission to the Communist Party. One of the forms required someone to certify the high school listed on the applicant's résumé—Jiang Lili immediately thought of Wang Qiyao. Wang Qiyao seemed so far away in her past, she almost doubted if the memories of her were real. For more than ten years now, Jiang Lili had been leading a radically different life. She had redirected her passion toward accepting everything that she had once found repugnant. Where she had been impulsive and self-indulgent, she was now self-critical and disciplined. Her ardor left everyone else straggling far behind. She took everything to the brink—and then some. To make up for her bad political background, she was determined always to go against what her heart truly desired—the more she abhorred something, the more she insisted on doing it. Marrying Old Zhang was one example, choosing to work at the cotton mill in Yangshupu another. As time went by, the old Jiang Lili grew increasingly distant; it was as if she was playacting, and her whole life was the play.

Her application for admission to the party was deemed problematic. The authorities conceded that she was a revolutionary—but not in the way they hoped. The reports she wrote nearly every six months overflowed with confessional passion—the feverish prose was a bit too melodramatic even for the party. In 1960 the disease of zealotry was spreading fast—most of those accused of it were petty bourgeoisie. In truth, it is difficult to pinpoint just where the disease originated; each class had its own disease, and most people couldn't even figure out where they themselves stood.

Leaving the building, Jiang Lili and Mr. Cheng got on the trolley and rode in silence, listening to the clanking bell. The sound seemed to conquer time and space, remaining constant in the midst of a world in constant flux. Likewise, the trolley tracks were like time tunnels that never moved no matter how many roads they traversed. The three o'clock sunshine had a familiar glow—it was difficult to say whether it belonged to the past, the present, or the future—for thousands of years it had remained unchanged, so it certainly was not going to be fazed by a few decades of human vicissitudes. They got off the trolley, crossed two intersections, and arrived at Peace Lane. There light and sound came in bits and pieces, jumbled together like fabric remnants haphazardly snipped off from the outside world. As they walked silently down the *longtang,* windows rattled and drops of water from the laundry hanging out overhead dripped down onto their necks.

Arriving at Wang Qiyao's back door, Mr. Cheng reached into his pocket and took out a key. Focusing on that key, Jiang Lili's eyes suddenly took on a piercing gleam, but when Mr. Cheng noticed her expression, she quickly looked away. Embarrassed, he wanted to explain, but Jiang Lili stepped briskly ahead of him and went inside. Upstairs, Wang Qiyao was awake but still resting in bed. Inside the darkened room, Wang Qiyao did not immediately recognize Jiang Lili. By the time she did, Jiang Lili was already standing in front of her, looking down at her. Their faces were close—almost touching—their eyes met and each held the other's gaze. It was only for a split second, but all of the sights and sounds they had experienced during all those years apart seemed to pass through their eyes. Wang Qiyao sat up in bed and called out, "Jiang Lili!"

Jiang Lili caught sight of her protruding belly under the blanket and the piercing gleam returned. Wang Qiyao drew back instinctively, but this only emphasized her condition. Jiang Lili blushed; staggering backward, she took a seat on the sofa. She turned to face the window, but didn't utter a word. The threesome had parted under awkward circumstances; they were united again under equally awkward circumstances—fate was not done collecting its debts, it seemed. The light on the curtains shifted, the noises filtering in through the window became quieter, more intermittent, and Jiang Lili announced she had to leave. They made no attempt to detain her, partly because they felt ashamed, but also afraid of being spurned. Mr. Cheng saw her out before going back upstairs. The two avoided eye contact—they both knew that Jiang Lili had gotten the wrong idea about their relationship, but were actually rather pleased with the misunderstanding.

That evening they sat across the table from one another, shelling walnuts. Shanghai opera came in erratic bursts from the radio next door. They were perfectly calm. No longer did they demand anything of life other than what they presently enjoyed. Perhaps it was not all that they wanted, but they had learned to be content with what they had. One cracked open the shells while the other removed the nuts; they ate all the broken pieces, saving the whole ones for later. That was one of the rare nights that Wang Qiyao didn't feel drowsy and her back was not sore as it had been. Mr. Cheng brought her a pillow to lean against.

"When is the baby due?" he asked.

Wang Qiyao counted on her fingers. It was going to be sometime in the next ten days. Mr. Cheng couldn't help feeling anxious; in the end, it was up to Wang Qiyao to put *him* at ease.

"Childbirth is the most natural thing in the world—just look at all the people out there walking the streets."

"I'm worried that you might be alone when the baby comes and won't have anyone to help you get to the hospital."

"Childbirth doesn't happen instantaneously," Wang Qiyao explained. "The process takes at least half a day."

Mr. Cheng was somewhat relieved at this, especially seeing how calm she looked.

After a pause, he mused, "I wonder whether it's a boy or a girl."

"I hope it is a boy," she said.

"Why?"

"A woman has so little control over her fate. . . ."

They fell silent. This was the first time they had discussed the unborn child, a taboo subject they had both tried to avoid. Now that they had broached this once-forbidden subject it felt like a hurdle had been overcome. A new intimacy arose between them and they suddenly felt closer. It was ten o'clock by the time they finished shelling all the walnuts. Wang Qiyao waited as Mr. Cheng descended the stairs; only after she heard the downstairs door close did she go around to make sure the doors and windows were locked. Then she washed and went to bed.

Childbirth

ONE DAY MR. CHENG went to Wang Qiyao's after work to find her pale and flustered, lying down every so often and then getting up to pace around. She even knocked over a glass, which shattered on the floor, but didn't bother to pick up the pieces. Mr. Cheng hurried out to call a pedicab, came back in to help her downstairs, and then rushed them off to the hospital. Having arrived at the hospital, she seemed to improve, and Mr. Cheng went out to get something for their dinner. By the time he got back, Wang Qiyao had already been taken into the delivery room. It was a baby girl. She was born at eight o'clock. They told Mr. Cheng that she had long arms and legs and a full head of black hair. This set him wondering, *Just who does she look like?* When, three days later, he brought mother and daughter home from the hospital, the threesome attracted quite a few curious stares down the *longtang*.

Mr. Cheng had fetched Wang Qiyao's mother the day before, setting up a place for her on the sofa, and even going to the trouble of preparing a set of toiletries. Mrs. Wang was silent the whole time, but, as Mr. Cheng busied himself with the household chores, she blurted out, "If only you had been the child's father . . ."

Mr. Cheng trembled and almost lost hold of the things in his hands. He wanted to say something but his throat had closed up. By the time he was able to speak, he had forgotten what to say. So he simply pretended that he had not heard. When Wang Qiyao came home the next day, her mother had already prepared a pot of chicken broth and the customary bowl of soup with red jujube and longan, which was supposed to be so nourishing for new mothers. She handed the bowl to her daughter in silence. She did not bother to even look at her granddaughter; it was as if the child did not exist. Neighbors began to call on them, but they were only the most casual of acquaintances—the only contact they normally had with Wang Qiyao was waving hello as she went in and out of the *longtang*; now they came out of curiosity. Each one went on about how much the baby looked like Wang Qiyao, all the while wondering who the father was.

Going into the kitchen to fetch the hot water thermos, Mr. Cheng found Mrs. Wang standing in front of the window, looking out at the overcast sky and quietly wiping away the tears. Mr. Cheng had always thought her a calculating woman. Back when he used to call on Wang Qiyao, she would never even bother to greet him but always sent the maid down to talk to him at the door instead. Now, he sensed, she was much closer to him, perhaps more understanding and sympathetic even than her daughter.

He stood behind her for a moment before offering a timid attempt at consolation. "Don't worry, Auntie. I'll take care of her."

With those words he could feel the tears welling up and hastened back into the room with the hot water thermos.

The next day Madame Yan, who had not visited for ages, came to see Wang Qiyao. She had long heard of the pregnancy from her servant Mama Zhang, who had seen Wang Qiyao coming and going with that protruding belly of hers; Wang Qiyao obviously wasn't worried about the rumors her pregnancy might stir up. Kang Mingxun and Sasha had by this time long vanished from the scene, one hiding out at home while the other fled far away. Then, out of nowhere, appeared this Mr. Cheng, who suddenly started coming by at least three times a day. Although Madame Yan wasn't exactly sure what had transpired, she wasn't in the least bit taken off guard; in fact, she fancied herself one imbued with keen insights into the situation of women like Wang Qiyao. Still, she was intrigued by Mr. Cheng. She could tell from the fine quality of the old suit he wore that this Mr. Cheng had been a stylish man back in the old days. She took him to be some kind of playboy whom Wang Qiyao must have known back in her dance hall days. Madame Yan imagined all kinds of things about Mr. Cheng. She had run into him a few times in the alley: he was always on his way to Wang Qiyao's with snacks like "stinky tofu," and would always rush briskly past lest the food get cold. The grease from the tofu had already soaked the bottom of the bag and was about to drip through. Madame Yan was touched, even somewhat jealous of Wang Qiyao for having such a devoted friend.

Hearing that Wang Qiyao had given birth, she was moved to sympathy; being a woman, she could relate to how difficult things must have been for Wang Qiyao, and decided to go over to see how she was.

Mrs. Wang, sensing that Madame Yan was a cut above the others, felt favored by the visit and tried to make herself pleasant. She even brewed some tea and sat down with Madame Yan.

With Mr. Cheng away at work, these three women of different generations compared notes about the hardships of childbirth. Wang Qiyao mostly just sat and listened, as if the shady circumstances surrounding the father of her child prevented her from claiming her share of the glory. Her mother and Madame Yan, on the other hand, vividly recalled every detail from earlier decades. When Mrs. Wang started to speak about how hard it was giving birth to Wang Qiyao, the irony of the present situation was not lost on her and her eyes reddened. She quickly found an excuse to scurry off into the kitchen, leaving the other two in an awkward silence. The baby had just been fed and was deep in sleep, her outline barely visible in its swaddling clothes. Wang Qiyao had been looking down as she picked her fingernails, but she abruptly raised her head and laughed. It was a tragic laugh that affected even Madame Yan.

"Madame Yan, I really appreciate you coming to see me . . . especially after all that's happened. I was worried you would look down on me," Wang Qiyao said.

"Oh, cut it out, Wang Qiyao!" replied Madame Yan. "Nobody is looking down on you! I'm calling on Kang Mingxun in a few days and I'm going to see to it that he comes to see you."

At the mention of his name, Wang Qiyao turned away. It was only after a long silence that she replied, "That's right, it's been ages since I've seen him."

Madame Yan grew suspicious, but was forced to keep her thoughts to herself; instead she casually suggested that they all get together again. "It's a pity that Sasha's no longer around. He must be off in Siberia eating his Russian bread! But that's okay, you can bring along that new friend of yours and we'll have a foursome for our mahjong games."

She took the opportunity to ask Wang Qiyao the gentleman's name, his age, where he was from, and where he worked, all of which Wang Qiyao responded to matter-of-factly.

At that point Madame Yan asked bluntly, "He is so loyal to you, and neither of you is getting any younger. . . . Why don't you just get married?"

Wang Qiyao responded with another laugh. Raising her head, she looked Madame Yan straight in the eye. "A woman like me. . . . How could I talk of marriage?"

The next day, Kang Mingxun indeed came by to call on Wang Qiyao. Although she had expected him to show up after Madame Yan's visit, she was still caught by surprise. Standing there face to face, neither knew what to say. Mrs. Wang sized up the situation and decided it was best to give them some privacy, but slammed the door shut on her way out to register her disapproval. But Wang Qiyao and Kang Mingxun didn't even notice. This was the first time they had been together since their parting. It felt like thousands of years since they had last seen each other. They had appeared in each other's dreams, but the images in their dreams were so far from the real person that they would have been better off not even dreaming. They had, in truth, resolved not to think of each other—and succeeded. But, face to face once again, they discovered that letting go was not as easy as they had thought. They stood there for a moment before Kang Mingxun walked around to the other side of the bed to take a look at the baby. Wang Qiyao stopped him. When he asked why he shouldn't see the baby, she said, "Because I said so. . . ."

Kang Mingxun pressed for an explanation. Wang Qiyao said that it wasn't his baby. They fell silent for a while before he said, "Well, whose is it then, if it isn't mine?"

"Sasha's."

At that, the two of them broke down in tears. All the sorrow they had suppressed back when they had to make that difficult decision suddenly came rushing back; they wondered how they had ever got through everything that had brought them to this point.

"I'm so sorry . . . I'm so sorry. . . ." Kang Mingxun kept apologizing, knowing it would do no good even if he said it a thousand times over.

Wang Qiyao kept shaking her head, aware that if she did not accept the apology, she would have nothing at all. They were both in tears, but it was Wang Qiyao who stopped crying first.

Wiping away her tears, she insisted, "She really is Sasha's child."

Hearing her say this, Kang Mingxun also pulled back his tears and sat himself down. There was no more mention of the baby; it was as if she had ceased to exist. Wang Qiyao had Kang Mingxun make himself some tea and, as he busied himself, she asked him what he had been doing of late—did he still play bridge? Was there any news on the job front?

"For the past few months, it feels like I have been doing only one thing—waiting in line. I get in line at nine thirty every morning to get into the Chinese restaurant. Then I line up again around four at a Western restaurant. Sometimes I have to line up just to get a cup of coffee or a quick bite, like a bowl of rice with salted pork."

He explained that he was the one who usually got stuck holding a place in line for the rest of the family; once it got to close to his turn, everyone else would show up.

"Everyone talks about there not being enough to eat, but I feel like all I do all day long is eat!"

Wang Qiyao took a closer look at him and jokingly observed, "You've been eating so much that you're starting to grow gray."

"I don't think that's from eating too much—it's from missing someone too much. . . ."

Wang Qiyao rolled her eyes. "Oh no, I'm not singing *Rendezvous at the Pavilion* with you again!"

They seemed to have slipped back into their old ways—except that there was this new addition asleep on the bed. Sparrows were pecking at crumbs on the windowsill and they could hear someone forcefully shaking out a comforter on a nearby balcony.

Kang Mingxun was just on his way out as Mr. Cheng came back from work. Passing on the stairs, they exchanged a quick glance but neither left much of an impression on the other. It wasn't until he got inside that Wang Qiyao explained that the man was her neighbor Madame Yan's cousin, the one she used to spend time with.

"It's almost dinner time. How come you didn't ask him to stay for dinner?" Mr. Cheng asked.

"We really don't have anything special to entertain a guest . . . so I thought it would be rude to invite him," she explained.

Mrs. Wang kept quiet but had a disgusted look on her face. She went out of her way to be nice to Mr. Cheng, who wondered who had crossed her—he knew it wasn't him. As usual, he spent some time playing with the baby after dinner. Seeing the baby fed and contentedly asleep with her tiny fist in her mouth, he took his leave. It was around eight o'clock. People and cars passed back and forth under the bright city lights. Instead of taking the trolley, Mr. Cheng draped his fall coat over his arm and walked home. He took in the familiar scents of the city and soaked up the evening scene. Now that the burden weighing on him for so long had been finally lifted, he felt relaxed: mother and child were safe and sound and the baby didn't bother him as he had originally feared. In fact, Mr. Cheng was struck with a peculiar happiness; it was as if he, and not the child, had been given a new lease on life.

The late show was about to begin at the cinemas, which added a feeling of excitement to the night air. The city still had the spirit of a night owl, and the same energy of years ago was still there. The tricolor revolving pole outside the barbershop was the emblem of this unsleeping city. The strong aroma of Brazilian coffee wafting out of Old Chang's gives the impression that time is flowing backward. How exciting the night is! Desire and contentment abound and, despite the compromises that have to be made, everyone gives their all, living life to the fullest. Mr. Cheng's eyes grew moist and a strange excitement welled up in his heart, the like of which he had not experienced in a long time.

The next time Kang Mingxun showed up, Mrs. Wang did not go into the kitchen to avoid him. She sat on the sofa reading a cartoon version of the *Dream of the Red Chamber*. Wang Qiyao and Kang Mingxun couldn't help but feel awkward and fell back on making small talk about the weather. When the baby woke up crying, Wang Qiyao asked Kang Mingxun to hand her a clean diaper. To her dismay, her mother got up and, taking the diaper out of Kang Mingxun's hand, scolded her.

"How could you have the gentleman do this kind of thing?"

"I don't mind," explained Kang Mingxun. "It's not like I'm busy with anything else. . . ."

"Right, let him help out," Wang Qiyao added.

Mrs. Wang drew a long face. "Don't you have any manners? How could you ask a gentleman like him to lay his hands on these filthy articles? He is decent enough to treat you with respect and come to visit; but don't take it as a sign that you can walk all over him. Show some tact!"

Stunned by the innuendo in her mother's sudden attack, Wang Qiyao burst into tears. Mrs. Wang became even more incensed.

She flung the diaper in her daughter's face, screaming, "I try to help you save face, but you just don't seem to care! You demean yourself, and it's all your own doing! If you want to lead a life of shame, go ahead! Nobody's going to be able to help you if you don't help yourself!"

With that, Mrs. Wang also burst out crying. Kang Mingxun was thoroughly bemused; he had no idea what had brought this on. Not knowing what else to do, he set about trying to mollify Mrs. Wang, "Please don't be upset, Auntie. You know that Wang Qiyao has a good heart. . . ."

His words made Mrs. Wang laugh.

She turned to him, "Mister, you are very perceptive. Wang Qiyao does indeed have a good heart. She has no choice. Where would she be if she didn't have a good heart?"

Suddenly Kang Mingxun realized that *he* was the object of her wrath. He stepped back and stammered something inaudible. At this point, the baby, whom no one had been tending to, began to howl. Of the four people in the room, three were now in tears. Aghast at the chaos, Kang

Mingxun felt impelled to say, "It is less than a month since Wang Qiyao gave birth. She should still be resting and we should try not to make her upset."

Mrs. Wang laughed coldly. "Oh, so Wang Qiyao should be resting this month, should she? That's funny, I didn't know. With no man around to rely on, how is she supposed to be able to rest? Will you explain that to me?"

Those words brought an abrupt end to Wang Qiyao's tears. When she had finished changing and feeding the baby, she said, "Mom, you said I lack tact; but what about you? How do you think it looks when you say such things in front of our guest? After all, it's not as if he has anything to do with our family. You're the one who is demeaning me—and yourself! At any rate, I'll always be your daughter!"

Mrs. Wang was dumbstruck. By the time she was ready to respond, Wang Qiyao cut her off. "This gentleman has the decency to come by and pay his respects. I would never dream of making any unseemly demands on him—and neither should you! All my life I've had no one to rely on but myself; I make no other claims besides that. I'm sorry to have troubled you to help out during this difficult time, but I promise you that I will repay you for your trouble."

Her remarks were directed at her mother, but they were also meant for Kang Mingxun. Mother and daughter both fell silent for a time, until Ms. Wang wiped away her tears and murmured bleakly, "I see I've been worrying too much. Well, you are almost through your first month, and it looks like I'm no longer needed here."

Even as she spoke, she began to gather up her personal effects. Neither Wang Qiyao nor Kang Mingxun dared say a word to persuade her to stay. They watched in shock as she packed her things and placed a red envelope on the baby's chest. She went out the door and down the stairs; then they heard the sound of the downstairs door closing, and she was gone. Inside the red envelope were 200 *yuan* and a gold pendant.

When Mr. Cheng arrived, he found Wang Qiyao out of bed cooking dinner in the kitchen. He asked where Mrs. Wang had gone. Wang Qiyao told him that her father was not feeling well and, since it was already almost a month since the birth, she had persuaded her mother to go home to look after him. Mr. Cheng noticed her swollen eyes and guessed that she had been crying, but he decided not to press her and simply let things go at that. With Mrs. Wang gone, the mood that evening was a bit dull. Wang Qiyao was not very talkative and answered Mr. Cheng's questions absentmindedly, leaving her guest rather down. Mr. Cheng sat off to one side and read the newspaper. He read on for quite some time and the apartment grew quiet. He thought that Wang Qiyao must be asleep, but when he looked over he saw that she had propped her head against the pillow and was staring up at the ceiling, lost in thought. He quietly approached to ask what she was thinking. The last thing he expected was for her to jerk back and ask him what he wanted. There was alarm in her eyes and a distant look that made Mr. Cheng feel like a stranger. He retreated to the sofa and went on with reading his newspaper.

All of a sudden, rowdy noises broke out from the *longtang* outside. Opening the window to look out, Mr. Cheng saw that a crowd had gathered around a man holding up a weasel he had caught in his chicken coop. After recounting the beast's crimes, the man carried it toward the entrance to the *longtang* with the crowd following close behind. Mr. Cheng was about to close the window when he caught the scent of osmanthus blossoms in the air; it wasn't terribly strong, but the fragrance went straight to his heart. He also noticed the narrow span of sky above Peace Lane—a deep, deep blue. He felt exhilarated.

Turning to Wang Qiyao, he said, "Let's have a banquet to celebrate the child's one-month birthday."

Wang Qiyao did not say anything at first. Then, breaking into a smile: "Is that cause for celebration?"

"Yes," Mr. Cheng said more earnestly. "A first-month birthday is always a happy and auspicious occasion!"

"What's so happy and auspicious about it?"

Mr. Cheng did not know how to answer. Although she had been the one to crush his excitement, he pitied her. Wang Qiyao rolled over away from him.

After a pause, she continued, "Let's not fuss over this one-month celebration. Let's simply make a few dishes, buy a bottle of wine, and invite Madame Yan and her cousin over. They have been good to me, coming to see me and all."

That was enough to put Mr. Cheng back in high spirits. He pondered what kind of soup and dishes they should serve. Wang Qiyao objected to virtually every one of his suggestions, and he had to start from scratch. They became more animated as they argued back and forth about the menu and gradually things went back to normal.

On the afternoon of the dinner Mr. Cheng left work early to pick up the food for that evening. They put the baby to bed early and chatted as they cooked. Mr. Cheng saw that Wang Qiyao was in a good mood, which also put him in a good mood. They arranged the cold dishes in a delightful pattern, garnishing the plate with purple radishes.

Wang Qiyao declared, "Mr. Cheng, you're not only a great photographer, but you can cook too!"

"And you didn't even mention what I'm best at . . ."

"What's that?"

"Railroad engineering."

"I practically forgot your true calling. You see, all along you have been entertaining us with your hobbies, and hiding your real talent!"

"It's not that I was trying to hide it. . . . I just never get the chance to show it off!"

Their jovial banter was interrupted by the guests, who had come bearing gifts. Madame Yan brought a pound of cashmere yarn, and Kang Mingxun a pair of gold ingots. Wang Qiyao wanted to tell him that he shouldn't have given such an expensive gift, but was worried that Madame Yan would take that as a sign that her gift wasn't lavish enough, so she decided to accept them both and save her misgivings for another day. Everyone went inside to see the baby before dinner and they all commented on how precious she looked. Since there were four of them, it worked out perfectly when they sat down at the table, one person on each side.

This was the first time that Mr. Cheng had met the evening's guests. Madame Yan had taken note of him, but he had never noticed her, and he had only passed Kang Mingxun on the staircase, when neither could get a good look at the other. Wang Qiyao made the introductions and they proceeded with dinner as if they were all acquainted. Madame Yan already had a good impression of Mr. Cheng and was especially friendly toward him; it wasn't long before she felt like they were old friends. Although Mr. Cheng was a bit overwhelmed by her warmth, he realized she had nothing but the best intentions. Kang Mingxun, on the other hand, was stiff and subdued. He said little, focusing on the warm rice wine. They finished off the first bottle rather quickly and started on a second. Mr. Cheng excused himself so he could go to the kitchen to prepare another dish, but seeing he was a bit tipsy, Wang Qiyao put her hand on his shoulder, motioning him to sit back down, and insisted that she take care of it. He gently caressed the hand on his shoulder, but she instinctively pulled it away. Kang Mingxun, in spite of himself, flashed Mr. Cheng a rather sharp glance. The effect on Mr. Cheng was instantaneously sobering.

Wang Qiyao returned to the table with the new dish she had just whipped up. By then even Madame Yan, whose cheeks were red, was getting a bit tipsy. She proposed a toast to Mr. Cheng, declaring him a rare gentleman and even quoting the old adage, "It's easier to find ten thousand ounces of gold than a true friend who can really understand you." Her words were inappropriate to the occasion; obviously, alcohol was bringing out some hidden truths. Not content to propose a toast on her own, she insisted that Kang Mingxun also drink to Mr. Cheng. Kang Mingxun raised his cup but didn't know quite what to say. As the rest of the party waited anxiously, he finally came out with something that sounded even more inappropriate.

"Here's to Mr. Cheng soon finding matrimonial bliss!"

Mr. Cheng accepted their toast with equanimity and a "thank you." Then, turning to Wang Qiyao, he asked if she had anything to say. Wang Qiyao was a bit disconcerted by the unfamiliar glint in his eyes—she wasn't sure if it was the alcohol or something else—so she put on a placating smile.

"Naturally, I should have been the first one to toast Mr. Cheng. Just as Madame Yan said, it is easier to find ten thousand ounces of gold than a true friend. No one else here understands me the way Mr. Cheng does. He has always been there for me during my most difficult times. And for all the mistakes I have made, he has always forgiven me. I owe him a debt of gratitude that I will never be able to repay."

Conscious that it was the alcohol that had emboldened her to open up, Mr. Cheng couldn't help being at once deeply disappointed and hurt by her words; all she spoke of was gratitude, with not a word about love. On the brink of tears, he lowered his head. Only after a long pause did he manage to force a smile and say, "Hey, we're not here to celebrate *my* one-month birthday! Why is everyone toasting me? Drinking to Wang Qiyao would be more like it!"

And so, with Madame Yan leading the way, they all toasted Wang Qiyao. But, perhaps because they had all talked too much already, no one had much left to say. So they just drank, one cup after another. Mr. Cheng's eyes met Kang Mingxun's once again. They stared mutely at each other, neither fully understanding the circumstances. But the seeds of suspicion had been planted.

Everyone drank more than they should have that evening. Mr. Cheng couldn't remember how he had seen the guests out or whether he had washed the dishes after they left. He woke up to discover himself on Wang Qiyao's sofa, a thin blanket draped over him. Leftover food was still on the table, and the room was filled with the sweet and sour fragrance of rice wine. The moon shining through the curtains on his face was cool as water. He felt utterly at peace as he watched the moonlight dancing on the curtain; he decided to let his mind go blank and not worry about anything that had happened that night.

Suddenly he heard a gentle voice ask, "Would you care for some tea?"

He followed the voice and saw Wang Qiyao lying in bed across the room. She had also woken up, but her face was obscured by the shadows and Mr. Cheng could only make out her silhouette. Mr. Cheng did not feel awkward; on the contrary, he was filled with a sense of serenity.

"I'm so embarrassed!" he said.

Wang Qiyao responded with a silent laugh. "You fell asleep with your head on the table. It took the three of us to get you onto the sofa."

"I drank too much," he said. "But that was only because I was happy."

After a silence, Wang Qiyao responded, "Actually . . . you drank so much because you were upset. . . ."

Mr. Cheng laughed. "What's there for me to be upset about? I was really happy."

Neither of them spoke and gradually the moonlight shifted a bit closer. Bathed in the moonlight, Mr. Cheng had the sensation that he was lying in water. Quite some time passed, and he was certain that Wang Qiyao must have long fallen asleep, when she suddenly called out his name. He was surprised to hear her call him.

"What is it?"

Wang Qiyao hesitated before asking, "Can't you get to sleep?"

"I think I got all the sleep I needed when I passed out earlier!"

"That's not what I meant. . . ."

"I think I know quite well what you meant," insisted Mr. Cheng.

"I don't think so. . . ."

Mr. Cheng laughed, "Of course I do."

"If you understand what I meant, then why don't you tell me . . . ?"

"If that's what you want, I will then," replied Mr. Cheng. "You meant that all this time we have been but just one step away from taking our relationship somewhere else. And if I were to take that step, you would not refuse me."

Wang Qiyao marveled at Mr. Cheng's perceptiveness, especially since he usually came off so stiff and bookish. Embarrassed, she tried to find an excuse to explain things away. "I know I don't deserve you . . . and that's why I wanted to wait for you to make the first move."

Mr. Cheng laughed again. He felt extremely relaxed, as if floating on air. When he spoke, it felt almost as if someone else was doing the talking, but the words that came out were indeed his deepest and most honest inner thoughts.

"We talked about taking that one last step. . . . Well, I have been waiting practically half my life to take that step. But it's not as easy as it sounds. Have you ever heard the saying, 'People can be a short distance away, yet poles apart'? There are a lot of things in life that simply can't be forced."

Wang Qiyao remained silent and Mr. Cheng, unconcerned as to whether she was really listening, continued to pour out the feelings he had accumulated inside himself all those years. He explained how he had long ago come to understand this principle. So long as they could be close friends, confidants, he thought, his life would not have been in vain. But once people are together, it is as the saying goes: "A boat sailing against the current must forge ahead or else be driven back."

"I would be lying if I said that I didn't have the desire to forge ahead . . . but when the boat won't go forward anymore . . . all I can do is turn back."

After a long silence, he suddenly asked, "Kang Mingxun is the father, isn't he?"

Wang Qiyao laughed, "What does it matter whether he is or not?"

Mr. Cheng grew a bit self-conscious. "I was only asking."

The two of them turned over, away from each other, and before long they were both fast asleep, snoring lightly.

The following day Mr. Cheng did not show up at Wang Qiyao's after work—he went to see Jiang Lili instead. He had called her at her office, and they agreed to meet on Tilan Bridge. By the time Mr. Cheng arrived, Jiang Lili was already standing there waiting, constantly looking at her watch. She had clearly arrived too early but insisted on blaming Mr. Cheng for being late. Mr. Cheng refused to argue with her. They found a small restaurant nearby, went in, and ordered a few dishes. As soon as the waiter turned away, Mr. Cheng bent over the table and started to cry, a stream of tears falling steadily on the bleached table cloth. Jiang Lili could pretty much figure out what had happened, but made no effort to comfort him. All she offered was silence as she silently fixed her gaze on the ashen wall, which had recently been stained a pale white. At that moment, all Mr. Cheng was focused on was his own pain, and he made no effort to understand what Jiang Lili might be feeling. Even people as good-natured and generous as Mr. Cheng can become extremely selfish and unfair in love. They tiptoe around their loved ones, fearful of giving offense; but with the people who love them they are thoroughly inconsiderate and arrogant, behaving like spoiled brats. This was what had motivated him to seek out Jiang Lili.

Jiang Lili did not speak for a long time. Then, seeing that he was still crying, she sneered, "What's wrong? Went out and got your heart broken, did you?"

Mr. Cheng gradually stopped crying and sat in silence. Jiang Lili had the urge to taunt him further, but, taking pity on him, softened up. "You know, it seems like the harder we try to get something, the more elusive it becomes. But when we don't want something, it ends up falling into our lap."

Mr. Cheng asked softly, "And what if one gives up on something but it still remains elusive?"

Jiang Lili was livid. She raised her voice, "What, are all the women in the world dead? Don't tell me that I'm the only one left? Sent here to listen to you ramble on about your grievances over her?"

Mr. Cheng lowered his head contritely and was silent. Jiang Lili also gave up speaking to him, and the two of them sat for some time in an awkward silence.

In the end, it was Mr. Cheng who continued. "Actually, I came here to ask a favor of you. . . . I'm not sure what made me break down like that. I'm so sorry."

Somewhat mollified, Jiang Lili told him to go ahead and say what he had to say.

"I've been thinking about this for a long time, and you are the only one I can go to for help. I know it's not right, but there is no one else I can turn to."

"Whatever it is, let's hear it!"

Mr. Cheng explained that he would never again visit Wang Qiyao. He wanted to ask Jiang Lili to look out for her. Jiang Lili did not know whether to be angry or bitter.

It took a long time before she managed to say, "Well I guess all the women in the world *are* dead . . . even me."

Mr. Cheng took her ridicule in stride and Jiang Lili stopped herself from saying more.

Wang Qiyao waited for Mr. Cheng's return. She waited several days, but in the end it was Jiang Lili who came to visit. She had come straight from work in Yangshupu and had had to transfer several times on the bus. By the time she got there, her hair was disheveled, her shoes were covered with dust, and she was quite hoarse. She carried a netted bag stuffed with fruits, crackers, milk powder, and a barely used bed sheet. She emptied everything out onto the table before Wang Qiyao could stop her, and with several forceful motions, ripped the bed sheet into several small pieces to be used as diapers.

An Old Friend Flew Off on a Yellow Crane

Eventually, Wang Qiyao also paid a visit to Jiang Lili. By that time Jiang Lili had moved from the model village on the outskirts of town to the Huaihai district, where she was only two bus stops away from Wang Qiyao's place. It was a Sunday and Wang Qiyao went out to pay the water and electric bills after putting her daughter down for her afternoon nap. The day was fine and, with time to kill after her errands, she decided to do some window shopping on her way home. Suddenly, she heard someone calling her—it was Jiang Lili. She was holding a roll of dark blue material; she was on her way to the tailor to have a pair of pants made, she said. Wang Qiyao took a closer look at the fabric and, seeing that it was common polyester, volunteered to make the pants for her.

"Are you sure?" Jiang Lili asked. "Well, in that case, let's go to your place so that you can measure me."

After a few steps, she suddenly stopped. "On second thought, why don't you come to my place instead? You have never been there."

So they turned around and headed in the direction of the Huaihai district. Jiang Lili's apartment was on the ground floor, with a pair of large south-facing rooms and one smaller room facing north. She also had a small garden in the front courtyard, but instead of plants there were only a few bamboo poles for hanging out the laundry.

The walls of the apartment had been whitewashed unevenly, and looked as though they were not dry. The floor, waxed on a regular basis by arrangement with the property management office, was marred here and there by uneven water stains that made it too look wet. With the doors of the apartment left wide open and all the rooms connected, the constant traffic up and down the staircase, situated right outside the front door, made the apartment feel like a busy alley.

Over everything hung the heavy smell of onions and garlic, which even the ample ventilation in the apartment was unable to dispel. Although it was already October, mosquito nets were still hanging around the beds. The sparse furniture made the place feel like a public dormitory. Jiang Lili employed a wet nurse as well as a maidservant. Previously stationed outside the back door, the two, who obviously did not get along, followed the visitor inside, where, standing in opposite corners, they eyeballed Wang Qiyao. A strange expression came over the faces of Jiang Lili's two older boys when they saw Wang Qiyao. They were around seven or eight years old and couldn't stop whispering and giggling as they found excuses to scurry in and out of the room. Old Zhang, Jiang Lili's husband, was not home. There weren't even any pictures of him hanging up, so Wang Qiyao had no idea what he looked like.

Jiang Lili did not own a tape measure and had to ask the maids to borrow one from one of the neighbors. The maids argued back and forth about which of them should go out to try to borrow one; eventually they agreed that none of the neighbors could possibly have such an item. In the end they decided that a ball of yarn would have to suffice as a makeshift replacement. Wang Qiyao cut two pieces of string, one for the waist and one for the pants length; placing them carefully in the folded fabric, she announced that she had better be going. Jiang Lili saw Wang Qiyao to the door, her maids following close behind. Wang Qiyao didn't feel quite herself the whole time she was there and completely lost her sense of direction as soon as she left. When she reached the first intersection down the lane, she heard a child shrieking from behind, "Hustler!"

She turned around to see Jiang Lili's sons racing away, which left her feeling even more lost and confused.

As they had agreed, Jiang Lili arrived two days later to pick up her pants. Wang Qiyao had her try them on; they were a perfect fit and Jiang Lili was quite satisfied. The one thing that Wang Qiyao was confused about was why Jiang Lili would want a pair of polyester pants just as the weather was turning cold. Jiang Lili said she liked to wear polyester pants over her heavy cotton pants, which Wang Qiyao found inconceivable—how could she wear polyester over cotton? After they folded up the pants, they sat down for a leisurely chat. It was well after dinner time and Wang Qiyao's daughter was in bed playing with a doll. Wang Qiyao made some tea and brought out a plate of watermelon seeds, but Jiang Lili reached into her pocket and took out a pack of cigarettes. Only then did Wang Qiyao realize the cause of the yellow stains on her fingers. When she asked her friend when she had started smoking, Jiang Lili responded by offering her a cigarette. Wang Qiyao declined but Jiang Lili insisted. They kept pushing each other until they collapsed in laughter; it felt like they were schoolgirls again. Watching the way she gestured as she smoked, Wang Qiyao couldn't help but be reminded of Jiang Lili's mother and asked about her.

"You know her . . . she'll never change," sighed Jiang Lili. ". . . always stubbornly hanging on to the habits of the old society. All she's doing is making things difficult for herself."

Wang Qiyao inquired after her brother, who as a teenager always shut himself up in his room. From all that time with Jiang Lili, she couldn't remember ever really getting a good look at her brother. Jiang Lili said he had not changed either; but at least he was now earning a living for himself as a high school teacher. But she spoke disapprovingly of his riding a motorcycle to work. According to Jiang Lili, her entire family reeked of mothballs; in this new era they were all remnants at the bottom of an old chest. Wang Qiyao had the uncomfortable feeling that she too was included in the description, and asked, somewhat testily, if an affidavit from someone like her would really be taken seriously when Jiang Lili applied for membership in the Communist Party. Jiang Lili laughed at the question and gave her a lecture on the charter of the Communist Party that Wang Qiyao found incomprehensible.

After Jiang Lili finished her lecture, Wang Qiyao asked if her application had been approved. Any trace of gaiety immediately drained from Jiang Lili's face. After a minute, however, she smiled indulgently at Wang Qiyao's ignorance and explained that the application was a long process, requiring unbending determination and unconditional faith. She told Wang Qiyao that joining the Communist Party is like being reborn, remade into a new person. The decision does not rest on consent from any one person. The Communist Party does not offer salvation—that is something everyone must find for themselves; loyalty and diligence are the only means to salvation. Listening to her, Wang Qiyao could almost see the old Jiang Lili, that romantic poet she had known in her youth, reappear before her eyes. Times had changed, however, and Jiang Lili's odes to the wind and moon had been replaced by devoted words about steely determination and selfless sacrifice. Now, as then, however, the style smacked of theatrical exaggeration and was not entirely persuasive. Nonetheless, Jiang Lili's sincerity and dedication were not to be doubted. After listening to her lecture, Wang Qiyao was at an utter loss as to what else she could say.

From this time on Jiang Lili began coming by to visit Wang Qiyao every two weeks or so. She told herself that she was merely holding true to the promise she had made, but that was only the half of it. The other thing that kept drawing her back was nostalgia; this nostalgia was so strong that it even allowed her to overlook the fact that Wang Qiyao was actually her rival in love. At the same time, however, she fancied herself as a product of the new society, someone who had made a clean break with the past. These conflicts playing out inside Jiang Lili came to the surface as resentment whenever she saw Wang Qiyao; it was as if someone had forced her to go and she had no other choice. Sometimes she would visit but barely say a word; when Wang Qiyao asked her something, she would respond with short, contemptuous answers. Even when she was in a better mood and allowed herself to talk casually with Wang Qiyao, she would suddenly grow stern, injecting a note of unease into their conversation.

Thus Wang Qiyao was always tense whenever Jiang Lili called, always struggling for things to say and prepared for a rebuke or a chilling glare at any moment. Nonetheless, she did not view Jiang Lili's visits with distaste, and even welcomed them. To her also Jiang Lili represented the past—Wang Qiyao had nothing against nostalgia. But even more important was the subtle feeling of satisfaction she got from those visits; standing before Jiang Lili, Wang Qiyao knew that she was the victor. She might have lost everything, but as far as Jiang Lili was concerned there was one thing that Wang Qiyao had won—Mr. Cheng. For this reason she felt she could well afford to take whatever abuse Jiang Lili might heap on her. It might look on the surface as if Wang Qiyao had gone out of her way to please Jiang Lili, but in fact it was Jiang Lili who had given in. No wonder she was annoyed. When it came down to it, Wang Qiyao had indeed claimed her paltry share of the moral high ground; but how pitifully insignificant is a plot of moral high ground when one stakes it on an abyss of emptiness? Jiang Lili very early on had accepted defeat, giving Wang Qiyao the upper hand; but what did that matter when all was said and done? Between the two of them, there was such a deep mutual understanding, even mutual consideration . . . but neither of them ever knew it existed.

But for all her icy haughtiness, Jiang Lili always showed her pleasant side when she was around Wang Qiyao's daughter. Jiang Lili had three boys—all diminutive copies of Old Zhang. They spoke Mandarin with a thick rustic accent, reeked constantly of onions and garlic, and had smelly feet. All three were rambunctious, foul-mouthed, disorderly, and dirty; and if they weren't quarreling or making a ruckus, they were out getting into a fight somewhere. The mere sight of them disgusted her, and the only time she opened her mouth when they were home was to yell at them. But the boys were not in the least bit intimidated, nor were they particularly fond of her—they were close only to their father. As sunset approached, the boys would walk hand-in-hand to the entrance of the *longtang*, where they would gaze at the darkening sky as they waited for their father to come home. The moment his silhouette appeared against the colors of the dusk, the boys would rush up to greet him. Home he would come, with one boy on his shoulders, the little one in his arms, and the third held by the hand. By that time, Jiang Lili would have already finished dinner alone and settled down to read the newspaper in bed; all the excitement her husband and the kids were enjoying seemed to have nothing to do with her.

Every six months or so Old Zhang's mother would come down from Shandong province to visit; she would help out with the housework and taking care of the children. Whenever her mother-in-law visited, Jiang Lili felt like even more of an outsider. The old lady loved to entertain, and she would fill the house with relatives from her hometown as well as all the neighbors. Jiang Lili, holding her head high, would walk around the house as if no one else was there. Amid the crowd of relatives and guests, her three boys might as well have been strangers.

But the moment Jiang Lili laid eyes on Wang Qiyao's little girl in that little yellow wool jumpsuit and saw the soft tuft of hair peaking out from beneath her bonnet, she was charmed. She held out a finger to stroke the baby's fat chin, and the tiny face lit up like a blossoming flower. Babies always have that innate ability to awaken the pure and gentle side in people. Life was a confused mess, and amid this chaos Jiang Lili felt like a hopeless knot, impossible to unravel. It was not exhaustion that was wearing her down, but frustration. By contrast, a baby's world is simple, and they open up a window into that world when they smile at us. Whenever she was around that baby, Jiang Lili's heart was set at ease, at least momentarily. But when her face betrayed some of the frustration and anger she always kept bottled up inside, the baby would inevitably grow frightened and sometimes might even cry. Jiang Lili would try to sooth her, but the harder she tried, the more violently the child would wail. Helpless, she would eventually give up in despair.

Wang Qiyao always waited until Jiang Lili was at the end of her rope before intervening. Once Wang Qiyao took over, the child would quiet down in an instant.

"Didn't you learn anything after giving birth to those three boys of yours?" Wang Qiyao teased.

"I may have given birth to them, but this is the first time I've actually held a baby in my arms."

Wang Qiyao's heart went out to her. "Here, take her as your daughter!"

But as soon as the words were out of her mouth, she started to worry that she might have offended Jiang Lili, so she quickly added, "I'm just afraid that she hasn't the good fortune to be raised by someone who would be as good to her as you."

But Jiang Lili wasn't in the least bit offended. "Actually, if we were Christian I could be her godmother. . . ."

"And Mr. Cheng could be her godfather . . ." Wang Qiyao blurted out.

The blood rushed to Jiang Lili's face. Wang Qiyao thought she had offended her at last, but to her surprise the redness gradually faded from Jiang Lili's face and she suddenly smiled. Then, in a tone that was both sardonic and somewhat melancholy, she asked, "And what if Mr. Cheng really wants to be this baby's father?"

Now it was Wang Qiyao's turn to blush. It took quite a while before she said, "She'd *really* be fortunate if that were the case!"

Together they gazed at the baby in silence. Having just been fed, the child blinked her eyes with a look of contentment; her serene gaze had the power to make so many uncomfortable situations feel completely natural.

One warm, sunny spring day Jiang Lili managed to drag Mr. Cheng over to take a picture of them with the baby. They all felt as if they had gone back in time; the presence of the child was the only thing that spoilt the illusion. They took the baby for a stroll in the park; all three were in high spirits and kept commenting on how beautiful the scenery was. Under the brilliant sun, the trees, flowers, and grass seemed too weak to withstand such praises, expressing an air of helpless struggle despite the care that had been bestowed on them. Only the sight of children waddling on the grass was enough to rally the spirit, their tender footsteps making up for the dry withering grass. An array of toys spread out on the grass got the children excited. Wang Qiyao put her daughter down on the grass; under the watchful eyes of the three adults, she stumbled and picked herself up.

Kang Mingxun and Wang Qiyao continued to see each other intermittently. Now that the problem of the child was resolved, there didn't seem to be any reason they should stay away from each other. However, the passion they had was nothing in comparison to what it used to be. Sitting side by side, they no longer set each other aquiver, and even when they slept together it was more out of habit than anything else, a matter of routine. They were like a pair of old buddies who knew everything about the other, but at the end of the day they had their own separate lives. So, when she heard that Kang Mingxun was seeing other women, Wang Qiyao did not feel terribly hurt; she only teased him a bit. Seeing that she didn't seem to mind, he didn't feel it necessary to break things off. In fact, he took his time dating all kinds of different women, thoroughly enjoying his freedom. Although he was always going out, he never found a steady girlfriend and in the end wound up dating less. Finally his relationship with Wang Qiyao began to feel almost stable; it lacked the passion they had once shared, but now they could even be said to be a steady couple.

If it were not for the child, Kang Mingxun would probably have come more frequently, but she made him uncomfortable. She raised too many disturbing memories. Once she started talking, she would call him "Uncle Maomao," which startled him. In her gaze he detected a desire to exact something out of him, and this filled him with panic and a certain disgust. Wang Qiyao sensed all of this and, to avoid those awkward encounters, would send the child outside to play or to one of the neighbors whenever Kang Mingxun came to visit.

Jiang Lili's visits also made Kang Mingxun uncomfortable. The first time he saw her she was wearing a blue khaki uniform and a pair of shabby pigskin shoes—like those worn by high school students—under a pair of baggy pants. He would have sworn that she had come from the police department to check their residence permits. He was even more surprised when she opened her mouth—half the words that tumbled out were political phrases lifted straight from the newspaper. He had heard Wang Qiyao mention Jiang Lili and knew about her family background, but the woman before him did not conform to the description at all; he couldn't figure out which side of her was real and which was merely a show. The way she looked at him was also intimidating. Since she usually came by in the evenings and on Sundays, he tried to avoid her by staying away at those times. This also resulted in his having less time with Wang Qiyao. Nevertheless, the infrequency of his visits did not really affect their relationship, which, like themselves, had simply settled.

And so time gradually slipped by. Had it not been for their daughter, who was growing up, they would never even have noticed the years slipping by. In addition to giving injections, Wang Qiyao now took on occasional side jobs knitting sweaters for the neighborhood factory. Only once did she tap into the gold bars that were still stowed away in her chest drawer, and that was when her daughter had the measles. She had asked Kang Mingxun to exchange one gold bar for cash, but by the time the money arrived, she found she no longer needed it, due to an unexpected order for sweaters. Working day and night to finish the order on time and pay for her daughter's medicine and treatment, she nearly collapsed, but the idea that she had left the money from the gold bar intact was an added source of comfort. Ever since she had realized that her chances for marriage were bleak, those gold bars were the only thing that gave her a true sense of security.

Deep in the night she would often think of Director Li, but, try as she might, she could no longer picture him. Parts of his face—his eyes and his nose—remained distinct in her mind, but she simply could not put the pieces together. It was as if her mental image of him had been shattered along with his body in that plane crash. The nights she had shared with him had also grown hazy—even her first time, when she had suffered such pain, was obscured by the repetitive lovemaking that came later. When she thought about the last time she saw Director Li and how they had said good-bye, it felt like a nightmare, now long buried beneath the reality that had taken its place. Her later experiences were like layers upon layers of bricks that had been built up over the years, forming a wall that sealed her off from the past. She knew the past was still there but no longer felt it. The only thing left that she could see, that she could touch, was the mahogany box with its Spanish-style floral carvings. That was the only thing that set her mind at ease. Wang Qiyao couldn't help but think back in sadness that her relationship with Director Li was probably the closest thing to a real marriage she would ever know. It had not been a formal marriage, nor was it an "eternal love," but at least emotion had been answered with real emotion.

Time ticked by in slow and meticulous detail. Living under the rooftops of Shanghai, one needed to be careful and attentive. It was as if one might not survive unless one concentrated one's whole soul on the most concrete and down-to-earth details. One couldn't get by simply looking at the big picture—it was the details that mattered. Beneath the meticulous care was a stubborn tenacity: not the kind of tenacity that impels one to brave a storm, but the kind that enables one to get through the long Jiangnan rainy season. Outside the drizzle went on interminably while inside all was damp as mold silently crept along the floor and walls. The small flame used alternately to heat pots of soup or a small caldron of medicinal broth was dry and warm, the only thing holding out against the dampness of the room. But even the flame held fast to the principle of frugality: there were limits to heat and warmth, which need to be used sparingly, broken up and shared out equally among modest people to achieve their modest objectives and live out their modest lives.

The noise of things stirring in the night deep in those winding alleys was the sound of people living out their modest lives. Their steps are smaller than the movement of the second hand on a clock, but with each forward movement they still make a slight squeaking sound; and though they are lighter than a feather, they still leave behind their footprints, which are always moving steadily forward. The sounds of their songs and tears are barely audible, because they keep their emotions pent up inside. It is only when you lift your eyes to the mist enveloping the sky above the *longtang* that you discover their sorrow and their sweetness.

1965 was a good year for the city. Its stability and prosperity provided solid resources and a stage against which people could live out their dreams of having a comfortable life. Currents of happiness and warmth flowed through the city skies, nothing ostentatious, just a simple, healthy urge for enjoyment manifesting itself. With the coming of spring, bright colors once again lit up the street scenes, nurturing a vanity that was entirely wholesome. Although it was concealed, one could still sense the pulsating feeling of being alive flowing through the streets. At night the city lights were far from brilliant, but each one had its place, highlighting the people, places, and things of the city—no light was wasted on spurious glamour. It was as if the entire city had been baptized, regaining an air of normality in the process. That is what the heart of the city was like in 1965, once all the dust had settled.

Mr. Cheng started using his photo studio again and spent his holidays there. When he turned the studio lights back on, his heart felt easy; he was like a wandering son who had finally come home. He began to regain interest in what had always been his specialty—portrait shots. It started when some of the neighborhood beauty salons asked him to take photographs of different hairstyles that they could use as samples to show their customers. His reputation soon spread, and a new wave of beautiful young girls began frequenting his studio. He was forty-three years old—an old man in the eyes of these young models. A grave and conservative man, Mr. Cheng was not one to fall in love easily—such romantic feelings as he had harbored had mostly been thwarted by a woman named Wang Qiyao, and there was not an ounce of romance left in his heart. In his eyes, those beautiful young models might as well have been made of wood or clay; for Mr. Cheng, their sole value was as objects of admiration.

It was hard to say if this was owing to his age and experience or to the living hell Wang Qiyao had put him through—but he found himself even more capable when it came to capturing the true beauty of each model.

Consequently, he was often able to find beauty in the mundane and so produced exceptional results. He was not one to accept assignments lightly, but once he did, he poured all his effort into producing the most exquisite images. Every photo that came out of his studio was a masterpiece. Each night he would sit alone in his darkroom, where the only source of light was the glow of a single red lamp—everything else was swallowed up by the darkness, himself included. The only things that really existed in this world were the stunning images that emerged from the fixer solution; but these were like cicada shells, empty on the inside. He would focus his energy on finding the most balanced relationship between darkness and light in each composition, and as he completed each task he would heave a soft sigh of relief. Ignoring the cup of coffee, now cold, that he had meant to drink, he would switch off the red lamp, feeling his way out of the darkroom into his bedroom. After climbing into bed, he would light a cigar—his latest indulgence, a gift bestowed on him by the prosperity of 1965. The smoke from the cigar worked like a sedative and before long Mr. Cheng would be asleep.

This was the year that things seemed to be getting back on the right track. The unproductive upheavals of the intervening years seemed to have passed, evaporating like a cloud of mist; it was as if the previous years had been a dream. Because of all the buildings, the Shanghai sky was always divided up into narrow slits through which light and rain would seep in. The Shanghai streets were bustling like always. People who did not live there would probably have noticed signs that the city had aged: the layers of ivy climbing the gables to bathe in the sunlight, the flow of the Suzhou River growing more sluggish as the water became choked with accumulated garbage, even the sliver of sky that hovered over the city growing darker as a result of the carbon dioxide being constantly spewed into the air. Every spring the new leaves on the plane trees seemed to be less shiny and healthy than the previous year. However, the city's inhabitants had no way of seeing this, because they too were aging along with their environment. They were surrounded by these things whenever they had their eyes open . . . and whenever they had them closed.

On a few occasions Mr. Cheng completely lost track of time while working in his darkroom. Time seemed to have concealed itself in the stillness of the night, and yet the stillness of the night is when time is most active. It wasn't until he heard the sound of the milk truck making its morning delivery in the back alley that Mr. Cheng snapped out of it and realized that he had spent the whole night working. He did not feel in the least bit exhausted. After developing the last photograph, he pulled open the heavy drapes covering the window in the darkroom and saw the dawn creeping up over the Huangpu River—this was a scene that had always been dear to him, but it was something he had nearly forgotten. He choked up a bit as he thought about how long it had been since he had laid his eyes on this familiar vista, knowing full well that it had always been there, waiting for him to come back to it. At that moment a flock of pigeons suddenly took to the air from the small crevices on the side of the building on which they were perched. *Is this the same flock of pigeons from years ago? Have they too been waiting for me?* he wondered.

Over time Mr. Cheng lost touch with most of his friends. He even stopped keeping in contact with Wang Qiyao and Jiang Lili. Living in those penthouse apartments of Shanghai were a lot of reclusive men like Mr. Cheng. The details of their daily lives were a mystery—their pasts, an even greater mystery. They always moved about alone. Their apartments were like giant shells: who knows what kind of exotic creatures inhabited them. 1965 was a good year for those individuals who hid in their shells. That was a time when society was relatively free, even though many things were secretly playing out beyond the eyes of man. Only the pigeons that flew overhead knew.

Then came one night when Mr. Cheng couldn't help being irritated by the ringing of the doorbell. He had no photo shoots scheduled; who dared to show up unannounced, he wondered. As he made his way to the door, he thought about how he should turn them away. Though a bit eccentric, Mr. Cheng was a mild-mannered man and quite refined by nature. But he immediately realized upon opening the door that he didn't need to turn anybody away—standing at his door was Wang Qiyao. He never dreamed that Wang Qiyao would show up at his apartment. In fact, he had not thought about her for a long time. He was taken completely off guard, but was also quite pleased and very calm. The storm of emotion that had once consumed him had given way and all that was left were memories of a heart-warming past. He invited Wang Qiyao inside and made her tea. It was only then that he noticed that she was quite worked up about something. She gripped the tea cup tightly in her hand without seeming to realize how hot it was.

"Jiang Lili is dying. . . ." Those were the first words out of her mouth.

Mr. Cheng was taken aback.

". . . she has a malignant tumor," she added hastily.

At that time cancer was not yet common and people did not know much about it. In fact, no one back then even used the word "cancer" instead referring to people who had such conditions as having a "malignant tumor." The thing had a frightening reputation, and although many people had heard of it, no one ever imagined it would strike them or someone close to them. But once it did, it was enough to break one with terror. Jiang Lili had actually been suffering from a liver disease for quite some time, only no one knew it. Because she had always looked pale, was a notoriously picky eater, and had a short temper, no one really noticed when her health started to deteriorate. Even Jiang Lili herself ignored the symptoms at first. Growing up in a well-to-do family, she always enjoyed the best food, which gave her a good constitution and a strong immune system, which over time lessened her sensitivity to illness. She realized that she didn't have much of an appetite, was easily exhausted, and felt some discomfort around her liver, but it was nothing she couldn't tolerate and she just wrote her symptoms off as a minor ailment. Then one day she suddenly found that she could not get out of bed; she was too weak even to lift up a piece of paper, and her husband, Old Zhang, carried her off to the hospital on his back.

The diagnosis was swift. They held her for observation over three days, during which time they kept her on an intravenous glucose drip, before Old Zhang was allowed to carry her back home. As Jiang Lili clung to her husband's back, she could smell the strong scent of Old Zhang's hair oil and a feeling of warmth filled her heart. She pressed her face against her husband's neck and wanted to tell him something, but couldn't find the words. The tenderness she felt was so unusual that she felt it was ominous. All Old Zhang could think of doing was to call in his family from Shandong province so that they could help out. One could not ask for more genuine and generous folks, but for some reason Jiang Lili always felt alienated around them. Filled with sadness and compassion, they would sit outside her bedroom, whispering from time to time. They resembled mourners at a funeral, and the atmosphere in the apartment became stifling. Jiang Lili felt suffocated by this air of bereavement and her tiny bit of tenderness evaporated, as did her will to resist the disease. There she lay, surrounded by a cast of strange faces carrying on in strange rural accents who crept in whenever someone opened the door. Several times she got so annoyed that she broke down and screamed at them, accusing them of trying to hasten her death. Her husband's family received these outbursts with understanding, taking them simply as the ravings of a sick person going through terrible suffering.

Wang Qiyao didn't know that Jiang Lili was sick. Before taking ill, Jiang Lili had been in charge of running a socialist education program in the suburb of Chuansha and came home only four days a month. It had been quite some time since she and Wang Qiyao had seen each other. But then one day Wang Qiyao walked past Jiang Lili's *longtang* and ran into her mother-in-law, who was on her way out to buy noodles. Wang Qiyao went up to greet her; although the old lady couldn't remember ever having met her, she was friendly, and liked being close to people, and moreover had been having such a difficult time with her daughter-in-law, that once she got started talking, there was no stopping her. Wang Qiyao was utterly flabbergasted by the news of Jiang Lili's illness and the color immediately drained from her face. Instead of comforting old Mrs. Zhang, who was in tears, Wang Qiyao headed straight down the *longtang* toward Jiang Lili's apartment.

She walked past the silent crowd outside the bedroom, pushed open the door, and went into see Jiang Lili. The curtains were drawn and Jiang Lili was sitting up in bed leaning against a pillow, reading *Life in a Branch of the Communist Party.* When she saw Wang Qiyao she smiled. That was an expression Wang Qiyao was not accustomed to seeing on Jiang Lili's face, whose brow was usually knit in anger. There was something pitiful about her smile at that moment; it was as if she was looking for forgiveness. The sight was enough to move Wang Qiyao to tears. She sat down on the side of the bed, her heart quivering; it was hard to believe the toll this disease had taken on her friend in so short a time. The truth about her illness had been kept from Jiang Lili, who was told she had hepatitis. Afraid that Wang Qiyao would have reservations about being so close to her, she explained that it was a chronic form of hepatitis and assured her that it was not contagious—that was why she didn't need to be placed in isolation. She inquired after Wang Qiyao's daughter and asked her to bring the little girl to visit sometime, repeating once more that she was not contagious. Wang Qiyao was too grief-stricken to speak; she could see that Jiang Lili was drained by talking, and soon excused herself. Meandering aimlessly down the sunny streets, she bought several things she really did not need and didn't get home until around lunchtime. Not feeling hungry herself, she warmed up some leftovers for her daughter and sat down to knit a winter hat. Her mind gradually settled as she knitted; once she had calmed down, her first thought was to go see Mr. Cheng.

That night Mr. Cheng saw Wang Qiyao all the way downstairs when she left. They strolled along the Bund for a while; inside they were both deeply troubled but they kept their conversation away from what was bothering them. A few aquatic birds were flying low over the river and they heard the faint sound of a ferry's whistle sounding as it made its way to Pudong on the other shore. With their backs to the water, they couldn't help gazing up at the grand fortress-like buildings created by the British during the days of the treaty ports. The overweening style of the architecture could be traced back to the Roman empire; it was designed to look down over everything, impressing viewers with an air of tyrannical power. Fortunately, behind these magnificent buildings was an expanse of narrow streets and alleys that led to the *longtang* houses, whose spirit was democratic. The Huangpu River too stood as a symbol of democracy. The ocean breeze, coming in through the mouth of the Suzhou River, tries to blow inland, but is thwarted by the tall buildings along the Bund, which turn it back, causing it to increase in intensity. It is a good thing that the surface of the river is wide enough for the wind to spread out so that the opposing currents do not collide too violently; the consequence, however, is that the wind constantly rages around the Bund at all hours of the day and night.

"How's your daughter?" Mr. Cheng inquired.

"She's fine," said Wang Qiyao.

But then she suddenly implored: "If something should happen to me one day, I would like you to take care of her."

Mr. Cheng found himself smiling. "Jiang Lili is the one with the incurable disease, so why are *you* seeking a guardian for your child?"

The mere thought of Jiang Lili made their hearts heavy. After a few minutes, Wang Qiyao said, "It's better to make arrangements now rather than later."

"And what if I refuse?" asked Mr. Cheng.

"It's not your place to refuse; I've already chosen you."

There was a solemn despair in her tone that prevented her words from sounding flippant. Mr. Cheng turned to face the river, which glimmered faintly in the dark. He recalled how the three of them, Jiang Lili, Wang Qiyao, and himself, had gone together to the Cathay Theater to see a movie. *How many years ago was that? How could it be possible that we are already approaching the end of the story?* But the end is nothing like what they had imagined. It seemed as if nothing had been truly resolved, and yet everything was resolved.

Wang Qiyao and Mr. Cheng also discussed whether they should try to persuade Jiang Lili to move back to her mother's house, where she could have some peace and quiet and would be able to eat better. They didn't know that the day before their visit, Jiang Lili's mother had visited her and was nearly driven out of the house by her daughter. By that time, Jiang Lili's father was back in Shanghai and had divorced Jiang Lili's mother, who got the house and a share of his assets. He and his mistress from Chongqing were renting a house on Yuyuan Road. Jiang Lili's brother, who had never married and had no friends, still locked himself in his room every day after work listening to music. He was still at home, living like a stranger under the same roof with his mother; they often went for days without even seeing one another. The woman servant was Mrs. Jiang's only company, but she too viewed Mrs. Jiang with contempt; with her own active social life, even she had little time to spend with her mistress.

Their little house came to feel like a huge lonely place. All of the flowers and plants in the garden had withered and died, leaving behind broken branches and rotten leaves. Eventually even those dead plants gave way to garbage and dirt, making the courtyard appear even more desolate. It was a good thing that Mrs. Jiang was not a sensitive person who took special notice of her surroundings, otherwise she would have suffered more. She only wondered why time hung so heavily on her hands. Her immediate reaction when she first heard about Jiang Lili's illness was to shut herself up at home and cry her heart out. For simpleminded women like her, incapable of seeking understanding, crying was an effective way to relieve anxiety. Tears gave her a measure of consolation, and usually elicited a positive response. Once her tears had dried, she would find new hope and feel much better. Wiping her face, she changed into going-out clothes, but as soon as she got to the door she started to feel apprehensive about her outfit. She was afraid that her nice clothes might offend her daughter and son-in-law's good Communist beliefs. She went back inside to change into a plainer outfit before setting out again.

All the way to her daughter's house she was weighed down by heavy thoughts. She disliked visiting her daughter and had been there only a couple of times. During each visit her three grandsons had looked at her as if she was a monster. Her daughter never treated her with respect; she didn't even bother to open the door for her when she arrived or to see her off when she left, and couldn't seem to open her mouth without saying something hurtful. The only one who had some manners was her son-in-law, a genial man, but *him* she regarded with disdain. She had difficulty understanding his Shandong accent and could not abide the smell of onion and garlic always on his breath. She treated him with indifference; he, for his part, not being in the habit of ingratiating himself, had simply put up with her giving him the cold shoulder.

Mrs. Jiang saw her daughter's illness as the perfect opportunity to assert her own rights. Strutting into the apartment with an authoritative mien, she went straight into Jiang Lili's bedroom, completely ignoring the rustic crowd outside. Within less than five minutes, she had already listed more than a dozen things that she thought were wrong about the household and voiced an equal number of suggestions. Her criticisms negated virtually everything as it presently was, and even she knew that her suggestions were impossible to carry out. Initially, Jiang Lili tried her best to put up with her, but her mother kept on pushing. Taking her daughter's silence as acquiescence, Mrs. Jiang became even more animated; she flailed her arms about, declaring that she was going to change the bedding and give her daughter a proper bath. She looked as if she was getting ready to revamp their entire living situation. Jiang Lili had no patience to argue with her: she simply flung the bedside lamp across the room. Emboldened by the commotion, Jiang Lili's Shandong mother-in-law rushed inside to find the room in total chaos. The glass thermos had been shattered, the medicine spilled all over the floor; Mrs. Jiang, her face ghostly pale, was still trying to reason with the patient as if she were a normal person, but Jiang Lili kept throwing everything within her reach, including her blanket and pillows. The mother-in-law grabbed the blanket and, throwing it around Jiang Lili, tried to restrain her that way, while Jiang Lili struggled in her arms like a threshing flail. She had no recourse but to urge Mrs. Zhang to go home and come back after Jiang Lili had calmed down. Jiang Lili collapsed the moment her mother was out the door. After that incident, her mother-in-law made a point of clearing all visitors with Jiang Lili before letting them in.

When Mr. Cheng and Wang Qiyao went to see Jiang Lili, they were turned away at the door. Mrs. Zhang came outside to explain that Jiang Lili was not receiving visitors because she was weak and needed her sleep. The old lady felt so badly about turning them away that she could barely bring herself to look them in the eyes, as if this was somehow her fault. Although neither of them dared say so out loud, each had an idea about why Jiang Lili refused to see them, and both were vexed. Jiang Lili's decision not to let them in was a form of reproach—an eternal condemnation from which they would never be free. Neither dared to look into the old lady's eyes—they even avoided one another's eyes as they parted hastily and went back to their respective apartments.

On two separate occasions after that Mr. Cheng and Wang Qiyao paid visits individually to Jiang Lili's house. Mr. Cheng was rebuffed a second time. After leaving in disappointment, he walked east on Huaihai Road until he came upon a bustling wineshop, with common laborers sitting around square softwood tables. Outside the entrance was a pot of "stinky tofu" simmering in a pot of boiling oil. Unable to resist the aroma of food and wine, he took a seat at one of the tables and ordered a small bottle of rice wine and a plate of shredded tripe. The others sitting at his table were strangers, and each ordered basically the same thing—one or two dishes and a bottle of wine. As they ate, the conversation of the party at the next table grew louder and louder. Once the rice wine had got into his system, Mr. Cheng felt warm and his eyes began to sting; before he knew it, tears were trickling down his face. No one around him seemed to notice. The smoke from the steaming wok enveloped everyone at the table in a hot, oily mist; no one could see clearly, and Mr. Cheng was free to wallow in his misery.

At this very moment, Wang Qiyao was sitting on the side of Jiang Lili's bed. Wang Qiyao had arrived at the mouth of the *longtang* leading to Jiang Lili's just as Mr. Cheng left it, and Jiang Lili had asked her in.

Wang Qiyao's first impression when she entered the bedroom and saw Jiang Lili was how much better she looked compared to the last time. Jiang Lili's hair had been carefully combed back behind her ears, she was wearing a freshly laundered white shirt, her cheeks were a rosy red, and she was sitting up in bed, propped up on a pile of pillows. Instead of greeting Wang Qiyao, she turned her back to her. Wang Qiyao sat down on the edge of the bed, wondering what to say; Jiang Lili's profile showed clearly that she was crying. The curtains were half-drawn and the westering sunlight crept in, gilding her hair, clothes, and the blankets, giving the room a melancholic air. After a long interval, Jiang Lili suddenly laughed, "Don't you think the three of us are ridiculous?"

Wang Qiyao, at a loss for words, gave a little laugh in response.

Hearing this, Jiang Lili turned around and gazed at her. "He was here earlier, but I wouldn't let him in."

"He really feels badly," explained Wang Qiyao.

Jiang Lili's face tightened. She exclaimed indignantly, "What the hell do I care if he feels bad?"

Wang Qiyao did not dare to respond. It suddenly dawned on her that Jiang Lili's rosy cheeks, which were by now bright red, were the sign of fever. She extended her hand to feel her friend's forehand. Jiang Lili pushed it away violently, but from the touch of her hand Wang Qiyao knew that she was burning up. Sitting up in bed, Jiang Lili leaned over and pulled a loose-leaf binder from the drawer of the desk next to the bed and flung it at Wang Qiyao. Inside were lines of handwritten poetry. Wang Qiyao recognized the poems as Jiang Lili's and was immediately taken back to their high school days. Those pages could have been burned to ash and she would have still recognized the flowery language—it had Jiang Lili's name written all over it. But as maudlin as they were, the words still exuded a touching sincerity. There is something about such sentimental poems that always awakens nausea in the reader—a combination of sincerity and exaggeration that leaves the reader at a loss as to whether he should laugh or cry. Wang Qiyao had never been able to stand this kind of poetry, and that was why she didn't want to be close to Jiang Lili. However, staring at those poems that moment, she was overcome by tears. She realized that even if this had been a show, the way Jiang Lili had invested her entire life into it had made it all real. Behind every line of poetry, whether good or bad, she could see the shadow of Mr. Cheng. Jiang Lili snatched the folder from Wang Qiyao's hands and, quickly flipping through the pages, read aloud the most absurd sections, often bursting into laughter before she could finish each line. Her mother-in-law peeked through the crack in the door to see what all the commotion was about. Jiang Lili laughed so hard that she could no longer sit straight and doubled over on the blankets.

"What do you make of this one?" Jiang Lili's eyes glimmered with sharp brightness and her voice took on a shrill new tone. Wang Qiyao couldn't help feeling apprehensive; she went to take the binder from Jiang Lili's hands so that she wouldn't be able to read any more. But Jiang Lili resisted, and in the course of their struggle she even scratched the back of Wang Qiyao's hand, drawing blood. But even then neither would give up; Wang Qiyao insisted on taking the binder away from her and even pushed her back down on the bed. As she struggled, Jiang Lili's laughter eventually dissolved into tears, which flowed copiously down her cheeks from behind her glasses.

"You're just the same as him! You both want to hurt me! You both say you want to see how I'm doing, but all you do is provoke me!"

Stung by the injustice of her remarks, Wang Qiyao momentarily forgot that she was talking to a dying woman.

"Well, you can rest easy because *I* will never marry him!" Wang Qiyao shouted in agitation.

Jiang Lili too became agitated. "Go ahead and marry him. Why should I care? What sort of person do you take me for, anyway?"

"Jiang Lili . . ." Wang Qiyao spoke through her tears. "It's not worth it. Don't throw your life away for a man. How could you be so foolish?"

Jiang Lili's tears were coming down in a steady stream. "Well, let me tell you, Wang Qiyao. . . . It's the two of you who have ruined my life, totally ruined it!"

Wang Qiyao couldn't suppress the desire to console her; she reached out to hug her.

"Jiang Lili, do you think I don't know? Do you think he doesn't know?"

At first Jiang Lili tried to push her away, but Wang Qiyao pulled her back into her arms and held her tight. They embraced and both were crying so hard that they could barely breathe.

"Wang Qiyao, I have had such wretched luck . . . such wretched luck!" Jiang Lili sobbed.

"If your luck is wretched, then how about me?"

All their pent-up bitterness surged up from deep inside them. But, alas, all of that was water under the bridge, and there was no way anything could be undone.

Neither knew how long they sat crying and hugging like that; their bodies ached from so much crying. Eventually, it was the smell of Jiang Lili's breath—a sweet fishiness that carried the stench of rot—that reminded Wang Qiyao that her friend was dying. Swallowing her grief and holding back her tears, she let go of Jiang Lili and gently laid her back down in bed before going to get a hot towel to wipe her face. Jiang Lili continued to cry; there seemed to be no end to her river of tears. By then it was starting to get dark outside. At the wineshop, Mr. Cheng had drunk himself into a stupor and was slumped over on the table, unable to get up. He heard the sound of the ferry in the distance and, in his drunken daze, thought he had boarded and was gradually pulling away from the shore. He could almost see the vast ocean, boundless, as it spread out around him.

The exultations and lamentations of 1965 were all like this, grand in an insignificant way. Tempests in a teacup, they yet had a beginning and an end, and were enough to take up a whole lifetime. The noises they made were petty and weak; even exerting their greatest effort, they were unable to make the sound carry. Only when holding one's breath could one hear the faint buzzing and droning, but each sound was enough to last a lifetime. Gaining strength in numbers, they converge into a large mass hovering over the city sky. They form what is known as a "silent sound," which sings its melody above the raucous noises of the city. One calls it a "silent sound" because it is tremendously dense and enormously large, its size and density equal to if not exceeding its "silence." The same method is found in traditional Chinese landscape paintings, where shading and texture in rocks and mountains are created by using light strokes of ink. And so, this "silent sound" is, in truth, the greatest of all sounds, because it is where sound itself begins.

Just one week after their meeting, Jiang Lili's spleen ruptured and she died of a massive hemorrhage. At the time of her death she was surrounded by Old Zhang, her three sons, and the whole family from Shandong. She had been in a coma before she died and did not leave any last words. At the factory where she used to work, a memorial service was held in which she was remembered for her courage in breaking off relations with her family from the exploiting class and for never giving up her dream of joining the Communist Party. Neither her parents nor her brother attended the memorial service. Apparently they realized that their presence would constitute a stain on Jiang Lili's lifelong ideals. But her family did hold all of the traditional funerary rites, from the "initial seven," performed over the first seven days after her death, to the "double seven." The "double seven" was held every seventh day, ending with the seventh ceremony, which took place on the forty-ninth day after her passing. During each ceremony, the family would sit together, sometimes in silence and sometimes quietly talking, creating an atmosphere of understanding and forgiveness. Jiang Lili, however, was gone forever and fated never to share in the tranquility of their communion.

Mr. Cheng and Wang Qiyao did not attend the memorial service; they actually did not find out about Jiang Lili's death until after it had taken place. By the time they learned of her death, they seemed to have gotten over the terrible grief they had been feeling and were more relieved than anything else: Jiang Lili was now released from her pain. They themselves had nothing worth celebrating, but they were the kind of people who had grown accustomed to making concessions to reality. They knew how to be satisfied with whatever cards life dealt them, unlike Jiang Lili, for whom life was a constant struggle, because she always refused to conform, always stubbornly insisting on doing things her own way, all the way to the bitter end. The two decided, each without letting the other know, to pay special homage to Jiang Lili, but both chose the same day to carry out their memorial, waiting until Tomb-Sweeping Festival of the following year. Mr. Cheng went alone to Longhua Temple and swept the ground in front of the vault where Jiang Lili's ashes were kept. Wang Qiyao waited until the middle of the night when everyone was asleep before she burned a cut-out of spirit paper for her lost friend. Although she did not believe in such superstitious practices—neither did Jiang Lili—it provided a small fraction of comfort in an otherwise helpless situation. What else could she have done?

At the memorial service Jiang Lili's mother-in-law's incessant wailing almost drowned out the eulogies delivered by the factory leaders. Her weeping evoked a chorus of answering tears; the mournful wails of the family from the countryside gave the entire service a feeling of genuine sorrow.

All That Remains Is the Tower Whence It Flew

Mr. Cheng was among of the first batch of people to commit suicide in the summer of 1966. Looking back on the previous year, all the nonstop merriment seemed like a bad omen; when the cup overflows, disaster follows. But the coming storm was something that took most city dwellers completely unaware. Only a few people of the older generation sensed what was to come and had been quietly brewing. Thus one might say that the gaiety of 1965 was only enjoyed by those common city dwellers who did not sense the danger in the air. To them, the catastrophe of the following summer came out of the blue. Strangely enough, the oleander blossoms in the *longtang* that summer were as gorgeous as they had ever been; the gardenias, magnolias, tuberoses, impatiens, and roses were in bloom everywhere, filling the air with their fragrance. Only the pigeons were on edge. They would rise abruptly from the rooftops, tracing circles in the sky before returning briefly to their rooftop perches, only to fly away again in panic. They stayed in flight until their wings were nearly broken and blood almost ran from their eyes; they had witnessed too much. No tragic scene—whether causes or consequences—escaped their eyes.

Longtang alleys of all shapes and sizes ran all over the city, and it was during the summer of 1966 that the red- and black-tiled rooftops riddled with protruding dormer windows and concrete terraces were all pried open suddenly, their secrets laid bare for everyone to see. These secrets, conciliatory or compromising, damp and moldy, reeking of rat piss, were in the process of rotting away, destined to become so much fertilizer to provide nourishment for new lives—because even the most insignificant of lives must pay the price of sacrifice. These secrets, light but copious, could creep between the bricks and through the cracks in the walls, dispersing throughout the city's air. But before anyone could notice the stench of their decay, they would already have transformed themselves, giving rise to new life. Now, when what lay underneath all those rooftops was revealed, the scene was shocking. Dubious tales, unveiled, went on to pollute the city's air. One such tale told of a headstrong girl who, failing to heed the family rules, was locked away for twenty years. By the time she was released, she could no longer walk, her hair had grown gray, and her eyes could no longer withstand the sunlight. Who could have imagined that hidden beneath these rooftops lay private prisons, no better than rat holes, where prisoners scurried around in the dark?

This was also the setting in 1966 for the Great Cultural Revolution, which played out in the streets of the *longtang* of Shanghai. The revolution was a force that swept away everything in its path; it had the power to touch people down to their very souls. It penetrated into the hidden hearts of the city. From this point forward there was no place to hide, everything was caught in its grip. Those hidden hearts had largely relied upon the cover of darkness provided by the city in order to survive. Although they existed in secret, unknown to most, they were the greater part of what kept the city alive—its life-force. They were like the submerged portion of an iceberg. The city's brilliant lights that sparkled in the night, and the bustling activities carried out during its day, all had their foundations in these secrets; these secrets were the fuel that fed the flames of the life on the surface, only no one saw them. Well, now that the curtains have been torn open, these hearts are already half dead. Don't just look at the dark, corrupted side of these hearts, for within they are shy, sensitive, and full of humility; they can endure suffering but not being exposed. You could almost call this a sense of dignity.

That summer all of the city's secrets were laid bare, paraded throughout the streets. Due to the size and variety of the population, the secrets accumulated over the previous hundred years in this city exceeded what most cities accrue in a thousand. Just one secret wouldn't have amounted to anything, but, put together, the whole was massive—a huge secret. These were secrets that could not be spoken, they were secrets that could not even be revealed through tears; these secrets were the beginning—and the end—to so many songs of joy and sorrow. Look, if you will, at the shattered glass vessels, the smashed antique porcelain, and the books, phonograph records, high-heeled shoes, and store signs all going up in flames! Look at the mahogany furniture, men and women's clothing, pianos and violins that, virtually overnight, ended up piled high at all the second-hand stores! These are the leftover carcasses of those secrets, the fossilized remains of people's private lives. You could also see the torn photographs scattered about the garbage cans; the torn faces in the ripped pictures looked like ghosts of the wrongly accused. In the end, actual corpses did appear, strewn along the crowded city streets.

Once all the secrets were exposed, the sediments that had been dug up along with them floated through the air, and gossip proliferated. The stories of illicit passions that we heard were only half true. And although we only half believe them, that does not stop us from perpetuating them. The alleys, lanes, streets, and roads of the city were all enveloped in a living hell. The gossip that was released had been chewed over by the toughest of tongues, which twisted and warped the words until they were unrecognizable even to the speakers themselves. You should never wholeheartedly believe the gossip you hear, but neither should you completely discount such rumors; because underneath the sensationalism there is always a grain of truth. That grain of truth is, in fact, quite simple, because it always stems from human nature—it all depends on how you listen to what you hear.

Thousands of monstrous people and events seemed to be born overnight. From the placid waters of yesterday to the terrifying calamities of today, everything was instantly transformed. You need only look at the black-and-white big-character posters displayed beside the road. Then there were the crudely printed colored handbills tossed down from high buildings, which scattered throughout the city. Those alone were enough to leave one completely confused as to what was happening. The city's heart had been warped beyond all recognition; its eyes too had gone askew, so that no matter what it looked at, nothing was what it had once seemed to be.

The roof hanging over Mr. Cheng's world was also torn open. In this new era he was made into a cunning special agent; his camera was his weapon and the women who came calling to have their portraits taken were actually his stable of spies, whom he personally trained to seduce victims and extract their secrets. That summer practically any plot was plausible. The floor of his apartment was ripped out and the walls smashed, but the mystery surrounding him only deepened. He was interrogated for several days and nights, but they couldn't get anything out of him. In the end they locked him up in the toilet of an institution for an entire month. During that month, Mr. Cheng was reduced to a zombie. All he did was eat, sleep, and write confessions, all in accordance with the whim of his captors. His mind became a blank. All night long he had to put up with the dripping sound of the leaking toilet, which was like an hourglass counting off the time.

One night, after being locked up for a month, Mr. Cheng was suddenly released at two o'clock in the morning. As the public buses had stopped running at that hour, he had to walk all the way home. The streets were deserted, as was the Bund alongside the river. When he arrived at his building, he found it deathly silent. The elevator was locked on the ground floor and a lamp hanging from the domed ceiling projected ashen light down onto the lobby floor. As he climbed the stairs that wound around the elevator, the echo of his footsteps rang out under the dome. Through the windows, he could hear the sound of the water lapping on the shore and see the navigational lights on the pitch-black river. When he reached the top floor and pushed open the door to his apartment, he was surprised to find it quite bright inside. All the curtains had been torn down and the moonlight was shining down on the floor. It was so bright that he didn't even remember to turn on the light. Instead, he walked over to stand in the moonlight for a while before sitting down on the floor.

That night the moonlight shone throughout the city into many curtainless windows, where it shifted across the floor. Whether occupied or not, the rooms into which the moonlight shone were always empty—rooms where piles of old items were stacked up in the corners, items all dating from long ago, long forgotten by their owners. The scene was reminiscent of abandoned ruins. The rooms were empty, as were the people who lived there, shells of their former selves—everything had been ransacked and taken away. In truth, the grinding away had begun decades earlier and most of the damage was already done; why should this recent episode matter? That night, the moonlight moved through many empty rooms and into the hearts of those shells of men, its light shining even into the cracks in the floor. Then a wind picked up, initially along the foot of the walls, but eventually it began to gather strength and emit a harsh whistling sound. Occasionally there would be a door or window not properly shut that would slam as the wind whipped through; the loud bang was like applause extolling the power of the wind. Loose pieces of paper and fabric were picked up by the wind and blown across the floor. These were the broken relics of the past, about to be swept into the trash, performing their final dance.

Nights like that were cold and desolate; those were nights devoid of thoughts, devoid of dreams—they were like death itself. When the sun comes up, things are bound to be better; one can then go out to see and hear what is going on. But at that moment there is nothing to see, nothing to hear. The streets are filled with stray cats that have formed packs to wander all over the place. Their eyes resemble human eyes; they are like exiled souls sleepwalking through the night. Sometimes they hide in dark corners, wailing mournfully as they gaze up at those empty rooms. No matter from how high a place they leap down, they always land silently on their feet. And once they step into the darkness, they disappear, leaving behind not a trace or shadow; in truth, they are those unfortunate souls driven out of the empty shells of flesh they once inhabited. Another creature that may very well be an exiled soul is the water rat running through the sewers. Day and night, these rats traverse the sewer lines running beneath the city's alleys, lanes, roads, and streets on their way to the Huangpu River. But they often die before reaching their destination. Even so, the day always comes when their carcasses eventually find their way to the river, where they are flushed away. Rarely sighted, this animal never fails to shock those who actually see it. But on that moonlit night, there is a commotion brewing in the underground sewers, a veritable parade of water rats. On that night, we were the ones to be pitied. No longer were we free to act as we pleased; those hearts that were once free have been exiled to a place far, far away. Fortunately, everyone was asleep, lost in a state of numb ignorance; and by the time they woke up, a boisterous new day lay waiting, with so much for them to see, hear, and do.

Mr. Cheng slept with his eyes open that night. As the moonlight and the wind passed before his eyes, he thought he was caught in a dream of the past. He did not notice his surroundings, nor what had happened to his home. It was the ferry whistle that first woke him up; then the shadow of the dying moon; and, finally, the first rays of the morning sun. He lifted his head and heard a voice speak to him: *If you are going to go, go quickly. It is already late.* Without stopping to consider what this meant, he stood up and climbed over the windowsill. The window was already open, as though it was waiting for him. The wind whipped past his ears. He felt as light as a feather and seemed to swirl around in the air as he fell to the ground. At that hour not even the pigeons had awakened, the first milk truck of the morning had yet to set out on its route, but there was a ship that had left shore, making for the mouth of the Suzhou River.

No one witnessed Mr. Cheng's flight, and his empty shell of a body struck the ground in silence. His time in the air was quite long, more than enough for him to reflect on a few things. The moment he left the window, his mind seemed to come back to him. He thought: *Actually, it was all over a long time ago. . . . It's just that the ending dragged on much too long.* It wasn't until the moment his body hit the ground that he finally heard the sound of the curtain falling.

Have you ever seen a building with one of its walls torn down, leaving all of the rooms inside naked and exposed? The people are gone, and the rooms they once lived in are reduced to nothing but empty boxes. It is difficult to imagine the kinds of scenes that must once have played out in those empty boxes, places that were once the stage for stories of life and death. Those empty boxes appear so small, so crude; it is almost impossible to imagine someone living there for even a day. They look so flimsy—the staircase looks like it was built for a mouse and would collapse under a human footstep. Take a look at the blue sky outside the rear window; there might just as well be no window. The doors, too, appear pointless; they look silly being there. Yet these are precisely the kinds of wooden and brick boxes within which we live our lives, playing out the good days and the bad.

Let us put the wall back in place; otherwise we will hear cries of mourning, mourning the loss of those vanished days. Let us stack those boxes back up the way they were, into tall buildings, and connect them into a *longtang*, in front of which runs a main street and behind which lies a small alley, both of them bustling with people and cars. No matter how many rooms are left empty and abandoned in the city, there will always be more people to fill them. The people in this city are like water that finds its way into every open crevice.

In this city one never has the leisure to mourn what has been lost; everyone is too busy fighting for a spot in line. That would be like cramming a century into a single year and a year into a single day; but, with an approach like that, you could use up someone's entire life and not even fill the slightest gap hidden between the teeth of history. If one is intent on mourning, one can dedicate a lifetime to it. But even if one mourns for an entire century, on the hundred and first year everything will disappear like clouds and mist. One need not have long-term goals to live in this city; but then one must not be too fixated on the present either: to plan for a hundred and one years into the future is just about right. Then one should simply enjoy life in one of those brick or wooden boxes, accepting the good days along with the bad. Although there is a certain resignation to this type of life, what other choice do we have? How else can we find happiness for ourselves? You should know that there lies, in those densely packed boxes, a basic and most sanguine article of faith. And even when all the boxes are empty, that faith shall remain. There was chalk writing scrawled all over the windowsills, the floor, the walls, the outside of the building and in the stairwell. The messages were in the hand of a child and they read, "Down with Wang the Mongrel Dog!"

That is what faith is all about.

Part III

Weiwei

WEIWEI WAS BORN in 1961. By 1976 she was fifteen, the age when most girls blossom. If you suppose, because her mother Wang Qiyao was beautiful, that Weiwei must have been pretty too, you would be gravely mistaken. Weiwei was not particularly attractive; although she did inherit her mother's eyes, they were the kind of eyes that look dull unless lit up by charm and emotion. The period in which Weiwei grew up, however, was incapable of providing the environment for honing those qualities. She couldn't help but be dull; there was even a rather coarse air about her. To be attractive during those years, a girl needed to rely on genuine merit: there was no room for weakness. Weiwei obviously did not qualify as "good-looking." She would often overhear people discussing her, saying how she wasn't as pretty as her mother. Such comments fostered a jealousy in her, especially as she entered puberty. Seeing how young and graceful her mother still appeared, she felt that she was being robbed of her own beauty. Those comments also had an effect on her mother, allowing her to maintain the psychological upper hand. Wang Qiyao could calmly face her maturing daughter without the oppressive feeling that her own time was ticking away. As soon as Weiwei was old enough to fit into Wang Qiyao's outfits, she began fighting with her mother over clothes. Occasionally Wang Qiyao would, with the best intentions, tell her daughter that a certain dress was too old-fashioned for her; but that would only make Weiwei want to wear it even more. She acted as if her mother had only said that as a dirty trick to prevent her from wearing the dress.

With two women in the house and no man to smooth things over, things often got difficult. If, however, you were to think that they might have been ostracized because Weiwei did not have a father, you couldn't be more wrong. Even though people whispered behind their backs, no one ever gave them any trouble; in fact, some people even pitied them and tried to help. As far as trouble went, they had only themselves to blame. Like all women locked in a power struggle, they were always scheming against each other. In 1976 Wang Qiyao was forty-seven years old, but she looked at least ten years younger. This was even more noticeable when she was with her daughter, for she appeared to be the handsomer older sister. But beauty is one thing, youth another. There is nothing one can do to turn back the clock. In the end youth always has the upper hand, for it confers privileges that are absolute and uncontestable—and those were always there for Weiwei to draw upon. And so Wang Qiyao was also jealous of her daughter—Weiwei had something on her mother after all. Mother and daughter had the upper hand at different times, depending on which perspective you viewed the situation from.

Every year, on the hottest day of summer, Wang Qiyao would air out all her clothes. She would open her camphor chest, hang the clothes out on bamboo poles, and spread her assortment of leather shoes on the windowsill. The entire room would be filled with particles of dust swirling in the sunlight. For a time Weiwei looked like she was walking on stilts when she tried on her mother's shoes. Her feet could only fill out the points of the shoes; after taking a few steps, she would fall down. But as the years went by her feet gradually filled out the high-heels. The laddered silk stockings at the bottom of the chest also excited her: putting her hand inside them, she would stretch them out in the sunlight to view the translucent silk, which resembled the wings of a cicada. Her hands grew bigger each year and eventually ripped through the stockings. And then there was the beaded handbag, the broken pearl necklace, the brooch with a missing diamond, and the moth-eaten flannel beret, scattered in the corners of the chest, which together composed a colorful and exotic portrait of another time. In the sunlight the portrait was a bit dull, even depressing—a peeling oil painting whose faded paint had lost its original luster but still held on to some of its splendor.

When Weiwei tried on those old clothes and accessories and looked in the mirror, she saw not a person but a witch! Affecting what she took to be the poses of a bad girl, she giggled until she doubled over. She couldn't imagine what her mother had looked like back then, nor could she fathom the kind of world her mother had lived in. Today's world may have been insipid and boring, but it was superior because it was hers. Occasionally Weiwei would intentionally damage some of the items at the bottom of her mother's chest; she might pinch a few tufts of fur off a collar, or pull out a few strands of silk from the satin *cheongsam*, and wait for her mother to scold her so that she would have an opportunity to talk back. But come sunset, when Wang Qiyao put her things away, she wouldn't always notice; even when she did, her reaction was always rather mild. She would hold the damaged article up to the light and examine it carefully before folding it up again and putting it away.

"Who knows if I'll ever have the chance to wear this thing again . . ." she would say.

This made Weiwei a bit depressed; she felt sorry for her mother and was even slightly remorseful, not out of compassion and kindness, but from the wanton arrogance of youth. The world belonged to her—why should she bother to harass an old lady like her mother? In her eyes anyone even ten years older qualified as "old." Sometimes she referred to someone as an "old lady" or "old man" when they were actually still in their thirties—we won't mention what she must have thought of people in their forties!

But deep down Weiwei had a slight inferiority complex that often led her to overlook her own positive qualities. That's the way young people are: lacking the requisite experience to take advantage of their best traits, too impressionable, and short of self-confidence. The result of all this was that she became reluctant to go out with her mother. Whenever her mother was around, Weiwei couldn't help putting on a look of dissatisfaction, an added detriment to her appearance. As a little girl, she depended upon her mother and had to suppress her sense of frustration. But as the proverbial wings got stronger, her feelings of dependence faded, her frustration intensified, and mother-daughter conflicts escalated.

In 1976 Weiwei, now a high school freshman, continued to be lackadaisical in her studies and so naturally had no political aspirations. She was a typical girl from Huaihai Road for whom window-shopping was a daily routine. What she saw displayed in the shop windows represented a life-style she could reach out and touch, with nothing of the grand illusion about it. It represented a life beyond the bare necessities to which she could aspire; you might call it the aesthetics of living—a spiritual dimension to enhance her material pursuits. Girls like Weiwei are molded by a distinctive aesthetics of living. In Shanghai, nowhere will you find girls with a better fashion sense than those who lived around Huaihai Road. The way they wear their clothing is a concrete manifestation of this aesthetics of living. The special charm they lend to a simple blue blouse simply by the way they wear it could take your breath away.

Back in the era when people were deprived of entertainment and excitement, the slightest thing was enough to light up a young lady's life. These girls were in no way less impressive than people who fought heroically against the currents. Moreover, they spoke less and took action more often. They devoted themselves to promoting a life based on passion and a "tell-it-like-it-is" philosophy. If you were to walk down Huaihai Road during the late sixties or early seventies, you would sense, beneath the hypocritical and empty political lives people were leading, a heart that was beating vigorously. Of course you would have to look closely to see it. You could find it in the slight curls at the tips of otherwise straight hair, in shirt collars peeping out from underneath blue uniforms, and in the way scarves were tied with fancy shoestring bows. It was remarkably subtle, and the care people put into those details was moving.

Weiwei's dream for after high school was to work behind the counter selling wool sweaters at a local government department store. To be fair, career choices in that era were limited, and Weiwei was not the ambitious type, nor was she a great thinker. Her plans for the future were based on what she thought others were doing. In this respect she was no match for Wang Qiyao, but naturally this also had to do with the limitations of her time. In short, Weiwei was a typical Huaihai Road girl; she didn't stand out, but neither did she lag behind—she was one of the masses, a face in the crowd.

1976 was a year of epochal change; the impact it had on Weiwei lay all within the realm of the aesthetics of living. The return of classic movies was one area, of high-heeled shoes another, and of perms yet another. It was only natural that Wang Qiyao too should get a perm. Maybe the hairdresser's skills were rusty, or maybe she just wasn't used to curly hair after so many decades of seeing only straight hair, but when she reached home, Wang Qiyao was extremely upset. Her new perm looked like a chicken's nest, sloppy and unkempt, and it made her look old. No matter how she combed it, she just couldn't get it right. She scolded herself for having gone and the beauty salon for advertising something they obviously couldn't deliver.

It was right around that time that Weiwei and her classmate went to have the tips of their pigtails and their bangs permed. Their new haircuts were quite sharp and they looked cute. Weiwei came home in high spirits, never expecting that her mother would say she looked like a Suzhou maid from the old days. But her mother's comments didn't bother Weiwei too much. She knew that her mother had been in a bad mood ever since the perm turned out badly. She not only let her mother speak her mind without talking back, but even tried to help Wang Qiyao roll and set her hair. Standing behind her mother in the mirror, Weiwei saw that she now had the upper hand. Wang Qiyao, recalling that the Buddhists had referred to hair as the "strands of vexation," went back to the beauty salon a few days later to have her hair cut especially short, which made her look smashing in a completely new way. Leaving the beauty salon, she noticed the deep blue sky and the glowing red sun, and felt the gentle wind caressing her face. Weiwei took one look at her mother and realized that by comparison she really did look like a Suzhou maid. She couldn't help but feel cranky. This time it was Wang Qiyao's turn to help fix *her* hair. But deep down Weiwei held on to her belief that all her mother's words of advice were just ploys to make her look bad. She went against everything that Wang Qiyao said. Eventually Wang Qiyao lost her temper and walked off, leaving Weiwei to gaze at herself in the mirror alone; before long she began to cry. After a scene like that, at least three days of mutual avoidance would pass before mother and daughter spoke to each other again.

The following year the clothing industry began to prosper and numerous new designs began to crop up on the streets. Old timers could see the root of these new designs in old pre-liberation outfits. Wang Qiyao mourned the clothes in her chest that she had sold or allowed to deteriorate because she thought she could never wear them again. Weiwei listened patiently as her mother went on and on, describing the style and material of each item and where she had first worn it. She thought back to all those times when her mother hung those outfits out to sun, and realized that her mother's good days were in the past, while her own were reaching out to her. She rushed forward to answer the call of the new world. She and her classmates nearly wore out the doormats of all the clothing stores and tailor shops in Shanghai. They spent more time talking about fashion than they did on studying. They watched foreign films over and over again as if they were fashion albums. Coming from a world where consumers had no choices, they were overwhelmed by the rich, colorful world they were entering.

A small minority instinctively found their direction and strutted out onto the front lines of fashion, and so took on the role of leaders. But average girls like Weiwei couldn't avoid a few wrong turns and had to pay their dues. Had Weiwei been willing to listen to her mother's advice, she would have probably been able to get on the right track a bit quicker. But she was determined always to be different from her mother. When her mother said "east," she would say "west." She worked hard at keeping up with the trends but invariably failed. Every so often she would come sulking to Wang Qiyao for more money to have new outfits made. When the finished products turned out to be different from what she had hoped, she would go sulking again to her mother. As she watched with resentment how her mother, simply by combining different items from the chest, easily took her place at the head of the crowd, Weiwei paid dearly in money and feeling, struggling every step of the way.

But hard work will eventually pay off, and just a year later Weiwei began to get the gist of this fashion thing. You needed only look at her to know what the hottest fashion on the street was. And once she caught up, Weiwei lightened up quite a bit. She developed the power to differentiate between the false starts and the genuine trends that she needed to keep up with in order not to fall behind. Looking back on the year before, she was relieved to have emerged from that state of confusion. One should not look down on this eagerness to be trendy—it belongs to the heart that is common to all. Day after day, night after night, it is this desire that holds up and sustain this city's prosperity. This common heart, being pure and clear, is best able to take stock of the changing times. Like the evergreen, it is eternal.

After her high school graduation Weiwei didn't go on to sell wool sweaters, but rather enrolled in an institute of hygiene; it was situated in the suburbs of Shanghai, so she came home only once a week. There were many more girls than boys at the institute, and when a bunch of girls get together, competition becomes inevitable. Everyone was vying to buy nicer shoes and clothing. Every Saturday, when she came home, Weiwei would hit the streets to catch up on the latest styles, as if making up for her time away from Huaihai Road. Wang Qiyao had long since retired the sign advertising inoculation shots and only took on some light knitting jobs at the factory. There used to be a shortage of people to handle this kind of work, but once the educated youths came back from the countryside at the end of the Cultural Revolution there wasn't enough work to go around. Of course, that meant less money.

To cover Weiwei's clothing expenses and occasionally buy something new for herself, Wang Qiyao had had to dip into Director Li's legacy. She would wait until Weiwei was not around before taking one of the gold bars down to the Bank of China on the Bund and exchange it for cash. She sighed to herself, *Even when I was starving I never touched that money. How ironic that I should turn to it now that we don't have to worry about bare necessities anymore.* She was aware that once she cashed in the first gold bar, it would be hard to stop; like losing your teeth, once one has dropped out, you know the rest will follow. This left her with a feeling of emptiness. But all the stores on the street were reaching out to her; even if she could make it through today, would she be able to resist tomorrow? The world in Wang Qiyao's eyes was not the new world that Weiwei saw but an old one in which there was a chance for her to relive her dreams. So much gaiety that she thought was lost had suddenly returned! Her happiness exceeded that of Weiwei because she knew better than Weiwei the price and meaning of that happiness.

Wang Qiyao had always kept the story of the gold bars from Weiwei. Just think of all the clothes Weiwei would have demanded if she had known her mother's secret! So whenever Weiwei asked for money, Wang Qiyao would remain tightfisted. At those moments Weiwei would think of her father—how many more outfits she would be able to get if she had had a father's income to help support her. Otherwise she never really felt she needed a father. Ever since she was little, Wang Qiyao had told Weiwei that her father was dead. That's what she told others as well. By the time Weiwei was old enough to ask questions, there were virtually no male visitors frequenting their home; female visitors were scarce as well, with the exception of Madame Yan from down the street at 74 Peace Lane. There was Grandma too, but they visited her no more than once a year.

All this meant that Weiwei's life was quite simple. She looked mature for her age, but inwardly she was still a child. She didn't understand anything besides fashion. But you can't blame her, because there was no one there to teach her those other things. In this she stood out as an exception to the other girls on Huaihai Road, who tended to be quite ambitious. Most families living in the central district of Huaihai Road belong to the middle of the economic spectrum. Exposed to the greatest opulence Shanghai had to offer, it was only natural for the girls to feel the sting of inequality, and they were prepared to do whatever it took to get what they felt entitled to. Heading west, the shops thinned out; here the quiet streets were lined with luxury apartments and Western-style houses—another world altogether. This is where the true masters of Huaihai Road lived, and that was where all those young girls from central Huaihai Road dreamed they would one day live. Weiwei never figured this out. She had a one-track mind—to hit her mother up for more money. Occasionally, when Wang Qiyao complained about how tough things were, Weiwei would cry about her family circumstances. But before long all of that would be forgotten and she'd be back for more money. Whenever her begging paid off, she was so ecstatic that she never even thought to ask where the money came from. As long as Wang Qiyao didn't volunteer the information, Weiwei would never know about the gold bars.

Now when the time came to sun their clothes, Weiwei would have her own pile—from the wool cape draped over her when she was still being breastfed to the trendy bell-bottom pants she had worn the previous year—these were like the cast-off shells of a molting cicada. For Shanghai women old clothes are the shells they shed during their metamorphoses. Their age is shown through their clothing; but the heart lying beneath the garments sometimes forgets to grow up. Wang Qiyao examined her clothing carefully for signs of mildew. Most of her outfits were still in fairly good shape—she had only stopped wearing them because they had gone out of style. But she knew that before long they would be back in fashion again. That is the law of fashion, which is based on the principle of cycles. Over decades of experience, she had learned that no matter how much fashion changes, some principles remain constant; every outfit has one collar and two sleeves, and no amount of creativity can make it end up with two collars and three sleeves. There are only so many designs, and their rotation is what defines fashion. Only sometimes a cycle drags on too long; Wang Qiyao was more than willing to wait it out, until the arrival of the next cycle, but she was getting older and knew all too well that time waits for no one.

She thought of that pink satin *cheongsam*: how thousands on thousands of hearts had been used up in the making of that dress, and how she had been the very incarnation of beauty when she wore it. For so many years it had languished at the bottom of the chest as she waited for the day to wear it again—that day was fast approaching, but how could she possibly wear it? She was much too old. Just thinking about such matters brought tears to her eyes. Time is hardest on a woman. Days pass, one by one, unnoticed, never to return. How could they have so quickly turned into ten years, twenty years? Airing out the clothes often made her sad; each outfit was a shadow from the past. As her clothes showed holes left by moths, started to fall apart, or became mildewed, she knew that the past was growing more and more distant.

Wang Qiyao let Weiwei try on her pink *cheongsam* once. To recreate her own youth, she even helped her daughter put her hair up. But when Weiwei stood before her wearing her dress, Wang Qiyao felt bewildered. What she saw was not herself, but Weiwei all grown up. Weiwei was much bigger and taller, and the *cheongsam* was tight on her and a bit short. The fabric had begun to yellow and had lost its luster; anyone could tell that it was old just by glancing at it. It just didn't look right on Weiwei, who paced back and forth in front of the mirror, giggling until she doubled over. The old *cheongsam* had not made her into a proper young Shanghai lady. Instead it set off her unrestrained youthful gaiety, which literally was bursting through the seams. Weiwei clowned around in front of the mirror until, having gotten her kicks, she took off the *cheongsam*. Instead of putting it back into the chest, Wang Qiyao simply threw it aside. She caught sight of it several times after that while cleaning, but always pretended not to see it. And gradually, over time, it was forgotten.

Weiwei's Era

From Wang Qiyao's perspective, Weiwei had a warped view of Shanghai. The electric trolleys that were the true heart of the city are now gone. You can no longer hear their clanking sounds against the hum of the city as they rumble down their tracks. The tracks themselves have long been pulled up; more than two decades have passed since the *nanmu* wood slabs paving Nanjing Road were pried out and replaced with cement. Along the Huangpu River, the stone walls on the Georgian buildings have all turned black, their windows masked by a layer of gray dirt. The river water has grown murkier and more polluted, and the sound of the breakwater seems to grow fainter by the year. And let's not even mention the Suzhou River, whose stench you can smell blocks away—scooped up, the water can probably be used directly for fertilizer.

The Shanghai *longtang* have grown gray; there are cracks in the streets and along the walls, the alley lamps have been smashed by mischievous children, the gutters are clogged, and foul water trickles down the streets. Even the leaves of the sweet-scented oleanders are coated with grime. Green bristle grass covers the courtyard walls and creeps out between the bricks in the ground; watermelon seeds scattered about in previous years have sprouted. . . .

But all of this is secondary to the changes that have taken place in the heart of those dwellings. Let's begin with the high-rise apartment buildings. With armies of people rushing up and down the stairs, the edges of the marble steps have all been worn down—decades of footsteps approximate the force of water dripping upon rock. Once saying that even the marble is worn, we need not mention the wooden staircases in the *longtang* houses. In the large buildings the coffers on the vaulted ceilings are usually broken, if not worse; they would have been better off without those Roman-style floral carvings, whose sole purpose seems to be to collect dust and cobwebs. The elevator, with its rusty cable and its mechanism in disrepair, emits loud groans every time it goes up or down. Never touch the stair rail unless you want several decades of accumulated dust on your hands. If you climb up to the roof, you will see that the iron shell of the water tank has gone rusty. The felt covering on the asphalt is tattered and pitted with holes from the battering rain. The wind raging on the rooftop terrace whips up dirt and sand. Who knows the origin of the abandoned items randomly strewn about? Holding on to the railing as you walk past these objects, you look down to see that the bricks and tiles of every balcony and rooftop in the city are damaged. Should you peer into some of the dormer windows, you would see that the wood panels inside have been eaten away by termites.

The Western-style garden homes are the most intriguing of all. Even before entering you can tell how drastically things have changed. There are more clotheslines in the gardens than at a laundry facility. Kitchen stoves are set up in the flowerbeds. Lovely large, semicircular terraces have been cut in half and made over into kitchens. If you should then venture inside, you would find yourself in a labyrinth. If it happens to be nighttime, you will be plunged into darkness, and your ears will be assaulted by the cacophony of woks cooking, water boiling, children crying, and radios playing. Every time you step forward or to the side you run into a wall. The smells of cooking oil seep out from the cracks between the walls. You can't even reach out to feel your way along the walls unless you want to get your hands all greasy. The place is completely transformed. The most luxuriant of yesteryear is today the most cramped, the most exquisite architectural designs no longer bear mentioning.

At least the *longtang* houses are subject to some restraints and so have succeeded in retaining their basic appearance. But once you look inside, you realize everything is different there too. Every hallway and staircase is piled up with junk no one ever uses anymore, but asking people to throw these things away would be like asking them to part with their own flesh. These old knickknacks have taken on a life of their own. They proliferate and sprawl out all over the floor before gradually making their way toward the ceiling. Some get stuck there, while others hang dangerously, threatening to fall down and hit you on the head. One glance and you know how many months and years have passed. The floors are buckling and the planks are ready to give way; the toilet is almost always leaking, unless it is clogged; the electrical wires are exposed in a tangled mess; the door bearings have been stripped off their tracks and resist being moved; the windows, if made of wood, are crooked—either they do not close properly, or, if they do, it's impossible to get them back open. These are all damages inflicted by time. However, the innermost heart of the *longtang* is actually more aged and worn than its appearance. It is only through sheer patience and self-control that it holds itself together, otherwise it would simply explode. It seems to understand that nothing good would come of exploding.

Aside from its being chaotic and timeworn, what troubled Wang Qiyao about this era of Weiwei and her friends was its vulgarity. The streets are suddenly flooded with people spouting profanities and spitting everywhere. On Sunday the deafening noise and the surging crowds inundating the shopping districts are terrifying. You feel afraid that if you made one wrong move, you would be drowned in this ocean of humanity. With bicycles and cars zigzagging every which way, it is frightening to cross the street, each step is a challenge. All the elegance of old Shanghai seems to have been wiped out by a violent storm. Everything has become a challenge—taking a bus, going shopping, getting a shower, having one's hair cut—all involve doing battle with the crowds. The arguments and fights that break out on the streets make the environment even more unsettling. Only a few quiet streets remain in the whole city, but even when you are strolling there under the shade of the trees, quietude seems elusive.

Food served in Western-style restaurants has also deteriorated. The plates and cups are all chipped, stained and crusted with bits of caked-on food, and seem not to have been washed in twenty years. The chef's apron, spattered with grease, likewise looks as if it has not been washed for at least twenty years. The cream was made the day before and the potato salad is already spoiled. At the tables, the old leather seats have been replaced by manmade material, and fresh flowers with plastic ones. Secret recipes for Western-style pastries are disclosed, and suddenly you can buy them everywhere, but none are authentic. Chinese restaurants rely on lard and MSG to season their dishes—the flavor is strong enough to take the hair off your eyebrows. Eateries jack up their prices for giving out hot washcloths, and even more for service with a smile. The vegetable-and-lard fried rice at Ronghua House is either watery or burnt; the soup dumplings at the Qiao Family Restaurant either leak or else are short of stuffing. The varieties of mooncakes sold during Mid-Autumn Festival have expanded many times over, but if you were to break open one of the most standard variety, you would find that no one has even bothered to remove the shells from the beans before making the paste filling.

The shoulders and back on Western-style suits no longer drape properly; neckties are worn all over the streets, but the fabric from which they are made is mediocre and even the facing is third rate. Young girls wear their hair long, and it is disheveled for lack of proper care. The heels of their shoes have been jacked up in defiance of the principles of physics, so nine out of ten heels are crooked and the girls wobble around perilously as if walking on stilts. Nothing could escape the prevailing crudeness and mediocrity in the general rush to produce instant results. Looking back, Wang Qiyao felt that people were much better off during the Cultural Revolution, when they had to wear the same blue cloth jackets rather than these outlandish outfits that did not fit them. At least back then they had the elegance of simplicity.

One could barely stand to look at the street scenes of Shanghai, which, having been suppressed, now erupted in a fiery ball of noise and clamor. They say that everything has returned to its former condition. But what comes back is not what was once there but something else. You can make out only the faintest outline of what it used to be. The neon lights are flashing again, but the night has changed; the old store signs are back up, but the stores are not what they once were; the street names have been changed back, but the pedestrians on those streets bear no resemblance to the people who once walked there.

Even so, Weiwei had a deep fondness for her era. After all, who doesn't like the era in which they live? It is not a matter of choice; even if you don't like it, you'd better learn to, because once it is gone, there is nothing left. Weiwei was not exposed to any radical ideas—her every move was in pace with the times. Virtually everyone in Shanghai was in step with the era, sometimes even driving it on. The tide was overpowering. Who could tell what kinds of crazy things Weiwei would have done if she didn't have Wang Qiyao to pick on from time to time? As she walked along the crowded streets, her heart swelled with joy for having been born during this glorious time. When she saw her own blurry image reflected in the storefront windows, that was the shape of modernity. She was always in a good mood because she was able to project all of her unhappiness onto her mother. If she was upset at home, the moment she stepped out the door she would be all smiles. The streets were hers and she had the right to say anything she wanted. What she hated seeing most were provincial people from outside Shanghai; she always gave them dirty looks. As far as she was concerned, being one of those people must have been the cruelest fate one could endure. So besides the satisfaction she got from being born to her generation, she was also very proud of her city. Her lips bubbled over with all the latest hip expressions; when she spoke like that at home Wang Qiyao could not understand a word of what she said, but the vulgarity disgusted her. Out in the streets Weiwei was always full of spunk. Anyone who might happen to step on her foot was in for a scene—and heaven forbid if that person happened to be from out-of-town. Most people don't dare mess with girls her age—cocky, supercilious, sarcastic, and full of themselves. But if they were to cross paths with a few hooligans looking for trouble, that would be another story. That is why they always traveled in groups of four or five. And if one of them happened to have a boyfriend, their haughtiness would know no bounds—what you would call "fearing nothing and no one."

Weiwei and the other girls of her generation who own the streets of Shanghai have one quality never displayed by previous generations—gluttony. Looking carefully, you will see that, virtually without exception, they are always chewing on something with a look of pleasure etched on their faces. Their lips and teeth are abnormally nimble, adept at separating sunflower seeds from their shells. Their sensitive tongues can discriminate an endless palette of flavors. Their strong stomachs are able to handle a variety of snacks in addition to the usual three meals a day. Actually, girls from past generations were gluttons too, they just had better sense than to show it; but not anymore. This generation's gluttony actually endears them to us—they are almost cute. In the movie theaters those noises of mice nibbling in the night are today's modern girls munching away. They don't pretend to have good manners, for theirs is a bold new attitude. If you can leave your ego aside and put up with their rude behavior, you will be able to make friends with them before long, and then you will have someone with whom to exchange all of your thoughts about modernity.

Another characteristic of these modern girls is their propensity for making a scene. Wherever they go, they like to announce their presence with nonstop chattering, like a nestful of magpies. Most of them have clear, high-pitched voices and take special pleasure in laughing out loud. They don't like to reveal their deepest thoughts at home, saving that for when they are out in the open, and half of what they say ends up being overheard by someone else. Their agile mouths are good not only for eating, but also for talking. Even those gossipy old *amahs* are no match for them, munching away in between their chitchat. One marvels how their tongues can keep up with all that talking and eating. But most of what they say is of little consequence; scarcely a word of all their prattle remains when they are done. But the girls of today have simple, sincere hearts; with the obstinacy of peasants, they set their sights on the road to modernity, and nothing will stop them.

Ballroom-dance parties began to come back into fashion. In the early days of the comeback, the scene at these dances was enough to move anyone. The participants were so shy and yet full of perseverance, their determination to dance waging valiant battle against their fear of making fools of themselves. Sometimes, even after several sets had been played, no one worked up the courage to get up and dance. Everyone sat against the wall in a circle, staring at the empty dance floor with a mixture of solemnity and excitement. As soon as someone started to dance, everyone tittered, giggling to conceal their envy. Back then dance parties were almost exclusively organized by government work units. People who wanted to dance a lot would have to have very good social connections, so as to organize their own parties. They could then bring one of the new cassette players that had just become available to an empty site and hold the dance there. Dancing was the sole purpose of these parties. No one went there with ulterior motives—you could tell by the way they danced. The fashion in the late seventies and early eighties wore its heart on its sleeve.

Weiwei's Girlfriend

Weiwei had several classmates she was quite close to; they were all great shopping companions. Whenever something new appeared on Huaihai Road, they would quickly pass the news on to one another. They would help and encourage each other, never letting anyone fall behind the latest trend. It was only natural that there should nevertheless be some competition between them, and jealousy was inevitable. But this never got in the way of their friendship; in fact, it actually inspired them to keep forging ahead.

Although they seemed to know nothing except how to follow the latest fashion, this is not to say they didn't have any original ideas. After a long period, during which they merely imitated what they saw, they gradually developed a perspective on fashion that was all their own. This was what they discussed when they were together—how else would you explain all they had to talk about? Actually, if you were to transcribe their conversations, you would have the materials for a handbook on how to predict fashion trends. Such a record would also reflect the simple dialectical thought process of these girls. In predicting the next craze, they usually applied the principle of "go against the trend." If, for example, black is what's in, then white will be next; when length is in fashion, short will soon follow; the pattern is to go from one extreme to another. "Extreme" could also be used to describe the spirit of their style. In order to capture the public's attention, fashion needs to wave a flamboyant flag and sport a unique spirit. But this is where contradiction arises—how can one be unique and remain in the mainstream? Their discussions were quite profound; had they kept at it, they might have ended up philosophers.

Out of all of Weiwei's girlfriends, the one she adored the most was her middle school classmate Zhang Yonghong. Zhang Yonghong stood out among Weiwei's friends and can be said to have reached a distinguished place in fashion. Her fashion instincts were simply uncanny: you couldn't deny that she had a born sense of beauty. Zhang Yonghong had the ability to take style as far as it could go; surrounded by a thousand other fashionable young girls, she would still be able to set the trend. She did not go counter to fashion, but took a complementary approach that pushed the current style to its pinnacle. It was a good thing that the streets of Shanghai had a girl like Zhang Yonghong to keep them up-to-date, because most people have a tendency to distort fashion, twisting it until it is almost unrecognizable. Zhang Yonghong couldn't avoid inspiring jealousy. Everyone thought she was stealing the show, but they had to concede that she deserved the limelight. They tried to stay on good terms with her because simply being in her company was a learning experience. Zhang Yonghong was aware of all this, which made her arrogant. She took no thought for anyone but herself, with the exception, that is, of Weiwei, whom she was willing to accommodate. She occasionally even went so far as to fawn on Weiwei, but the way she did it carried a touch of condescension.

Actually, it is all quite simple. Even the proudest people are afraid of loneliness, and everyone needs a companion. Zhang Yonghong had decided on Weiwei. Although her decision wasn't the product of conscious deliberation, gut feelings have their own internal logic. Weiwei's simple heart and nonthreatening nature made her the perfect companion for Zhang Yonghong. Seeing how well Zhang Yonghong treated her, Weiwei was overwhelmed by gratitude. She couldn't have been more ecstatic, because, deep down, she was insecure. She had only one enemy in the world—her mother. Everyone else was her friend and she went out of her way to please them, most of all Zhang Yonghong, who was so exceptional. Whenever she was around Zhang Yonghong, Weiwei felt a bit like the jackal strutting next to the lion. If Zhang Yonghong stood out from the crowd, she did too.

It is difficult to imagine what kind of family a fashion queen like Zhang Yonghong could have come from; that in itself was the most astonishing miracle ever to befall the central district of Huaihai Road. On either side of the bustling Huaihai Road are many narrow streets. Some, such as Sinan Road, were quite nice, covered by a canopy of trees, an island of tranquility amid the chaos. There you would find small buildings whose doors seemed invariably to be closed, as if they were showcases with no tenants. Inside, people lived lives that the common imagination could never have conceived. By comparison, even the splendor and excitement of Huaihai Road appeared a matter of bluster, being the splendor of ordinary people—all show and no substance.

Understanding this, you might be better prepared for what you saw in the smaller streets. The classic street of this type was Chengdu Road, a thoroughfare running north to south, rather than east to west, as did virtually every major road in the city, so that it ran at right angles through many prestigious streets! Even so, it wasn't affected by the flashiness that surrounded it. Chengdu Road was a bastion of everyday living. Life there was stable and solid as a rock. Take one whiff of the smells there and all will become apparent. The odor from the food market was a potent mixture of fish, raw meat, rotting vegetables, and tofu products fermenting on wooden shelves, as well as the smell left behind by the bamboo broom that swept the street. The houses alongside the street were constructed from thin wooden planks and the second-floor windows were so low you could almost reach up to them from the ground. The gutters were corroded, rusted black by the rain. The ground floors were occupied by small shops, which locals called "tobacco shops," selling odds and ends.

Once you left Chengdu Road and ventured into the *longtang* neighborhoods, things got worse. Those alleys were crooked and winding, many still paved with cobblestones, and most of the homes were makeshift shacks. You would never guess that tumbledown shacks like those existed in the heart of the city. By Weiwei's time most of these had been torn down to make way for new concrete structures, which made the area even more chaotic, and the *longtang* alleys even narrower, barely leaving room for the pedestrian to turn around. Who could have guessed that the glamour of Huaihai Road was built on a way of life that had its feet so firmly planted on the ground?

Between Huaihai Road and Changle Road, tucked into the folds of the long and winding Chengdu Road, there was a small door opening onto the street. The door was usually left ajar, but seldom did anyone take notice. That is because not only was the door very small, but it was extremely dark inside. If you happened to stand outside the doorway for a moment, you would immediately be assaulted by a strange odor. The identifiable part of that strange odor was Glauber's salt, but there was another, more mysterious smell—the breath of tuberculosis. The door was like a black hole, there was no rear window, and the front window was blocked by a discolored floral curtain that only allowed a hazy light to penetrate inside. If you were to turn on a light, you would discover that the room couldn't possibly have been any smaller than it was. Piled up all around were old leather shoes and the tools of a tanner. The shoemaker sitting in the middle of the room was Zhang Yonghong's father. Facing the door was a steep, narrow staircase without a railing that went directly up to the second floor. Although we call it the second floor, it was actually an attic; the center of the room was the only place where you could stand erect without bumping your head on the ceiling. Lying in the attic were two sick people—Zhang Yonghong's mother was one, and the other was her older sister. They were both victims of tuberculosis.

If Zhang Yonghong had gone to the hospital to be examined, it is very possible that she would have been diagnosed as well. Her skin was unusually fair, almost transparent, taking on a red glow every afternoon at around two or three o'clock. She was as beautiful as a plum blossom. Since childhood she had never had much to eat and thus learned to suppress her appetite, eventually developing severe anorexia. She ate like a bird; meat and fish made her especially nauseous. To pay for the clothes she wore, she took on all kinds of odd jobs, including taking apart discarded fabric to extract the thread, walking school children to school, and supervising their homework until their parents get home. She was never short of cash, but even so never spent money on buying herself food.

The first time Weiwei brought Zhang Yonghong home with her, Wang Qiyao could immediately tell what was wrong with her. At first she prohibited Weiwei from spending time with her, fearing contagion. But Weiwei was never one to listen to her mother's advice; Wang Qiyao was just wasting her breath. Moreover, Zhang Yonghong looked so gorgeous that tuberculosis only enhanced her elegance, covering up the ugly stamp a life of poverty had left on her. She also touched Wang Qiyao in a way that made her feel sympathetic toward the girl; Zhang Yonghong reminded her of all those old stories about beautiful young maidens fated to live short and difficult lives. Zhang Yonghong's elegant style of dressing also won Wang Qiyao's approval. The same fashions that on Weiwei appeared humdrum took on a new look when Zhang Yonghong tried them on. Eventually Wang Qiyao stopped interfering with their friendship; but she never invited Zhang Yonghong to stay for dinner and, naturally, didn't have to worry about Weiwei eating over at her friend's house.

Wang Qiyao left a deep impression on Zhang Yonghong. When she asked Weiwei what her mother did for a living, Weiwei didn't know what to say. Asked about her mother's age, Weiwei was certain that, like everyone else, Zhang Yonghong would say how she could pass for her older sister. She was surprised to hear Zhang Yonghong remark, "Look at the cotton overall your mother is wearing. It's actually a men's overall with vented sides and the front buttons on the opposite side—that's so hip!"

Weiwei wasn't as offended by her comments as she normally would have been; in fact, she was a bit pleased. She had felt indebted to Zhang Yonghong for her kindness but had always regretted that she had nothing to give in return. Seeing Zhang Yonghong's respect and admiration for her mother made Weiwei feel a bit better. Even though she knew her mother did not want her to bring her friend home, her qualms were outweighed by her eagerness to repay Zhang Yonghong's kindness. And so Weiwei invited her friend over almost every other day. Zhang Yonghong was happy to accept every invitation, never missing out on a chance to get closer to Wang Qiyao. As they learned more about each other, they both secretly wished they had met earlier; for they really saw eye to eye on almost everything—one look and each knew what the other was thinking. As Weiwei sat beside them listening to their conversation, she was often dumbfounded.

"You know, Auntie Wang," Zhang Yonghong said on one occasion, "when it comes to fashion, you're the real thing. We're all fakes compared to you."

"What do I know about fashion?" Wang Qiyao laughed. "All I know is how to recycle the old and try to make it new again."

"That's right!" exclaimed Zhang Yonghong. "Your fashion sense comes from recycling the old."

Wang Qiyao nodded. "Actually, that's what all fashion is—recycling the old and making it new."

"All you guys do is repeat yourselves," laughed Weiwei. "You sound like you are playing a word game!"

Because of her adoration for Zhang Yonghong, Weiwei gained a new respect for her mother. She even eased up a bit and ceased to be so hostile.

Zhang Yonghong's aesthetic sense was untrained. Everything she knew she had picked up on the streets, and the fact that she was able to distinguish herself was proof of her talent. But she was still young and had not experienced many fashion cycles. Gifted as she was, she still had her limitations. She was able to avoid falling behind but could never see past the current trend, and was not capable of developing her own distinctive style. Wang Qiyao opened up a new world for her. It had never dawned on Zhang Yonghong that, prior to her own time, Shanghai fashion had already known a glorious age. Like most young people, she thought history began with her generation, but unlike Weiwei, she wasn't thickheaded and moreover Wang Qiyao had won her over with her discriminating taste—truly she was a living portrait of the fairy-tale resplendence of bygone years.

Zhang Yonghong was exceedingly thankful that Wang Qiyao had come into her life and gladly became a disciple at her feet. Wang Qiyao also felt lucky to have Zhang Yonghong in her life. It had been years since she was able to talk freely to someone, and best of all, on a subject dear to her heart—clothes. Wang Qiyao could recall at will decades of fashion, all of which came back to her without bidding. One might call fashion the product of vanity, but one must never underestimate it, for it carries with it the spirit of the age. Were it able to speak, it would speak volumes. As Wang Qiyao described in detail all the changes that had taken place over the past several decades, images of beauty passed before Zhang Yonghong's eyes, and she was humbled to think of all that she had missed out on. It dawned on her that the fashions of her era were only a continuation of what had gone before. There was so much she had to catch up on.

Weiwei was also present for these discussions, but she heard all this unmoved. She still preferred the fashions of her generation: as far as she was concerned, the things her mother described might as well be costumes in an old opera, preposterous and laughable. She conceded defeat only when, with a shift in fashion, some of the old styles came back before her eyes. She was the kind of person who wouldn't weep until she actually saw the coffin—she didn't use her brain. All that seemed to matter was the present: for Weiwei, neither the past nor future had any meaning.

Shanghai fashion in the early eighties had an air of dogged determination. It strutted boldly forward, keeping one eye on the past and the other on the future. Having undergone an era of distortion and suppression, its mind was now liberated, but it really didn't know where to go! And so it felt its way as it went along. The street scenes at this time were oddly exaggerated and a little out of control, but the painstaking care and hard work behind them were plain to see; and those who understood what had gone into their making were quite moved. Under Wang Qiyao's influence, Zhang Yonghong began to break away from the mainstream. At a casual glance, she looked as if she was falling behind, but closer scrutiny revealed that she was already far ahead, leaving the mainstream in the dust. But girls with real vision like Zhang Yonghong were few and far between; even her good friend Weiwei had a hard time understanding her, and so she began to feel estranged. Her rivals congratulated themselves, supposing her to have stepped out of the race, leaving the stage to them. If anything, they should have felt sad, because they had lost their leader. Without Zhang Yonghong, each new fashion cycle now fizzled out in mediocrity. Fashion is a good thing in its own way, but when the elite abandons it, it inevitably descends into banality. Zhang Yonghong became a solitary figure, with Wang Qiyao her sole confidante. Sometimes, even when Weiwei wasn't home, she would drop by to chat with Wang Qiyao; if Weiwei happened to return in the middle of their conversation, the two of them would glance up at her as if she was an intruder. After graduation, Weiwei went on to nursing school but Zhang Yonghong, having come from a poor family, had to take a job as a meter reader at the gas company. That enabled her to visit Wang Qiyao more frequently; she would stop by almost every day, and in Weiwei's absence the two of them became even closer.

"Why don't you just trade me in for Zhang Yonghong!" Weiwei would occasionally say to her mother.

However, the nature of Wang Qiyao's relationship with Zhang Yonghong was not at all that of mother and daughter; it was a relationship between two women who overcame the barriers of time and experience to form a strong bond.

Of the two, one had a heart that would never grow old and the other was born with an innate understanding; their hearts were both ageless—they were the hearts of true women. No matter how much their bodies might change, their hearts would always be the same, carrying with them an intimate self-understanding and a sense of longing. Don't belittle the fact that they put their hearts into a few articles of clothing. Do you know what clothing is? To them clothing is life itself. You might accuse them of vanity, but if they were not supported by an inner strength, they would not be able to sustain the external beauty. They know their destiny better than anyone else; they know that they will never have a share of the world's larger glory; all they can do is fight for their moment in the limelight, when they adorn the world's larger glory. They don't entertain illusions and extravagant dreams, but that isn't to say that they are not ambitious; you would be hard pressed to find anyone as conscientious and meticulous. When they examine a skirt, they take in every seam and every stitch. They are extremely demanding when it comes to the color and texture of the fabric. Their carefree appearance belies their intense attention to detail; this is what you would call "seamless perfection." When they start thinking about a new outfit, their hearts fill with pleasure and they take swift action. They go down to the fabric shop to pick out material and lining, making sure that the buttons match. The first fitting is the moment of truth, and not even the minutest error escapes their discerning eyes. Upon completion, as they stand before the mirror to survey their new outfit, taking notice of every thread and stitch, they cannot help but feel a spell of melancholy, wondering who they have gone through all this trouble for. It is during those moments of emptiness that they need each other most.

Each in her distinctive outfit, the two of them would stroll down the bustling Huaihai Road, Zhang Yonghong's arm locked in Wang Qiyao's. There was a unshakable aura of desolation in the sight of them walking side-by-side—the desolation that holds sway at dusk and again at dawn, when only a single ray of faint light shows against a world enshrouded in darkness. One of them was reaching her end with no future left to speak of. The other had a future, but there was no guarantee that her future would be any better than the one that was just ending; everything was hazy. If it weren't for the difference in age, they could truly have passed for sisters.

But they never shared the kinds of things close friends talk about; their intimate exchanges all consisted of conversations about clothing and fashion. It was only after one particular incident that their relationship began to change. On that day, Zhang Yonghong had just left Wang Qiyao's and was already at the edge of the *longtang* neighborhood when she suddenly remembered that she owed Wang Qiyao two *yuan* and went back to repay her. Stepping in, she saw that the teacup she had been drinking from had already been put aside, with a piece of paper placed inside it, clearly in imitation of the practice used by restaurants and teahouses of putting a strip of red paper in the cups of customers suffering from infectious diseases to remind employees to take extra care in disinfecting these items. Zhang Yonghong didn't say anything. She repaid Wang Qiyao and left. The following week she did not call on Wang Qiyao. When Weiwei came home from school that Saturday, she asked her mother why Zhang Yonghong wasn't coming over. Wang Qiyao said she didn't know, but privately she had already guessed. Weiwei went to look for Zhang Yonghong, but her sister stuck her head out the window to say that she was working overtime. Weiwei ended up spending that weekend with some of her other girlfriends.

Two days later Zhang Yonghong suddenly reappeared. Without saying a word, she placed a medical report on the table before Wang Qiyao. Written in the sloppy hand of the doctor was the result of her examination, stating that there was no evidence of viral infection or tuberculosis in the lungs. Wang Qiyao turned red from embarrassment and hesitated for a moment before regaining her composure.

"Zhang Yonghong, you have raced ahead of me," Wang Qiyao said. "I've been wanting to take you for an exam for a long time! Now I can finally stop worrying. But even though you do not have tuberculosis, I still think you may have too much internal heat in your lungs. How about I take you to see a herbal doctor in a few days?"

Zhang Yonghong was taken aback at first, but she soon turned away and started to cry.

At her age, Zhang Yonghong's favorite conversation topic was, naturally, boys. She didn't have a boyfriend, and whenever she talked about boys who liked her, it was with an air of ridicule. Wang Qiyao knew that girls like Zhang Yonghong were prone to making the mistake of being too picky. They think that, just because they are pretty, wear nice clothes, and are pursued by a few boys, they can have their pick of anyone they want. They flaunt this attitude, not realizing that most boys are not terribly patient and quickly retreat when things do not look promising. If there is a persistent one among them, he always seems to be the least desirable of the lot. In the end, girls who know themselves not to be a prize catch tend to fare better. Harboring no illusions about their situation, they manage to seize opportunities as they arise. Wang Qiyao felt it her responsibility to share this truth with Zhang Yonghong; deep down she also wanted to put a damper on her arrogance. *Nobody really has endless time to fritter away,* she thought.

But that was not how Zhang Yonghong saw things. She remained unconvinced and thought Wang Qiyao had underestimated her. And so the next time she shared her boy stories with Wang Qiyao, she embellished them a bit, even including several boys who didn't in fact qualify as suitors to boost her story, and in the end wound up believing these lies herself. As she told the stories, they all seemed true to her. This naturally did not escape Wang Qiyao, who worried lest Zhang Yonghong be misled by her own fantasies. Seeing that Zhang Yonghong did not heed her advice, Wang Qiyao would sometimes deliberately refrain from concealing her disbelief. Infuriated, Zhang Yonghong would grow even more intent on proving that she was telling the truth, which only made her lies more transparent. The interesting thing was that when she was not talking about boys, Zhang Yonghong never stretched a single truth, but whenever her favorite topic came up she couldn't help letting a few lies slip in. She was always cordial when they discussed other things, but once the conversation turned to boys, a rift would immediately open up and they would grow testy with each other. Of the two, Wang Qiyao exercised more self-restraint and was much more composed, while Zhang Yonghong was always ready to be at daggers drawn. She was young, after all, and it was only because she couldn't see Wang Qiyao's weak spots that she was so tenacious. And then one day, in order to prove that everything she had been saying was true, she brought over a boyfriend.

Weiwei was home when Zhang Yonghong came over with her boyfriend; when she saw him, Weiwei became spunky and garrulous. Wang Qiyao gritted her teeth, silently cursing Weiwei for not behaving with more dignity. She tried to throw meaningful glances, but Weiwei took no notice and continued chatting up a storm. Zhang Yonghong sat silently off to one side, looking magnanimous. Indeed, the boy wasn't half bad; he had a nice clear complexion and was very well-mannered, and this was enough to vex the mother even more. However, the boy was so likeable and had so many interesting things to say that Wang Qiyao burst out laughing as he went back and forth with Weiwei as if performing a cross-talk comedy routine. As she went into the kitchen to prepare some hot snacks for the kids, her ears ringing with their laughter, Wang Qiyao lightened up. *They are young people after all, what do they know of "yours" and "mine"? They're just having fun,* she told herself. *This is a good thing. Adults shouldn't rain on their parade.*

After they finished the snacks, Wang Qiyao sent them off to the movies and sat alone in the quiet room, watching the spring afternoon sun as it moved across the western wall. She recalled many such afternoons in her life. The light with which she is so familiar has shone for hundreds and thousands of years, and it will always be there. People, on the other hand, can never escape the trap of time. She followed the light, watching it until it disappeared and the room gradually grew dark. There was no sign of Weiwei—*Who knows where she might be having fun. It seems to be an unwritten rule on Sunday evenings that nothing ever gets started on time, a special time when nothing is set in stone.* It was the hour people normally cook dinner and yet it was particularly quiet. Soon the lights would come on, one by one, and night would arrive; and all those people out for a good time would have even less reason to return home.

Wang Qiyao didn't wait up for Weiwei. She woke up in the night to find a light on; Weiwei was getting her things together to go back to school the next morning. *At least she hasn't completely forgotten about school,* thought Wang Qiyao as she closed her eyes. In her half-sleeping state, she could hear the pigeons on the neighbor's balcony cooing in their dreams. Before long the light went out and Weiwei, too, had gone to bed.

The next time Zhang Yonghong came over, Wang Qiyao made a point of complimenting her on her boyfriend, not expecting her to state the disclaimer, "He's not my boyfriend, just a friend who's fun to hang out with."

Having been rudely brushed aside, Wang Qiyao couldn't finish what she had intended to say. After a brief pause, she went on with a smile, "Just don't spend all your time having fun . . . or you might regret it."

"Don't worry," replied Zhang Yonghong. "Having fun is how we are supposed to spend our time."

"And you think you can take all the sweet time your heart desires?" asked Wang Qiyao. "It all flashes by in an instant. No matter how much fun you may be having, there always comes a day when you suddenly have to look back and reflect on what you have done."

"So what? If I have to look back, I'll look back," Zhang Yonghong responded coolly.

Neither was in the best of spirits when they parted. Zhang Yonghong brought her boyfriend over again the following visit—only this time it was a different boy. This one was darker, a bit taller, and not as outgoing. Stiff as a ramrod, he sat in silence as Zhang Yonghong chatted and giggled; he couldn't have been more different from the last one. Wang Qiyao knew that she was "just having fun" and didn't take the trouble to make them any snacks; Zhang Yonghong and her boyfriend left before dinner.

The following day, Zhang Yonghong came by to tell her that this one was a "real boyfriend," although they were still in their trial period. Wang Qiyao took her words with a grain of salt. But the next time Zhang Yonghong brought the same boy along, and the two soon became frequent guests. Although this boy wasn't as agreeable as the first one, he was quite capable. He knew how to fix everything, from faucets and toilets to light switches and the belt on the sewing machine; all problems mechanical and electrical were solved instantly. Moreover, he seemed to be devoted to Zhang Yonghong. Whenever Weiwei was home, the three of them would go out to eat at one of the new Western restaurants, and he would always foot the bill. But then one day Zhang Yonghong suddenly announced that she was breaking up with him. The reason she gave was quite strange; she said that he had athlete's foot . . . and that it had spread between his fingers. After the breakup, the boy came to Wang Qiyao with a mixture of shame and anger and ended up sobbing. He wasn't the only one who felt bad, for even Wang Qiyao felt she had been led along.

"From now on, don't bring your friends around," Wang Qiyao told Zhang Yonghong, "I don't have time for them."

That was indeed the last time Zhang Yonghong brought her boyfriends over. But occasionally she would get up in the middle of a conversation, saying that she had to go because someone was waiting for her. Before she even finished her sentence, one could hear the sound of a bicycle bell ringing outside the window. Unable to hold back her curiosity, Wang Qiyao would rush over to the staircase window and look down as soon as Zhang Yonghong had gone down the stairs. She saw her leaving the *longtang* slowly on the back of a bicycle. Although she couldn't quite make out the boy on the bicycle, she could tell it was someone new. She heard from Weiwei that Zhang Yonghong had gone through several more new boyfriends.

Zhang Yonghong changed boyfriends faster than most people change light bulbs. She had different sources to draw upon when looking for a new boyfriend: people from the same work unit, middle-school classmates, and neighbors who lived on the same street. One was even a customer of the gas company she met when she went out to read his meter. It is hard to say how much she liked them. There was actually only one reason she agreed to go out with any of them—that was because *they* liked her. Having men around who liked her bolstered her up; to that end she felt the more, the merrier. Aside from thus adding to her glory, she had no use for them, and felt she was better off relying on herself. She set herself off from the crowd by her stylish dress and surrounded herself with servile boys only too willing to obey her every wish; jealous gazes followed her everywhere. This was the portrait she had composed for herself; even if it was off by a few strokes, it was still hers. She was unusually good at catching admiring gazes and, with a few deft maneuvers, could turn that admiration into attachment. But this was as far as that would go, and she would move right on to the next one. Her superb ability to chew boys up and spit them out—without any fear of running out of new candidates—rivaled that of any army recruiter. The boys fell into a trap that had a beginning but no end; what they were left with were memories of a transient beauty that could not be erased. Being young and impressionable, most of them went on believing for the rest of their lives that women were complicated and mysterious creatures. And what of Zhang Yonghong? Boyfriends drifted past her like scenes from a revolving sideshow; she was content with a taste of the subject at hand but didn't let herself be drawn too deeply into the joys and sorrows of the experience. Gradually her heart grew numb and could no longer feel any real excitement, as if she had grown a protective shell around herself. So, although on the surface she looked animated, underneath, she was as calm as still water.

Over time Zhang Yonghong came to prefer dragging Weiwei along when she went out on her dates. Weiwei was there to serve as a "light bulb"—the current slang for an unofficial chaperone—but she could also be the audience and turn the date into an exhibition, which was just what Zhang Yonghong wanted. Other girls wouldn't have agreed to serve as the "light bulb" so readily, but Weiwei didn't mind. She enjoyed having a good time and even repeatedly thanked Zhang Yonghong for bringing her along. She was also at the age when she was beginning to notice boys. Boys and girls at her school didn't speak to one another. They put up a front of being reserved while secretly hoping for interactions with the opposite sex. Weiwei could hardly contain her excitement whenever Zhang Yonghong brought her along on her dates, and, often forgetting her role as the "light bulb," would get into the conversation, but Zhang Yonghong never got upset with her; in fact, she seemed pleased. At first the boy thought Weiwei was too pushy and calling too much attention to herself; Zhang Yonghong seemed to be deliberately pushing her toward him, and he felt frustrated that his solicitude was being wasted on the wrong girl. Gradually, however, he came to realize that he was getting nowhere with Zhang Yonghong. Facing the pain of rejection, and prompted by Weiwei's bubbling enthusiasm, he unconsciously began to shift his interest onto her. He was aware that he was settling for second best—but then young people are adept at finding things to be cheerful about. This did, however, lead to a subtle change in the ranking of the girls in his estimation. How could Zhang Yonghong fail to notice? As soon as she became conscious of what was happening, she immediately dumped him. It is always best to be the first to act. That way she could console herself with the thought that Weiwei's boyfriend was one of her rejects.

Weiwei was surprised and delighted whenever she was asked to go out on a date alone with the boy, although she feigned reluctance. That wasn't because she was worried about selling herself short by picking up one of Zhang Yonghong's rejects; this was simply the way a girl was supposed to respond when a boy asked her out, or so she thought. This much she had learned from Zhang Yonghong. She also learned from her about switching boyfriends, but all of her boyfriends came only after Zhang Yonghong culled them out of her herd. Still Weiwei continued to admire Zhang Yonghong deeply, following her every move and observing her dating strategies, and could not wait to put them into practice. But no matter how hard she tried, what she learned from Zhang Yonghong was all very superficial, and she could not change who she was deep down inside. First, unlike Zhang Yonghong, she had trouble resisting the kindness of others; moreover, she herself was naturally inclined to treat people with courtesy and warmth. She didn't have the heart to chew men up and spit them out the way her friend did, and she was never good at putting on airs. Being in the position of the observer, moreover, she was able to judge whom she really liked with detachment. And so, after a succession of dates, she found herself a steady boyfriend. He may not have been a raging bull of passion, but he appeared stable and there seemed to be a future between them. They saw each other once or twice a week, going window shopping or out to the movies. Their good-byes were never drawn out, but neither of them ever blew off a date. It was the kind of love that could preserve its purity all the way up until their wedding night. You say it sounds boring; well, perhaps it was. But that is how countless happy and harmonious marriages begin. By this time Weiwei was already interning at a local city hospital, where she was a surgical nurse.

Weiwei's Boyfriend

Weiwei's boyfriend was named Lin, and he was three years older than she. His father, an engineer at the gas company, wasn't that old, but he had suffered greatly during the Cultural Revolution and had taken early retirement because of his poor health, letting his son, working under him as a repair technician, take his slot. Xiao Lin worked during the day and studied on his own at night. He had applied to college but unfortunately didn't make the cut. He was now preparing to reapply the following year. Because he had failed in his pursuit of both higher education and his first love, Zhang Yonghong, he tended to look gloomy and subdued—a perfect complement to Weiwei. Her lively and uncomplicated nature was without doubt exactly what he needed, while his silence toned down Weiwei's impetuousness, making her more sedate. They were a perfect couple and couldn't have gotten along better.

Girls like Weiwei may not be the most sophisticated thinkers, but they know how to follow that voice inside them. This instinct never deceived her and seldom let her down, leading her to reap unforeseen benefits. Instincts do not work for girls with the intelligence and sensitivity of Zhang Yonghong, yet their intelligence and sensitivity are insufficient to prevent them from making mistakes. The truly wise know how to transform instinct into its own breed of logic; that way they can still follow their inner voice. The way this works is like a double negative coming out as a positive. Maybe Weiwei was better off not having to go around in circles.

The first time Wang Qiyao saw Xiao Lin, she couldn't help thinking: *Now this is what you call, "a fool ends up with a fool's luck!"* Weiwei did not need to tell Wang Qiyao that Xiao Lin had been one of Zhang Yonghong's boyfriends. She didn't think there was anything necessarily wrong with that, and actually felt sorry for Zhang Yonghong, wondering how she could have been so unperceptive as to spurn such suitable husband material.

Xiao Lin lived in an apartment on New Happiness Road, a quiet, shady street, one of the rare places in the city where you could hear the sound of birds, chirping in a nearby garden that had belonged to a tycoon back in Shanghai's glory days. This endowed Xiao Lin with a serenity and clarity of mind lacking in his peers, who were stamped by the agitation and restlessness of the noisy city. It was plain from his face that he came from a good family. Just by looking at the copper street number sign hanging outside their apartment, Wang Qiyao could guess the kind of lives that were living behind that door. Life in such a place should have been solid as a rock, but even a place like that could not withstand the passage of time and was showing a tendency to disintegrate. Some of the pressures came from without, such as the forced accommodation of additional families into the building during the Cultural Revolution. Others were internal, such as dissension between brothers leading to the establishment of separate households. If it had been spared those two kinds of catastrophes, life there probably could have continued for at least one more generation—and it would have been a good life, filled with happy, healthy, and peaceful days without harassment, the kind of life so many people struggle for and never achieve.

On this day Wang Qiyao sent a solemn invitation asking Zhang Yonghong to come over so that she could learn more about Xiao Lin. In reality, this wasn't exactly her intention; she had already heard most of what she wanted to know from Weiwei's own loose lips. What Wang Qiyao really wanted to do was to give notice to Zhang Yonghong that Xiao Lin was now Weiwei's boyfriend. She was wary that Zhang Yonghong might change her mind and interfere with the new relationship. Wang Qiyao understood that Weiwei was no match for Zhang Yonghong, especially given how easily the embers of love could flare up again among young people. Partly too, she wanted to offer Zhang Yonghong a bit of consolation. Zhang Yonghong had sensed the nature of the invitation and, as soon as the subject was broached, she immediately declared her enthusiastic support for the new couple, even taking credit for introducing them. Wang Qiyao couldn't help but marvel at the girl's intelligence and arrogance. But she was still a child after all, and lacked an adult's suavity. Her performance was far too exaggerated and seemed unnatural. Wang Qiyao could see her disappointment and her heart went out to this girl who had no adults looking out for her and had now to contend with an adult adversary. Out of guilt, she changed the subject and asked her if she had found a steady boyfriend. Zhang Yonghong was surprised by the question, but didn't say anything.

"Don't tell me that, out of all those boys," said Wang Qiyao, "none of them suits your fancy?"

Zhang Yonghong remained silent, but her eyes started to turn red. Wang Qiyao's comments seemed to have touched off something inside her.

Wang Qiyao heaved a sigh. "I'll say what I've said before: they may all be clamoring for you today, but in the blink of an eye they'll be running like startled animals. Women have only so much time to settle down. Those who miss the boat are mostly smart, beautiful girls like you."

Zhang Yonghong lowered her head and remained silent for a long time before replying, "Which one of them did you think was good for me?"

Wang Qiyao laughed at her childish mannerisms. "Why does what I think matter? It's what *you* think that is important!"

Zhang Yonghong also laughed. "Please . . ." she implored with a touch of childish beseeching, "I want to hear your opinion."

"Well, I don't have an opinion," responded Wang Qiyao.

"You gave Weiwei your opinion about her boyfriend. How come you can't help me?" Zhang Yonghong pleaded.

Although she didn't mean anything in particular by this question, it made Wang Qiyao uncomfortable. After a brief pause, she replied, "If you want to know the truth, I never told Weiwei half the things I shared with you. You are much sharper than her, but sometimes I'm afraid that you are too smart for your own good."

Zhang Yonghong didn't say anything more. The two of them sat facing each other in silence for a while before Zhang Yonghong took her leave.

In the meantime, Weiwei's boyfriend Xiao Lin was at a critical phase in his preparation for the college entrance exams, which naturally meant that he had less time to spend with her. Wang Qiyao noticed how bored and lonely Weiwei was and couldn't help worrying that all this talk of "preparing for the exam" was merely an excuse. But then again, she realized that her daughter was not in immediate danger of becoming an old maid; even if it didn't work out with Xiao Lin, she would still have plenty of opportunities to find a proper man. But she was still worried. At ten o'clock that night, after Weiwei had already showered and gone to bed, Xiao Lin unexpectedly called out to her from the *longtang* below. Weiwei went down in her nightgown and didn't come back up. Wang Qiyao figured that she wouldn't go far in her nightgown, but went to check up on her under the pretext of going to buy mosquito-repellent incense. At the end of the *longtang* she saw two figures standing at the intersection under the streetlight. There was a bicycle between them and they were talking. Weiwei was, as was her wont, acting silly, bearing her fangs and brandishing her claws to show how tough she was; the sound of her laughter carried deep into the night. Wang Qiyao sneaked back home. As she opened the door and stepped inside she felt calm, but was also struck with a feeling of emptiness. The feeling was set off by the empty room, where the only other presence was her shadow. The mirror on her nightstand was even more unbearable; standing outside the mirror and reflected within it was the same lonely soul. She should not have looked. Just as she was standing there, she heard Weiwei come flapping up the stairs in her slippers.

"Why did Xiao Lin come by so late?" asked Wang Qiyao.

"He got sick of studying and needed a break. He thought seeing me would help him relax."

"Next time invite him up for some watermelon," suggested Wang Qiyao.

"Who cares about watermelon?"

The next time Xiao Lin came over, he called Weiwei outside again for another evening chat under the streetlight. This time, however, Wang Qiyao walked over to them and told Weiwei that she had to pick up a few things at the store. She said she had left the door open and asked if Weiwei and her friend could go back and keep an eye on the place. Weiwei felt she had no choice but to drag Xiao Lin home, grumbling the whole time about how senseless her mother was to have forgotten to lock the door. The two of them went upstairs and talked about all kinds of things, and in the absence of Wang Qiyao they both felt much more at ease. Xiao Lin walked around the apartment; pointing at the walnut chest, he commented, "This is an antique."

He went over to the mirror on the nightstand. "This is too, and it's still in good shape."

"Since when do mirrors go out of shape?" Weiwei replied.

Xiao Lin laughed but didn't argue with her. Examining a pearly bed curtain he concluded that this too was an antique.

"So, to you," Weiwei retorted, "our house is a second-hand store?"

Xiao Lin knew she had misunderstood him, but didn't try to explain. It was at that moment that Wang Qiyao came upstairs carrying several blocks of ice cream; she went into the kitchen for plates and spoons to serve them. The two young people were a bit edgy after their last exchange and neither spoke. Wang Qiyao asked Xiao Lin a series of questions, such as how his preparation for the exam was going and where the exam was to be held. Weiwei took the liberty of answering most of the questions for him. Xiao Lin couldn't seem to get a word in edgewise and resorted to staring down at the floral patterns and gold rims on the plates; he was thinking to himself how rare it was to see such fine china these days. Xiao Lin may have been young, but he had a deep nostalgia for the past and was fond of everything old, not because he had ever enjoyed those things, but precisely because he had never had the opportunity. Everything he knew of the old days he learned from stories his parents told him; it was inevitable that they should have a few good memories, living in that old apartment of theirs. Xiao Lin saw in the things at Wang Qiyao's apartment the remains of the old days;

though they were just odds and ends, he could perceive that they were real.

"From now on, just come up when you want to talk to Weiwei," said Wang Qiyao. "Don't worry about being polite. What's the point of standing outside under the streetlight like that—do you want to feed the mosquitoes?"

Xiao Lin laughed but Weiwei retorted, "He's not trying to be polite—he doesn't even know you."

Wang Qiyao felt Weiwei's comments were a bit out of line and ignored her. She took the dirty dishes into the kitchen and Xiao Lin got up and said goodnight.

From that point on, Xiao Lin stopped calling up to Weiwei through the window and would come directly upstairs, calling out to her from the staircase. Wang Qiyao would always find some excuse to go out so that they could have some time alone. When she eventually returned, it was only to fix them some snacks. When they were done eating, it would be time for Xiao Lin to go home. Those peaceful evenings they spent together were crucial to Xiao Lin, who was facing a potentially life-changing exam. They took his mind off the stress and allowed him to focus on some of the smaller details in life, which had nothing to do with fate, but are the underpinnings of fate. Under normal circumstances, they usually go unnoticed—the stuff of everyday life. Wang Qiyao had a talent for making everyday life special. She could transform things usually taken for granted and make one feel as if they were a gift. When that happened you would think: *As bad as things may get, I will still always have this gift.* To your average person, like Weiwei, the benefit of such a gift was negligible, because they have no aspirations in life. But to people eager for success, like Xiao Lin, it was magic.

During the final stretch before the exam, Xiao Lin came by almost every day. He was extremely nervous and, out of anxiety, became more gregarious than usual. Because Weiwei was childish and often pretended to understand even when she didn't, Xiao Lin directed most of his remarks to Wang Qiyao. He told her that his father was an orphan and had been raised in a Catholic orphanage founded by Xu Guangqi. One day an elderly man came to the orphanage school, saying he would adopt whoever was best at memorizing passages from the Bible—the boy he wound up adopting was Xiao Lin's father, who received a first-rate education and went on to study in America. All he ever wanted was for his children to have the opportunity to go to college and have successful careers. But neither of his two older children were fated to go to college—one was sent down to the countryside and the other became a factory worker. Now all of his hopes rested on Xiao Lin.

"Parents tend to exaggerate when they speak of their aspirations for their children," Wang Qiyao laughed. "I'm sure all they want is what's good for you, so you shouldn't worry too much about them. Just concentrate on doing your best. What's more, Xiao Lin, they only want a college education for you because that's what you're cut out for; in the end, their only hope is to help you achieve your own dreams. But if you spend all your time worrying about them, you'll end up overlooking yourself."

She wanted to lighten his load without relieving him of his responsibility, so that he could go into the exam without too much psychological baggage. Her words had the intended effect; Xiao Lin seemed to brighten up and grow calmer. But once this topic had been broached, there was no turning back: Xiao Lin went on to tell Wang Qiyao about his mother. She had been born into a middle-class family that skimped to scrape enough money together to put her through the Chinese-Western Girls' Middle School. Sitting beside them, Weiwei began to grow impatient. She begged Xiao Lin to take her out for a walk, and he had no choice but to cut short his conversation with Wang Qiyao, albeit with a great deal of reluctance. Weiwei pranced down the stairs with Xiao Lin trailing behind her.

"You and my mom sure have a lot to say to each other!" Weiwei said as soon as they got to the end of the *longtang*.

"What's wrong with that?" asked Xiao Lin.

"Everything! It's all wrong!" declared Weiwei.

Seeing how unreasonable she was, Xiao Lin turned and walked off, pushing his bicycle. The two of them parted in rancor.

Then just like that the day of the exam arrived. The afternoon after the exam, Xiao Lin went straight from the test site to Weiwei's apartment instead of going home. Wang Qiyao brought him a bowl of green bean and lily soup to help him cool off from the summer heat before rushing out to call Weiwei on the public phone to tell her to come home from work early. Xiao Lin had lost a lot of weight in the days leading up to the exam, but he was in high spirits. Asked how he had done, he responded with a perfunctory okay, but she sensed that he was waiting for Weiwei to get home so he could tell her all the details. Rather than asking him more questions, she handed him some newspapers to read. Before long, Weiwei returned, kicking off her high-heeled shoes and complaining how hot it was outside—looking as if *she* was the one who had just taken the exam. Xiao Lin was waiting for her to question him, but she didn't. Instead she wondered aloud what movie they were going to see, complaining that they hadn't been to the movies in ages. She went on to describe the latest style sweeping the streets, saying how she'd be out of fashion if she didn't catch up.

At this point, Wang Qiyao could no longer stand the discomfiture and started to question Xiao Lin on behalf of Weiwei—what was the exam like and how he did. Xiao Lin gave them the details in an even tone, but his enthusiasm and excitement still came through. He grew particularly animated when he started in on the foreign language portion of the exam—this touched on only about a third of what he had mastered, and he breezed right through. Weiwei got excited as she listened to him and clamored for a celebration at Red House. Wang Qiyao chided: "Xiao Lin hasn't even had a chance to go home yet. His whole family is waiting! What's more, it's not as if he's gotten accepted anywhere yet. Stop trying to fleece him!"

Xiao Lin, however, said it was all right. He could telephone home and, as to whether or not he would get accepted, that was out of his hands now. He had done his best and the rest was heaven's will. He spoke with nonchalance, but it was backed up by a strong confidence. Wang Qiyao decided to let them go ahead. As they were heading out the door, Xiao Lin suddenly turned around: "Auntie Wang, why don't you come with us!"

Wang Qiyao naturally declined, but Xiao Lin insisted. Weiwei, however, was impatient to get going, which made the situation rather uncomfortable.

"Okay then . . ." Wang Qiyao finally agreed. "But it's my treat! It'll be my way of congratulating Xiao Lin for his hard work!"

She sent them on ahead and told them she would meet them at the restaurant. By the time she had changed clothes, grabbed her purse, and made it over to Red House, it was already seven o'clock. Twilight during the summer always seems to last forever; the sun had already set, yet its glow was still rippling through the streets. A thousand years may pass, but sunsets like those never change, allowing us to forget the passage of time. Maoming Road is also a place that defies time; the plane trees lining the street on both sides meet in embrace and form a canopy overhead. Although the French-style edifices have seen many difficult days, they are basically unchanged. Farther down the road, the theater at the corner has the forlorn air that pervades after the curtain has fallen and the crowds are gone. Nevertheless, it still has enough glamour to call up its former splendor. Maoming Road is truly the eternal heart of Shanghai—even the sky above has Shanghai written all over it. Wang Qiyao caught sight of Red House behind a row of green trees and thought what an upbeat name it was, enabling people to feel ever-youthful. At that moment the streetlights lit up, emitting a yellow glow that set off the night scene, against a sky veiled by a layer of thin mist.

Wang Qiyao could distinguish Xiao Lin and Weiwei through the glass door of the restaurant. Under the light of a lamp, their heads were almost touching as they bent down to read the menus. Unconsciously, Wang Qiyao hesitated for a moment and thought to herself: *How could all those decades have passed by in the blink of an eye like that?* She pushed open the door and went inside.

When she got to their table, the first thing Weiwei said to her was, "And I thought you weren't going to show up!"

Her tone clearly indicated that she would much rather that her mother did not.

Wang Qiyao pretended not to notice and replied, "I promised to take you two out—how could I not show up?"

Weiwei ordered. She picked out the most expensive dishes, partly to show off to Xiao Lin, but also to wring out her mother. Initially Wang Qiyao was ready to go along with this, but, seeing how her daughter completely disrespected her, she decided to assert her authority by canceling some of the dishes Weiwei had ordered and replace them with others that were just as tasty but less expensive. Weiwei tried to argue, but Wang Qiyao retorted, "Don't make the mistake of thinking that something is good just because it is pricy. That couldn't be further from the truth. Oxtail soup is highly acclaimed, but it is best eaten in France where oxen are raised especially for their meat; we don't have anything like the quality of that meat here. You'd be better off ordering French onion soup, which tends to be much more authentic."

This barrage left Weiwei speechless. She lowered her head and didn't open her mouth again for the rest of the dinner. Xiao Lin, however, appreciated the knowledge and experience evident in Wang Qiyao's words, which he attributed to the "old days." He asked a string of questions, which Wang Qiyao was only too happy to answer, patiently explaining everything she knew.

In the blink of an eye the table was covered with large and small dishes, the white china giving off a soft glow under the lights. Their eyes grew moist from the steam rising from the food. Outside the sky had turned completely dark and the streetlights shone like stars; under them the people and cars passed noiselessly by. The trees swayed gently in the evening wind, projecting their dreamlike shadows toward them. This corner could be said to be the most romantic spot in Shanghai: shatter that romance and you will still find its broken shards here. For a while Wang Qiyao did not speak. She sat staring out the window as if she was searching for someone or something she knew. But all she saw was the reflection of the three of them in the glass, moving like characters in a silent film. By the time she turned back around, the sound and color had returned. They may not have been aware of it, but the couple sitting before her was a match made in heaven. Wang Qiyao sat in silence, barely moving her fork or knife. She couldn't drive away the oppressive feeling that her world had returned, but she was now only an observer.

Chapter 2

The Dance

THE WOMAN SITTING in the corner at the dance, content in her loneliness—that is Wang Qiyao. Keeping an eye on a pile of jackets and purses, a charitable smile lighting up her face, she watched the dancers on the floor. She seemed to be saying: *You're doing the steps all wrong, but it's okay.* Each night she too would take to the floor every so often; her partners were always young men and women. Once you got close to her on the dance floor you would hear her whispering instructions to her partner, and only then did it become clear that she was the one teaching them. You wouldn't have enough experience to rate her dancing skills, but her calm and assured manner was evident. Maintaining her poise like that in a roomful of young people wasn't easy. At every dance there would always be at least one or two people her own age who were there to turn back the clock. They brought back the air of gallant gentlemen and proper ladies from thirty or forty years before; although they weren't the most eye-catching ones present, they embodied authenticity. When they got out on the floor, they always looked solemn; the movements they made were exact. Seeing them for the first time, you might think that dancing was work for them and that they approached the floor with a sense of duty. But closer scrutiny would reveal that they were dancing joyously. Their joy did not overflow in the way of young people; it was more like water coursing steadily down an irrigation ditch—quietly, without calling attention to itself, yet full of stamina.

Compared with this, the happiness of the young could only be described as "getting wild." The thing that is beguiling about Latin dance is its ability to take raw emotion and channel it into precise movements, giving it a rational, almost philosophical expression. It takes a special understanding to appreciate Latin dance, and this was why the older dancers held themselves somewhat aloof. This was back in the days before disco became popular in China, but the young people were already getting impatient. When they danced, their movements were coarse and impulsive, and they liked numbers with a fast tempo that made it easier to gloss over their mistakes in front of others—and themselves. They were overeager for the excitement of dancing and did not care whether they knew how to dance; all they wanted was to get out on the floor; the rest they could worry about later. They failed to understand the principle of restraint, which is what makes excitement grow and endure. Their inclination was to squander everything; the money they made was never sufficient to cover their expenses, nor was a single night of song and dance ever enough. And so they danced night after night, drawing on the happiness that was their due, not realizing that they were depleting their accounts prematurely. Nevertheless, their excitement was contagious; one could hardly sit still beside them without feeling one's heart pounding and blood racing.

On one occasion the district political consultative committee organized a dance, and Xiao Lin, who was able to get tickets, took a few friends along. It was here that Wang Qiyao first witnessed true Latin dance. This dance stood out from the others because more than half the dancers were past fifty. Wearing everyday blue and gray outfits, those who knew each other sat together, chatting. The dance was held in a dining hall and the air was filled with the smell of grease. The floor, which had been mopped and sprinkled with powder, only managed to look squalid. The ceiling was stained yellow from accumulated smoke, but the molding was a Renaissance-style floral pattern, the hall was lined with Roman columns, and a semicircular French window looked out into the garden. The blazing lights did nothing to hide the age of the building. Under their glare, one could count every old-age blemish on peoples' hands and faces. The static-laden music sounded hollow and pathetic as it rang out through a four-speaker boom box in the large open hall, and everyone looked tiny under the great dome.

Only after several bars of music had been played did a few couples make their way onto the dance floor. Under the large domed ceiling, they looked as if they were Lilliputians. But these little people were great dancers with decades of experience, and they burned up the floor with their consummate skill. Their demeanor was cool, but they all knew exactly what they were doing. Thirty years away from the dance floor—yet they had not forgotten a step, for they had been properly trained and had spent the necessary time practicing. And even though this was a kingdom of little people, the look on their midget faces was expressive of a solemn dignity. Can you tell what they are thinking? Do you know what they see? Something unfathomable. Their expressions contained a mixture of sorrow and joy; but what was it that aroused these feelings? The young people all fought their shyness of the dance floor; when they did dance, they felt intimidated in this atmosphere enshrouded by a somber gravity. The graying dancers were timeless, like the hall itself. Latin dance has this truly amazing power to transcend time—to transform the old, timeworn, dejected, battered, foul, and rotten into something noble and ethereal.

Wang Qiyao encouraged Weiwei and her friends to dance while she sat off to one side watching. A draft stole in from the French window. She felt as if the scene before her had been transported from thirty years earlier—the only difference was that, having gathered thirty years of dust, it looked somewhat grayer. She even fancied that she could see whole strands of dust drifting down from the old curtains onto the scene before vanishing without a trace. Once more of the young people got up to dance, however, the scene grew livelier.

A few of them were really decked out; although they looked out of place and their dancing skills were dubious, they certainly grabbed your attention. All it takes to liven up the atmosphere is a little eye-catching youthfulness. Some of these young people are dancing frantically, getting all out of rhythm but still carrying on till the bitter end, when the music stops. Some mistake dancing for walking and end up traipsing all over the hall. In the middle of the dance two men suddenly come in carrying two cartons of soda pop, instructing everyone to show their ticket stubs before claiming their bottle. Impatient dancers walk straight across the floor to get theirs. The hall suddenly fills with the sound of bottle caps popping. A few even take the liberty of going over to the boom box to stop whatever is playing in mid-song and put on their own tape instead, leaving no time for the dancers either to stop or to get in step up with the new tune. Before long it turns into a free-for-all, with people dancing the four-step to folk melodies, and the formerly decorous scene evaporates.

Wang Qiyao was sitting by herself when she was asked to dance, as it turned out, by an older gentleman. By then things were getting a bit out of control and everybody seemed to have the right to ask anyone they wanted for a dance. Slowly Wang Qiyao was led out onto the floor, surrounded by people who were oblivious to all but their own movements. Dancing to the same song, everyone did it their own way. The older gentleman wavered a bit before finally getting into rhythm; his steady steps were like a coral reef in a tumultuous sea. Wang Qiyao could ascertain the kind of person he was from the way he danced: an honest, dutiful, hard-working man with solid assets and a virtuous wife, the sort who would set foot in a dance hall only for social engagements related to his work. Back in the old days he was the kind of man that parents of unmarried girls kept a sharp lookout for. Now his hair was gray and he no longer dressed the way he used to. At the end of the dance he saw Wang Qiyao back to her seat, gently shaking her hand and bowing slightly before turning to leave. Right after that came the last song of the evening, the theme from *Waterloo Bridge*, "Auld Lang Syne."

Besides dances organized by different work units, there were also dance parties held in people's homes. All that was needed for these was a large room and a tape player. Zhang Yonghong's latest boyfriend, Xiao Shen, was a frequent organizer of such parties and held them at his friend's house. He invited Wang Qiyao to one of them, saying he wanted her to teach them how to dance. Wang Qiyao insisted that she had nothing to teach them; but she went anyway. Xiao Shen's friend lived in the Alice Apartments, in a ground-floor flat two doors down from where Wang Qiyao used to live. Although it was dark when they arrived and the surroundings had dramatically changed in the years since she had last been there, Wang Qiyao recognized the place as soon as she set foot inside the compound. She thought it strange that over the years she had never once been back—if it hadn't been for the dance party that night, she might never have gone back as long as she lived. The place was only three or four bus stops away from where she now lived, but it felt like a world separated by mountains and oceans. Occasionally, when her thoughts drifted to the Alice Apartments, it had seemed a previous life.

Xiao Shen's friend's apartment, though also on the ground floor, had a different layout from Wang Qiyao's old place. It had two bedrooms and an extra area in the living room. His parents and sisters had, one after the other, emigrated to Hong Kong, so he was the only one left in Shanghai and had the entire place to himself. It was clean and had all the amenities, but didn't have a lived-in feeling. The friend didn't boil hot water for tea for the guests, but simply set out bottles of soda and beer on the table. By the time Wang Qiyao and the others arrived, several couples were already dancing slowly to the music. It was hard to tell the host apart from the guests, as people seemed to know each other very well.

Everyone helped themselves to ice cubes from the refrigerator; when the doorbell rang whoever was closest opened the door; new arrivals made themselves right at home. One guest, apparently uninterested in dancing, even went to take a nap in the master bedroom.

Wang Qiyao had been invited as their dance teacher, but no one seemed interested in learning anything from her; they were all focused on themselves. She felt awkward at first, but seeing how everyone took care of themselves, she relaxed a bit. As no one else was playing host, she went to boil herself a pot of water in the kitchen and poured it into a thermos. Then she found a box of tea leaves and made herself a cup of tea before sitting down in a quiet corner. Others followed suit and made tea, but no one bothered to ask who had boiled the water, as if it should have been there in the first place. By then there were about two dozen people in the room, and someone had turned off the lights, leaving on only a single desk lamp. The shadows of people, thrown onto the wall by the hazy yellow light, resembled a black forest. Wang Qiyao sat alone in an unlit corner, content that no one was taking any notice of her. She had returned to Alice, but Alice was now a different Alice—and she was a different Wang Qiyao.

As she sat on the sofa, the teacup she was holding gradually grew cold. Amid the thick forest of shadows, her own shadow had been swallowed up. She almost forgot who she was. But she is the heart of the party! She may have been the only one not dancing, but she was the essence of the party. That essence came in the form of the memories she held within. Never mind the people waving their arms, shaking their hips, and stomping on the dance floor. They wouldn't know a real dance move if it was staring them in the face. The music they knew was merely the cast-off shells of true music, shed in a century of metamorphoses since the days of Johann Strauss, a whole heap of them. Those swirling motions that once turned circling skirts into blossoming lotus flowers—turn and turn as they might, the figures they trace are empty air, for not a jot of romance remains. All that was left of the old romance was memories in the hearts of a select few—Wang Qiyao being one of them. The memories were fragile and could not endure being put on display, like ancient tombs best left unexcavated; once unearthed, their contents disintegrate with the first breath of air. *There is no point in such a party,* thought Wang Qiyao. Between two numbers, she heard the sound of the trolley coming from the direction of the Paramount. *Just another night at Alice's?* she wondered.

Vacation

When Xiao Lin received his college admission notice, Wang Qiyao offered to send him and Weiwei on vacation to Hangzhou by way of congratulations.

"Aren't you coming too, Auntie?" Xiao Lin asked.

Wang Qiyao thought for a moment. It occurred to her that, though Hangzhou is so close to Shanghai, she had never been. She decided to go with them. Shortly before their departure, she called Xiao Lin over while Weiwei was at work and gave him a gold bar to exchange for cash at the Bank of China. Weiwei was not to know. She had more faith in Xiao Lin than in her own daughter; he was the one she went to when she had important matters to discuss or when she was looking for advice. As for Xiao Lin, he went to Wang Qiyao for everything and turned only to Weiwei when he wanted to horse around and have a good time. But whenever he was down, he always shared his innermost thoughts with Wang Qiyao: only she could comfort him. To him she was more his friend than his future mother-in-law. She in turn regarded him at least partially as a friend; she would sometimes forget his age and tell him personal things about herself. She hesitated for a moment as she handed him the gold bar, wondering if she should tell him the story of its origin. But that was a huge secret. How many secrets had she accumulated over the decades! She listened to Xiao Lin's footsteps as he went out the downstairs door. Around noontime he returned and handed her a stack of bills. She felt that she was cashing out her hidden past. Perhaps it was best not to bring it up after all. Xiao Lin didn't pry. How people accumulated their wealth was one of this city's unverifiable secrets: an old Shanghai native like Xiao Lin knew this all too well. Wang Qiyao kept him for lunch before sending him home.

During their three days in Hangzhou Wang Qiyao did her best to make herself scarce. In the mornings she would wake up before them and go out for a walk around the hotel. Their hotel was right on Inner West Lake, and she would walk along its banks all the way to Bai Causeway. The sunlight lit up the surface of the lake and she worked up a light sweat before heading back. On the way she would run into Weiwei and Xiao Lin, who were also going for a morning stroll.

"See you at breakfast," she would say before going back inside the hotel. By this time the hot water would have been turned on and she would take a shower, change clothes, and go down to wait for them in the hotel dining room. They would show up about fifteen minutes later.

Whatever activities they had planned for the day, Wang Qiyao made sure to stay behind part of the time, as well as giving them rein to spend the evenings as they wished. Weiwei didn't come back to the room until midnight; Wang Qiyao would close her eyes and pretend to be asleep as soon as she heard the door opening. She would listen to Weiwei bump into things as she showered and brushed her teeth, turned the light on and then off again, and finally got into bed. It was not until she heard her daughter quietly snoring that Wang Qiyao felt it was safe to turn over and open her eyes, which had grown tired from being kept closed so long. The room was actually quite bright and everything was clearly visible; the light fluctuated slightly as it reflected off the surface of the lake. Wang Qiyao thought about the Nine Creeks and Eighteen Gullies they had visited earlier that day; a Zen-inspired place of nature and solitude, and wondered what it would be like to live there as a hermit. *How wonderful it would be not to be bothered by the annoyances of the world! It would be nice to live in an isolated place where a century is like one day and there is no past or future.* But then it was a bit late for her to become a hermit. She had already paid a heavy price during the first half of her life; was it all to have been for nothing? Were there to be no harvest to be reaped from all that she had been through? Wouldn't she be losing out by giving up halfway? When she went back to ponder what that harvest might be, her mind began to drift and she couldn't focus any more; gradually, she fell asleep.

On the third morning she woke up to find the room bathed in sunlight and Weiwei gone without a trace. She realized that she had overslept, but she wasn't anxious. Instead she decided to take it easy. She rested her eyes a bit longer before getting out of bed to comb her hair and head down to the hotel dining room to wait for her daughter and Xiao Lin. She waited for quite some time, and it wasn't until the dining room was about to close that she quickly nibbled a few bites. She went to wait for them in the reception area, but they still didn't show up. Finally she went outside to wait for them. It was already muggy on the lake; all along the Bai Causeway and the Su Causeway, tourists were out strolling, their reflections shimmering on the lake. A few wispy clouds floated overhead, but soon disappeared. The sound of cicadas rang out, but there was still no trace of those two.

That morning Weiwei and Xiao Lin had gone for tea at Park Number Six, then directly from there to rent a boat on the lake. They didn't get back to the hotel until noon. They thought they would run into Wang Qiyao when they got back, but when they didn't they simply had lunch and went upstairs to grab a few things before going out again. Xiao Lin, who was sharing a room with someone else, went to put his belongings in the women's room. Opening the door, they were startled to see Wang Qiyao sitting up in bed reading a comic book, a whole pile of comics stacked up beside her.

"Did you have something to eat, Auntie?" Xiao Lin asked after taking a moment to compose himself.

Wang Qiyao, however, responded with silence, pretending not to hear him. She kept her eyes on the comic book and turned the pages with a smile on her face. Weiwei grabbed some clothing and went into the bathroom to change as Xiao Lin said, "This afternoon we're going to see the bamboo groves at Yellow Dragon Cave. Why don't you come along!"

"I'm not going!" Wang Qiyao replied, the smile on her face suddenly vanishing.

Xiao Lin paused a moment before he tried to explain. "This morning Weiwei and I went for a walk along Su Causeway. We ended up pretty far out and that's why we didn't make it back for breakfast."

Wang Qiyao could no longer contain the bitterness welling up inside her. Her eyes turned red and she struggled before responding, "Well, I also went out for a walk."

As soon as the words came out of her mouth she got angry at herself for showing her weakness. "You need not report to me," she added.

At that point Weiwei emerged from the bathroom and asked, "Are we going or not?"

She directed her question at Xiao Lin and didn't even look at Wang Qiyao, as if there was no such person in the room.

Looking up from her comic book, Wang Qiyao demanded, "Who are you talking to?"

Weiwei was taken off guard. She rolled her eyes. "I wasn't talking to you."

Wang Qiyao flashed a cold smile. "If you're not talking to me, then just who are you talking to? What makes you think that just because you have a man you can ignore everyone else? You think men are reliable? Just you wait, one day they'll step all over you and you'll come running back to me. Maybe you don't believe what I'm telling you, but just you wait!"

Her comments, which seemed to come totally out of the blue, caused Weiwei to panic. "Who's got a man?" she retorted. "And who's the one ignoring everyone else? Today I'm going to set the record straight! And I'm not going to Yellow Dragon Cave either!"

With that, she sat down on the other bed, folded her legs, and stared at Wang Qiyao, affecting the posture of one ready to settle scores. The two of them always treated each other as equals, rather than as mother and daughter; the fact that Wang Qiyao looked so young was not the only reason people took them for sisters. They quarreled frequently, so that even an outsider like Xiao Lin had witnessed their bickering on more than one occasion. But today the scene was something out of the ordinary. It seemed to have come out of nowhere, and even when there was nothing left to argue about they were both determined to carry on. In fact, trouble had been brewing for some time, and Xiao Lin, conscious of the great embarrassment a full-blown eruption would cause all three of them, went over to pull Weiwei away. But she knocked his hands aside.

"You're always taking her side! Just what is she to you?" Before Weiwei could finish the sentence, her mother slapped her across the face.

Weiwei was brassy enough to exchange harsh words with her mother, but she was far from the point of being able to trade blows. Beside herself with rage, she could only take refuge in tears. Xiao Lin tried to pull her away, but she only sobbed, "The two of you are ganging up on me!"

No one went out that afternoon. The beautiful sunny day, amidst the gorgeous scenery of lake and mountain, passed by under the shadow of anger, tears, and resentment.

Xiao Lin's roommate wasn't around, so he took Weiwei back to his room, where he did everything he could to console her and try to cheer her up. After a great deal of whimpering, Weiwei gradually calmed down.

"Xiao Lin," Weiwei raised her teary eyes and gazed at her boyfriend. "You be the judge: was all this my fault or hers?"

Xiao Lin wiped away her tears. "What's all this talk about 'my fault or hers'? It's your mother we're talking about! Even if she was wrong, she's still your mother."

Weiwei was upset again. "So, according to you, there is no such thing as right or wrong in the world?"

Xiao Lin laughed. "I wasn't talking about the rest of the world!" He was silent for a moment before continuing, "You know, there is something quite sad about your mother."

"What's so sad about her?" Not wanting to risk a row, Xiao Lin stared blankly out the window. It was only after a brief pause that Weiwei turned him around and asked, "Are you in a relationship with her or with me?"

Weiwei's stern expression gave the ludicrous question a serious tone. Xiao Lin kissed her. "Is it really necessary for me to answer that question?"

Weiwei laughed, and then became embarrassed. She hid her head under a pillow and wouldn't let Xiao Lin look at her. The two of them kept on like this and the time slipped away. Before long it was dinner time.

"Let's go down and get her for dinner. But you have to try and smile!" he said.

Weiwei intentionally drew a long face. "I don't know how to smile."

Just as they were getting ready to leave, there was a knock on the door. It was Wang Qiyao. She had changed clothes, had her handbag with her, and looked perfectly serene. She said she wanted to take them out for dinner at the Louwailou and waited patiently for them to collect their things.

The sun was hanging low over the streets, bathing all of Hangzhou in a golden glow. Bicycles glided by as if they too were fish swimming in the shining lake. The few boats remaining on the water drifted to the shore, where they seemed to exchange glances of surprise with the pedestrians. Soon the sky turned a gorgeous hue, dyeing the clouds on the horizon a rainbow of brilliant colors. It was so beautiful that Xiao Lin decided to take some photographs, including shots of the women, singly and together. After the colors had faded from the firmament, they proceeded to the restaurant and sat down to dinner. Wang Qiyao let the two of them order and refrained from interfering. Gradually Weiwei became her old vivacious self. She grew talkative and Wang Qiyao chimed in a few times, putting what had happened earlier that afternoon behind them. Only then did Xiao Lin, who had been walking on pins and needles all day, finally heave a sigh of relief.

"Weiwei," Xiao Lin said earnestly as he poured out the beer, "you should toast your mother. It mustn't have been easy raising a girl like you!"

"That was her decision," Weiwei rejoined perversely. "It's not as if I forced her!"

Wang Qiyao laughed. "All right, so I forced you, okay?"

"Here's to Auntie, who really broke the bank paying for this vacation!" Xiao Lin exclaimed.

He had not expected his words to make Wang Qiyao blanch. Although she managed to hold on to her smile, her expression changed, growing colder. She took a sip of beer and, without saying anything, began to eat. Weiwei naturally didn't notice anything wrong, but Xiao Lin felt uneasy, sensing he had said something wrong—only he wasn't sure what. He was already exhausted from having spent most of the day trying to patch things up between the mother and daughter, and now it all seemed to have been a wasted effort. Disheartened, he addressed himself to the food and drink. Only Weiwei was still in high spirits, blithely unaware that anything was different. In the end, she was the only one who enjoyed the meal.

That night Wang Qiyao returned alone to her room and, for lack of something else to do, began packing her things for the return trip the following day. In the middle of her packing she suddenly smiled, thinking, *So he thinks of me as his private bank!* Then, after a pause, *And what does she take me for?* Putting down her things, she decided to take a shower. It was too early for hot water and all that came out of the shower head was air. Forgetting to turn it off, she lay down on the bed and dozed off. She awoke to the sound of rushing water and clouds of steam billowing out from the bathroom door.

The following day they took the afternoon train back to Shanghai's North Station, arriving at ten in the evening. The square in front of the station was bustling with people. Lining the square in every direction were lamp posts that shone a murky yellow light onto the swarming crowds. Weiwei and Xiao Lin walked ahead, with Wang Qiyao lagging a few steps behind. Every so often Xiao Lin would turn around to make sure she was okay and didn't need any help. Wang Qiyao said she was fine, thinking scornfully that she wasn't so old as to need his help. After they had crossed the square and stood at the curb, they were still surrounded by an endless stream of people. Arriving home, they found the apartment covered in a layer of dust, even though they had been gone for only three or four days. Several moths, hatched while they were away, fluttered around the room.

Christmas

That year saw the revival of Christmas celebrations in living rooms scattered around Shanghai. On Christmas Eve the lights stayed on in those houses till well past midnight. People played Christmas songs on their pianos all night. Festivities such as these invariably involved food and drink, but with Christmas candles and music setting the mood, even the most mundane food and drink took on a special air. There were no Christmas trees to speak of, as there was no place to buy them. For midnight chimes, one had to rely on the time signal coming over the radio, a lonely sound in the still of the night, but even so it made Christmas Eve stand out.

The people who celebrated Christmas were not necessarily Christians; in fact, most could barely tell you who Jesus was. The majority had come to know about this holiday from Christmas cards sent to them from abroad. True churchgoers, who had been living their lives according to the gospel, probably didn't give much thought to Christmas. They were, for the most part, quite old and had long fallen behind the times. Christmas was observed by the city's trendiest residents. The sharp eyes of these residents scanned the city for what it lacked and nothing escaped them. They pushed their city aggressively into the mainstream to bring an end to its isolation. Christmas at this time had not yet won mass acceptance, but you could already sense its power and sincerity. The finest china was trotted out, a new tablecloth was laid on the table, fresh roses were put in the vase, and the smartest people were invited as guests—one look and it was clear that these were the new masters of this city. "Merry Christmas" rolled off their lips as they came inside. It was a bit cold out and there was no heating, but they were in such high spirits that they didn't care; everyone wore spring clothes. Eating and dancing, they would start to warm up and lose their inhibitions. Christmas Eve celebrations generally began around nine o'clock. As most of the people who had stayed home were preparing for bed, others who had gone out were on their way home, and dances were wrapping up elsewhere; at Christmas parties guests were only just arriving. With all the lights out in the neighbors' homes, the radiance emanated by those parties resembled a beacon light—never again would the city lose its way.

During these years Shanghai was like a huge sponge that, having been dried up too long, opened its pores to soak up all the pleasure it could. There was still a long way to go before it was saturated. There was more darkness than light in the sky above the buildings; behind those tightly closed windows and doors, most people were sleeping—such paltry sums of pleasure were not enough to go around. If that pleasure were to flow down the street, it would only leave the ground a bit damp. You don't realize how much pleasure this city needed! Old as those living rooms may have been, they were still functional and large enough to accommodate the singing and dancing of Christmas Eve parties. The pianos were all out of tune, but they were all classic instruments made by J. Strauss & Son. And what about the piano tuners of yore? They needed to be tracked down one by one to resume their old profession—all the old pianos in the city were counting on them. Otherwise what would come of the Christmas songs? And what about all those sonatas and serenades: how would they ever manage?

Weiwei went with Xiao Lin to his classmate's place for Christmas, leaving Wang Qiyao home alone. She wondered, *What Christmas is there to celebrate on a dark gloomy night like this?* Sitting down under the lamplight to knit a baby's wool jumpsuit, she was suddenly struck by the silence all around her. The sounds of people talking and moving about that normally filled the air had completely stopped. Could they have all gone out to celebrate Christmas? At that moment she heard the clock chiming; counting to ten, she realized how late it was. How stupid the whole Christmas holiday was! *Who wants to sit together with a bunch of people and listen to the clock strike midnight? Doesn't it strike midnight every night?* Wang Qiyao went to bed well before Weiwei crept back in later that night. When she got up the next morning and set out for the market, Weiwei was still fast asleep, her new boots and clothing strewn around the bed, looking as if she had been on an all-night revel.

Wang Qiyao descended the stairs quietly and went out. The streetlights had just been extinguished. The gloomy sky, portending snow, conveyed a weariness, as if it too had been partying all night. Pedestrians walked briskly past, and Wang Qiyao could see the mark Christmas had left on their faces. She thought: *Everyone but me has been celebrating Christmas, but I don't give a damn!* She bought vegetables, milk, soymilk, and deep-fried twisted doughsticks for breakfast. All the way back she walked past children on their way to school, their faces crimson from the cold as they munched on their cold breakfast. Their parents must have just returned from an all-night party and didn't have enough time to fix them a hot meal. The sun projected its sluggish rays from beyond the haze. When Wang Qiyao got back, the apartment looked exactly as she had left it. Weiwei was still in a deep slumber. The bittersweet odor of the night before filled the room, leaving her feeling vexed. It dawned on her that it was Weiwei's day off and she wondered how late she would sleep in. She retreated into the kitchen to make herself breakfast. Through the window, she could see the neighbors across the way busily cleaning their apartment, scurrying in and out. A drying pole with clean laundry was pushed out from another window, which quickly shut again. The clothes looked as if they would never dry in the damp cold air. Then came the boy with the morning paper, ringing his bicycle bell. The *longtang* started to bustle—another day begins.

Weiwei slept well into the afternoon, missing both breakfast and lunch. Wang Qiyao didn't want to get into a fight with her and let her sleep in. As the clock struck one, Zhang Yonghong arrived. Weiwei turned over and opened her eyes, listening to them talk from under the bedclothes, but she didn't interrupt. It was rare for Wang Qiyao to see her daughter so peaceful. She asked her if she was hungry, but Weiwei wasn't. Her face was flushed from sleeping so much and her hair was all messy—she looked like a lazy cat.

"Did you go out for Christmas Eve last night?" Wang Qiyao asked Zhang Yonghong.

Zhang Yonghong looked bewildered. "What do you mean, 'Christmas Eve'? I've never heard of such a thing."

Wang Qiyao patiently told her the story of Christmas. Zhang Yonghong listened intently, occasionally asking a few ignorant questions. Weiwei was also listening, but she didn't say a word. It was a gloomy day and dark inside as well, not the kind of darkness that comes at night, but the kind that seals off the outdoors, leaving people with a feeling of warmth. After listening to Wang Qiyao explain Christmas at some length, Zhang Yonghong exclaimed, "Just think how many exciting things we've been missing out on!"

"At least you still have time," replied Wang Qiyao. "Look at me, I don't even have that."

"But you already experienced all of that!" Zhang Yonghong demurred. "How can we compare with you?"

"It is like the theater," Wang Qiyao consoled her. "The first act may be over, but after an intermission, act two will begin."

"I hope the intermission doesn't last too long," said Zhang Yonghong.

"How could it?" Wang Qiyao replied. "The bells and gongs have sounded. Look at this one!" She pointed to Weiwei, who sank back into her comforter, leaving only her eyes exposed. "She was out being wild all night long!" Weiwei still didn't say a word.

She told Zhang Yonghong how Weiwei had gone out to celebrate Christmas Eve with Xiao Lin last night. "I don't even know what time she came back."

Zhang Yonghong glanced at Weiwei but kept quiet. The room grew a bit darker, and a bit warmer. Wang Qiyao went into the kitchen to boil some water, leaving the two of them in silence, one sitting, one lying down, neither speaking. Weiwei closed her eyes and seemed to fall back asleep. Zhang Yonghong lowered her head, lost in her own thoughts. By the time Wang Qiyao came back from the kitchen, the room had grown so dark you could barely make out the outlines of the two girls. Nobody made a sound for quite some time, each wrapped up in her own concerns. Suddenly, a sharp cackle erupted from the bedclothes. Wang Qiyao and Zhang Yonghong looked over to discover Weiwei had buried her head under the comforter.

"What are you laughing at?" Wang Qiyao asked.

At first there was no answer, but after a while Weiwei offered a giggly response. "What, I'm not allowed to laugh?"

Wang Qiyao paid no heed to Weiwei's antics. She turned to Zhang Yonghong and asked how things were going with her boyfriend. Zhang Yonghong seemed reluctant to get into the subject and simply said they had broken up. Wang Qiyao had known that this was going to happen, but still was surprised. She wanted to say something, but realized that she had already gone over everything before. But then Zhang Yonghong started to open up. She listed all the bad qualities of the last boyfriend, and each item on her list was a deal breaker.

When she reached the end of her recital, Wang Qiyao smiled. "Zhang Yonghong, you've really built up a lot of experience when it comes to judging people. You see right through them, don't you?"

Oblivious to the irony, Zhang Yonghong responded in a dejected tone, "That's right. There must be something wrong with me. After ten minutes of passion, nothing about them seems to sit right with me."

"You've had too much, you know," remarked Wang Qiyao. "It's like medicine. If you take too much, you build up a resistance and the medicine becomes useless. After too many boyfriends, it is difficult to stick with any one."

"In any case, I dumped him when I had had enough," Zhang Yonghong said.

That's what she said, and her voice showed the pride that she felt deep down in her bones. After all, she was the one who was picky and not the other way around, and she was the one doing the dumping, showing that she still had other options. Wang Qiyao could tell what she was thinking and knew that the day would come when she would look back with regret. She looked at Zhang Yonghong's colorless, almost transparent, face and saw there the shadow of emaciation; her experiences had begun to leave their mark on her. The affairs were over and done with, so she claimed, but they remained etched on her face. How does a woman get old? This is how. Rouge is useless as the vicissitudes of life draw their lines, the result of which is age. The more you try to hide it, the more it shows. Wang Qiyao watched Zhang Yonghong as she wound the yarn ball with her delicate fingers. The nail polish emitted a seashell-like glow and the veins in her arms showed light-blue under the light, giving one the impression of too much effort expended. Wang Qiyao felt sorry for her. Zhang Yonghong started to retell some of the rumors she heard on the streets—all sex scandals and murders. Weiwei's head emerged from the comforter and her eyes widened as she listened.

Wang Qiyao chided her. "Did you go out for Christmas Eve, or did you work the night shift? What are you doing? Waiting for us to serve you?"

To Wang Qiyao's surprise, Weiwei did not talk back. This lack of reaction was very unlike her. Wang Qiyao glanced at Weiwei, but she just lay lazily in bed without moving.

Before long it was truly nightfall. As soon as they turned on the light, the entire room filled with a radiant glow. Even when Zhang Yonghong announced her departure, Weiwei still didn't get up. Wang Qiyao saw Zhang Yonghong as far as the landing and went into the kitchen to make dinner. Only when she saw the thick fog outside the north window and heard a crisp rustling sound did she realize that it was snowing. Gazing out the window, she thought how much it really did seem like Christmas. She heard Weiwei calling to her from the bedroom. At first she ignored her, but finally she went in to ask her what she wanted. "Don't tell me you want me to bring your dinner to you in bed?"

Instead of answering, Weiwei pulled the comforter up to her chin. "Xiao Lin proposed."

Wang Qiyao sat down slowly. "When did he say he wants to get married?"

"During the Spring Festival," Weiwei responded, her back to her mother.

Although Weiwei's relationship with Xiao Lin had seemed a set thing, they had never discussed marriage. Wang Qiyao had known it would be coming sooner or later, but now that it was here it still took her by surprise. She thought, *Weiwei's getting married—how times flies!* She couldn't tell if she was happy or sad and for a moment didn't know how to respond. She sat there in a daze for she didn't know how long, until she heard Weiwei saying with irritation in her voice, "His parents have invited us for dinner next week. So, do you approve or don't you?"

Wang Qiyao snapped out of her trance. "What's there for me to approve? The two of you have decided this on your own. Since when have you ever asked me for advice?"

But Weiwei pressed her for an answer.

Wang Qiyao heaved a light sigh. "How could I be against it? This is a good thing!"

"What do you mean, 'a good thing'?" Weiwei asked.

Wang Qiyao did not reply. Instead she got up and walked over to the corner of the room, where she cleared the things lying on top of her camphor chest, and opened the lid. One after another, she took out wool blankets, down quilts, eiderdown pillows—whole sets of beddings, which she put in a neat pile.

"I prepared all of this for you years ago." As she spoke, tears trickled down her cheeks. Weiwei also cried, but she couldn't bring herself to say anything sweet.

The Wedding

The trousseau Wang Qiyao prepared for Weiwei could just as well have been prepared for herself. Each and every article was a mark of striving for a bright future—but bright futures come by chance and cannot be counted on. Everybody is supposed to have one, and this gives people something to look forward to. The dragons, phoenixes, and peonies woven in jacquard on the damask bedding, the broad-pleated furbelows, and the vines and branches in cutwork—all these were blueprints for the future. Most of the women crowding around the linens section of the department store were there to buy articles for trousseaus, whether for themselves or for their daughters. They might shop ten stores only to emerge empty-handed, so when they finally find what they have been looking for, they make it into a big event! Who can fathom their dedication?

Wang Qiyao had never prepared herself a trousseau—she had bypassed that moment in her own history. Now, stepping back and taking everything in from a distance, she discovered that she had arrived at a place in life where none of that mattered anymore. She was now in a position to prepare a trousseau for Weiwei, but sometimes she wondered just what business it was of hers. Her enthusiasm fluctuated; but over time she managed to purchase enough items to fill two or three chests. Opening the chests to air out the clothes under the blinding glare of the summer sun, she could barely bring herself to look at these brand-new items: these had no history, no roots, only a future of which she could not partake. She opened the windows to let in the sunlight and fresh air. The room filled with the distinctive smell of those new things untouched by human hands, and for a split second she was filled with the kind of joy that lets one momentarily forget oneself. New things always fill people with delight, with the excitement that comes just before something is about to begin.

As Weiwei took the trousseau bundle from her mother's hands, she felt as if a great fortune had suddenly been bestowed on her and contentment filled her heart. She went through the articles on a daily basis, examining them and discussing them with her mother. Whenever they suspected that a fabric might not be what it was alleged to be, they would conduct a little test. To see if something was pure wool, they would tease out a small clump and, setting it on fire, watch the rate at which it burned. They looked like children as they huddled together, gazing intently at the flames.

Zhang Yonghong also came over to inspect Weiwei's trousseau. As she looked the items over, she secretly compared them to her own trousseau. At some point unknown to the others, Zhang Yonghong had started to put aside half the money she normally spent on clothes for her trousseau. Although her boyfriends came and went like fleeting clouds, her trousseau grew with the passing months and years as steadily as if vows of everlasting love had been exchanged. It was only when accumulating items for her trousseau that Zhang Yonghong could faintly make out her future, a future that otherwise utterly bewildered her. One of the items in Weiwei's trousseau was a bed net made of beaded gauze; Wang Qiyao spread it out with the help of Zhang Yonghong, who took the other end. When Weiwei crawled inside, she really did look like a bride through the sheer netting. As Wang Qiyao and Zhang Yonghong exchanged glances, a feeling of commiseration welled up between them, and they quickly looked away.

Then it was time for Weiwei to have new clothes made. Wang Qiyao picked out some woolen suit material in magenta and asked Madame Yan for a good tailor. The day the tailor came over to take the measurements, he was besieged with vociferous opinions about the design from Wang Qiyao and Zhang Yonghong, as well as Madame Yan, who had brought him over.

Thoroughly exasperated, the tailor demanded, "Excuse me, but who's the tailor here, you or me?"

They all laughed. "Okay, okay! We'll keep quiet from now on!"

But before long they were at it again. Weiwei, the only one who remained silent, stood with demure composure as they maneuvered her around—that day she was the star of the show. The lead role had fallen into her lap and she accepted the part in a muddleheaded way. You could say that she had no clue as to what marriage really was, but storybook romances with happy endings always seem to fall into the laps of people like that; the more one pursues the perfect marriage, the more elusive it becomes. This is what they mean when they say, "Follow love, and it will flee; flee love, and it will follow thee." They also spent a great deal of time trying to figure out what shoes would match the magenta suit. At first it seemed logical that she should wear white shoes, but these made her look top-heavy and somewhat provincial. Black was the next color they tried, but although the proportions seemed right, the somber color had a deadening effect that took away from her gorgeous outfit. After racking their brains and running all over Shanghai, they finally found a pair of leather shoes in a slightly deeper shade of magenta: that did the trick, and they looked perfect on her. Next came the issue of hairstyle. Wang Qiyao had the final say here. She suggested that Weiwei get a permanent wave one month before the wedding, then go back for a trim every other week after that. By the time of the wedding, her hair would look naturally curly and no one would be able to tell that it had been permed, and it would look just right whether put up or hanging down.

By that point Weiwei had already tried on her bridal gown in front of the mirror countless times. Each time Wang Qiyao couldn't help but be secretly surprised at how even an average-looking girl could be transformed into a glowing beauty as her wedding approached. This was that magic moment when the petals open up and all the beauty in the world steps aside to clear a path for the flower in full bloom. It is the instant at which a woman becomes a real woman; everything leading up to this is preparation for this day, when it all comes to fruit. The beauty and essence of womanhood are concentrated at this turning point.

Next it was time to sew the wedding quilt. Wang Qiyao went over to Madame Yan's and said to her, "You know, it would be bad luck for a woman like me to embroider a pair of mandarin ducks on Weiwei's wedding quilt. Madame Yan, you've been blessed with both a son and a daughter and have had a life of great fortune. I would be so grateful if Weiwei could enjoy even a fraction of the good fortune you have enjoyed."

Madame Yan didn't need any more convincing; she immediately ordered the nanny to come along with her to Wang Qiyao's apartment. There she had the nanny help her spread out the quilt as she began her needlework. Wang Qiyao watched from a distance, but didn't lift a finger to help, even when Madame Yan asked her to thread a needle. "Madame Yan, you know I mustn't touch it . . ." she said.

"You finally found yourself an excuse not to help!" exclaimed Madame Yan, who nevertheless felt sorry for her, but refrained from saying anything further in front of the Shaoxing nanny. Instead she simply lowered her head and went hard at sewing. The nanny left around noon and Madame Yan stayed on to dinner. Smelling the aroma from the kitchen, she suddenly felt as if the clock had turned back and she was transported to a scene from many years ago. All kinds of old secrets rushed up, but they were the kinds that could never be broached. Once dinner was on the table and the two women were sitting face to face, Madame Yan cut to the chase. "Weiwei's getting married . . . Don't you think you should let her father know?"

The blow was cushioned by a lapse of more than twenty years and the question didn't come across as abrupt.

"Her father's dead," Wang Qiyao said with a smile. Then she added, "He died in Siberia."

The two of them laughed so hard they almost spit out their food.

"You should get yourself a new dress to wear on Weiwei's wedding day," Madame Yan said.

"For someone as old as I am, what good is a new dress?" replied Wang Qiyao.

"Then maybe you should take a hint from Weiwei and do something to make yourself into a whole new you!" With that, they both laughed again. Once their giddiness had passed, Madame Yan turned serious. "Actually, I was partly serious about what I said before. Once Weiwei leaves you'll be lonely. You should find yourself a companion!"

"And where should I look?" Wang Qiyao asked.

Madame Yan finished the embroidery on the quilt, marking the end to yet another day; Weiwei's wedding was now another day closer. As the Spring Festival drew near, everyone got busy preparing for the New Year, to see off the old and welcome in the new, all of which added to the gaiety surrounding the wedding. Xiao Lin was on winter break, but had signed up for an English class. His father had an old friend in America who had already agreed to act as his sponsor. Xiao Lin was planning to finish out his sophomore year in Shanghai before going on to the United States to complete his studies. Getting married was one step in his plan to go to America—it was much easier to get an entry visa as a married man. The idea made Wang Qiyao nervous. But not Weiwei—she had the opposite reaction, and was even more excited about Xiao Lin going to the States than she was about getting married. Sooner or later, everyone gets married, but not everyone gets to go to America—never mind the prospect of Xiao Lin one day taking her there; just the thought of *his* going was exciting enough.

Because Xiao Lin was slated to leave, they had a short-term perspective when it came to some of the wedding preparations. Their bridal chamber was set up in a small west-facing room in his parents' apartment, and none of their furniture was new. But marriage always makes people happy; no matter how often this old ceremony is repeated, it never loses its flair. Whatever time Xiao Lin didn't spend cramming English he spent with Weiwei—shopping, eating out in Western restaurants, or going to the movies. Knowing that marriage was right around the corner, they couldn't help crossing the line once in a while, but that was okay. Just how far could they really go standing in dark doorways or in the corner of the public park at night?

They also spent some of their time together at Wang Qiyao's place. They would talk about America and it was as if their hearts had already flown there. Wang Qiyao, too, was a fan of America—the America she liked was the one she had seen in Hollywood movies. But, fond as she was of the America on the silver screen, she knew that it was all make-believe; her America was a place within sight but far beyond reach. Xiao Lin and Weiwei, however, took their America for real and they had all kinds of plans to carry out there. Wang Qiyao couldn't get a word in as they talked about their American dreams, but their America was boring to her—it didn't even come close to her Hollywood movies.

One day Xiao Lin came over while Weiwei was still out.

"Come on in," Wang Qiyao said. "Weiwei should be back right after lunch."

Xiao Lin picked up the evening newspaper from the previous day. Wang Qiyao, who went on knitting a sweater, asked where the wedding reception was going to be held and whether he had booked the room. Xiao Lin said that his mother was just about to inquire about how many tables Wang Qiyao's family wanted for the reception. Wang Qiyao figured that, even if she invited people from her mother's side of the family, they might not come. Besides them, no one else really mattered, except Madame Yan. Although they didn't always see eye to eye, they had never fallen out of touch all these years and could be said to be lifelong intimates. She told Xiao Lin that she wouldn't even need a whole table; it would just be herself and Madame Yan.

"Of course we'll invite Madame Yan," Xiao Lin replied. "But she's only a friend. Aren't there relatives you'll be inviting?"

Wang Qiyao was silent for quite a while before responding. "Weiwei's my only relative . . . and now I'm giving her to you."

As those words left her lips, they were both moved.

"In the future, you'll come to live with us," said Xiao Lin.

Wang Qiyao stood up. Putting down the cashmere, she cried, "That won't do! What about your parents?"

With that, she ran out to the kitchen. Xiao Lin became a bit depressed, as if his impending happiness was suddenly shrouded by a melancholic shadow. He realized at that moment that all the old furnishings he had admired in her apartment—everything from the chest to the vanity mirror—carried that same shadow. "Old" was not the right word; it was "melancholic sadness." He didn't sense it when Weiwei was around, because she was the flighty sort that likes to be free and easy with life. But "melancholic sadness" reaches out to grasp at the vanishing years. This was yet another difference between mother and daughter—Weiwei didn't stop until she had used everything up, whereas Wang Qiyao made it a point to take stock carefully as she went along, and couldn't let go even after it was all used up. But what good did that do? It's not within our control anyway, so why make life more difficult by refusing to let go?

The wedding day finally arrived. In the morning the young couple went to Wangkai Photo Studio for their wedding portrait, accompanied by Wang Qiyao. The gown and tuxedo, rented out by the studio, had already adorned countless couples. Pins were used to adjust the same dress—cut to the largest possible size—to fit virtually any client, and the time they spent adjusting all those pins for Weiwei was no less than it would have taken to tailor make a brand-new one. But that white dress retained a virginal look; it may not have fit properly, but it still looked perfect. Weiwei became extremely quiet as Wang Qiyao made the adjustments. The train heaped up on the floor over her feet like a pile of snow. However, Wang Qiyao's fingers could feel the dampness of the gown and she had trouble getting the pins to work right because they had become dull from overuse. Before long her palms became sweaty and beads of perspiration appeared on her forehead; she grew dizzy and momentarily forgot that the woman in the gown was her daughter. Raising her head, she saw in the mirror a princess, beautiful and proud. The top of the mirror reflected the glow of an electric lamp, the window had been covered by a heavy curtain, and there was a hairbrush with tangled strands of hair caught in it sitting on the dressing table. A curious air of mystery reigned in the studio's dressing room with its arsenal of little-known tricks, such as those two rows of closely spaced safety pins just below the armpit and others hidden in the folds of the skirt. The hair, too, had been manipulated, as the bobby pins littering the floor attested. Her wedding gown now near perfect, the veil flowing down over her face like a gentle waterfall, Weiwei could almost pass for a fairy descended from heaven.

As the studio lights turned on, Wang Qiyao sat in a dark corner and became almost invisible. The lights shone onto another world only a few feet away from her, but it could just as well have been at the other end of the universe. It suddenly occurred to Wang Qiyao that she never should have come. She had ended up an onlooker at a spectacle that she didn't want to see. She knew quite well that photo studios were all dens of deception, yet she had still walked right into their trap—after so many decades, she still hadn't learned her lesson. Her heart rose and sank as the studio lights turned on and off. Those lights were the most familiar sight in the world to her, yet at that moment they felt so far away. She could clearly see the photographer's lips moving but couldn't hear a word he said, nor could she hear the voices of the young couple. When they were finished, they stepped away so that another couple could begin their shoot. As Wang Qiyao helped Weiwei out of the gown, a pile of pins dropped to the floor, emitting an odd clinking sound. Then, in taking off the dress, Weiwei accidentally smeared lipstick onto the white crape, adding another stroke to the history of the gown, which, piled up on the floor, looked like the empty shell of a giant cicada.

It was already afternoon by the time they left the studio and went to the eleventh floor of the Park Hotel for lunch. All three were worn out from the photo shoot and no one spoke much. Outside the window, there wasn't a single cloud in the boundless sky, but, looking down, they could see an unbroken expanse of rooftops and the noises of the city assaulted their ears. The sky above and the city below were of two different worlds and each went about its own business, as did the Huangpu River, which was constantly flowing, never an end to its moving current. Who is to say who holds the truth?

They spent the afternoon at Wang Qiyao's apartment, where Xiao Lin had followed them. As it was only the second day of the New Year, firecrackers were still going off intermittently in the *longtang.* The second day of the New Year is traditionally a time for calling on friends and relatives, so Peace Lane was bustling with the rituals of receiving guests and seeing them off. After things quieted down, the apartment took on a lonesome air. Weiwei and Xiao Lin sat in silence, physically and psychologically drained by several days of nonstop hard work and excitement. Now that the ceremony was almost upon them, they both found themselves instinctively pulling back a bit. They sat at the table eating melon seeds; before they knew it, the table was filled with a pile of shells and their lips were stained black. The sunlight projected a checkered pattern on the floor, and the young couple looked a bit pale and couldn't think of any better way to pass the time than sitting around eating more watermelon seeds. Wang Qiyao tried to make small talk, but neither of them responded.

Going into the kitchen to boil some water, she noticed that light of the sinking sun was showing through the north window; yet another day had slipped by, like all the rest. The sunlight on the north window had indeed completed its day's journey and, with its acquired wisdom, shone on her with understanding and compassion. A sparrow looking for food landed on the windowsill and took a few pecks before flying away. Wang Qiyao opened the window and placed a few grains of leftover rice there so that the bird would have something to eat when it came back the following day. Returning from the kitchen, she was surprised to see the young couple fast asleep in separate beds. Seeing how late it was, she quickly woke them up and hurried them to get ready. Before long, the taxi they had reserved pulled up in the back alley and beeped its horn.

Even as they got into the taxi, their faces looked numb with exhaustion. This day felt like the longest day in their lives, and they had little confidence that they could see things through to the end. All three felt daunted by the grand occasion ahead. The young couple had stage fright: the curtain was about to rise on a show that would come only once in their lives, and they realized that they were not fully prepared. At a complete loss, they could hardly remember the script. Wang Qiyao too was struck with stage fright; she was as yet unprepared for her role of spectator. The prior scenes had been full of surprises, and now the final and most dazzling act was about to be performed before her eyes. At the entrance to the hotel they could see lights flooding the ground, just waiting for the couple to bask in their radiance. As the taxi pulled over to the curb, a few pedestrians stopped to look as the bride and groom stepped onto the stage. Wang Qiyao got out of the car first and stood off to one side, waiting for the couple to step out. Taking Xiao Lin's arm, she guided Weiwei's hand to grab hold of it before giving them a gentle nudge from behind. As they approached the entrance, shoulder to shoulder, their retreating silhouette was indeed the image of a perfect couple!

Off to America

Weiwei was married. She took all her clothing away with her, leaving the dresser half empty, and also the chest. Twenty-three years Wang Qiyao had spent raising Weiwei, and now her daughter was gone—and all she had left was her gray hair. Her skin and figure still looked young; it was only recently that she had begun to dye her hair. If it hadn't been for the fact that she had an adult daughter, no one would have guessed her age. She also used her daughter to remind herself about her own age, or else she would have never believed how old she was either. Dyed hair is even darker and shinier than natural hair, so it made her look even younger. Wang Qiyao gazed at herself in the mirror, a bit disoriented, wondering just what era she was living in.

Once Weiwei was gone, there were days when Wang Qiyao ate only a single meal. Sometimes she would go to sleep in the afternoon and not wake up until the same time the following day, when she would finally get up at one or two o'clock in the afternoon. The sun would be exactly where she had left it the previous day. But all this changed on Sunday, because that was when Weiwei and Xiao Lin came to visit. They would arrive in the morning and leave after dinner—it was only then that Wang Qiyao's life regained a semblance of normalcy. But the very next day everything would start to slip away again; the power of her daily routine was obviously far from enough. But at least she had Sundays to add some rhythm to her disorganized days; otherwise her entire life would have dissolved into chaos.

Now that they were married, Weiwei and Xiao Lin became guests. Wang Qiyao would ply them with food and liquor, making full-course dinners; when the evening was done, they would go home, leaving her with a pile of dirty plates and bowls. As she stood by the sink washing the dishes, she would heave a sigh of relief that the day was finally over. Once she was finished straightening up, she would turn on the television, take out a pack of cigarettes from the drawer, and light up. Sitting down, her elbow leaning on the table, she inhaled, slowly and deeply. The smoke clouded her vision, and her heart was clouded too. One cigarette was enough. After putting the pack of cigarettes away, she needed to sit for a while longer, listening to all the sounds of the changing seasons coming from outside. The sounds crept in from between the cracks in the concrete, and one had to be extremely quiet to hear them. They were but whispers of sounds, enmeshed in smoke and mist. Who understood time better than Wang Qiyao? She may have passed her days in a muddled haze, but that was only because she wanted to. When the window curtains moved gently, you might say that what you saw was the wind, but what Wang Qiyao saw was time. When small holes appeared in the wooden floor and staircase, you might say that what you saw was the work of termites, but what Wang Qiyao saw was time. Sunday nights, Wang Qiyao was never in a hurry to get to bed. It wasn't that she wanted to hold vigil over the lonely night: she was floating on time.

There was no reason to keep track of the days. The winter clothes came off and then out came the spring clothes, which before long began to feel heavy. Xiao Lin got his visa and would be leaving for America in August, just in time for the fall semester. In the days leading up to his departure, their schedule was quite erratic. For a while Xiao Lin and Weiwei ceased their Sunday visits, and then there was a period during which they came over almost every day. The reason they visited so often was to get Wang Qiyao's advice about what Xiao Lin should take for the trip. The impression they had of America was that it was one big nonstop party; how could he not bring along a few nice outfits? At the mention of clothing, Wang Qiyao would spring to life. She took Xiao Lin to Baromon to have a suit made, giving him tips about the proper way to wear a suit along the way. Wang Qiyao grew animated when she talked about clothing. What are clothes? she would say. Clothing is like a diploma, providing conclusive proof as to what is inside so that it won't get buried. Xiao Lin found her ideas about clothing interesting and amusing.

"Don't laugh," Wang Qiyao warned him. "I'm not exaggerating one bit. At the very least, for a woman, clothing is her diploma—and it's a much more important diploma than any earned in school!"

Xiao Lin laughed and turned to Weiwei. "Do you have a diploma?"

Wang Qiyao made a wry face. "Weiwei's diploma is the kind anyone can get from a few years in school. What I'm talking about is something you have to work on all your life. Don't bother asking Weiwei about that—she's too spoiled to understand. Go ask Zhang Yonghong."

"Zhang Yonghong may have a 'diploma,'" replied Weiwei. "But even now she still can't find a 'job'!"

Those were harsh words, the kind spoken only by one who is blinded by her own happiness. Even someone as resilient as Wang Qiyao felt the sting.

"You don't need to worry about Zhang Yonghong," she retorted just as they were arriving at Baromon. "She's stronger than you!"

They started by looking at fabrics and then moved on to pick out a style. Another clash seemed inevitable. Weiwei was leaning toward the double-breasted jacket with wide lapels that was the latest thing. Wang Qiyao, on the other hand, insisted that he go with a more traditional style, which she felt would be more appropriate. If he went with the more conventional suit she suggested, he would be able to wear it on virtually any occasion, whereas the more modish style was only good for the moment and would quickly go out of fashion; moreover, just because it was popular in Shanghai didn't mean it was popular in America. Although Weiwei didn't have a convincing argument, she still stubbornly insisted on her choice. With her natural aversion to anything old-fashioned, she was always drawn to the newest and latest fashion; also, because she lacked vision and couldn't see what was coming in the future, all she knew was to follow the current trend and so she always looked at things out of context. Weiwei grew quarrelsome and was on the verge of yelling at her mother.

"Let Xiao Lin decide for himself!" Wang Qiyao had no choice but to declare.

Xiao Lin followed Wang Qiyao's advice.

Weiwei was so angry that she turned and headed for the door. Xiao Lin chased after her, leaving Wang Qiyao alone. It was awkward for her to stay in the store, but equally embarrassing to follow them outside, so she stood there for a while before deciding simply to go home. She got on a public bus, thinking how pathetic it was that the three of them had gone out together and now she was going home alone. The bustling excitement on Nanjing Road seemed to be mocking her. It was almost noon by the time she finally arrived home. The other two didn't return until much later that afternoon. They pranced in, giggling and carrying a bunch of shopping bags, all the unhappiness of the morning long forgotten. Wang Qiyao didn't even bother asking about what had transpired with the suit. She pretended not to care, although she did notice Xiao Lin wink at her when Weiwei wasn't looking—that was his way of trying to smooth things over. Wang Qiyao felt misunderstood. *Why should I care about what kind of suit you get anyway?* she thought.

For Xiao Lin's upcoming trip, nothing but the best would do, as if anything less would be an embarrassment to the Americans. He didn't take any of his old clothing; everything he packed was brand-new. He cared for quantity as much as quality, buying everything by the dozen, as if he were preparing for a long career in the remote countryside, where nothing could be purchased, rather than going to study abroad. However, it was indeed a rare opportunity to go to America. Everyone thought it must be a wonderful place, although no one really knew what made it so wonderful. All Xiao Lin could do was prepare as best he could. It was a bit like preparing a trousseau—something tangible you could do against a bewildering future; whether or not it would ever come in useful was another matter altogether. As those two humongous suitcases gradually filled up, Xiao Lin began to feel more at ease.

One day Weiwei came over alone and insisted on helping her mother with all sorts of chores, even hand washing the two articles of clothing Wang Qiyao had been soaking in the basin. Wang Qiyao knew that Weiwei had a favor to ask and was pretty certain it had to do with borrowing money. Weiwei was behaving the same way she used to when she wanted her mother to buy her new clothes. But this time she was even more solicitous than usual and a bit more hesitant about saying what she actually wanted. She had already left the nest, and going back to her mother for handouts now was a bit out of line. Wang Qiyao couldn't help sighing as she wondered what would happen to Weiwei after Xiao Lin left—it was uncertain when the newlyweds could reunite and in the meantime she would have to live with her in-laws. Technically, they were her family now, but she really had very little in common with them and Wang Qiyao dared not speculate on what might be in store for her daughter. When Weiwei came back inside from hanging out the wet clothes, she saw some money lying on the table.

"Take it and buy Xiao Lin a new pair of shoes," said Wang Qiyao. "Think of it as a gift from me."

Weiwei didn't touch the money. "We've already bought him shoes for every season. He doesn't need any more."

Wang Qiyao could tell that she wanted more. She added, "If not shoes, then something else. But that's all I've got right now. Take it as my way of congratulating him."

Weiwei still didn't touch the money. She lowered her head. Wang Qiyao's spirits sank; she walked away without saying anything. She had not expected Weiwei to break the silence by telling her that she had heard about someone who had gone to America with nothing but a gold locket. When he got to America he sold it; with the help of that money, he managed to get through those first few months and finally got on his feet. Wang Qiyao grew anxious as she listened to the story. *What is she trying to say?* And then she remembered the day she asked Xiao Lin to exchange a gold bar for her at the bank. Her heart skipped a beat and she turned red.

"Never in my life have I failed to do my duty by you. . ." Her voice trembled.

Weiwei raised her eyebrows in surprise. "Who ever said you failed us? We're just asking to borrow it. We'll pay you back, I promise!"

Wang Qiyao was almost in tears. "Weiwei, you must have been blind to marry a man like that!"

Weiwei started to lose her temper. "Xiao Lin doesn't know anything about this. I came here to discuss this with you on my own. Actually, I have a few rings, but they are only fourteen carat gold. They were only expensive because of the craftsmanship, but I wouldn't get much if I tried to sell them. Buyers only care about the quality of the gold. How about this—I'll leave these with you and you give me just one of your nicer ones?"

It was only then that Wang Qiyao realized that Weiwei was after the antique ring with inlaid stones that Director Li had given her back when they first met, the one that he had let her pick out at the famous Lucky Phoenix Jewelers. It would have been her wedding ring had they married. Instead it was a mere memento that at best commemorated a vanished world and the vicissitudes of a difficult life. She might as well give it to her! Wang Qiyao paused for a moment before unlocking her desk drawer.

As she handed the ring over to Weiwei, Wang Qiyao only said, "No good will ever come to you if you treat men too well."

Weiwei ignored her, took the ring, and left.

Prior to his departure Xiao Lin hosted a farewell banquet at the Jinjiang Hotel. He booked four tables for his friends and relatives—it was an even grander occasion than their wedding reception. Wang Qiyao looked at the way Weiwei radiated happiness and wondered how she could possibly be happy when she was merely being used as a tool to help Xiao Lin go abroad. She sat amid the Lins and their friends and, though no one paid her much attention, she kept a smile on her face. Xiao Lin and Weiwei made the rounds, toasting all the tables; when they reached Wang Qiyao's table, she felt like laughing. Instead, tears began to trickle down her cheeks, making everyone feel a bit awkward. Her tears eventually gave way to a strange depression that seemed to come from nowhere—she just felt the whole thing was pointless. The merriment around her appeared to be edged with grief, as if everyone was in mourning for unknown causes and the smiles on their faces were forced through tears.

The table where Xiao Lin's young friends were sitting was the most convivial of the lot and the noise they made was deafening, but Wang

Qiyao felt their laughter was but the extremity of sorrow and that all that their faces showed was grief. A boy at the next table knocked over a glass belonging to one of the adults, spilling red wine—to Wang Qiyao the stain on the tablecloth was the color of blood. She could barely make it through the banquet—her heart ached, though she couldn't figure out why, nor could she find a release from the pain. The banquet felt like the last supper; everything seemed to be coming to an end. This kind of despair comes on suddenly, in a torrent, and for some reason seems especially to favor grand occasions as its setting. The more magnificent the occasion, the more overwhelming the grief that attends it. Over at the next table, she could hear Xiao Lin and Weiwei singing a song. Their gleeful voices nearly shattered her last line of defense, but the ensuing rowdiness held down her grief. By the time everyone got up to say good-bye, Wang Qiyao could barely speak—she could only bow her head to the guests. It was a good thing that hardly anyone there knew her and she was simply brushed aside. Walking past the clusters of people saying their good-byes, she went home by herself.

This unexpected assault of misplaced emotion was followed by a long string of quiet, peaceful days. Xiao Lin left. Weiwei began to visit home more frequently again, and sometimes, when Zhang Yonghong was there too, it almost felt like the old days. Laying out a piece of new fabric on the table, they would discuss it endlessly before they set about cutting out the pattern.

By this time a new breed of younger and more fashionable girls had come on the scene on Huaihai Road, making Zhang Yonghong's generation look conservative. But their conservatism wasn't what we usually think of as conservative; it was in fact a strategy of conserving one's strength for future attacks, of stepping back in order to spring forward. Having lived through many trends, they had gradually formed their own perspective. They had progressed beyond blindly following the latest trend and were now stepping aside to let a new generation take over the cutting edge. You could say that they had finally secured a foothold amid the raging torrents of shifting fashion. Just because they were no longer driving the trend didn't mean they were no longer a part of it: they were the ones who controlled when fashions came and went. In contrast, though the fashions on the street may have looked explosive, they were rootless and fleeting.

Weiwei, always a step behind Zhang Yonghong, was the kind who instinctively looked to someone else for guidance. If she hadn't had Zhang

Yonghong and Wang Qiyao to steer the ship for her. Weiwei would probably have spent her entire life as a slave to fashion. But there they were, the three of them together again, heatedly discussing cuts and alterations, just like old times. Each of their outfits was the end result of extensive research and discussion. As they tried on new clothes, one would stand in front of the mirror while the other two stood on either side, carefully looking her over. Every now and then, one would turn around and find a look of loneliness on the face in the mirror, at which point she would quickly find something to say to the others in order to cover it up.

The three spent Christmas together that year. They put on newly tailored jackets, applied some makeup, and showed up for the Christmas dinner at a hotel that had just opened in the new Hongqiao Development District, where they had made reservations ahead of time. Before the taxi even reached the hotel, they were already struck by its splendor. It took them a minute to get their bearings after stepping out of the taxi. Overhead, a weblike arrangement of Christmas lights hung from the trees, which appeared to be aflame with silvery flowers. Moving on into the hotel, they were greeted by an attendant dressed like Santa Claus. The lobby was a-bustle with well-dressed visitors. They went up to the restaurant and found their seats next to a long table for twenty, where they were surrounded by young couples and parents out with their children, everyone carrying on as if they were by themselves. The three of them usually never had a shortage of things to say, but now found themselves at a loss for words and sat prim and proper in their seats. There was nothing terribly fancy about the cuisine and, because there were so many people, it actually felt like they were having cafeteria food. There was a constant flow of Christmas songs and the guests were repeatedly reminded that the bells would ring at midnight, whereupon Santa Claus would give out presents—the lucky recipients to be determined by a raffle.

The three women sensed they had come to the wrong place—this had been an utterly unsuitable choice. They could only avert their eyes as young lovers cozied up to one another. The small children were friendlier; they weren't afraid of strangers and would come up to chat with them, livening up the atmosphere somewhat. But the forbidding parents avoided their gazes and they had to check any impulse to socialize. In any case, they felt totally out of place and ill-at-ease. They could not bring themselves to stay until midnight and, having talked it over, decided to go home. No one took any notice as they got up from their seats and left. At the door they ran into waitresses on their way into the dining room, carrying trays of ice cream, but none of them was in the mood to go back for dessert. The hallway was quiet and the elevator quietly ascended as soon as they pushed the button. When the doors closed before them, they saw that the walls on all three sides were made of mirrors, but seeing their own faces was unbearable. They remained silent, staring at the numbers over the door as they lit up, one after the other, until they finally arrived back on the ground floor. Lacking the presence of mind to ask for a cab, they walked straight out of the lobby onto the road. The roads in this new district were broad and straight, with few pedestrians, only a quiet flow of traffic coming from the direction of the airport. They walked on awhile before they thought of hailing a cab.

"Why don't you come over?" suggested Wang Qiyao. "We can celebrate Christmas at my place."

The girls agreed and they walked back to get a cab at the hotel entrance. It was now eleven o'clock. The city was silent, but behind its locked doors and windows all kinds of festivities were taking place. One would have had little inkling of what was going on in the city until someone came out, bringing with him the sights and sounds of the gaiety, which spilled over the sidewalks like seeds. The threesome capped off Christmas Eve at Wang Qiyao's apartment. Coming from the raucous celebrations at the hotel, they found Peace Lane extraordinarily quiet, as if the people there were holding their breath. But the silence set off the excitement in their hearts, which had been suppressed and stifled all this time. Here was their world. They munched on snacks and exchanged gossip, telling stories they usually didn't share with one another as the spirit moved them. Zhang Yonghong related her latest argument with her boyfriend; the occasion itself had been minor, but it had been pivotal in deciding whether they would one day get married. Realizing that Zhang Yonghong was finally thinking of marriage, Wang Qiyao encouraged her to lower her standards. She had, of course, given the same advice many times before, but because of the special mood that night, her words seemed to come straight from the heart. Not only did Zhang Yonghong hear her out; she even opened up, releasing some of the pain she had bottled up. It wasn't that she had overvalued herself, she said, but that she looked on marriage as her only shot at getting a second chance in life.

"You all know the kind of family I was born into. . . . That's why I've always felt that marriage was my one chance to rewrite history."

"But you can't expect to just walk into a situation where everything is already taken care of for you," said Weiwei. "If you want to rewrite history, you'll have to do it together with your husband."

"It's not that I want to walk into a situation where everything is already taken care of," explained Zhang Yonghong. "What I want is some capital to live off of. If both of us start with nothing, we'll be decrepit before we begin to see the light at the end of the tunnel. But speaking of having everything already taken care of, the one who fits that description is Weiwei. You've got an apartment to live in rent-free *and* a hubby in America."

"I would have been more than happy if he didn't go to America!" Weiwei protested. "You have no idea what it's like being in my shoes!"

This was the first time since Xiao Lin's departure that Wang Qiyao had heard her daughter complain. It surprised her a little, but on second thought she understood why.

"Of course things may be difficult for the time being, but all of that will pass," said Zhang Yonghong.

"But *I'm* the one who has to get through it every single day! No one else can do it for me," said Weiwei. "Do you know why I keep running back to Mom's house? Because I can't stand the sight of his parents' snotty intellectual faces!"

Zhang Yonghong laughed. "What's wrong with intellectual faces? I wish I could see some, but there aren't any around!"

The three of them laughed. Zhang Yonghong stayed over that night on the sofa. They lost track of the time and fell asleep only when the morning light was already peeking through the curtains.

The sympathy they shared that night was enough to last them quite some time. After that they saw each other several times a week, and Weiwei had practically moved back in with her mother. As long as Zhang Yonghong was around, mother and daughter were able to maintain an atmosphere of mutual tolerance and understanding. Zhang Yonghong was the lubricant in their relationship. Before long, however, she met a new boyfriend and her visits became scarce again.

Six months later, Xiao Lin successfully completed the paperwork for Weiwei to join him in America, and she too left. Although it had taken only one year, the process exhausted Weiwei's patience. She wasn't even in the mood to prepare for the trip; all she did was to pack two suitcases, one with clothing and the other with daily necessities such as cooking utensils and a large box filled with crucifix necklaces, which she had bought on Huating Road for just pennies each—Xiao Lin had said in one of his letters that they would go for two dollars each in America.

Wang Qiyao agonized over whether to give her daughter one of the gold bars. In the end she decided against it. Weiwei had Xiao Lin to rely on, but who did she have? Wearing a plain cotton outfit and a pair of old shoes, Weiwei boarded the plane for San Francisco.

Chapter 3

Old Colour

"LAO KE-LA" REFERS to a specific breed of debonair figures active during the fifties and sixties. These were the keepers of old-style Shanghai fashion in the new society, at a time when holding on to the past was considered radical. The term probably originated with the English word "old colour," or perhaps "old classic," a remnant of the colonial culture of Shanghai in the day of the treaty ports. As the lingo of the city incorporated bits and pieces of foreign languages, words became dismembered and, with the passage of time, grew increasingly distant from their original meanings. By the eighties, people who fell into the category of "Old Colour" were virtually extinct. The surviving handful were all fairly advanced in age, their erstwhile shape completely transformed; eventually even the term itself was forgotten. But then something odd happened. In the mid eighties, a new generation of Old Colours emerged quietly upon the scene. Lacking their predecessors' craving for notoriety, they were not compelled to behave ostentatiously and appeared more easygoing. It was not even easy to spot them in the crowd. Where might one go to find such a specimen?

These Old Colours—when everyone was out buying a stereo, they were listening to old phonographs. When Nikon and Minolta cameras equipped with auto-focus features were all the rage, they were busy fiddling with their vintage Rolleiflex 120s. They sported wind-up watches, drank coffee brewed in small pots, shaved with old-fashioned razor blades and shaving cream, took great delight in antique slide projectors, and wore large leather shoes shaped like boats. When you saw these markings, you could be certain that you had found one. Then, having found one, you couldn't help but notice just how crude and boorish the so-called fashionable were in comparison. The rush to be trendy left no time for elegance or refinement. One was driven about by a succession of waves. Speed and quantity were all that mattered, and the result was that corners were cut and things got done in a slipshod manner and had eventually to be discarded. You could tell this by looking at the clothing shops where advertisements for markdowns were posted all over the walls, shelves, and counters—even the stalls outside. Before the last season's clothes had sold out, they were two steps behind the latest fashion, which had already arrived. What choice was there but to run constant sales and markdowns?

In this crude and uncultured fashion world, the "Old Colours" were the stewards in charge of safekeeping refinement. They were the only ones paying attention to the things that mattered; though they never advertised themselves or talked about what they were doing, they had their feet firmly planted on the ground. They took things one step at a time; men of action, they let others do the talking. They didn't even have a name. The term "Old Colour" was given to them by the few who remembered the old days, but it never gained wide circulation. A small minority called them Western-style "Yuppies," but that never caught on either. And so they remained nameless, silently tilling their little plot of land. We could, if we chose, refer to them as nostalgic "lovers of the past," although they were all young and didn't have a past to love per se. But they had all been to the Bund and seen, riding on the ferry, what it looked like from out on the water: there they saw the ramparts formed by the Georgian buildings, the Gothic bell tower with its pointed steeple, and the dark forbidding windows staring back at them—all of which sent them down the tunnel of time. They had also climbed up to the rooftops to release pigeons and fly kites, and there, looking out over the sea of rooftops, a few of which jutted out like sails, felt as if they were navigating against the currents of time. Besides these, the ivy crawling up the sides of the walls and the sounds of someone playing the piano in the Western-style house next door also came to feed their nostalgia.

Wang Qiyao knew one of these "Old Colours." He was twenty-six years old, so calling him an "Old Colour" was a bit ironic, a way of emphasizing his youth. A gym teacher at a local middle school, he normally dressed in sweatpants, and his hair looked like the bristle end of a scrub brush. He had a dark complexion from years of working outdoors. At school he kept to himself and never fraternized with his colleagues. Who would have guessed that he was an accomplished flamenco guitar player with a collection of more than a hundred jazz records? This "Old Colour" lived in a traditional *longtang* in Hongkou, with parents who were honest, hardworking government employees and watched what they spent;

his sister had left home to get married. He himself occupied the third-floor *tingzijian*: his palmwood cot lay on the floor along with his record player. As soon as he entered his room, he would take off his shoes and, sitting on the bare floor, enter into his own little universe. Outside his dormer window was a slanted portion of the roof. Occasionally, during the summer, he would climb out the window with a backpack, spread a mat out over the roof tiles, and, tying himself to the windowsill with a rope around his waist, spend the evening lying outside. Looking up, he would see a sprinkling of stars suspended in the deep blue sky above. He could faintly make out the rumbling sounds of the machinery from a factory in the distance, and the smoke from the factory's smokestack billowed white against the sky. The scattered sounds of the night seemed to have sunk down to earth, while he himself had dissolved into the air, empty of thoughts and desires.

Old Colour was still without a girlfriend. Although he got on quite well with some of the girls in his regular circle of friends, things had never developed past the point of ordinary friendship. As there was nothing further he needed, he had no particular aspirations and was content just to have a job. However, he recognized that he had only himself to rely on, and this made him approach things with a positive attitude. And, though he lacked long-term goals, he did have some short-term plans. This meant that, while never vexed by major problems, he was struck by the occasional fit of inexplicable depression. For these depressions he found an antidote in his collection of old jazz records from the twenties. The sound of the saxophone, mixed with the hissing sound of the needle against the vinyl, gave him a feeling of an almost palpable intimacy. Old Colour was a bit old-fashioned: nothing new suited his taste, because to him it lacked substance and smacked of the nouveau riche; but then neither was he a fan of things that were *too* old, which would have felt antiquated and dismal. A hundred years was just about enough. He longed for a time back when, like the sprinkling of stars in the night sky, only the elite prospered—for a European-style house on a smooth cobblestone road, and the spiraling sounds of the phonograph twisting their way up through an otherwise perfect silence. This was, when all was said and done, what all those old jazz records stood for.

His young friends were all modern individuals at the cutting edge of fashion, quite the opposite of Old Colour. When Shanghai inaugurated its first tennis court, his friends were the first customers standing in line; when a certain luxury hotel opened up a bowling alley, they were the first to try it out. All of them were college classmates of Old Colour from the phys-ed department; they prided themselves on their athletic spirit and prowess, which happened to be right in tune with worldwide fashion. Just look at the most popular brand names of the day—Nike and Puma—you could see that they were all athletic apparel, whereas brands like Pierre Cardin had long been on the way down. This cohort would appear on the streets on motorcycles, a girl seated at the back with her hair streaming down from her helmet, and you could feel the rush of wind as they flew past. They were the wildest ones on the dance floor at the discos. They always managed to get hold of a foreigner or two to give their gatherings an international flavor—which, incidentally, gained them entry into all kinds of exclusive places where only international guests were welcome.

Among them, Old Colour was always the quiet one: he never really contributed to the group. When everyone else was having a great time, he would be off standing in one corner as if he did not count. He seemed a bit lonely, but it was precisely such loneliness that provided this fashionable, happy-go-lucky crowd with a certain substance. So it actually *wouldn't* have been the same if he hadn't been there. As for himself, he needed a modern backdrop to set himself off from everyone else; had he been thrown into the sea of people unattached, his old-fashioned style would have been completely drowned out. Because his style appeared outdated on the surface, people had a hard time identifying it for what it was; but it really stood out against a super-modern background, like an antique placed on a velvet mat. Without the mat, someone would probably have thrown the piece away, thinking it was junk. Therefore Old Colour had to run with that crowd, lonely as he may have been. If he had left, he would have lost even the distinction of being lonely—he would have simply disappeared among the teeming masses.

Old Colour's parents always thought of him as a responsible son; he didn't drink or smoke, had a steady job and a healthy hobby, and never got mixed up with the wrong sort of girl. They themselves had been fairly conservative in their youth; going to the movies once a week was their sole entertainment. There was a period when his mother became obsessed with collecting movie pamphlets, but during the Cultural Revolution she took it upon herself to burn her entire collection; later the movie theaters stopped putting them out. Once his parents bought a television set, they stopped going to the movies altogether. Every night they would turn on the television after dinner and watch until eleven o'clock. With this television set, their golden years seemed perfect. The music their son played up in the *tingzijian* had a familiar sound, which tended to confirm their opinions that he was steady. The fact that he was taciturn also put them at ease. Even when they had dinner together at the same table, the entire meal would pass with barely a few words. When it came down to it, they were all strangers to each other, but seeing each other, day in, day out, they didn't think much about their state, as if this was how it was supposed to be. But they were, in truth, decent people; their thoughts and actions were always in line and, whether it be spiritual or material, just a little bit of space was enough for them.

Crammed in under the rooftops of the Shanghai *longtang* were countless people living out their frugal lives just like that. On occasion you might feel that it is rather noisy—as soon as the windows were opened, your ears would be assaulted by all kinds of sounds. But don't be offended: what you hear are the accumulated sounds of the activities of prudent people over their lifetime; at least the noise shows that they are lively. And Old Colour certainly wasn't the only one stargazing from the rooftop on those summer nights; the hearts of all these people are restless and unsure of where to go—and so up they go to the rooftops. There everything is wide open; even the knowing pigeons are bedded down for the evening, leaving the sky empty of their flight. All the noise and clatter remain below, but they have floated to the top and it feels good to drift for a while. In these *longtang* with the dormer windows, the songs of the heart have quite a distinctive sound, and the dormer windows are the throats through which the songs are forced out.

Old Colour finds true understanding in the neighborhoods on the west side of Shanghai, and he likes to wander there along the tree-lined streets. Even the canopies of the trees there have a history, having filtered out the sunlight for a century. Maoming Road passes from a roaring hubbub on one end to quietude on the other, both of which have the vintage of years. Old Colour loved traversing this area, where he had the feeling that time had been turned back. Examining the trolley tracks on the street, he tried to imagine what it was like when the cars were still running; he could picture two rows of wooden benches facing each other inside the trolley, just like the ones he had seen in old silent films. There seemed to be writing on the brick and stonework of the old hotels; as he patiently read them, the words recounted trials and tribulations from the past. The areas on the east side of the city also understood Old Colour. Every major street there leads to the river. Though the scene is less refined, it has a sharpness about it. The silent film being played here is more like a sweeping epic, the action coming on like a hurricane. Time has stopped for the seagulls soaring across the sky, as it has for the pigeons.

That's what he, too, wanted—for time to stop. That's not too much to ask, is it? He didn't ask for an eternity, only the last fifty years. His request was restrained, like the sunrise in the city, which does not come up over the sea or the horizon, but from the rooftops—its beginning and the end curtailed. In fact, the city is still a child and doesn't have many days to look back upon. But a child like Old Colour was already an old man, who, bypassing experience, went straight to reminiscence. All of his deepest thoughts were dialogues with the past. At least the clock in the Customs House was still ringing, in a world where everything else seemed to have vanished like clouds and mist, and the sound he heard was the very sound heard decades ago. As Old Colour walked down the street, the wind blowing against his face was a draft squeezed through the space between two buildings. He may have looked calm on the surface, but his heart was vibrant, almost dancing with joy. He loved the sunset over Shanghai; the streets at dusk were like a faded oil painting, a perfect match for the mood of the city.

One day a friend of his told Old Colour about a party someone was having. All kinds of people were supposed to be coming, including a former Miss Shanghai from the old days. He hopped onto the back of his friend's motorcycle, and they headed west to the new residential area near the airport. The man lived on the thirteenth floor of a building that he was managing for the owner, a relative of his who was living overseas. He didn't normally live there, but every few days he would invite friends over for a fun-filled afternoon or evening. Gradually, his parties started to gain some notoriety: word traveled fast, as one guest brought ten friends and each of them brought along others—but he didn't mind, everyone was welcome. As the numbers started to build up, it was inevitable that some questionable individuals would weasel their way in, and sometimes unpleasant things, such as thefts, would happen. But with so many people, the probability of someone extraordinary showing up was also quite high. Occasionally, real celebrities would appear, such as movie stars, the first violin from a famous orchestra, and reporters, as well as the children and grandchildren of powerful Communist and Nationalist leaders. This friend's parties were like small political meetings, where old stories and the latest gossip were passed around the living room, the whole place abuzz with excitement.

In this new district, all you saw when you opened the windows was a forest of buildings. Some of the windows were lit up while others remained dark; the sky was unobstructed, but this made the stars seem more distant. Below, the cars speeding down the straight broad roads looked like a chain of pearls. Not far off there would always be a construction site, where the lights blazed through the night and the noise of pile-drivers, hammering away in rhythm, filled the entire space below the heavens. The air is choked with particles of chalky cement and the wind is especially strong as it whips between the buildings. The lights over in the hotel district look a little lonely due to the heights of the buildings around it, but theirs is a resplendent loneliness that pierces the heart with rapture. This was indeed a brand-new district that greeted everything with an open heart, quite unlike the downtown area, whose convoluted feelings are more difficult to grasp. Arriving in the new district, one has the feeling that one has left the city behind. The style of the streets and buildings—built at right angles in a logical manner—is so unlike downtown, which seems to have been laid out by squeezing the emotions out from the heart.

Under the sky of the new district, the joyful laughter coming from the thirteenth floor of this joint-venture construction suddenly dissipates and the music fades away. But how much does that bit of happiness really matter in this new district? Playing out behind the honeycomb-like windows of those tall buildings is a fresh new form of happiness. In hotels so new that they have yet to acquire their four or five stars, there are buffets, dances, and receptions every night, as well as brazen games of passion that offered no excuses as they announced themselves to the world with "do not disturb" signs. With people of all races and colors taking part, it feels like a party of universal jubilation. This is especially so around Christmas time: as soon as the Christmas carols break out, you are hard pressed to discern whether you are in China or abroad. When you first arrive here, the place seems to lack a heart because it is so carefree—but that is because it hasn't yet had time to build up a reservoir of recollections; its mind is blank and has not begun to feel the need to call on its memory. Such is the spiritual state of the entire district. The laughter and gaiety coming from the thirteenth floor form but a drop in the ocean. The only one who seems a bit annoyed is the elevator attendant, as people come rushing in and out of the elevator, in couples or crowds, holding wine and flowers—mostly strangers, in all shapes, sizes, and colors.

More than a dozen groups of guests had already arrived by the time Old Colour got to the party. The door had been left half-open and the room was filled with people moving about. No one paid the newcomers much attention as they came in; the stereo was blaring loud music. A few people sat around watching a television miniseries in the first room, which led out to the balcony. The door to the balcony was ajar and the wind was agitating the curtains. In a corner of this room sat a woman with fair skin, wearing light makeup, in a pinkish-purple suit made of raw silk. She was leaning forward slightly toward the television screen with her arms crossed. The curtain brushed against her skirt from time to time, but this didn't seem to distract her. Only when the screen suddenly lit up did her drooping eyelids show, giving away her age. But the stamp of age passes in a flickering instant: she carefully wrapped hers up and tucked it away inside her bones. The years had tiptoed around her, careful not to leave too many traces, but in the end they couldn't help leaving a few. This was Wang Qiyao in 1985.

Around this time the opulence of 1946 was revived in a few essays reminiscing about old Shanghai, and the name Wang Qiyao suddenly came into the spotlight again. One or two nosy reporters even went so far as to investigate what had happened to Wang Qiyao in the years following the pageant; several articles were published in the back pages of the newspapers but failed to generate much interest, and the whole thing eventually died down. A lot of time had indeed gone by. No matter how glamorous a woman has been, once she has entered the black hole of time, she is lucky to generate even a few flickers of light. The aura surrounding the beauty pageant, no less than Wang Qiyao herself, had also faded after forty years, and it only served to date her by revealing her age. It was like the old clothes at the bottom of her chest: though many were still in good shape, wearing them only made her look older, because they were from the wrong era.

The only one who seemed to be moved by any of this history was Zhang Yonghong. She didn't believe the story initially, but once she had accepted it she had an endless array of questions for Wang Qiyao. Wang Qiyao, for her part, resisted answering them at first, but once she began to open up, she had an endless series of revelations for Zhang Yonghong to uncover. There were many things that Wang Qiyao thought she had completely forgotten, but as soon as she got started, all of those tiny bits and fragments of detail came together to make a flowing river of memories. The stories she told were those of a woman who had stood in the limelight; but wasn't that the goal of all those girls on Huaihai Road trying to outdress one another? Wave after wave of fashion that came and went—weren't they all vying for their moment in the spotlight? Zhang Yonghong, who understood the magnitude of the splendor Wang Qiyao was describing, exclaimed, "I'm so envious!"

Zhang Yonghong introduced Wang Qiyao to all of her boyfriends and invited her to all kinds of parties. These were mostly parties for young people, and, knowing her own place, Wang Qiyao would usually sit off to one side. Nevertheless, her elegance would still add a touch of distinction to the party. Barring the occasional glance, people didn't pay her any attention, but everyone was aware that there was a "Miss Shanghai" in their presence. On occasion there might even be a few people eagerly awaiting her arrival, not realizing that she had been sitting in the corner all along—she sat there alone until the music stopped and the show was over. Wang Qiyao was always well dressed and elegant; she was never awkward and never got in the way. She was an ornament, a painting on the wall to adorn the living room. The painting was done in somber hues, with a dark yellow base; it had true distinction, and even though the colors were faded, its value had appreciated. Everything else was simply transient flashes of light and shadow.

It was under these circumstances that Old Colour first met Wang Qiyao. *Could that be the "Miss Shanghai" everyone was talking about?* he wondered. Just as he was about to walk away, he saw Wang Qiyao look up and scan the room before lowering her head again. The look in her eyes had a hint of panic, but she was not at all looking for sympathy or forgiveness. It was then that Old Colour realized how callous he had been. He thought, *The Miss Shanghai pageant was nearly forty years ago.* His vision grew blurry as he stared at Wang Qiyao, as if his eyes couldn't focus properly, and through that hazy vision he saw an image of her from more than three decades ago. Gradually the image became clearer, taking on depth and new details. But none of those details looked real; they floated on the surface, piercing Old Colour's heart. He came face to face with a cruel reality—the corrosive power of time.

At twenty-six years of age, Old Colour should have been too young to care about the passing of time; time had yet to teach him such truths, but that is precisely why he longed for the past—that is the only reason he dared to extol the fruits of time! The passage of time associated with those old jazz records was indeed a good thing; it had smoothed things out until they were strong and fine, rubbing off the superficial layers to reveal the inner grain, like gold emerging when the fire has burned away the dross. But what he saw that day was not an object, like an old jazz record, but a person. He was at a complete loss as to what to say, because the situation had an element of the tragic. He had finally touched the heart of that bygone era, whereas before he had only paced back and forth on its surface. Something halted his steps and Old Colour couldn't bring himself to walk away. He picked up a glass of wine and leaned up against the door, fixing his gaze on the television. Eventually Wang Qiyao got up from the corner to go to the restroom. As she walked past him, he flashed her a smile. She immediately accepted his smile, responding with a look of gratitude before smiling back at him. When she came back, he asked her if he could get her a drink. She pointed to the corner and said that she already had a cup of tea, so there was no need. He asked her to dance. She hesitated for a moment . . . and accepted.

Disco music was blaring in the living room, but they danced the four-step at half speed. With all manner of wild movements swirling around them, only they were stationary, like a lone island in a rushing torrent. She apologized, suggesting that he go back to disco dancing rather than waste his time with her. But he insisted that he was having a good time. He put his hand on her waist and could feel the slight pulsations of her body. It was a strategy of nonmovement in response to the myriad changes taking place around her, of finding her own rhythm, no matter what the tempo of her surroundings might be, a rhythm that could carry her through time. Moved by this, he remained lost in silence until she suddenly complimented his dance skills; they were now doing a traditional Latin number. When the tune changed, someone else invited Wang Qiyao to dance. During the next number, they each danced with their respective partners but their eyes occasionally met, whereupon they exchanged a knowing smile, lit up with the joy of this chance meeting. The party took place on the evening of National Day and fireworks were being set off from one of the balconies. A single rocket shot up into the darkness and slowly unfurled its fiery petals in the night sky before breaking up into a stream of falling stars, which vanished slowly, leaving a faint white shadow in the sky. It was some time before the last of the light was absorbed into the blackness.

After that evening Wang Qiyao ran into Old Colour at a few other parties and they gradually got to know each other better. One time Old Colour told Wang Qiyao that he suspected he was the reincarnation of someone who had lived four decades earlier. This person had probably died a violent death in his youth, but because he hadn't properly finished out his previous life, was now left with a strange attachment to the past. Wang Qiyao asked him if he had any proof of this. He replied that his proof was based on his endless longing for the Shanghai of the forties, a world that otherwise had nothing to do with him. Sometimes, walking down the street, he would slip into a daze that seemed to transport him back to the past. The women would all be wearing *cheongsams* and dresses, the men had donned Western-style suits and hats, the trolley bell would ring out, and girls crying "Gardenias for sale!" sounded like orioles, while the apprentice at the silk shop made crisp noises with his scissors as they cut through pieces of fabric. Amid these sights and sounds he would slip into the past, becoming a person of that bygone era, someone who parted his hair in the middle, carried a leather briefcase, and supported his virtuous wife and family by working at a Western firm. Wang Qiyao laughed at this.

"Virtuous wife? Tell me, just how is she virtuous?"

He ignored her and continued on with his story. He said that in his vision he had taken the trolley to work as usual when a gun fight broke out inside the trolley car. A spy from Wang Jingwei's puppet government was trying to assassinate a man from the Chongqing faction. They chased each other around the car and in the end he was shot by a stray bullet and died there on the trolley.

"You got all that from a TV show!" Wang Qiyao challenged him.

Still disregarding her comments, he continued, "I was unjustly killed and my soul refused to accept what happened. That's why even though I seem to be here, my heart is in the past. And look at the way I always make friends with people much older than me, and when I first meet them I always have a feeling of déjà vu."

At that moment the music came back on and the two of them went back out onto the dance floor. Halfway through the number, Wang Qiyao suddenly smiled and said, "Actually, it's funny how *I* lived through that era and, much as I want to, I can't go back. But here you are, able to go back whenever you want!"

Her words moved him, but he didn't know quite how to respond.

"Even if it is a dream," Wang Qiyao continued, "It's *my* dream! You don't get to have those dreams and make them seem so real!"

With that, the two of them broke out in laughter. Before they left for the evening, Old Colour invited Wang Qiyao out to dinner the next evening. Seeing him play the role of the gentleman, Wang Qiyao thought him ridiculous, but she was also touched. "Why don't I be the host? But not at a restaurant. Why don't you come over to my place for a simple dinner? Anyway, you decide."

The next evening Old Colour arrived nice and early for dinner at Wang Qiyao's apartment. He sat on the sofa and watched Wang Qiyao as she trimmed the bad ends off the bean sprouts. Wang Qiyao had also invited Zhang Yonghong and her new boyfriend, whom everyone called Long Legs; they arrived just before dinner was supposed to start. By then the dishes were already on the table and Old Colour was putting out the plates and chopsticks as if he was one of the hosts. Because Wang Qiyao was a whole generation older than her guests, she felt no need to stand on ceremony and put out all of the cold and hot dishes together, leaving only a pot of soup simmering on the gas stove. Zhang Yonghong and her boyfriend had seen Old Colour around, but didn't really know him well enough to connect a name with his face. They couldn't help feeling a little awkward, and the conversation didn't get off the ground until Wang Qiyao smoothed things over. Since they were eating, the subject at hand naturally turned to food. Wang Qiyao mentioned a few dishes that they had never heard of, such as Indonesian coconut milk chicken. Since they were no longer able to buy coconut milk, she said, she couldn't make that dish. Another one was Cantonese-style barbecued pork, which she couldn't make because some of the ingredients were also unavailable. Then there were French goose liver pate and Vietnamese fish sauce . . . the list went on.

"That's what dinners were like forty years ago," Wang Qiyao explained, "a veritable United Nations conference. You could get food from any country! Shanghai back then was a little universe of its own. It was a window onto the rest of the world. But what could be seen outside the window was not half as important as what happened inside. What you saw outside was mere scenery; what happened inside was the foundation of everyday life. Forty years ago nobody ever flaunted this foundation, no posters or advertisements were needed. Every grain of rice and every piece of vegetable was accounted for. Today people carelessly grab things by the handful, and everything tastes like cafeteria food cooked in vats. Did you know that, forty years ago, when you ordered noodles, they would make them one bowl at a time?"

Old Colour could tell that Wang Qiyao's words were meant for him. She wanted to show him what life was really like forty years ago—to remind him how little he really knew. He knew that he was being mocked, but he didn't feel insulted; he actually welcomed that type of criticism, because it gave him entrée into real knowledge. He also got a taste of how astute she was. That was a quality from four decades ago: it was about silently putting up with wrongs rather than fighting for a better position, because in her world there was no place for displays of strength or cries of emotion. There was more consideration for others and less calculation for oneself. It was about understanding, something that was missing from the prevailing astuteness that has taken root forty years later.

After that night Old Colour started to come by quite often. On one occasion, when Zhang Yonghong was asking Wang Qiyao's advice about making a coat, he sat beside them, listening. Although he understood little about dressmaking, what she said seemed to contain some more abstract truths that could be applied to all kinds of things. He realized that he had been completely ignorant before; those old jazz records he listened to were intended as an accompaniment or background music; the real melody and action lay elsewhere. The saxophone might snatch at your attention with its dazzling displays of virtuosity, but the real star of the show always maintained its composure. Simple and unadorned—it was the common heart with which one lives the everyday. He gazed out the window at the neighbor's closed window across the way and wondered what lay concealed. Perhaps romantic stories were being played out. He walked slowly around the room; with each step he heard the sound of floorboards creaking and knew that here too were stories. There was so much indeed that he neither knew nor understood. In fact, the romance of forty years ago had lain right under his eyes, scattered in every corner.

Old Colour was an extremely quick-witted young man, and it took only a little effort for him to comprehend what the world had been like back then. Nothing authentic could slip past his eye, and nothing fake could fool him. He could almost smell the air from back then, carrying the scents of Rêve de Paris perfume and gardenias. The former belonged to the elite while the latter captured the banal tastes of the commoner, but even those gardenias had been romantic in their own way, each one carefully planted and cared for. And while that French perfume strove to rise above the rest, it still had its feet firmly planted on the ground. They represented the romance of the everyday world, which was quite enduring; even after its shell was cracked, the kernel remained.

"Whenever I come over to your place," Old Colour commented, "I really get the feeling that I have gone back in time."

"If you go back in time," Wang Qiyao mocked him, "I'm afraid there isn't that far you can go! Your mother's belly?"

"No," he explained, "I'm talking about going back to a previous life."

Afraid that he was about to carry on again about his previous life, Wang Qiyao quickly waved her hand for him to stop.

"I know all about your former life as a gentleman working at a foreign firm and married to a virtuous wife!" she snorted.

He laughed for a while before continuing, "I'm afraid that I even saw you once in my previous life. You were a student at a middle school, wearing a *cheongsam* and carrying a bookbag with a lotus-leaf shaped border . . ."

"And so you followed me, right?" She picked up where he left off, "and said, 'Miss, would you like to see a movie? Vivien Leigh is in it.' . . ."

With that, both of them keeled over in laughter.

That was the beginning.

From that point on, they often began their conversations that way, taking roles in a Hollywood-type movie. Naturally, love, which was the requisite theme, had to be part of the story. And so the two carried on rather recklessly, one fuelled by recollection, the other by aspiration, both fully immersed in their respective roles. From time to time they would forget it was mere playacting and take their fantasy as real. They even injected real feelings into the scenarios and grew melancholic as they ad-libbed. That's when Wang Qiyao would have to put a stop to it: "All right already! Stop carrying on as if this was real!"

"I wish it were real," declared Old Colour.

These words were followed by a long silence. They both felt a bit awkward and only then realized how far things had gone. He was after all still quite young and wasn't always capable of finding the proper words for the occasion. He tried to explain by adding, "I really love the whole atmosphere of that time."

Wang Qiyao didn't respond immediately. It was only after a brief pause that she replied, "Oh yeah, the atmosphere back then was great! A pity that the people involved are now so old that their teeth are falling out!"

Old Colour realized that he had said something wrong, but he couldn't find the words to explain himself any better and his face turned red in frustration. Wang Qiyao extended her hand to caress his hair.

"Such a child!"

He felt a lump in his throat and dared not look up. He couldn't get rid of the feeling that he had been misunderstood, yet didn't know how to express himself. Nor could he say for sure what exactly he had done wrong. As Wang Qiyao ran her hands through his hair he could sense the hurt this woman felt and her understanding. A well of compassion opened up in his heart, which brought them closer together.

They sat down next to each other and tried to avoid the previous topic of conversation by talking about some trivial things. Although the conversation wasn't as animated as before, neither of them was uncomfortable, as they felt something existed between them that transcended the occasional silences. It was those made-up stories from old Shanghai—the kind that linger, clinging to the heart. That night Old Colour invited Wang Qiyao out to dinner again; she wanted to accept, but she didn't. She thought, *Just what is this? He's forty years too late!*

She smiled. "There's no need for that. You usually eat better food at home than you do in some of those restaurants."

Sensing that she was heading off in a different direction, Old Colour decided not to press the issue. From that point on, he would call on Wang Qiyao every three days or so. He would usually stay for a meal, and her apartment eventually became almost like a second home to him. Sometimes Zhang Yonghong would come over and wind up joining them for dinner. Other times she brought Long Legs along with her, but they wouldn't necessarily stay for dinner, often just sitting and chatting for a while before leaving Wang Qiyao and Old Colour to have dinner alone. At such times the atmosphere would grow very still, as if signifying something. By tacit agreement, they avoided parties, which they found unwieldy because it was difficult to talk. Spending time at home may have been a bit too quiet, but there was a solidity to the quietness; they spoke when they had something to say, and kept silent when they didn't. It was a setting more appropriate to two people who knew each other well, whereas parties were designed to make strangers feel more comfortable with each other.

Whenever Wang Qiyao tried out a new dish she would ask Old Colour, "How does this measure up to your mother's cooking?"

Once, when she said this, Old Colour replied, "I never compare you to my mother."

Asked why, he responded, "Because you are ageless."

Wang Qiyao didn't know what to say. After a pause she asked, "How can someone be ageless?"

Old Colour persisted, "You know what I mean."

"You're right, I know exactly what you mean . . ." said Wang Qiyao. "But I don't agree with you."

"You don't have to agree with me," Old Colour responded, before lowering his head in dejected silence.

Wang Qiyao paid him no heed, but deep down she was laughing wryly, thinking that this fellow really didn't know when to quit. She wasn't sure if she liked that feeling or not. She stood in front of the stove waiting for a pot of water to boil as she stared at the scenery outside the window. Dusk was falling and the last rays of the sun seemed reluctant to leave. This was a scene she had been looking at for years; it had been etched into her heart. She knew that feeling so well that it was clear at every moment what the next moment would bring.

Wang Qiyao went back into the room and put the freshly brewed tea on the table. Seeing the gloomy look on his face, she said, "Now don't go making a big deal out of nothing! Everything is fine, so why spoil it?"

He turned away with a peevish look.

Wang Qiyao continued, "You're a nice boy who is really smart and polite and I really like you. But I don't like boys who let their minds run wild thinking about crazy things!"

"Who are you calling a boy?" he shouted as he jerked his head up. "Stop calling me a boy—as if I was just a child!"

"What a temper!" said Wang Qiyao, as she got up to walk away.

But Old Colour called her back. "Where do you think you're going? What are you trying to run away from? If you have something to say, then say it!"

"You want me to talk to you? About what?"

He pushed things even further. "You are the one being unreasonable. You're always running away!"

Wang Qiyao laughed. Turning around, she sat back down. "So let's hear what *you* have to say. Go on!"

He pressed on with his accusations. "You don't even have the guts to look reality in the face!"

She nodded her head in agreement, signaling for him to continue, but he didn't know what else to say.

Wang Qiyao snorted. "And here I was, thinking you had some great truth to set me straight on!"

Those words really set him off. Ready to explode, he opened his mouth but nothing came out . . . ; he pressed his head into Wang Qiyao's bosom, wrapping his arms around her waist. Wang Qiyao was shocked but didn't dare to reveal her surprise. She didn't push him away or get mad; instead she raised her arm and began to gently caress his hair, whispering consoling words. He refused to raise his head, however, and after a while Wang Qiyao ran out of reassuring things to say and had to stop. The two of them sat in silence.

Dusk slowly crept in, covering everything with a veil of darkness, but leaving the delicate outlines still visible; all was still. They, too, remained motionless. There was no future for them to look forward to; they could only remain stationary, eking out the moment as long as they possibly could. All they had was silence; what was there to say when they would probably only end up arguing as before? In truth, they were just blindly letting off steam, but they could have just as well have been speaking different languages, like an ox trying to reason with a horse. In the end, both were left more confused than ever. Eventually they calmed down and things seemed finally to be getting back on track. But time was slipping by and they couldn't just keep carrying on like that until old age! It was only after it was completely dark and they could barely make each other out that their silhouettes could be seen rising and separating. Only then was the light turned on in the last window to light up on Peace Lane that night.

After that evening, both of them seemed to forget what had transpired; they put it aside and never mentioned it again. However, Wang Qiyao stopped asking Old Colour things that might upset him, such as "How do I compare to your mother?" which under the circumstances would have taken on a provocative overtone. They also stopped talking about how old they were and whether or not she was "ageless"—all these became taboo subjects. The results of that day's confrontation seemed to be a loss, as they now had fewer topics they could discuss; but that loss was actually a way of purging the impurities in their relationship, like pruning away dead branches. After that, their relationship became purer and simpler; they might not have always had things to say, but sometimes silence is better than speech. There were also times when they talked nonstop—always about important things, such as Wang Qiyao's reminiscences of the past. Her stories were so splendid that they made everything happening in the present pale in comparison. But the splendor was all linked with heartbreaking losses, like a ceremonial robe bathed in neon light.

Wang Qiyao showed him a forty-year-old hand-carved box from Spain; she let him examine the floral engravings on the outside, but wouldn't open it up, as if the contents were not meant for his eyes. The designs on the box and even the style of the lock were all quite dated; it was a useful prop to help him get into the forty-year-old role he was trying to play. To a certain degree, he even viewed Wang Qiyao as an old Hollywood star, but he never looked at himself as her male counterpart. He was more like an adoring fan, the kind that thinks what they see on screen is real. He loved those old movies from that era—he couldn't get enough of them. And though all he did was watch, it was often enough to make him forget where he was.

Emerging from Wang Qiyao's stories and coming back down to reality, Old Colour felt the same feeling of letdown he had at the end of a movie. Although what was being recounted wasn't his own experience, he was so consumed by the story that it seemed to affect him even more than her. That's because she had to use part of her energy to cope with the changes in her life and keep herself together. The next time he lay on the rooftop outside his dormer window and stared up at the sky, images began to appear before him. One after another, they rolled over the horizon formed by the rooftops. Oh, how this city resembles a sunken ship! That telephone pole is like a mast jutting up from the bottom, still hanging on to a bit of tattered sail—the sail is actually the remains of a child's kite that got caught in the wires. Old Colour was so sad he could almost have wept. The clouds suspended over the ship's hull were the bearers of illusions and mirages.

The distant sound of the pile-driver reached his ears, echoing throughout the sky; that pile-driver seemed to be driving this city down to the bottom. He could feel the roof shaking, and the tiles beneath him made a rattling sound from the vibrations. Not even jazz could console him anymore; his records were all dusty and the needle on the record player had lost its point, producing a hoarse sound that only deepened his sorrow. Before he knew it, he fell asleep. When he awoke the stars had come out to disperse his illusions, but the pile-driver was hammering away even more fiercely, its sound rising and falling like a great choir. This choir was a new all-night program in the city. The sounds would only die off as the dew formed with the coming of dawn. He instinctively drew back; as he opened his eyes, a flock of pigeons flapped past overhead. *Where am I?* he wondered. He watched the pigeons with a dazed stare as they receded, to become spots on the horizon, and imagined himself one of them. The sun rose, its light shining down on the roof tiles. It was time to get up.

"Do you ever feel that this city has aged?" he asked Wang Qiyao.

She laughed. "Is there anything that doesn't age?" She went on after a pause, "Look at me, I'm evidence of that! What right do I have to expect other things not to age too?"

He looked at Wang Qiyao and his heart was seized with pain. No matter how young she appeared, she still could not conceal her puffy eyelids and those delicate wrinkles. *How could time be so heartless?* he thought, and pity welled up inside him. He raised his hand to caress Wang Qiyao's hair like an older friend offering consolation. Wang Qiyao laughed and tried to push his hand away, but he resisted and firmly took hold of her hand: "You always look down on me."

Using her free hand to smooth down his hair, she replied, "I never do . . ."

"You do!" He held his ground.

But so did she. "I never once looked down on you."

"It actually has nothing to do with age," he added.

Wang Qiyao thought for a moment before responding, "That depends. . . ."

"On what?

Wang Qiyao didn't answer and it was only after he pressed her that she finally said, "On the timing."

The archness of her reply drew laughter from both of them; he was still holding on to her hand. And though the whole scene was rather silly, even pointless, underneath lay something very serious. What that something was it was difficult to say, and to attempt to find out would only cause more pain. Who ever saw a courtship like this? Was that any way to flirt? With more than a quarter of a century between them, the timing was completely off, and so was the rhythm. If it hadn't been for that mysterious something, the whole thing would have been disgusting. They held hands for a while but stopped short of anything else. It was a good thing that they were both patient; but more than patience, they didn't seem to have any real objective, so what was the point of rushing? And so they eventually let go of each other's hands and let everything go back to the way it was before. Even though one of them might still say something absurd from time to time, they found their way to deal with it and went on just as before.

"You can't blame me!" he said on one occasion.

"I don't!" she replied.

"But deep down you do! You blame me for coming into your life too late," he argued.

Wang Qiyao laughed and responded, only after a pause, "Should we start practicing for the next life?"

"What for?"

"Haven't you heard? It takes a hundred years of self-cultivation if you want to be on the same boat, and a thousand years if you want to share the same pillow."

As soon as she said "pillow," they both felt a tremor of the heart and fell immediately silent. Wang Qiyao started to turn red, aware that she had spoken out of turn and injected something prurient into the conversation. When she saw him sitting there in silence with his head hanging low, she thought he was upset and was so embarrassed she started to cry. To prevent him from seeing her tears, she quickly turned around and walked into the kitchen, where she stood for a few moments, putting away various odds and ends in a state of abstraction. By the time she came back he was gone. There was a note on the table: *Together in this life—who needs a next life?* Reading those words actually calmed her down a bit; it was, in a way, ridiculous, and she wondered: *What is he thinking? Can he be serious?* She took the note and crumpled it into a ball. The incident eventually passed, and, in its wake, so did several equally tense moments. But fear lingered every time she thought about their clashes. She was living on the razor's edge; she knew she couldn't take one false step, but she didn't know how to get off. It was like walking a tightrope—and it was exciting. But you can't stay up on the tightrope too long or you'll lose your footing. Whenever they were alone together, the atmosphere would grow tense, and they both seemed to have their daggers drawn.

Zhang Yonghong's visits were especially welcome during these tense moments. With a third party present, they could get down from the tightrope for a while. The three of them could talk about almost anything, and no matter how far off the topic was, Wang Qiyao and Old Colour always seemed to be on the same page. With Zhang Yonghong there as an outsider, they became one—her lack of a direct connection to them seemed to strengthen their connection to each other. In this way a tacit understanding arose between them. The addition of Zhang Yonghong seemed to solve the quandary they were facing about whether to move forward or step back—with her there, they could simply drag out the status quo. Gradually Zhang Yonghong became an essential part of their relationship.

When Old Colour invited Wang Qiyao out to dinner yet again, she couldn't refuse because Zhang Yonghong was also included. She brought Long Legs, and the four of them went to the Western restaurant on the ground floor of the Jinjiang Hotel for steak. Even though Long Legs only came along at the last minute, he was the most gregarious one at the table and so took center stage. He knew all the latest slang and told them all the popular gossip, recounting all kinds of amazing stories—old news to Old Colour and Zhang Yonghong but a revelation for Wang Qiyao. She had no idea that there were people in the city who made their livelihood out of burning, killing, looting, and pillaging, living their days amid the glimmer of knives and pools of blood. She listened in a state suspended between belief and disbelief, pretending that what she was listening to was just tall tales.

Dinner ended in a flutter of excitement as Long Legs insisted on paying the bill, and wouldn't take no for an answer. Old Colour tried to pay, but gave up after a few attempts. Zhang Yonghong couldn't care less about who paid. However, Wang Qiyao and Old Colour were not happy, feeling that they had just eaten off the wrong plate. They had intended to use Zhang Yonghong as an agent to help them resolve a long outstanding issue between them; but not only had they been thwarted, they were now left with their feelings still dangling. Zhang Yonghong and her boyfriend hopped in a cab to go to their next engagement as soon as they left the hotel. The other two were left standing on the street and, for a moment, didn't know where they should go. It was only after they had walked for some time along the covered corridor outside the hotel that they became less awkward.

"I really wanted to treat you to dinner this time," said Old Colour, "But I still didn't get to."

Wang Qiyao laughed. "I guess you weren't sincere enough!"

"Then I'd better keep trying. . . ." With those words he put his hands in his pockets and extended his elbow toward Wang Qiyao, who slipped her arm through his. The shady streets of Maoming Road are a place of endless romance. You say those trees lining the street are there to provide shade from the heat? You're wrong. They are there to create a dreamscape, a world where people are shrouded in shadow, insulated from the brilliant light on the outside.

Long Legs

Zhang Yonghong and Long Legs managed to keep their friendship up for quite some time. One reason for this was that he was always willing to spend money on her, and another, that a suitable replacement had yet to show up. According to Long Legs, his grandfather was the famous Soy Sauce King known throughout Shanghai and, as his only grandson, Long Legs was the legal heir to his estate. Grandfather, he said, had soy sauce factories all over Southeast Asia and a few in Europe and America. Besides the soy sauce business, the old man held interests in a rubber plantation, farmland, even a virgin forest; he had his own private dock on the Mekong River and his company stock sold on Wall Street in New York. It sounded like a story right out of the *Arabian Nights.*

Zhang Yonghong didn't take it seriously, but one thing she knew was true—he *did* have money. The way Long Legs threw his money around was astonishing; Zhang Yonghong had to adjust the way she looked at money by several digits. Unable to control her excitement, she would occasionally describe their extravagant spending habits to Wang Qiyao. When Wang Qiyao asked her where all that money was coming from, she repeated the fabulous story Long Legs had told her. In retelling the story, she herself began to believe it. But Wang Qiyao didn't. She suspected something was amiss but didn't want to be the one to break the news to Zhang Yonghong; she had had the opportunity to observe Long Legs and noted several things that didn't sit right with her.

There were always people like Long Legs who hustled their way throughout Shanghai. Most of them didn't have a normal job, yet somehow they got all their basic needs pretty well taken care of. These were the men one saw drinking and making merry in the lobbies of fancy hotels during the day. There's no need to mention what they did in the evenings—without them, the city's nightlife would never get off the ground. But don't make the mistake of supposing that all they ever did was have fun, because they were also working to earn their keep. They did such things as playing tennis with foreigners and giving motorcycle-riding lessons. They helped travel agencies to arrange tours and, while they were at it, made sure to exchange some foreign currency on the side. To establish these relationships with foreigners on the streets and in hotel lobbies, they usually spoke some English, at least enough for simple greetings, exchanging money, filling in as a tour guide, and making small talk. The international nature of their work tended to broaden their horizons, and eventually they came to display a level of sophistication in their manners and dress that was right up there with the rest of the world. They were a group of the most liberal-minded of men, completely unrestrained in their style. In Shanghai society, there were all kinds of necessary but minor details that people were too busy to deal with: that's where these men came in—to fill in the gaps. They were perhaps the busiest of all; virtually all the cabs in Shanghai relied on them for their business, as did the restaurants. How prosperous the city appeared—and all thanks to them!

Long Legs was six foot two and had a long thin face that caved in somewhat in the middle, slightly protruding front teeth, and eyeglasses. He looked extremely thin, but was actually fairly well built. His buck teeth gave him a bit of a lisp, but this didn't really get in the way; it actually made him sound more refined. He was quite the talker and would open up to everyone, whether he knew them or not, which always left people with a warm impression. He loved to treat friends to dinner; so much so that when he ran into old friends at a restaurant he would sometimes settle up for them when paying his own bill. Whenever he took Zhang Yonghong out shopping, he made sure that they went for the best, and he never showed up empty-handed at Wang Qiyao's, always remembering to bring along a house gift. His usual gift was most elegant—a dozen roses. On cold winter days he bought roses flown in from the south at ten *yuan* a stem. Wang Qiyao's apartment was unheated and the flowers would wither before long.

Long Legs was so busy running around that he never had time to spend the money he was making, so he ended up spending most of it on others while he wore the same old pair of dirty blue jeans all year round. His sneakers were also dirty and beat up. But it was part of his style not to pay attention to himself. This was especially true in winter: he'd rather stick with his accustomed single layer and huddle up, his nose blue with the cold, than put on a thick winter jacket. Even so, he would still be in high spirits, always laughing and joking. Happiness was in his nature—he liked noisy, festive occasions with a lot of people around, and when others were having a good time, he had a good time. In order to create a fun atmosphere he was even willing to make himself the butt of people's jokes; he didn't think twice about putting himself in what other people would have thought of as an awkward situation. The world doesn't have many people like that, now, does it? Over time, he slowly won over everyone's hearts. Whenever his friends went out, they always made sure to bring him along, and when he wasn't around they would instantly start looking for him: "Where's Long Legs? Where'd he go?"

That was Long Legs, patiently cultivating his interpersonal relationships. People like him, who know how to get by in society, may look on the surface as if they are always on the move, but in fact they are, relatively speaking, quite stable, and they have accepted principles to which they adhere. Like people who commute to work every day, their comings and goings are governed by fixed routine. Their day usually begins around eleven o'clock, when most factory workers start their second shift, and finishes up around midnight. When they say goodnight, each goes his separate way and gradually disappears into the shadows under the trees.

Riding his beat-up old bicycle, Long Legs would head toward the southwest corner of the city. There were few people out on the streets as he slowly pedaled past. At first he would hum some tunes as he rode, but that gradually ceased. The only sound left was the rattle of his bicycle chain. As the streets grew more desolate and the streetlights became more spread out, his light heart began to sink. If one of his friends could have laid eyes on him at that moment, they wouldn't have believed that he was the same person. Joyless and melancholic, he knit his brows in a fury of impatient frustration that made him look ferocious. His face darkened and lost its usual glow. By then he had arrived at a residential area built in the 1970s, which, due to the shoddy construction and low-quality building materials, already looked old. Under the moon, which came out abruptly from behind the clouds, it looked like a series of massive cement boxes—there wasn't a single light on in the whole complex. This was a place where nightmares lurked; only one sentient soul walked here—that was Long Legs. If you could have seen him from above as he rode through those cement boxes, you would have thought he looked like an insect crawling among the tombs in a graveyard.

Long Legs stopped in front of one of the buildings and leaned his bicycle against the wall. As he stepped inside, the darkness consumed him. Poor Long Legs: it was going to take a mighty effort to walk up a staircase cluttered with all kinds of random items that left the passerby barely a foot-wide space to squeeze through. But then at that moment he changed into a nimble cat, silently making his way upstairs, two or three steps at a time. From this you can imagine how long he must have been living here. He opened the door onto a dimly lit interior; the only light inside was coming in from the hallway window. There was also the sound of water coming from the broken toilet. The hallway was filled with various odds and ends. Two families had shared this unit for years; the cobwebs in the corner were proof. The first thing Long Legs did was to go into the kitchen and open up the small screen door to the cabinet, where fresh leftovers were kept, to look inside. He did this from force of habit—he wasn't really hungry. Inside the cabinet were a few bowls, their contents coated with a thin layer of mold. Closing the door, he grabbed a jug of water from under the stove before going into the bathroom. A few minutes later came the sound of water gently splashing as Long Legs washed his feet in the basin. He did all of this by the faint light of the moon coming through the window; he didn't need to turn on the light—he could have done it with his eyes closed. He sat on the toilet with his feet soaking in the basin, the dry towel in his hand draped over his knees, and stared straight ahead. A few insects scurried over the damp concrete floor. What was Long Legs thinking?

If you hadn't seen it with your own eyes, you would have never believed where Long Legs slept. His bed was set up outside one of the bedrooms. At the head of the bed was a square dinner table smelling of grease. Above it was a makeshift shelf used to store winter blankets in the summer and bamboo mats in the winter, as well as an assortment of items kept there all year round even though they all should have been thrown away. Thus it looked as if Long Legs was crawling into a hole to sleep. As soon as he had squeezed himself in, he would cover his face with the blanket and, within moments, would be whisked away by his nightmares deep down into the darkness of night. He wouldn't move after that, consumed by a dark silence that lay beyond words. The darkness of the nights there was the real thing; bottled up inside those cement blocks, it became even more concentrated. Coming in from the bright world, how could Long Legs possibly bear all of this? That's why he covered up his head and went into a deep sleep that was akin to weeping, like a weeping ostrich. If you witnessed the sorry sight of his bent waist and scrunched up legs as he tried to tuck his body into a bed where it would never fit, you would cry too.

In the light of day, the same spectacle would take on an air of the ridiculous. That's because a late-riser like Long Legs usually didn't get out of bed until quite late. Even if he got up early, where could he possibly go? That was when all of Shanghai's night owls were still in bed! And so he too stayed in bed. Everyone in the apartment who had to get up early for school or work walked around his bed, talking loudly as if he wasn't there. They sat down on the edge of his bed to eat breakfast, their chopsticks clanking against their bowls all the while. Through the open windows and doors the morning sun shone directly down on Long Leg's sleeping form—this was the nightmare he had to endure when the sun came up. Who ever said that nightmares only come at night? Some don't. As if they were deliberately trying to distance themselves from the intense quiet the night before, they made as much noise as possible, with noises of all kinds—now that was a bona fide ruckus! But Long Legs slept right on through it, the sole creature asleep in a world of boisterous beasts. The ruckus usually lasted for at least an hour; then came the sound of doors closing, followed by the echo of footsteps going down the stairs, and the sound of bicycle bells gradually dying off in the distance. But just before the descent of that final silence there came an assault of music—morning calisthenics at the neighboring elementary school; the overpowering rhythm of the music made its way into Long Legs' ears, transporting him back to his childhood.

As a boy, Long Legs was accustomed to another kind of music. Every day, around four o'clock in the afternoon, a bell would ring along the intersection at the railroad tracks near his home. As soon as the bell started to ring, his two older sisters would take him over by the tracks to wait for the train, and he would stand between them, holding each one by the hand. He had some faint memories of the old house they lived in back then, one among a row of bungalows. He and his two sisters would rush down the small footpath past these makeshift homes, as if they were late for some important meeting. As they approached the intersection, the hazard light would be blinking, warning pedestrians and vehicles to stop;

the bell would still be sounding. Then came the toot of the whistle and the train would come rumbling toward them. At first it seemed to take its time, but as it got closer it suddenly flew past like a bolt of lightning. The carriages flashed by in a blur; there were people inside, but he could never make out their faces. Long Legs used to wonder: *Where are they going?* Once the last carriage had passed, there would be a brief pause before the mechanical arms blocking the road would slowly rise, letting a flood of people and vehicles onto the tracks. Long Legs would recognize a familiar face in the crowd—his mother. He was the only boy in the family; one sister was seven years older than he, the other one six, and both were his babysitters. At one time they tied a rope to the tree outside their house, affixing a stool to the end of the rope to make a swing. That was their playground. There were also the ants crawling on the bricks outside and the worms slithering through the mud—these were their playmates.

He still had faint but fond memories of those happy days. Later his family moved into the factory housing complex where they were still living. All that those cement boxes ever brought Long Legs was boredom and, however good-natured his disposition, it wasn't enough to prevent a feeling of oppression from developing inside him. The dust collecting in the corners and under his bed, the water stains on the walls, the cracks in the ceiling, and the ever-accumulating clutter around the apartment—all added to his growing frustration. He couldn't say exactly what it was: he just felt as if everything was pointless, so pointless. After graduating from middle school, he was assigned to a fabric dyeing plant as a machine operator. His second year there, he was diagnosed with hepatitis. He took some time off to recuperate and never went back to work. During his extended sick leave, he would take long, leisurely bicycle rides every morning and gradually, without realizing it, he found that he was able to shake off that oppressive feeling.

Taking in all the street scenes as he rode his bicycle around town, his happy and carefree nature returned. The sun shining down on the streets was bright and beautiful, as was everything he saw during those bike rides. Leaning forward and slowly pedaling, Long Legs was like a fish swimming in a river of sunshine. It was usually eleven-thirty by the time he reached downtown. He would stop by the side of the road, a confused look on his face—only for a moment, though, before it was replaced by a look of determination. Having fixed on one direction, off he rode. The sharp rays of the sun reflecting off the tops of the buildings excited him. The area he was in was right around Wukang Road and Huaihai Road, a haven of quietude in the midst of the bustle of the city. It was also a quiet moment in the midst of the hectic hours of the day, as if harboring a dormant happiness and confidence. Long Legs' heart began to lighten up and the shadow of the nightmares disappeared; he felt relaxed and free. Everyone who saw Long Legs was sure that he was a successful man with important things to do; but what was Long Legs going to do? He was on his way to take his friends out to lunch.

Long Legs' desire to please was incredibly strong; so long as they were outsiders, all, near or far, were his friends. Together these people constituted the Shanghai that he loved. They became the masters of the beautiful streets of Shanghai. He and his family had come from the provinces and were not highly regarded by the natives, but now, through his own efforts, he had made it into mainstream Shanghai society. Walking down the streets, he truly felt at home; the other pedestrians were his family and they shared his thoughts. What was displayed in the store windows on either side of the street may not have been his, but the fact that they were there made a big difference. Perhaps only one individual out of ten thousand on the streets harbored such thoughts; but this rare individual was the backbone of the Shanghai streets, their spirit. As frivolous as it may have seemed, such a life force is irreplaceable. You may call it blind, but its innocent naiveté is sufficient to carry one back to the realm of truth.

Long Legs had been making his living exchanging money on the black market for quite some time. Don't look down on currency exchange, it's a real job—he even had business cards printed up! These money changers were all men of integrity; if you go and check, you'd find that they weren't the ones who swindled people—it was always the small-time players who had somehow weaseled their way into the business who did that kind of thing. Every profession has its imposters. But real money changers have regular clients who can attest to their character. Nevertheless, this was a high-risk business, and whether business was good or bad the risks were always there. When the going was slow, they would lie low for a while, waiting for the right moment to jump back into the game. Long Legs always put friendship first in doing business. When his friends came knocking, he would always cut them a deal even if it meant losing money. This created the impression that he had solid financial backing. His business cards were all over the city—virtually everyone had one. People were apt to suggest that he should use his connections to get into big-time trading, to which Long Legs would smile without comment, and this too strengthened the impression that he was a force to be reckoned with.

Zhang Yonghong met Long Legs at a time when changing money on the black market was going quite well. The way Long Legs threw money around was nothing short of shocking. Spending money always gives a man a feeling of achievement, especially when he is spending it on a woman. Long Legs had a kind and generous disposition, but he had had little opportunity to experience the warmth that a woman can give; so he kept buying things for Zhang Yonghong, and eventually seemed to have bought himself into some genuine feeling. During this period he brushed his business and friends aside, focusing his warmth and sincerity on Zhang Yonghong. He appeared so kind and faithful, he had such a gentle look in his eyes—everyone who saw him was moved. He was really the kind of man who could lose himself completely, devoting his entire being to someone else. He bought a pile of clothes for Zhang Yonghong, never giving a thought to how slovenly he himself usually was. He saw only the good in her and only the worst in himself. He wished he could give every piece of himself to her, but figured that everything about him, body and soul, was utterly worthless. There were so many heartfelt things he longed to share with Zhang Yonghong, but all that came out of his mouth was big talk and petty lies.

When Long Legs first started dropping by Wang Qiyao's apartment, his sole motivation was to see Zhang Yonghong, but that eventually changed. He started to like the place . . . and Wang Qiyao. Although she was a bit older, he didn't feel any distance when he was around her. There was no gap between her and the spirit of this new generation. Unlike Old Colour, Long Legs knew nothing about the past, nor was he sentimental about it—he was always looking ahead, and the farther ahead the better. But because he wasn't as bright as Old Colour, his actions were the result not of choice but of going with the flow. If the wave was surging forward, then that's where he was heading, and he let it sweep him up and carry him along. But he did have good intuition and sometimes intuition is more perceptive than reason, taking you right to the heart of the matter.

Being around Wang Qiyao gave him a certain peace of mind, and he didn't need to hustle to get that feeling, which was reassuring for him. It was as if he had quietly discovered that things go in cycles and that underneath all the apparent change, everything remains the same. All the empty and evanescent grandeur of the streets of Shanghai had found a home in Wang Qiyao's apartment. The meat and vegetable dishes on Wang Qiyao's table represented the heart of fancy banquets served in hotels and restaurants, the clothes that she wore were the heart of what was displayed in fashionable shop windows, and her simplicity was the heart of extravagance. In short, she provided a place where he could feel solid, where he could see something akin to the essence of this city. He shared with Old Colour the same love for the city. One loved the old face of Shanghai while the other loved its new face; but this was actually only a difference of labels, at its heart was the same love for its glory and splendor. One was a sober love while the other was more muddled; but the degree to which they loved was the same, devoting every piece of their hearts and souls to this romance. Wang Qiyao was their teacher and guide. With her leading them, all of their dreamlike illusions transformed into something tangible and real. That was the mysterious appeal of Wang Qiyao.

Long Legs also had questions for Wang Qiyao, but they were usually a hundred times more childish than the sorts of questions Old Colour used to ask; sometimes they were almost laughable. But Wang Qiyao would always patiently answer each one, at the same time sighing to herself at how adorably silly his questions were. *I'll bet he is putty in Zhang Yonghong's hands,* she thought. Perhaps it was Zhang Yonghong's good luck. But then she would smile wryly to herself: *The only question is how long can Long Legs keep this up. No one in the world spends money the way he does. Most people are careful about how they spend their hard-earned money, but Long Legs throws money away as if it isn't even his!* Yet her thinking this way only showed that she did not understand him. This was a man only too willing to spend his money on others. In fact, that was precisely his motivation for making money; otherwise he would have never bothered putting himself through so much grief and unrest. He himself had virtually no expenses. As mentioned earlier, he only needed the very basics when it came to clothing and was even less concerned about eating—a bowl of thick gruel with preserved cabbage was enough for a meal. Even at fancy banquets he spent most of his energy serving others and barely even touched what was on his plate. His personal needs were minimal; all he needed were the clothes on his back and a bite to eat. His happiness came from providing others with food, drink, and merriment; on the few occasions when someone else tried to pay the bill after dinner, he became furious because he felt they were cheating him of his enjoyment.

Nevertheless, Long Legs often fretted about being short of cash. Currency trading was a business always in flux and he couldn't rely on it for a steady income. His family would occasionally give him money, but that was never enough. A friend once got him a job showing around a group of overseas Chinese who wanted to go sightseeing and shopping, but in the end he insisted on treating them to meals and ended up spending more than what he took in. His friend tried to tell him that the meals were covered under the agreed-upon package, but he replied, "I'm just making friends!"

That's how much emphasis Long Legs placed on friendship. But people didn't know that, behind that magnanimous façade, he worried about money day and night. In truth, the money he had already borrowed from his sisters added up to a small fortune; he tried to avoid thinking about that. He would sometimes dip into the money he had set aside for trades, telling his clients he would come with the cash a few days later. Luckily, his credit was good and everyone knew how loyal he was to his friends, so they would let him slide for a few days. But he knew only too well that he couldn't make a habit out of doing this, or the floodgates would break wide open. When he really got into a bind and had nowhere else to turn, he would tell everyone he was going out of town for a few days to stay with a relative who had just come back from abroad; that would buy him a few more days of extra time. During those days, no one would see him at those convivial dinner parties or hear him fighting to pay the bill. Who would have thought that he was actually sitting on a bench in a small isolated park in the northeast corner of the city? There he watched the children play on the slide, their high-pitched screams of joy ringing out in the open air and echoing far, far away in the outskirts of the city. Sparrows pecked at the sand at his feet and kept him company. He would sit there the entire day, heading home only after dusk when the park closed. Reaching home, he would eat the leftovers that his family had kept covered for him. On days like this, he didn't even have money in his pocket for a small bowl of dumplings.

Prosperous Shanghai was in every sense of the term a place where power was everything; people without money or power had no place here. Long Legs, in spending money on his friends, was actually paying his dues in this power market. The flashing neon lights, the new fashions that came and went with blinding speed, and now new additions—like pop songs and discos—made Shanghai a place frothing with incessant excitement; would you be willing to sit and watch it pass you by? For people like Long Legs, who spent their days and nights sauntering through the city's splendor, every day was like Christmas: how could they be expected to endure a boring, uneventful lifestyle like the common herd? Even with their eyes closed, they could still differentiate light from the dark. Walking down a dark, shady street, they could sniff out through the walls where all-night dance parties were raging and where people were only sleeping. They were the sharpest sort of people—how could they possibly settle for "ordinary"? Only after understanding this can one sympathize with the sufferings of Long Legs as he sat there by himself in that park; then one would know what he was thinking without even having to ask.

The park was actually only around a half-hour's ride from downtown, but it was another world; there even the wind and the air were lonely, not to mention the people. He wondered what his friends were doing. *What was Zhang Yonghong doing?* When he was with her, all he thought about was how to please her. Now that he was alone, he found himself thinking about his future with her. This was a state of mind quite alien to him. To people like Long Legs, who got through life by means of hustling, the future is something that arrives on its own and there was no point in thinking about it. Now that he sat down to ponder it, Long Legs discovered that his mind was blank. His confusion about the future was partly because he simply didn't know, but also because he had no plans. His mind went in circles as he realized that he and Zhang Yonghong had no real future to speak of—all they had were the days ahead of them. These days could be reduced to eating out and going to dance parties and on shopping trips—things that made up the essence of life, the most important things—but all of those things required money. And so his thoughts came full circle. . . . Everything came back to money.

When Long Legs made his return, it was with a new, completely refurbished appearance. He was in high spirits, smiling from ear to ear, had a sharp new haircut, and was wearing fresh clothes, and his wallet was stuffed with cash—even his posture was better than it had been in years. He wanted to invite everyone out for barbeque at the Beer Garden, the new restaurant that had just opened in the Jinjiang Hotel. It was an early autumn night. The candles on the tables flickered in the wind, as did the flames in the barbeque pit, the wine inside the glasses had a shiny luster, and the faint smoke from the pit faded into the breeze. Tears almost came to Long Legs' eyes as he thought: *Am I dreaming?* The canvas canopy above them was like a sail, billowing up from time to time, as if carrying them off to some warm place far, far away. That was how an evening in Shanghai ought to be—all other occasions were the dregs of this one. Such a sudden departure followed by a dramatic return surely meant adding an exciting new chapter to his family myth. On nights like this, in a place as beautiful as a crystal palace, people tended to believe whatever they were told—adults too need a place to exercise their imagination. A few insects nibbled gently on people's feet on the lawn, all around them was Western-style architecture, the leaves of French parasol trees hung down over them, and melodious music played. But all of this was only secondary: what was most important was inside their hearts—what they were feeling in their hearts! They didn't seem to be people at all, but celestial beings. But the words deep inside Long Legs' heart didn't form complete sentences, his song was out of tune; his knees were knocking gently and his fingers tapping against his leg could not keep time. What's intoxication? This was intoxication. It had only been a few days, but Long Legs had already experienced two different lives.

Long Legs hadn't come by in several days and Wang Qiyao was almost certain he was a fraud; but when he showed up at last, she was confused again. Long Legs didn't bother explaining where he had been; instead he carelessly put down a bag of gifts on which DUTY FREE was printed in both Chinese and English. Wang Qiyao wondered where he had been, but instead of inquiring about that, asked him why he hadn't brought Zhang Yonghong along. Even before she had finished her question, Zhang Yonghong came up the stairs—she had been out in the *longtang* making a phone call. As it turned out, Old Colour was there too, and the four of them sat down to chat. After his brief absence, Long Legs looked around Wang Qiyao's apartment and felt quite moved: *It hasn't changed one bit.* He felt as if he had been gone an eternity, but all the people and things here were still the same; it was as if they had all been awaiting his return and he felt a warmth surging into his heart.

In order to get his life back, Long Legs had become a swindler. Two nights earlier, in a *longtang* off Lujiazui Road in Pudong, he was exchanging money with a client when he secretly replaced a stack of ten twenty-dollar bills with one dollar bills. There was nothing new about this type of scam, but for Long Legs it was the first time: a shameful blemish on his record as a currency trader. On the ferry from Pudong back to Puxi, Long Legs gazed up at the moon veiled in clouds and his heart sank. If he hadn't had nowhere else to turn, he would have never gone down that path. Part of Long Legs' good-natured disposition was his purity, but now that purity had been tarnished and his heart ached silently. At that moment he looked out across the water and saw the lights and majestic architecture of Shanghai on the opposite shore. The buildings were like a mountain range rising before his eyes, gilded by the lights of the city. The night was calling out to him and oh, how it captivated his soul!

Misfortunes from Within

AGAINST THE CLAMOR of the city, who could hear the prayers being uttered in Peace Lane? Who would notice people whose dearest wish in life is not to be praised for merit but only to avoid making mistakes? Here a lean-to shed has been added on to the terrace and the courtyard roofed over to make a kitchen. If you were to look down upon the rooftops of the city, you would find them in utter disarray, worn and dilapidated, structures built on top of structures, taking up every bit of free space. This was especially true of the older *longtang,* like Peace Lane—it's a miracle that they haven't collapsed yet. About a third of the tiles were broken, patched over in places with bits of felt, the wooden frames on the doors and windows were blackened and rotting, with everything in view a uniform ash gray.

But though it was falling apart on the outside, the spirit of the place remained; its inner voice, though stifled, was still audible. But amid all the noises of this city, just what did this voice amount to? There was never a moment of peace and quiet in the city; the day had its sounds, as did the night, and between them they drowned that voice out. But it was still there—it couldn't be silenced because it was the foundation upon which the hubbub and commotion fed; without it all of those noises would have been nothing but an empty echo. But what did this voice say? Two words: *to live.* No matter how loud the noise became, no matter what a rumpus it made, or how long it carried on, it could never find those two words. Those two little words weighed a ton, so they sank, and sank—all the way down, to the very bottom; only immaterial things like smoke and mist could float up to the surface. It was impossible to listen to this voice without crying. The prayers whispered in Peace Lane went on day and night, like an ever-burning alter lamp, but they weren't burning on oil: inch by inch, they were burning thoughts. In contrast, the chaotic noises echoing in the city's air were nothing but the scraps and leftovers of life, which is why they could be so liberally strewn about. The prayers concealed throughout those thousands of Shanghai *longtang* rang out louder and clearer than all the church bells in Europe: they created a rumbling thunder that seemed to emerge from the earth itself, the sound of mountains crumbling. A shame we had no way of participating in this ourselves, but just looking at the abyss they created was enough to make the heart grow cold. See what they have done to this place! It is hard to say whether this was a form of construction or destruction, but whatever it was, it was massive.

What Peace Lane prayed for was peace itself. You could hear it even from the bell that was rung every night to warn people to mind their kitchen fires. Peace is not something ordinary, but Peace Lane had an ordinary heart and its prayers were quite humble as well; these modest requests, however, were not easily granted. No major disaster had befallen Peace Lane in many years, but little things kept coming up, such as someone falling off the balcony while bringing in their laundry, another getting electrocuted when he turned off a light switch with a wet hand, pressure cooker explosions, rat poison accidentally ingested. If all these, who died wrongful deaths, had cried out, their howls would have been deafening. So how could one not pray for peace and security?

In the early evening, when the lights came on, you could see in all the windows the watchful eyes of frightened people looking out for signs of trouble. But whenever something bad did happen, no one ever saw it coming. This was where Peace Lane had gone numb and where it displayed its pragmatism. The residents were never prepared for the closest dangers. Yes, they understood the dangers of fire and electricity, but beyond that they had no imagination. And so if you were to see the people of Peace Lane praying, they would be like idiots reciting a book from memory, chanting with their lips but not their minds, repeating the same incantations over and over again. Meanwhile the flowerpot sitting on the windowsill was just an inch away from falling down, but no one ever bothered to move it; the termites had already done their work on the floors, but no one ever seemed to care; illegal structures kept being added one on top of the other, causing the foundation to sink, yet another one was about to be built. During the typhoon season, when Peace Lane shook and rattled and it appeared as if the entire neighborhood was going to pieces, people curled up in their rooms, complacently enjoying the cool breeze brought by the storm. What people in Peace Lane prayed for was to be able to live in a fool's paradise—they would rather turn a blind eye and never ask questions. The pigeon whistles sounding in the morning sang of peace, announcing the good but never the bad; but even if they had, would that have made a difference? You might be able to escape it in the first round, but would you escape in the second? Put that way, those prayers must imply an acceptance, a sort of Daoist resignation to reality. For want of anything else to pray for, night after night they pray for peace, but that was just wishful thinking.

The wind whistles across the street and down the alleys, picking up handfuls of dead leaves along the way. Sunlight, also in handfuls, seemed reluctant to leave the long, winding *longtang* behind. Summer was gone, autumn waning. The houses at the end of *longtang* had their doors and windows all tightly shut. The sweet-scented oleander shed its petals; stories that never got a chance to be told were swallowed back down and kept quiet. This was the moment when the Shanghai *longtang* showed their solemn side; their solemnity carried weight and from it you could feel the pressure of time. This *longtang* had already built up its own history and history always shows a stern face, making the *longtang* put its frivolous side away. How unruly it used to be!—Seductive eyes peeking out of every corner, one false step and you would be ensnared.

But now the story seems to be coming to an end. Even those who attempt brazen acts with a smiling façade are met with sober, straight faces: the time for equivocation was over. The tide was receding and the rocks would soon be exposed. Counting on one's fingers, one finds that the Shanghai *longtang* have quite a few years on them—a few more and they'll be treading on thin ice. Going up again to the highest point in the city and looking down, one sees that the crisscrossing *longtang* neighborhoods are already beginning to look desolate. If these had been large imposing building, that desolation might be mitigated by their grand proportions. But *longtang* buildings all have low walls and narrow courtyards, filled with ordinary people carrying out their mundane tasks: could places like these be thought of as desolate? Desolation takes on a comical aspect in such places, and that only makes the people living there all the more dejected. Putting it in harsher terms: the whole place bore a certain resemblance to a heap of rubble. With the leaves falling in early winter, all we see are broken bricks and shattered tiles. Like an aging beauty who retains her alluring profile, it can no longer bear scrutiny. Should you insist on searching for a trace of her former charm—after all, not everything is erased—you would have to look for it in the turn of the alley. Left here, right there, as if glancing coquettishly from side to side, but the eyes that are so flirtatious are also getting on in years, they have lost their luster and are incapable of grabbing hold of your attention. Soon, sleet began to come down—that was the frigid past accumulated over generations—turning to water before it even hit the ground.

Let's now look into the *longtang* windows to see what is happening inside Peace Lane. In the quarter built right over the entrance lives the family of the old man who used to sweep the streets in the *longtang.* A Shandong native, he passed away year before last and his funeral portrait is hanging on the wall. At the table beneath his portrait his grandson is doing homework; he is supposed to write each Chinese character twenty times over, but he is so drowsy that nothing can pry his eyes back open. Downstairs, in the apartment with the lean-to shed, the dinner party is still going on. They have not had that much to drink, just a quart of Shaoxing wine, but they are taking their time, savoring each and every drop. Going deeper into the neighborhood, we look through a kitchen window and see two women whispering in hushed tones, their eyes making dramatic gestures—it is a mother and daughter exchanging nasty words about the new daughter-in-law. Following the street number signs hanging over the doors, we arrive at the next household, where the front room is filled with people playing mahjong—one can hear the clacking of the tiles as the players shuffle them and their voices calling out different hands. The players look as if they belong to the same family, but their grim expressions show they are playing for real stakes. The couple next door is in the middle of an argument, exchanging insults and curses. It's clear they can no longer stand each other—not even one more night; so back and forth they go on a violent seesaw. The lights are out in the next apartment over: maybe the people are asleep, or maybe they have yet to come home. At 18 Peace Lane, the retired tailor, now working on his own, is busy cutting fabric as his wife carefully threads a needle; the television is on, but they are both too preoccupied to watch.

That's right. Although each family was busy with their own affairs, there was one thing that they all had in common—television. Whether they were playing mahjong, drinking, arguing, or reading, the television was always on. It didn't matter whether or not they were watching or even listening, they just liked to have it on. Most of them kept it on the same channel, usually one of those with endless miniseries that dominated the evening's activities. Finally, we reach Wang Qiyao's window. Perhaps you expected it to be lonely on the inside, but it is surprisingly packed with people, some sitting on the sofa, some in chairs, and even a few on the floor, while others stood or leaned up against the wall, and the whole room was filled with the aroma of fresh-brewed coffee. They were having a party and oh, how exciting it was!

Once again Wang Qiyao's apartment had come alive with people, mostly young friends of hers. Pretty, refined, bright, and fashionable: just seeing them there was enough to make one light up with joy. They appeared in Peace Lane like a flock of golden phoenixes alighting in a nest of grass. Staring at them as they disappeared into Wang Qiyao's apartment, the neighbors marveled at her ability to bring together the best and brightest of Shanghai's fashionable elite. Everyone forgot how old she was, just as they had forgotten how old Peace Lane was. They even forgot about her daughter, taking her for a single woman who had never borne a child. If there is such a thing as an evergreen tree, she was one, untouched by the seasons. And now she had a new set of carefree young friends; they made themselves at home in her apartment, which became a palace of youth. Sometimes even Wang Qiyao herself wondered if time had stopped and everything was still as it had been forty years before. It was easy to get carried away, to focus on the pleasure at hand and leave reality behind.

The visitors to Wang Qiyao's apartment were actually people we run into every day—we just didn't make the connection. If you went to Market 16, for instance, you would surely recognize one or two of the dockworkers bringing in the crabs. Or you would discover that one of the guys selling crickets in the small local market looked awfully familiar. The scalpers outside the movie theater, the hustlers trying to purchase bonds on the stock exchange . . . they came from every profession and you could see traces of their activity everywhere. They spent their free time at Wang Qiyao's apartment, drinking coffee and eating the exquisite dim sum she had prepared—they couldn't have wished for a nicer place. They would always bring along their friends; Wang Qiyao didn't even know all of their names and then there were others whom she knew only by their nicknames, and still others whom she never even got a good look at. There were too many in this mixed crowd, and she couldn't give everyone equal attention. Her salons were beginning to gain a degree of notoriety in Shanghai; people from all over the city came to see what all the fuss was about and as a result spread the word even farther.

But Wang Qiyao's regular visitors were still that same trio of old friends—Old Colour was one, and Zhang Yonghong and Long Legs were the other two. They had grown closer and would often go out together for tea or dinner while on other nights they would all go out dancing or to the movies. In the winter Wang Qiyao would set up a hotpot in her apartment and they would sit around eating and telling stories; time would fly by and the sky would gradually darken, but that hotpot only got hotter. Suddenly Wang Qiyao was struck by a feeling of déjà vu: all of this had happened before, only the faces had changed, and a feeling of sadness would hit her. Then, as a fresh piece of charcoal beneath the pot burst into flames, a crimson glow illuminated Wang Qiyao's face. The light accentuated the wrinkles on her face. It was only for a split second, but Old Colour saw everything. Shock was followed by anguish. *She's an old woman....* They ate until they were stuffed, at which point they all fell silent. Even Zhang Yonghong and Long Legs quieted down, each consumed by their own thoughts, which carried them far away. It was quite some time before Wang Qiyao suddenly let out a gentle chuckle, and the others were startled to find how dark it had got. Wang Qiyao rose to turn on the light and added more water to the hotpot.

"How come no one's talking?"

"Why don't *you* say something then?"

Wang Qiyao chortled again. When they asked her what was so funny she didn't answer. It was only after they pressed her that she responded, "Seeing the three of you reminds me of something..."

But when they asked what it was, she blew it off, saying it had nothing to do with them. This felt as if she was intentionally trying to push their buttons, and her guests insisted on an answer. Only after much pressing did Wang Qiyao finally burst out, "I was just wondering what kind of future lies in store for the three of you!"

They were all taken aback. After a pause, Zhang Yonghong asked, "And what about *your* future? You don't know what will happen to you either...."

"What future do I have?" asked Wang Qiyao. "For me the future is now!"

Everyone said that she was just being modest, but Wang Qiyao laughed it off and continued, "Everything is crystal clear today, but who knows what tomorrow will bring."

Baffled, the others looked at each other and began to feel a bit awkward, especially Old Colour. He felt that he had been lumped in with Zhang Yonghong and Long Legs, which made him feel like a third wheel; he wondered what kind of fish Wang Qiyao was trying to catch by stirring up the water like that. He sensed that she was directing her words at him, that it was an inquisition of some sort, as if she were trying to test him. Feeling exceedingly uncomfortable, he tried to change the subject, but Wang Qiyao wouldn't hear of it, and continued to talk about how unpredictable fate was: if the mountain doesn't shift, then the water will, and when the water doesn't, people will. Zhang Yonghong and Long Legs were befuddled by all this, but Old Colour was growing impatient and had just about had all he could take.

He laughed sarcastically. "If I understand you correctly, the two of them are heading for a breakup, and Zhang Yonghong and I will eventually start dating, is that it?"

Putting everything so bluntly made them all laugh. Wang Qiyao didn't try to defend herself at first, simply saying that he had misunderstood her.

"But you were referring to the three of us, so what other combination could there possibly be?"

Wang Qiyao was speechless and simply smiled. Long Legs was smiling too, but deep down he was angry—not at Wang Qiyao, but at Old Colour, whom he felt had taken a cheap shot. Zhang Yonghong accused Old Colour of being crazy, but an odd quiver passed over her heart.

Laughing, Wang Qiyao nodded at Old Colour. "You've got a sharp tongue—you win this time. . . ."

A few days after their hotpot dinner, Old Colour dropped by Wang Qiyao's again; he went straight upstairs, where he found the door ajar and Wang Qiyao sitting on the sofa with a blanket over her legs as she knit a wool top. He tapped on the open door and stepped inside. But Wang Qiyao didn't even look up—she went on knitting as if no one was there. Old Colour knew that she was upset at him, but pretended not to notice and paced slowly around the apartment. He was wearing a tunic suit with a white silk scarf carelessly flung around his neck, with both hands in his pockets—the very image of an idealistic May Fourth youth. After pacing around the apartment for a while, his eyes fell on the checkered pattern of sunlight coming through the window and realized that winter was approaching. Suddenly he heard Wang Qiyao's cold voice behind him, accusing him of disturbing her peace with all his pacing back and forth. Old Colour sat down on a chair and looked out at a sparrow pecking at tidbits on the windowsill; the bird was obscured by the window frame and he could only see half its head. Soon Wang Qiyao announced that she wasn't feeling well and didn't intend to cook, so she wouldn't have anything to offer him.

"You think I came here to eat?" he sneered.

Only then did she raise her head. "What did you come here for then?"

"What do you think I came here for?"

Wang Qiyao withdrew her gaze and went back to knitting, trying to ignore him.

Old Colour was getting angry. He sat sulking with his hands still in his pockets. His posture indicated that he felt aggrieved, but he was unable to speak up for himself to get the justice he felt was owed to him. A bit later Wang Qiyao got up from the sofa, made a pot of tea, and set a cup out on the table in front of him.

"What's there to be angry about?" she asked as she turned around and went back into the kitchen to make lunch.

Now it was Old Colour's turn to ignore her. He sat in his chair silently stewing in anger. He couldn't figure out how he could have let Wang Qiyao come out with the upper hand again. It was times like this that the advantages of life experience really showed. That kind of experience takes time to build up; no amount of cleverness is a match for time. The difference of a day or two, or even a year or two, might not matter much, but several decades did.

Lunch that afternoon was much more elaborate than usual. Wang Qiyao swallowed her irritation and was extremely attentive to Old Colour, casually telling him all kinds of interesting stories she had never shared with him before. Old Colour gradually cooled down, till he almost forgot that he had been upset—but then Wang Qiyao brought it up again.

"You really think those things I said the other night over dinner just came out of nowhere? As if I had nothing better to do?"

Old Colour stopped eating, uncertain of what she was trying to say.

"I was thinking back to many years ago, on a day like this one, when it was cold and bleak outside and there were four people sitting around a hotpot. One of the women was just an onlooker, but you would not believe what happened between those two men and that other woman."

Wang Qiyao paused for a moment before continuing. "That woman was me."

Old Colour put down his chopsticks and glanced up at Wang Qiyao. She had an indifferent expression, as if she were talking about someone else. What happened between her, Uncle Maomao, and Sasha some twenty years earlier seemed so alien, it didn't even feel like a part of her anymore. She didn't know if the details had faded with time or she had blocked them out, but she had trouble remembering the sequence of how things had happened. Her nonchalant air only made the tragedy more shocking. This was the first time that Old Colour had heard Wang Qiyao talk about her past; up till then she had described only the settings, but the participants were elusive, disappearing and reappearing like phantoms. But now those phantoms had come to life. They were real people; ironically, this knowledge only made Old Colour feel more perplexed, lost in a massive cloud of mist. Wang Qiyao's face was like a reflection in water—it seemed to ripple and sway. He realized that he was crying, partly out of sympathy and partly because he was deeply moved.

"Even *I'm* not crying," protested Wang Qiyao, "so what are you crying for?"

"I don't know . . ." he murmured as he put his head down on the table.

From that point on, Wang Qiyao began to reveal her secret life over the past several decades to him. They spent the next few days together, Wang Qiyao telling her buried stories, Old Colour silently listening. The stories were accompanied by cigarettes and the room became enveloped in thick smoke. Their faces grew hazy, their voices too. It was a story that began forty years ago, about a life filled with splendor and turmoil—where would one trace the beginnings of such a story? Although it was a tragedy, it was a tragedy laced with grandeur and elegance—how was such a story going to end? Wang Qiyao's voice grew quiet, and all was silent, only the cigarette smoke thickened and dissipated freely in the air. Then the sound of someone clapping thrice softly broke the silence—it was Wang Qiyao. Taken aback, Old Colour immediately looked over to see her smiling at him through the smoke.

"Our little game is coming to an end too, isn't it?" she said.

He trembled slightly, struck by an ominous sensation.

"After all, life is like a game, right?" she continued.

He didn't know whether to agree or disagree, but he saw her stand up and walk toward him through the smoke. She began to caress his hair, which took him off guard. She ran her hands through his hair several times and he heard her whisper, "You silly boy."

He reached up to guide her hands but before he could touch her, she was gone. Wang Qiyao had already left the room, and as he watched her receding into the door he began to feel feverish. Upon her return she found him shivering, his teeth chattering loudly. She put down the bowl in her hand to feel his forehead, only to be caught up in his arms, like vines wrapping around a tree. When she asked him what was wrong, he didn't say a word, but keeping his eyes closed, pulled himself against her body. She could feel that his whole body was burning and helped him over to the bed to lie down. Clamped down on her waist with both arms, he pulled her down on top of him. Wang Qiyao kept telling him to let go, but he just held on more tightly. In her panic, she slapped him in the face. But he just kept his eyes closed and held on tighter still. She continued hitting him until her hand ached. His face was coming out in red welts, and taking pity on him, she gently caressed his cheeks. To this he responded by pushing his face against hers. They lay like this for quite some time went by. As she leaned on his chest, Wang Qiyao let out a sigh, and he took advantage of her momentary passivity by turning over suddenly and pressing down on top of her.

As his fever subsided, he broke out in a cold sweat, but continued to shiver. Strange, incoherent mumblings spilled out of his mouth and Wang Qiyao had no idea what he was saying. She did all she could to sooth him, treating him like a child who needed to be comforted. She consented to whatever he wanted, doing all she could to please him. At certain moments he grew frustrated because he didn't know how to do what he was yearning to do and ended up throwing a tantrum. In the end it was Wang Qiyao who guided him with her hand. He sobbed a few more times, desperately, as if his world had come to an end. So Wang Qiyao consoled him and did her best to encourage him. That was a long, distressful night, and many things occurred that should never have been. The lights went on and off all night as they tried to go to sleep but kept getting up. There was something odd about Peace Lane that night, it was so quiet, empty of all the usual sounds of things stirring about—the only noises were those they made. And even these sounds seemed to get swallowed up, so that the noisier they were, the lonelier it felt. They were both plagued by nightmares, emitting muffled cries. Their breath came heavily, and their eyes felt sore and dry. It was an exhausting night, and felt as if they were both being crushed under some enormous weight.

They prayed for the morning to arrive, but as the first rays of light shone on the curtain, they started to worry how they would get through this new day. He was utterly spent, so exhausted that he could barely move. But she forced herself to get up before sunrise. She couldn't bear to look at herself in the mirror as she washed her face and brushed her hair. Quickly getting herself together, she tiptoed like a thief out of the apartment with a basket. It was still dark outside, the streetlights were still on, and there was virtually no one on the streets. Wang Qiyao walked briskly toward the market, where people were beginning to stir. By this time the sky was brightening and she felt that she had finally got past the previous night's ordeal. The streetlights went off one by one, but a few stars were still faintly visible in the sky. She asked herself what time it was. When she got home, the bed was empty and Old Colour had gone.

Old Colour did not come back. Wang Qiyao thought it was probably just as well. With him gone, the first thing she did was to pull open the curtains to let the sunlight in, letting it dissolve the darkness from the night before. Her mind seemed to skip over that night; she kept thinking,

Nothing happened... nothing happened. The ensuing days were quite peaceful, as were the nights that followed. Her social life was calmer, as everyone was busy with different things. She started a new cashmere sweater that required some very complicated knitting work. She knitted from morning until night, stopping only to eat. She kept the television on constantly, all the way until "Good-bye" appeared on the screen. Only then would Wang Qiyao put her knitting away and go to bed. She tried not to think of him, erasing his name from her mind as if he had never existed. Sometimes she would wonder, *What's the difference? I still live my life exactly as I did before.* But then one day Long Legs came by and casually asked, "When is Old Colour coming back to town?"

Wang Qiyao was taken aback. She didn't even know he had left.

"He went to Wuxi, didn't he?" said Long Legs.

Wang Qiyao didn't say anything, but inside herself she couldn't help laughing a cold, mocking laugh. She cooked several dishes for Long Legs, heating up some high-grade Shaoxing wine for him, and listened to him carry on with his tall tales. Long Legs had been doing well of late; several of his business deals had gone smoothly and he told Wang Qiyao about every one of them. She listened carefully, occasionally asking questions. Long Legs was quite touched to see someone paying so much attention to him—combined with the wine, this even made him a bit teary-eyed.

"Auntie Wang, if you or any of your friends ever need to change money, come to me. I guarantee I'll give you a better rate than the Bank of China," he said, and went on to quote the different rates and make the calculations for her.

"But I don't have any foreign currency. . . ." She hesitated for a moment before continuing, "Do you trade in the yellow stuff?"

"Of course!" declared Long Legs. He quoted her the price for gold on the black market as compared to the official price, rapidly calculated the difference, and cited some examples of recent transactions.

To his disappointment, Wang Qiyao said, "Well, I don't have any gold either. . . ."

"It's actually a very good deal," he added, and then moved on to another topic. By the time they finished lunch and Long Legs left, it was already three o'clock; the sun was still bright, but it was beginning to wane. Long Legs was a bit tipsy and couldn't quite walk straight. He could barely keep his eyes open. Standing there on the bustling street, he wondered, *Where should I go now?*

That night Wang Qiyao sat on the sofa knitting and listening to the noisy television. Feeling utterly bored, she closed her eyes, and before she knew it she had fallen asleep. When she awoke there was white static on the screen and the room was filled with the empty buzz of the television. Opening her eyes wide, she found the room larger and emptier than usual; the lights seemed brighter too, bathing the room in a harsh white. She forced herself to get up and turn off the television and the light before crawling into bed; but as soon as the light was switched off, the moonlight shone down at the foot of her bed and she was suddenly wide awake. She gazed at the floral patterns on the curtains in the moonlight and wondered what day of the lunar month it could be for the moon to be so full. She blamed herself for dozing off earlier, because now she wouldn't be able to get back to sleep—how was she supposed to get through the night? When people wake up alone in the middle of a quiet night, it is only natural for their thoughts to stray. The strange thing was that she didn't remember anything important, only an insignificant night from long ago.

One night, many years ago, two men from the provinces had knocked on her door hoping to find a doctor for the patient they were carrying on a stretcher. That sharp, insistent rapping in the stillness of the night rang in her ears—at the time she didn't know if that knock was the bearer of good news or bad. Wang Qiyao's hearing had grown keen at this moment and she could hear everything that went on in the *longtang*. There was nobody knocking now, the entire *longtang* was deathly silent, and one could even hear the thump when a cat jumped down from a wall. Wang Qiyao took in all of these minute sounds and carefully analyzed them. This was a little game she played with herself on quiet nights to pass the time. That night Wang Qiyao ended up staying awake almost the entire night; she did doze off a few times, but it was a light sleep and the slightest sound was enough to startle her awake. Worried that the same thing might happen the following night, she forced herself to stay awake until late; but she couldn't fight off her exhaustion and the moment she crawled under the covers she was out like a light.

She suddenly woke up to a knock on the window. Once fully awake, she heard it again—it sounded like someone throwing pebbles against the window. She got up and went over to pull the curtain back, only to discover the empty moonlit alley of the *longtang*. She stood there a moment and was about to close the curtain again when someone suddenly emerged from the shadows, stepping out into the moonlight, and looked up at her. They gazed at each other for a long while before Wang Qiyao turned to put on a jacket and went downstairs. The back door opened and the man scurried inside; no words were exchanged as they walked one behind the other up the stairs.

No lights were on inside, but the moonlight was there. They both stood facing it in order to avoid looking at each other. One sat down on the bed while the other stood, arms folded.

"You came back?" she, standing, asked after a long silence.

He, sitting, lowered his head.

"What were you running from? Don't tell me you were afraid that I'd come after you?" This was followed by a cold laugh.

Wang Qiyao walked over to the sofa and lit a cigarette. Her moonlit face was ashen, her hair was disheveled, and the smoke rose into the air, once again obscuring her. Without speaking, he took off his clothes and crawled into bed, covering his head with the blanket. Still smoking her cigarette, she turned to face the window. The moonlight picked out her profile, which in the haze of the smoke appeared like the silhouette of a creature from another world. She was uncertain about the hour, which must have been late, as there was not a sound, not even from a stray cat. Finishing her cigarette at last, Wang Qiyao put out the butt in the ashtray before coming back to bed. This was a quiet night: everything was carried out in silence. There were no tears, no moans, even their breath seemed to be stifled. Eventually the moon moved west and the room grew dark; lying in bed, the two of them seemed to sink down to the very bottom of the earth, completely silent and still. No one could have predicted what ended up happening on that dark silent night. This is what is known as a dark secret, a secret that must not be seen, spoken of, or even thought of—nothing whatsoever can be done about it. There was but one source of noise on that silent night—the pigeons on the rooftop, who were making disturbing sounds all night as if their nests had been invaded.

At nine the next morning, on one of the few sunny days they had seen all winter, Old Colour rode his bicycle down the street. *Could I be dreaming?* he asked himself. Everything around him seemed bright and alive, making his nightmares from the night before seem insubstantial, and this terrified him. He couldn't remember how everything had started or how it had ended. He was drawn to crowded places, as if they could bolster his confidence. He also liked the daylight and felt relaxed when he saw the sun rising. What he feared most were those moments just before dusk; he would be seized by a sudden panic and unable to sit still. He would often line up various meetings and things to do just before that time, but after dinner, around seven or eight o'clock, just before all the evening activities were about to start, he would feel compelled to get on his bike and ride toward Wang Qiyao's apartment—it was as if the demons from his nightmares were beckoning him.

How long had it been since he had been to the record store? He didn't even listen to the records he already had at home, which had all grown dusty. And on nights that he insisted on returning to his *tingzijian*, he would usually stay up, unable to rest. Outside the dormer window was the open empty sky; he felt if he gazed at it long enough, his heart would fall into it. At moments like this, the nightmares would return with a vengeance to his fully conscious mind; they were particularly vivid at this time and too much for him to handle alone. He couldn't do it by himself—he had no choice but to go to Wang Qiyao. But that only created a new nightmare. Knowing that he would be restless no matter what, he became resigned to his predicament. One morning, instead of creeping away from Wang Qiyao's bed right away, he decided to lie there watching the room slowly grow brighter. He glanced at Wang Qiyao with her head resting on the pillow, and she looked back at him. They smiled at each other.

"What should we have for breakfast?" Wang Qiyao asked, as if they were an old married couple.

Without answering, he reached over Wang Qiyao's body for the pack of cigarettes on the headboard. Wang Qiyao handed it to him, taking one for herself; the way they lit up was also like an old couple. By that time the first rays of sunlight had come into the room, but stopped on one side of the window frame. There was a note of weariness and desolation in the thin mist shrouding the morning sunlight. As if the day was almost over before it had even begun.

"What time do you have to be at work?" Wang Qiyao asked.

He said that he wasn't working—he was on winter vacation. It dawned on Wang Qiyao that Spring Festival was right around the corner, but she hadn't done a thing to prepare for it.

"How are you going to spend your vacation this year?" she asked.

"Just like always," he responded.

"I really don't know how you usually spend it. Why don't you tell me?"

He could hear the petulance in her words but decided not to play along.

Wang Qiyao got the message. Putting on a smile, she said, "What about inviting Zhang Yonghong and her boyfriend over right after the New Year?"

He agreed. They lay there smoking and didn't say anything further. The sun had already bathed the curtains in a crimson glow and filled the room with light, in which the cigarette smoke shimmered and danced. They stayed in bed until noon. Wang Qiyao fixed them a simple bowl of noodles and asked him to help with the spring cleaning. They hung the comforter out in the sun, soaked the sheets in detergent, and pulled the drawers out of the chest to dust them. The work gave them a sense of exhilaration. The dark atmosphere of the previous day and night was swept entirely away and their mood brightened. When they were done sweeping and dusting, Wang Qiyao went back to scrub the bedsheets that had been soaking. She sent Old Colour off to take a shower, asking him to pick up some smoked meats for the New Year dinner on his way back. It was already early evening by the time he got back with the groceries. Although it was late, the apartment was bright, clean, and freshly aired, and dinner was ready on the table. Wang Qiyao was sitting on the sofa knitting a sweater and watching the television.

"Dinner's ready!" she said as he walked in.

That night was exceptionally peaceful. Old Colour even thought to himself: *Isn't this what everyone aspires to in life?* He regaled Wang Qiyao with stories of his childhood, how he hit his head trying to climb over a wall, how he tried to trap a chicken but it ended up eating the bait and getting away, and all kinds of other trifling tales. Wang Qiyao listened quietly with a pleasant smile on her face. But his stories grew increasingly broken and rambling, against which the television sounded like an off-screen commentary. They were startled when an impatient devil in their neighborhood couldn't wait to set off the first firecracker in celebration of the coming New Year. The bang scared them half to death—it too was like an off-screen sound effect. That was a night that could almost be called sweet and cozy; the nightmares had retreated and insomnia had released its grip. They fell into a deep slumber, undisturbed by fitful sleep-talk. The room was silent, with the exception of the sound of their gentle breathing. The nights of struggle had finally disappeared, leaving a peaceful evening on Peace Lane.

In this atmosphere of peace Spring Festival arrived. This was the Lunar New Year of 1986, an auspicious holiday, and all around were hopeful signs of change. You could tell from the firecrackers going off on New Year's Eve, the explosions rising and falling with no signs of letting up. When the clock struck midnight, the entire city was filled with the sound of firecrackers and the sky turned red. Shredded remnants of firecracker paper rained down like a riotous collection of flower petals, transforming the streets into crimson highways; this too was a harbinger of good fortune. Had there ever before been so spectacular a New Year celebration? The joyous explosions seemed to declare the coming of a new world.

Just as the firecrackers sending off the old year had died down, more explosions erupted to greet the new. Breaking through the morning fog, the first firecracker of the day reverberated through the sky like a cock crowing at daybreak; this was the sound of a new era being unveiled. It was answered by a chorus of explosions near and far. They weren't as earthshaking as the night before, but they spread with growing density, not dense like porridge but like a string of large and small pearls being dropped into a jade bowl with crisp ringing sounds—almost like choral music. The music has a polyphonic quality, like a fugue that gradually shifts without the listener even realizing it. Everyone sings in counterpoint, one group harmonizing with the melodies of another. They are actually singing a canon, one wave following the last. Such is the great chorus of the city, with voices chiming in from every crevice and corner. When one gets tired, another takes over, and the music never stops. Listening to that chorus, one realizes that in this city strength lies in unity.

As Wang Qiyao had suggested, Zhang Yonghong and Long Legs came over for dinner on the second day of the New Year. Contrary to their usual routine, Old Colour decided to try his hand in the kitchen. He strapped on Wang Qiyao's apron and oversleeves and started preparing the day before. Wang Qiyao, playing his assistant, teased him, "Look who is doing the grunt work for you!"

"Only the best are qualified to work for me !" he rejoined.

Wang Qiyao nodded, laughing. "Look who's talking! If you keep flaunting it, you'll end up flat on your behind!"

"Don't worry, if I do, I'm sure someone will pick me up."

"Who?" Wang Qiyao demanded. "I'll tell you who . . . YOU!"

They worked the whole of that evening and all through the next morning; it was only around two o'clock on the afternoon of the dinner that things started coming together. Wang Qiyao was quite surprised at how well things were turning out. When she asked Old Colour where he had learned to cook, he just smiled. When she pestered him further, he said that he had learned on his own. In the middle of this conversation, the other two showed up. As always, Long Legs came bearing all manner of gifts, even a bouquet of roses. Although Wang Qiyao chided him for bringing such expensive flowers, she was really quite pleased, thinking this a good omen. One glance at the dishes on the table and Zhang Yonghong immediately knew something was different. She asked if they had hired a new chef. Wang Qiyao shot out her lips in the direction of Old Colour, who smiled but wouldn't admit to anything.

"Wow! This must have been one expensive chef!" Zhang Yonghong exclaimed.

"Not in the least . . ." Old Colour modestly replied.

Wang Qiyao and Old Colour busied themselves with a few last preparations, and the four of them soon sat down to eat. It was still a bit early for dinner, but things tended to get chaotic around the New Year and they didn't mind eating early.

Once they had all sat down, Zhang Yonghong and Long Legs toasted the host and the chef before everyone exchanged new year wishes. Next it was Old Colour's turn to introduce the dishes to them; as he prefaced each with an elaborate preamble, Zhang Yonghong was prompted to taunt him, but he didn't bother to argue—he knew the food would speak for itself. Although visibly impressed, she refused to concede, and this provoked him to take her to task, and so they parried back and forth. Not only were both extremely intelligent, but each had learned a thing or two from Wang Qiyao about how to get a point across; their playful exchanges elicited cries of approval as the other two watched with pleasure. Inspired by their audience, they pushed their performance up another notch and set upon each other with redoubled energy. After who knows how many rounds, there still seemed no end to their resources. Gradually, however, the enthusiasm of the audience flagged, which showed in their lagging applause and waning laughter. Zhang Yonghong and Old Colour eventually had to bring an end to their show even though they could easily have gone on.

This exchange gave each of them a taste of how clever the other could be, which left both exhilarated and wanting another chance to compete. Even as they tried to scale back to a more polite tone, they couldn't help seasoning their remarks with playful sarcasm. Every time one opened his mouth, out came a provocation, to which the other would respond by taking up the challenge. Over the course of the meal, there were at least two or three times when their exchanges were so brilliant that they seemed perfectly matched. Both relished the excitement of the battle and neither was anxious to declare victory as they reveled in the sheer delight of performance. Wang Qiyao had to call a halt. "Okay, time for a break. You two can pick up again after we have some fruit."

It was only then that the two snapped out of it and realized they had been ignoring Wang Qiyao and Long Legs. Long Legs appeared especially out of sorts, pacing around the room with a dejected look on his face. Wang Qiyao maintained a smiling composure as she handed out plates of fruit, avoiding Old Colour's eye as she handed him his portion.

Although she politely replied whenever he spoke to her, she made a point of looking away, as if there was something more pressing on her mind. He knew she was upset, but that didn't seem to spoil his mood; in fact, it seemed to put him in even higher spirits. He eagerly challenged Zhang Yonghong to another round of combat, looking happy and animated, clever in the extreme. But Wang Qiyao refused to look at him. She concentrated on the knitting in her lap, but the smile never left her face. Long Legs, however, had lost patience and was clamoring to leave. When they finally looked at the time, it was already eleven o'clock. Zhang Yonghong got up to leave.

"I'll leave with you . . ." Old Colour said, and headed out the door with Zhang Yonghong and Long Legs.

One could hear the sounds of their footsteps going down the staircase before everything fell silent. Wang Qiyao walked over to the kitchen and was getting ready to wash the dishes when she heard the rattling of their bicycles as they pushed them through the back entrance under the window. Someone said he couldn't find the key to his bicycle lock. It was only after a search that the key was found, and she heard a sharp click as the lock snapped open and they all rode away. Wang Qiyao looked at the sink full of dishes and was at a momentary loss as to where to begin. After staring a while at the dirty pile, she turned off the light and went into her bedroom.

After Old Colour parted with the others outside, he rode around the block before making his way back to Wang Qiyao's place. There was hardly anyone out and only a single public bus rumbled down the deserted streets. He could hear the hissing sound of his bicycle chain going around; the excitement that had kept him going all evening began to quell. He was quite the child who, having had his share of pranks, wanted to go home now. Having got his kicks for the evening, he was feeling exceptionally relaxed. He admired the dark silhouettes of the buildings on the streets and the shadowy outline of the parasol tree branches. Various scattered thoughts raced through his mind as, gradually, he found himself approaching the *longtang* that he knew oh, so well.

Old Colour saw there was a single light on down the alley of the *longtang.* A stray cat scurried by in front of his bicycle, its paws making a soft sound on the cement. He silently parked his bicycle outside the back entrance to Wang Qiyao's building; after feeling for his key, he unlocked the door. When he got upstairs, he took out the other key to unlock the apartment door, but it wouldn't open. He put his ear up against the door, but all he heard was a deathly silence—Wang Qiyao had bolted the door.

He paused for a moment before tiptoeing back downstairs and scurrying out through the back door. Though he had been locked out, he wasn't in the least bit upset. *It's not my fault!* he thought as he rode out of the *long-tang*. As he peddled out of Peace Lane, his shadow suddenly appeared on the ground beneath his feet and for some reason this made him ecstatic. Taking one foot off the pedal, he straightened his back and looked up to the sky—what a quiet night it was! He pedaled home, riding like the wind, and from far off he had already caught sight of his dormer window extending out from the rooftop. He could almost hear the sound of jazz music playing, the saxophone echoing in his ears.

He didn't leave his apartment for the next two days. For the third and fourth day of the New Year, Old Colour sat in his third-floor *tingzijian* listening to jazz records. Everything seemed to be back the way it had been a few months earlier. The phonograph needle made a scratchy sound as it went over the grooves on the record—that was the sound of it welcoming him back, pleasantly surprised that he was suddenly paying it attention again. He carefully went through his collection, using a fine brush to dust off all his records. He ate all his meals at home: the taste of his mother's cooking was another reunion. His parents expressed their joy that he was back home with a childlike bashfulness; when father and son sat across from each other at the dinner table, they avoided one another's gaze. The fact that no friends came to visit him during those days showed just how long it had been since he had last spent time at home. He lay on his mattress, staring up at the triangular ceiling, and felt at ease. The peace he felt was not the kind that comes after everything has been resolved; it was tinged with anticipation, but he didn't yet know what it was that he was waiting for.

Outside the window, children were still occasionally setting off firecrackers and he could hear the neighbors exchanging formalities with the visitors who were coming and going. That was what the New Year was all about! Family's family, after all, and visitors are visitors. He spent the fifth and sixth days of the New Year at home as well; his parents went back to work, the firecrackers grew less frequent, the *longtang* became more peaceful, and things got back to normal. Because everyday life had been sorted out by the holidays, they were better able to take hold of their emotions, to let bygones be bygones and start afresh. The seventh day of the New Year fell on a Sunday and the festive spirit of the holiday enjoyed a momentary revival, inspiring a few ripples of excitement. Old Colour decided to go out and rode his bicycle unhurriedly down the streets. Some of the shops were open, but some were still closed for the holiday.

Between the paving stones were burnt-out remnants of firecrackers still waiting to be swept away, and a burst balloon that hadn't quite made it to heaven was hanging on a tree branch. As he approached Peace Lane, Old Colour noticed the sun shining on the building that stood at its entrance; on the cement slab bearing the inscription of the year the building had been completed, the numbers were worn and appeared dispirited. The gray and dilapidated entrance too had a dispirited air. Old Colour's bicycle glided past the entrance to Peace Lane without going in; he wanted to test himself to see just how stubborn and unreasonable he could be. He rode faster, swaying slightly as he went—he no longer looked like Old Colour, but rather a modern youth surging forward with an indomitable will.

A few days later the schools were back in session and he went back to work. He had a full schedule and would leave early and not return home until late. He went to bed early every night and slept peacefully. Spring had begun to adorn the dark roof tiles outside his dormer window. The wild grass that sprang up from between the tiles was nameless, but it grew thick. The sunlight was warmish and had a moist feel. Even the songs of birds sounded richer, as if they had endless things to say. Waking up in the morning, he would wonder, *What good things are going to happen today?* Even people who are wise to the ways of the world can't help being infected by this strange hope. That was the benefit of spring: everyone looks on the bright side of things and feels more lighthearted.

That Sunday, he finally went to Wang Qiyao's apartment. As he entered the back alley, he suddenly began to feel lost, and even asked himself, *What kind of place is this?* Had he even been there before? But his bicycle seemed to know the way and he rode right up to Wang Qiyao's building. He left his bicycle outside the back door and went straight up the stairs. Her door was closed. He knocked but no one answered. He took out his key, but before he could get it into the keyhole, the door opened. The curtains were all pulled shut, but the noon sun had managed to creep in, filling the room with a hazy glare that mingled with the cigarette smoke in the air. Wang Qiyao had got up and put on her nightgown before opening the door, but once she had let him in, she went back to bed.

"Are you sick?" he asked.

She didn't answer. He approached, intending to console her, but as soon as he saw the stains on her pillow from her hair dye, his heart sank. There was a stale odor lingering from the previous day, which also brought his spirits down.

"It's stuffy in here," he said as he went to open a window. The glare of the sun blinded him as he pulled the curtain back.

"We should start preparing lunch . . ." he said, trying to put on a cheerful air.

He had not expected his words to find an echo in Wang Qiyao, who said quietly, "You've always talked about taking me out for a meal . . . well, how about today?"

Those words were the equivalent of calling out "checkmate." Both of them understood the significance of eating out together like that, but one of them had always refused to go. Times have changed, and the tables have turned; she, who had once refused, wished to go, while he, who had been so aggressive, now refused. He stood with his face toward the curtains for a moment before turning around and walking out.

From the Blue Sky Down to the Yellow Springs

As we have mentioned before, Long Legs was a god of the night, never returning to his lair until past midnight. One evening, after wrapping up his nightlife early but not feeling like going home, he decided to ride past Peace Lane and somehow found himself going in. Seeing the light on in Wang Qiyao's window, he figured there must be people up there having a grand old time, and rode over toward the back alley with eager excitement. At that moment he saw someone getting off his bicycle outside the back door of her building. It was Old Colour. Long Legs was about to call out to him when he saw Old Colour unlock the door and head straight upstairs, quietly closing the door behind him. *How could he have a key to Wang Qiyao's building?* Long Legs may have been naïve, but he wasn't stupid; he knew better than to knock on the door, and instead turned around and rode out of the back alley. As he passed by the front on his way out, he looked up again at the window and saw that the light had already been turned off.

Looking down at his watch, Long Legs saw that it was midnight. There was not a single light on in Peace Lane and the apartment buildings threw a jagged silhouette against the curtain of darkness. It was a strange night. There was something mysterious about that night, even to someone as deeply embroiled in the city's nightlife as Long Legs; it made him feel oppressed and somewhat perturbed. Strange demons seemed to have taken over the narrow night sky between the buildings, and the night air rang out with premonitions. Long Legs was suddenly struck by how distant and strange this city really was to him. In these streets, empty of cars and pedestrians, the traffic lights at the intersections changed from red to green to red again, as if controlled by some alien force. When an occasional pedestrian chanced on another, they were fearful and couldn't wait to get away. The night was a massive net and Long Legs felt like a fish trapped inside it; no matter how hard he swam, he couldn't escape. It was like something from a nightmare. But Long Legs was a man without a memory: every morning he would awaken and everything from the night before would disappear like clouds and mist. By the following evening he would be just as lovable and friendly as ever; it felt good to be together with his friends and even the neon lights were all practiced in singing and dancing.

However, that was back before the Spring Festival. On the second day of the Lunar New Year, when he was at Wang Qiyao's apartment watching Old Colour and Zhang Yonghong parrying with each other, the incident he had witnessed never even crossed his mind. That New Year was a tough time for Long Legs; the day after the dinner, he disappeared. Everyone thought that he had gone to Hong Kong to see his cousin—Zhang Yonghong was expecting him to bring back the most fashionable outfits for her. But what was really up with Long Legs? Bundled up in a factory-issue cotton overcoat, his hands drawn back inside his sleeves, he was, in fact, braving the cold in the passenger seat of a three-wheel pedicab on his way to an aquatic products supplier at Hongze Lake. The cars on the highway were all trying to overtake each other; their glaring headlights, swinging this way and that, shone harshly on the night traveler curled up in the back of the pedicab. Blaring in his ears were the sounds of truck engines mixed with the sharp blasts of horns; occasionally they passed by pedicabs broken down by the side of the road, the occupants standing next to their vehicles with a blank look on their faces.

That was indeed another world. Between unbounded heaven and the limitless earth, human beings crawled like small insects, and could be crushed by a single step. When one finds himself in such circumstances, it is easy to act out of desperation. The aquatic products business was exceedingly risky and uncertain, but Long Legs went ahead and threw in his last bit of money. In doing so, he effectively burned all of his bridges—there was no turning back now. If he failed, how could he ever go back to Shanghai to face his friends? How could he face Zhang Yonghong?

At this very time, the story about his trip to Hong Kong was spreading all over Shanghai. You know what happens once people start talking—everyone tells their friends, their friends tell their friends, and before you know it the story gets blown completely out of proportion. People started to say that Long Legs was never coming back: his cousin was sponsoring him to emigrate. Others said that he had gone away to claim his inheritance and that even if he did come back, he wouldn't be the same person. Zhang Yonghong began to grow anxious and silently counted the days since his departure. She couldn't help but feel uneasy when she thought about how old she was; she was already well past marrying age. For the past year or so she had set her sights on this one man—he was her sole candidate. The more she worried about her future, the more she missed Long Legs. With no news from him, and the rumors flying all around, she could no longer sit still. She decided to visit Wang Qiyao to try to take her mind off the matter. Just as she was about to open the back door to Wang Qiyao's building, Old Colour stepped out.

"Wang Qiyao's not home?" she asked.

Instead of answering, he asked whether she had time to get a bite to eat. Zhang Yonghong figured she might as well find distraction at the restaurant and went along with him. They didn't go far, just over to Nocturnal Shanghai in the adjacent *longtang,* where they found a quiet and secluded table in a corner. Zhang Yonghong thought that Old Colour would ask after Long Legs and was wondering what she should say, but to her surprise he never even broached the subject. Deep down her gratitude was mixed with a feeling of being cheated, as if he had let her get off easy in a game of chess. His magnanimity, however, only made her all the more determined to bring up Long Legs. She said that he had been incredibly busy since arriving in Hong Kong and had only had time to send one postcard.

"Has Long Legs gone to Hong Kong?" Old Colour asked.

It was only then that she realized Old Colour hadn't even heard about the trip. She cursed herself for assuming too much and felt a bit awkward. Old Colour, however, took no notice, and simply asked her what they should order. As they were talking, someone wove past the other tables toward them and stopped in front of them. They looked up and saw Wang Qiyao. Her hair was freshly washed and neatly done up in a tight bun. She was wearing light makeup and had on a light green cotton jacket, and looked exceptionally youthful.

"What a coincidence!" she chirped brightly, "running into you two here!"

Although Zhang Yonghong didn't understand all that was going on, she sensed that something was wrong. Her heart pounded. Old Colour was barely able to maintain his composure; the color drained from his face and only after a pause did he manage to say, "Please have a seat."

"That's okay, I wouldn't want to disturb the two of you."

With that she sat down at a small table for one by the window in the opposite corner. As she sat down she turned to them and smiled. And so the three of them sat at two different tables; soon other customers came in and started filling up the restaurant, blocking their view of each other. But it was no use: they had eyes for only one thing—even with all the people there, not a single gesture or movement at the other table across the room escaped their eyes.

That was a difficult lunch to get through. None of them knew what they were eating, let alone what they were talking about or what the other people in the restaurant were doing. By the time they finally emerged from Nocturnal Shanghai, the streets were filled with passing cars and pedestrians and they became even more confused. Old Colour wasn't quite sure how he had said good-bye to Zhang Yonghong, but they each went their separate way. He decided to call on some of his friends. He had been away from them for a long time, but Old Colour could still guess what they were up to on a Sunday afternoon like this and rode off in pursuit. Sure enough, he managed to track them down as they were on their way for a swim at some luxury hotel that had a heated pool. There were five or six in the group and he decided to tag along.

In the layer of mist that hovered above the water, all the objects and people on the other side of the pool shimmered like apparitions. The sounds also had an illusory quality as they echoed and bounced off the high ceiling. Old Colour swam laps; through his goggles he could see the blue water flowing past him like a current. The water felt good rolling off his body, serving as a measure for his strength and flexibility. He swam away from his friends into the deep end, where their cries of laughter seemed to be a world away. As he swam, all the filth inside him seemed to be cleansed away, and his mind cleared up. Afterward they took the open glass elevator downstairs; a few lights were already lit, sparkling in the waning light of dusk. Looking down on the city at that moment, one could feel the embracing warmth of Shanghai, as if the city was ready to forgive anything. The colors of sunset grew dim but the warmth lingered. He felt exhilarated and his spirit soared. As much as Old Colour was enamored with the world of forty years ago, he couldn't escape the fact that his heart belonged to the present. By the time the elevator arrived on the ground floor, his excitement had calmed, leaving behind an intimate feeling that moved him. It was at that moment that he thought of Wang Qiyao; the image of her sitting alone in the corner suddenly appeared before his eyes. His heart twitched gently and he thought: *It's about time I brought things to a close.*

The dinner hour had long passed by the time he arrived at Wang Qiyao's. She got up to make tea when he came in. As she placed the teacup before him, the calm look on her face showed no trace of what had happened earlier. That made him feel somewhat at ease, even though he suspected that she was still angry. Just as he was trying to decide how to break the news, he saw Wang Qiyao walk over to her chest and unlock one of the drawers. She took out a small wooden engraved box and, turning back toward Old Colour, placed it on the table in front of him. He had seen this box before, he remembered the floral engravings, and he knew the story of its origin—he just didn't understand why she was taking it out at this moment. After a pause, Wang Qiyao began to explain. She said that if she had learned one thing all these years, it was that she couldn't rely on anything; but *this*—she motioned towards the wooden box—was the only exception. In all the dark, hopeless days, this had been her only source of consolation. But now, she said, she wanted to give it to him. She didn't have much time left, she could see that. He wouldn't have to worry, for she wouldn't take up too much of his time; she just wanted him to be there for her, and it wouldn't be for long. If he had never come into her life it would have been easier, but now that he had come, she felt that losing him would leave her with nothing. Her words gradually became incoherent and she started to speak more and more quickly. She was smiling, but a tear trickled down her cheek. She cried, not a sea of tears, just a single drop from her left eye, as if the rest of her tears had dried up. As she spoke, she pushed the wooden box toward Old Colour, who tried to push it away but, feeling her resistance, had no choice but to apply some force.

"You don't want it? You probably don't know what's inside . . . let me show you," she said.

She was about to open the box when he reached over and held the lid down to prevent her from opening it. As their hands touched, he felt how cold she was. Taking her hands in his, he too began to weep, struck by the tragedy and wondering how things could have ended up like this. Wang Qiyao wrestled her hands free, determined to open the box, saying that he was sure to like what was inside and that once he saw it he would understand how reasonable her proposition was. She was willing, in all sincerity, to give him all she had—how could he refuse to give her just a few years? Wang Qiyao's words were like a knife cutting through his heart. Old Colour couldn't say a word—all he could offer were his tears. He should never have come back: he had not realized how pitiful Wang Qiyao had become. Forty years of romance and it all came down to this pathetic ending. He had missed the splendid climax and only caught the ending: how ill-fated was that? Finally he struggled free of her and got away. In one short day he had run away from her twice, each time more desperate than the last. His hands still carried traces of her icy skin—it left him with a premonition of death. He promised himself, *Never again can I go back to that place!*

Spring arrived without mercy, as did the spring rains. A warm humid haze encompassed the city and open umbrellas were the blooming flowers of this rainy season, as the pedestrians under the umbrellas scurried down the damp streets. Long Legs finally returned. He had been gone so long that the rumors about him had eventually died down. Zhang Yonghong had almost lost hope waiting for him; if it hadn't been for Old Colour, who helped her pass the time, who knows how she would have got through those days of waiting. She had even considered turning her attention to Old Colour, but was sensitive enough to recognize the state of his emotions. She could tell that he was only spending time with her to help him get through a difficult phase in his own life. He never talked about it and she never asked, which he always appreciated. But just because he appreciated her understanding didn't mean that he appreciated her in *that* way. She therefore nipped that idea in the bud.

One day Old Colour said he had a favor to ask of Zhang Yonghong. When she asked what, he placed two keys tied together on a string in her hand, saying all she had to do was give these keys to Wang Qiyao the next time she went to see her. Zhang Yonghong refrained from asking why he didn't deliver them himself, knowing that they must have had some kind of falling out. She didn't dare let her imagination run wild; the whole thing was way too complicated and she had her own problems to deal with. She took the keys and put them in her pocketbook. They had dinner together and parted ways after leaving the restaurant. On the way home Zhang Yonghong passed by Peace Lane and thought she would go in to drop off the keys; seeing that the lights were out in Wang Qiyao's apartment, she decided to come back some other time. Over the next few days, she kept forgetting to go back. When she remembered, something else came up, so she decided to go the next day. But then the next day Long Legs made his quiet return.

Long Legs brought Zhang Yonghong a set of French cosmetics and a sleek woolen hat. The two went to Café Dream, where they sat at a candlelit table. Zhang Yonghong told him everything that had happened in his absence, but Long Legs had changed—he had little to say and seemed distracted. Although he was looking directly at Zhang Yonghong, he may as well have been gazing at her from the other side of the ocean: he had returned, but his spirit was still wandering. The candles flickered gently as they spoke in whispered tones; as they drank more wine, everything took on a surreal aspect, emerging and dissolving, running together into a rainbow of hazy brilliance. Long Legs, however, stood on the margins of this brilliance, in the darkest spot, and no matter how hard he looked he couldn't see himself—he had disappeared. Café Dream was indeed a place where one could go to lose oneself.

Slowly, Long Legs lightened up and started talking about his adventures in Hong Kong. He was struck by a bolt of inspiration and Hong Kong suddenly appeared before his eyes—he could see it all so clearly! He told Zhang Yonghong all the amazing things he had done since he left. A brilliant prospect lay ahead of him—he even broached the subject of marriage. He said that they should get married in either Bangkok or San Francisco, where his father's mansions would be the perfect place for a ceremony. Zhang Yonghong was infected by his excitement; tears of happiness glimmered in her eyes. Although they were both practical minded, they couldn't fight the dreamlike atmosphere of the café. The candle on the table floated in a small dish of water, never sinking, and seemed to be burning for all eternity. The melted wax stuck firmly together, feeding the flame of their fantasies.

Who knows how much wine the newly reunited lovers consumed that night? After they paid the bill and were getting up to leave, Zhang Yonghong suddenly remembered the keys and took them out of her pocketbook.

"Isn't it strange?" she said with a laugh. "Old Colour asked me to give these keys to Wang Qiyao—as if he couldn't do it himself!"

Long Legs took the keys and examined them. Suddenly something lit up inside him and he sobered up instantly.

"I don't want to go back to her apartment either," said Zhang Yonghong. "Who's to know how she'd react . . . ."

She went on to tell Long Legs about what had happened that day at Nocturnal Shanghai. Long Legs wasn't really paying attention to her story; his whole attention was focused on examining those keys.

"Why don't you return them for me?" Zhang Yonghong suggested.

He consented and put the keys in his pocket as they left Café Dream. After seeing Zhang Yonghong home, he rode alone down the streets and somehow found himself heading in the direction of Wang Qiyao's apartment. As he rode into the *longtang*, he seemed to see the shadow of Old Colour standing there in the darkness, slipping in through the back door. He rode over to the door and, putting one foot down on the ground to steady the bike, took out the keys and selected one to try in the lock. The lock turned easily. He rotated it back to its original position and pulled it back out. At this moment he noticed that there was still light, even on that starless, moonless night—it was bright enough for him to make out the cracks and the grain on the wooden door. The city was never completely dark: think how many lights burned throughout the night, and how many people stay awake even during its darkest hours! There you will find the sources of this light. Long Legs held the key in the palm of his hand and rode out of the *longtang*. The lights were out in Wang Qiyao's apartment.

At three o'clock the next day Long Legs paid a visit to Wang Qiyao, bringing along a box of cosmetics for her. As soon as he got upstairs, the bitter smell of Chinese herbs assailed his nostrils; a pot of medicine was simmering on the stove. Wang Qiyao had been taking a nap and got up only when he arrived. Long Legs noticed her dry skin and yellow complexion and asked her what was wrong. Wang Qiyao said she had too much cold energy in her stomach and too much heat in her liver. She wanted to make him some tea, but Long Legs insisted on helping himself, and offered to bring her medicine over to her. Wang Qiyao said that it still needed ten more minutes, so Long Legs sat down. They chatted about how important it is to take care of one's health, and Long Legs told her about his trip to Hong Kong; before they knew it, ten minutes had gone by. He went into the kitchen to turn off the stove and pour the medicine into a bowl for her, almost scalding himself in the process. He set the bowl of black bitter liquid beside her bed.

He waited until she had finished the medicine and was sucking on a piece of candy to get the bitter taste out of her mouth before he placed the two keys on the table. He told her that Old Colour had asked him to drop them off for him. The instant she laid eyes on the keys, Wang Qiyao spat out the candy and spit up a mouthful of her medicine into the bowl. Long Legs rushed over to pat her on the back; after the fit had passed, he helped her to lie back down.

"That's life for you," Wang Qiyao laughed. "I'm sorry for not being a good host today, but I'll have you over some other time."

Long Legs insisted that none of that was necessary—after all, they were old friends. He was only concerned that here she was, sick, with no one to take care of her. He decided to keep her company, and sitting down beside her, he regaled her with all kinds of stories. At dusk he went into the kitchen to cook dinner, but didn't even know where to start and ended up just standing there in front of the gas stove. Finally Wang Qiyao staggered in and said that she would handle it. Long Legs wanted to help but, not knowing how, just stood beside her, lending a hand when needed. Before long, two bowls of noodles were ready; Wang Qiyao also steamed a bowl of salted fish patty especially for him. After she finished half her noodles, Wang Qiyao's face seemed to regain its color. She appeared to be in better spirits and smiled wryly as she looked around the room. "Look at this room! The instant I fell ill, all the dust started to accumulate, as if it wants to bury me!"

"What's the big deal about dust? You just wipe it away and it's gone!"

With that, he actually picked up a rag and started wiping the furniture, which really did brighten up the place. He also turned on the television and the room finally began to feel alive with the music.

Long Legs came back first thing in the morning for the next two days, exhausting every ounce of his energy in taking care of Wang Qiyao. Watching him, Wang Qiyao couldn't help wondering, *Why is he bothering with all this?* But then she figured, *Why else?* And then, mocking herself: *Why should I care about his reasons anyway?* Nevertheless, she deeply appreciated Long Legs being there for her at such a difficult time, and tried her best to share all kinds of gossip to keep him amused. Long Legs was spellbound by her stories and became even more solicitous in hopes of hearing more. When she grew tired from talking, it would be his turn to tell her stories. He finally got around to the price of gold, telling her that its value on the black market was several times what was quoted on the official exchange.

"But isn't that illegal?" asked Wang Qiyao. "I remember people getting executed for doing that in the fifties!"

"There is the old saying, 'The government can get away with arson, but the people aren't allowed to light a lamp'!" joked Long Legs. "If you want to talk about illegal dealings, well, the state is the biggest crook out there! What we do on the black market is small time compared to them!"

Wang Qiyao smiled. "The way you put it makes sense."

"Even so, everything comes down to timing. Right now things are fairly open, but who knows when the authorities might clamp down," remarked Long Legs.

"So what do you suggest?" asked Wang Qiyao.

"Well, if you have gold, I'd say that now is the best time to exchange it."

"That may be, but who has gold lying around in this day and age?"

"If I had to hazard a guess," said Long Legs, "I'd say that at least one out of every hundred has some gold stashed away somewhere. When we were ransacking people's homes during the Cultural Revolution, we even found two gold bars hidden in the home of a rickshaw coolie!"

Wang Qiyao laughed, "I wish I was that rickshaw coolie!"

Long Legs laughed too, and that marked the end of that conversation. Over the next few days, Wang Qiyao gradually regained her strength and started to feel better.

"It's been a long time since everybody got together. What do you say about having a party this Saturday night?" she suggested.

"Sounds great!" Long Legs readily assented. "I haven't really seen any of my friends since getting back from Hong Kong, so this is a good opportunity to see everybody."

"I'll take care of the food, and you can be in charge of inviting the people," Wang Qiyao said.

Long Legs agreed and headed for the door. When he got to the stairs, he suddenly turned around. "Should we invite Old Colour?"

"Why ever not?" asked Wang Qiyao. "He should be the first one on the list!"

After that, they each began making preparations. Because Wang Qiyao was still weak, she decided to take the easy route; so instead of doing all the cooking, she put in an order with the privately owned restaurant that had recently opened on the corner. She had everything delivered so that she would only have to prepare some beverages, fruit, and pastries. The day of the party, all she did was rearrange the furniture slightly and put out a new tablecloth and some fresh flowers; suddenly the entire room felt different. Wang Qiyao suddenly thought to herself, *It has been so long since I hosted a party. For so long there has been only one person coming in and out of this apartment, but tonight we'll have some fun!*

Everything was ready by three o'clock; all that remained was for the guests to arrive and the food to be delivered. The tidy room felt a bit empty. Wang Qiyao sat all alone, and her heart also felt a bit empty. The sun shone into the window, creating a powerful glare. The children didn't have to go to school on Saturday afternoon, and they were all playing outside in the *longtang*, singing songs, some new and others several decades old and familiar to Wang Qiyao. The potted oleanders on the rooftop terrace across the way were sprouting new leaves, green and glossy. After all, it was spring and the days were getting longer. It seemed as if the sun would never set. The staircase was silent, the guests had yet to arrive, but the crisp sounds of footsteps reverberated down the *longtang*, now approaching, now fading away. But there was no need to worry: an exciting night was approaching—it would be here soon enough.

Old Colour never showed up. In his heart he knew that Wang Qiyao was throwing the party especially for him; he also knew that going would bring him nothing but discomfort and sadness—those were the delicacies that Wang Qiyao was preparing for him. But he still couldn't resist riding around Peace Lane that night at around ten o'clock, when most parties reached their climax. Coming down the alley, he saw a flickering light in Wang Qiyao's window—not, he knew, a light bulb, but candlelight. Gazing up at the window, he was lost in a daze for several minutes, wondering, *What year is this scene from?* He could hear the sound of music but couldn't date it. Then he turned around and left, reassuring himself that no matter what, he now could say that he had dropped by. That was his way of replying to her invitation! That was their official good-bye, accompanied by music and dance. He was neither happy nor sad: he just numbly turned his back on the gaiety and left. The partygoers caught up in the excitement of the music and dancing were creatures of illusion—if he were to reach out to try to grasp at them, his hands would come up empty. As for the past that flowed like water—he could cross bridges and ferry his way across rivers, but in the end it would always elude him.

Wang Qiyao actually knew that he wouldn't show up. Her invitation was simply a message, a way of telling him that she couldn't let go of him, and that without him all gatherings were pointless. She ran around the apartment busying herself with making the guests comfortable, but all that was just to fill the emptiness in her heart. After she had turned off the lights and lit the candles, she felt some of the good times from her past coming back to her. The apartment filled with young friends singing and dancing made her forget that time was passing. Everyone was carrying on about what a wonderful time they were having. Then before they knew it, the clock had struck twelve and the night was gone. The wine bottles were empty and all that was left of the enormous cake was messy bits and pieces. Her friends bid her an affectionate farewell and, one after the other, filed down the stairs. Long Legs was the last to leave; he wanted to stay behind to help her clean up the plates and cups.

"Don't worry. I'll take care of it tomorrow. I'm too tired to worry about it tonight," she told him.

As soon as Long Legs was out the door, she blew out all the candles; silence fell over the apartment and the stairway was plunged into pitch-black darkness.

"Good-bye," Long Legs called out as he went softly down the stairs. He closed the door behind him as he exited through the back. When he got outside, a shiver suddenly came over him. A handful of scattered stars emitted a dull light, and there was a chill in the wind. Long Legs continued to shiver slightly as he undid his bicycle lock and peddled out of the *longtang*.

That night's excitement left its mark on Peace Lane. All those who were accustomed to turning in early went to sleep thinking that the lights would be burning all night long at Wang Qiyao's apartment. This was something quite out of the ordinary for Peace Lane, and it spiced up their dreams that night. The first thing anyone who happened to wake up in the middle of the night did was to look up at Wang Qiyao's window to see if the party was still going on. People coming home from the late shift and those leaving for the night shift also gazed up at her window and thought, *They're still at it*! Actually, it was only midnight then, and they had no idea of what transpired after that. The hours between two and three o'clock in the morning are the most peaceful hours, a time when even the insects are dreaming. The dreams of that hour are the soundest of all dreams—airtight, so that not even the wind can creep in—this is the hour people need to recover from the exhaustion of the previous day. The streetlights on Huaihai Road continued to shine quietly, lighting up the deserted road.

At the far end of Peace Lane there is only a single rusty iron lamp. It has been there for many years and emits a dirty, dull glow. It was during that hour of deathly silence that a long shadow crept into Peace Lane—it was Long Legs. Long Legs quietly parked his bicycle by the rear entrance to Wang Qiyao's building, took out a key from his pants pocket, and unlocked the door. There was a sharp click as the lock popped open, but it was far from enough to break the deep silence of the world that night. Like a cat, he tiptoed up the stairs. Halfway up the staircase there was a small window, through which the moonlight shone down on him, but Long Legs was not himself that night and the light seemed to be shining on someone else. He surprised even himself with his own dexterity as he navigated around the staircase cluttered with junk. But he didn't bump into a single thing and continued on up the stairs until he found himself standing outside Wang Qiyao's door. The door to the common kitchen was ajar, letting in a little light and projecting his shadow onto the apartment door; his shadow too looked like someone else's shadow. He paused for a moment before feeling for the other key.

Long Legs pushed open the door to find the interior bathed in moonlight, which projected the flower patterns from the curtains onto the floor. He felt calm and completely at ease. It was the first time that he had seen the room in the middle of the night like this and it looked completely different, yet he was able to find his way smoothly, without a single misstep. He saw the walnut chest against the wall, shimmering in the moonlight like a bride waiting to be taken to the altar. Anticipation overcame Long Legs. *That's it! So elegant and mysterious, it's there waiting for me.* It was like an assignation, at once stirring and tormenting. Long Legs' heart pounded as he approached the chest; he pulled a screwdriver out of his pocket, itching to get it open. But in the moment that he fitted the screwdriver into the drawer lock, the light suddenly turned on.

The sight of his own shadow leaping onto the wall caught Long Legs by surprise, but as he scanned his surroundings, his eyes were reassured by the familiar scene. Even now he still hadn't realized quite what had happened; out of habit, he wedged the screwdriver further in and, pressing down, popped open the drawer. Under the lamplight, the sound that it made was quite pronounced and it was only then that, startled, he turned around to find Wang Qiyao. She had gone to bed fully clothed, and was now sitting up, propped against the pillow. This had been a difficult night for Wang Qiyao to get through, and she had been awake the whole time. She had been counting the minutes, counting the seconds until sunrise, hoping that some miracle might turn up with the coming day. When she first saw Long Legs come in, she wasn't in the least scared. She was aware that all kinds of bizarre events take place deep in the night, when even the most devilish of behavior seems normal. Even when she saw him pry open the drawer she wasn't at all surprised, the middle of the night being a queer time when people witness all kinds of outlandish things with perfect composure.

"I told you," Wang Qiyao said, "I don't have any gold."

Avoiding her gaze, Long Legs laughed in embarrassment, "But that's not what everybody says."

"What does everyone say?"

"Everyone says you were once Miss Shanghai and caused quite a stir on the Bund back then. Then later you got involved with some rich guy who left all his money to you before running off to Taiwan. They even say that he still sends you remittances in U.S. dollars every year."

Wang Qiyao listened with curiosity to his version of her story. "And what else?"

Long Legs went on, "You have a chest filled with the yellow stuff, but you've only tapped into a fraction of it over the past several decades. You cash in a few bars at the Bank of China at regular intervals. If not for that, what would you live on?"

Wang Qiyao didn't know what to say. After a brief pause, she said, "That's the most ridiculous thing I've ever heard!"

Long Legs took a step closer and fell forward, kneeling before her bed. His voice trembled as he begged, "Please help me. Just loan me a little bit. I'll pay you back double as soon as I get back on my feet."

Wang Qiyao laughed. "Long Legs, has there been a time when you were *ever* on your feet?"

Long Legs' pleading voice betrayed a hint of desperation, "Look at what I've been forced to resort to. Why would I lie to you? Please, Auntie, help me. Everyone knows what a good heart you have and how generous you are."

Wang Qiyao had originally been ready to continue this little conversation, but as soon as she heard him start calling her "Auntie," she found herself losing her temper. Her face became stern and she scolded him, "Who are you calling 'Auntie'?"

Long Legs leaned on the edge of the bed and clung to Wang Qiyao's leg as he pleaded yet again, "Please help me. I'll write you an IOU."

Wang Qiyao pushed his hand away. "Why are you coming to me for help and not your father? Everyone says that your father is a millionaire! Didn't you just come back from Hong Kong?"

Those words pierced Long Legs to the heart. His face turned ashen and he withdrew his hands. Getting up from the floor, he brushed the dust off his knees, "What does this have to do with my father? If you aren't willing to help me out, then just forget it!"

With that, he strutted toward the door.

But Wang Qiyao stopped him.

"You think it's that easy to just walk out of here? I've never heard of someone trying to borrow money by sneaking into people's homes in the middle of the night!"

Long Legs had no choice but to remain standing there.

Deep in the night, when people should be sleeping, their thoughts often wander off to strange places: they utter words that do not make sense and everything tends to degenerate into a farce. It seemed as if Wang Qiyao had successfully headed off a disaster and the story would end there, but just as the curtain was falling, she called "Stop" . . . and forced the action to go on.

"What do you want from me?" asked Long Legs.

"Go to the police station and turn yourself in," replied Wang Qiyao.

Long Legs began to grow anxious. "And if I refuse?"

"Then I'll go report you to them."

"You don't have any proof."

Wang Qiyao smiled complacently. "What do you mean, I don't have proof? You pried the drawer open and your fingerprints are everywhere."

Long Legs suddenly felt as if he had been struck by a train—he felt dizzy and his forehead broke out in a cold sweat. He stood there for a while and then a sinister smile appeared on his face. "Looks like the result will be the same whether I do it or not, so I might as well finish what I started."

With that, he walked over to the chest and pulled the wooden box out of the drawer. Unable to lie still any longer, Wang Qiyao got up from the bed to take back her possession. Long Legs ducked out of the way and held the box behind his back, out of her reach.

"What are you worried about, Auntie? Didn't you say you didn't have anything?"

Now it was Wang Qiyao's turn to feel anxious. She began to perspire and screamed at him, "Put it down! You thief!"

"If you call me a thief, then that's what I am!" A shameless, even brutal, look came over his face.

She tried to twist the box out of his hand, and he let her struggle all she wanted, but he wasn't letting go. By then he had got a sense of the box's weight. Excitement swelled inside him because now he knew that he had not gone through all this trouble in vain.

Anger contorted Wang Qiyao's face. Gnashing her teeth, she cursed him. "You wretched thief! You're a thief! You think I believed all that garbage you tell everyone? I saw through you a long time ago—I just didn't want to embarrass you!"

The words made Long Legs swallow his smugness. He put down the box and grabbed hold of Wang Qiyao's neck.

"Say it again! I dare you!" he screamed.

"Thief!" cried Wang Qiyao.

Long Legs wrapped his large hands around Wang Qiyao's throat. *Look at how thin her neck is, just skin and bones, it's enough to make me sick!* Wang Qiyao struggled to break free of his grip, cursing him all the while. His grip tightened. He looked at her face: so ugly and desiccated. Her hair was brittle and the roots were gray, but the rest was dark and shiny with hair dye—how comical! Wang Qiyao's lips quivered, but no sounds came out. Long Legs hadn't finished getting his kicks. He had exerted only a fraction of his strength and her neck was too skinny for his hands to dig into. That feeling of excitement rushed into his heart again and he squeezed tighter and tighter until the neck grew soft and lost its elasticity. He sighed a little regretfully, gently put her down, and released his grip.

Too impatient even to take a second look at her, he turned his attention to the box. The floral engravings on it indicated that it was high-class and expensive—a prized object. It didn't take much effort for Long Legs to pry the lock off with his screwdriver and get the box open. He couldn't help being a bit disappointed, even though it wasn't a complete loss. He took out the contents and put them into his pockets, which felt heavy. He remembered what Wang Qiyao had just said about fingerprints and found a cloth with which he wiped the whole place down. He then turned off the light and quietly crept out of the apartment. Over the course of the entire episode, the moon had barely shifted; everything had transpired during the dead hour between two and three o'clock in the morning, a time when even the darkest of deeds can be carried out in absolute secrecy. Who would ever know what had happened here on this night?

Only the pigeons would bear witness. They are the offspring of those birds of four decades before; generation after generation, their line never stops and everything is recorded in their eyes. You can hear them cooing and know that their nightmares are born of the nights of man. How many unsolved crimes there are in this city, all committed during those late-night hours in the long, dark *longtang* alleys that run like cracks through the city, never to see the light of day. When day breaks and the flocks of pigeons take to the sky, you will see that the moment they suddenly leap into the air carries with it a sudden terror. The eyes of these mute witnesses are filled with blood; countless injustices remain sealed away in their hearts. The whistles of the pigeons are clearly cries of mourning; it is only thanks to the vastness of the sky that they do not sound so harsh. The pigeons fly circles in the sky, but never go far; they are expressing their condolences for all the lost souls in this old city. Amid the forest of new skyscrapers, these old *longtang* neighborhoods are like a fleet of sunken ships, their battered hulls exposed as the sea dries up.

The last image caught in Wang Qiyao's eyes was that of the hanging lamp swinging back and forth. Long Legs had pushed against it with his shoulder and sent it swinging back and forth. There was something familiar about this picture and she was trying hard to figure out where she had seen it before. Then, in that last moment, her thoughts raced through time, and the film studio from forty years ago appeared before her. That's it: it was in the film studio. There, in that three-walled room on the set, a woman lay draped across a bed during her final moments; above her a light swung back and forth, projecting wavelike shadows onto the walls. Only now did she finally realize that *she* was the woman on that bed—she was the one who had been murdered. And then the light was extinguished and everything slipped into darkness.

In another two or three hours, the pigeons would be getting ready to take flight again. They would leave their nests and dart into the sky, their strong shadows flashing onto her drapes as they flew past. The potted oleanders on the balcony across the way were beginning to bloom, opening the curtain on yet another season of flowering and decay.

September 23, 1994–March 16, 1995

Afterword

Wang Anyi and *The Song of Everlasting Sorrow*

Wang Anyi came to prominence during the early eighties with a string of award-winning short stories, such as 1981's "The Destination" and "The Rain Patters On," and over the course of the next few decades came to establish herself as one of the most prolific, dynamic, and imaginative fictional stylists on the Chinese literary scene.

Born in Nanjing in 1954, but raised in Shanghai—the setting for so many of her stories—Wang Anyi hails from a literary family. Her father, Wang Xiaoping (1919–2003), was a noted dramatist. Her mother, Ru Zhijuan (1925–1998), was an important writer in Mao's China who caused waves with her 1958 short story "Lilies," whose graceful style boldly broke with the party line on literature of the day.[1] Wang Anyi spent two years (1970–1972) in Anhui as an educated youth before joining a song-and-dance troupe in Xuzhou, where she played the cello. She began writing in 1975, publishing her first short story, "Pingyuan shang" ("On the plains"), in 1978. As the restraints that stifled creative freedom for her parents and so many writers of their generation began to lift in the 1980s, Wang Anyi's literary career began to flourish. With a string of important short story collections (*Lapse of Time)*, novellas (*Love in a Small Town, Love on a Barren Mountain, Brocade Valley*), and novels (*Baotown*), Wang emerged as nuanced writer unafraid to challenge literary conventions and push the boundaries in her bold portrayals of sexuality and female desire.

As Wang's literary vision continued to expand and mature during the 1990s, many of her works took on a markedly more experimental approach. *Jishi yu xugou* (Facts and fictions), a sprawling fictional exploration of her family's matriarchal lineage, was matched by an equally powerful examination of her father's Singaporean family line in *Shangxin de taiping yang* (The sorrowful Pacific). 1990's *Shushu de gushi* (Uncle's story) was a influential offering that became a representative work of Chinese postmodern fiction in the post-Tiananmen era. An interesting counterpoint to this string of experimental writings was *Mini* (Minnie), a disturbing tale of two educated youths who return to Shanghai after the Cultural Revolution only to descend into a dark web of addiction, prostitution, and betrayal. *Minnie* provided Wang with ample scope to flex her storytelling muscles while crafting an unsettling postscript to the tales of educated youth she had written more than a decade earlier.

In the years following the landmark publication of her 1995 novel *The Song of Everlasting Sorrow,* Wang Anyi has shown no signs of slowing down when it comes to her own ever-expanding fictional universe. She has published more than half a dozen volumes of new fiction, from 1995's *Wo ai Bier* (I love Bill), which explored the effects of a university student's series of relationships with foreign men in the wake of her breakup with an American diplomat, to 2005's *Biandi xiaoxiong* (The fierce and ambitious), a landmark novel that traces the radical moral and psychological transformation of a Shanghai taxi driver after he falls victim to a random carjacking. In between, Wang's astonishingly prolific fictional output has included such novels as *Meitou* and *Fuping* and numerous collections of short fiction, including *Youshang de niandai* (The age of melancholy) and *Xiandai shenghuo* (Modern life).

Always known primarily for her novels and short stories, in recent years Wang has also been gaining increasing notice for her rich array of nonfiction genres, which range from travelogues, diaries, and transcripts of university lectures to essays on literary technique, music, and masterworks of world fiction. These essays have been collected in such books as *Gushi he jiang gushi* (Stories and telling stories), *Xiaoshuojia de shisan tangke* (Thirteen classes with a novelist), and *Xinling shijie* (The world of the mind). And while serving as chair of the Shanghai Writers Association and as professor of Chinese literature at Fudan University, Wang has also ventured into literary translation, with a Chinese edition of Elizabeth Swados' *My Depression.*

But among her rich body of work, which now contains more than three dozen volumes of fiction and essays, it is *The Song of Everlasting Sorrow* that stands out as her crowning literary achievement. Completed in 1995 and published the same year, *The Song of Everlasting Sorrow* tells the story of Wang Qiyao, a Shanghai girl enraptured by fashion and Hollywood movies who, after being discovered by an amateur photographer, competes in the 1946 Miss Shanghai beauty pageant. A recent high school graduate at the time, Wang Qiyao becomes second runner-up and is awarded the title of "Miss Third Place"—a fleeting moment of stardom that is the pinnacle of her life. For the next forty years Wang Qiyao clings to that moment and the glamorous lifestyle of pre-liberation Shanghai, in all its glory and decadence. Throughout the historical vicissitudes of modern Chinese history, Wang Qiyao survives and perseveres, secretly playing mahjong during the anti-Rightist Movement, giving birth to an illegitimate child, and carrying on fleeting romances on the eve of the Cultural Revolution. She emerges in the 1980s as the purveyor of "old Shanghai"—a living incarnation of a new commodity called nostalgia—only to be murdered by a petty scam artist in a tragic climax that echoes the films of her youth.

In 2000 the novel was awarded China's highest literary honor, the Mao Dun Prize, which is given only once every five years, among numerous other literary awards in Taiwan and Hong Kong. It was around the same time that *Asia Weekly* assembled a panel of literary critics from around the world to determine the one hundred best works of twentieth-century Chinese fiction and *The Song of Everlasting Sorrow* was ranked number 39 on the list. Further testimony to the novel's importance comes in its multitude of popular-culture manifestations. The year 2003 saw a major stage adaptation of the book by Zhao Yaomin, which received starred reviews after its Shanghai premiere. In 2004 the novel became one of the first Chinese titles to be released on compact disc as an audio book. And 2005 saw the release of a major motion picture adaptation under the title *Everlasting Regret*, directed by Hong Kong filmmaker Stanley Kwan and produced by Jackie Chan. The film, which starred Sammi Cheng, Tony Leung Ka-Fai, and Hu Jun, offered stunning cinematography and sumptuous set design, but lacked the nuances, narrative breadth, and emotional power of the original novel. The same year, Kwan also produced *To Live to Love*, a thirty-five-episode television miniseries adaptation (directed by Ding Hei), which was accompanied by the publication of a teleplay novelization penned by Jiang Liping and a separate illustrated edition with drawings by Weng Ziyang. In all their stunning array, the popular reinventions of Wang Qiyao in the decade since Wang Anyi brought her to life have not only offered new alternatives for this character's fictional universe, but also placed her alongside real-life icons like Ruan Lingyu and Zhou Xuan as one of the most potent cultural symbols of old Shanghai.

One of the key pitfalls encountered by both the film and television adaptations of the novel stems from the need on the part of the producers to continually reintroduce characters—such as Mr. Cheng, Jiang Lili, and Director Li—for increased dramatic effect and continuity of story, even when those characters pass away in the novel. This stands in contrast to the character Wang Qiyao, who, as conceived by Wang Anyi, is a woman incapable of maintaining enduring human relationships. People come and go throughout her life, but she can never hold on to them—not even her own mother or daughter—and this is precisely one of the qualities that make this character so unique . . . and stain her life with sorrow.

Cycles of Sorrow and Copies of Nostalgia

Whereas visual adaptations of *The Song of Everlasting Sorrow* have gone to great lengths to strengthen the interpersonal relationships in Wang Qiyao's life (such as her virtually nonexistent bond with her parents) and reintroduce secondary characters back into her life (such as Mr. Cheng and Director Li, who both die in the novel), the original work already has its own internal philosophy of narrative continuity, one far more subtle and sophisticated. In contrast to the rather forced reintroduction of characters in the film and television miniseries, Wang Anyi's novel instead weaves a complicated web in which relationships, scenarios, and even characters serve as counterpoints to earlier incarnations of themselves. The effect is a form of literary déjà vu that works simultaneously on the interior as well as the exterior levels of the text as both the novel's characters and we the readers try to navigate through the complex human networks that Wang Qiyao alternately constructs, abandons, and reconstitutes by way of proxy throughout her life.

One of the earliest examples of this narrative pattern occurs in part I, when Wang Qiyao's best friend Wu Peizhen is "replaced" by Jiang Lili. What may appear on the surface as a new bond formed in the wake of a fallout with her former best friend actually serves as a prelude to a cyclical pattern of relationships that will recur throughout Wang Qiyao's life. As the novel progresses, these patterns become most evident in the series of love triangles that dominate each respective section, involving Mr. Cheng and Director Li in part I, Uncle Maomao and Sasha in part II, and Old Colour and Long Legs in part III. These romances are, in each case, further conflated by the women in Wang's life—for instance, when Weiwei and Zhang Yonghong appear in part III as shadowy reminders of Wu Peizhen and Jiang Lili from the novel's opening.

The situational motifs that echo and reverberate throughout *The Song of Everlasting Sorrow* are not so much base repetitions as subtle de-evolutions that further illustrate the inner world of the heroine. Cycles of repetition reflect not only Wang Anyi's ingenious literary design, but the heroine Wang Qiyao's tragic quest to reclaim her memories, revisit her past, and relive her lost loves. It is tragic because, with each affair, with each romance, more of herself gets stripped away and destroyed. From innocence (Mr. Cheng) to practicality (Director Li) and from deception (Sasha) to becoming a true object of "imaginary nostalgia" (Old Colour), in the end Wang Qiyao is no longer even the object of desire, but merely a means to an end (Long Legs). This is, once again, not simply the author's literary technique at work, but an expression of the psychology of Wang Qiyao, who is continually searching for vehicles to relive her past, no matter how futile that attempt may be. Her song of everlasting sorrow is a canon that, instead of growing stronger with each refrain, grows increasingly weaker and desperate.

The same cyclical logic also manifests itself through characters who appear as hazy reflections of figures from earlier chapters that have long since faded from Wang Qiyao's life and hence the novel's narrative. Just as the author observes, "Everything in this city has a copy, and everything has someone who leads the way,"[2] the characters, too, have their copies and clones. One of the most interesting examples comes in the form of Zhang Yonghong, Weiwei's best friend and Wang Qiyao's confidante. If there is a true double for Wang Qiyao herself, it is not her daughter but Zhang Yonghong, the most fashionable girl on Huaihai Road in the eighties. But even as Zhang Yonghong masters all the fashion secrets, dance steps, and kernels of Western culture from Wang Qiyao, she can never truly measure up. And how can she? Born during the Cultural Revolution—more than two decades too late to experience the real "old Shanghai"—her identity is branded by her name, "Yonghong," or "Eternally Red," a permanent reminder of the socialist cradle from which she came.

The longing for Shanghai's pre-liberation days, which form the setting of part I and the object of Old Colour's obsession in part III, has led many critics to comment on the place of nostalgia in the novel's framework. These, however, are readings that Wang Anyi sees as detracting from the work's original vision:

> The part of the book in which *The Song of Everlasting Sorrow* provides the most nostalgic material appears in the section set during the 1940s, but that is entirely fictionalized. I have absolutely no personal experience relating to that era and therefore absolutely no psychological reason to feel nostalgic. All I wanted to do was to create a most majestic stage for Wang Qiyao to live out the few good days she had in her life. . . . And so *The Song*

> *of Everlasting Sorrow* was not completed under the thrust of simple nostalgic sentiments; moreover, what it contains and represents cannot be embraced by the term "nostalgia."[3]

While Wang Anyi has repeatedly rejected descriptions of her novel as a work of nostalgia—referring to the glorious world of old Shanghai as embodied by foreign concessions, calendar girls, and the bright lights of the Bund—the drive to recreate relationships throughout the novel points instead to her heroine's own very personal form of nostalgic longing. It is a nostalgia that drives Wang Qiyao to ceaselessly attempt to re-create earlier moments in her life. In Wang Anyi's literary world, history seems to repeat itself . . . but it doesn't. And in the end it simply produces flawed copies and imperfect replicas of itself, wherein the original patterns and scenarios appear increasingly distant. But isn't that what nostalgia is all about? An incurable longing for what is lost but can never be recovered.

It is in the final scene of the novel, when Wang Qiyao is strangled by Long Legs in her apartment on Peace Lane, that she is struck by an otherworldly epiphany and the true meaning of the simulated death scene she witnessed as a teenage girl at the film studio suddenly becomes apparent.

> Then, in that last moment, her thoughts raced through time, and the film studio from forty years ago appeared before her. That's it: it was in the film studio. There, in that three-walled room on the set, a woman lay draped across a bed during her final moments; above her a light swung back and forth, projecting wavelike shadows onto the walls. Only now did she finally realize that *she* was the woman on that bed—she was the one who had been murdered.[4]

It is in that moment that it suddenly becomes clear that even Wang Qiyao's own life is but a copy, an attempt to recreate a fleeting fantasy/nightmare of her youth. And if it is, then perhaps the sorrowful song of the ensuing four decades was all part of a necessary plot to produce the perfect tragically stained reproduction?

Writing Literary History and Erasing History

The Song of Everlasting Sorrow borrows its title from one of the most famous literary works of the Tang dynasty, Bo Juyi's (Bai Juyi) (772–846) extended narrative poem "Chang hen ge," which forms the single most important subtext to the novel. Dating from 809, the original poem tells of the epic romance between the Tang emperor Xuanzong (685–762) and his beloved concubine Yang Guifei (719–756), whose stunning beauty is legendary in Chinese historical lore. Beginning with Yang's entry into the palace, the poem recounts the emperor's passionate love for her, which eventually leads to his dereliction of state affairs and a full-scale rebellion (the leader of which, An Lushan, gained power through Yang's influence). In the wake of the rebellion and growing unrest, Xuanzong is pressured to order the execution of his beloved consort, and the final section of the poem describes his quest to find her in heaven, concluding with the famous couplet, "While even heaven and earth will one day come to an end, this everlasting sorrow shall endure."

Some readers may see similarities between the imaginary Wang Qiyao and the legendary Yang Guifei, from their status—Wang was "Miss Third Place" but not Miss Shanghai while Yang was a concubine but not the empress—to their shared tragic fate by strangulation. But the way Wang Anyi cements her indebtedness to Bo Juyi throughout her novel is through numerous and subtle textual referents, such as when she describes Wang Qiyao's discriminating fashion sense in language directly quoted from the Tang masterpiece, thereby further equating her heroine with the prototypical tragic beauty.[5]

Wang Anyi, however, does not stop with "Chang hen ge" and actually laces her novel with intertextual references, such as to the work of tenth-century poet Li Yu and the Tang poet Cui Ying's famous "Yellow Crane Tower" ("Huang he lou"), from which the chapter headings "An Old Friend Flew Off on a Yellow Crane" and "All That Remains is the Tower Whence It Flew" are borrowed. The way Wang Anyi seamlessly weaves this myriad of textual references into her novel, using them to comment on her story, is part of what makes *The Song of Everlasting Sorrow* such a powerful literary work. But the novel's attachment to Chinese literary history does not stop with the Tang dynasty.

David Der-wei Wang was among the first critics to link Wang Anyi's literary recreation of old Shanghai with one of the twentieth century's greatest Chinese writers, Eileen Chang (Zhang Ailing) (1920–1995).[6] And while his influential essay "A new successor to the Shanghai School" argued that *The Song of Everlasting Sorrow* secured the author's place as Eileen Chang's literary successor, Wang Anyi has downplayed any similarities to work of the iconic writer, instead claiming that the closest thing to a literary model was actually Hugo's *Notre-Dame of Paris.* While *The Song of Everlasting Sorrow* situates itself within a rich literary history of Chinese and Western classics from which it draws and to which it has often been compared—from Bo Juyi and Cui Ying to Eileen Chang and Victor Hugo—Wang Anyi's conception of history itself is quite different.

In stark contrast to the rich literary history in which Wang Anyi brilliantly anchors her fictional universe lies the seeming weightlessness of "history" against which her novel plays out. Although *The Song of Everlasting Sorrow* spans four crucial decades of modern Chinese history, from 1946 to 1986, many of the historical landmarks we naturally expect are absent. All of the keywords that seem inevitable in modern China—the Civil War, Liberation, the Great Leap Forward, the Anti-Rightist Campaign, the Cultural Revolution, the Gang of Four, Mao Zedong, Deng Xiaoping, the Open Door Policy—are virtually nonexistent in the novel's narrative. This significant absence points to a new conception of history that is formulated by subtle changes in fashion and popular culture rather than politics and historical movements, an approach that stands in stark contrast to other works of contemporary Chinese historical fiction. In discussing the historical vision of her novel, Wang Anyi writes:

> Some people accuse me of "avoiding" the impact that large-scale historical events have on practical life. But I don't feel that is the case at all. I personally feel that the face of history is not built by large-scale incidents; history occurs day after day, bit by bit transforming our daily lives. For instance the way women on the streets of Shanghai went from wearing cheongsam dresses to Lenin-style jackets—*that* is the kind of history I am concerned with.[7]

This is not to say that the historical forces that surround the characters in *The Song of Everlasting Sorrow* do not affect them—think of Director Li's fatal plane crash toward the end of the Civil War or Mr. Cheng's death during the Cultural Revolution—but history never takes center stage: instead it quietly plays out in the shadows on the periphery of the everyday. As the novel opens, Shanghai does not appear on a massive canvas, but gradually takes form from a series of dots and lines, signaling a fictional universe built on the details of daily life. Unlike Bo Juyi's famous poem, which is written on a grand stage of politics, rebellion, and dynastic crisis, Wang Anyi's tragic ballad quietly plays out in the back-alley *longtang* neighborhoods of Shanghai, where "tell-it-as-it-is," "less-is-more," and the cycles of fashion rule the (every)day. And where two-thirds of Bo's poem is devoted to the emperor's mourning and his quest to find his lover in the netherworld after her death, who is there to mourn Wang Qiyao? In the end, the death of "Miss Third Place" is perhaps simply another piece of gossip to float through the labyrinthine back alleys of Shanghai.

This afterword is aimed at introducing Wang Anyi and her *Song of Everlasting Sorrow* and providing a series of different perspectives from which to approach—or reflect upon—this seminal literary work. From cycles of recurrence to the politics of nostalgia and from literary history to a new historiography of the everyday—these are but a handful of the themes to which *The Song of Everlasting Sorrow* takes us. And while critics have described her work with many labels, including nostalgic, Shanghai-school, and feminist, Wang Anyi has rejected them all, a stance that has only increased the complexity of ideas with which we must approach her work. The novel has been alternately read as a postmodernist showcase and a postsocialist testimony to the fate of Shanghai in the twentieth century.

In the years since its initial publication, *The Song of Everlasting Sorrow* has come to be recognized as one of the true classics of contemporary Chinese fiction. At the same time, just as Wang Qiyao inspired Old Colour's nostalgic longing for an "old Shanghai" he never knew, so *The Song of Everlasting Sorrow* has itself helped give rise to a new "Shanghai fever" that has swept China since the late nineties. In this context, new meaning is brought to the life (and death) of Wang Qiyao as she is posthumously transformed into a true "Miss Shanghai," a fictional incarnation of this Paris of the Orient's imagined past and a new icon for it as it looks toward the future.

M. B.
Santa Barbara, California
March 2007

NOTES

1. See Perry Link, "Rebels, Victims, and Apologists," in *New York Times,* July 6, 1986. "Lilies" and other representative works by Ru Zhijuan are available in the collection *Lilies and Other Stories* (Peking: Panda Books, 1985).
2. Page [orig 46].
3. Wang Anyi, "*Chang hen ge* bu shi huaijiu" ("*The Song of Everlasting Sorrow* is not a work of nostalgia"), in *Wang Anyi Shuo* (Wang Anyi speaks) (Hunan: Hunan wenyi chubanshe, 2003), 121.
4. Page [orig 771].
5. Page 554. The original Chinese refers to the "rainbow skirt and feathered coat" (*ni shang yu yi*), a description that actually appears twice in Bo Juyi's original poem to describe Yang Guifei's clothing and which has come to be equated with the tragic consort. Thanks to Alice Cheang for this observation.
6. See Wang Dewei (David Der-wei Wang), "Shanghai xiaojie zhi si: Wang Anyi de 'Chang hen ge'" ("Death of Miss Shanghai: Wang Anyi's *The Song of Everlasting Sorrow*"), in Wang Anyi, *Chang hen ge* (*The Song of Everlasting Sorrow*) (Taipei: Maitian, 1996), 3–10; and Wang Dewei, "Haipai zuojia, you jian chuanren: Wang Anyi lun" ("A new successor to the Shanghai School: On Wang Anyi"), in *Kua shiji fenghua dangdai xiaoshuo 20 jia* (Into the new millennium: Twenty Chinese fiction writers) (Taipei: Maitian, 2002), 35–54.
7. Wang Anyi, "Wo yanzhong de lishi shi richang de" ("The history I see is that of the everyday"), in *Wang Anyi Shuo* (Wang Anyi speaks) (Hunan: Hunan wenyi chubanshe, 2003), 155.